Tombland

C. J. SANSOM

Tombland

MULHOLLAND BOOKS

LITTLE, BROWN AND COMPANY

NEW YORK   BOSTON   LONDON

Copyright © 2018 by C. J. Sansom

Hachette Book Group supports the right to free expression and the value of copyright. The purpose of copyright is to encourage writers and artists to produce the creative works that enrich our culture.

The scanning, uploading, and distribution of this book without permission is a theft of the author's intellectual property. If you would like permission to use material from the book (other than for review purposes), please contact permissions@hbgusa.com. Thank you for your support of the author's rights.

Mulholland Books / Little, Brown and Company
Hachette Book Group
1290 Avenue of the Americas, New York, NY 10104
mulhollandbooks.com

First United States Edition: January 2019

Originally published in the United Kingdom by Mantle, a division of Pan Macmillan, in October 2018

Mulholland Books is an imprint of Little, Brown and Company, a division of Hachette Book Group, Inc. The Mulholland Books name and logo are trademarks of Hachette Book Group, Inc.

The publisher is not responsible for websites (or their content) that are not owned by the publisher.

The Hachette Speakers Bureau provides a wide range of authors for speaking events. To find out more, go to hachettespeakersbureau.com or call (866) 376-6591.

ISBN 978-0-316-41242-1

LCCN 2018962432

10 9 8 7 6 5 4 3 2 1

LSC-C

Printed in the United States of America

Tombland

AUTHOR'S NOTE

The seismic events of the 1549 English rebellions are surprisingly little known; but *Tombland* is based on the known evidence, and the huge camp on Mousehold Heath actually existed.

Some events, such as those concerning the gentleman prisoners in Part Six, and one incident that takes place in Chapter Seventy-five, may appear too far-fetched to be true, but they actually happened.

More detail is given in the Historical Essay.

CONTENTS

I did well in keeping Kett's camp and thought nothing but well of Kett. He trusted to see a new day, for such as I.

Ralph Claxton, Norfolk parish clerk,
prosecuted for speaking these words, 1550

Prologue

January 1549

I HAD BEEN IN my chambers at Lincoln's Inn when the messenger came from Master Parry, asking me to attend him urgently. I wondered what might be afoot. He was the Lady Elizabeth's Comptroller, head of the financial side of her household, and I had worked under him since I was recommended to Elizabeth by Queen Catherine Parr two years before, following King Henry's death. The old king had left a huge income – £3000 a year – to each of his two daughters, with the intention that they should convert the income into landed property. Lord Protector Somerset had decided to let the Lady Mary have first choice of what was available on the market; though her religious conservatism was entirely at odds with his Protestant radicalism, as Henry's elder daughter, Mary was heir to the throne should anything happen to young King Edward. Her welfare was also important to her cousin the Holy Roman Emperor Charles, with whom Somerset needed to keep on good terms. Elizabeth, on the other hand, counted for little. But Mary was settled now, the bulk of her estates in Norfolk, and Parry was starting to build up blocks of land for Elizabeth, mostly in Hertfordshire. Some juicy piece of ex-monastic land had probably come his way, and he was keen for me to secure it quickly.

I thought how much I owed to that dear lady, Catherine Parr. I had been distressed when, shortly after King Henry's death, she had married Thomas Seymour, the Protector's brother, a charming, handsome, unscrupulous and ruthlessly ambitious man. Lady Elizabeth had lived with them, but had left the house under a cloud the previous May, amidst rumours that Seymour had made advances to the then fourteen-year-old girl. And then, last September, Catherine Parr herself died

I

giving birth to Seymour's child. It had been a great shock, which still lay heavy on my heart.

Telling my clerk John Skelly I might be gone a while, I set out from Lincoln's Inn to walk to Master Parry's offices off Knightrider Street — he was not a lawyer, so not a member of the Inns. It was a cold, icy day; dirty snow still lay at the sides of the streets, and I watched my footing carefully among the busy Londoners. I shook my head at how many beggars there were now, crouched in doorways, muffled in whatever rags they had gathered against the cold.

The growing desperation of the poor was one of the many changes that had come to pass these last two years. Henry had left control of the country to a nominated Council until King Edward, now eleven, reached his majority. The Council, however, had quickly devolved power to Edward's elder uncle, Edward Seymour, now Duke of Somerset, who ruled as a virtual king. Perhaps after sixty years of firm, centralized rule by Henry VII and Henry VIII, those in power could only conceive of government by a single man.

After five years of war with France and Scotland, Henry had left the kingdom at peace when he died. It was much needed; his wars had bankrupted the country, and had been paid for by the debasement of the coinage, adulterating silver with copper. These coins were no longer accepted at face value by traders, and prices were now almost double what they had been a decade ago. The effect on the poorer classes, especially, was catastrophic, for wages remained the same.

But Protector Somerset had promptly launched a massive war against Scotland, hoping the growing number of Scottish Protestants would support him, and that the marriage of the six-year-old Mary, Queen of Scots to King Edward would take place, uniting the kingdoms. He had built a series of forts in the new Italian style which he believed unassailable, throughout the Scottish lowlands and up as far as the River Tay. But the Scotch had resisted everywhere; the forts, poorly built, had been taken one by one, while Mary herself had been sent to France, Scotland's ally, which had also provided troops. Although the war was a disaster, the Protector refused to accept defeat, and was said to be planning yet another campaign even while his soldiers in the remaining forts were deserting for lack of pay.

I dropped a coin into the cap of yet another beggar shivering against a wall. The man was missing a leg, probably a veteran of the wars. The Protector made much of his claims to be a friend to the poor, and blamed the economic problems on the illegal enclosures of rural manors by landlords, and the turning of tenants off their land to make way for the more profitable sheep. There had been rebellions in Hertfordshire the previous year, and remedies were promised.

I walked downhill, the great spire of St Paul's Cathedral starkly outlined against the cold blue sky. I was reminded of how, when the cathedral's great rood screen had been taken down, two workmen had been killed, which religious traditionalists had said was a punishment from God. For religious change, greater by far than under King Henry, was convulsing the country. Under the Protector, Protestant radicals were now firmly in charge. Images were being removed from the churches, wall paintings whitewashed. The chantries where prayers were said for the dead had been abolished and their revenues appropriated to the Crown. And soon there would be a new prayer book in English. It was said that in it the Mass − with the belief that the priest turned the wafer and wine into the actual blood and body of Christ − would be replaced by a Communion commemorating Christ's sacrifice − a view punishable by burning to death only three years before. I shuddered at the memory of the execution of Anne Askew at Smithfield, which I had been forced to witness.

I entered Knightrider Street and arrived at Parry's chambers, kicking the snow from my boots before entering the building. To my surprise, the outer office was empty, so I went in and knocked on Parry's door. A voice called me to enter. I went in, then almost staggered back with surprise. The chair behind the broad desk was occupied, not by the stout figure of Thomas Parry, but by a thin, greyhaired man in black silk robes, the gold chain of the Lord Chancellor of England round his neck. Lord Richard Rich, my oldest enemy. Standing behind him I saw, with almost equal surprise, the spare brownbearded figure of William Cecil. I had worked with Cecil three years ago, when he was employed by Catherine Parr. His rise since then had been very fast. Not yet thirty, he was one of the Protector's senior secretaries, already a powerful man. When I worked with him before, he had been a friend.

But even then I knew that he put his own success, and the Protestant cause, before anything else. And now he was in company with Rich. I looked at him. Cecil's protuberant grey eyes fixed on mine, but he said nothing as Rich sat studying me, wolfishly.

Taken utterly by surprise, I blinked, and asked, 'Where is Master Parry?'

'In the Tower,' answered Rich, in a voice as icy as the weather.

I stared at him. He continued, in severe, accusatory tones, his eyes never leaving my face. 'As is the Lady Elizabeth's chief gentlewoman Kat Ashley, and sundry others, accused of conspiring treason with Lord Thomas Seymour. The Lady Elizabeth herself is under interrogation by Sir Robert Tyrwhit at Hatfield.'

My heart pounded. Grasping the back of a chair with a trembling hand to steady myself, I asked, 'Of what treason is Seymour accused?'

Rich smiled and turned to Cecil. 'See, Master Secretary, he is unmanned now all is discovered.' Cecil continued to stare at me impassively. Rich leaned forward over Parry's desk, clasping his long fingers together. His voice deepened with indignation.

'You ask what treason? Better to ask what treason he is *not* accused of. Conspiring with the pirates he is supposed to clear from our seas as Lord Admiral, to share their profits. Suborning the head of the Bristol Mint to put coin at his disposal. Filling his castle at Sudeley with armaments. Conspiring to abduct the King and make himself Protector in his brother's place. And, finally, conspiring with Master Parry and Mistress Ashley to marry the Lady Elizabeth without the consent of the Council. Will that do, Serjeant Shardlake? Perhaps there is more you can tell us in due course, but in the meantime we wish to know what knowledge you have of Thomas Seymour's plan to marry the Lady Elizabeth. Mistress Ashley has already confessed to talking of a marriage with him, and Master Parry to discussing her purchases of land with Seymour.'

I glanced at Cecil. He spoke gravely. 'All this is so.'

I turned back to Rich. 'My Lord Chancellor, I know nothing of this.'

Rich continued as though I had not spoken, 'You are responsible under Master Parry for dealings pertaining to the Lady Elizabeth's lands. Parry must have consulted you in order to answer Seymour's questions fully. Tell me what was said between you on the matter.' He had a blank sheet of paper before him. He dipped a quill in the inkpot and held it ready to write.

'Nothing,' I answered, truthfully. 'Master Parry never told me of any talks with Seymour, certainly not of any proposed marriage to Elizabeth. How can you imagine he would have?' I added, my courage returning. 'You know full well that I have ever despised Thomas Seymour, who has always been capable of the wildest and most fantastical talk.' I glanced again at Cecil. This time, he gave me the faintest of nods.

Rich sneered. 'You did not despise Lord Thomas's late wife, the former Queen. I know of your closeness to Catherine Parr. It was her patronage that got you your current post. What correspondence did you have with Catherine Parr concerning Elizabeth in the months before her death?'

'Again, my Lord, none. We never wrote, nor met again, after my appointment to the household of the Lady Elizabeth after the old king's death.'

Rich gave a scoffing little laugh. 'You expect me to believe that? You were her confidential adviser.'

'Not since the old king died. She was soon married to Seymour.'

'You seriously expect me to credit that?' Rich said, in a courtroom tone of mock outrage. 'Given your old closeness to her, and your service to Elizabeth? She said nothing to you of what happened between Elizabeth and Seymour? Of Seymour's advances to Elizabeth while his wife's belly was heavy with child?'

I took a deep breath to steady myself. 'I swear I knew nothing of any of these alleged matters before today.'

'Not alleged,' Rich snapped. 'Kat Ashley is singing like one of the late Queen Catherine's songbirds. She cannot say enough about Seymour's advances to Elizabeth.'

'I know nothing of any of this.'

Rich smiled. 'So said Master Parry. Before he was shown the instruments in the Tower.'

Fury and bitterness suddenly overcame my fear. 'I have seen them too, Lord Rich, and thanks to you. But you will not entrap me. If Thomas Seymour has been such a fool as you say, may he receive the justice he deserves. You talk of conversations with Parry and Mistress Ashley, but you have said nothing of any actual agreement to encourage a marriage without the Council's consent. And the Lady Elizabeth must have said nothing either, or you would have told me about it. So, I repeat, I know nothing of this.'

Rich's pale face reddened, angry in his turn. Then, behind him, Cecil held up a hand for me to see, palm down, and lowered it gently. A warning to me to still my tongue.

Rich had seen me glance at Cecil, but not his gesture. He turned to him. 'Young Master Cecil is come with me to make a search of Master Parry's offices. He will be going through all his documents. You can help him.' Rich paused. 'Before we do, is there anything here to which you would direct us? Helping us voluntarily now might go in your favour later.'

'I know of nothing.'

Rich smiled nastily. 'Afterwards, I may carry out a search of your own chambers, and your house.'

'You will need a warrant, Lord Rich,' Cecil reminded him gently.

Rich frowned. 'That is easy, I am Lord Chancellor.'

'Please,' I said quietly, 'do not wait on a warrant. Make any search you like. I would not wish to slow your investigations.' I realized now that Rich had come on no more than a fishing expedition, hoping to trap me in his nets.

The Lord Chancellor threw down the quill, spattering Parry's desk with ink. 'We shall make the search, and a deposition will be required of you.'

'As you wish, my Lord.'

Rich set his thin lips, then stood up. 'I am wanted at the Tower. Seymour is to be questioned again.' He looked narrowly at Cecil. 'Conduct the search of Parry's offices thoroughly. I have others working at his home. Shardlake's premises can be examined later.'

'Yes, my Lord.' Cecil bowed, as did I. Rich gave me a look of pure malevolence, then walked swiftly to the door, his silk robe rustling. He slammed it behind him – he ever had a streak of petulance. Cecil and I were left alone. He did not speak until he heard the outer door slam, too.

'You truly know nothing of any of this?' he asked quietly.

'Nothing, I swear.'

'I did not think so. Master Parry knows well when to keep things to himself.' He smiled thinly. 'Rich is one of those in charge of the interrogations; when your name came up he insisted on questioning you himself. The Protector asked me to accompany him, to make sure he did not — exceed himself.'

'Thank you, Master Cecil.'

His face became grave. 'Seymour's plotting, though, is a desperately serious matter. And if the Lady Elizabeth did indeed consent to marry him without the Council's agreement, which would never have been given, that *is* treason.'

'But unless the Lady Elizabeth agreed to an illegal marriage, she is innocent. That is also true of Parry and Kat Ashley.'

'It is.' Cecil's shoulders relaxed slightly. 'I think Parry and Ashley may be found guilty only of careless gossip, and Elizabeth of nothing.'

I hesitated, then asked, 'Is it true, then, about Seymour's advances to the Lady Elizabeth?'

An expression of distaste crossed his thin features. 'I fear, according to Ashley, that it is. It was when the late Queen Catherine caught them embracing that she sent Elizabeth away.'

I shook my head. 'I would not have thought the Lady Elizabeth would ever be so — thoughtless.'

He sighed. 'Young girls are impressionable, and Seymour has the charm of the devil.'

'The evidence against him on the other matters —'

'Irrefutable. It will be public knowledge very soon. He intended to take control of the King. I do not think anything can save Thomas Seymour now. The Protector will have to execute his own brother.' Cecil shook his head. 'It is dreadful for him.'

'Yes.' I sighed. 'Poor Queen Catherine. Poor Elizabeth.'

'You do not say, "poor Thomas Seymour".'

'As I told Rich, if he is guilty, let him get what he deserves.'

'It will be the axe.'

There was a moment of silence, then Cecil rubbed his slim hands together. 'Will you go and call Parry's servants? Rich sent them out, they will be huddling in the inner hall. It is cold in here. We should get them to light a fire if we are to go through Master Parry's papers.'

✝

IT WAS A STRANGE, uncomfortable thing to go through my employer's documents. Master Parry and I were not friends, but I respected him. To my relief, we found nothing. Afterwards, as we donned our coats to leave, Cecil paused thoughtfully and glanced towards the window. Dust motes, stirred by our searching, whirled in a ray of winter sunlight. 'Master Shardlake,' he said quietly, 'I do not think the Lady Elizabeth is in any real danger, but she has never been in great favour with the Protector, and this scandal will only make him more suspicious of her. His is not –' he paused, and sighed – 'a trusting nature, and his own brother's treason will make it even less so. When you see Master Parry, tell him to warn the Lady Elizabeth to be careful no breath of scandal touches her again.'

'Thank you, Master Cecil. I will.' Then I added, curiously, 'Why would you help her?'

He inclined his head, then raised both palms and held them up in perfect balance. 'The King has two sisters. Mary an enemy of true religion, Elizabeth a friend. For now, political reasons mean the Lady Mary has the Protector's favour. But perhaps, when she is older, Elizabeth may be used to redress the balance.'

Part One

LONDON

Chapter One

June 1549

IT RAINED THROUGHOUT our journey to Hatfield Palace; hard, heavy rain that dripped from our caps and made our horses' reins slippery and slick. Occasionally, a gust of cold wind drove it at us slantwise; as though even now, in early June, the chill of the hard winter and cold spring was reluctant to let go of the land.

There were six of us in the party that set out from London in the grey morning; myself, my young assistant Nicholas and four sturdy men in the service of Master Comptroller Parry, swords and knives at their waists. Their leader, a taciturn middle-aged man named Fowberry, had arrived at Lincoln's Inn the previous morning, bearing a letter from his master requiring me to attend the Lady Elizabeth at Hatfield on a case of urgency and delicacy. I was to return there with him, stay the night at an inn outside the town, and meet with Parry and the Lady Elizabeth the following morning. The letter added that he was sending Fowberry and his men to accompany us back as a precaution, given the unsettled state of the country after the risings in May. It was unlike Parry, a naturally verbose man, to be so brief, and I wondered what it augured. The purchase and sale of lands, the business I had conducted for him on behalf of the Lady Elizabeth these last two years, occasionally involved delicacy, but seldom urgency.

We spoke little on the journey; the weather did not encourage conversation. Nicholas rode beside me, his long slim body bent over his horse, Fowberry on his other side and his three men behind. The traffic was mainly in the opposite direction, carts bringing supplies to London and a few lone travellers. Once though, a fast post-rider brightly arrayed in the King's livery and accompanied by a pair of armed servants rode up behind us, sounding a trumpet and waving at us to move to the side of the road. The party overtook us, spattering us with mud from the highway. Nicholas looked at me, rats' tails of red hair on his brow dripping water into his eyes and making him blink. 'I wonder what that was,' he said. 'Another proclamation from Protector Somerset?'

'Perhaps. I wonder what about this time?'

'Perhaps he decrees that blind men shall see, or fishes fly through the air.'

I laughed, but Fowberry, on my other side, looked at him askance.

☩

EVENING CAME ON, the grey sky darkening. I turned to Fowberry. 'We must be at the inn soon, I think.'

'Ay, it can't be far now, sir,' he replied in his deep, lilting voice. Like Parry, and many others in Elizabeth's service, he was Welsh. He sat solid astride his horse, ignoring the weather; a soldierly bearing. Perhaps, like many of his countrymen, he had fought in the French wars.

I ventured a smile. 'A good idea of your master, that we should spend tonight at this inn. Otherwise I should be presenting myself to the Lady Elizabeth as soaked as a drowned rat, and bespattered with mud.'

'No, sir, that wouldn't be right at all.' His face remained expressionless. I had hoped to coax him into revealing something of what our summons portended, but if he knew anything, he was not saying.

Nicholas drew his horse to a halt, pointing over to the right of the road. At a little distance, across a field of growing barley, a light was visible. 'Master Fowberry,' he said. 'Look over there. Could that be the inn?'

Fowberry halted, signalling his men to do the same. Wiping the rain from his eyes, he peered into the deepening gloom. 'That's not it. We've another mile to go.' He leaned forward, screwing up his eyes. 'And that's an open fire, it's not coming from a window. I think it's in that copse of trees behind the field.'

One of his men put a hand to his sword. 'Not another camp of rebel peasants?' he asked.

'I've heard there's been more trouble in Hampshire and Sussex,' Fowberry replied quietly.

I shook my head. 'That's a small fire. Probably just another crew of masterless men wandering the countryside.'

'They could be watching for lone riders to rob.' Fowberry spat on the ground. 'The Protector should have these rascal knaves branded and made bond slaves under the new law Parliament passed.' He nodded. 'We'll warn the innkeeper, he can alert the constable and send the town watch out.' He turned to me. 'You agree, Master Shardlake?'

I hesitated. Nicholas gave me a warning look. He knew my views on the current unrest, but this was no time or place for an argument. 'As you think best, Master Fowberry. Though whoever is over there may be about some honest business.'

'Best to be safe, in these dangerous times. Besides, Hatfield Palace is close, and we would not wish trouble near the Lady.'

I nodded briefly in acknowledgement. We jerked at our tired horses' reins, and rode slowly on. Whoever was setting a campfire in this weather, I thought, would have a sorry night of it.

✝

THE INN, JUST outside the little town of Hatfield, was a fine, comfortable-looking place. We dismounted in the yard and a couple of ostlers led our horses away. Fowberry's men followed them, leaving him with Nicholas and me. I was stiff and sore; bone-tired after the journey. My back hurt, as it did more and more these days on long rides. But an ageing hunchback of forty-seven could expect no less. A servant came out of the inn and shouldered our packs, leading us into the large old building. The interior was bright with candlelight, for it was now full dark. A stone-flagged hall gave on to a large taproom from which some fellow-guests, traders of the better sort from the look of them, regarded us curiously. A plump, bald man with an apron over his doublet left a conversation with one of them and bustled over.

'Master Fowberry,' he said cheerfully. 'We were told to expect you.' He bowed. 'And you must be the legal gentleman come to consult with Master Parry.' Sharp, nosy little eyes studied us.

I said, 'I am Serjeant Matthew Shardlake, of Lincoln's Inn. My assistant, Master Overton.'

The innkeeper nodded cheerfully, then turned back to Fowberry. 'I am pleased to see you, sir.' He leaned closer and spoke quietly. 'I would be obliged, sir, if Master Parry could pay your guests' charges in gold coin. The silver coinage is so debased –' He shook his head.

'We always pay in gold at Hatfield Palace,' Fowberry said proudly.

The innkeeper bowed again, gratefully. 'We are always honoured to trade with the palace –' He paused. 'We have not seen you for some time, sir. The Lady Elizabeth is well, I hope.'

Fowberry smiled tightly. 'Indeed yes, my good man.'

'And over her recent troubles, I hope.' He looked at each of us in turn, like an eager raven keen to see what trinket of gossip it might pick up. The room behind him had fallen quiet.

Fowberry spoke coldly and steadily. 'I do not chatter abroad the business of the household I serve, Goodman.'

The innkeeper stepped back a pace. 'Of course, sir. It's just – business with Hatfield Palace has been slack.'

'It'll get slacker if you go nosing for information about the Lady's affairs,' Fowberry replied brutally. 'But here's something that is your business. A mile south we saw the lights of a camp in the fields. To the left of the road. You might do well to let the constable know.'

'Probably only a few men grouped around a fire,' I explained.

The innkeeper, though, looked serious. 'I'll send word.'

'Do that,' Fowberry said. 'And now, we're all soaked. We want rooms with fires, and towels. Then bring some food for the gentlemen.'

'Will you eat down here?' The innkeeper indicated the taproom. 'Good company, and a fire lit, given the weather –'

'We'll eat in private, thank you,' I answered.

☦

MASTER PARRY HAD arranged a room each for Nicholas and me; he had spared no expense. He could afford to, the Lady Elizabeth being one of the richest people in the country. A fire was already lit in my room and it was bright with candles. I changed out of my wet clothes, setting them before the fire to dry. My bag had been brought up and I laid out my lawyer's robe carefully on the bed.

The food came, thick mutton pottage, bacon with bread and cheese, and a jug of beer. Rough fare, but good. Shortly afterwards there was a knock at the door and Nicholas entered, bending his head to pass through the doorway. He, too, had changed, and had dried his red-blond hair. He wore a green doublet tied with silver aiglets, with a fashionable high collar showing a little ruffle of shirt above.

'Sit down, lad,' I said.

'Thank you, sir.'

We set to our food with a will. When he had taken the edge from his hunger, Nicholas put a hand to his purse and took out a little silver coin, laying it on the table. 'I was given one of these in London yesterday,' he said. 'The latest shilling.'

I picked up the bright new coin, stamped with the head of our eleven-year-old king, a serious expression on his face. Around the edge was stamped *Edward VI by the Grace of God* in Latin. I weighed the coin in my palm. 'It's bigger than the one they put out at the beginning of the year. But more copper in it?'

'I think so.' Nicholas frowned. 'God's death, does Protector Somerset take us all for fools as he robs the country of its silver? All this chopping and changing just raises prices even further. Beer is up another farthing.'

I smiled wryly. 'He needs silver from somewhere to pay for his Scottish war. Along with this latest round of new taxes Parliament has granted him.' I shook my head. 'When the old king died, I thought all this pouring money into unwinnable wars would stop, not that things would get even worse.'

Nicholas grunted. 'Do you think we're beaten up there?'

'It looks like it.'

'That will be a great dishonour for England.'

I looked at the coin thoughtfully. 'I have never seen prices rise so fast as this year. If you are a poor workman —' I shook my head. 'With that, and grasping landowners raising rents and enclosing lands —'

Nicholas interrupted me. 'What else are they to do? Prices go up for them too. I know my father found it hard to turn a profit, which

was why –' Nicholas broke off, shrugging, a frown crossing his freck-
led brow.

I looked at him. Three years before, when he was twenty-one, his
Lincolnshire gentry parents had disinherited him for refusing to marry
a woman they had chosen for him, but whom he did not love. The
bitterness caused by their rejection still haunted him, I knew, though
he seemed happy enough as my assistant, and looked forward to the
prospect of soon being called to the bar. He worked hard and skilfully,
though his heart was not as wholly in the law as mine had been at
his age, and spent much time carousing with other young gentlemen –
he remained acutely conscious of his gentleman status – in the London
taverns and, I suspected, the brothels, too. I thought sometimes that
what he needed was a wife. Although not conventionally handsome,
Nicholas was a striking young man, and not lacking in confidence;
but he did lack money, being reliant on his limited earnings, and
that would count. Currently, he was paying court to another barrister's
daughter, Beatrice Kenzy. I had met her a couple of times, and did not
like her.

Changing the subject, Nicholas asked, 'Is it possible I shall see the
Lady Elizabeth tomorrow?'

'Unlikely. I see her rarely enough.'

He smiled. 'You brought me because her status means you should
not arrive without someone to serve you.'

'You know that is the way of it. Though there may be documents
to copy. But access to the Lady Elizabeth is strictly controlled by Master
Parry and her ladies.'

Nicholas leaned forward, his green eyes alive with interest. 'What
is she like now?'

'I have not seen her these eight months,' I replied. 'Not since I went
to deliver my condolences when – when Queen Catherine died.' I
stumbled slightly over the words, swallowed, then continued, 'Elizabeth is fifteen, but you deal with her as with an adult. She has never
known a secure childhood.' I smiled sadly. 'She is extraordinarily
clever, though, quick with words, and she can use them sharply. When
I was first appointed to work under Master Parry, she told me that her
dogs would wear her collars. And so she expects.'

Nicholas hesitated, then said, 'This business – do you think it might be connected with what happened in January – her trouble?'

'No,' I answered firmly. 'The scandal involving Thomas Seymour died with that wretched man. That I do know.' I looked at him firmly. 'Remember, the Protector publicly acknowledged that the Lady Elizabeth was involved in no illegal marriage plans with Seymour. That is all I can say on the matter, Nicholas. I have my duty of confidentiality.'

'Of course. Only—'

'Only everyone from that innkeeper to every lawyer at Lincoln's Inn would love to know the details,' I answered with asperity.

'No, sir.' He looked a little uneasy. 'It is just that, this matter we are summoned on being urgent and confidential, I wondered if there might be some connection. Whether –'

I nodded. 'Whether there might be politics involved. No, I am sure not. And I am sorry to have snapped just then, only so many have fished for gossip, knowing I work with Parry.' I shook my head. 'Better sometimes, Nicholas, to know as little as possible. There, a free piece of advice from an old lawyer.'

✟

LATER, WHEN NICHOLAS had returned to his room, I went and opened the window. The rain had stopped, though the sound of water dripping was audible through the still night. A half-moon cast a dim silver glow over the fields surrounding the inn. People were already saying this would be a bad harvest, the first in four years. I wondered what would happen if there was a dearth of grain on top of everything else.

I turned from the window. I should really do the exercises my doctor friend Guy had prescribed before going to bed, but I was too tired. I worried about Guy. For the last month he had been ill, with a low fever it seemed nothing could abate, and for a man now in his mid-sixties that was serious. I would visit him again as soon as we returned to London. In truth, I feared him dying. I had lost so many people these last few years, not only Queen Catherine. Jack Barak, my former assistant and friend, I saw seldom – and clandestinely – for his wife Tamasin, once also a friend, had never forgiven me for leading him, three years before, into an affair where he had lost a hand, and nearly died. Their little boy, George, nearly four now, was my godson, but Tamasin would not allow me to visit the house. I had never even seen their daughter. My former servant boy, Timothy, was gone to be an apprentice, my old servant girl, Josephine, was now married and far away in Norfolk. Her last letter to me had suggested that she and her husband were in difficulty; I had sent back some money and asked her to let me know how she fared, for I knew she was pregnant, but there had been no reply, which was unlike her, and it worried me.

I sat on the bed and thought, I am become melancholy. And then the realization hit me, starkly: It is because I am lonely. I had seen Timothy and Josephine almost as the children I had never had. It was foolish, foolish. And I was becoming bored with my work, the endless land conveyances, the negotiations to buy farms and manors that sometimes petered out into nothing. I had been much happier in the years when I represented poor men at the Court of Requests. I had looked forward to getting Nicholas to assist me in such cases, perhaps knocking some of his gentlemanly prejudices out of him, but when, two years ago, Rich became Lord Chancellor, it was indicated that my post was needed for another. I shook my head sadly.

✢

AS I READIED FOR BED, I remembered that frightening day in January again. Elizabeth had escaped the accusations against her, as had her servants; Parry had been allowed to return to Elizabeth's service, though Kat Ashley was still kept away. Thomas Seymour had died by the axe in March; the execution of his own brother for treason had caused much gossip, and weakened the Protector. I had not seen Rich since. My office had indeed been searched by his men, probably more to make a nuisance than anything else. I had had to tell Nicholas and Skelly, who had been present when the searchers arrived, what had happened. I had seen fear in Nicholas's face then, and had understood it; he was remembering the last time I had been involved in the savage world of court politics, during the plot against Catherine Parr three years before. Through me he had been drawn into its coils, though he was only a lad just up from the countryside. We had seen terrible things.

I saw myself reflected in the window; the candle picked out the deepening lines on my face, the growing stoop of my hunched back, my hair still thick but completely white. I seldom prayed these days but that night I knelt and asked God's help for my sick friend Guy, for Josephine in her unknown troubles, for the Lady Elizabeth, and for those unknown men out in the countryside on whom Fowberry had set the Hatfield Watch.

Chapter Two

NEXT MORNING, WE ROSE early and, after breakfasting, rode the short distance to Hatfield Palace with Fowberry and his men. The weather had turned warmer, with a light wind and fleecy clouds high in the sky. Nicholas wore his short black robe, and I wore my hood, white serjeant's coif, and dark silk summer gown, the breeze stirring the fur collar. My horse, Genesis, had been reluctant to set out that morning, and I realized he was getting too old for such long journeys.

Hatfield Palace was modern and commodious, built in bright red brick around a central courtyard, with a park beyond enclosed by high walls. It was Elizabeth's main residence now, containing her household of some hundred and fifty people. Standing in the main doorway to meet us was a middle-aged woman with a round face, keen eyes and an air of confident severity. She wore a black dress and old-fashioned gable hood. A large bunch of keys hung at her waist. I had met Blanche apHarry before; Welsh, like Thomas Parry, she had served Elizabeth since babyhood and controlled the running of the house and access to her mistress. We dismounted and bowed to her. With a nod and a wave of her hand she dismissed Fowberry and his men, who led our horses to the stables. She looked hard at Nicholas, who carried a folder containing paper for making notes, then turned to me with a brief smile.

'God give you good morrow, Serjeant Shardlake. I fear you will have had a wet journey yesterday.'

'We did, mistress, but made it safely.'

She nodded. 'Good. Master Parry awaits you. The Lady Elizabeth will receive you later.'

She led us into the building. It was decorated with tapestries and good furniture, but in a sober style very different from the colourful, rather overblown decoration the old king had favoured in his palaces. The servants, too, were dressed in blacks and browns; a Protestant style for a Protestant mistress.

We came to a corridor I recognized, and stopped outside Master Parry's office. Turning to us, Mistress Blanche spoke quietly. 'As Master Parry will tell you, I know about the matter on which he wishes to instruct you. Nobody else in the house does, and nothing –' she looked sharply at Nicholas again – 'nothing is to be said outside Master Parry's office.' Nicholas bowed his head in acknowledgement. Mistress Blanche knocked at the door. Within, Parry's deep voice called us to enter. Mistress Blanche drew the door shut behind us, and I heard the chink of the keys at her waist fade as she walked away.

Thomas Parry was a tall man in his early forties, a once-powerful body now running to fat. His rubicund face was dominated by a large nose and small, penetrating blue eyes, his black hair cut fashionably short. Elizabeth's Comptroller, her man of business. Like many in official positions he had cut his teeth working for Thomas Cromwell, helping him intimidate the monasteries into surrender the decade before. He came over to us, his manner bluff and cheerful as usual.

'Matthew. Good morrow. I am sorry to bring you out here at such short notice. Good thinking to bring a change of clothes with that pissing rain. God knows what the harvest will be like, the barley is weeks behind.'

'I was thinking the same yesterday, Master Parry.'

'Fowberry tells me you spotted some men camping not far from here. Turned out to be a crew of masterless men. Northampton shoe workers whose trade had gone under, making for London, according to their tale of woe. They had clubs and knives about them though, so I wonder. Anyway, the Hatfield Constable and Watch kicked their arses out of the parish.'

'I see.'

'Ah, don't look so disapproving, Matthew. I know you Common-wealth men would have all the beggars given gold.' He winked at Nicholas.

'Work, at least.'

'Ah, Matthew, if all were given jobs, wages would rise, prices even

more, and then where would we be?' Parry smiled again, the know-
ledgeable man of affairs arguing against the idealistic lawyer. Looking
at his plump, cheerful face, though, I remembered what Rich had said
in January; when he was shown the instruments in the Tower he had
been happy to tell all he knew of Thomas Seymour. But who, in those
circumstances, would not start talking? And nothing Parry confessed
had implicated Elizabeth. He was shrewd, and loyal.

He turned to Nicholas, who had accompanied me on visits to his
London office before. 'What of you, lad, do you read all the pamphlets
and sermons against the greedy rich men?'

'No, sir,' Nicholas replied. 'I think such talk threatens the right
social order.'

'Good lad.' Parry nodded approval. 'How far on with your studies
are you now? Called to the bar yet?'

'Before long, I hope. I began my studies late.'

'Well, your work has always seemed conscientiously done.' His face
changed suddenly and, like Mistress Blanche, he gave Nicholas a hard
look. 'Can you be trusted with confidential matters? With depraved,
revolting details that would titillate all the gossiping lawyers?'

'Depraved, sir?' Nicholas's eyes widened. He had not expected
that. Neither had I. But Parry's face remained set.

'Yes, about as nasty as you can get.'

'I have never broken a client's confidence, Master Parry.'

The Comptroller turned to me, his voice suddenly hard. 'Can
he be fully trusted, Matthew, in all matters? This thing is out of the
common run.'

'Master Overton has kept serious confidences before. When I
worked for the late queen.'

Parry nodded, then smiled, all bonhomie again, and clapped
Nicholas on the shoulder. 'I had to be certain.' He went behind his desk
and sat down, motioning us to chairs set in front. 'Then we had best
begin. There is none too much time.' He slid an inkpot across the desk
towards Nicholas. 'Take notes, Overton, but only of names and places,
and keep them safe. What I am about to tell you is known only to
myself, Mistress Blanche, and the Lady Elizabeth, who has personally
requested that you undertake this investigation.' He frowned, as though

doubtful of her wisdom, then continued, 'She will speak with you afterwards, Matthew. But do not mention the more gruesome aspects of the story. We had to tell her, but I fear it near turned her stomach.'

Nicholas and I looked at each other. This was indeed no query about land ownership.

'Have either of you been to Norfolk?' Parry asked.

'No, sir,' Nicholas answered. 'I come from Lincolnshire, but over by the Trent.'

'And I have never been,' I replied. 'Though I had a goodly number of clients from the county in the days when I represented poor folk at the Court of Requests.'

'Ah yes.' Parry smiled cynically. 'You'll know the saying, then, "Norfolk wiles, many men beguiles". I've heard the commons there are the most litigious in the country, forever suing gentlemen over rents and enclosure of common land. What's that other saying? "Every Norfolk man carries Lyttelton's Tenures at the plough's tail".'

'Certainly Norfolk people have good knowledge of their rights. And are ready to club together to obtain representation in Requests where the common law won't help them.'

'Did you win many cases for these oppressed Norfolk commons?'

'Some. Despite the law's delays and the landlords' own wiles.'

Parry grunted. 'Well, the people this matter concerns are gentry; I would say as little as possible about your old days at Requests.'

I observed, 'The gentlemen of Norfolk have a reputation for being as quarrelsome with each other as with their tenants. Particularly since the old king destroyed the Howards and stripped them of their lands. They used to be masters there.'

Parry nodded. 'I know. The old Duke of Norfolk kept a certain rough order. Now he sits in the Tower year after year, under that sentence of treason trumped up by the old king. The Protector hasn't the balls to execute him; he's waiting for him to die. He won't, though, from sheer obstinacy, though he's past seventy-five.' Parry laughed brusquely, raising his eyebrows. 'As you know, his lands have mostly been sold to the Lady Mary, and she is building up a landed interest in East Anglia. She has taken up residence at Kenninghall, the Duke's Norfolk palace. I believe she is there now.'

'The Lady Elizabeth wanted to build an estate in Norfolk, did she not?'

'I know several proposed purchases there fell through,' Nicholas said. 'I wondered at the Lady Elizabeth's interest in that county.'

'The Boleyn family are from Norfolk,' I explained.

'I thought their home was Hever, in Kent,' Nicholas said.

Parry shook his head. 'They were Norfolk gentry originally. I have wondered if Mary has looked to build up an affinity there to spite her sister. She hates her enough. She truly believes Elizabeth isn't Henry's daughter at all, that Anne Boleyn had her by her lover Mark Smeaton. *Pentwyr o cachu.*'

Nicholas looked puzzled.

'Pile of shit,' Parry translated.

I looked at him in surprise. 'I've not heard that story.'

He smiled tightly. 'Oh, I have one or two – shall we say observers – in Mary's household at Kenninghall, as, no doubt, the Lady Mary does here.' He leaned forward, clasping his plump hands together. 'Which is one reason I stressed the importance of keeping this matter close. I know the Lady Mary was mighty sore when Elizabeth escaped charges in January.' He frowned again and shook his head. 'Having Mary at Kenninghall now is a complication. The story is not widely known yet, but when the Norfolk assizes start, it will be.' He looked at me hard. 'It concerns members of the Boleyn family; distant relatives, but relatives of the Lady Elizabeth nonetheless. That is why it is delicate.'

'And you said, depraved –'

Parry leaned back. He said quietly, 'The Boleyns have been minor Norfolk gentry time out of mind. Living on their estates, collecting their rents, occasionally sending a clever son to make his way in London, like Anne Boleyn's great-grandfather. But they were never big fish until the old king set his cap at the Lady Elizabeth's mother. When Anne Boleyn and her immediate family fell, the Norfolk Boleyns continued as out-of-the-way landowners, keeping quiet. The family name had acquired a certain notoriety.'

'Yes,' I agreed quietly. 'Which it still has.' Thirteen years after Anne Boleyn's execution, some people, especially religious traditionalists, still screwed up their faces at mention of her name. I had been present at her execution and for a moment saw again in my mind's eye that grey spring morning, the silent crowd, the sword flashing through the air and the spray of blood as the Queen's head was severed. I suppressed a shudder.

Parry continued, 'But the Lady Elizabeth is rich now, and occasionally people come here asking favours, claiming to be poor kin from Norfolk fallen on hard times.'

'As always happens when people come into much money, and have a large household full of positions.'

'Exactly. Mistress Blanche and I have always discouraged such visitors. The Lady Elizabeth has sometimes wanted to meet one of these so-called relatives, but we have always advised against. Even now, Boleyn associations are best avoided.' He raised his bushy eyebrows. 'Frankly, we usually do not tell her when someone turns up claiming distant kinship.' He gave a short, barking laugh. 'A couple of times she has found out from other servants that we have turned people away. Then Mistress Blanche gets the sharp end of her tongue. And I get the inkpot thrown at me if I'm lucky, the paperweight if not.' He rubbed one cheekbone reminiscently, then continued. 'I always investigate these people afterwards, and they have nearly always turned out to be fraudulent. I have a barrister who acts for me on such matters, Aymeric Copuldyke, together with a Norfolk man in his employ, Toby Lockswood.'

I said, 'I met Copuldyke at your office last summer. He had called to see you. We only exchanged a few words.' I remembered a short, fat man, perspiring and irritable in the heat.

Parry grunted. 'Toby Lockswood is more useful than his master. You will need to speak to both when you return to London.'

Nicholas said quietly, 'It must be hard for the Lady Elizabeth, to have no close family.' I glanced at him. He knew better than most.

Parry answered sharply, 'In the Lady Elizabeth's case, it is politic to keep Boleyn relatives at a distance –' He hesitated. 'Mistress Blanche tells me she wears a locket round her neck containing her mother's image. Such loyalty could be exploited by some fraud. Make another scandal.' Parry sighed deeply, and I realized he was under strain. He paused, then continued, 'Just a month ago, on the fourth of May,

Mistress Blanche brought me news of a woman who had turned up in the servants' hall. She claimed to be a distant cousin by marriage to the Lady Elizabeth, who had fallen on hard times since her husband died and their landlord ended his tenancy. Normally Mistress Parry would have thrown her out, but there were things about this woman that led her to suggest we both see her.'

'What things?' I asked.

'She was about fifty, to begin with, while most who try that game are young. She had blonde hair turning grey, cut short, against nits no doubt. And, though she was dressed in rags, she spoke in refined tones, not that incomprehensible Norfolk draunt, which showed she came of good stock. So Mistress Blanche brought her to me.' Parry shook his head. 'By Jesu, she was a poor-looking creature. She looked half starved. She had a thin face pinched with cold and hunger, hair dirty under her coif, and was wearing a cheap wadmol dress.'

Nicholas observed, 'A real gentlewoman would surely have had clothes of fine material, even if they were worn with use.'

Parry nodded. 'Well observed.' He paused. 'But this woman's accent sounded genuine. And she seemed worn out, truly desperate. She said she was sorry to trouble us, she was only distant kin by marriage, but had nowhere else to turn. Those who come here with such claims usually gawp at the house with awe, or at least interest, but this woman hardly seemed to notice anything. So I invited her to sit down and tell me her story. She did so, and it sounded plausible. At first,' he added grimly.

'She said her name was Mistress Edith Boleyn, and that until the death of her husband last November she had been mistress of a goodly farm near Blickling, fifteen miles north of Norwich. That's where Anne Boleyn's family came from, though there are other Boleyns scattered around Norfolk. I asked for details about the farm and she said it was a large one, but the lease ended with her husband's death and the lord of the manor would not renew it. He was turning his lands over to sheep. She was given three months to quit.' He smiled sardonically. 'Just the sort of thing your friends the Commonwealth men rail against, though it can happen to wealthy tenants as well as poor ones.'

'Did she not have children, relatives?'

'She said she had no children and both her parents were dead.' A flicker of compassion crossed his heavy features. The plight of Edith Boleyn had evidently moved Parry, hard man of affairs though he was. 'If I had known then –' he said, quietly, then lapsed into uncharacteristic silence.

'Did she say exactly how her late husband was related to the Lady Elizabeth?' I asked.

Parry nodded. 'She said he shared a common great-great-grandfather with Anne Boleyn.'

In my work I dealt often with matters of family descent, and made a quick calculation. 'Making him third cousin once removed to Elizabeth.'

'She had the family tree off pat. Wrote it down for me on a sheet of paper, all the way back to Geoffrey Boleyn, who came to London in the 1420s and became Lord Mayor. It was obviously painful for her to write, her fingers were bent and the knuckles of both hands badly swollen. She wrote in a good hand, though, which showed she was educated. I noticed she wore no wedding ring, and asked her about that. She said that when her fingers became swollen she had to have it cut off as it was pressing painfully into the skin. I was starting to believe her.' Parry raised his bushy eyebrows again, and his voice hardened. 'But then I asked for some more details, and her story began to fall apart.'

'How?'

'When I asked the name of the lord of the manor who had dispossessed her, the details of the tenancy, the name of the nearest town and the local families, she came out with a list of sheer fictions. She had rehearsed them well but had not taken into account that my past experiences have given me, with lawyer Copuldyke's help, a detailed knowledge of Norfolk geography. When I challenged her she began to stammer and trip over her words. Mistress Blanche and I were both looking at her hard by then, and she saw she was in trouble. In the end she blurted out that her husband was truly kin, and she asked for no more than the humblest place in the household – a maid, a cook's assistant, anything the Lady Elizabeth could give her. She was red in the face by now. I noticed then that her fingers were calloused as well as swollen. This woman had known hard manual labour.' Parry shrugged his broad shoulders. 'Well, after her lies about where she came from, there was nothing to do but turn her out. I thought, whoever she is, she came of gentle stock once, and had fallen on bad times, but that can happen to the best of people these days and does not justify telling such lies. I told her to leave.'

'And did she?'

'I expected her to burst out crying and weeping but she didn't; she only slumped in her chair. I asked Mistress Blanche to show her out. As she led her to the door I put my hand to my purse – I was going to give her a few coins – but Mistress Blanche shook her head. She was right, we cannot encourage liars. The woman left the house as she came, by the back door.' He paused, then looked at me. 'Yet, as I was to discover, though Edith Boleyn was a liar where her personal circum/ stances were concerned, what she said about being related by marriage to the Lady Elizabeth was quite true. And that is why, Master Shard/ lake, we are in trouble.'

'Trouble made by her?' I asked.

Parry gave a humourless laugh. 'Only if you consider getting your/ self murdered in the foulest way imaginable to be making trouble.'

I said quietly, 'So it is a murder you wish me to investigate?'

'It is, I fear.' He looked me in the eye.

People in high places had made that request of me before. It usually provoked a clutch of anxiety at my heart. But in Parry's office in Hat/ field Palace I felt, unexpectedly, a quickening of excitement. I glanced sideways at Nicholas. His face was alive with interest too.

'What happened to her?' I asked.

Parry opened a drawer in his desk, took out a folder and removed a sheet of paper. It was a deposition, a witness statement for a court case. He looked at it. 'I told you that Edith Boleyn – and that *was* her real name – came here on the fourth of May. Eleven days later, early on the morning of the fifteenth, a shepherd named Adrian Kempsley left his cottage in the parish of Brikewell, south of Norwich, to go and tend his master's sheep. The master's name is Leonard Witherington, and he is one of those who has been building up flocks of sheep on his lands, and, yes, encroaching on common land. He is unpopular with his tenantry, and with his neighbour, another landlord.'

I nodded. 'As I said, if they are not quarrelling with their tenants, the Norfolk gentlemen fight with each other.'

Parry continued. 'Between them, Witherington and his neighbour had purchased a large parcel of monastic land when the abbeys went down ten years ago. Apparently, the old monastery deeds were unclear about the boundary and Master Witherington recently claimed a good portion of his neighbour's land.' He raised his eyebrows. 'The neighbour's name is Master John Boleyn, he is Edith's husband, and he is not, as she told us, dead. Though he may be, within the month, dangling on the Norwich gallows.'

Nicholas's eyes widened. 'She had a husband living! Then why come here?'

Parry raised a hand. 'Wait, young man. To continue, according to Adrian Kempsley, whose deposition this is, Witherington's sheep were kept on a large meadow, which slopes down to a stream, which forms the boundary between Witherington's land and that of John Boleyn, though as I said, that boundary is disputed.'

I said, 'There have been many such cases since the monastic lands were sold off, title documents often centuries old and plans faded, or unclear.'

'Indeed,' Parry agreed. 'There has been much rain this spring, as you know, and the stream was full, a good deal of mud around it. Kempsley saw something white sticking out of the stream, and in the early light thought a sheep had got itself trapped. When he came closer, though, he got the shock of his life.' He paused. 'I warn you, this next part is, as I said earlier, depraved and revolting. It was no sheep that Kempsley saw but, sticking up from the water, the naked body of Edith Boleyn. She had been shoved into the stream head first, her head and the upper half of her body buried in the water and the mud beneath. Her lower half stuck up in the air, her legs pulled apart so that her private parts were displayed to the heavens.'

There was a moment's silence. 'Someone must have hated her very much to do that,' I said quietly. 'What was the cause of death?'

'No question about that,' Parry answered. 'She had been struck on the head with something very heavy. Kempsley says the top of her head fell to pieces when they pulled the body out. It must have been placed in the stream the night before. And yet Edith Boleyn had, according to law, already been dead for two years.'

Nicholas had been taking notes, a paper on a wooden board on his knees, but now his quill skittered across the page, dropping blots. 'What?'

Parry laughed bleakly. 'That was my reaction when lawyer Copuldyke told me.' He drew a second deposition from the folder. 'According to John Boleyn, his wife Edith, mother of his two sons, simply vanished one day in 1540, nine years ago. He says they had never got on, but her disappearance was sudden and unexpected. She vanished one winter day with nothing but the clothes she stood up in. John Boleyn enquired of her family – and she does have family, despite what she told us – her servants and the neighbours, but nobody had seen her or could explain her disappearance. She was never seen again. Two years ago, seven years having passed, Master Boleyn applied to the coroner to have Edith declared legally dead. An order was granted, and last year he married his current wife – with whom he had already been living for some years, somewhat to the scandal of the community.'

I considered. 'The courts usually investigate such claims thoroughly, where a spouse has disappeared.'

'They did. The local coroner, apparently, is a man of probity. He found that nobody in the neighbourhood had seen or heard anything of Edith since the day she vanished. During his enquiries the question of her state of mind was raised. Everyone agreed she was a strange, surly woman. According to Boleyn, there were times when she would refuse to eat, and become very thin – she looked starved when she came here, though I thought that was from being penniless on the road.'

'And nobody had seen her in nine years, until she arrived here?'

'Nobody. Apparently, John Boleyn had been carrying on with his current wife even before Edith vanished, and some gossiping woman had told Edith not long before she disappeared; John Boleyn's deposition says that in the period before she left she was full of melancholy and was refusing to eat properly again.' Parry took a deep breath. 'The coroner's view was that Edith had most likely committed suicide, perhaps by drowning herself in a river, the body carried out to sea and never found.'

I said, 'If John Boleyn had been seeing another woman nine years ago, and his wife discovered it and made trouble, that could have given him a reason to murder her then.'

Parry nodded agreement. 'So people said back in 1540. But there was no evidence, no body. John Boleyn left it a year before he moved his lover' – Parry glanced at the depositions – 'Isabella Heath, into his home, but after that they lived together quite openly. She worked in a tavern, would you believe? The neighbouring gentry were outraged, and there were mutterings that such behaviour was only to be expected of a Boleyn. And always the suspicion that he had done away with his wife. Recently, by the way, there had been serious trouble with his neighbour Witherington over the land dispute, involving some sort of violent affray. And there are rumours he is in financial difficulty – he owns several manors, but recently he bought an expensive London house.'

Nicholas said, 'So his wife was actually not dead at all, she had only left him?'

Parry spread his hands wide. 'That is how it appears. She must have been somewhere these last nine years, but God knows where. All we do know is that she was found horribly murdered less than a fort-night after she visited this house.'

'And your lawyer Copuldyke told you about the murder?' I asked.

'He learned of it through his man in Norwich, Lockswood. Copuldyke thought I should know as I had made enquiries about her after she visited Hatfield.'

'And John Boleyn has been arrested?'

'Yes. Edith was identified by her father, and John Boleyn arrested the next day.'

'That is quick,' Nicholas said.

I said, 'In a murder investigation, if you don't find the killer – or a credible suspect – within a few days the trail quickly goes cold.' I turned to Parry. 'What were the grounds for his arrest?'

'Strong ones. There were footprints in the mud around the body, made by large, heavy shoes, well clouted with nails. John Boleyn is a big man and when a search of his house was ordered, a pair of such shoes, covered with mud, were found in the stables, where he keeps a horse so unruly that no one but him dare approach it. Together with a large, heavy hammer, with blood and hair on it.'

Nicholas looked at me. 'Someone could have put them there, to incriminate Boleyn,' he said.

Parry produced another document. 'According to the coroner's report, apart from a stable boy who was apparently half-witted, Boleyn had the only key to the stables. But he will plead not guilty when he appears before the Norwich Assizes this month. The judges have already started out on their circuit tours.'

'Yes,' I said. 'I heard some of them wanted the summer circuits postponed, because of the disturbances last month, but Lord Chancellor Rich would have none of it. The judges are to travel as usual, and show their power.'

'Is Barak on circuit?' Nicholas asked.

'Yes, and on the Norfolk circuit this time. He did the Home circuit last year.'

'Who is Barak?' Parry asked.

'My former assistant. He is now a jobbing solicitor, and works part-time assisting the judges on the summer and winter circuits near London.' I considered. 'The circuit will probably be trying cases in Buckinghamshire now, on their way out to East Anglia.'

Parry said, 'The Norwich Assizes opens on the eighteenth of June. Less than a fortnight away. Could this Barak be useful?'

I answered carefully. 'He might be able to help with information. He worked with me for many years, and is quite trustworthy.'

Parry considered. 'Then I agree that you talk to him about the case. But not about Edith Boleyn's visit to Hatfield.'

'Of course.' I considered. 'Surely there is a good chance of Boleyn being found innocent. If his vanished wife had turned up at his house again after nine years, and he had remarried, that would give him a motive to kill her, but quietly and secretly. Displaying the body publicly like that, showing she had been alive the day before – that automatically invalidates his new marriage, and opens an investigation where he must be a suspect. Why would any sane man do that?'

Parry shrugged. 'Perhaps she returned home and he was so overcome with rage and hatred he temporarily lost his reason. But I agree,

it sounds more like someone wanting to get Boleyn into trouble. As I
said, he is unpopular locally, and I do not need to tell you that counts
for much in a jury trial.'

'What of his family?' I asked. 'His new wife? Has he any children
from his marriage to Edith?'

'His new wife is holed up at his house, I believe. John Boleyn had
twin boys by Edith, they are in their late teens now.' Parry frowned.
'The authorities in Norfolk seem convinced Boleyn will be found guilty
and his lands forfeit to the King. Officials of the Norfolk feodary and
escheator have already been sniffing around his properties. He is rich
enough for his lands to interest the royal officials. I've got Copuldyke to
go on the record as Boleyn's attorney, and warn them off, remind everyone the case is *sub judice*; he is innocent until proven guilty, and his family
should be left alone until and unless he is convicted.'

'Indeed.'

Parry grunted. 'The escheator and feodary, the officials responsible
for the King's properties in Norfolk, are Henry Mynne and, as feodary,
the Lady Mary herself. Both delegate their work to local officials –
Richard Southwell is steward of many of Mary's Norfolk properties
while Mynne's official in that part of Norfolk is John Flowerdew. A
nasty pair. Perhaps you have met Flowerdew? He is a serjeant-at-law
like you, though he concentrates his efforts on grasping as much Norfolk land as he can.'

'No, we've never met.'

'As for Southwell, he is the Lady Mary's creature.' He raised his
eyebrows again. 'Yes, this damned case reaches out to her. I wouldn't
be surprised if she set Southwell on the family.'

I considered. 'Boleyn's indictment for murder is public. From what
you said, there is already gossip in Norwich.'

'Indeed. But that will be nothing to the open scandal if he is found
guilty and hanged. The family name, the foul details of the crime – the
pamphleteers will have the time of their lives, they'll be selling versions
of the story from London to Northumberland.' Parry's voice deepened
with anger. 'I despair when I look at the stuff that floods out of the
printing presses now; Commonwealth men ranting against the rich,
Calvin's people's warning of hellfire and the Apocalypse, the mad

prophecies and lewd stories, the biting and slandering. I wish the damned press had never been invented.'

Nicholas broke the silence that followed by asking him, 'Do you think Master Boleyn guilty, sir?'

Parry gave him an irritated look. 'God's pestilence, lad, how on earth should I know? I have no idea. I know only that Copuldyke's man Lockswood has visited him in Norwich Castle gaol and said he makes a sad and sorry figure.'

I looked Parry in the eye. 'Are you certain nobody knows Edith Boleyn was here? Apart from you and Mistress Blanche?'

'Certain. So far as the other servants noticed her, she was just another poor beggar come to the door. Nobody else knows her name. And they mustn't,' he added with emphasis. 'The Lady Elizabeth cannot be associated with this.'

I asked, 'Then why do you wish us to go to Norfolk?'

Parry sighed, long and hard. '*I* do not wish you to go anywhere. But I had to give the Lady Elizabeth the news of the murder – she would likely have found out through tittle-tattle when it came to trial. Her first reaction was that we must tell the authorities Edith Boleyn had been here. That might mean her movements could be traced back, and then perhaps something could be found out about where she had been these last nine years.'

'Lady Elizabeth was right,' I observed quietly. 'Strictly speaking, if you, or she, know about Edith Boleyn's visit here so soon before her murder, and say nothing, that could be construed as withholding evidence.'

Parry looked at me hard. 'I persuaded the Lady Elizabeth that Mistress Edith, a most distant relation, was no concern of ours, and the last thing she needed, after the Seymour business, was direct associ-ation with a scandal involving murder. Mistress Blanche supported me. Thank God, the Lady Elizabeth is a realist at heart, and eventually agreed we would say nothing and let justice take its course.' He leaned forward, speaking slowly and deliberately. 'Outside this room, Edith Boleyn's visit to this house never happened. Do *not* forget that.'

'Very well.' I was glad that as lawyers in Elizabeth's employ,

Nicholas and I were protected by legal privilege from revealing any-thing Parry told us.

'However –' Parry shook his head – 'the Lady Elizabeth has set two conditions. First, a legal representative of hers should be sent to Norfolk to enquire – delicately – about events. That would be no more than showing legitimate concern that justice was done to John Boleyn. Her wish is that the representative, given your – experience – in such investigations, should be you.'

I considered. 'As it is a criminal trial, Boleyn cannot have represen-tation by counsel because, the burden of proof being guilt beyond a reasonable doubt, the law considers the facts should be so plain that counsel is not needed. Nonsense, of course, but there it is.'

'Complete nonsense,' Nicholas agreed. 'I was shocked when I began studying law and learned that.'

Parry looked at us. 'Personally, I thank God for it, or the Lady Elizabeth would have you arguing John Boleyn's case in court. But we agreed you will only make enquiries about the case, and present any relevant evidence you may find to the authorities. I told her Copuldyke and his man could do that, but she insisted on you.'

'What if I were to find evidence confirming John Boleyn's guilt?'

'Then the law must take its course.' Parry narrowed his eyes. 'It would be convenient for all, Master Shardlake, if you were to find nothing of significance either way. We do not wish to be seen to rock the boat.'

I did not answer directly. 'You said the Lady set another condition.'

'Yes, and I am still trying to dissuade her from it. I hope' – he shook his head, wearily – 'it does not arise. But here it is. If you find evidence to support Boleyn's innocence, but a jury convicts him none-theless, she says she will fund an application for a royal pardon.'

I took a deep breath. The King had the power to grant a pardon nullifying even a verdict of murder. When very wealthy people were convicted of capital offences, there often followed a greasing of palms in the royal household, all the way up to the King. But nowadays, given Edward's youth, in practice that meant a pardon from Protector Som-erset, with whom Elizabeth was already in bad odour.

'I can see why you would dislike that course, Master Parry.'

'She thinks that if the request for a pardon comes from her, the King himself will intervene. But Edward won't lift a finger. He is mildly fond of his sister, but no more. He doesn't see her from one season's end to the next, and he is completely in the power of the Seymours. The family, you will remember, who displaced the Boleyns.' He looked at me hard again. 'I said the Lady Elizabeth was a realist, and she is cautious, but where anything to do with her mother is concerned, her heart begins to rule her head. She is still only fifteen, remember. Help me bury this business, Matthew. For her sake. Let Boleyn be found guilty or not, as the evidence and local politics dictate. I want no application for a pardon.'

'I see,' I said slowly. 'You said your man Copuldyke and his assistant will help me with local information?'

'Yes. Both are now in London, you can speak to them when you return. You will act as Copuldyke's agent, and his man will go to Norfolk with you. Take the lad' – he nodded at Nicholas – 'but use careful judgement if you talk to your friend Barak. Base yourself in Norwich. The Boleyn property is only about a dozen miles from there.'

I did a quick calculation. Today was June the sixth. I would have to get back to London, talk to Copuldyke and Lockswood, and make speedy arrangements to go to Norfolk, a three or four days' journey. It was irritating that I had to return to London, for Hatfield was on the way to Norfolk. I said to Parry, 'It will be a week before I get there. That leaves only a few days to investigate before the Assizes start.'

Parry inclined his head. 'One can only do what one can in the time,' he said, an evasive note in his voice. I wondered whether he had deliberately delayed telling Elizabeth of Edith's murder, to make it less likely that I would have time to find anything that might prove troublesome.

I asked, 'May I have copies of all the documents you have? It will save me having to get them from the court in Norwich.'

'Very well. Your lad can make copies of the case file while you see the Lady Elizabeth. She will be expecting you by now. I will call Mistress Blanche to accompany you.' He rang a bell on his desk. A servant entered, and was sent to find her. 'There is a bench just down the corridor, wait there till she comes. I will have the papers put in a room for

Master Overton to do the copying.' He stood, came over and shook my hand, looking at me as seriously as ever he had. 'Remember, Matthew, the Lady Elizabeth is young, she is learning care and caution in a hard school, but still does not always see what is in her best interests. Do not work this case overmuch, Matthew. Talk to people, as discreetly as you can, attend the Assizes. Keep me informed of developments. But do *not* overwork it.'

Chapter Three

WE FOUND THE bench Parry had indicated, opposite a window giving onto an intricately designed knot garden. There were still a few daffodils in the flowerbeds, extremely late in the season though it was.

'Daffodils are a Welsh emblem, aren't they?' Nicholas observed. 'No doubt they gladden Master Parry's heart.'

I spoke quietly, keeping an eye out for passing servants. 'I think it has needed gladdening these last months. First Seymour's treason, now this murder.'

'He just wants us to check everything is done properly, doesn't he?'

'He'd rather steer clear of the whole business. I see his point of view.'

'Should not justice be done?'

'Of course. But we both know that it can be – hit and miss.'

'The Lady Elizabeth wants us to do what we can.'

I looked at him. 'You do not like Master Parry much, do you?'

'He is too much the politician.'

'He is loyal. I have always respected that. And young as she is, Elizabeth commands here now. He must obey her, but protect her, too.'

'So what if we get to Norfolk and discover John Boleyn is innocent?'

'Then we tell the authorities. But come, let us not think too far ahead. We know only the bones of the case so far.'

Nicholas smiled. 'A change from land conveyances, isn't it?'

'Yes. It certainly is.' I smiled. 'I see you are drawn to this.'

'It will be good to get out of London for a while.'

I sighed. 'I too have become weary of late. And I confess this is – intriguing. And it should hold no danger for us. At least,' I added, 'I hope not.' For a moment I remembered the terrors I had suffered in the past from my involvement with the great ones of the realm, but reflected that this was hardly in the same league. And I genuinely felt the need for a change. I said to Nicholas, 'As I told Master Parry, we have none too much time. It is a long way to Norwich.'

'At least this rash of local disturbances is over.'

'Remember the new Book of Common Prayer is to be used in all church services from Sunday. A lot of people won't like it.'

Nicholas looked at me. 'You have a copy, don't you?'

'Yes, I bought one when it first came out in March.' I was silent a moment, then said, 'The services and psalms in English at last. And Cranmer's translation of the services from the Latin is beautiful.'

'Does the new service truly say the bread and wine do not become the flesh and blood of Jesus on consecration by the priest?'

I shook my head. 'No, the Prayer Book does not go so far. It is deliberately ambiguous. I think Cranmer and Protector Somerset do believe the Communion service is only a commemoration of Christ's sacrifice. But they dare not say that publicly – not yet. This is a compromise, which they hope all will accept.'

'Something people can interpret in their own way?'

'Yes. But no traditionalist will like it. They will want the old Mass, in Latin.'

'So there may be more trouble, over religion this time?'

'These last two years people have accepted things I would once have thought impossible – the taking down of all the images and stained glass, the closure of the chantries. But this may be a step too far for some.'

We sat quietly a moment. Nicholas had an open-minded tolerance in matters of religion, which I admired when so many young people cleaved to extremes. As for myself, once an ardent reformer, I had scarce known what I truly believed for some time.

Nicholas asked, 'Do you think Thomas Seymour went – well – all the way with the Lady Elizabeth last year?'

'I think even he would not have been foolish enough to do that, which is some comfort. But tush, we should not discuss that here.' I had heard the chink of keys, and a moment later Mistress Blanche appeared round the corner, hands clasped before her. She directed Nicholas to an office to do his copying, and ordered me to follow her.

⳿

THE LADY ELIZABETH sat behind a wide desk covered with books and papers. Unlike her brother the King or her elder sister Mary, as his heir, Elizabeth had no canopy of state to sit under. She was dressed in black, a French hood on her head from which her long, auburn hair fell to her shoulders, a token of virginity. I wondered if she wore black still for Catherine Parr, or whether, like the relative austerity of the Hatfield furnishings, it was more a sign of her loyalty to Protestant sobriety. Her face, a long oval like her mother's but with the high-bridged nose and small mouth of her father, made her remarkable, if not beautiful. The square front of her dress showed the full breasts of a girl almost grown, but otherwise she was thin and pale, with dark rings under her brown eyes. She was studying a document as I entered, her long fingers playing nervously with a quill. Blanche announced, 'Serjeant Shardlake, my Lady,' and I bowed deeply as she moved to take a position beside Elizabeth. Blanche kept her eyes on me; I had no doubt everything we said would be reported back to Parry.

Lady Elizabeth studied me a moment, then said in her clear voice, 'Serjeant Shardlake, it is many months since I have seen you.' A shadow crossed her face. 'Not since you called to give me your condolences after the Queen Dowager died.'

'Yes. A sad day.'

'It was.' She put down the quill, and said quietly, 'I know you served that sweet lady well. And I loved her. Truly, despite what some have said.' She took a deep breath. 'I remember when I first met you, four years ago was it not? You were with the Queen Dowager, come to discuss a case.'

'That is right, my Lady.'

She smiled. 'I recall that I asked you about justice, and you said that all deserved it, even the worst of people.'

'You remember well.'

She gave a pleased nod of acknowledgement. Always she liked to show off her memory, her intelligence. She continued, 'How are you faring with turning the money my father left me into land?'

'Matters go quicker now your sister has chosen the land she wants.'

'Oh yes, Mary must always come first. Though we will see how she fares when the Prayer Book comes in. She will have to get rid of all her popish chaplains.' Elizabeth smiled grimly, then waved the matter aside and sat back in her chair. 'Justice, Serjeant Shardlake, I know you have always believed in it, and have sometimes sought it in dark corners. Perusing documents about my lands must seem dull by comparison.'

'I grow older, my Lady, and am content with quieter work. Most of the time,' I added.

'I would have you see justice done now, to my relative and to his poor dead wife. Master Parry will have told you the horrible details.'

'He has. And that you would have me go to Norfolk to' – I chose my words carefully – 'examine the details, satisfy myself that justice is done to Master John Boleyn.'

'Yes. Blanche and Master Parry should never have sent that poor woman away.' She glanced at Blanche, and I was surprised to see that formidable lady colour. Elizabeth's tone softened. 'Oh, I know they only seek to protect me, they fear scandal and the lies told about me round the Protector's court. But I will have this matter properly inves⁄tigated. Parry will have told you of his man, Lawyer Copuldyke.'

'His eyes and ears in that part of the world, I believe.'

'Parry suggested I employ him to deal with this matter. Well, I hold no great opinion of Copuldyke. A puffed⁄up fool. I think you will do better.'

'Thank you for your confidence in me, my Lady.'

'Master Parry has told you to go to Norfolk as soon as possible.'

'He has.'

'And would be glad, I think, if you came back with nothing.' Her voice hardened. 'But if you *do* find something, Serjeant Shardlake, which may affect the outcome of this matter, you are commanded to inform the courts in Norwich. And to tell me.' Elizabeth looked at Mistress Blanche again. 'I will tell Master Parry I am to see all corres⁄pondence.'

'I shall do all I can.' I hesitated, then added, 'Of course, Master Boleyn may be guilty.'

'Then justice must be done,' she said. 'If it can be proved. But if Master Boleyn be found guilty, and you find evidence that he did not kill his poor wife, I will make application to my brother for a pardon. Before you leave I will give you a copy under my seal, which you are to give to the judges should the need arise.' She looked firmly at Blanche, then continued, 'I understand you are to take Lawyer Copuldyke's assistant with you. Rough though he is, I hear he is capable. Also that long lad you came with. I saw him arrive with you from my window. He looked to be trustworthy enough.'

'I trust Master Overton entirely.' I thought, This fractured royal family, how they plan, and calculate, and watch from windows.

'Good.' Elizabeth closed her eyes a moment, and I sensed how tired she was, and weary. She continued, in a sombre tone, 'Master Parry is to give you a copy of all the documents in the case.'

'Master Overton is copying them now. I will do my best to ensure justice is done – you may be sure of that.'

Elizabeth nodded. She sat thoughtfully a moment, then said, with a sad smile, 'You have never married, have you, Serjeant Shardlake?'

'No, my Lady.'

'Why is that?' she asked, with genuine curiosity.

I hesitated. 'I have a certain – disability – in the marriage market.'

'Oh tush,' she said, waving a hand. 'I have known many hunch-backs who have married, and far worse-looking than you.'

I caught my breath. Nobody else would have dared address the matter with such brutal frankness. Mistress Blanche gave a warning cough, but Elizabeth waved it away, those brown eyes on mine.

I laughed uneasily. 'I have perhaps been too demanding where matters of the heart are concerned. More than once I have admired women who were – above my station.' I regretted saying that immediately, for Catherine Parr had been one of them. I wondered if Elizabeth had guessed, but her look was hard to read. I added lamely, 'And I am an old whitehead now, I think it too late for me.'

I had expected her to contradict me again, but instead she nodded, her expression hardening. She said, 'I have decided that I shall never marry.'

'My Lady –' Mistress Blanche began.

Again Elizabeth waved her away imperiously. 'I am telling everyone, so my intentions may be known.'

I ventured, 'But if you should change your mind –'

'Never.' Elizabeth's voice remained calm, but her tone was intense now. 'I want all to know, so there will be no more plots to take me to the altar for the political gain of some man.' She continued looking at me. 'I know what marriage can mean, for women of royal station. I saw what happened to Catherine Parr. How the papists plotted to blacken her good name with my father, and have him do away with her. As you well know. And then, her marriage to Thomas Seymour.' She coloured, the blood rising into her pale face. 'He married her for her position, and behaved without honour, so that she cursed him on her deathbed.'

'My Lady!'

Blanche's voice was insistent now, but still Elizabeth ignored her. She said, 'First there is love, then marriage, then betrayal, then death. That is what happened to Catherine Parr.' She added quietly, 'And one before her.'

I lowered my eyes. She meant her mother. Elizabeth should not be talking to me like this. As though reading my thoughts, she smiled sadly. 'I know I can trust your confidence, Serjeant Shardlake. I have known that since I first met you, and I have come to learn how rare a quality that is. And I know that you will ensure – this time – that a Boleyn is given justice, and the murderer of that poor woman who came to me seeking succour, is punished. Whoever it may be.'

Chapter Four

WHILE NICHOLAS completed his copying I was permitted to take a walk through Hatfield Palace Gardens. Under the blue sky, following the pathways between the trees, I could believe that summer had, at last, arrived. Entering a patch of woodland I spied a deer, feeding on the leaves of a low-hanging branch. Two tiny fauns, just learning to walk on spindly legs, stood beside her. I stood stock-still, watching until the doe moved deeper into the trees, the fauns tripping uncertainly after. I sighed, not welcoming the thought of the long ride back to London.

It was early afternoon when we left; a night's accommodation had been booked for us at an inn at Whetstone, somewhat over halfway back. Parry's man Fowberry brought the horses round and saw us off. As we rode down the drive I glanced back, looking at the windows glinting in the sun, and wondered whether the Lady Elizabeth was watching.

After a few miles my back and legs were already sore. I thought of the coming journey to Norfolk, the longest I had undertaken in several years. I would have an uncomfortable time. I wished I had been less remiss of late in the exercises Guy had set for my back. I wondered whether he himself was better; the next few days would be busy, but I would make time to visit him.

The road to London was quieter than on the way out, and there were no other riders in sight when Nicholas, beside me, said quietly, 'Ho, ahead there.' I saw, walking along the road with their backs to us, a group of a dozen raggedly dressed people. They included a woman and a couple of children, but most were men, one wearing the tattered rags of a soldier's jacket, the white cross of England on the back. Some of the men had staffs, no other weapons visible save the knives all men carried at their belts.

Nicholas said, 'I wonder if those are the people who made the fire we saw last night, that the constable moved on.'

'Perhaps. There are so many on the road these days. They don't look dangerous.'

'All the same, let's get by. They shouldn't be taking the middle of the roadway.'

'There are hedges on either side,' I remonstrated, but Nicholas shouted, 'Make way, there,' and spurred his horse on. I followed. As I passed the little group I had a quick glimpse of faces raw and red from living in the open, straggly beards, scowling expressions. Then we left them behind us.

✝

THE INN AT WHETSTONE, as at Hatfield, was a regular stopping-point on the Great North Road, and again our accommodation was comfortable. We took supper in the parlour, where a few other travel-lers also dined. Unlike at Hatfield, here at least we were anonymous. We dined at a table beneath a window, the long June twilight obviating the need for candles. I had spent an hour before dinner going through the papers Nicholas had copied out in his clear secretary hand, and over dinner we discussed them, in quiet tones, both careful to make no reference to Edith Boleyn's visit to Hatfield.

The information in the papers was sketchy enough – the coroner's verdict of murder, the indictment of John Boleyn for the murder of his wife Edith on the fifteenth of May, his deposition proclaiming his inno-cence, the coroner's report and, potentially fatally, the deposition of the local constable reporting the finding of a pair of mud-encrusted boots and a heavy hammer with blood and hair on it in the stables on Boleyn's property. There were also depositions from the labourer who had found the body, and one from Boleyn's new wife stating that she believed her husband had been at home that evening. She could not swear to his whereabouts the entire time, however, as he had gone to his study for two hours before coming to bed, and had asked specifically not to be

disturbed as he wanted to peruse his land deeds and other legal documents. He was concerned about the dispute with his neighbour
Witherington.

'I wonder what that work was,' I mused. 'It was a boundary dispute. And the body was found in the ditch forming the disputed
boundary. Yet to leave the body in that ditch – it draws attention to the
dispute, as well as to Boleyn. Why would the neighbour do that?' I
shook my head. 'The key to this case is the fact of the body being left
in that state in that ditch. It makes one less likely to suspect Boleyn – if
he killed her, surely he would have made sure the body was well and
truly buried. The only purpose I can think of in leaving it where it was,
is to cause maximum humiliation to the dead woman.'

Nicholas said, 'Boleyn's new wife would have had reason to hate
her.'

'Wife no longer. Legally, since Edith was alive all the time, the
prior declaration of her death is invalidated, and so is Boleyn's new
marriage. Again, if his new wife were involved, she would have
wanted the body well hidden.'

Nicholas thought a moment. 'There are no depositions from
Boleyn's sons by Edith. Twin boys of eighteen, are they not?'

'Yes. Perhaps they were not at home. What must they have made of
it all? Their mother abandoning them – for that is what she did – when
they were small, and then her being found like that after all this time. I
wonder what the second wife's relations with them were like.' I leaned
back. 'Well, we shall find out more from Lawyer Copuldyke tomorrow.'

'When do we leave for Norfolk?'

'I should think Monday.' I smiled. 'Do not worry, we shall keep
our dinner engagement on Saturday, and you will get to see Mistress
Kenzy. But after that we may be away a couple of weeks. I must check
with Skelly that all the work is kept in hand.' I sighed. 'I am not looking forward to the ride. And I must hire another horse. Genesis is
getting old, like his master, and I should have a younger animal for this
journey. Your horse should do, though.'

He smiled. 'Yes. Lancelot is a fine beast.' It was two months since
Nicholas had bought a sturdy young gelding which, I suspected, had

denuded his savings. He looked at me, hesitated, then asked, 'Sir, is it
only the long journey that worries you?'

'Yes. I want to go. I need something for my mind to —' involuntar-
ily, I clenched a fist — 'to bite on. Even if the details are nasty.'

'We may meet a murderer.'

I nodded. 'We shall certainly meet John Boleyn.'

'And if it is someone else?'

I smiled. 'Then I will have you there to ensure I am not knocked
on the head.' I looked at him, then added more seriously, 'Unless you
would rather not.'

'No. So long as there is no politics. No mixing with the rulers of
the realm who would kill men as easily as a fly.'

'Ay, and I regret that it was through me that you learned how they
can behave. But we are not going to Norfolk to play a political game,
rather we play down Elizabeth's interest. Not that she is of great
moment in the political scheme of things just now.'

He considered. 'We should bear in mind that quarrels over land
can also be vicious.'

'Yes. They make fat purses for us lawyers. And they're not always
resolved through the law. Parry said Boleyn and his neighbour had
been involved in some sort of violent affray.'

Nicholas picked up a piece of bread from his plate and crumbled
it between his long fingers, suddenly looking thoughtful, and sad. 'My
father —' he broke off.

'Yes?'

'Five years ago, he had a quarrel with a neighbouring landowner,
who, like my father, had the right to pasture beasts on the local
common land. My father — for he began the trouble — started overstocking. There is only grass for so many beasts. His neighbour went to
the manor court, but my father had greased the palm of the lord of the
manor, and so his right to graze was upheld.'

'If his neighbour had gone to the higher courts, pleaded manorial
custom—'

'You know how long that can take. Seasons pass, and beasts need
to eat. The neighbour got together with the poor tenants of the village,
whose grazing rights were also affected, and drove out my father's

beasts, threatening to set about him with cudgels if he came back. My father barked about hiring men of his own, but the local Justice of the Peace stepped in, settled the matter against my father and said he would have no battles between bands of ruffians in his jurisdiction.' Nicholas's face set in hard lines. 'My father can be fierce, but he is not brave enough to get himself in trouble with the Justice.' He wiped the remaining crumbs from his fingers.

I looked at him, wondering not for the first time what it must have been like for him, only child to a hard, unjust man. Nicholas smiled wryly. 'My father was furious, said that allowing himself to be intimidated by a gang of peasants impugned his honour.'

'His status, at least,' I said.

'It was no matter of honour. Honour is a right behaviour, honest dealing between gentlemen, and recognition of the right order of society. He was right at least that his neighbour should not have descended to hiring common folk to brawl with each other.'

'From what you say, the poor tenants' interests were under threat as well.'

'They have their rights, but also their place.' He looked down at the table. 'Well, I am out of that now.'

'It sounds like a similar affair in Norfolk.'

'But at least here I can take a lawyer's impartial view.' He laughed, a bitter laugh for one so young. He washed his fingers in the bowl of water provided for us and wiped them on his napkin. 'I think I shall go to bed. It has been a long day.'

'It has. But, strangely, I am not tired. My mind has been working too hard. I think I shall go for a walk, clear my head.'

✝

OUTSIDE IT WAS still light, the air fresh and clear. Whetstone village consisted only of a few houses straggling down the road to an old church. The church doors were open, and I walked towards them, entering the lychgate and following the path between the gravestones.

Within, a man was whitewashing one wall, broad brushstrokes covering a painting of angels in bright flowing robes. The other walls were already whitened over. The stained-glass windows had gone as well, replaced with plain glass in accordance with Archbishop Cranmer's injunctions. The rood screen was down, the altar open to the body of the church. On one wall the Ten Commandments had been painted in black Gothic script; the idolatry and imagery of the past replaced with the Word of God, though most of the parishioners would be illiterate.

I sat on one of the chairs set out for elderly members of the congregation, and watched the painter work on. I thought, Here is the faith denuded of papist ceremony and ritual that I had argued for so fiercely as a young man. And yet I remembered too, as a country child, how in the grey bleak months of winter it was wonderful to experience the colour and brightness of the church on Sunday, smell the incense and see the paintings; a feast for the senses, attuning the mind to things of the spirit. Even the mumming of the Latin Mass had once sent a thrill through me. Well, I had rejected all that. I had got what I wanted and now it seemed cold, and hard, and stark.

The workman ceased his labours and began washing his brushes in a pail of water. He jumped when he saw me sitting there in my black robe, then took off his cap and approached, bowing.

'Forgive me, sir, I did not see you.' He looked to be in his fifties, his lined face flecked with paint.

I smiled. 'You are working late, fellow.'

'Ay. And must start again at first light tomorrow. Our new vicar wants all done for the new Prayer Book service on Sunday.'

'You are doing a thorough job.'

'I'm being paid well enough, though—' The man broke off and stared at me with bright blue eyes, a bold look from a working fellow to a gentleman. 'In a way I'm being paid with my own money, and that of my ancestors.'

'How so?'

'Because this work is being paid for from church funds, we couldn't afford it if it weren't for the money from the sale of all the old silver plate we were ordered to remove. There was one candle holder, beautifully carved, it was bought by my great-grandfather's family for a candle dedicated to him, perpetually lit in the church.' He looked at one of the many empty niches, then lowered his eyes and said hastily,

'I know, we must obey King Edward's orders as we did King Henry's. I am sorry if I offended at all.'

'Change is sometimes hard,' I said quietly.

'Did you have business with the vicar, sir?' He looked anxious now, afraid he had said too much.

'No, I am just a traveller who wandered in.'

He nodded, relieved. 'I must lock up now, for the night.'

I left the church. When I closed the door it made a hollow, echoing noise.

✝

I DID NOT FEEL like returning to the inn; there was a wooden bench beside the church and I sat down, watching the sun set. I reflected that old King Henry himself would not have approved of what was happening, but power rested now with the Duke of Somerset and with Cranmer, who were taking England halfway to the continental radicals like Zwingli and Calvin. Though there were, of course, plenty who did approve, especially in London where some churches had even replaced the altar with a bare Communion table. Yet it had all been imposed from above, like every religious change these last sixteen years, whether people liked it or not. I recalled the sudden fear in the painter's eyes after he spoke to me about the candle holder. I remembered Jack Barak's total cynicism, his disrespect for both sides of the religious divide. 'Balls to it all,' he had said when we last met for a drink a couple of weeks before, in a tavern near the Tower where we were unlikely to see anyone who knew his wife Tamasin.

Tamasin. I shook my head sorrowfully. I had been present the day she met her husband, and for years we had been good friends; I had shared her sorrow at the death of her first child, her joy at the birth of the second. But for three years now she had been my open enemy. I recalled the terrible night when she learned Barak had been maimed, and might die, after I had got him, behind her back, to help me in a dangerous enterprise. I remembered her balled fists, the fury in her face as she cried out, 'You will leave us alone, never come near us again!' She blamed me for what had happened, as I partly blamed myself, though Barak stoutly insisted he was responsible for his own actions.

When Barak had recovered sufficiently Guy had worked to find a suitable prosthesis for his missing right hand. They had settled on a device, strapped to his arm above the elbow, with a little metal stump at the end, from which a short knife protruded. Underneath it was a curved half-circle of metal, with which Barak could carry things and even, after practice, ride, while the knife could be used at table, to manipulate latches and open boxes, and in the last resort, in the dangerous London streets, serve as a weapon. It was a clumsy-looking thing, but he had learned to use it with dexterity. And, to my amazement, he had taught himself to write with his left hand. It was a scrawl, but perfectly readable.

As Tamasin had forbidden him to work for me again, Barak had looked for work among the solicitors – some respectable and others less so – who found work for the barristers around the Inns of Court. He found employment easily, for he had gained a high reputation as my assistant. He now worked for various solicitors; finding witnesses, taking depositions, rooting out evidence, no doubt with a little bribery and perhaps threats along the way. He had also gained a place as a junior assistant to the judges when, twice a year, they made their circuits of the localities, trying civil and criminal cases, and ensuring the magistrates were carrying out the Protector's instructions. Barak's work was in assessing jurors, rooting out reluctant witnesses, helping with the paperwork, and sniffing out the local mood in the taverns. He worked on the two nearest circuits to London, the Home Counties and the Norfolk circuit, which travelled from Buckinghamshire to East Anglia. Each circuit lasted a month, and though it paid well, he had refused work on the more distant circuits as Tamasin did not like him spending too much time away from her and the children. I suspected, too, that with his disability riding to the longer circuits would be tiring. Though he never mentioned it, when we met I could sometimes tell that his arm was painful.

I remembered him telling me, at our recent meeting, that he was coming to dislike circuit work. People in the localities feared the judges, arriving in the towns in their robes red as blood, with pomp and ceremony. 'It's the way the criminal trials are going,' he said. 'The judges don't encourage jurors to give the accused the benefit of the doubt on capital charges the way they did. There are more hangings every time. And that comes from orders at the top.'

'From Chancellor Rich?' I asked him.

'I think from the Protector and those around him. The Calvinists, who want to root out and punish sin.'

'So much for the Protector's promise of milder times when he abolished the old Treasons Act.'

Barak spat in the sawdust on the tavern floor. 'Milder climes for radical Protestants. Bishop Gardiner's in gaol, and all unlicensed preaching's forbidden. Funny sort of mildness.'

'Who are the judges on the Norfolk circuit this summer?'

'Reynberd and Gatchet.'

'Watch Reynberd,' I said. 'He has the air of an easy-going, sleepy old fellow but he's sharp and watchful as a cat.'

'I've been on circuit with Gatchet before,' Barak said. 'He's clever, but cold and hard as a stone. He's one of Calvin's followers. The hang-man will be busy.'

✞

THE SUN WAS ALMOST below the horizon now; I stood up, wincing at the stiffness in my back and legs. There was barely enough light now to see my way down the church path. I thought that if I saw Barak in Norfolk, and Tamasin learned of it, she would consider it a betrayal on his part. And then, with a burst of anger, I reflected that chance had taken us to the same Assizes, which was hardly uncommon in the small legal world, and we could not just ignore each other. And why should I not seek his help in gathering information? There was nobody better at keeping his ear to the ground.

I stumbled over a projecting oak root, and cursed. Watching my way carefully, I went through the lychgate and headed up the street, the flickering candlelight from the inn windows guiding me back.

Chapter Five

THOUGH WE LEFT Whetstone village early the following morning, we did not enter London till after midday, for a couple of
miles out of the City we found ourselves stuck behind a row of gigantic carts, each drawn by eight heavy horses and laden with new-cast
bricks. The drivers wore the Protector's red and yellow coat of arms
and we followed at a snail's pace as the carts lumbered on, making deep
ruts in the road.

'More bricks for Somerset House,' Nicholas observed sourly.

'Ay, Edward Seymour's palace will eat up half of London before
he's done.' Since becoming Protector, the Duke of Somerset had
begun work on a vast new palace on the Strand, clearing away rows of
old tenements and even digging up part of the ancient St Paul's Cathedral charnel house, sending cartloads of bones of ancient distinguished
Londoners to be buried with the rubbish out in Finsbury Fields.

Nicholas said, 'I hear he's ordered two million bricks for rebuilding
that crumbling old family place of his in Wiltshire – what's it called,
Wolf's Hole?'

'Wolf Hall. All paid for by the public purse, empty though it is.'

We had to halt outside the Moorgate, for there was scarce enough
space for the carts to enter. I saw a new proclamation in the King's
name posted outside: from now on the gates were to be closed during
the hours of darkness, and a good night watch to be appointed in each
ward.

'Are they expecting trouble after the new service on Sunday?' Nicholas asked. 'Even though most of London is Protestant.'

'Not everyone,' I replied. The atmosphere in the city that spring
had been tense, pamphlets against the Pope and the Mass everywhere.
The performance of plays and interludes was already prohibited, and

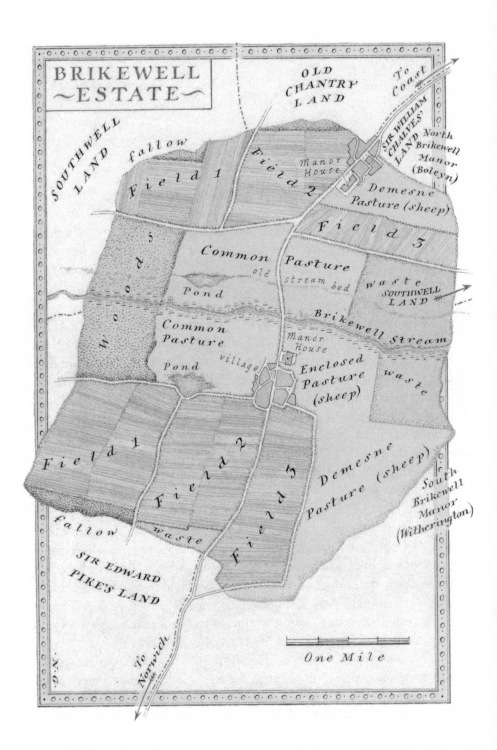

BRIKEWELL ~ESTATE~

SOUTHWELL LAND

OLD CHANTRY LAND

To Coast

SIR WILLIAM CHALVES' LAND

North Brikewell Manor (Boleyn)

fallow

Field 1

Field 2

Manor House

Demesne Pasture (sheep)

Field 3

Common Pasture

old stream bed

waste SOUTHWELL LAND

Pond

Woods

Brikewell Stream

Common Pasture

Manor House

village

Enclosed Pasture (sheep)

waste

Pond

Field 1

Field 2

Field 3

Demesne Pasture (sheep)

South Brikewell Manor (Witherington)

fallow

waste

SIR EDWARD PIKE'S LAND

D.N.

To Norwich

One Mile

servants and youths required to keep off the streets after dark. The May disturbances in the countryside, and the unruly behaviour of soldiers from the encampments outside the city waiting to go up to the Scottish war, had added to the authorities' concerns.

The last cart passed through the city gates, almost flattening one of the city guards as it lurched sideways over a deep rut. The man stared after it, white-faced.

'Come on,' I said. 'We're through.'

✝

WE RODE DOWN TO Cheapside, making for my house at Chancery Lane. The city was busy and noisy as ever, blue-coated apprentices and workmen in leather or wadmol jackets jostling with goodwives in their coifs and aprons, while gentlemen with swords and bucklers at their waists, retainers beside them, pushed their way through. The view from the saddle showed plenty of hollow cheeks and anxious faces. This was a hard time of the year, with last year's store of winter food running low, two months until the new harvest, and prices raging ahead. Beggars in ragged blankets crouched in doorways, a host of them around the great Cheapside Cross, crying for alms, trying to catch the eyes of those who passed.

I said to Nicholas, 'Come with me to my house and change, then we can go to see Copuldyke. He is a Lincoln's Inn man, so thank God is nearby. You can go back to your lodgings after our meeting.'

✝

WE PASSED ST PAUL'S Cathedral, then went under Newgate to my house in Chancery Lane. There, I ordered my steward John Goodcole to take our packs, see to the horses and prepare some water for us to wash. I went to my bedroom to lie down and ease my back; from below I heard the familiar sounds of bustle in the house. Since the death of my housekeeper Joan four years before, I had had to sack two stewards in succession for serious misdemeanours. Two years ago, however, John Goodcole, his wife and their twelve-year-old daughter had come to work for me after their old master, another Lincoln's Inn lawyer, died. He had been a man with a large family, and in working for me, a bachelor, the Goodcole family had found an easy berth. But they did their work diligently, and as a family were a contented trio, at ease with each other and genuinely keen to do good service. I gathered from gossips at Lincoln's Inn that they favoured the old religion, but was happy to turn a blind eye to that.

There was a knock on the door. I heaved myself up and bade John Goodcole enter with my washing-bowl. It was time to make myself presentable again. And I needed to ask him to hire a horse to take me to Norfolk on Monday.

✝

AYMERIC COPULDYKE practised from an office in a corner of Lincoln's Inn Square. I knew most of my fellow barristers to some extent, but as I told Parry, had only met Copuldyke once. His main practice was in Norfolk, and he was often away. He did not look very pleased to see Nicholas and me when we arrived, but bade us enter. He was a short, fat man in his fifties with a beaky nose, a wobbling double chin and a fussy, discontented air. As he asked us to sit he waved casually at a well-built young man in a neat grey doublet sitting at a small desk under the window. 'My solicitor for business in Norfolk, Toby Lockswood.' Lockswood rose and gave us a quick bow before sitting again. He had thick, curly black hair, an equally thick beard, and a round, snub-nosed face. His bright blue eyes were keen. This was the man Parry had said was sharper than his master.

Copuldyke leaned back in his chair and said, in tones of peevish irritation, 'This is a nasty business Master Parry has got us involved in.' He shook his head. 'I was reluctant to have my name associated with it, but Master Parry – well, his mistress has deep pockets, as you know.' He shot me a calculating glance. 'But I will be only too glad to have you act as my agent in this, Serjeant Shardlake, and myself stay here in London. I have no civil matters on at the summer Assizes,' he added. 'As a Norfolk man, Serjeant Shardlake, I know how unpleasant disputes can get up there.' He narrowed his eyes. 'Also the Protector's commissions to investigate illegal enclosures will be setting out soon, I'm told, and the Norfolk peasants will all be claiming land rights, saying Jack is as good as his master. I want to stay away from all that.

Though I understand you used to practise at the Court of Requests, so you will have first-hand experience of representing these churls,' he ended pointedly.

Copuldyke was not worth the trouble of getting into an argument with. I ignored his remark and said, 'I have agreed to act for Master Boleyn, so I must get myself up to East Anglia. I will need authoriza-tion in writing from you, sir, to act as your agent, your name being on the record as acting for him.'

'I have it prepared. Toby —' Copuldyke waved haughtily at his assistant, and the bearded young man passed me a document.

'Thank you,' I said. 'That appears in order, Brother Copuldyke. If you could just sign.'

'Happy to.' Copuldyke took the paper and signed with a flour-ish. He let out a sigh of relief as he passed the authorization across the desk. I turned back to Lockswood. 'I gather you are to come with us.'

'I am, sir,' the young man said quietly. Though Copuldyke had no trace of an accent, Lockswood spoke with a deep burr.

'Master Parry said you had good knowledge of Norfolk.'

Copuldyke interrupted before Lockswood could reply. 'Oh, Toby knows Norfolk inside out. Spends more than half his time there on work for me. His father's a yeoman farmer, though he hasn't enough land for his sons, so I took Toby on when he decided to try the law.' Copuldyke spoke condescendingly, then turned to Nicholas. 'And you, young man, you are going, too?'

'I am, sir.'

'Not called to the bar yet, by your short robe.'

'I hope to be called soon, Master Copuldyke,' Nicholas replied, a slight edge to his voice.

'We must leave on Monday,' I said. 'I know the basic details of the matter from Master Parry. But perhaps you and Lockswood could tell me a little more.' I turned to the young man. 'I understand you visited Master Boleyn in gaol.'

Lockswood turned to his master, who nodded his agreement, then said, 'I visited him last week in the castle gaol, where he is held until trial. An unpleasant place, sir, and Master Boleyn was in a sorrowful

state. He seemed shocked by what had happened to him, kept dod-
dering—'

'Toby!' Copuldyke snapped. 'How many times have I told you not
to use Norfolk slang in this office?'

'I'm sorry, sir.' Despite his apology, Lockswood's eyes flashed
angrily for a moment. 'I meant he was shivering, very upset. He kept
repeating that he was innocent. And he was concerned for the welfare
of his wife. I promised him the Lady Elizabeth's Comptroller had
taken an interest in the case, and would be sending a lawyer experienced in matters of blood. If I may venture an opinion —'

I glanced at Copuldyke, who shrugged and waved a hand. Lockswood continued, 'I thought, sir, that a guilty man who had left Edith
Boleyn's body in full view would not be so shocked at finding himself
in gaol.'

'Unless he was a good actor,' Nicholas said.

'That's true, sir.'

'Have you visited his family home?' I asked.

'Yes, sir, at his request. It's a fine old manor house, though most of
the servants have left since their master was arrested. His second wife
was there, and Master Boleyn's sons by his first wife. Poor Mistress
Boleyn was in a piteous state. She said the neighbours shun her.'

'Best not refer to her as Mistress Boleyn now,' Copuldyke said.
'The return of Edith Boleyn, even if recently dead, invalidates this
subsequent marriage. What is her maiden name again?'

'Heath,' Lockswood answered. 'Isabella Heath.'

'Formerly serving girl at the White Hart Inn in Norwich,' Copuldyke said. He gave a little bark of laughter. 'No wonder eyebrows
were raised when Boleyn took her into his house after his wife disappeared, and then married her. I hear she's a saucy strumpet.'

Lockswood did not comment on the remark, but went on quietly,
'Some have wondered if Isabella might have been involved in Edith's
murder. Like her husband, she has a motive for killing her if she turned
up out of the blue. But, of course, she would have no more motive than
John Boleyn for displaying the body so grotesquely.'

'We thought it sounded more like a crime committed by some third
party who hated Edith,' Nicholas observed.

'And who perhaps hated John Boleyn and Isabella as well,' I added.

'When I went to visit Isabella at the house, to tell her a lawyer was coming from London to look at the case, she was full of gratitude,' Lockswood said. 'She said she did not know what would become of her, otherwise. She must have suffered for years from all the muckspouts – I beg your pardon, gossips, regarding her low status.' There was a note of anger in Lockswood's voice, quickly suppressed. He glanced at Copuldyke, then continued, 'From what I hear she and her husband were close.'

'And what of the twin boys?' I asked. 'Edith's children?'

Copuldyke interjected, with some fierceness, 'Spoiled brats run wild. The Boleyns couldn't keep a tutor because of their antics. Once when I was riding near their home they threw stones at my horse, and knocked my cap off. Ill-conditioned brats.' He frowned. 'But what would you expect, with their mother leaving them to be brought up by a serving woman?'

Lockswood waited till his master had finished, then answered me. 'Their names are Gerald and Barnabas. Apparently, they have always been difficult, even before their mother left. They are like as two peas, save Barnabas has a large scar running down one cheek. Both resemble her, fair-haired and strongly built.'

'How were they with Isabella?' I asked curiously.

'They just ignored her. They were preparing to set off on a journey when I arrived. They asked me if I thought their father would get off, and when I said I didn't know, they wanted to know whether the King would take his property if he were hanged, told me the escheator's and feodary's men had already been round to take a look. I had to tell them their father's property was forfeit if he were found guilty. One said to the other that they'd have to go to their grandfather about that.'

'Who would that be?'

'Their mother Edith's father, Gawen Reynolds, he's a wealthy Norwich merchant and alderman. John Boleyn's parents are long dead; he inherited their property – not just the North Brikewell manor where they lived, but two other manors in Norfolk. He has some wealth, which is why Southwell's people and the escheator's man

Flowerdew were sniffing around. Although there are rumours his finances are not in sound order. His income from rents has been falling because of the inflation, and he overstretched himself by buying a large house in London a couple of years ago.'

I considered. 'The boys sound more interested in the property than in their father.'

'Yes,' Lockswood agreed. 'They did not even ask whether I thought him guilty.'

'Did they show any sign of mourning their mother?'

Lockswood shook his head as he looked at me. 'They did not mention her. I remember Isabella stood in the doorway as I spoke with them, watching them with a strange look – dislike, but fear too, I think.'

'Did you see Master Reynolds, the grandfather?' I asked. 'He and his wife must have suffered a shock, believing their daughter had disappeared nine years ago, then learning she had been murdered just days before.'

Lockswood shook his head again. 'There was no point in my trying to see them. The Reynolds are a rich family, I doubt they'd see a mere solicitor. They might talk to you, sir. Though apparently Reynolds and his wife have shut themselves away since news of their daughter's death. Word is the old man is convinced John is guilty, and wants to see him hanged.'

I glanced at Nicholas. When Edith came to Hatfield she had said her parents were dead. If she had landed in dire straits, and did not want to return to her husband, surely her parents were the obvious people to appeal to. Yet she had not done so. I could not discuss the Hatfield visit with Copuldyke or Lockswood, but made a note to talk to Edith's parents as soon as I could.

'Of course one can understand the interest of the King's officials,' Copuldyke interjected. 'The estate was originally monastic land, held by Boleyn on knight tenure when the old king sold it. Thus if Boleyn is executed, the boys become wards of the King, and he'd have the right to make their marriages – or, rather, the Lady Mary would, as feodary. Although she delegates that work to Sir Richard Southwell. Not that the boys sound very marriageable, especially if the Boleyn lands are forfeited.'

'And the agent of the escheator, responsible for the administration of the lands if they are forfeited, I believe that is a man called John Flowerdew.'

Copuldyke chuckled throatily again. 'Flowerdew is a serjeant like you, Brother Shardlake. A busy, quarrelsome fellow. Has his nose into everything, and always on the make. I wish you the joy of meeting him.' His manner became serious. 'As for Southwell, you should be careful how you deal with him. He is one of the leading men in Norfolk now, runs twenty thousand sheep and is in line for the King's Council.' He shifted in his seat. 'He is a dangerous man. He has been the subject of many accusations – embezzlement, conspiracy to abduct an heiress, a false witness in the case against his old master the Duke of Norfolk, along with a narrow escape from an accusation of murder.'

'Murder?'

'Yes, indeed. Getting on for twenty years ago he was involved in a quarrel with another Norfolk landowner, and ended up knifing him in a fight in London. It was a clear case of murder, but he made an appli-cation for a pardon from the old king, and got it.'

'As the very rich do,' Toby said quietly.

Copuldyke went on, 'Do not get into bad odour with him, sir. Especially as he represents Mary, and your instructions are from Eliza-beth.' His voice rose anxiously. 'Remember that officially you are my agent. I want no trouble with Southwell.'

'He is no man to meddle with,' Lockswood agreed.

Copuldyke said, 'Perhaps if John Boleyn is executed Mary will buy his lands, add them to her Norfolk estates. To spite her sister.'

I answered, 'Yet these visits by agents of Southwell and Flowerdew seem very – previous. John Boleyn has not yet even been convicted.'

'The common view is he will be,' Lockswood said gravely. 'He's not popular, especially since marrying Isabella. Then there is the dis-pute with his neighbour.'

'What can you tell me about that?'

Copuldyke bridled a little at my addressing his assistant directly rather than him. 'Tell him, Toby,' he said. 'Give Serjeant Shardlake

the benefit of your great knowledge of the law of property in Norfolk.'
He turned to me. 'He's even gone to the trouble of making a sketch
map for you.'

Lockswood reddened at his master's patronizing tone. 'If it would
help you, sir —'

'I am sure it would.'

He produced a paper from a drawer and placed it on the desk. We
leaned forward to look. It was not an exact plan, but had been carefully
drawn.

'That's good, Lockswood,' Nicholas said appreciatively.

The older man frowned slightly; he was half a dozen years older
than Nicholas, and probably far more experienced in the law. But as a
clerk his status was distinctly junior. 'This is a map of John Boleyn's
manor, North Brikewell,' Lockswood explained. 'He owns other
properties, as I said, but this is his largest property and his residence' —
he pointed to the top of the map — 'is the manor house here, next to the
village, which is quite small. And down here, see, the Brikewell
stream. It divides the manor from South Brikewell, which is owned by
his neighbour Leonard Witherington. Both manors are farmed on the
usual three-field system, two fields planted with crops and the third left
fallow each year, on a rotating basis. Each field is divided into strips,
and each tenant holds one or more strips in each field.'

'Serjeant Shardlake is a land lawyer, Lockswood,' Copuldyke said
heavily. 'I imagine he and even his young assistant know how the three-
field system works.'

Nicholas pointed to the fields. 'There are quite a few larger patches
among the strips. Is that where tenants have brought together several
strips and enclosed them as a separate farm?'

'Yes, that is correct.'

'There are one or two tenants who have done the same on my
father's estate, in Lincolnshire.'

'We have more enclosed lands, often freehold, in Norfolk than
most counties. And as you will see, if you look at the bottom right,
Witherington has enclosed parts of one of the common fields for
sheep, opposite his own demesne land. And there is also an area of

enclosed pasture which used to be part of the common pasture of South Brikewell.'

'How did he get hold of it?' I asked.

'I don't know,' Lockswood answered. 'Probably argued that as lord of the manor he is entitled to a share of the common pasture, proceeded to enclose it, and was able to enforce his will.'

I smiled wryly. 'Like a Roman emperor gradually extending his territory. How many sheep has Witherington on his lands?'

'Maybe three hundred. With the high price of wool, this shearing time he will make a tidy profit. Far more than if the land were put to crops. It is happening all over Norfolk,' Lockswood added seriously.

Copuldyke stirred in his chair. 'Landlords must turn a profit if they are to live like gentlemen,' he said irritably. 'With the rise in prices, a rent set thirty years ago will hardly provide much income.'

'And so you get landlords enclosing tenants' land where the leases have run out, or enclosing part of the common pasture and running it for sheep, not always in accordance with manorial custom.' I smiled grimly.

Copuldyke waved a dismissive hand. 'If the tenants think it has not been done correctly, they can always go to the courts.'

'Which often takes years as well as money. While a poor farmer needs to work his land from year to year, from day to day.'

'You sound like a Commonwealth man,' Copuldyke said disap-provingly. 'I've had to tell Lockswood here off for some of the things he comes out with.'

'I speak only from many years' experience in Requests.' To avoid further argument, I turned to look at the plan again. 'This is an un-usual layout for a manor. The woodland, common pasture and waste are set between the manors, not surrounding the main fields.'

'That is because the stream dividing the manors runs through the middle,' Lockswood explained. 'The land on either side gets slabby – muddy – in wet weather, though to ease the problem over the years drainage ditches have been dug along it. Over to the eastern end it is quite marshy, used as common waste from which the villagers take reeds, and wildfowl. And the west is given over to woodland.'

'What is the X?' Nicholas asked. 'Is that where Mistress Boleyn was found?'

'It is.'

I said, 'The spot is very near the only bridge across the stream. So perhaps her killer met her at the bridge, and killed her there. Otherwise she would have had to be carried quite some distance.'

There was silence for a moment, then Copuldyke said, 'The two estates are almost mirror images of each other.'

'Not quite, sir,' Lockswood ventured. 'North Brikewell is a good bit smaller. When the Benedictine abbey that owned it was dissolved in 1538, John Boleyn and Leonard Witherington were local men looking to expand their properties, and each bought one manor. There was only one manor house there originally, for the monks' steward, the one which John Boleyn bought. Leonard Witherington built his own house there, as you see. Like John Boleyn he owns other lands, and he is the wealthier of the two.'

I looked again at the map. 'I see Richard Southwell has land to the north, and also to the east.'

'Yes,' Copuldyke interjected. 'And runs sheep on both manors. If John Boleyn is found guilty Southwell may wish to buy North Brikewell, link his lands together. The bigger the sheep run, the greater the profits. He might not even need an extra shepherd.'

Nicholas said, 'He'd have to get the existing tenants off the land.'

Copuldyke waved a hand. 'That is future conjecture, and not our business.'

'What is the average size of a tenant's holding?' I asked.

'Small, ten to fifteen acres,' Lockswood answered. 'Some have larger holdings, like the tenants who have managed to enclose their lands, but at the other end of the scale there are many small cottagers who supplement their income by hiring themselves out as labourers or craftsmen to make ends meet. But with both Boleyn's and Witherington's areas of demesne land, which was once farmed, being put to sheep, there is less demand for labour. There are around twentyfive families in North Brikewell, somewhat over thirty in South Brikewell.'

I traced a dotted line which cut through the middle of the North

Brikewell woodland, pasture and waste, marked *old stream bed*. 'Is that the line which Witherington claims is the proper boundary?'

'Yes,' Copuldyke answered. 'According to the original grant to the monks – a centuries-old piece of parchment like all the monkish title deeds – the boundary between the two manors is described as "the Brikewell stream". There is evidence of an old stream bed there, but some time over the course of the past four hundred years, the stream has shifted its course, as happens in that sandy country. It is an interesting legal problem. Is the proper boundary today the present course of the stream, or the stream as it was when the document was made? Of such matters are long and profitable court cases made, eh, Brother?' He smiled and rubbed his hands together.

I considered. 'When Boleyn and Witherington bought the manors ten years ago, they obviously accepted the modern boundary.'

Copuldyke raised a finger. 'But Witherington says the old deeds were not delivered to them until after purchase. Otherwise he would have questioned it. You know what the Court of Augmentations is like for delay.'

'I'm sure a court would say that it was Witherington's responsibility to check the boundaries.'

Lockswood interrupted with a gentle cough. 'The present issue, I believe, is that Witherington's tenants have been discontented with him over the enclosure of part of the common pasture. The tenants say they have not enough left to graze their animals, the horses and bullocks they need to pull their ploughs, the cows to give them milk –'

Copuldyke barked with laughter again. 'And so on and so on, tenants always scream nowadays if they lose an inch of common land. But Witherington has proposed a remedy to his tenants – if he can gain control over the land between the current stream and the old stream bed, he has promised to turn half of it over to common pasture for the tenants, keeping only half for sheep.'

'*If* he can gain control of it,' I observed.

Lockswood turned to me. 'If Witherington won his argument, the North Brikewell tenants would lose a good deal of their common land. There is now a good degree of enmity between the two villages, though some of the tenantry in both blame Witherington's plans. A few months ago there was a fight between tenants of the two villages when Witherington tried to move some of his sheep onto the North Brikewell common pasture. I believe the Boleyn boys were involved.'

'Yet Witherington has not taken the matter to court,' I said. 'Perhaps his lawyer advised him he will lose. It certainly gives Witherington a motive to get John Boleyn out of the way. He could then try to buy up North Brikewell and be done with it.'

Copuldyke said, 'But if Southwell wanted it, I doubt Witherington would dare do battle with him.' He shrugged. 'Though perhaps he and Southwell could arrange some exchange of lands.'

'Thank you, Lockswood,' I said pointedly. 'I see the situation on the ground more clearly. And I look forward to your coming with us.'

Lockswood gave a little bow. 'I shall be glad to give what help I can.'

Copuldyke sighed and looked put upon. 'I can't really spare Toby just now, but Master Parry is an important client. There's one more thing that needs doing,' he added. 'When Toby visited John Boleyn in prison he asked if someone could go and ensure his London house was secure, and remove the deeds and associated documents relating to his land from there. When he is not in town he pays the local watch to keep an extra eye on the place. It's not far, on the north side of the Strand opposite Somerset House. Toby has the key.'

'Perhaps we could go there now,' I said. 'Get things underway.'

'All right. But come straight back after, Toby, I've some errands for you before you disappear to Norfolk.'

I rose and bowed to Copuldyke. 'I thank you for your assistance, Brother.'

He gave me a weary look. 'Just keep this matter out of my hair, Serjeant Shardlake. That is all I ask.'

We went out. And I thought, If John Boleyn had his deeds and documents in London, what did this do to his claim that the night Edith was killed he had spent two hours studying his deeds and legal matters in his North Brikewell study?

Chapter Six

JOHN BOLEYN'S TOWN house lay on the north side of the Strand, opposite the huge construction site of Somerset House. As Nicholas, Lockswood and I walked down Chancery Lane, I studied the young man who would be our guide to what was happening in Norfolk. The light breeze ruffled his black hair and beard, but his round face was expressionless.

'Have you worked for Master Copuldyke long?' I asked.

'Five years.'

'And you are a farmer's son? My father was a yeoman in Lichfield.'

'A good farming area, from what I hear,' Lockswood answered neutrally. I remembered Copuldyke saying his father's farm was too small to support his son, and changed the subject. 'The papers at John Boleyn's house are connected with the Brikewell manors?'

'I believe so. When I visited him in prison, he said he'd brought them down to London as he planned to consult a lawyer.'

'So,' I said, 'perhaps Witherington planned to go to law over the stream boundary after all.'

'Yes. Maybe he hoped to wear John Boleyn out with a long battle through the courts.'

Nicholas said, 'This Witherington sounds as though he has an interest in seeing Boleyn hanged.'

'I do not know. But John Boleyn seems to have been content to live quietly on his lands, spending part of the time at his London house, while Master Witherington is one of those who would pile land on land, money on money, and hope for a knighthood at the end of it. As the saying goes,' Lockswood added, sadly, 'never in England were there so many gentlemen and so little gentleness.'

'Come, fellow, you exaggerate,' Nicholas said, adopting the

patronizing tone he sometimes used to those of lower status. 'There are many fine and honest gentlemen in England.'

'I'm sure you are right, sir,' Lockswood said, blank-faced again.

We turned the corner into the Strand, passing under the arch of Temple Bar. A pall of dust hung in the air, which set me coughing, and there was the sound of sawing and hammering from the southern side of the road where hundreds of men were working on Somerset House. The huge palace, fronted with high columns, was almost complete, but work continued on the many lesser buildings; trenches were being dug, foundations laid, timber was being sawed, masons in aprons worked on great blocks of stone. As we passed on the other side of the road Nicholas said, 'Remember last year, when they blew up part of the old St Paul's charnel house with gunpowder, sending the bones of ancient aldermen flying across the town?'

'I do, indeed. An ancient thigh bone with part of a shroud attached landed in my neighbour's garden.'

Nicholas grasped my arm, bringing me to a halt. 'Look!' he said excitedly, pointing across the road. 'Is that not the Protector?'

I followed his gaze, and saw a tall, thin man with a long, pointed fair beard, a richly coloured robe, and a guard of three swordsmen in Seymour livery. He was bending over a plan laid out on a trestle table, where an architect in a long robe was indicating features with a pointer. I had met Edward Seymour, Duke of Somerset and Lord Protector, briefly, in the old king's time, and was struck by how much older he looked, his thin face hollow-cheeked, his expression severe. He stroked his long beard as he followed the architect's words.

'Is that him?' Lockswood asked curiously. 'The Good Duke?' He used the name which Somerset had gained by his professed friendship for the poor.

'It is.'

'He looks as though he has all the cares of the world on his shoulders.'

'Those of the kingdom, certainly,' Nicholas remarked. 'You have not seen him before, Lockswood?'

'Yes, now you point him out. I went to watch the procession to open the Parliament two years ago, and saw him riding next to the King. It was the King I watched, of course, dressed all in purple and gold, so many jewels on his clothes they shone in the sun.' He shook his head in reminiscence. 'Such a little boy. They say he is much grown now.'

'Still six years till he comes to his majority,' I said.

Nicholas said, 'Perhaps Somerset House may even be built by then.'

'Perhaps. Come on,' I said. 'We should not stand staring, and the dust hurts my eyes.'

✟

THE SOUTH SIDE of the Strand was where the great men of the realm had their houses, gardens running down to the river making an easy boat ride to London or Westminster. The buildings on the north side were older and less grand, lanes between them running up to the open fields beyond. Boleyn's house was at the top of such a lane, a rambling house built round a central courtyard, probably an old farmhouse. I noticed loose tiles and chipped paintwork. Lockswood produced a key and opened the heavy front door. We followed him in. The place was only half furnished, everything covered with dust from the Protector's building site. I smelled damp, too.

'Looks as though it needs some work to make a gentleman's town house,' Nicholas said.

'Maybe Boleyn's eyes were larger than his purse.' I turned to Lockswood. 'I think we should look for those papers.'

'Master Boleyn said his office was upstairs. We can find them, make sure everything is secure, and then I must find the local constable. Master Copuldyke has given me a half-sovereign to grease his palm, make sure he continues to keep a good eye on the house.' Lockswood smiled tightly. 'He'll be sure to enter it in the ledger to claim back from Master Parry.'

We climbed the staircase. A number of rooms gave off the landing. One door was half open, the room within furnished as an office – a desk, a few stools, and a large wooden chest. The walls were bare except for an old portrait of a stern-looking, black-haired man in the red robes of a London alderman. On the frame was a plaque, *Geoffrey Boleyn, 1401–1463*.

'Anne Boleyn's great-grandfather,' I said, 'who came to London and made his fortune.'

'He was brother to John Boleyn's great-grandfather,' Lockswood explained.

'You know something of the family?'

''Tis my business to know about the Norfolk gentry, sir. When claimants call on the Lady Elizabeth, my master sends me out to find their antecedents.' I noticed again the keenness in Lockswood's blue eyes, contrasting with his cautious expression. He went to the chest, producing another key. It would not turn. Frowning, he attempted to lift the lid. It opened, showing compartments filled with paper, documents and writing materials. 'That's odd,' he said. 'Master Boleyn said I'd need the key.' He looked among the papers, then pulled out a folder containing an ancient plan along with some parchment scribed in Latin and Norman French. 'I think this is it,' he said.

I held out a hand for the plan and opened it carefully. It was a faded, yellowed parchment, hundreds of years old, with a coloured plan of the North and South Brikewell manors. The stream boundary, I noticed, followed the course of the old stream. 'Yes,' I said. 'Here it is—'

I broke off at the sound of running feet from the corridor outside, coming from the back of the house. I glanced at the doorway, then turned to the window, my eye caught by a movement outside. To my astonishment I saw a dirty, barefoot, ragged boy of about ten running frantically across the stone flags of the courtyard. Suddenly he gave a cry and fell over, blood welling up through the dirty linen of his shirt. He struggled to rise but as he got to his feet he howled and fell over again, grasping one arm.

'Got him!' a voice cried.

'Me too! One hit each!' The voice which answered was almost identical, educated but with a slight lengthening of the vowels. Then two stocky fair-haired young men ran past the door of the office, not seeing us, and clattered down the stairs. I realized that from the back of the house they would not have heard us enter.

Nicholas and I stared at each other in surprise, and Nicholas's hand went to his sword hilt. 'What on earth – ?' I asked.

Lockswood looked suddenly grim. 'It's the twins.'

We watched as the fair-haired lads, dressed in good-quality doub-lets, ran from the inner door into the courtyard. In build they were identical. Each carried a sling; they must have used them to hurl stones at the child from the windows. The little boy was trying to get up again. One of the twins kicked him in the ribs and he cried out in pain and fear.

Lockswood's face was suddenly grim. 'We must stop this.' He headed for the door. I grasped his arm.

'Are those John Boleyn's sons?'

'They are, sir. They must have made their way to London, perhaps to seek what they could steal from here. If we don't stop them,' he said seriously, taking a deep breath, 'they might kill that child.'

The three of us rapidly descended the staircase and stepped into the morning sunshine. The ragged child was still trying to escape, but each time a well-aimed kick sent him falling over again. 'Think you can camp out in our father's house, you little beggar thief?' one of the twins asked.

'What have you stolen, eh?' The other was talking now. 'Hope it's enough to have you hanged.' Their tone was jesting, mocking, their voices hardly raised.

'Master Gerald, Master Barnabas!' Lockswood called out. 'Stop that, please.'

The two boys looked up. Their faces were square, with wide, flat noses, thin lips and small blue eyes. They could be told apart only by the long, narrow scar which one had running from his mouth to his ear, standing out pale on his suntanned face. They stared at us coldly, while the injured boy lay on the cobblestones, weeping now.

The scarred twin grinned, showing square white teeth. 'Here, Gerald,' he said. 'It's that nosy clerk Lockswood. Maarnin' there, Toby Lockswood,' he said in an exaggerated Norfolk drawl. 'What's frampling yew, bor?'

'How yer diddlin, Toby?' The other followed his brother's lead. 'Brung a pair o' laawyers, have yer? A hunchback an a long streely lad.'

'Did you not hear us come in?' Lockswood asked.

'We were busy having fun,' the boy without the scar answered, reverting to his educated voice.

Lockswood reddened, but spoke firmly. 'We are here to secure your father's premises, and fetch some documents. What are you doing to that poor child?'

'Poor child?' the one without the scar answered. 'He's a little thief and burglar. We, too, came to see how the house fared; we were just leaving when we found him camped in the kitchen, little mitcher. Did your job for you, I reckon.'

'Did your father authorize you to come here?' I asked sharply.

'Who are you, Master Hunch-fuck?'

Nicholas put his hand on his sword hilt. 'You'll show my master some respect,' he said.

The boys stood shoulder to shoulder and met his stare, quite unintimidated. 'Don't go threatening us, you long streak of piss.'

Nicholas stepped forward, but I clutched his arm to hold him back. I said to the boys, 'I am Master Shardlake, appointed by Master Copuldyke to represent your father. I am coming to Norfolk next week to help with his defence in the case of your mother's murder.' I hoped that by speaking directly of the terrible things that had happened to their parents the boys might be cowed, but they shrugged in unison, as though they could not have cared less. I looked at the little boy on the ground. 'What were you doing to him?'

Gerald – the boy without the scar, according to Lockswood – answered with chilling casualness. 'Just hunting him around the house. We felt like a bit of sport, and there's no deer or game here in London.'

'Take him to the constable, if you like.' Barnabas added. 'There's some silverware missing from the house, enough to hang this little rabbit.'

'Or have him branded and put to service at least, under the new law,' Gerald said.

The boy looked at me. 'I've stolen nothing,' he said frantically, 'by Christ's wounds!'

I noticed that Barnabas and Gerald had full pouches at their waists, remembered what Lockswood had said about them coming here to steal, and stared hard at them. 'Maybe you'd like to show us what you have in those pouches,' I said, glancing at Nicholas, whose hand was still on his sword hilt.

The twins looked at each other. Perhaps realizing the odds were against them, Gerald said, 'Naah. I think we'll fetch our horses and go back to Brikewell.'

I thought of forcing them to open the pouches, but sensed they would fight and I did not want to start this investigation by dragging Nicholas and Lockswood into a scuffle with Boleyn's sons. I asked, though, 'Did you open the chest in your father's office?'

'Yes,' Gerald answered truculently. 'Why shouldn't we? If they hang him we're his heirs. We wanted to see what we might get, but we couldn't make much of the Latin and French rubbish written in those papers.'

'If they hang your father, his lands go to the King, and you become the King's wards,' I said.

Gerald's eyes narrowed, 'I've heard that sometimes, if the heir's a minor, the King will grant the land back to him.'

'And Protector Somerset's known to listen to a sob story,' his brother added.

'You'd have to get past the escheator first,' Lockswood said. 'John Flowerdew is his local agent, he'd be responsible for the lands. You'll have heard what he's like.'

Gerald shrugged. 'Well, whatever happens, that bitch Isabella won't get anything. Come on, Barney, let's get away from these leeching lawyers.'

The two boys turned and went back into the house. I heard the outer door slam. The little boy they had been hunting had got to his feet and stood shivering, his back to the courtyard wall.

'Have they hurt you?' I asked gently.

'They got my side with a stone, then my ribs.'

I looked at the ground and saw a couple of small, pointed flints. 'They came in and when I tried to escape they chased me all over. I heard one shout that the first to break my head open would get a half-sovereign.' He tailed off, crying again. 'I was only looking for shelter. It's been so cold and wet till this week.'

I sighed, and gave the boy two shillings from my purse. 'Be off now. We're going to lock up the house, and it's probably safer not to come back.'

'I stole nothing, sir. I promise. I was asleep in the room next to the kitchen and heard sounds like metal clanking. Anything that's gone, they took it.'

'All right. Just go now. Straight through the house and out the front door.' It was hard to look at the child, rake-thin, his dirty shirt blood-ied, spots and scabs on his face. As he limped away I realized I had not even asked his name.

We stood in silence in the sunny courtyard for a moment. 'So those are John Boleyn's sons,' I finally said.

Lockswood nodded. 'A nasty pair. They've had a bad reputation since childhood.'

Nicholas said, 'They seemed to care nothing for their father's imprisonment, or their mother's death.'

I looked at Lockswood. 'Was that bravado, do you think? Pretend-ing not to care?'

He sighed. 'I don't know. But hunting a helpless child as though he were a rabbit – that does not surprise me.' His round face was set now, and angry. And indeed there had been a coldness about those boys that chilled me. He continued, 'A few months ago they took part in the scuffle with Leonard Witherington's men over the estate bound-ary. They mix with a crowd of gentlemanly ruffians, some of them Sir Richard Southwell's servants. They've hired themselves out more than once to landlords who want to get tenants off their land. There's stories of cattle maimed, ricks set on fire, people hurt.'

Nicholas asked, 'How did that one – Barnabas, is it? – get his scar?'

'There's a story that has gone about for years, though nobody knows if it is true.' Lockswood took a deep breath. 'Apparently, Edith Boleyn, God save her soul, was no good mother to the boys. As soon as they were born she handed them over to a wet-nurse and wanted nothing more to do with them. As they grew up she ignored them as much as possible, although both of them took after her, fair-haired, strong in build.' I remembered Parry telling me the woman who had visited Hatfield had been thin and scrawny, but also the story that sometimes Edith starved herself. Lockswood continued, 'She never behaved like a mother, for all they sought her attention. All she did was criticize and chastise them, and one thing that made her angry was that she was unable to tell them apart. One day they were pestering her in the kitchen and she said she'd give anything to tell one from the other, to know who to punish when one was rude to a servant or reported for stealing apples. Apparently, the boys went outside into the yard. A servant saw them talking, heads together, then one took a couple of pieces of straw from the yard and held them out to the other. He picked a straw, and it turned out to be the short one. Then there was a flash of metal and a scream. A moment later the boys reappeared in the kitchen doorway, standing side by side, only Gerald had ripped Barnabas's face open with a knife taken from the drawer; he was covered in blood. Edith screamed, asking what they had done now, and Gerald just said, "We did it for you, so you can tell us apart now."'

Nicholas gave an uneasy laugh. I looked at Lockswood, aghast. 'Do you think the story true?'

He shrugged. 'It's what people say, the common fame of the district. But the twins never talk about how Barnabas got that scar, they don't like people asking. They're such devils, perhaps they started the tale themselves. All I know is they were the despair of their father. People have often said those two were born to hang. Yet it is their father in gaol on a charge of murder.'

Nicholas and I looked at each other. If that was what their childhood had been like, it gave the twins a twisted motive to kill Edith Boleyn, and I could easily imagine them capable of leaving her body in a position of grotesque humiliation. Yet I was aware of how much I had heard was gossip and 'common fame', and knew how a story can become embedded like a rock in its neighbourhood of origin, when it contains but a wisp of the truth.

✝

WE LOCKED UP the house, and Lockswood left to find the constable and ensure a close eye was kept on the property. We arranged to meet him on Monday morning at the Moorgate, to commence our journey to Norwich.

Nicholas and I walked slowly back to Temple Bar; he was to return to his lodgings, while I decided to take the opportunity to go and see Guy. The visit to Boleyn's house had given us both food for thought.

'There seem to be more and more people with a possible motive to kill her,' Nicholas said. 'John Boleyn, his second wife Isabella Heath, his neighbour, and now those boys. But everyone would have been safer if they'd just buried her.'

I said, 'Those boys are hardly' – I struggled for a word – 'normal.'

'No, they're not.'

'If that story of them drawing lots to see who would get his face carved, just so their mother could tell them apart, is true, that needed an extraordinary degree of control. Was it a gesture of love, I wonder. Or hate?'

Nicholas shook his head. 'It seems they consider themselves gentle-men, but they behave like ruffians.'

'What do you think of Lockswood?'

'A loyal servant, and not afraid to stand up to those boys.'

'And his master, friend Copuldyke?'

He laughed. 'A lazy fat slug.'

I said, 'I wonder how Lockswood stands him.'

Nicholas shrugged. 'Copuldyke pays his wages. And Lockswood gets paid for putting up with it. 'Tis the way of things.'

I smiled. 'Then perhaps I'll start talking to you like that.'

He matched my mocking tone. 'Ah, but I am more than just a clerk.'

'You weren't when you started with me.'

'Perhaps Lockswood will rise in the world. Copuldyke's indolence means Lockswood has the contacts, the knowledge of Norfolk affairs, and that's a saleable quality.'

'He's going to be useful to us, I know that. The more I learn of the Boleyn family and their neighbours, the more grateful I am to have a guide through this cesspit.' I shook my head. 'I will ask him what he thinks might have happened to Edith during the nine years after she vanished. We are hobbled by being unable to mention that she ended up at Hatfield just before her death.'

'Those were Parry's conditions.'

'I wonder if we will be able to be loyal both to the Lady Elizabeth and to discovering the truth. By Jesu, I pray that we will.'

Chapter Seven

WE REACHED Temple Bar; Nicholas then returned to his lodgings, while I went to visit Guy. I walked down Cheapside. At the busy market stalls with their striped awnings, the usual frantic haggling was going on between the stallholders and the goodwives in their white coifs. These days, though, frequently it was not the good-natured haggling of earlier times but desperate, angry arguments as buyers tried to persuade stallholders to part with their goods for at least a good part of the face value of the new shillings. Amidst the old cabbage leaves, rotten apples and other discarded rubbish, I noticed a pamphlet, and picked it up. It was one of the many anti-enclosure pamphlets, exhorting the King:

> . . . truly to minister justice, to restrain extortion and oppression, to set up tillage and good husbandry whereby the people may increase and be maintained. Your godly heart would not have wild beasts increase and men decay, ground so enclosed up that your people should lack food and sustenance, one man by shutting in the fields and pastures to be made and a hundred thereby to be destroyed.

I put the pamphlet in my purse.

Guy lived in the apothecaries' district, in the maze of alleys between Cheapside and the river, the apothecaries' shops displaying stuffed lizards from the Indies and curled horns they claimed were from unicorns. Guy was a licensed physician and could have afforded somewhere much grander than his little shop with rooms above, but he had lived there for years and, like many old men, disliked change. I saw his shop windows were shuttered; for the last couple of months, since he had been ill, Guy had taken on no new patients. It was a worrying sign, for his profession had always been the centre of his life.

I knocked at the door, which was answered immediately by Guy's assistant, Francis Sybrant. Like Guy, Francis was in his mid-sixties, and like him was a former monk. Always inclined to plumpness, he had grown very fat this last year or two. He carried a satchel over his shoulder.

'Master Shardlake,' he said. 'God give you good morrow. We were not expecting you.' He looked a little flustered to see me.

'Good morrow. How fares your master?'

'The same, sir,' he said sadly. He looked tired. 'No change. If you will excuse me, I have to deliver remedies to some of his patients.'

'I thought he was taking on no more.'

'The existing ones still pester us for remedies and cures, and I make them up at Master Guy's instruction. If you forgive me, I am late — there is so much to do — please, go up and see him. He is awake.' He bowed me inside, then waddled off up the street.

I stood a moment in Guy's consulting room, looking at the neatly labelled jars and flasks of herbs on the shelves, then climbed the stairs to his bedroom. My old friend lay in bed reading in a nightshirt, his big old Spanish cross with the carved figure of Christ above his head. Such crosses had been taken from the churches now and burned; even displaying one in a private house might earn official suspicion, but Guy remained resolutely Catholic.

He looked up and smiled, with teeth that were still white. Otherwise he looked bad. He had always been slim but now the bones of his temples and his large, thin nose stood out. Even his brown Moorish skin seemed to have a sickly, yellowish cast. He had always been prone to fevers, which he blamed on the bad air of the marshland on which his former monastery had stood, but recently he had had one after the other, with only brief periods of respite, and I could see they were wearing him out. I could only hope they would pass.

'God give you good morrow, Guy,' I said.

'Matthew. I was not expecting you today.' He hesitated, as though about to say something else, and glanced briefly at the door, but then smiled again.

'I have just got back from Hatfield, and thought I would call. How are you?'

He raised a thin hand, then let it fall to the quilt. 'Weak, and tired. And physician though I am, I have no idea what to do about it.' He smiled wearily. 'I have been reading.' He held out the book. 'Thomas More. *A Dialogue of Comfort Against Tribulation*. I know you never liked him, but he had great learning.'

'A great burner and torturer of heretics.' It was an old argument between us. I took the book and glanced at the page Guy was reading. I quoted, ' "The rich man's substance is the wellspring of the poor man's living." Ah yes, that theory, that as the rich grow richer their wealth trickles down to the poor like sand. Well, I have been practising law twenty-five years and all I have seen is it trickle ever upwards.' I remembered the pamphlet I had just picked up earlier. 'See,' I said, handing it to him, 'this writer makes just complaint.'

Guy looked at it. 'Enclosures have been going on for years. Thomas More wrote against them.'

'And when Cardinal Wolsey tried to enforce the laws against them in court, More ruled against him.'

Guy laughed gently. 'Ah, you are such an arguer, such a lawyer. But I am too tired for debate just now.'

'Forgive me. Have you been out of bed today?'

'Only to visit the jakes. At the moment even sitting in a chair tires me. Well, at least I shall not be expected to go to church on Sunday, to listen to Cranmer's English Communion service in a bare church.' He shook his head. 'I never thought England would come to this.' Tears welled in his brown eyes.

'I saw a church being whitewashed on my way back from Hat-field,' I said quietly. 'It seemed – cold, heartless somehow, even with the Scripture verses on the walls.'

'So,' he said gently, 'things have gone too far now for you, as well?'

'Yes. I think they have.'

'What were you doing in Hatfield?'

'Visiting the Lady Elizabeth.'

He smiled wryly. 'Ah, the Protestant Princess. But no, she is still just the Lady, like her sister Mary. Both their mothers' marriages annulled. Unlike Jane Seymour's. I wonder if her brother the Protector is making a point by denying them the title of Princess.'

'Perhaps.'

'Are you still working on the Lady Elizabeth's lands?'

'Yes. In fact, I have to go to Norwich on Monday, Guy, on business for her.'

'Norwich?' He sounded surprised. 'What sort of business is it?'

I hesitated, but I had always valued Guy's insights. 'Unusual. A distant Boleyn relative of the Lady Elizabeth is on trial for murder at the Assizes. She wishes me to investigate, quietly, and ensure justice is done.'

Guy looked at me keenly. 'It is a long time since you have involved yourself with such a matter. Not since Jack Barak lost his hand.'

'This is quite different. It involves the Norfolk gentry, not high politics.'

'Will you take young Nicholas?'

'Yes. He wishes to go. And frankly, Guy, so do I. I am tired of pen-scratching. And this man may have been accused unjustly of his wife's murder, though I do not know that yet.'

A spark of interest came into his eyes. 'Do you want to tell me the story? I could do with distraction.'

I was glad of Guy's interest, and I briefly recounted the facts, leaving out Edith Boleyn's appearance at Hatfield. When I had finished, Guy lay back, and I thought perhaps I had tired him, but he had only been thinking, for he said, quietly, 'Perhaps the twins' pranks as small boys were done to gain their mother's love, or at least her attention. Drawing lots for one to disfigure the other may have been a last, frantic attempt to do that.'

'Frantic indeed.'

'And yet her reaction was anger?'

'So I am told. Though all I have heard so far is at second and third hand.'

'If she reacted to one child disfiguring himself only with more anger, perhaps that led the boys to think the shedding of blood a light thing.' He considered. 'What is the father like? The man accused of killing his wife?'

'I do not know. He scandalized his neighbours by moving in a woman who served at an inn after his wife disappeared. And he also has a quarrel over land with one of them. And the name Boleyn still carries a stigma. All those things may go against him with the local jury. I will learn more next week.'

'Come back safe,' Guy said quietly.

'I will, to see you well again.'

He raised a thin brown hand, then let it fall. 'I wonder if my pilgrimage on earth is nearly over. I am sixty-six now.'

'The Bible allows three score years and ten.'

'Few enough reach that, as we both know. Seeing what England has become, the church to which I gave my life finally, completely destroyed, perhaps it is time.'

'Nonsense.' I spoke with deliberate lightness. 'You have your patients to treat. I confess, I have not been doing my exercises diligently. I will suffer for it on the way to Norfolk, and may need to consult you again when I come back.'

He looked at me. 'When you ride out, remember to sit high in the saddle, on the bones of your pelvis. Do not stoop nor cast your eyes down, I know the cast of your body inclines you to do that but you should look up, proudly.'

'I will try.' I leaned forward and grasped his hand, which felt like little more than bones. There was a moment's silence. Then I heard a knock at the door. Guy flashed me a quick look, in which I saw apprehension, but called, 'Come in.'

Tamasin Barak stepped into the room, holding a full basket in one hand and leading a little fair-haired boy by the other. She said, 'I have everything you asked for—' She broke off at the sight of me. Her pretty, full-lipped face, framed by a white coif from which strands of blonde hair drifted, turned, in a moment, as cold as ice.

I had not seen her in three years, and I saw that she had aged, new lines around her mouth and eyes. Her little boy George, nearly four now, was officially my godson; he had been born before the breach between us. I had never seen her daughter. George stared at me with wide-eyed curiosity.

I said quietly, 'God give you good morrow, Tamasin.'

She turned to Guy as though I were not there, and spoke in a hard, flat voice, 'I will take these things into the kitchen, and leave the meat and vegetables out for Francis to prepare a pottage when he returns. The meat is scraggy, the price has gone up again and I did not have enough money for a good cut.'

'Matthew called unexpectedly,' Guy said. 'I did not tell him you were out shopping for me. I thought that perhaps if you saw him again—'

She cut across him, a tremble in her voice now. 'I have to get back. Mistress Marris is looking after Tilda—'

'Tamasin, Tamasin,' Guy said beseechingly. 'Matthew is about to go on a journey to Norfolk, it would delight my heart if the two of you could reconcile before he leaves. Remember Christ's injunctions to us to forgive.'

There was a moment's silence. Then little George piped up, 'Who is that man in the black robe?' He pointed to me. 'His body is bent. Is that a hunchback?'

'Tush, George,' Tamasin said, pulling the child to her. Then she turned to face me, her face still cold, her voice low but harsh. 'I can never forgive the injury my husband suffered because you led him into danger. Every evening I remove that wretched device he has for a hand, rub oils into that cruel stump. I see the pain he is often in. Then sometimes I think of you, but not forgivingly.' Her voice trembled slightly.

'Jack made his own decision,' Guy said.

'It was I that led him into that, I know,' I said to Tamasin. 'But we were friends once. Cannot we be so again – or at the least be civil to each other?'

'Would you want that?' she asked. 'Civility, when all my heart feels is anger?' She looked at Guy. 'You should have told him I was coming, and asked him to leave.' She turned her gaze back to me. 'So, you are going to Norfolk?'

'Yes. A case is taking me to Norwich.'

'My husband will be there, for the Assizes. You had best leave him alone. I shall ask him if he has been with you when he returns, and by God, he had better answer that he has not. Now, I shall go to the kitchen.' She turned, and as she left the room with George, the little boy looked over his shoulder at me. Guy slumped back in his bed, defeated.

'I am sorry,' he said. 'She has been shopping for us, all the work is too much for poor Francis. I hoped if you were brought together –' He shook his head. 'I should not have mentioned Norfolk, I forgot Jack was going there.'

I sighed. I was smarting inwardly with shame, and hurt, but also the stirrings of anger.

'Tamasin has ever had an obstinate streak,' Guy said.

'Yes,' I agreed, 'she has.'

He shook his head slowly to and fro on the pillow. 'And since what happened to him she has been over-protective of Jack. I think he begins to resent it. I should have told you she was coming, given you the chance to leave. Selfish of me.'

'No, you did your best.'

He smiled. 'I know you and Jack still meet, but he has to do it in secret.'

'Yes, and I intend to see him in Norfolk.'

He looked at me seriously. 'Don't get him in any more trouble.'

'I won't, but I will see him, given the chance.'

Guy nodded. I saw his eyes were closing with tiredness. 'I think I had better go,' I said. 'I will see you in two, maybe three weeks.'

'I look forward to it, Matthew.'

I turned to leave. As I descended the staircase I heard, from the kitchen at the back, the sound of things being moved on a table. Quietly, for Tamasin was never one to give way to temper. I hesitated for a moment, then turned and left the shop.

Chapter Eight

NEXT MORNING, Saturday, I rose early. It was a lovely June morning, but I had little leisure to enjoy it; I had to visit Lincoln's Inn and find friendly barristers to look after my cases for the two or three weeks I would be in Norfolk. Fortunately, especially at Assize time, such arrangements were common. And I must ensure my clerk John Skelly was properly briefed. Then in the evening there was supper at my friend Philip Coleswyn's house.

Over breakfast John Goodcole told me he had hired four good horses to be available early on Monday morning, to transport Nicholas, Lockswood, myself and our baggage to Norwich. I thanked him gratefully. He also handed me a letter, just delivered by a rider from Hatfield. I opened it. It was from Parry:

Master Shardlake, greetings.

I send this letter to reach you before you depart for Norfolk. I have arranged rooms for you and Master Overton for two weeks from the thirteenth of June, which should be the earliest you will arrive. They are at the Maid's Head Inn, by the cathedral, one of the best in Norwich. It is in Tombland district, at a little distance from the market square below which stand the castle gaol and the Shire Hall, where the trial will be held. Most of the lawyers will be staying at the market square inns, so you will be away from all the gossip.

Yesterday I had occasion to meet with Master William Cecil, Secretary to the Protector, with whom I know you are acquainted. He is my distant relative and is to be trusted on matters concerning the Lady Elizabeth. I mentioned the Boleyn case to him, and sought his discretion should any rumours reach him. I also mentioned you were going to Norfolk to carry out discreet enquiries.

Please write and let me know when you are safely arrived in Norwich.
Your loving friend,
Thomas Parry

I had not realized that Parry was related to William Cecil. I guessed he had asked Cecil to keep any rumours about John Boleyn from the Protector. And he was lodging me at an inn some distance from where the other lawyers would be. I understood his desire for discretion, but that would be difficult if I were to investigate things properly as the Lady Elizabeth wished. I was conscious of the sealed application for a pardon which Elizabeth had handed me before I left Hatfield, and which was carefully locked away at my house. I hoped I would never have to use it.

✝

I SPENT THE MORNING at Lincoln's Inn, where, fortunately, I man-aged to find people to deal with my cases temporarily, then went into my chambers with a list of instructions for Skelly. Nicholas was already there, finishing some work of his own.

'Looking forward to tonight, hey?' I asked.

'I am, sir. It was good of you to ask Master Coleswyn to invite the Kenzy family.'

'Well, I know you are keen to see the delightful Beatrice.'

Nicholas flushed slightly, and Skelly lowered his head to hide a smile. I reflected again that there was something about Beatrice Kenzy that I did not like, but it was not for me to lay rocks in the path of my assistant, who seemed genuinely smitten.

'Do you know who else is coming?' Nicholas asked.

'I think it is just Philip Coleswyn and his wife, us and the Kenzys. And Philip's old mother, who lives with them now, to make up the numbers.'

'Has he not invited a lady to pique your interest?'

'Not unless the old woman piques it. But I believe she is over seventy.'

Philip was a good friend; I had met him when we were on opposite sides in a particularly unpleasant case, and he had shown himself an honest and compassionate man. He was a strong Protestant, but open-minded enough to mix with people with differing views. Philip knew Beatrice's father, another barrister, from work, and with typical kindness he had agreed to invite us all to supper so that Nicholas could further his pursuit of Beatrice.

✝

THE SUPPER WAS arranged for six o'clock, and I walked from my house to Coleswyn's residence in Little Britain Street, off Smithfield. It stood in a row of old dwellings, their overhanging jettied roofs giving welcome shade from the sun, which late in the afternoon was hot still. Summer, it appeared, had arrived at last.

Before setting out I had begun packing for Norwich, and had looked out my last letter from my old servant Josephine. I remember it said that she was pregnant, that she and her husband were in difficulty, and I had sent some money. I realized it was six months since then. The address they gave was Pit Street, St Michael's Coslany, Norwich. I had no idea where that might be. I thought, Pit Street; Tombland. Neither name seemed to augur well.

I was a little late, the last to arrive. I had dressed in my black summer robe with a brown doublet beneath, silver aiglets on silk cords the only concessions to colour, remembering this was a Protestant house where modesty in dress was favoured. And indeed, when I was shown into the parlour and Philip stepped forward to greet me, he wore a dark doublet beneath his robe, the white collar of his shirt the only contrast. He had grown the long beard fashionable among radicals. He took my hand. 'Matthew. God give you good evening.'

'I am sorry to be late.'

'Just a little, no matter.'

His wife, Ethelreda, came forward and curtsied. She was a fair-haired, attractive woman, like her husband nearing forty. She wore a brown dress, her hair bound under the blue circlet of a French hood. I thought how different she looked from the worn, frightened figure I had first met three years before, when the old king's final hunt against Protestant heretics was in full swing.

'Ethelreda. You look well. How are your children?'

'Growing fast. But we have a good tutor, who keeps them in order.'
Unlike the Boleyn twins, I thought, with whom no tutor would stay.
'Come,' she continued. 'This is my husband's mother.' An old
woman with white hair under a gable hood, a discontented expression
on her plump, wrinkled face, sat in a chair. 'Mother,' Ethelreda said,
'this is Serjeant Matthew Shardlake, our good friend. My mother-in-
law, Mistress Margaret Coleswyn.'

The old lady turned a keen, wintry gaze on me, then gave a crooked
smile. 'I see you are an old white-head, like me. Young people are
too quick to show off their hair these days, headgear is not as modest
as it was.'

Edward Kenzy stepped forward. In his fifties and a fellow-barrister
at Lincoln's Inn, he was a political and religious conservative, a sea-
soned cynic about both the law and the world, who enjoyed good conversation, food and wine. I had met him several times in the course of
business, and despite our different opinions I rather liked him. Under
his lawyer's robe he wore a dark red silken doublet; the collar of his
shirt was decorated in elaborate blackwork. Old Mistress Coleswyn,
for whom, no doubt, he was too gaudily dressed, frowned. Cheerfully
ignoring her, Kenzy shook my hand. 'Brother Shardlake,' he said. 'It
is a while since we have seen you in the courts. The Lady Elizabeth
must be keeping you busy. Young Master Overton tells my daughter
you are off to Norfolk on her affairs on Monday.'

'Yes, we are.' I looked across to where Nicholas stood in conversation with Beatrice Kenzy. He was not wearing his robe, but a new
doublet of light green satin and a black belt with a decorated golden
buckle at his waist. Both looked costly. Beatrice wore a blue dress with
a high collar, a jewelled pendant round her neck. She was a pretty girl,
black-haired like her father, her face white with powder. She was listening to Nicholas with wide-eyed attention, her small mouth set in a
slight simper. It was that simpering expression, I realized, that had set
me against her, unfairly perhaps, for I had always favoured strong-
minded, intelligent women. Standing just near enough to hear the
conversation was a middle-aged woman so like Beatrice that she had

to be her mother. She wore a fashionable little hat on her greying hair instead of a hood, and a yellow dress with contrasting black sleeves.

Kenzy took me to her. 'My wife, Laura. My dear, this is Serjeant Matthew Shardlake, Nicholas's employer.'

Her expression as she listened to her daughter's conversation had been sharp, but it softened into a smile as she curtsied. 'Serjeant Shard-lake, I have heard much about you,' she said in gushing tones. 'How you used to work for the late Queen Catherine, God save her soul, and now for the household of the Lady Elizabeth.'

'Yes, though I used to work at the Court of Requests as well.'

'Such connections must bring you good work.' She glanced at Nicholas and Beatrice. 'And of course, working for you, young Nich-olas must be making good connections too.' Her blue eyes were calculating, and I now began to understand something that had puz-zled me – why a successful, prosperous barrister would encourage a penniless young man like Nicholas to court his only daughter. Mistress Kenzy, who I realized was probably the prime mover, had been dazzled by the names of my patrons, and hoped Nicholas would soon be mixing with the highest in the land. I looked at Beatrice, still listening with rapt interest to Nicholas's account of his visit to Hatfield Palace, and wondered if that was her motivation, too.

A steward appeared in the doorway, and Philip clapped his hands. 'Come everyone, let us eat.' We passed through to the dining room, where the table was set with plates, fine glassware and napkins. We seated ourselves and placed our napkins over our shoulders. I was next to Laura Kenzy, while on my other side Philip sat at the head of the table. Opposite me old Mistress Coleswyn settled herself down with the aid of a servant. Grace was said, and Philip offered a toast to the health of 'The King, our little shepherd'. Servants brought in a first course of salads, eggs and cheese, with plates of good manchet bread and butter.

Philip said, 'This is the first supper this year where we shall not need candles.' And indeed the light from the windows giving on to the pretty garden outside was quite sufficient to dine by. 'The weather has been dreadful this spring,' he continued, 'I fear a bad harvest, and much suffering for the poor later in the year.'

'The poor are always with us,' Edward Kenzy said. 'It was always so, and always will be.'

'They have seldom suffered so much as now,' Philip replied. 'A penny loaf is but half the size it was two years ago.' Philip was a strong Commonwealth man, as ardent for reform in society as in religion, believing like me that the State owed a duty to rectify the abuses that had caused such a rise in poverty. He turned to me for support.

''Tis true,' I agreed. 'Prices go up faster than ever, but the wages of the poor remain the same.'

'Prices have gone up for everyone,' Laura Kenzy said, righteously. 'It is no easy thing for those like me who have to run a household. Or my brother, who owns houses at Bishopsgate. His costs go up, but the tenants' rents were set years ago. Is that fair?' She turned to me, flushing slightly. 'Begging your pardon, Serjeant Shardlake.'

'No need, madam. You have the right to an opinion like everyone else.'

Ethelreda said, to change the subject, 'Is anyone going to St Paul's Cathedral tomorrow, to hear Archbishop Cranmer preach from the new Prayer Book?'

'My wife and daughter will be going to the Lincoln's Inn Chapel, but I shall go to St Paul's,' Edward Kenzy answered neutrally. 'I suppose it will be, at least, a historic occasion.' I looked at him, remembering his reputation as a religious traditionalist. He met my eye. 'What of you, Brother Shardlake?'

'I shall go. As you say, a historic occasion.'

'I believe you have worked for the archbishop, too, in the past,' Laura Kenzy said, any traditionalist reservations of her own overcome by snobbery.

'Yes,' I agreed. 'In the old king's time. Whatever else, Archbishop Cranmer is a man of sincerity.'

Ethelreda, her face alight with enthusiasm, joined in. 'Last week our family went to hear Master Latimer preach at the Cathedral Cross. He spoke of the sickness in the body of the State, and the need to ensure the bodily welfare of all within the Commonwealth.'

'You speak wrongly, Ethelreda, sometimes I think you have not the brains of a flea.' Old Margaret Coleswyn's voice rasped with contempt. 'Yes, Master Latimer spoke of reform that is needed in the Commonwealth, but that was for ten minutes in a speech of two hours. He spoke far more of what is truly wrong in England, its devotion to the sins of the flesh, gaming and whoring, its failure truly to root out the remnants of papistry. And he condemned those who rose up against their landlords last month.' The old woman glared around the table, inviting challenge.

Ethelreda went red. 'Mother –' Philip said, warningly.

Edward Kenzy chuckled. 'The Commonwealth men and pamphleteers will have noted down only what he said about land reform, I'm sure, and distributed it far and wide. I hope Master Latimer did not condemn fine dining, or we are all condemned to hellfire. Though I think he believes most of us are doomed to it anyway, and is quite cheerful about it. This egg sauce is delicious, Coleswyn.' An uneasy titter went round the table, though old Mistress Coleswyn sat stony-faced.

'Latimer was right at least in condemning those peasants who rose up against enclosures last month,' Kenzy continued, more seriously. 'There was a bad business in Wiltshire, too, where they tried to take down the fences round Sir William Herbert's new park, and he had to gather two hundred men to rout them, not without bloodshed, I hear.' He looked at me. 'Herbert's wife is sister to the late Queen Catherine. Did you hear any news of the affair?'

'No, I met the Herberts only once,' I said carefully. 'One can surely understand the anger of Herbert's tenantry against huge amounts of good agricultural land being fenced off so the great lords may go a-hunting. This passion for parkland has its consequences for the poor of the Commonwealth.'

Kenzy looked at me levelly. 'What is your definition of the Commonwealth?'

'The whole nation, held in economic balance, the rules ensuring that none are too poor to live.'

Philip added, 'The Protector issued a strong proclamation against illegal enclosures in April, and I believe he has asked John Hales to organize a whole new series of commissions to go around all England this summer, and reverse all illegal enclosures of land since 1485. Many old injustices may thus be remedied.'

I considered, then said, 'Many old injustices there are, and new ones too with the enclosure of common land for sheep.' I thought of the Brikewell manors. 'But to disentangle all enclosures since 1485 –' I shook my head sadly – 'that is a job that could occupy a hundred lawyers for years. Any return of lands to the common people will be challenged in the courts by the landlords, even if they are not seized back as soon as the commissioners move on – the magistrates and gentlemen will be united against them. I do not think the Protector has thought this through. He may indeed wish serious reform, but careful planning is needed.'

Kenzy said, 'Yes. How are the commissioners supposed to know what was common land fifty years ago, if documentary evidence is lacking, which, probably, it is?'

Coleswyn said, 'Then evidence will be taken from aged persons who were alive at the time –'

'Anyone who was an adult in 1485 would be eighty now, if still alive,' Kenzy replied scoffingly.

'They may have told their children, who could give evidence.'

'Come, Philip,' Kenzy said impatiently. 'You know that would be mere hearsay, inadmissible in court. And who are these people the commissioners will be asking to testify? Tenants, leaseholders, squatters; are they to be the ones who decide who is to own what land in England? Against the will of the local landholders? Does Protector Somerset wish the foot of the body politic to rule the head against all natural and biblical precedent?'

'He only wishes to do justice,' Philip said, gravely.

'He wishes to keep his reputation as the Good Duke with the poor, is nearer the truth,' Kenzy retorted. 'As Serjeant Shardlake says, he does not think things through. And in truth Somerset cares for nothing but conquering Scotland.'

'I have occasionally wondered whether perhaps it might be better if the foot of the body politic had the rule,' I said, greatly daring, 'given how the head treats the foot.'

Old Margaret Coleswyn was scandalized. 'You would deny the social order ordained by God? You sound like an Anabaptist, sir, who would bring the land to murder and anarchy!'

I gave her a wintry smile. 'I recall just three years ago, when accusations of Anabaptism were thrown at every Protestant by religious
traditionalists. Strange how readily reformers themselves now throw the
name Anabaptist around. Mistress Joan Bocher has been found guilty
of Anabaptist heresy, has she not? I believe she is in the care of Lord
Chancellor Rich, who tortured Anne Askew. Perhaps she too will be
burned. It is strange how the wheels turn.'

The old woman did not reply, but simply looked at me in outrage.
There was silence round the table. Then, to the relief of us all, the
second course was brought in; a platter of roast beef on a bed of herbs,
plates of chicken in lemon juice. Everyone set to with a will.

'I congratulate you on the fine meal, Mistress Coleswyn,' Edward
Kenzy said eventually.

'Thank you. It was hard to get everything, things are either scarce
or expensive. The merchants hoard goods one month, then sell them
the next when prices have risen again.'

'I know,' Kenzy said. 'I think everyone round this table would at
least agree the rise in prices is a serious problem.' He looked around.
'But what is the cause, hey? Merchants withholding goods so prices
rise, yes, but the real problem is the debasement of the coinage. It is no
accident we have had two re-coinages this year alone, and that prices
rise faster than ever. The root problem is the waste of money on that
war in Scotland, which can never be won. The six-year-old Mary,
Queen of Scotland is gone to France, now she will never marry King
Edward, and there are French troops in Scotland too. I believe that is
all the Protector cares about, fighting this unwinnable war to the cost
of everyone.'

Nicholas spoke up from his end of the table. 'But sir, England
must protect itself. Every time we have gone to war with France, the
Scotch have attacked us in the rear. If we take control of Scotland, we
shall have secured our back door.'

'But the Protector's campaigns have been disastrous,' Kenzy
replied, irritably. 'His chain of Scottish forts have fallen one by one,
support from Scotch Protestants is non-existent, and our soldiers are
deserting. That is the root cause of our troubles, Master Overton.
Silver taken out of the coinage and used to finance a failed war. King

Henry started this ruination of the coinage, but that is nothing to what the Protector has done since.'

'I disagree the war has failed,' Nicholas persisted. 'A fresh campaign is being prepared even now.'

Ethelreda said, 'I saw a troop of Switzer mercenaries passing through London last week, mounted and in armour and carrying arquebuses.'

'I saw them too, madam.' Nicholas's face was alight with the youthful enthusiasm for war. 'A remarkable sight.'

'A fearsome sight,' Ethelreda answered quietly. 'What if they turn on us?'

'They are pledged to the King.'

I said, 'They will pledge themselves to anyone for money. On this matter at least I am with Master Kenzy.'

'An honourable nation should never be afraid of war,' Nicholas said firmly.

I looked at Beatrice, sitting opposite him. Until the talk had turned to the war, she had been talking with Ethelreda Coleswyn, turning her head away to rebuff Nicholas's attempts to join in the conversation. It looked to me like a womanly tactic, so he would be grateful when she did deign to converse with him. I said, 'Good Mistress Beatrice, what think you of the war? Do you agree with Master Nicholas, or your father?'

Beatrice looked disconcerted. She blushed and turned to her mother. Laura Kenzy smiled. 'My daughter has no views on such things. She has been taught to concern herself only with matters appropriate to a young lady.'

Beatrice looked relieved. 'You see, Nicholas,' she said, 'what a poor girlish wit I have.' She gave me a sudden look of pure anger before turning back to Nicholas. 'Let us talk no more of war,' she said lightly. 'Though you will be gone north yourself next week. I shall fear for you.'

'Only to Norfolk, Mistress Beatrice, it is very far from Scotland.' Nicholas spoke reassuringly, though I was sure Beatrice was perfectly aware Norfolk was a long way from Scotland. Nicholas touched her fingers with his. She smiled round the table, as though to say, how stupid I am.

But, I thought, you are not.

'I wish you were not going,' she told Nicholas. 'Perhaps when you come back you will be speaking the local tongue, and I shall not understand you.'

'Well, at least we have taught our daughter to speak properly,' Laura Kenzy said. I looked at her, realizing she was humourless as well as a snob. I caught her husband's eye, and he winked.

I said, 'Norfolk people cannot be so different. Norwich is the second city in England, after all.'

'And has some of its finest buildings,' Edward Kenzy said. 'The great cathedral, the fine guildhall.'

'You know it?' I asked.

'Yes. I once had a case which took me there, although that was many years ago. I hear its economy is greatly decayed since then.'

Just then Philip reminded us that curfew time was near, and no one was supposed to be out after ten. We parted, none of us altogether sorry to end the rather fractious supper. It was almost dark now, and candles had been lit during the meal. Philip sent his steward out to fetch some link-boys to guide us home with their torches. We waited for them outside in the balmy evening. I stood next to Edward Kenzy. 'An interesting evening, Brother Shardlake,' he said. 'I am glad we agree on the debasement, but tell me, would you really have the social order overturned? Do you not, like all gentlemen, fear the rabble, feel easier when accompanied in the streets by your assistant with his sword? Do you not turn your eyes away in disgust from the hordes of beggars as they thrust their hands at you, showing welts and sores that half the time are painted on?'

'I turn away with shame, Brother Kenzy, not disgust. But I do turn away, so perhaps indeed I have no right to preach. Still, I would see the wrongs of the common people righted.'

Kenzy did not reply, merely rocked a little on the balls of his feet as he smiled and inclined his head to where Nicholas was bowing over Beatrice's hand, making an elaborate farewell.

'Young Nicholas is a good lad, if a little brash.' He looked at me, keen eyes glinting in the candlelight from Philip's window. 'My wife is dazzled by the range of your contacts at court. You once worked for Lord Cromwell himself, did you not?'

'Those contacts were never easy, Master Kenzy. Only the Lady Elizabeth is left, and I am only assistant to her Comptroller, Master Parry.'

'That's enough for Laura.' He chuckled, and I realized Kenzy did not really care whether the relationship between Nicholas and Beatrice prospered or not, so long as it kept his wife from bothering him. I looked again at the young couple. Laura Kenzy was saying that she hoped Nicholas would come to dine with the family when he returned from Norfolk. 'Oh, yes,' Beatrice agreed, looking up at Nicholas with her large eyes. I saw something false in her fond look that he did not see. But who can see clearly when they are in love?

Chapter Nine

NEXT DAY WAS WHITSUNDAY, the ninth of June. From that morning all church services were to be from the new Prayer Book. I dressed in my robe and serjeant's cap, took my copy of the Prayer Book, and set out for St Paul's. I was alone; Nicholas avoided church services so far as possible, and though I had asked John Goodcole if he and his family wished to attend with me, he'd replied apologetically that he and his wife would be attending their own church. I did not press them. For myself, I wanted to see a historic occasion.

As I passed under Temple Bar I considered whether my thoughts about Beatrice Kenzy had been unfair. I hardly knew the girl, and it was not really my business to approve or disapprove Nicholas's choice. However, if the opportunity came while we were in Norfolk, I would raise the matter with him gently.

I passed under the Ludgate, the great spire of St Paul's Cathedral looming ahead. Around the gates were the usual group of beggars, children holding out stick-like arms, men with missing limbs calling out that they had been injured in the wars. Remembering my discussion with Edward Kenzy the evening before, I reached for my purse and gave a shilling to an emaciated little girl. As I walked on I heard others call, 'Sir, spare something for us, we starve!' I quickened my step, fearing they might follow, and aware I was alone.

✝

I WAS EARLY for the service, but the great cathedral was already crowded. I noticed that members of the King's Yeomen of the Guard lined the walls at intervals. All the great men of the city were there – Lord Mayor Amcoates and the London aldermen resplendent in red, the heads of the trade guilds in their colourful coats, and many of the Royal Council in furred robes and bright gold chains – Richard Rich was there in his Lord Chancellor's robes, a severe expression on his thin features, William Paget, recently ennobled, with his hard, square face and long forked beard, looking plumper now, Catherine Parr's brother, the Marquess of Northampton, a thin-faced man in his thirties with an auburn beard. Parr was glancing idly through the pages of his Prayer Book. I thought how unlike his late sister he was. His reputation was of a man of polished manners but little ability, his rise to the Council table a consequence of his relationship to the late queen. Then I saw William Cecil, his narrow face alert, protuberant eyes roving over the crowds. He caught my eye and nodded briefly. I nodded back, remembering that cold and frightening day in January. I saw Philip Coleswyn and his family, but he was on the far side of the nave, a crowd of people between us.

Heads turned as a procession of clerics entered at the main door and processed up the nave. At their head was Thomas Cranmer, Archbishop of Canterbury, with his long white beard and large, keen blue eyes, his sallow face set in an expression of calm authority, the Prayer Book in his hands.

He mounted the lectern and went through the Whitsunday service, every word declaimed in English in his loud, clear voice. In the new service there was no invocation of saints. People looked stealthily around, wondering whether someone might shout out in favour of the old Latin, but there were no disturbances, only a sense of growing tension as Cranmer approached the climax of the service – 'the supper of the Lord, and the holy Communion, commonly called the Mass', as the new Prayer Book worded it cautiously. During the preparatory prayers there were none of the old ceremonies associated with preparation for the Mass – the washing of hands, crossings, blessings. The archbishop lifted the bread and wine and chanted, not in Latin but in clear English: 'Grant us therefore, gracious Lord, so to eat the flesh of thy dear son Jesus Christ, and to drink his blood in these holy Mysteries, that we may continually dwell in him, and he in us.'

And so it proceeded, every word in English through to the end of the service. I saw many look almost numinously happy, some sad and frowning, but as Cranmer spoke, in that great space a pin could have been heard to drop. When the service ended and Cranmer stepped down, there was a chorus of sighs and rustling clothing, everyone look, ing around to gauge their neighbours' reactions. I kept my face expressionless as I moved away with the crowd.

I saw two men moving towards me, both dressed like me in law, yers' robes and coifs. The smaller was Cecil, and behind him was a tall, stocky man in his mid-forties, clean-shaven, with a face whose handsomeness was marred by the haughty expression in its heavy, lidded brown eyes and downturned mouth. The tall man had the trick of looking down at you as though you were a supplicant who had wronged him, and had been brought in for correction.

Cecil, however, smiled as he wished me good morrow. There was colour in the cheeks above the young secretary's wispy beard, enthusi, asm in his eyes. 'Well, Serjeant Shardlake, how did you find our new service?'

'A great change,' I answered noncommittally. Cecil's companion frowned slightly, and I guessed he was not an enthusiast. Cecil, his manner turned brisk and businesslike, introduced us. 'Serjeant Shard, lake, this is Sir Richard Southwell. He is associated with the Council, and works for the Lady Mary in her duties as feodary of Norfolk. As I believe you are going there tomorrow, I thought you might welcome an introduction.'

I bowed to Southwell, who gave me the briefest nod in return. And I remembered Parry saying that he had spoken to Cecil. Cecil must have some purpose in making this introduction.

Southwell spoke, his voice as haughty as his expression, 'I gather you are retained on this business of John Boleyn. You may have a wasted journey; the word is he will almost certainly be hanged.' I saw he clasped a pair of gloves in his large, meaty hands.

'I know little as yet, Sir Richard.' I hesitated, then added, 'I under, stand you yourself own some land adjoining Boleyn's.'

'I think so.' Southwell waved the gloves dismissively. 'But I have over thirty manors in Norfolk, I can't keep track of them all.'

I smiled graciously before replying, 'I believe some of your officials have already visited his wife.'

Southwell frowned, looking down on me with cold appraisal through those half-closed eyelids. 'Those are standing instructions where lands may be forfeit through a landowner's execution. And whatever else the woman living at his house may be, she is not his legal wife. His whore, I think, would be more exact.' He laughed harshly, showing bad teeth.

Cecil said, 'The discovery of Edith Boleyn's body certainly raises legal complications.' He turned to Southwell. 'I am sure Brother Shardlake understands that. His enquiries are intended only to ensure justice is done as it should be.'

'That's what juries are for, Master Cecil. And now I need some fresh air, gentlemen. Perhaps we shall meet in Norfolk, Master Shard-lake.' His tone was slightly threatening. He turned on his heel and walked away.

Cecil raised his eyebrows and smiled briefly as we joined the crowds heading for the door. He spoke quietly, 'I apologize for South-well's manners, but that is what he is like. I thought you should know.'

'I know Comptroller Parry's lawyer, Copuldyke, is afraid of him.'

Cecil lowered his voice. 'Southwell is one of the most wealthy and powerful people in Norfolk, he runs around fifteen thousand sheep on his lands. For a long time he was a client of the Duke of Norfolk, but three years ago when the old king wanted the family gone, Southwell gave perjured evidence against them. His reward was a place as assistant executor of the old king's will, and an alternate member of the Council should another member die. Now that the Lady Mary has bought the Duke's land, and has the position of feodary, she has become Southwell's patron. All in all, he is a very powerful man.'

'So he is no friend to the Lady Elizabeth, or the Boleyns.' I hesi-tated. 'I have wondered if he has designs on John Boleyn's land.'

Cecil gave me a hard stare. 'If Boleyn is convicted and Southwell wants to buy the lands, then let him. His fondness for the old ways in religion – and he does not hide those – means he has not risen as far as he might, but he has the Protector's confidence. The Lady Mary has refused to adopt the Prayer Book service in her household; she will need to be negotiated with, and Southwell will be important.'

'It seems I am not to cross anybody,' I said ruefully.

'That is in the Lady Elizabeth's best interest. And when it comes to Southwell, in yours.'

'I heard that he was once convicted of murder.'

Cecil glanced around him, then answered quietly. 'Yes. Seventeen years ago he murdered a fellow Norfolk landowner at Westminster over some quarrel, stuck a knife in him, I believe, but he paid large sums to the old king to gain a pardon. And last year, by the way, he connived with a servant of his, John Atkinson, who abducted a fourteen-year-old Norfolk heiress, and put her through a form of marriage against her will. The girl's family appealed to the Protector, and it ended up on my plate. The heiress went back to her family, and Southwell had harsh words from the Protector.' He looked at me. 'He is an exceptionally rough and brutal man, with powerful contacts. So yes, do not cross him.'

'I have wondered,' I replied, 'given that he owns neighbouring land on both sides, whether he might have had something to do with this murder. And if he is capable of the things you say —'

Cecil shook his head. 'Southwell has had to be careful since the abduction last year.' His voice deepened. 'For Jesu's sake, don't set any rumours like that running.'

'I won't. I shall make every effort to keep out of his way. I am not going to Norfolk *looking* for trouble, Master Cecil.'

Cecil smiled thinly. 'But trouble has a habit of finding you.' He stopped, and looked back at the pulpit from which Cranmer had spoken. 'We took a great step today. Before long, we shall go further, and have a service that makes clear the bread and water are only a commemoration of Christ's sacrifice.'

'That is what the Protector wishes?'

He looked at me seriously. 'It is what the King wishes. Their minds are as one.'

We had reached the door. Cecil turned and shook my hand. 'Take some time to enjoy Norwich, Master Shardlake, it is a beautiful city. And the Norfolk people mostly favour the reformed faith, Southwell and the Lady Mary notwithstanding. And keep a low profile, eh?' He walked down the steps to where a little group of servants stood waiting for him. I stepped out into the sunshine. Philip Coleswyn came across, with Ethelreda and their two young children. Like Cecil's, his face was alight with enthusiasm. 'So, it is done,' he said.

'Cranmer is certainly a great preacher.'

'It was good to see you at supper last night,' Philip said. 'I am sorry if the conversation became a little – fractious.'

I smiled. 'Conversations tend to, in these days. No, it was a fine meal, and interesting company. Thank you for inviting the Kenzys.'

'Edward Kenzy is a man of reaction, though, oddly, I cannot help liking him.'

'I like him too. He says what he thinks, with candour.'

'Though his wife –' Ethelreda stopped herself.

Philip raised his eyebrows. 'Perhaps the less said about her the better.' We laughed. 'When you return from Norfolk you must come and dine again.'

'I will.'

I watched them go, envying their family happiness, then walked away. I thought suddenly of Edward and Josephine Brown. Their child would have been born by now. I would have to seek them out when I got to Norfolk.

I had not been concentrating on where I was going, and looked up at the sight of a crowd gathered at the head of an alley leading to Carter Lane. In the middle of the group a man was on his knees. His hands covered his face; blood seeped through his fingers and there was a bright red stain on the grey cobbles. He was surrounded by half a dozen grinning soldiers wearing white tunics with the Cross of St George. I remembered the Boleyn twins and the beggar boy they had tormented. This, though, was worse. The crowd, mostly apprentices but a few workmen and a couple of women too, looked on appreci-atively and called approval as a soldier aimed a kick at the man's side with a boot. He groaned and put a hand out to the wall to stop himself from falling.

'I'm no a spy,' he said in a thick Scotch accent, 'I've been in London these ten years, an honest worker—'

Someone from the crowd called out, 'If you're Scotch, why aren't you up fighting with your countrymen?'

'Yes, have you no honour?' The soldier who had aimed the kick, a large fellow who seemed to be the ringleader, drew his foot back for another. 'Come, spy, uncover your face! I'll make it so your mother won't recognize you!'

There was a bustle of movement, and to my relief I saw the stout figure of Lord Mayor Amcoates approaching, in his red robes and huge gold chain, half a dozen constables with clubs at his side. He stepped forward, face red with fury above his long grey beard. Beside him walked another soldier; about forty, tall and slim, with a seamed face, beaky nose, and short brown beard. He had an air of authority, though his expression was one of irritation.

'In the name of the King, stop this brawling!' the mayor shouted at the soldiers. 'God's death, I'll have you all hanged for riot and deser-tion! Captain Drury, bring your men to order!' He glared at the soldier beside him, who gave the mayor a narrow-eyed look but called to his men to stand to attention, which they immediately did, stepping away from the Scotchman. The mayor turned to the crowd, which was already melting away. 'Be off with you all!' he shouted. 'Go find a cockfight!' The Scotchman, meanwhile, made an attempt to stand but fell back; I caught a glimpse of his blackened eyes. He spat out a couple of bloody teeth. Seeing this, Captain Drury gave a smile that sent a chill through me.

'What's this hurly-burly, men?' Drury asked the soldiers in a jesting tone.

'We came into town, sir, to see what was happening,' the man who had kicked the Scotchman answered. 'That Scotch ape came out the tavern and called us English hogs! It was a stain on our honour, sir.'

The man lifted his shattered face, looked at the mayor, and desper-ately tried to speak, his voice muffled by the blood that dripped from his mouth. 'I didnae! I was buying a chapbook from a peddler, the soldiers heard my accent and set on me! I've lived in London ten years, I earn my bread honestly —'

Mayor Amcoates looked down at him with distaste. 'How? What do you do?'

'I work for a grain merchant, sir. Master Jackson at Three Cranes Wharf. I fetch grain from the docks, help in the warehouse — I've a wife and children —'

The mayor turned to Captain Drury. 'Your men should be in camp, not wandering the city causing trouble.'

Drury said, 'This man insulted them. He could be a spy.'

'A spy would not draw attention to himself.' The mayor raised his voice. 'God's bones, Drury, you may lead the King's chief company, but I will have no more of these soldiers' commotions! I warn you, Protector Somerset is aware of them. Now, take your men and get back to your camp at Islington.'

Drury looked at his men, then spoke boldly to Amcoates. 'And what of this Scotch dog, sir? Should he not be prosecuted for insulting His Majesty's soldiers?'

Amcoates met his gaze with fury, but Drury did not flinch. The mayor sighed, then nodded to a constable. 'Take him to the Fleet, hold him for questioning.'

Captain Drury showed that nasty smile again, then bowed and ordered his men to fall in behind him. They marched away. Two constables took the Scotchman under the arms and dragged him off, feet bumping over the cobbles, drops of blood falling from his face. I thought of my old friend George Leacon, who had been a captain in the French wars and had gone down on the *Mary Rose*. He would have been ashamed to see men under his command act like that. But we had been at war so long, perhaps it had turned men into brutes. I glanced at the blood on the cobbles, glistening bright red in the sun. I wish to God it could have been the last such sight I was to see that summer.

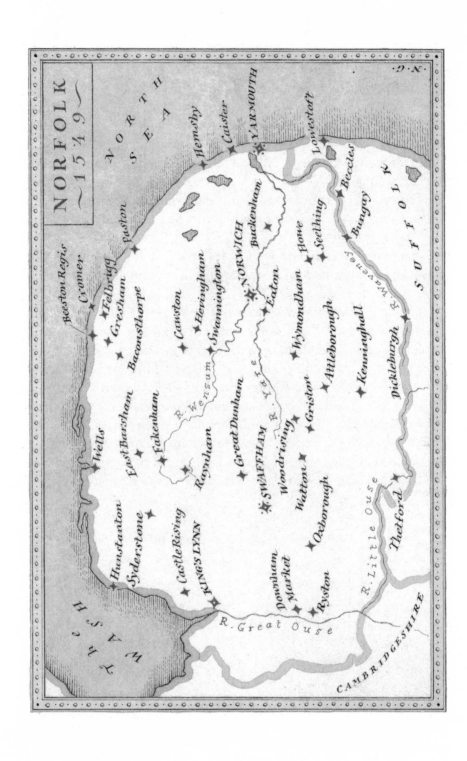

Part Two

NORWICH

Chapter Ten

WE WERE DUE to arrive in Norwich early in the afternoon of Thursday, the thirteenth of June, five days before the Assizes were to begin. It was a long ride, north through Middlesex and Hertfordshire, then north-east to Norfolk. The weather continued warm and sunny, but the roads were in a poor state after the frosty winter followed by the wet spring. Many times we had to plod slowly through mud. I found the journey increasingly hard on my back, as I had feared, and was in some pain by the time we crossed into Norfolk. Nicholas was solicitous of my condition, though Toby Lockswood was keen to proceed as fast as possible and did not appear to notice. Pride prevented me from ordering him to go more slowly, but Nicholas must have spoken to him on our second day, for afterwards he did go at an easier pace. The only times we all speeded up were when we saw groups of masterless men on the road, of which there were a good many, always heading south towards London.

I had already observed that Toby and Nicholas, who lodged together at the inns we slept at, did not get on well. They spoke to each other little, though with me Toby was civil and helpful, if self-contained; he was quiet, though, with something cold about his manner. Nicholas's gentleman's habit of talking down to those of lower station, even if he had to work with them, was reasserting itself with Toby.

We entered Norfolk at Thetford, and at first the road cut through forest and woodland country, with many small farms and areas given over to pasture. Much of the woodland was ancient oak, green and verdant, but we had no time to take pleasure in it, slogging steadily on. Shortly after leaving Thetford, Toby pointed to our right and said the Lady Mary's palace of Kenninghall lay a few miles off in that direction.

We followed the long straight road through Attleborough and the larger town of Wymondham, names which meant nothing to me then. As we approached Wymondham, Toby referred to it as 'Windham', which puzzled me as I had seen the longer name on the route plan we carried.

'But it is spelt Wymondham,' I said.

'We do that sometimes in Norfolk,' he said. 'Miss out the middle syllable when a word's too long. Take the easy way round.'

I smiled at this rare sign of humour.

After Wymondham the nature of the countryside changed. There was less woodland; the flat land stretching to the wide horizon was intensively cultivated, apart from occasional areas of sandy heath dotted with forget-me-nots and rabbit burrows. It was what I had expected, a patchwork of open fields divided into strips, but with a good number of self-contained, enclosed farms carved out of them, some quite large. What surprised me were the large areas given over to sheep, more than I had ever seen. Strange-looking creatures too; they had wool curling down in long braids, rather than the short fleeces familiar from the fields round London. They were penned in by strong wicker hurdles about five feet high, connected to each other with metal braces, which sometimes stretched a mile or more along the roadway, often with ditches outside. On the farms the fields were dotted with people weed-ing the crops, which had not grown nearly as high as one would expect in mid-June. The sheep-runs, though, were empty of people except the occasional shepherd with a boy or dog. One dog ran alongside us for a while, barking wildly on the other side of the fence, scaring the sheep so the silly creatures ran away, huddling together and bleating in panic.

We passed through several villages. Through open windows I saw weavers at their looms, and many women and children stood in the doorways spinning wool on wooden spindles, turning them endlessly. Many people gave us sour looks, and hardly any doffed their caps or bowed as country people customarily did to gentlemen passing through. At one village a cart full of hay, pulled by a bony nag and led by a man in a smock, turned out of a farmyard in front of us. The cart was in the centre of the road and there was room for him to move to one side to let us pass in single file. I thought perhaps he had not seen us and called out, 'Please, fellow, let us pass!'

The man ignored me. Nicholas frowned and called out angrily, 'Out of the way, churl! We're on urgent business!' The man set his shoulders firmly and continued to proceed along the middle of the road. Toby gave Nicholas a cold stare. 'Rudeness won't help you here, master,' he said. There was a bite on the last word I had never heard before. He called to the man in front, emphasizing his Norfolk accent, 'Pardon that fellow's antrums, bor. Be good-doing and let us through, we're in a hurry to reach Naaritch.'

The farmer looked round at Toby, nodded, and moved the cart to the side.

On the far side of the village Nicholas asked Toby, 'What are antrums?'

'Airs and graces,' Toby answered tersely. ''Tis a good thing neither of you are wearing your legal robes. Lawyers are not popular in Norfolk these days.'

✟

WE SPENT THE night at an inn in Wymondham. My back was now so painful I found it difficult to walk without the stick I had brought with me. In the inn yard, as the horses were led away, Nicholas said solicitously, 'You look uncomfortable, sir.'

'I'll be all right when we get to Norwich tomorrow. No more riding.' I lowered my voice. 'I think you would do well to be more friendly to Toby. His local knowledge is important to us.'

Nicholas frowned. 'I do my best, but he makes it clear he dislikes me. In the evenings he tries to lecture me as though he were my equal, saying the ills of the country are caused by greedy gentlemen. It is boring, and insolent. Dangerous, too, with this talk of trouble in the West Country.'

His talk of trouble there was true. At each inn we stopped at, the talk was of the sudden uprising in Devon, which apparently had now spread to Cornwall, with rumours of troubles in Hampshire, too. Nobody seemed sure whether these protests were against the new Prayer Book, or the abuses of the gentlemen, or both.

'He's never spoken like that to me,' I said.

'You pay his wages. I understand now why Copuldyke speaks roughly to him.'

I said gently, 'Well, Nicholas, you have told me your own father is no great example of gentlemanly behaviour.'

'I seek to do better, to live up to my station,' he answered proudly.

'Then humour Toby. You'll get on better without what he sees as' – I smiled – 'your antrums.'

Nicholas did not smile in return; he only said grimly, 'I'll try.'

✢

THE NEXT MORNING, we set out early. Some miles from Norwich Toby pointed up a sandy lane. 'That leads to the Brikewell manors,' he said. I looked up the lane; in the distance I could see the roof of a two-storey house, perhaps John Boleyn's.

Around midday we crossed the River Yare. By now we could see the great spire of Norwich Cathedral ahead. As we came closer we saw other spires, and the battlemented city walls, which stretched along a wide area, except where the River Wensum flowed through the city, brown and fringed with reeds.

The road was busy with carts bringing goods into the city and we halted as we approached the largest and most ornate of the gatehouses set in the walls, with double round towers on each side of a wide-arched door. There was insufficient room for more than one cart to pass through at a time, and there were several carts ahead of us. We halted before a low ditch with a wooden bridge in front of the gatehouse, half-filled with stinking rubbish like the ditches outside London Wall. There was a gallows, too, where the half-rotted body of some malefac-tor hung in chains, a pair of rooks picking at the blackened flesh. I turned and looked along the walls. They were of dark flint, studded with many projecting towers. I noticed that in some places they were in a state of disrepair, half tumbled down. 'These walls are in no good state for defence,' I said to Toby. 'And they are lower than I expected, lower than London or York.'

He nodded. 'They were built for civic pride, not defence. In the days before the Great Plague two centuries ago. The city was larger then.'

✟

WE ENTERED THROUGH the gate, and rode into the city. I was surprised by how much open ground there was – to our right was an area of grass, where earthen butts stood for Sunday archery practice, while to the left were the grounds of a large building undergoing demolition. 'St Mary's,' Toby said. 'Used to be a big chantry college. The government has sold it to the Spencers, one of the big Norwich families.'

We rode on. There were more buildings now, houses and shops with glimpses of courtyards behind them. A small, malodorous stream ran down the centre of the road. Many shops were selling leather goods, and there was a strong smell of new-tanned skins in the air. The streets were busy, though not as thronged as London, with the same mixture of workmen in leather or wadmol jackets, blue-coated apprentices, goodwives in their coifs and the occasional gentleman with decorated doublet, codpiece and sword. I noticed the gentlemen were accompanied by a good retinue of armed servants, while many citizens looked poor; shoeless, their clothes ragged and dirty, their cheeks hollow. Beggars and workless men leaned on walls, watching those who passed by. Some gave us hostile looks. I thought of Josephine and her husband, and wondered how they fared.

To our left, atop artificial grassy mounds built one on top of another, stood a Norman castle, a gigantic battlemented cube of stone, faced with flint at the lowest level, the higher levels of limestone, dirty with age. Like all the Norman castles it was a brutal, solid statement of power. Most now served as gaols. Toby pointed to one of the smaller buildings beside it. 'That's the Shire Hall, where the Assizes will be held.'

'And Master Boleyn is in the castle prison.'

'No escape from there,' Nicholas said, staring at the huge, solid block. 'His only road is to trial.'

'And from there,' Toby said, 'to freedom or to the gallows on hanging-day afterwards. You are right, Master Overton, there is no other road.'

I did not answer, but thought of the Lady Elizabeth's application for a pardon in my pocket, and again hoped desperately it would not be needed.

We rode on, into the largest market square I had ever seen, rect-angular and with a downward slope towards the river. We passed a magnificent church, where I noticed that the stained-glass in the east window, beautifully coloured, was still in place. 'St Peter Mancroft,' Toby said. 'Where the rich city fathers gather on Sundays.'

On the grassy mounds leading up to the castle a cattle market was in preparation, the beasts in a series of pens, men walking around, inspecting them. The marketplace itself, with permanent booths and shops at the top and an open cobbled space at the bottom, was closed; men in leather aprons were clearing rubbish from the cobbles. 'Wed-nesday and Saturday are market days,' Toby said. 'On Saturday, there won't be room to move here.'

We rode through the marketplace. In its centre stood a huge, ornate market cross, two storeys high. At the top of the square I saw an impres-sive building of flint and limestone, one wall decorated in an alternating pattern of black and white squares. 'The Guildhall,' Toby said, 'where the city business is done, the tolls are added up, and the guildsmen meet.' By the doors I noticed a small group of gentlemen in richly decor-ated gowns attended by armed retainers, looking down over the marketplace and talking quietly. 'The city aldermen and sheriffs,' Toby explained. 'Representatives of the great city families. The Stewards, the Anguishes, the Sothertons. That fat little fellow in the red robes is this year's mayor, Thomas Codd.' I noticed that next to the Guildhall another gibbet stood, though without a dangling corpse this time, and beside it were the town stocks and a canopied well.

'You said John Boleyn's father-in-law was an alderman.'

'Yes, Gawen Reynolds. But he and his wife have shut themselves up in their house in Tombland since the news of their daughter's murder. Reynolds is well known as a haughty old fellow with a vicious temper, but if you attend him in your serjeant's robes, he may speak to you.' Toby smiled wryly. 'He married his daughter to John Boleyn when Anne Boleyn was set to become Queen; he thought association with her name would add to his status. But of course she didn't last.'

Before I could reply a crowd of beggarly children appeared, seem-ingly from nowhere, and surrounded our horses, lifting stick-thin arms with cries of 'Charity, gemmun!', 'We're clammed half ta dead!'

To my surprise it was Toby who waved them away, calling fiercely, 'Shut that rattock! Begone!' We rode on, followed by a stream of insults. 'Bent hunchback! Doghearts! Snudges!' I looked at Toby. 'You have to be firm here, sir, even more than in London,' he said quietly. 'If you are marked out as charitable, you'll get no peace. It's hard, though, many of them are truly near starving. The city set a new poor rate last month, but what they raise makes little difference.' There was an angry tremor in his voice.

A number of inns stood at the top of the marketplace, just above the Guildhall. Little groups of people stood talking outside. The inns where the lawyers would stay when the Assizes arrived, I thought. As we approached, a stocky man in his late thirties detached himself from one group and marched towards us. He wore a green doublet and black hose, a wide red cap covering his brown hair. The thing that drew Toby's eye towards him, though, was that he lacked a right hand, having instead a metal rod with a curved handle, below a pointed end covered in a leather sheath. With the handle he held a leather bag.

'Jack!' I said, leaning over to take his proffered left hand. 'I hadn't expected to see you in Norwich so soon!'

'I hadn't expected to see you at all! But when I saw a gentleman surrounded by a crowd of eager beggars, I thought it must be you. And Nicholas, how fare you, long lad?'

'Well enough.' Toby looked a little surprised at their familiarity, but though my former assistant had started life as a child of the streets, he had helped train Nicholas up, and the three of us had lived through the events that ended with Barak losing his right hand to a swordsman.

I indicated Toby. 'This is Goodman Lockswood, a Norwich man assisting us on the case that brings us here.' They shook hands.

'You're here on a case?' Barak asked. 'At the Assizes?'

'Yes.'

'One of the civil law matters? A land case?'

I hesitated. 'Not quite. I'd welcome the chance to discuss it with you, if you have time. But why are you here now? Surely the trials are not due until next week.'

'No, the judges are still in Cambridgeshire. I'm one of those sent ahead, to sniff out the air in Norwich, see which of the Protector's proclamations are being properly observed – which is pretty well bugger all – how folk are reacting to the Prayer Book, what sort of people might be suitable for jury service.' He inclined his head back to the group he had been talking to. 'That's what I'm doing now.' Then his eyes narrowed. 'What sort of case *is* this one of yours, then? A criminal one? You won't be allowed to represent the accused.'

'Later,' I said quietly. 'Where are your lodgings?'

'An inn down by the river. The Blue Boar. At the far end of Holme Street. It's a bit of a hike from here, but the likes of me don't get the best quarters. Where are you staying?'

'The Maid's Head, in Tombland.'

'Very nice. I pass it on my way into the city.' He paused, and looked at me. 'You look pale, are you feeling all right?'

'Yes, yes,' I answered irritably. 'Just a little trouble with my back. Can I meet you for a drink at the Blue Boar later? Say at seven.'

'All right. You can tell me what trouble you've got yourself into now.' Barak winked at Nicholas, gave Toby a salute with his artificial hand, then turned and walked back to his fellows.

✝

WE RODE OUT of the marketplace, into the busy, tangled alleyways of the centre of the city, and through the clanging noise of the metal-workers' district. I remarked that many of the buildings looked new. Toby said, 'There were two great summer fires in central Norwich forty years ago. It could happen again, the new houses are mostly lath and plaster. It was mostly flint buildings, like the churches, which survived.'

'The city seems full of churches,' Nicholas observed.

Toby replied with a rare smile, 'They say there are more churches and alehouses in Norwich than anywhere in England.' He turned to me. 'So that was the man who used to work for you.'

'Yes. Jack Barak.'

We passed a large, ancient stone building where workmen were carrying in bales of cloth. Toby told me it had been a great Dominican friary before the Dissolution, and had been sold to the city by old King Henry. Then we rode down a street of new houses, built since the fires, mostly dwellings of richer citizens, which Toby said was called Elm Hill. At the far end, just below where a flint church stood, the street crossed a broader highway. Nearby I saw a bridge over the brown, muddy river. Toby turned in the opposite direction, downhill. The huge cathedral with its high, narrow spire now dominated the view. Beyond, in the distance, I saw a large heath, surprisingly high in the flat Norfolk landscape, the grass dotted with sheep.

We rode down towards the cathedral. Toby stopped just before the highway ended in a broad space fronting the walled cathedral precinct. 'That is Tombland,' he said.

'Why is it called that? Was it once a burial ground for the cathedral?'

'No. It's always been called Tombland, perhaps the name comes from the old Saxons. Only the richest have houses there.' He nodded to his left, where a wide gateway set in the wall of a large building stood open. 'And this is the main entrance to your inn, the Maid's Head.'

✝

THE GATEWAY LED into a stableyard. A plump middle-aged man in a fine black doublet appeared and gave us a pleasant smile. He reached up and took my hand. 'Welcome to the Maid's Head, sir. I am Augustus Theobald, in charge of the finest inn in Norfolk.' A mounting block was brought for us. I found it hard to dismount, and then to stand – Nicholas had to hand me my stick, which was tied to the back of the packhorse. I leaned against the pump of a well which stood in the yard, a disabling knot of pain between my shoulder blades. Master Theobald looked concerned. 'Are you all right, sir?'

'Yes. It is just that we have ridden from London. If I lie down for a little I will be all right.'

'Are you sure?' Nicholas asked. He had never seen me in such difficulty.

'Yes, don't fuss!' I turned to the innkeeper. 'We have rooms booked by Master Thomas Parry, for three.'

The innkeeper looked embarrassed. 'I fear he only booked rooms for two.'

'It's all right,' Toby said. 'I wrote and cancelled my room. My parents' farm is only three miles off, I can stay with them, and still ride here to assist you every day.'

'There is no problem,' I told Master Theobald. 'Could you have our packs taken to our rooms? And the horses taken to the stables and given a good rub down?'

'Certainly,' the innkeeper replied, bowing.

'Stay with them, Nicholas, and see to things. I would like a word with Toby. Master Theobald, could you show me somewhere I can talk with Goodman Lockswood.' I grasped my stick. 'Somewhere I can sit.'

Theobald led us into the building, pointing out the large comfortable dining room and other amenities, and mentioned that in their time both Catherine of Aragon and Cardinal Wolsey had been guests. Then, bowing, he left us in a well-appointed parlour. A servant fetched two cups of beer, and some welcome bread and cheese. I sat in a chair with great relief, my back supported at last. I gave Toby a stern look.

'You should have told us you planned to stay with your parents. We have much to do, and little time, and need your knowledge of this city.'

'I apologize.' He stroked his curly black beard with a large hand, then fixed me with a direct gaze from those keen blue eyes. 'But my mother is ill, and wishes to see me. I promise I will rise early enough to be here at any hour you wish.'

'Is she seriously ill?'

'She is not strong, and lately finds the work on the farm makes her breathless. Not that there will be much profit from the harvest this year, given the size of the crops.'

'No,' I agreed.

'I hope you are not angry with me, sir,' he added.

I sighed. 'No, I understand. But I will need you here early tomorrow. I am going to visit John Boleyn in the castle gaol, then try and talk to Edith Boleyn's parents. The day after, I want to go and visit the Brikewell estates. This evening I have arranged to see Barak, as you heard, so you may go to your parents' farm now. How far from here is the Blue Boar Inn?'

'I will draw you a diagram.' He looked at me dubiously. 'But will you be able to walk?'

'With my stick, yes.' I heard that testy note in my voice again. 'And I shall lie down for a little first.'

'You should take Master Nicholas.'

'I thought I might go alone. There is a – personal – matter I wish to discuss with Barak.'

Lockswood looked at me seriously. 'A well-dressed stranger with a walking stick would be advised not to wander Norwich alone in the evening. There are robbers about, more than in London.'

'Very well.' I looked at him. 'For all its great buildings, there seems to be much poverty here.'

'There is. For years the great wool merchants have been moving cloth weaving out to the countryside, to avoid the guilds' regulations about manufacture. And centralizing the other processes of cloth production in their own hands. Often they ship the cloth illegally to Europe, to the Dutch. The great families we saw earlier today, by the Guildhall, they grow in riches. But for the poor it is different and now, with the number of farm labourers thrown off the land coming to the city, and the great rise in prices, the mood is fierce.' Toby spoke quietly, evenly, but again with that angry undertone.

'Perhaps the new enclosure commissions Protector Somerset is sending out soon will mend things.'

'Do you think so, sir?'

I remembered my conversation with Edward Kenzy last Saturday, and answered cautiously. 'I think in the little time the commissioners will have, and with the landlords against them, it will be difficult.'

Toby leaned back. 'So others say. My father relied heavily on his rights to graze his cows and oxen on the common land of the manor, but three years ago the landowner enclosed a large part of the common, which he said he was entitled to do, as the largest landowner. There's not a lot left for the village beasts. My father has got by with his crops

these last three years, when the harvests have been good. But this year –'
He shook his head.

'I am sorry.'

'I tell you so you may understand my concern for my family. Please, do not tell Master Copuldyke this, he would use it to make a mockery of me.'

'I shall say nothing.'

'Thank you.'

'In return, perhaps you may do something for me.'

'If I can.'

'Try to get on better with Nicholas. He is over-proud of his gentle-man status, but there are reasons for that. Otherwise he is a decent young fellow, conscientious, intelligent and, as I have reason to know, brave.'

Lockswood gave a wry smile. 'You are observant, sir.'

'So should all lawyers be. And, finally, I want you to help me with some local information.'

'Certainly.'

'First, I should like to speak to the coroner who investigated Edith Boleyn's murder. Where is he based?'

'At the Guildhall. The coroners, like the justices, are expected to be in attendance when the Assizes begin.'

'Good. Now, two years ago, I had a serving girl who worked for me in London. Her name is Josephine. She married a young man named Edward Brown, servant to an aged barrister named Peter Henning. Henning and his wife were retiring to Norwich, where they came from, and they took Edward and Josephine with them as servants. I was very fond of Josephine, I was able to help her once with some trouble, and gave her away at her wedding. She had no family, and nor did Edward.' I told him of the letter I had received, the money I had sent, and my anxiety at hearing no more. Finally, I told Lockswood her address.

'Cosny, eh? That's how common folk pronounce Coslany here,' he added. He looked serious. 'Those are rough parts. I doubt a barrister would live there. Perhaps the old man died?'

'Possibly. If Edward and Josephine are in trouble, I should like to help them.'

Lockswood nodded. 'I can make some enquiries.' His eyes narrowed as he spoke. I could tell what he was thinking, and said sharply, 'Josephine was just a servant to me, nothing else.'

'Of course,' he answered, smiling. 'When would you like me to return tomorrow?'

'At six in the morning? You can breakfast with us.'

'Then God give you good evening, sir.' He stood, bowed, and walked out to the stables with his solid, confident tread. I sighed, took my stick, and went to find someone to guide me to my room, thinking uneasily of what he had said about Norwich being an unsafe place for gentlemen to travel alone, even on a light June evening.

✝

ON THE RIDE I had been in more pain than I had admitted, and it was a great relief to stretch out on the feather quilt on the fine four-poster bed in my room. I lay there and looked through the window. I had a view of the church on the corner of Elm Hill, and of an elm tree with pale green leaves. I was much more comfortable lying down, but the journey had told on me. The space between my shoulder blades hurt badly.

I remembered an exercise Guy had given me when I had twisted my back some years ago. It involved lying on a rolled-up cloth placed under the affected area, and stretching my arms over my head. The bed was a little soft, so with some difficulty I lay on my back on the floor, a tightly rolled-up cloth under my shoulder blades, and gingerly raised my arms with an uncomfortable grunt.

For a moment nothing happened, then I felt a tremendous crack. I gasped with shock, then carefully rolled over and stood up. I feared I might have crippled myself, but in fact my back felt easier. 'Kill or cure,' I muttered, then, lying carefully on the bed, sent a mental 'thank-you' to my old friend. I lay dozing for some time, until the lengthening shadows cast by the elm made me realize it was time for me to go and meet Barak. I heaved myself to my feet, grasped my stick firmly, and went to find Nicholas.

Chapter Eleven

W E STEPPED OUT into the warm June dusk. With my stick I could walk normally, with a little care. We went down the street and found ourselves in Tombland. On three sides stood well-appointed houses, most three-storeyed, painted in a variety of bright colours, with gated courtyards in front. On the fourth side stood the high walls fronting the cathedral, where two massive doors, each set in magnificently painted and decorated arched gateways, were closed for the evening. Over the wall we could see the high, ancient cathedral church, built like Norwich castle of white limestone, and the huge, pointed stone spire. Men in servants' and traders' clothes went in and out of the houses and through little clicket gates in the cathedral doors. A couple of watchmen bearing clubs stood at a corner, their coats showing the city arms of a red shield with a castle and lion underneath. A butcher's cart rumbled by, stopping at one of the big houses. Two aproned men opened the courtyard door and helped the carter unload a bloody side of beef and several plucked geese.

'Someone's holding a grand dinner,' Nicholas observed. 'Tomb-land must be a fine place to live.'

'If you have the money,' I answered.

Lockswood had given me a roughly drawn map and we crossed Tombland and walked along a thoroughfare the plan called Holme Street, which followed the high outer wall of the cathedral precinct. There were a good number of pedestrians still about, mostly traders bringing baskets of produce into town, and the occasional cart, one loaded with new-shorn curly fleeces from the local sheep. As elsewhere in the city, there were many poor men in rags, one with an iron collar around his neck to mark him as an illegal beggar; one or two glanced at the good quality clothes we wore, then noticed the sword and buckler hanging from Nicholas's waist and looked away.

'How is your back, sir?' Nicholas asked hesitantly.

'Better now I have rested.' Thanks also to Guy's exercise, I thought. 'I'll be glad if I never see another horse again.'

We came to another open area, dominated by a large church. The houses here were smaller than in Tombland, but still substantial, with glimpses of gardens behind. Then the road took a turn, and became walled on both sides. Beyond the walls on the side opposite the cath-edral we glimpsed a high, square church tower which Lockswood had marked as the 'Great Hospital'. A pair of wooden gates gave entrance to what looked like an old monastic precinct; on each side half a dozen beggars, men and women, sat with begging bowls in their laps. They cried for alms as we passed. An old fellow with the marks of smallpox on his face stood up and waved his bowl in my face. 'I fare sick, sir,' he cried, 'dorn't pass by, be good-doing!' Nicholas put out an arm to thrust him aside but I reached into my purse and gave him a sixpence. All the others immediately struggled to their feet with outstretched bowls, and Nicholas grasped my arm and hurried me away.

'Don't pull at me like that,' I complained, but only when we were out of reach.

'They'd have mobbed you!'

'It was only Christian charity!'

We walked on to where an inn stood, next to a high, battlemented gatehouse guarding a stone bridge across the river, weeping willows on both banks. The high, bare heath loomed beyond, a large mansion visible on the top. I turned to Nicholas. 'At some point I'll give you a nod. Say you need the jakes. There is a – personal – matter I must dis-cuss with Jack.'

He nodded. 'There he is,' he said, pointing to where a number of tables had been set out in the inn garden. Groups of men were sitting there, mostly in the smocks and leather jackets of the artisan class. Alone at one table, a mug of ale in his left hand, sat Barak. He rested the other arm with its metal prosthesis on the table, where it caught the glint of the setting sun.

He rose, pleasure at seeing us evident in his face. I noticed he was continuing to put on weight. 'How fare you both?' he asked. 'God's bones, young Nicholas, I'll swear you've got even taller.'

'How are you, Jack?' Nicholas asked.

'Glad to be out of London for a bit.' Yet, looking in my old friend's eyes, I saw sadness and something more: weariness.

'I'll fetch some beer,' Nicholas said.

'Ay, I'm always ready for another,' Barak replied cheerfully. Nicholas went into the inn and I sat down. 'How goes your work in Norwich?' I asked.

'All right. I spend evenings in the taverns, listening to conversations, sounding out the local mood. The judges' clerks have people doing that on most Assizes.' He smiled wryly. 'The judges know I have a history of such work, back to when I worked for Lord Cromwell. Then I have to liaise with the sheriff, and make sure, very politely, that he is doing his work efficiently in selecting jurors for the Assizes. Though I've had to deal with his deputy this time; Sir Nicholas L'Estrange has been in Somerset.'

'And how do you find the mood in Norwich?'

'Bad.' He lowered his voice. 'Masterless men coming in from the countryside, jobs going from the city, much misery and anger. It's been decided that instead of the usual grand feast to welcome the judges, there's only going to be an ale for them. The city authorities fear too ostentatious a celebration might spark something.'

'Are things that tense?'

He nodded. 'They have been all along the circuit, though not so bad as here.'

Nicholas returned with three mugs of ale, and we drank each other's health.

I spoke quickly. 'Jack, there is something we need to know, if you can tell us. When will the criminal cases be heard? Will it be at the start of the Assizes, as usual?'

He shook his head. 'No, they're doing them on the third day, there are a couple of big land cases they want heard first. The criminal hearings will be on the twentieth.'

'Then we have a week to investigate,' Nicholas said. 'More time than we hoped for.'

Barak looked at us. 'So you are here on a criminal matter?'

'Yes. The case against John Boleyn, for the murder of his wife. Have you heard anything about it?'

'Indeed. It's roused some interest among the assize staff, on account of the name, and the nasty circumstances. It all sounds pretty horrible.'

'It is.' I told him what I knew of the Boleyn case, the Lady Elizabeth's interest, and Toby Lockswood's accompanying us to Norwich, though I had to leave out the story of Edith Boleyn's visit to Hatfield. When I had finished, Barak looked at me narrowly. 'I thought you'd had enough of political matters.'

'This is not political. The Lady Elizabeth only wants us to investigate the facts and ensure justice is done.'

'It may not be high London politics, but it's political around here. The Boleyn name isn't popular, I've learned that much, and John Boleyn setting up house with an alewife did him no good with the local gentry.'

'So I've heard.'

He looked at me sharply. 'Do you think him innocent?'

'I honestly don't know. My mission is to ensure all information comes before the court, and that he has a fair trial.'

Nicholas asked, 'Do you think they'll be able to find an impartial jury?'

Barak shrugged. 'It won't be easy. The name Boleyn isn't popular, as I've said. And the judges will be looking for a conviction on an outrage like this. Sentencing gets harsher every year; it's thanks to all these Calvinistic types in power.'

'You told me one of the judges on the circuit is a hard man. Judge Gatchet, wasn't it?'

Barak nodded seriously. 'He'll want a kill. You know the other judge, Reynberd; quiet, smiling. Sometimes he pretends to be asleep, but he observes everything, especially local politics. He can strike hard when he chooses but he's not as harsh as Gatchet. As usual on Assizes, they appoint two different types, to balance each other.'

'You sound out of sympathy with the Assizes,' Nicholas observed.

Barak leaned back in his chair. 'Ay, lad, I am. Seeing the judges entering the cities with their armed retinues, all pomp and ceremony, up there on horses in their red robes, the robes of blood, as people call them . . . Then watching them hurry through the capital cases, afraid of catching gaol fever. They're on to the next town before the hanging day. Some of the civil cases too' – he shook his head. 'Last year a land-lord brought a case against a blind widow with five children. Her husband was his tenant, but he died, and the landlord wanted to put the widow and children out on the grounds they couldn't manage the farm. He won, the judge saying the tenant had to be able to farm the land to pay the landlord his due rent, and the widow and children went on the streets.' He shrugged. 'I suppose he was right, as a matter of law.'

'Unfortunately, he was,' I agreed.

'That's hard,' Nicholas said quietly.

'Ho, Nick, I thought you were the landlord's friend.'

'Not where an injustice like that is concerned.'

'Spirit of the times,' Barak said bitterly. 'Pay the poor in worthless money, conscript them to serve in this mad Scottish war.'

I smiled. 'You are become a Commonwealth man.'

He shrugged. 'I see what I see. I was here in Norwich on the winter Assizes two years ago, and, by God, things are worse now. People are saying they wish King Henry was back, at least you knew where you were with the old bastard.'

'Usually in trouble,' Nicholas said feelingly.

Barak sighed. 'Well, I think I'll make this my last Assizes. Spend more time working with the London solicitors.' He smiled, brighten-ing. 'I can write a fair hand with my left now, it's taken a lot of practice and it's a bit of a scrawl but it's legible. I can take depositions again.'

'That is good,' I said, looking uncomfortably at his prosthesis, the attached knife sticking out, protected by its leather sheath.

There was an uncomfortable silence. I was conscious that a group of four young men, who had taken seats at an adjoining table shortly before, were looking at us. They were sunburned, wore wide hats and leather smocks, and long poles were balanced on their table. I took them for boatmen from the nearby river.

'The Blue Boar's coming up in the world,' one said, loud enough for us to hear. 'Look at yinder gemmen.'

'Even if they are a funny-looking crew.'

'Furriners here for the Assizes, probably. Come to see who's going to dance from market gibbet next week.'

'Yin's a hunchback, yin's got a metal hand. Can't see what's wrong with the third one.'

'Maybe he's missing his cock.'

They laughed coarsely and Nicholas reddened. 'You insolent churls,' he said, pushing back his chair. Barak put out a restraining hand, then laid his artificial one on the table with a loud clang, and pulled off the sheath covering the knife. It was not long, but sharp. He looked meaningfully at the men.

'We're just mardlin, sir,' one said, though a touch aggressively, and they bent their heads over their drinks again. Barak turned back to us. 'See what I mean,' he said quietly. 'Gentlemen aren't popular here now, and don't get the usual civilities.'

'Insults that children would make,' Nicholas said, still staring boldly at the men. One looked back at him threateningly, and Barak asked, to distract him, 'What are your next steps on the case?'

Nicholas answered, 'Tomorrow we'll see Boleyn in gaol, and the coroner, then visit the victim's parents, if they'll see us.'

'Any idea yet who might have done it, if not John Boleyn?'

I shook my head. Nicholas said, 'There's plenty of choice. Boleyn's sons, his second wife, the neighbour he had quarrelled with.'

I thought, but did not say, And Richard Southwell, who might be interested in Boleyn's lands, and from whom I was warned off by Cecil.

Nicholas said, 'If only Boleyn had an alibi for the two hours when his second wife said he was studying legal papers, but did not actually see him.'

'Especially as those papers were down in London,' I added. 'The crucial papers about Brikewell. I have them.' I looked at Nicholas. 'I think we should take Lockswood and visit the Brikewell manors on Saturday.'

'Mind if I come along?' Barak asked diffidently. 'I'm busy tomor-row, but free Saturdays.' I raised my eyebrows, and he said, 'Tamasin's down in London, isn't she? She won't know.'

I hesitated, then said, 'All right.' I gave Nicholas a quick nod. He said, 'I need the jakes. I'll be back in a minute.'

When he had gone, I said quietly to Barak, 'I had an encounter with Tamasin a week ago.' I told him what had passed at Guy's. He shook his head. 'She won't forgive or forget, will she? Three years now. I've tried to move her, but she won't budge.'

'She said she thinks of me when she rubs oils on your – your stump in the evening. She says it hurts then.'

He sighed deeply. 'It does, it hurts now. But pain is part of life, isn't it? I noticed you were walking very carefully when you came in.' Then he said, with sudden anger, 'She's always on at me not to do this, be careful with that. I think she would like to have me in swaddling clothes like a baby. The arguments we have when I say I'm going on Assizes duty – I get sick of it.'

I looked at him anxiously, remembering the time they had parted for a while. He read my look and said, 'I'd never be without Tammy and the children, the care she gives me is more than most men get, but – she's got to realize I can do most things I used to.' He shook his head. 'Women, eh? How's young Nick doing in that department?'

I smiled. 'He is interested in someone, and it may go somewhere, but I can't say I like the girl.'

Next to us the four boatmen stood up, taking their staffs. One tipped his hat to me, and bowed, but then made a loud fart. Laughing, he and his companions walked off towards the inn. Barak smiled. We sat in silence for a moment. I looked over at the high gatehouse, its battlemented towers a darker shadow in the growing dusk. A light glimmered in the diamond-paned windows twenty feet up.

'That's an impressive building,' I said.

'It was built to guard Bishopsgate Bridge. It's the only bridge over the river on this side.'

'What's that great mansion on top of the hill beyond?'

'Surrey Place. Built only a few years ago by the Earl of Surrey, the Duke of Norfolk's son. Since he was executed it's been empty, managed by the King's escheator. It's too grand a place for anyone else in these parts to buy. Beyond is Mousehold Heath, a big expanse of land

owned by the cathedral, too sandy for anything but light grazing. It has
its history,' he said, melancholy entering his voice.

'What's that?'

'Centuries ago they found a young boy murdered there. They
blamed the Norwich Jews, and they suffered for it. They made the boy
a saint, William of Norwich; there was a shrine to him in the cathedral
until all the shrines were taken down by King Henry. At least that's
one good thing the old villain did.' Barak's hand had gone to his shirt,
and I guessed he was fingering the old, worn mezuzah handed down
to him by his father, for he was of Jewish ancestry. He gazed up at the
darkening escarpment. 'And Mousehold was the site of a great camp
during the Peasants' Revolt.' He looked at me meaningfully. 'The other
day in a tavern I heard some working men talking about that. They
mentioned Wat Tyler, and Piers Plowman. That's the mood here.'
He looked round. 'Where's Nicholas, he's taking a long time over
that piss.'

'I could do with a visit to the jakes myself. And I'm hungry, do
they serve food here?'

'Ay, a reasonable pottage.'

'I'll get some.'

I stood, wincing a little as my back protested, and made my way
across the garden to the far end, where a horn lantern swung above a
wooden shed. 'Nicholas,' I called. 'Are you in there?' There was no
answer. I pulled the door open, then stepped back with a gasp. Nicholas lay face down on the filthy floor, next to the pit with two planks
on bricks over it. I grasped at the lantern and held it over him. There
was blood on the back of his head. I touched the pulse on his neck. To
my relief it was throbbing. I saw a paper had been placed on his back,
and raised the lantern to it. In scrawled capitals I read: *DEATH TO
ALL GENTLEMEN.*

Chapter Twelve

Nicholas groaned and stirred. I helped him to a sitting position, calling loudly to Barak. He hurried over, followed by several other patrons of the inn. By that time, to my relief, Nicholas was groaning and shaking his head.

'What happened?' I asked him.

'I don't know. I came in here, then someone hit me on the back of the head.' His hand went to his purse. 'It's still here,' he said in surprise.

Barak stepped forward and examined his head. 'Just a scalp wound. Lot of blood but no damage. They meant to humiliate you, I think, not to kill or rob. Did you see who it was?'

'No, but I think there were several of them.'

'Those boatman,' Barak said.

I held up the note. 'I think you're right,' I said quietly. 'Revenge.'

'Revenge for what?' Nicholas asked angrily. 'It was they who began insulting us.'

'Perhaps for calling them churls,' Barak said. 'People of low class, in other words. It's not an insult to use lightly around here.'

I said, 'They called us worse, and for no reason. Come, let's get out of this stink-hole.'

Watched by a dozen curious faces, we helped Nicholas outside and over to a bench. He blinked and shook his head again. Someone laughed. 'He's fair dozzled.'

'A's fine clothes is all shitty.'

Indeed Nicholas's clothes were mired with the filth of the cesspit floor, and he stank mightily. The inn landlord hurried up. 'What's going on?' he asked anxiously, addressing Barak, his guest.

'Our friend here was attacked when he went to the jakes.'

'Was he robbed?'

'No, but he was hit on the head.'

I handed the innkeeper the note. 'This was left. There were some boatmen insulting us earlier, I think it might have been them.'

'He said he didn't see nothing,' someone said angrily. 'Gemmun all right, accusing folk without evidence.'

'Furrinners, too. Why don't they go back to London?'

There was a murmur of agreement from the little crowd, and the innkeeper led us away. He lowered his voice.

'A lot of my customers are river folk,' he said. 'I'm sorry for what happened, but please, sir, don't throw accusations around, or there'll be trouble. Report it to the constable, if you like, but I doubt he will be able to do anything without evidence.'

I looked hard at the man, guessing the boatmen who had attacked Nicholas were probably regular customers, but Barak, after surveying the crowd, said quietly, 'I think you and Nicholas should go.'

'What about you?'

He smiled wryly. 'I'm only a gentleman by association with you two. I'll be all right.'

The innkeeper looked relieved. 'I'll call a couple of link-boys to light your way back. Where are you staying?'

'The Maid's Head.'

The innkeeper walked back to his customers. 'It's all right. Nobody is being accused. Come on now, no trouble, lads.' The men returned to their benches.

'How are you feeling?' I asked Nicholas.

'Just a sore head. But by Christ, I need a wash.'

I looked around the candlelit benches, receiving a couple of sour looks in return. I was glad when the innkeeper reappeared, accompanied by a couple of stout link-boys with flaming torches.

✝

BACK AT THE Maid's Head, we explained Nicholas's state by saying he had slipped on a turd in the street. After a thorough wash and change of clothes he looked much better, though still pale. He insisted he would be able to accompany me and Toby around Norwich the following day, and I left him to sleep. I had kept the piece of paper.

One of those boatmen – I was sure the attack had come from them – had been literate. This hatred of gentlemen – and boldness in attacking them – was something I had never encountered before, and I was careful to lock my door before going to bed.

✠

THE NEXT MORNING, I was up at five, and eating breakfast with Nicholas in the inn parlour before six. Fortunately, his colour had returned, and the nasty bruise on his head was concealed by a wide cap. I had repeated Guy's exercise last night, and my back felt much better. I would not have liked to ride again so soon, but I felt I could manage to walk without my stick. Punctually, as the cathedral bells sounded six, Toby Lockswood walked in from the stables. He bowed to us. 'God give you good morrow, sirs.'

'And you, Toby. How fare your parents?'

'My mother is better than she was. But my father is worried about the crops.'

I looked out of the window at the sunlit street. 'At least the wet weather is over.'

'Ay. It's hot already, it's going to be a swelking day.'

'And a busy one. I want to see John Boleyn at the castle, the coroner, and, if possible, Edith Boleyn's family.'

'I managed last night to arrange a meeting with the coroner. He will see you in the Guildhall at twelve o'clock.'

I considered. 'I would rather see him before Boleyn.'

'That was the earliest he could do, sir.'

'Then we'll see Boleyn first. And did you manage to find out anything about my old servant, Josephine Brown?'

He shook his head. 'Nobody recognized the name, nor that of the retired lawyer, Peter Henning. However, a solicitor's assistant, who is a friend of mine, will make enquiries. Even if Master Henning is retired, his name should be known. God willing, he's still alive,' he added.

'Thank you. It is – important to me. Well, we should go.' I glanced at Nicholas. 'Are you sure you're up to it, after that blow on the head?'

'Of course,' he answered, a little irritably.

Toby frowned. 'Blow on the head?'

I told him of events at the Blue Boar, and showed him the paper I had found. He flicked his black beard.

'You shouldn't have called those men churls,' he said seriously. 'Even if they did start it.'

'So my friend Barak said.'

'Just going to an inn not usually patronized by gentlemen would be enough.' He looked at Nicholas. 'You must take care to avoid any unnecessary quarrels.'

'I was thinking of reporting it to the constable,' Nicholas replied.

'It would go nowhere, and may get you a bad name.' He looked at me with those intense blue eyes. 'And sir, we have our work cut out as it is, do we not?'

✝

WE LEFT THE Maid's Head at seven. Nicholas and I had donned our legal robes. First of all Toby led us round the corner into Tombland. He pointed at a large house brightly painted in yellow. 'That is Alderman Gawen Reynolds's house, next to Augustine Steward's. I warn you again, he is a difficult and bad-tempered old man. His poor old wife always looks afraid of him, and he has ever had a reputation for pestering the female servants. But now, to get to the Guildhall, we should turn back and go up Elm Hill.'

We walked on to the wide market square, the great block of the castle looming over it. There people were cleaning their stalls and sweeping horse dung and rubbish away in preparation for the morrow's market. Goods were being carried into warehouses. Beside the market cross a man in a preacher's robe was addressing a crowd, mostly blue-coated apprentices, stabbing the air with a New Testament to emphasize his points. In his loud, deep voice, he said, 'St Paul tells us, "The body consists of not one member, but many. Now, they are many, but of one body."'

'Ay!' a boy called out. 'All the faithful are equal before God!' There were shouts of agreement.

The preacher, a tall young man, waved the Testament again. 'They are! But St Paul also reminds us we each have different parts to play in this world, like the parts of the body. "Having then gifts differing according to the grace that is given to us. If it is the gift of prophecy, let us prophesy—"'

An old man with a wild white beard shouted out from the crowd, 'I prophesy the commons shall have rule of the country when John Hales's enclosure commission comes. For together we are as great as the Leviathan in Job.' Eyes turned to him as he quoted, in turn, '"Can you draw out Leviathan with a hook? Or his tongue with a cord? Can you put a hook into his nose or bore his jaw through with a thorn?"' His voice rose. '"Will he make many supplications unto you? Will he speak soft words to you?" We, the common people of this land, are Leviathan.'

There were cheers. The preacher shook his head vigorously. 'No, brothers, there is justice that needs to be done in God's kingdom, and it will be done, by the grace of the King and the Lord Protector. But the body must have its head, some must rule. Again, St Paul says, "Let him that rules, do it with diligence."'

'Fuck the landlords!' an apprentice called out.

We walked on. 'The preacher walks a tightrope with the crowd,' I observed. 'It's the same in London.'

Toby replied, 'That's why the right to preach is strictly controlled now. That was Robert Watson, one of Cranmer's protégés, appointed as a canon at the cathedral to be a thorn in the side of Bishop Rugge.'

'Is Rugge a traditionalist?' Nicholas asked.

'Ay, and lazy and corrupt. Watson sings the Protector's tune. Though some, like that old man, want more. Old Zachary Hodge. He thinks himself a prophet of the Lord, he's been preaching around Norwich for twenty years. Done spells in the Guildhall gaol for it. Not that a lot of what he says isn't right.'

'So many think themselves prophets these days,' Nicholas said wearily. 'Preaching,' he continued, 'it's always slanted to somebody's politics.'

'That it is, lad,' I agreed.

We had reached the bottom of the market square. We paused beside a cart to allow a skinny, ragged lad in his mid-teens, with an unruly shock of brown hair and carrying a large bale of cloth, to cross our path. A plump middle-aged man standing in a doorway called out to him, 'Hurry up, Scambler! Ain't got all day!'

Though struggling under the load, the boy picked up his pace. Someone from inside the building approached the man with a list, and he turned away. At that moment three other boys, in apprentices' robes, who had been loitering near the cart, ran across to the boy, one of them kicking his feet from under him so that he fell forward. The bale, despite the boy's frantic attempt to grab it, landed in the mud of a puddle drying after the rains. The three boys shouted, 'Sooty Scambler's done it again!' The man in the doorway turned round, frowned mightily, and walked rapidly over. He looked with dismay at his bale of cloth. He dragged it from the mud, then stood over the boy, who was rising to his feet, a puzzled expression on his face. The three apprentices who had caused his fall stood around, serious-faced now. One shook his head disapprovingly.

Scambler's employer shouted, 'Look what you've done now, you shanny, buffle-headed—'

Nicholas marched over to him. 'If you please, sir! Those three tripped him, we saw it!'

Toby sighed. 'I've said before, we need to keep the peace.'

'Those boys should not be allowed to get away with that,' I answered, going to join Nicholas. Toby followed reluctantly.

The stallholder was glowering at Nicholas. 'You keep your nose out, young master lawyer! I've had six weeks of Sooty Scambler's non-nying about and I've had enough. Get out, Scambler! If you had any family left, I'd sue them in the mayor's court for damage to my cloth!'

'Excuse me, sir,' I said firmly. 'But my assistant is right. Those boys tripped your employee. All three of us saw it.'

'We did not,' the apprentices chorused in outraged unison. The boy Scambler stared at them, the startled expression on his face turning slowly to a frown. 'Did they?' he asked quietly.

I looked at him more closely, wondering if he was a wantwit, but his eyes, though full of perplexity, did not have the vacancy of a fool.

The stallholder was still furious. 'You think my poor Norfolk wit not up to knowing my own workers?' He pointed a shaking finger at the three boys. 'Those lads are apprenticed to respectable Norwich freemen. Scambler's a careless fool without the concentration of a sheep. His own father, that was a chimbly sweep, had to sack him because, little bag of bones though he is, he kept getting stuck up people's flues.' That explained the nickname Sooty.

One of the apprentices heaved up the muddy bundle of cloth and handed it to the stallholder. He nodded thanks. Scambler, tears in his eyes now, said, 'They must have tripped me. I was watching my footing, master!'

In reply, the stallholder smacked him hard round the face. 'Get out! Don't come near my stall again!' He glared at us. 'Lawyers! Furriners!' He spat viciously on the ground, then went into the warehouse and slammed the door. The three apprentices ran off, laughing. As they disappeared into one of the alleyways, one sang tunelessly, 'Sooty Scambler, Sooty Scambler! Little buffle-headed cunt.' Scambler stared after them with tears coursing down his face. I said gently, 'I did my best, lad, I'm sorry.'

'It was kind, sir, I thank you.'

I felt in my purse and handed the lad a shilling. 'Why did those boys do that?' I asked. Scambler shook his head, then blinked, the tears flowing faster now. 'People do things like that to me,' he said quietly. 'I don't know why.'

Toby said impatiently, 'Come, lad, stop weeping. Be a man.'

Scambler looked at him, then suddenly turned and ran off, up towards the castle. We stared after him.

'Little wretches,' Nicholas said. 'Why torment the boy so? Losing him his job.'

I said feelingly, remembering my own childhood, 'Because he's different. People don't like difference, children even less than adults. The preachers are right about one thing, mankind is fallen from grace.' I looked at Toby. 'You might have backed us up.'

'I said, sir, it is better not to attract attention. Master Copuldyke said that was Master Parry's instruction.'

'Come,' I said sharply, 'we are due at the castle.' As I turned away I thought, So there are limits to Toby's sympathy for the oppressed.

Chapter Thirteen

T O REACH THE SERIES OF enormous grassy mounds on which
Norwich Castle was built we had to cross an open area where
stalls for tomorrow's cattle market had been set up, then a filthy stream,
before following a long circular path to the causeway giving entrance
to the great building. The sun was higher now, and by the time we
reached the causeway, I was hot, my back beginning to hurt again,
though both Lockswood and Nicholas looked quite fresh, despite the
events of the night before. We then had to walk along the causeway
itself. Eventually, we reached the main doorway, a huge semicircular
arch. The great wooden doors were closed, but a well-built guard
carrying a polished halberd stood at a small clicket door set into one of
them. He wore a round helmet and the white tunic of a soldier, the
letters ER embossed on it, reminding me that authority over the castle
rested with the King, not the city. He was watching a man nail a large,
official-looking paper to the castle door. He finished and nodded to the
guard. 'Off to the Guildhall next,' he said and walked off down the
causeway.

Lockswood studied the official-looking paper. He stroked his black
beard, then whistled.

'Another proclamation from the Protector?' I asked.

'Ay.' We leaned forward to read it. Toby said, 'See, it offers a general pardon for all those who rioted against enclosures in the spring.
Against Sir William Herbert and his like.'

Nicholas frowned. 'What is he thinking? At this time? With the
rebellion in the West. It'll only encourage others to do the same.'

Toby answered, his face expressionless, 'Yes, it could, couldn't it?'

I went to the guard and showed him the letter of authority which
Copuldyke had given me in London. 'We are here to see a prisoner,

John Boleyn,' I told him. The man nodded and let us through the clicket door. We walked under a stone-flagged porch and a magnificently decorated arch into a huge, empty space, dimly lit by high windows. The place smelled, like all prisons, of sweat, urine and damp. Despite the heat outside, the air was chill and dank. Another couple of guards were playing cards at a trestle table. One came over, an enquiring look on his face, and when I explained my business he shouted, 'Oreston!' in a voice which echoed round the vast chamber. I heard footsteps ascending a metal staircase, then an inner door opened and a heavily built young man in a dirty smock, a club at his belt, walked over to us. 'A cartful of lawyers to see Boleyn,' he was told. The gaoler looked at us curiously. 'Someone is taking a great interest in Master Boleyn, I see.'

'His lawyer in London is unable to attend.' I nodded at Toby. 'This is his assistant, Goodman Lockswood.'

The gaoler led us through a door and down a flight of circular iron steps into another broad area, stone-flagged, dimly lit by high windows, containing several doors with small barred windows. Our footsteps made an echoing clang as we descended, and several pale, desperate men came and looked through the bars. The gaoler led us over to a door, opening it with a key from a large bunch at his belt.

John Boleyn's cell was small, lit only by a tiny barred window under the roof. I guessed we must be underground. There were dirty rushes on the floor, a stinking pail, a stool and a truckle bed with a straw mattress the only furniture. A man sat on the bed, squinting to try and read a New Testament by the light from the window. He looked up. I had expected someone fair and burly like the twins, but their father, though tall and athletically built, had black hair and a black beard. His lined, dirty face looked worn out, and there was a shocked expression in his wide blue eyes. It was hard to believe this was a substantial Norfolk landowner. I remembered Lockswood, in London, saying that Boleyn was in a sorrowful state.

The gaoler asked cheerfully, 'Making your peace with God, master, before you hang?'

Boleyn stared back at him contemptuously.

'Get out,' I told the gaoler. He shrugged and left, locking the door behind him.

I extended a hand to Boleyn. 'I am Serjeant Matthew Shardlake, sent to look into this matter on behalf of Master Copuldyke. My assistant, Master Overton. I think you know Goodman Lockswood.'

'Ay,' Boleyn replied in cultivated tones. 'You are a serjeant-at-law? I had not expected someone so senior.'

I smiled. 'There are those who would help you, Master Boleyn. I am not allowed to represent you in court as it is a criminal case, but I will investigate the facts further, see if new light can be thrown on the matter. Do you mind if I take the stool? My back has been troublesome of late.'

'Have you seen my wife, my Isabella?' Boleyn asked with sudden emotion.

'No, but I hope to go over to Brikewell and see her tomorrow.'

'They say she is my wife no more, the chaplain will not let her visit.' Boleyn sighed angrily. 'They will hang me. They don't like my name, they don't like my wife, my neighbour covets my lands —'

I spoke encouragingly. 'In court, it is facts that matter, not prejudices. I would ask some questions, if I may? I have your deposition here.' I took it from my bag.

'If you wish.'

'First, about your wife disappearing nine years ago. I understand she left quite suddenly, without any explanation.'

To my surprise, he laughed bitterly. 'Yes. And yet in some ways I was not surprised.'

'Why?'

He hesitated, then said, 'When I married Edith Reynolds near twenty years ago, she was a beautiful young woman, buxom and with lovely blonde hair, though quiet and shy — dominated by her father, I think. I believe now she only married me to get away from him. Though I loved her then. I did.' He fell silent again, biting his lip, then spoke softly. 'As soon as we were married, she changed. She was reluctant even to perform the most — essential wifely duties.' His face went red and he looked at me defiantly. 'A man does not like to admit such things, but I am past caring. She fell pregnant at once with the twins, but then refused to have more children. And she had no attachment to the boys, right from when they were babies. I have sometimes wondered if that is why Gerald and Barnabas have turned out the brutes they have.' A tremor of anger sounded in his voice. 'Living with her became a very hell. She was constantly ill tempered, the servants were afraid of her, apart from her maid Grace Bone, who became her confidante for a while, but even she left in the end. And her strange habits – as I told you, my wife was a buxom woman when we met, but sometimes, for no reason, she would starve herself until she was just skin and bone. I don't know why; she would just snap that she wasn't hungry. I tried kindness, I tried shouting at her, but nothing made any difference. I began to fear Edith was mad.'

'And then you met your present wife. Isabella.'

Boleyn lifted his face defiantly again. It was a mobile face, the face of an emotional man. 'Yes, the year before Edith vanished. Isabella worked at an inn I frequented. She was everything my wife was not – kind, cheerful, friendly, young, and – she liked me. It was strange to be liked by a woman after so many years. She became my mistress. Is that so unusual, in the circumstances?' he asked, a sudden note of anger in his voice.

Toby said, 'Then tongues started clacking, and somebody told Edith about Isabella.'

'Yes, Edith said nothing to me, but fell into one of her bad phases. It was not long since Gerald cut Barnabas's face, which angered and, I think, frightened her. She stopped eating again. It was a difficult time, a very hot summer. We had almost no harvest that year, I was worried about money. You may remember, it was the year Lord Cromwell fell. I confess I was harsh with Edith, and more than once lost my temper.' So, I thought, he did have a temper, but could it cause him to lose control to the extent of murdering Edith in that terrible way? He continued, 'Then one day at the beginning of December she simply disappeared, taking nothing but the clothes she stood in. A hue and cry was raised, but no trace of her was ever found.'

I asked, 'When did Isabella move in?'

Boleyn frowned, a stubborn expression appearing on his face. 'The next year, only when it was clear Edith was gone for good. You'll see that from my deposition, I've made no effort to hide it. Oh, that scan-dalized the fine gentry folk of Norfolk. Half of them believed I had murdered Edith and buried her somewhere; they were avoiding me anyway, saying I had no more morals than Anne Boleyn, my distant kinswoman. So I thought, to hell with them.'

'And you have no idea where Edith was, all those nine years?'

He shook his head wearily. 'I wish I did. Like everyone else, I thought she was dead, that she had killed herself.'

'Did she have any connections outside Norfolk?' I hesitated, then added, 'In Essex, say, or Cambridgeshire, or Hertfordshire?' Nicholas gave me a warning look. Mentioning Hertfordshire was getting a little close to Hatfield. But Boleyn only looked back at me blankly.

'No. She was Norwich born and bred.'

'I understand her father is a Norwich merchant.'

'Oh, yes.' Anger entered his voice again. 'Gawen Reynolds is a cloth merchant, as were his father and grandfather. They built up a fortune, partly by selling worsted cloth to the Dutch, illegal though that is. A hard man. I thought I'd better not put all that in my depo-sition. He's one of those who run Norwich, his wife is a Sotherton. A brutal, vicious man, high in city politics. He's gone to ground, con-cerned the case will hurt his status in the city.' Boleyn laughed. 'He had ambitions to be Mayor of Norwich. This case will put an end to that. He would not be sorry to see me hang.'

'I plan to see him later.'

'I doubt he will talk to you.'

'I can be persistent.'

Toby had begun to scratch his head, and Boleyn smiled mirth-lessly. 'I fear the bedding here is full of fleas.'

'Master Boleyn,' I said seriously, 'if we are to get you acquitted, we must consider who else might have had a motive to murder your wife. A motive to set you up for the murder. And identify who might have been able to put your boots and the hammer in the stables after the attack. Is it true that you and the stable boy had the only keys?'

'Yes.' His face softened. 'My horse, Midnight, is a fine steed, but temperamental. He will do anything I tell him, but is suspicious of others. I would not let the twins near him, he kicks at them on sight, and I feared he might do the same to Isabella or my workmen. He was safe only with the stable boy. But he could not have been involved.' Boleyn gave a mirthless laugh. 'The boy's a wantwit, though he had a remarkable way with horses. I took him on at the start of the year, though I had some doubts; he had a reputation as an unreliable scamp, but someone told me he had a feel for horses. It was true, he was very good with Midnight, and the horse liked him. I think young Simon preferred animals to people. The twins were always baiting him. He could no more have killed my wife than flown to the moon. He always kept the keys with him, at my instruction. After the murder he handed them in and left. I think Scambler was scared, he was scared of his own shadow, that one.'

Nicholas and I exchanged a look. I said, 'We saw a boy called Scambler in town on the way here. A skinny lad of about fifteen.'

'That's him.'

'Some apprentices tripped him while he was carrying a bale of wool, making him drop it in the mud. His employer sacked him on the spot. They called him Sooty.'

Boleyn nodded. 'He's always careering madly around the city, always in some sort of trouble because of his scatterbrained foolishness.'

'What happened today was not his fault,' Nicholas said.

Boleyn shrugged. 'Boys will be cruel. But you can forget about Scambler in connection with this.'

'That we cannot,' I answered firmly. 'If we are to investigate this matter thoroughly, we have to interview *everyone* who was potentially involved. You say he was the only one apart from you with a key to the stables. When he left you, where did he go?'

Boleyn shrugged, irritated now. 'I don't know. I believe he has an aunt around Ber Street. His parents are dead. Someone will direct you easily enough, Sooty Scambler is well known in Norwich. But you will be wasting your time.'

'The key to your defence is finding out who put those things in the stable,' I said determinedly. 'I need all the information I can get. I shall spend this week finding it.'

'Serjeant Shardlake has a great reputation for discovering murder-ers,' Nicholas stated proudly.

Boleyn looked at me. Clearly he did not believe it. 'Well, anyway, I thank you,' he said.

'Now,' I continued. 'What of others with a possible motive? I am afraid I must consider Isabella, and your sons.'

Boleyn spoke slowly and patiently, but with a deep underlying anger. 'Isabella, like me, obviously had a motive for killing Edith. But none whatever for leaving her body on gruesome public display, which could only throw suspicion on us.'

'I agree. And that is the strongest card you have. By the way, was Isabella questioned?'

'Yes. And convinced the coroner she had nothing to do with the murder.'

'No deposition was taken from her. Nor from Gerald and Barnabas. What if they had discovered that their mother, whom they had no reason to love, had returned to Norfolk?'

Boleyn looked me in the eye. 'I know my sons are ruffianly brutes. But they did not do this.'

Toby said, 'Master Shardlake met them. At your house in London.'

Boleyn looked surprised. 'What were they doing there?'

'I fear they had come to see what they could steal.'

Boleyn grunted. 'They have no love for me. I have always known that. And yet – after their mother left, both of them, believe it or not, were full of sorrow. They cried for weeks. I do believe that in their way they loved her.' He looked me in the eye. 'I am their father, but my eyes are not closed to what they are like. Yet I cannot believe they did this.' He sighed again. I could see he had had enough, yet we had little time, so I pressed on.

'That leaves your neighbour, Leonard Witherington. You and he had a quarrel over the boundary between your lands. If you were found guilty and the lands were to be forfeited to the King, he could buy them.'

Boleyn laughed bitterly. 'He'd have to contest that with Sir Richard Southwell, whose land adjoins ours on two sides. He'd lose that battle. No, it's the boundary Witherington wants changed.'

'Have you had any trouble with Southwell?'

'I'm too small a fish for him to bother with. It's Witherington; he sees changing the boundary as a way to stop his peasants protesting about his taking their land for sheep, he would use the extra land as common land or waste for them. But my own peasants would make trouble then.'

'I gather there has been a confrontation already.'

'Yes. In March. Witherington's steward got some of his tenants together to try and enter my land forcibly. I heard about it in advance from one of Witherington's men who was in my pay, and got my own steward, Chawry, to gather some of my people to throw him off, including my sons. I knew they would enjoy a bit of trouble. They brought some friends, and acquitted themselves well in that little ruffle, broke the head of one of Witherington's tenants for him. The man's been in a daze ever since. And that old bastard Witherington will have to think again.'

Toby said, 'No doubt the injured man was only trying to protect his livelihood, even if Witherington was making use of him.'

Boleyn looked at Toby, and for the first time I saw in his eyes the fierce superiority of the lord of the manor. 'If peasants start making trouble for their superiors, or their superiors' neighbours, they deserve all they get. Anyway, Witherington threatens to go to law now, but I doubt he will.'

I said, 'I understand you have other lands in the county, Master Boleyn.'

He shrugged. 'Other manors some way off. I would like to turn them over to sheep. It's the only way a gentleman can make a profit these days, with the rise in prices killing rents. But there are a lot of freehold farms I cannot touch and my bailiffs there tell me the tenants are prepared to go to law.' He sighed. 'I can't face the costs and trouble of that, on top of Witherington.'

'Your house in London must be expensive,' I said.

'Too expensive, if that's what you're getting at. I thought I could afford it, and planned to go and live there with Isabella, away from these infernal disapproving neighbours. Though I'd never sell Brikewell; my family came from near there.'

'There is one more thing I must ask you about, Master Boleyn,' I said quietly.

'Well?'

'On the night of the murder you said you spent two hours in your study, going over the papers relating to your estate. Between nine and eleven in the evening, according to your deposition. Unfortunately, neither your wife nor anyone else saw you during that time.'

'I needed quiet. I told her to leave me undisturbed.'

'What papers were you studying?'

'Old documents. Deeds and suchlike. If Witherington was going to law, I needed to study the papers myself before employing my own lawyer.'

When a witness has been clearly speaking the truth, as I believed Boleyn had been up to now, it is often easy to tell when he begins lying. His eyes would not meet mine, and he shifted uneasily. I said quietly, 'But I have all those documents. We found them at your London house.'

Boleyn's head jerked up. For a moment he hesitated. 'I took some of the papers to London because, as I said, I was going to consult a lawyer myself. I remember now, it was the old estate books I was looking at that night, records of the tenancies and so forth.'

I thought of challenging him further, but then decided, no, go to Brikewell first, let him think on it. 'I see,' I said, my tone intentionally doubtful. 'Well, I am sure we must have tired you. We shall come back and see you soon, but tomorrow I want to visit Brikewell. I might try to see Master Witherington.'

'He's a savage old brute.' Then Boleyn's expression changed, became imploring. 'Will you give Isabella my love? Tell her I think of her constantly. And thank her for the food she has sent me. Though the gaolers take their share, damn them.'

'I will.'

Then he said quietly, 'When he came before, Toby said the Lady Elizabeth has taken an interest in me. Is that true?'

'Yes. She has.'

'Is she paying your fees?'

'She would see justice done. But I would ask you to keep her involvement quiet.'

'I shall, believe me. Norfolk is Mary's territory now.'

I stood up carefully, my back creaking. Toby banged on the door and the gaoler came to let us out. It was a relief to walk out of the cold, dank castle into the sunshine. The three of us stood on the castle steps for a moment, looking over the city. I had never seen so many church spires.

'Well,' I said quietly. 'What did you make of him?'

'He was lying about what he did on the night of the murder,' Nicholas said.

'Yes. We must try to find out why.'

'So, he may be guilty after all,' Toby said.

'Indeed he may be,' I replied. 'And I think he has a temper, but whether that would be savage enough to do what was done to his wife is another matter. A ruthless streak, too, from the way he described that fight at Brikewell. And yet − in some ways he strikes me as a weak man; frightened of his tenants of his other manors taking him to court, and Witherington, too. He appears to me a man who would rather have a quiet life if he could. In either event, his lying is the most important matter we need to resolve. And we need to find Master Sooty Scambler.'

Nicholas shivered slightly. 'I've never been inside a prison. 'Tis a doleful place.'

'You don't have anything to do with the criminal law?' Toby asked.

'We are land lawyers,' I said. 'Though I myself do have experience of visiting clients in prison.' And two short spells in the Tower, I thought grimly. I looked at the sun, almost overhead. 'And now, to the Guildhall, and the coroner.'

Chapter Fourteen

IN THE MARKETPLACE, the preacher had gone. I saw one of the boys who had tripped Scambler, and wondered where he had fled to.

We walked up to the Guildhall. It was an impressive three-storey building, its doors guarded by two men in city livery. The flint facing of the wall was knapped smooth, the mortar between the flints inset with thin flint chippings. I was about to run my fingers over the surface when Toby warned, 'Careful, those gallets can tear your hands.'

I became aware of a faint crying sound from ground level. I saw a tiny grille through which dirty fingers waved. A voice called, 'Alms, for food, merciful sirs.'

'This place has a prison,' Toby said. 'The mayor's court and the justices sit here. Only Assize prisoners go to the castle.'

I passed some pennies through the grille. They were quickly snatched away, and more desperate fingers appeared from the gloomy interior. I straightened up with difficulty, and sighed. Turning to Toby, I said, 'But the city council meets here too?'

'Yes. It's the largest Guildhall in England, outside London. Built a hundred and forty years ago using forced labour from the city. My own forebears among them.' He moved to the porch and spoke to one of the guards, who bowed and waved a hand to usher us inside.

The building was lit by large windows, probably once colourfully decorated but now plain glass. The guard led us to a staircase. 'The coroner will meet you in the Swordroom, sirs,' he said.

'Swordroom?' Nicholas asked, interested.

'There aren't any swords on display,' Toby said. 'It's the council meeting chamber. But there's a false roof, and weapons are stored above in case the city constables ever need to deal with trouble.'

'Has that ever happened?' I asked.

'Not yet.'

The guard took us upstairs and knocked on a big wooden door. A voice within called us to enter and a servant opened the door, bowing.

We entered a sizeable chamber, with benches and chairs set in a semicircle. On a raised dais at the front a plump middle-aged man with a grey beard was leafing through a pile of documents. He stood and bowed. 'Serjeant Shardlake?'

'Yes. And Master Overton, and Goodman Lockswood.'

He studied us with shrewd blue eyes. 'I am Henry Williams, coroner for Norwich. My district includes Brikewell. I do not often meet a lawyer of your rank, sir. Do you know Serjeant Flowerdew, agent of the King's escheator?'

'No. Though I gather he is keen to have John Boleyn's family out of his property, even though the trial has not yet taken place.'

Williams grimaced. 'Perhaps he is interested in acquiring the land, for himself or another. He is a man who – well, let us say that his name does not suit him. Anyone less like the dew on a flower would be hard to conceive.' He laughed mirthlessly, then looked at me sharply again. 'You have taken over the Boleyn case from Master Copuldyke, I believe.'

'To act on his behalf in the matter, yes.'

'Copuldyke acts for Thomas Parry, the Lady Elizabeth's cofferer.' He looked at me narrowly.

I continued, 'I am instructed merely to look into the facts, with a fresh eye. I make no presumption about Boleyn's guilt or innocence.'

'That is for the jury to decide.'

'Indeed.' I smiled reassuringly, knowing the coroner would want his own court's verdict to be upheld. 'You will be giving evidence at the trial?'

'Of course. As the one responsible for the initial investigation. Where the jury's verdict was that Edith Boleyn was murdered by her husband John,' he concluded with emphasis.

'I understand. The evidence of the boots and hammer in Boleyn's stables?'

'Taken with the fact that only he had keys, apart from his wantwit stable boy. And nobody else could have gone into that stable, the horse he kept there was quite uncontrollable, as he admitted in his deposition.'

'That is indeed strong evidence. But could someone else have thrown the boots over the top or under the bottom of the stable door?'

Williams frowned. 'The constable did not mention it.'

I changed the subject. 'I cannot help wondering what motive John Boleyn could have for displaying his wife's body in such a public way? Have you any thoughts on that, Master Williams?'

The coroner shrugged. 'Who knows what went on in his mind, what rage he could have fallen into if Edith suddenly turned up? He certainly had a motive to murder her.'

'I agree. But I think that usually, if something does not make sense, it is unlikely to be true.'

Williams grunted. 'The older I get, the more I find that much of what men do makes little sense.' He smiled wryly, then looked at me sharply again. 'Have you been down to Brikewell?'

'I go tomorrow. Another thing that puzzles me, Master Coroner. Does anyone have any idea where Edith might have been these last nine years?'

He shook his head in genuine puzzlement. 'Nobody. I investigated that matter both recently and two years ago when John Boleyn applied to have his wife declared dead. And my predecessor investigated it thoroughly in 1540 after she vanished. But nobody could tell us any-thing.'

'Not her parents?'

'No. She never contacted them. It is as though she hid in a hole for nine years.' He considered a moment, then added, 'I remember when I took over from my predecessor – dead now, God save his soul – he told me about the case. There was one person then whom he wanted to interview, but could not trace.'

'Who was that?'

'Edith Boleyn's maid, Grace Bone.'

'Yes, Master Boleyn mentioned her earlier. He said that before her disappearance Edith was the terror of her servants, even her loyal maid left her employ.'

Williams shook his head. 'That is not the full story, according to

what my predecessor told me. When Edith's disappearance was investigated back in 1540 — with the marriage in trouble and Boleyn having a
mistress, there was naturally fear of foul play — the story he got from the
servants was different. Apparently, Edith and Grace had been very
close, as is sometimes the way with women and their maids, and when
she learned of her husband's adultery, Edith could often be heard weeping in her room, with Grace Bone trying to comfort her. If anything
during those last months they became closer than ever. So when she left
with only a week's notice, the servants were puzzled. Edith seemed more
distraught than ever, and herself disappeared shortly after.' Williams
looked at me seriously. 'My predecessor even wondered whether the
maid had secretly been done away with, like her mistress.'

'By John Boleyn?'

Williams shrugged. 'I know only that she was never traced. She
vanished as completely as her mistress. She had a brother in Norwich,
it was said, but he could not be traced. Of course, it is too late to raise
that matter now.'

I said incredulously, 'You mean a *second* woman disappeared at the
same time as Edith, and the matter was never investigated?'

The coroner frowned. 'It was investigated, sir, by my predecessor,
as I told you, but nothing was found. Possibly Grace Bone knew that
Edith planned to leave her husband, and left herself before trouble
blew up.'

'That could be. But where did she go?' I looked at Williams.
'There may be two murders here.'

Williams shook his head. 'There is no evidence. And without
evidence there is nothing to be done. But as for Edith's death last
month, there is clear evidence, and it points to John Boleyn.'

I said quietly, 'I see there is a very brief deposition from Edith's
father, Gawen Reynolds, saying only that he never saw his daughter
again after 1540 until he was called to identify her last month.'

Williams shrugged. 'That was all he had to say.'

'And no deposition has been taken from Simon Scambler, the
former stable boy.'

Williams laughed suddenly. 'I remember now, mad Sooty
Scambler. He wouldn't have the balls or brains to murder a chicken.'

'Nonetheless,' I said, 'I shall be speaking to him. And also to Master Gawen Reynolds.'

Williams looked me in the eye. 'Be careful with that old man, he is not to be trifled with.'

☦

WE LEFT THE Guildhall. 'What thoughts on the meeting with the coroner?' I asked.

Nicholas replied, 'He told a slightly different story than John Boleyn about the maid's departure.'

'Though with the state of the marriage, Boleyn may have assumed that when Grace left it was because she was tired of Edith's ways. We must question him again. And press him about where he was that night.'

☦

WE WALKED UP to Tombland. The sun had passed its zenith, and the tall houses in the prosperous central areas of the city provided welcome shade. We noticed a great Italianate mansion, the doors closed and secured with wooden bars. 'The Duke of Norfolk's former palace in the city,' Toby observed.

'The King's property now,' I replied. 'Or has it been sold to the Lady Mary like the Duke's other lands?'

'I think it is still in the King's hands.'

'And managed now by his escheator.'

☦

THE REYNOLDS HOUSE in Tombland looked lifeless, the shutters on the upper windows closed and the courtyard gates firmly locked. Toby knocked loudly on the door and we heard footsteps slowly approaching. The door was opened by a handsome, strongly built man in his thirties, with brown hair, a short beard and sharp green eyes. He wore a madder-red doublet and green cap. When he saw Nicholas and me in our lawyers' robes his eyes narrowed.

'Is this the house of Master Gawen Reynolds?' I asked.

'Alderman Reynolds, yes,' the man answered cautiously. 'I am his steward. He and his wife are seeing no visitors at present, they have suffered a bereavement.'

'It is about that we have come.' I introduced myself and the others. 'We are investigating the tragic death of your master's daughter.'

The steward did not move. He glanced across the courtyard to the house, then said, 'For whom are you acting, sir?'

'That is something for me to discuss with your master. Is he at home?'

A man's angry voice called from the interior of the house, loud enough to reach us. 'God's death, Vowell, who is it? Get rid of them!'

The steward hesitated. 'Wait here, please.' He closed the door.

'Doesn't want to see us,' Nicholas observed.

'He'll be curious,' I replied. 'A serjeant's robes can sometimes be useful.' Though hot, too, I thought, even my silken summer robe.

A minute later the steward returned. 'You may come in. Please wait in the hallway a moment.' He led us inside. The house was well furnished, a large vase of flowers on an expensive Venetian table. He left us and went through an inner door. I caught a faint murmur of voices. At the end of the hallway a door opened and a maid looked out. Seeing us, she quickly closed it again.

Looking round, I started slightly. A thin elderly woman was descending the staircase, moving so quietly we had not heard her. The three of us doffed our caps and bowed. She stood on the bottom step, examining us with cold, still blue eyes, her hands clasped together on her black dress. I saw that she wore white bandages on them. Under a black hood her hair was silvery. Her face was pale as parchment.

'Why have you come?' The old woman's voice was little more than a whisper.

'We are helping to investigate the murder of Edith Boleyn.'

'My daughter is dead and gone.' She spoke in a voice of utter weariness. 'In a few days her husband will be tried. What is there to investigate?'

The steward reappeared. 'Alderman Reynolds will see you, sirs, but I warn you he is much distressed since his daughter's death.' We approached the room. The steward raised a hand to bar Toby's progress. 'I am sorry, Goodman, he will see the lawyers only. You must wait here.' Toby shrugged. Mistress Reynolds still stood at the foot of the staircase, one hand grasping the banister.

Nicholas and I were shown into a large reception room. With the shutters drawn it was dim, candles alight on a large table. A tall, stringy man stood there, dressed in a long black robe. He, too, was elderly, about seventy. His white hair was worn long, almost to his shoulders, in an old-fashioned style. The lined face was long-nosed, square-chinned, the severe mouth turned down at the corners, the eyes dark and fierce. I guessed that Gawen Reynolds would be a hard man to deal with in business. His wife had come to stand in the doorway, looking apprehensive. The steward stood behind her.

Reynolds waved a hand at them. He said, his voice angry from the start, 'My wife, Jane, and my steward, Goodman Michael Vowell. They can stay there, we will not be long. What have you come for?' He stepped forward and I saw that he carried a gold-topped walking stick. Even with its aid he limped badly.

I said, 'We wondered if you might help us with a little informa-tion. We are investigating the death of your daughter—'

Reynolds's voice cut in sharply, 'That investigation is done. Who are you working for?'

'My instructions come from Master Thomas Parry—'

'Who the fuck is he?'

I took a deep breath. 'Cofferer to the Lady Elizabeth.'

Reynolds's lips tightened. 'Elizabeth. Of course, trying to save a Boleyn from the gallows. But it is too late, Master Hunchback Ser-jeant, John Boleyn is guilty, and in a few days will be dangling from the Norwich gallows.' He spoke this last sentence with satisfaction.

'We have been asked only to review the matter,' I answered quietly. 'Will you be giving evidence, sir?'

'I do not know,' Reynolds said, in a tone of quiet, fierce anger. 'I can hardly bear even to go out, to see all the nosy glances. As for my hopes of the mayoralty next year, those are finished.'

I thought, Was that all his daughter's death meant to him, but Nicholas said sympathetically, 'What happened must have been a great shock to you, sir.'

'A great shock?' Reynolds's voice rose in anger. 'Nine years ago my only child left her husband and disappeared without trace. She did not come to me, or anyone else, just – vanished.' He waved a hand angrily. 'Then last month that terrible discovery at Brikewell. Do you wonder we are shocked?'

'No, sir,' I answered, 'it must have been all the worse after hearing nothing for nine years.'

'Yes. Nine years,' he repeated, angry still.

I turned to Jane, hoping she might be more cooperative. 'Did she have any other relatives in Norwich? Or elsewhere? Or friends that she might have gone to?'

Her husband answered. 'Relatives, friends? You may as well know, Master Serjeant. My daughter was never normal, right from when she was a child. She did not like mixing with other people – she did not *like* other people. The trouble we had getting her even to play with other children, let alone attend social functions when she grew up, pretty girl though she was then. I hoped marriage might tame her, but she treated her own poor children badly, and probably Boleyn too.' He laughed suddenly. 'We were glad when John Boleyn showed an interest in her, for Anne Boleyn was on the rise then and we all hoped this could bring a link to the Royal Court. But John Boleyn had no real go in him, he was all at sea when he went to London and failed even to get to meet Anne Boleyn. As for Edith, she refused point-blank to go.' His voice rose again. 'And then Boleyn murdered her! Set up a damned common barmaid in her place! I shall see that bitch out on the road once this is over!' His eyes were almost wild with rage. Glancing at his wife I saw fear in her eyes.

There was a moment's silence, and then to my surprise I heard the faint sound of a woman's scream from the back of the house. Jane Reynolds frowned. 'What are those boys doing now?' she asked.

To my surprise Reynolds gave a barking laugh. 'Something with young Judith, by the sound of it.'

Jane left the room. A moment later I heard familiar mocking tones outside the room. 'Fucking hell, Lockswood, not you again. You'd better not have come to trouble Granfer, you prick.'

Nicholas and I glanced at each other. Barnabas and Gerald, the twins.

'What have you been doing in the kitchen?' The steward spoke angrily.

'Sticking our hands up young Judith's skirts. But she started squealing.'

'Your grandmother asked you to leave the maids alone.'

'Mind your business, if you don't want your cap knocked off.' The scarred boy, Barnabas, swaggered into the doorway. He saw us and for a moment stood still, frowning, before recovering his bravado and calling out, 'Hey, Gerry, the hunchback and the streak of piss are back.' Gerald came in, and looked at us threateningly.

Reynolds turned to us. 'You have met my grandsons?'

'They were at their father's house in London last week.'

'Just sniffing about,' Barnabas said.

Reynolds turned to us. 'I am protecting my grandchildren, they are all I have left. When their father is dead, I shall apply for their wardship.' He smiled with real affection at the twins. 'Find a pair of rich wenches for you to marry, eh?'

'Not yet, Granfer. We're having too much fun to settle down.'

Reynolds looked at me. 'By the way, in case your thoughts were tending in that direction, my grandsons have an alibi for the night my daughter was killed. Carousing with their friends, weren't you, lads? All drinking at John Atkinson's house, and they stayed the night there. A dozen witnesses. The coroner had that checked.'

Gerald flexed his broad shoulders. 'Do you want us to throw these two and Lockswood out, Granfer? It'd be a pleasure.'

Reynolds looked at us. 'I think it is time for you to go. Now, before I let them loose on you.'

Nicholas looked fiercely at the twins. Barnabas winked at him. I touched Nicholas on the arm and led him from the room. There was nothing more to be gained here. One of the twins called after us, 'I hear there's gypsies in town, Master Crookback. Take care they don't steal you for their exhibition!' Their grandfather guffawed. I thought, He had no grief for his daughter, none at all.

Outside Toby stood with the steward. Vowell was frowning, looking towards the kitchen door, from which a faint weeping could be heard. Jane Reynolds had gone.

He opened the door for us. Nicholas and Toby and I went out. To my surprise, Vowell accompanied us outside. He glanced quickly back into the house, then took my arm and said quietly, 'You should know, sir, my master did not tell you the full story.'

'What do you mean?'

His face twitched with anger. 'There is evidence he could have given, but did not. I was with him nine years ago, and I know that a few months before she disappeared Edith Boleyn came here to seek aid from her father. John Boleyn wanted more children, but she would not lie with him. Boleyn tried to force her, and beat her. She wanted her father to intervene. But you have seen what sort of household this is. He refused, and sent her on her way, saying she must settle her own affairs with her husband.'

'Why are you telling me this?' I asked sharply.

'Because I would have you know what sort of man Gawen Reynolds is, how what really troubles him is that he is unlikely to become mayor, after this scandal. And now the twins are here – well, soon I too may disappear.'

I nodded. 'How did he damage his leg? Old as he is, I thought he might come at us, till I saw he was lame.'

'Slipped in the mud in Tombland during the spring rains. I was with him at the time. He's not been able to walk properly since. Anyway, I have had enough of this household. I thought you should know.' And with that, he stepped back and closed the door. I went over to Nicholas and Toby. 'What was that about?' Nicholas asked.

I told them. 'If Reynolds says that Edith complained to him of violence from her husband, it would damn Boleyn further.'

'Why does he not do so?' Toby asked. 'He wants Boleyn hanged.'

'Because he ignored his daughter's appeal. If that became public, his reputation would suffer further. And that is what matters to him. Poor Edith,' I concluded heavily. 'What sort of life did she endure?'

✠

THAT EVENING, I made notes of the evidence we had gathered so far. There was no doubt, it all seemed to damn John Boleyn even further. Yet still the picture of a violent, brutal husband did not, to me, accord with the man in Norwich Castle. It was time for me to write to Parry and Elizabeth. I considered whether to tell them things were looking bad, that a guilty verdict looked likely and that the application for a pardon might be needed, and that I myself was unsure of Boleyn's guilt. However, though the trial was only a week away, there were still leads to follow. Tomorrow we would go to Brikewell. So I merely wrote to say I was investigating as thoroughly as I could, and would write again shortly. I sealed the letters, put them in a bag, and took them down to be given to tomorrow's post-rider to London. I wondered what reception the letters would get at Hatfield. Parry, I guessed, would not be too concerned at the lack of progress, but the Lady Elizabeth was a different matter.

Chapter Fifteen

THE NEXT MORNING, another fine sunny day, Toby again joined us for breakfast punctually at six. His mother, he said, was a little better. Scarcely had he sat down than Barak appeared in the doorway. The man waiting on the breakfast tables looked askance at his arm and cheap clothing, but Barak ignored him and came to sit with us. I said, 'You remember Toby Lockswood? He was with us when we rode in on Thursday.'

'Ay.' Barak shook Toby's hand. 'You're the local knowledge on the case.'

'Something like that.'

'Ears and eyes on the ground, that's what you need.' Barak added approvingly.

'Yes, and my Norwich contacts provided me with useful information yesterday evening.' Toby turned to us. 'I have an address for Scambler's aunt, down in Ber Street, and have also managed to trace Josephine and Edward Brown.'

'Josephine,' Barak said. 'Of course, she's here now. How is she?'

'Her husband works for a stonemason, she as a spinner. They have moved to a place in Conisford, south of the castle.' He hesitated. 'A poor area.'

I said, 'We shall go and see her, and Scambler too, when we return from Brikewell this evening. Thank you, Toby. How did you manage to trace Josephine?'

'My friend discovered that the retired lawyer, Henning, and his wife both died of smallpox last year. The executors sold his house and put the servants out. My friend got in touch with their old steward, who is living little better than a beggar now, but he was able to tell me about

Goodman Brown and his wife. They had kept in touch until a few months ago.'

Nicholas shook his head. 'You mean the servants were left with nothing? That's hard.'

'Happens more often than you'd think,' Toby replied.

Barak said, 'Good work.'

Toby gave him a careful look. 'I believe you are also acting as eyes and ears for the judges, weighing up the public mood in Norwich.'

I said, 'Jack did similar work for Lord Cromwell for many years.'

'Cromwell.' Toby looked, impressed. 'They say he would have been a friend to the poor, had Parliament or the old king let him.'

'Very true,' Barak agreed.

'But that is not so of the judges,' Toby said, his blue eyes still keenly on Barak's face.

'I'm just here to see what the general mood is. The judges have to report back to Lord Chancellor Rich and the Protector after the Assizes.'

'And what would you say the mood is?'

'Very discontented.' Barak smiled enigmatically. 'It's been the same all along the circuit, but especially here. I've never come across anything like it.'

✝

WE RODE OUT shortly after. My back was much better and I hoped the five-mile ride would be bearable. To avoid the marketplace, we rode out of St Benedict's Gate to the west of the city before joining the road south. Early as it was, the road was busy with people bringing goods to market, ranging from carters with loads of butter and cheese to peddlers with huge packs on their backs. There were also several gentlemen and lawyers riding in for the start of the Assizes, now only three days away, each with a small retinue of servants. Two elderly lawyers in black robes, surrounded by mounted servants, rode up to where a group of teenage lads heading for town were strung out across the road, talking loudly and cheerfully.

'Make way there, churls,' the lawyer shouted.

Normally the boys would have made way for such as they,

especially as their servants were large men with long knives at their belts. This time, however, although they moved to the side of the road, the lads then promptly turned their backs, lowered their netherstocks, and presented the lawyers with a view of six skinny white arses. The face of the man who had shouted at them reddened with fury, all the more since many other travellers laughed and there were shouts of, 'Well done, bors!' and 'Now shit on him!' Barak and Toby laughed too, although Nicholas and I, both also dressed in lawyers' robes, exchanged uneasy glances. 'Nobody had better try that with us,' Nicholas said.

The crowds thinned as we continued south. The land was flat, the cloudless blue sky wider than any I had seen. On a piece of pasture-land a little group of men was busy shearing, hurdles drawn together to pen in the sheep. The animals were pulled out one by one, thrown on their backs on a trestle table, and the long, curled fleeces removed with amazing dexterity by the shearers with their big shears. It was late in the season for shearing, but the cold winter and spring had doubtless delayed everything.

I was riding with Nicholas, Toby and Barak behind. I had not seen Barak ride since he lost his hand but he managed well enough, mainly using his good hand on the reins though the end of his prosthesis was curled over them, too. I caught snatches of his conversation, and was glad Toby seemed to be getting on well with him, if not with Nicholas.

'Never seen so many sheep,' Barak said.

'More land turned over to them every year. And more unemployed villagers as a result.'

'So I've heard around the taverns.'

I glanced back at them and asked, 'Have either of you heard any more about the rebellions in the West?'

Barak said, 'Some say they are against the new Prayer Book, others against the local gentlemen. I don't know, I'm not sure Protector Somerset does either. But it sounds as though it's spreading.'

We rode deeper into the countryside, then turned right into a sandy lane.

Behind me, Barak asked Toby if he was married.

'Me? No, I'm not ready to tie myself to a wife and children yet.'

'I've been tied down for seven years,' Barak laughed. 'It's good to get away now and again.' He called out to Nicholas. 'What about you, lad? How's your love life?'

'I am wooing the daughter of a Gray's Inn barrister. Her name is Beatrice.'

'Nice-looking, is she?'

'Fair as a rose, gentle as a dove.'

'Will there be wedding bells?'

'Who knows?'

I leaned back to join in. 'Beatrice's mother is dazzled by the range of people I have worked for. I think she dreams of one day meeting the Lady Elizabeth.' I would not have dared criticize Beatrice in front of Nicholas, but a dig at her mother would do no harm.

'A snob, then?' Barak answered, ever direct.

'All the better for me to advance my suit,' Nicholas said shrewdly.

We passed a small chantry church, where until last year a priest would have said Masses for the dead; the church and lands had now been appropriated by the King. Many of the stained-glass windows had been broken by stones, and someone had chalked *Death to the Pope* on the door. A little beyond, we saw a church steeple rising in the distance, and Toby pulled to a halt. 'We're nearly at Brikewell now. That's the Brikewell church. It may be useful, sir, to have the plan I gave you to hand.'

I pulled it from my pouch, looking at it as we rode on. The ploughland to our left belonged to the old chantry. I wondered if someone was negotiating to buy it, and noticed that Sir Richard Southwell owned the land beyond. We arrived at a small, poor-looking hamlet. Ancient cottages, most of them tiny, were clustered round a small pond. Again, to our left was ploughland, while to the right was green pastureland, dotted with the grey-white local sheep. 'That's demesne land, belonging to the manor,' Toby said. 'Boleyn farmed it directly till he put it to sheep. And beyond is his manor house.'

Brick walls abutted the lane now. We came to a pair of open iron gates, giving us a view of a modern red-brick manor house, long chimneys reaching to the sky. I noticed the knot gardens in front of the house were starting to run wild, the flowerbeds full of weeds.

'So this is where John Boleyn lives?' Nicholas asked.

'Yes,' Toby answered. 'A far cry from Norwich Castle gaol.'

We rode slowly up the path. As we approached the main door a tall bearded man in his thirties, with red hair and a solid body already starting to run to fat, came out. He was carrying a mounting block. 'I am Serjeant Shardlake,' I said. 'A lawyer appointed by Master Copuldyke to look into the case against John Boleyn. Is Mistress Isabella at home?'

The man frowned. 'We didn't know there had been a change of lawyer.'

'I am acting as Master Copuldyke's agent. I have a letter of authority. And you will recognize Goodman Lockswood.'

'Ay. God give you good morrow, Toby.'

'And you, Daniel. We are here to help if we can.' Toby turned to me. 'This is Master Boleyn's steward, Daniel Chawry.'

The steward bowed to each of us in turn. 'I fear when you have dismounted I must ask you to help me take the horses to the stables. There are no other male servants now.'

'Is it just Mistress Isabella at home?' I had feared the twins might have returned, but Chawry answered, 'Just her, her maid and me. The other servants left when the master was taken away.'

I nodded sympathetically. Association with scandal, particularly something as horrible as this, often drove servants to leave a house. We dismounted, a twinge below my shoulder blade reminding me my back had not quite settled down. Chawry led us round the side of the house to a stable block. There was a smaller, separate stable beside it, and as we passed it we heard a loud neighing and the crash of hooves. Barak asked, 'Is that the fabled Midnight?'

'It is. The only horse left apart from the mistress's. Thank God his stable is built of strong oak and he's well penned in; I throw his food over the top of his stall. I haven't dared go in there to muck it out.'

I passed the reins of my horse to Barak and walked across to the little stable. So this was where the boots and hammer were found. I glanced at the door; it was firmly chained and padlocked and I saw that it was flush with the wall at the top, and with the step at the bottom. Nobody could have flung the hammer and boots in there from outside. I walked round the building. There was a shuttered window at the rear; I pulled at it; it was locked from inside. My action set off another round of frantic neighing and kicking from within. I returned to the front of the building. There was a small gap of a quarter inch or so between two boards and I peered inside. It was almost totally dark, but as my eyes adjusted I caught a glimpse of the whites of the rolling eyes of a horse. I stepped away. 'Is it not cruel to keep the horse in darkness?' I asked Chawry.

'That window's bolted from the inside. To get to it you'd have to go past Midnight's stall, and that's within kicking range. But I have the key since Master Boleyn was taken away; I can let you in if you like,' he added, a little insolently.

'I think not,' I said dryly.

'Master Boleyn is very keen to sell Midnight as soon as possible for some reason; he has asked me, through Isabella, to arrange it. It is not proving easy.'

We tied up our horses in the other stable, then Chawry led us into the house, asking us to wait in the hallway while he went to find his mistress. It was a pleasant place, finely furnished, an expensive tapestry of an idealized rural scene, all nymphs and shepherds, dominating the hallway. I noticed, though, balls of dust in the corners.

Chawry returned and told us Mistress Boleyn would receive us. I noticed he used the name she was not strictly entitled to now. I signed to Barak and Toby to wait – I did not want to overwhelm the woman – and Nicholas and I followed the steward into a parlour, well furnished but with the same slightly neglected air as the rest of the house. An unusually pretty, buxom woman in her early thirties, with blonde hair under a sober black hood, stood with her hands clasped in front of her. We bowed, and I introduced myself and Nicholas.

'Master Copuldyke has asked you to help my husband?' Her voice had a strong Norfolk accent.

'He wishes me to investigate the whole case thoroughly, to see whether new light can be cast on the murder.'

'God bless her grace the Lady Elizabeth,' Isabella said feelingly. 'But there is so little time now. Only six days –'

'I know. I visited your husband in Norwich Castle yesterday; he asked me to send you his love, and thank you for the food you have provided him with.'

'I have some more. Could you take it back with you today? Otherwise he'll have no vittles to chaw, the prison provides nothing.'

'Most certainly.'

She raised a hand to brush away a strand of blonde hair. 'Since our cook left I have done nothing but prepare dishes for John. 'Tis as well I have experience from when I worked at the inn.' She fixed me with her large, dark blue eyes. 'You will know my former work. John's neighbours have despised him since he brought me to the house. Do you despise me, sir, for what I was, and for living in sin for years?'

This was remarkably direct, but also very brave. 'Certainly not. I will do anything within my power to help you.'

'And I,' Nicholas added. He looked at Isabella, obviously appreciative of her unusual beauty. I said, 'May we sit down, and ask some questions? Master Nicholas will make notes.' I added, 'They will inevitably be personal ones.'

'Of course. Daniel, would you leave us?' Chawry bowed and turned to go. He paused at the door and gave Isabella a look which seemed to me to have longing in it, though Isabella appeared not to notice. When he had gone she said quietly, 'Of course you know that at law I am no longer John's wife. Yet I know that if he is found not guilty, he will return and take care of us just as he did in the years before Edith was found dead.'

'That is good to know.' I coughed. 'I believe you first met your husband about ten years ago.'

'Yes, when I was working at the inn. John used to come there to escape his life at home. He told me of his troubles with Edith – though I would not have had this terrible thing happen to her – and with his sons, who, though no more than eight, were already' – her mouth twisted in distaste – 'cruel and vicious.'

Nicholas said. 'We have already had the pleasure of meeting Gerald and Barnabas.'

'I started by feeling sorry for John. I could see he was a decent man struggling with a sad fate. And over the months – we came to love each other.' She looked at me with a defiant air. 'People do, despite differ/ ences in age and status, you know.'

'Yes, I do know,' I answered feelingly. I smiled, then asked, 'Did you ever meet Edith?'

'Never. But I heard enough stories from John, and later from the servants and neighbours. About her sour disposition, her lack of care for her children, her sometimes starving herself for no reason. John said he had begun to think she was mad. And then some gossiping muck/ spout told her about us, and not long after she vanished. Later, when it was clear she was not coming back, John asked me to come and stay. Oh, he warned me the local gentry would be scandalized and the twins would be a trial. But I loved him, and agreed.'

I hesitated, then said, 'Did he ever tell you that he had asked Edith to give him more children?'

She looked at me boldly for a moment. 'Yes, but she refused. He had argued with her at first, but he told me that soon he came not to care, that long before he met me he had come to feel the same revulsion for his wife that Edith seemed to feel towards him.'

I exchanged a glance with Nicholas. This was not the story that Gawen Reynolds's steward Michael Vowell had told us yesterday. I said, 'Forgive me for asking this. Once you and John were living together, you had no children. Was that a deliberate decision?'

Isabella sighed. 'I did not want a child out of wedlock. John wanted more children. He hated the idea of the twins as his only heirs, and he tried to persuade me for a while' – she reddened, and looked down – 'but in the end accepted my refusal. We – we took precautions, in the ways countryfolk know. I told John that if ever we could marry, I should be happy to give him a child. And so, when we married after Edith was declared dead, we tried.' She sighed. 'But we have not yet been blessed with a child.' She shook her head wearily. 'If I had known what was going to happen this year, I would have tried to give him one years ago.' She took a deep breath, her face reddening again, and I realized how hard it must be to speak so frankly to a stranger. Again she struck me as brave, not bold.

I said quietly, 'And when you came to live at Brikewell, how were matters with the twins?'

She looked me in the eye. 'They hated me from the beginning, as I came to hate and then fear them. No matter what my husband did, they were uncontrollable.'

'I heard no tutor would stay.'

'They tied one poor young man up with ropes, and rolled him down the stairs. A wonder he didn't break his neck. Another tutor they stripped naked in the schoolroom, then took him out and dumped him on the lawn. He was the last. They were fourteen then, already strong as horses and pestering the women servants. Always the two of them acting together. Since John was taken, I have been afraid of them, but thank the Lord they have decided to throw themselves on the protection of their grandfather, fearing they will be made wards of the King if my husband is –' She broke off, finally losing control, and tears rolled down her cheeks. She wiped them away fiercely with a handkerchief and said, 'Go on, Master Shardlake. Forgive my womanish ways.'

'Do you know their grandfather, Master Gawen Reynolds? I met him yesterday. A choleric old man.'

'I have never seen him. He would have nothing to do with me, though the twins visited him often. Birds of a feather, I think.'

'He seems to indulge them.'

She shrugged. 'Let him. I will be happy never to see them again.'

I said, 'There is one other, very important matter. According to your deposition, on the night of Edith's murder your husband told you he was going to look at some documents in his study, and asked not to be disturbed. For two hours you did not actually see him.'

'Yes. He has a quarrel, as you will know, with his neighbour, Witherington. Poor John, always people conspire to make his life difficult.'

'Those missing two hours are very important.'

Isabella frowned. 'Do you think I don't know that? When John was first arrested and I went to see him in prison, I offered to say I had gone to his study during those hours and spoken to him. But he would not let me, he said it would be perjury and if I were discovered, I would be in trouble. You see, Master Shardlake, what a devoted husband John is.'

'And what a devoted wife you are.' I said softly. 'Nicholas, make no record of what Mistress Boleyn just said about perjury.'

'I heard her say nothing about that.' He smiled, and Isabella smiled faintly in return.

'Where do you think he was those two hours?' I asked.

Isabella looked at me hard. 'In his study.'

I asked, 'Will you alone be giving evidence in your husband's favour at the trial?'

Isabella set her mouth firmly. 'Yes. I shall say he was the best of husbands, and that I cannot believe he murdered Edith.'

'One final question. Have you any idea who *could* have killed her?'

She shook her head. 'Believe me, I have thought and thought on it but I can find no answer. Leonard Witherington wants part of our land, but surely not enough to put himself under suspicion of murder.'

'And the twins?'

She shook her head. 'No. Bad as they are, I believe that those boys loved their mother.'

'They seem to show no sorrow at her death.'

'That is their way. They would think it weak.'

'I see.' I smiled at her. 'Finally, let me give you a little advice. I admire the forthright way in which you have answered me. But in court you should be – perhaps a little more humble in manner, a little more subdued. And do not be afraid to be tearful. A tearful woman can make a jury sympathetic.'

'You think me too bold? Believe me, facing people down has been my lot these last nine years.'

'I understand, Mistress Boleyn. But remember, the jury.'

'I will. And when I come to think of what will happen to my husband if he is found guilty, the tears will come soon enough.' She bowed her head, then looked up. 'Find the murderer, please. For the sake of my husband, and that poor wretched Edith.'

Chapter Sixteen

I TOLD ISABELLA that I was going next to visit the scene of the murder, and asked if Chawry might accompany us. She agreed readily, and went to find him. Nicholas and I returned to the hall, and brought Barak and Toby, who were chatting amiably, up to date.

'She is a woman of courage and spirit,' I said. 'And obviously devoted to her husband.'

'A little too bold for her own good,' Toby said. 'I've heard she can be as fierce as any fine lady in dealing with complaints from the tenants. The jury may think her a hussy.'

'I have advised her to be humble. And I do not forget she had as good a motive as her husband to get rid of Edith, but not for displaying her body like that.'

Nicholas asked, 'Did you notice the look Chawry gave her?'

'I did. But she seemed not to.'

'If Boleyn hangs, it would be an opening for him. Then he, too, may have a motive.'

I sighed. So far, my visit to Brikewell had produced only another suspect.

Chawry appeared, and said he would take us to the stream forming the boundary between the Boleyn and Witherington parishes, where Edith was murdered. He had brought three pairs of heavy working boots. 'It's very gulshy by the stream,' he said.

'Muddy,' Toby explained.

I looked at the boots. They were all heavy, large in size. 'They belong to the twins and Master Boleyn,' Chawry explained. 'The pair found in the stable were taken as evidence.'

We thanked him, put on the boots, and he led us out of the house.

✝

WE WALKED DOWN the path through the middle of the Brikewell estate, ploughed fields on either side of us.

'Your mistress is very loyal to her husband,' I said to Chawry.

'She is a fine woman,' he answered stoutly, 'and a good mistress.'

'Do you believe Master Boleyn to be innocent?'

'I do. I have worked for him these five years past. He gets frampled sometimes, I mean he is a worrier, but a good master. I think all he has ever wanted is a quiet life.'

'Do you live at the manor house?'

'No, I have my own cottage a little way off.'

'Ah,' I said with apparent lightness. 'Enough space to bring up a family?'

'No, I am not wed yet.'

'Did you hear anything on the night of the murder?'

'No.' His mouth set. 'I have no alibi, if that is what you mean.'

I saw that most fields were divided into strips, but in one place several acres had been consolidated into larger fields, and a modest stone house built next to the road. Chawry looked at it and grunted. 'Yeoman Charlesworth's land. He exchanged his strips with those of other tenants, bought some others. One of those new-risen peasants who pays to send his children to school.'

I said, 'As my father did me. He was a yeoman, too, in the Mid-lands.'

Chawry looked embarrassed, and I saw Barak and Toby exchange a wink. I noticed that the people in the fields had stopped working, and, leaning on their implements, were staring at us.

'We'll be out of their sight soon,' Chawry said. 'Nosy knaves.'

A little further on, the fields ended, divided by a fence from an area of common pasture on both sides of the path. A few sheep grazed there, but many more bullocks and cows. Away to the right, beyond a pond, was some woodland, while to the left lay a marshy, reedy area dotted with trees. The sun blazed down; it was hotter today.

Toby halted, leaning over the fence, and looked at me. 'The com-mons, Master Shardlake. Which the landowners seek to enclose in many places. Each of those cows belongs to one villager, and provides a family with milk. The bullocks and horses pull their ploughs. The woodland provides timber, and foraging for the pigs in season. The marsh provides reeds, and waterfowl for the pot. Without the common land, no village can survive.'

Chawry said, 'True, though some villages have more commons than they need. Here it is Master Witherington who seeks to enclose his lands for sheep, and to make up the difference by taking some of my master's land.'

'Isn't common land protected by the customs of the manor?' Barak asked.

'Ay,' Toby retorted. 'But who runs the court, and keeps the books of record? The lord of the manor.'

Chawry turned on him. 'You sound like one of these radical Commonwealth men, Goodman. If you want to find a bad landlord, look to Master Witherington.'

I said, 'Goodman Chawry, do you see over there, a narrow strip through the commons where the grass is darker – is that the course of the old stream, which Witherington claims for the boundary?'

'Ay, it is,' Chawry said. 'No water flows there now, though the old watercourse fills in when it rains.'

'And down there, a third of a mile off, I see a stream, and a bridge.'

'That marks the boundary. Where poor Edith Boleyn's body was found.'

'Then let us go there, and see.'

We walked on, to where a bridge of wooden planks crossed a stream, the boundary with Witherington's land. On his side there was farmland to the left, sheep pasture enclosed by hurdles to the right. Further down we could see a village, and the church. Chawry said, 'In some places, the local priest might have been asked to intervene in a quarrel, but the man here is weak, uneducated, and keeps out of things.' He grunted. 'Favours the old ways, and keeps quiet.'

We stood on the bridge, looking down at the little stream flowing slowly between its muddy banks, overhung by the occasional willow. Chawry took a deep breath. 'You wish to see the place the body was found?'

'Please.'

We returned to Boleyn's side of the stream, and went through a gate into the pastureland. Chawry followed the stream for about fifty yards, then stopped, looking down the muddy bank. 'It was just there, by that young willow. I was called out when the old shepherd discovered her. It was an awful sight, that naked body sticking up for all to see: when they pulled it out the head was all pashed in. The top fell to pieces, dropping her brains in the water.'

I stepped down into the mud, glad of the boots. Each step released stinking bubbles. Nicholas followed, extending a hand to aid Barak, who found it hard to balance because of his arm. Chawry and Toby stayed on the bank. Chawry called down, 'Be careful, it sucks at your feet; you have to slod through carefully.'

'Easy enough to get a body in the water, if you're strong enough,' Barak said. 'Just need to hold it by the middle and drop it in.'

I looked back at the bridge, measuring the distance. 'But carrying it here, and then through this mud, would be hard. Even if we assume Edith was bludgeoned and killed at the bridge – and it's an obvious place for people to arrange to meet – the killer then had to carry the body here, and in total darkness. It would take a very strong man, and one who knew the ground, to do that.'

Nicholas nodded agreement. 'I doubt I could do it.' He looked at me. 'Perhaps there were two of them.'

'That's a possibility,' Barak agreed.

For a moment, we stood in silence in the mud, looking at the gently flowing water, a peaceful place now.

'We agree it would be difficult for one man to carry Edith here,' I said. 'Yet surely a madman acting out some hideous fantasy would act alone.'

'Or two brutal madmen who always act together,' Nicholas said quietly.

I looked at him. 'Gerald and Barnabas?'

'Their mother could have contacted them, arranged to meet them here.'

'Yet everyone has said they loved her, however they behave towards everyone else.' I bit my lip and stared over the fields and meadows. 'So many possibilities.'

We heaved ourselves out of the mud and returned to the path.

Chawry was stroking his red beard. I said, 'I am grateful to you, Master Steward, for showing us this place. One more question, if I may. Have there been any other murders, or disappearances, in this area in the last few years?'

He shook his head, looking puzzled. 'None. This is a quiet place – apart from the ruffle with Witherington's tenants a few months ago.'

'I just wondered,' I said lightly. I was thinking of the maid Grace Bone, who had disappeared as completely as Edith, just before her.

He shook his head. 'I don't know.'

I said, 'That ruffle, I understand the twins were there, and there was some violence on both sides. Did Master Boleyn ask you to organize matters on your side?'

Chawry's brown eyes glinted and he frowned slightly. 'It was Witherington who tried to occupy our land forcibly. I had a paid informer among his tenants, so we were ready for them when they came. Master Boleyn asked me to organize matters and, yes, it was my idea to bring in the twins. Despite their bad relationship with their father, they are always keen on any sort of trouble. They are part of a little band of young gentlemen who hire themselves out when there are quarrels between landlords, or between landlords and tenants. If things got rough, blame Witherington.'

'Did Master Boleyn know the twins were coming?'

His eyes glinted again. 'I thought it better not to tell him. I contacted them through their grandfather.'

'Probably best,' I said. I thought, There was a streak of ruthlessness in this man. 'Thank you for your help. I think you should return to your mistress now. We shall go on to South Brikewell and see if we can talk to Master Witherington.'

Chawry inclined his head. 'Be careful, sir. Witherington can be a brute.'

As we crossed the bridge I looked back. Chawry was standing on the path, staring at us. Then, ahead of us, we heard cries and shouts, voices raised in anger. On Witherington's lands, something was happening.

Chapter Seventeen

W E WALKED ON, towards South Brikewell village. The shout‚
ing continued, and on the rising ground beyond the village we
could discern figures running about in the fields, and white birds flying
up. We walked past the gateway of another manor house, newer than
Boleyn's, built of flint. In the courtyard men were running to and fro,
and a couple of horses were being brought from the stables. One man
stood holding a pair of enormous hunting mastiffs on leashes. They
saw us and began barking angrily, baring their teeth.

'Doesn't look like a good time to visit,' Barak said. 'There's trouble
of some sort going on.'

'We could see what's happening in the fields,' Toby suggested.

'Maybe that's best left alone,' Nicholas answered.

'No,' Barak said. He was holding his prosthetic hand up with his
left; the dragging weight of it told while he was walking. Nonetheless,
he was keen to discover what was happening. 'It may be useful to take
a look. We've all got knives,' he added, 'and Nick has his sword.'

'All right,' I agreed. 'But be careful.'

We passed through the village, again mainly poor houses built
round a pond, and somewhat smaller than North Brikewell. Behind it
enclosed pasture was dotted with newly shorn sheep. In the middle of
the pasture stood a shepherd's hut, and I wondered if it belonged to the
man who had found the body, Adrian Kempsley.

The village was deserted apart from a few chickens and goats
scrabbling around. Most windows were shuttered, but where they were
open we saw faces, mostly old people and children, looking out with
anxious expressions. We could now see, in the fields beyond, some
thirty people, mostly men but also women and some older children,
walking along the narrow ridges that divided the strips where oats

grew, green and short for the season. They carried nets and pitchforks, and three young men had bows and arrows. As the people moved slowly along, more white birds rose from the ground, flying in a disoriented way. People slashed at them, and one of the archers loosed an arrow, bringing a bird to the ground.

'Good shot,' Nicholas said admiringly.

'What are they doing?' I asked.

Toby smiled. 'Killing the landlord's doves that are eating their crops. Look over there.' He pointed to where, at the edge of the pastureland, a tall hexagonal building stood. 'A great dove house. Dove eggs and meat are a great delicacy for the rich, but they steal grain from babies' mouths.'

Nicholas said, 'My father has a dove house, but it is tiny compared to that.'

'Fashionable ones like this one can house hundreds of the wretched birds.' Toby laughed. 'See how they stagger. The people will have left out some seed well laced with beer.'

'It's not legal to kill them like that,' I said. 'They could get into trouble.'

'People have had *enough*,' Toby spat, with sudden violent emphasis. I stared at him hard. 'I'm sorry, sir,' he said.

Another dove rose dozily into the air, to be impaled by a pitchfork. People were looking at us now, no doubt puzzled by the sudden appearance of four strangers. I remembered the scene when the boys had bared their arses at the group of lawyers on the road. 'Maybe we should leave,' I said quietly.

At that moment, though, there was a barking and clatter of hooves on the path behind us. We stepped hurriedly aside as two horsemen rode past, followed by half a dozen burly men carrying swords and halberds, and two others, each with a mastiff on a lead. The horsemen dismounted at the fence enclosing the field, tethered their animals, and threw open the gate. Their leader was a short, plump red-faced man in his fifties, waving a sword. 'Stop that,' he roared. 'Knaves! Churls! Stop killing my birds! You're breaking the law, I'll have you all conscripted and sent to Scotland!'

Barak said, 'Master Leonard Witherington, I'd guess.'

Witherington led his party into the field. The villagers stopped attacking the birds and gathered together. They did not answer him, even when he slashed out angrily at the green barley with his sword, cutting off the ears of the crop. The villagers stood in a group, the men holding up billhooks, forks and other agricultural implements which could easily become deadly weapons. The three young archers strung arrows to their bows, but pointed them downwards as they eyed Witherington's approaching men.

The plump little man came to a halt in front of them, still yelling at the top of his voice. 'Dozzled plough-joggers! Knaves! I'll have you off your lands for this!'

'Shut your clack-box, Master Witherington!' someone called back.

'Ay, or I'll stick you with this gib-fork! And those dogs of yours!' An elderly man raised a two-pronged fork angrily.

'You'll bully-rag us no more!'

A villager pointed a billhook at the big hexagonal building. 'Burn down his duffus!'

Witherington's men raised their swords. In turn the archers raised their bows and aimed at them. Then a tall, middle-aged man stepped forward from the villagers. In contrast to the ragged, pinched look of many of his fellows he was well-fed, wearing a good-quality doublet and hose. He looked at Witherington and spoke in a loud clear voice. 'We want no violence, sir, but your birds are playing havoc with our crops. The harvest will be poor enough this year.'

'I'd not have expected you to side with these dogs, Yeoman Harris,' Witherington said angrily. 'You have fifty acres of your own land, half of them bought from me.'

'That doesn't stop your birds spoiling them!' Harris replied. 'It must stop!'

There was a moment's silence, the two groups facing off. People from both sides looked curiously at us. 'What yew doin' 'ere!' one of the villagers called out threateningly. Harris raised a hand to quiet him, then walked slowly down towards us. He had a large knife at his belt. Nicholas had been right, this could mean serious trouble. But as he approached, I saw the man was smiling.

He asked, eagerly, 'Are you the commissioners come to look into illegal enclosures? We knew the Protector was sending them out. We did not expect you so soon.'

I realized he thought we were part of Somerset's promised new commissions. It made sense, a senior lawyer and his men suddenly appearing in the village. I hesitated, then said, 'No, though I have heard they are to be sent. I am in Brikewell on private business, nothing to do with your lands. I came to speak to Master Witherington.'

Another man walked briskly down towards us. He was younger, poorly dressed in a ragged smock and carrying a scythe. The expression on his face was furious. 'You doddipoll, Harris, they're Witherington's men.' He raised the scythe threateningly. 'Think you can get us for clearing our fields of those pests! I could gut you like a fish, Master Hunchback!' Barak and Nicholas moved forward, but the man did not move. 'What've I left to lose, eh?' he shouted angrily. 'Two years in Scotland, harried by the redshanks, living in damp forts built of mud that couldn't even keep the rain out, and a year's pay owing! I come back and find my family near clammed with hunger, while that bag of shit' – he waved his weapon at Witherington – 'piles up profits from his sheep!'

'Wait, Melville!' Harris put a restraining hand on the man's arm, then looked at us, his expression hard now. 'What is your business with Witherington?'

I replied in a voice loud enough to carry up the field. 'I am working on the Boleyn murder case, I have come from his house, I wish only to ask Master Witherington some questions.' Witherington frowned at me. There was silence again. Barak spoke quietly to Melville. 'You've got numbers on your side, matey, but they've got the better weapons and those dogs, and you've women here. It's up to you, but if it were me, I'd leave off, for now at least.'

'Ay, he's right,' Toby agreed. 'More's the pity.'

Harris and Melville looked at each other, then Melville called out to the crowd. 'The lawyer isn't a commissioner, but he's not Wither-ington's man either. Come, let's leave it, we've done what we came to do, got most of these birds.'

The archer who had shot the dove retrieved his arrow and held it up, the bird impaled, its white feathers now a mass of blood. The villagers cheered, and Witherington went puce. Nonetheless, he allowed the crowd to walk past his men. But he shouted after them, 'Harris! You're a marked man! And Melville, I'll have your lands, you insolent churl!'

For answer, Melville turned and raised two fingers at him.

I took a deep breath. 'Thank God you were here,' I said to Barak. 'Otherwise there might have been blood spilt.'

'A mighty ruffle, at least.'

'By God, the way those peasants spoke to the manor lord,' Nicholas said. He shook his head and laughed, outrage tinged with reluctant admiration.

'Here he comes,' Barak said. Witherington had left his men and was stumping down towards us, sword in hand, his round, red face still furious. He halted before me.

'Who are you, sir? I heard you mention Boleyn.'

'Yes, we are reviewing the evidence in the case against him. Merely to make sure nothing has been overlooked.'

'On whose behalf?'

'I am appointed agent for Master Copuldyke.'

Witherington eyed me narrowly. 'You're here for the Lady Elizabeth, then.'

I took a deep breath. 'She only wishes us to examine the facts, and ensure justice is done. I do not say Master Boleyn is innocent.'

'As well you don't.' Witherington gave a sudden, scoffing laugh. 'The Lady Mary won't be pleased if she gets to hear her sister's sniffing around Norfolk business. Well, what do you want of me?'

'Only to hear events from your – perspective. And perhaps, if you permit, to talk to the shepherd who found the body.'

Witherington looked at Barak. 'What did you say to those churls, that made them go?'

Barak met his gaze. 'Only that you were better armed, and that they should have a care for the women among them.'

Witherington looked at me again. 'I shall be reporting this matter to the Justice of the Peace, I'll have Harris and Melville prosecuted for destroying my birds.' His anger rose again. 'You can be witnesses, you saw them killing those doves, you saw their insolence, and saw Melville raise two fingers at me!' For a moment he almost choked with anger.

'You are free to contact me,' I said. Toby opened his mouth to protest, but Barak gave him a wink. Allowing Witherington to contact me did not mean I would reply, nor give a reply to his liking.

Witherington, however, nodded with satisfaction. He was, I realized, a man of no great intelligence. He turned to his men. 'Shuckborough! Go and fetch old Adrian Kempsley to the manor house. He'll be dozing in his shed.' He paused, then added, 'And bring Lobley too. This man should see him. You two, bring the dogs back to the manor; the rest of you, about your business.' With that, the little martinet marched back to the road. We followed, passing his men, who looked at us dubiously.

✝

WE ARRIVED AT Witherington's house, and he led us into an echoing, stone-flagged hall. Servants peeped nervously at us from open doorways, and one approached his master. 'Is all well, sir?' he asked meekly.

'Not unless you count the killing of dozens of my birds as being well,' Witherington answered fiercely. 'Bring some beer to my study. You two lawyers, come with me.' Leaving Toby and Barak in the hall, Nicholas and I followed him into a study which smelled strongly of dog, and where account books and documents were piled untidily. He pushed them aside. 'This house is getting messy since my wife died.'

'I am sorry,' I said.

Witherington nodded acknowledgement. He put his sword on the desk, then sat behind it, waving Nicholas and me to stools. He looked at us, then gave a bark of laughter. 'That's some hand your man outside has got.'

'He lost the real one in an honourable fight,' Nicholas said.

'Against the Scotch barbarians?'

'No,' I answered. 'Some London ones.'

'Oh yes,' Witherington said, 'there's plenty of barbarians in England, as you've just seen. Christ's bowels, the times we live in. It's these damned Commonwealth men, and the Protector. By Jesu, I wish we had the old king back. I hear things are getting worse in the south-west, and there's trouble elsewhere. And that was not the first such scene in these parts. People here are too stupid to see what is in their own interest. They say I want to enclose more land here for sheep, which I do, but I told them that when I get part of Boleyn's land through the court, they can have it for pasture.'

I said, 'I heard there was an – incident – in the spring. Between some of your men and Boleyn's.'

Witherington looked at me narrowly. 'Yes. In March. I sought to assert my legitimate claim to the land up to the old stream bed by occupying it, but my men were driven off violently by Boleyn's people.'

In fact, his forcible entry onto disputed land was quite illegal, but I did not make the point. 'I understand you are now taking the matter to law.'

Witherington shrugged. 'It may not be necessary. If Boleyn hangs, his lands will go to the King, and I may be able to negotiate with the escheator.'

'His local agent being John Flowerdew.'

'I believe so,' he answered cautiously.

'I understand that Sir Richard Southwell owns land bordering both yours and Boleyn's.'

Witherington shrugged. 'No doubt some deal beneficial to all parties can be negotiated.' I wondered whether he was in touch with Southwell or Flowerdew already. Yet Boleyn had told me Southwell was not interested in Brikewell.

'I do not see what such matters have to do with the evidence for Mistress Boleyn's killing,' Witherington said, folding his plump hands on his stomach.

'I am just trying to see the whole picture. Tell me, did you know Mistress Boleyn?'

'Hardly at all. She disappeared only two years after Boleyn and I bought our lands from the old monastery. She came to dinner here once, and sat at table barely exchanging a word with anyone. When I tried to engage her in conversation, all I got was surly looks. And she ate barely more than a bird. We did not invite them again. Personally, I think she was not right in the head. Those damned sons of hers take after her, I think. Certainly they're not like their milksop father.' He curled his lip in contempt. 'When Edith disappeared and Boleyn took that whore to live with him, a lot of people thought he'd done away with his first wife. I never did, though; he wouldn't have the balls.'

'Where do you think Edith Boleyn might have been these last nine years?'

Witherington shrugged again. 'I've no idea. Someone must have been giving her shelter, I suppose. Somewhere far from these parts.'

'Strange that she was found dead on the boundary between your land and Boleyn's,' I said.

'What do you mean, sir?' Witherington's voice rose.

'Nothing. Only that it was a strange way, a strange place, for someone to dispose of a body.'

'Perhaps Boleyn met her on the bridge by arrangement, then lost his temper and killed her there and then. He does have a temper, by all accounts.'

There was a knock at the door, and the servant he had addressed as Shuckborough entered, followed by a thin, white-haired old man, obviously afraid, kneading a greasy cap in his hands. I guessed Shuckborough was Witherington's steward, in everyday charge of the estate as Chawry was on Boleyn's. He was a large, well-built man in his forties, with a square, hard face. He gave the cringing old man a look of contempt, then addressed his master. 'Kempsley, sir. He was asleep in his shed, like you said. Then he had the cheek to moan all the way here about how there are too many sheep for him to manage; he needs a boy to help him.'

'If it's too much for him, he can go out on the road,' Witherington replied. 'Is that what you want, old Adrian?'

'No, sir.'

'Then keep your clack-box shut. These two gentlemen are here about Boleyn's killing his wife. They want you to tell them what you saw that day.'

'I made a – what was it called, a deper—'

I smiled at the old man. 'Deposition. I have read it. You must have had a terrifying experience.'

'It was, it was. Like something come up from hell. At first I thought it was a sheep trapped in the mud, it was only dawn and the light was dimsy, but then I got close and saw it was that poor woman —' He shuddered at the memory.

'And you saw footprints in the mud?'

'Ay, sir, big ones, leading down from the grass on Master Boleyn's side. Made by big boots, you could see that.'

'You are sure the body must have been put there during the night?'

'Ay. I walked round the sheep just afore it got dark the evening before. About nine o'clock. There was nothing in the stream then.'

'Whoever did the deed must have known the lie of the land, do you think?'

Kempsley nodded firmly. 'Yes. Moving in the dark, carrying the poor lady.'

'And he must have been very strong.'

'Ay. I doubt one man could have done it alone.'

Witherington interrupted. 'We can do without your speculations.'

'On the contrary,' I said, 'they are most helpful. Tell me, do you think the prints could have been made by *two* pairs of boots?'

Kempsley frowned. 'The mud was so pashed up, sir, boot-prints everywhere. All were made by the same type of boots. That's all I can say, sir.'

'Thank you. That's all. I will leave you to your sheep.' The steward nodded, and Kempsley scuttled from the room. Witherington looked at Shuckborough, then at us. 'There is one more person I should like you to meet.' He nodded at Shuckborough, who went out, returning a moment later leading a young man by the arm. He was no more than twenty, tall and athletically built, with tangled brown hair and a scraggy beard. His expression was curiously vacant, and a dribble of saliva ran from a corner of his mouth.

Witherington said, 'This is Ralph, who works my lands with his father and brothers. They are my serfs. Last April, he was one of those I sent to stake my claim to the lands Boleyn says are his.' He laughed bitterly. 'Ralph was a good strong lad, said he'd give a good account of himself. You couldn't do that now, could you, Ralph?'

The boy stared at him. 'I – am – Ralph,' he said slowly. Then he smiled and said, 'I know a rhyme. Ring-a-ring-o-roses—'

'Shut up.' Shuckborough shook his arm. Ralph fell silent. Witherington said, 'Show the gentlemen your head, Ralph.'

'Don't want to,' the boy said, then squealed as Shuckborough pushed him down roughly, so that we could see the top of his head. I recoiled. On the crown was a large bald patch with scarring and an actual depression in the skull where he had been hit with something heavy.

'Not a pretty sight, is he, Master Shardlake?' Witherington said. 'Gerald Boleyn did that to him, when they led some of their friends and Boleyn's men to throw my men off the land. You'd expect a bit of punching, perhaps a couple of broken bones in such a tussle, but the Boleyn twins each had a great club and the one without the scar hit Ralph over the head with it. Amazing he wasn't killed; as it is, his wits are gone.' He waved a hand. 'Take him away, Shuckborough, before he starts blubbing.'

As the steward took the boy out, Nicholas said, 'If there were witnesses, surely Gerald Boleyn should have been prosecuted. He could hang for that.'

Witherington shifted uneasily in his chair. 'I didn't want that. Not when my men had been on what Boleyn claims is his land. Ralph's family are taking care of him, I give them some money.' He looked at me. 'But I warn you, Master Shardlake. I make sure my house is well guarded, especially at night. Master Boleyn may be one kind of man, but those sons of his are something else.'

Chapter Eighteen

WE ARRIVED BACK at Tombland late in the afternoon. During our ride from Brikewell the sky had gradually turned darker, 'greasy', as Toby called it. It looked as though a thunderstorm was coming. Outside the Maid's Head I saw, lying inside an alcove in the outside wall, a man covered in a large, ragged blanket. A little trail of vomit spilled from beneath the blanket onto the street; he was either drunk, or ill. People passing, especially those of the richer sort riding into the Maid's Head courtyard, gave him looks of disgust.

After leaving the horses, Barak and Nicholas were keen to go on to see Scambler, and I wanted to visit Josephine, but I had pulled a muscle in my back on the ride home, and could not face going out again. I said I needed an early night, and suggested we take dinner soon, so that Toby could return to his farm.

The place was busy with new arrivals, servants carrying heavy baggage upstairs, the innkeeper Master Theobald directing them with a self-important air. All the newcomers wore fine clothes, and some lawyers' black robes like ours, though I saw nobody I recognized. 'People coming for the Assizes,' Barak observed.

'Ay,' Toby agreed. 'All the Justices of the Peace and royal and county officials will be gathering.'

'Will we see Sir Richard Southwell, or John Flowerdew?'

'Yes, they'll be here,' Toby said. 'I'll point them out.'

'I've met Southwell briefly. He seems a formidable man.'

'He's a brute,' Toby answered, 'and the greediest man in Norfolk.'

✝

THE FOUR OF us sat down to dinner. Candles were lit, for the evening sky continued to darken, and we heard the occasional distant rumble of thunder. Quietly, we discussed the case.

Nicholas said, 'Isabella clearly loves Boleyn. I think Chawry likes her, but who would not?'

'Yes,' I agreed. 'I think he does.' I pondered. 'When she said she wouldn't give Boleyn a child until they were married, it certainly doesn't sound as though he tried to force her.'

'Witherington's a different matter from his neighbour,' Barak observed.

'Yes, a grasping bully.'

Toby said, 'Already he's got land that once supported dozens of villagers, which is worked now by one old shepherd, and he can't even treat him decently. So much for all the old nonsense about ties of honour and loyalty between landlord and tenant.'

Nicholas said, 'I agree with you about Witherington, but there are honourable men among the landowners, too, who recognize their obligations.'

'When it's a matter of making a profit, they're all the same. Bully, threaten, steal, enclose.'

'How strong do you think Witherington's case is over the boundary issue?' Barak looked at me, changing the subject, then speared a piece of meat from his plate with the knife on his metal hand.

'From the old deeds and the map we took from Boleyn's London house, pretty weak. I think it was because he knows his case was poor that he tried that bit of self-help in the spring.'

Nicholas asked, 'But would he go as far as setting up John Boleyn for his wife's murder?'

'What if he's in debt?' Barak suggested. 'That can make men desperate.'

Toby shook his head. 'I went into that for Master Copuldyke. Boleyn's finances may be in a poor state, but Witherington's aren't. Greedy snudge that he is, he knows how to turn a profit.'

'He didn't strike me as especially sharp,' Barak observed.

'I agree,' I said. 'Witherington struck me as stupid and obstinate. You could argue such a man might be so stupid that he would think he could get away with murder, but I can't see him facing a capital sentence over a small piece of land. Though we can't entirely discount the possibility.'

Nicholas sighed. 'So we're no further forward. Except that Isabella, and Chawry who has no alibi, must be added to the list of suspects.'

'Except for what we saw at the scene of the crime,' I said. 'The killer was local, knew the area well. And if it was one man, he was very strong.'

'Or two other people acting together,' Barak replied.

I said, 'Remember the twins have an alibi for the whole night in question. Carousing with a group of friends.'

Nicholas considered. 'Friends can be intimidated. Those two would be good at that.'

I winced at a twinge from my back. 'I wish I could see a way through this tangle.' I looked at Toby. 'Could you try and trace Grace Bone's family, see if anyone has heard of her in all these years? That has to be followed up.' I considered. 'And we should talk to those twins about their alibi.'

Nicholas said, 'They'll not do that willingly.'

'We need to get them off their own ground,' Barak said. 'Four of us to two of them.'

I nodded. 'Yes. But it needs thought.'

'They're dangerous,' Toby said warningly.

'Come on, they're just a couple of lads,' Barak said impatiently.

Outside, the thunder rolled nearer.

☦

DURING THE NIGHT the storm came, and I was wakened by a great crash of thunder and white flashes of lightning that lit up the room, followed by the sound of torrential rain. I wondered about the poor man lying in the alcove outside.

By morning, the storm had passed, and the air was fresher. Toby, Nicholas and I had arranged to meet Barak for breakfast at eight. None of us had expressed a wish to go to church; I suspected that Toby's commitment to religion was as distant as that of Barak, Nicholas and

I. Yesterday, Barak had said he particularly wanted to see Josephine again, but I saw he had also become caught up in the thrill of the chase. From tomorrow, Monday, he would be busy with Assize duties, which eased my conscience a little. I dared not imagine how Tamasin might react if she discovered that her husband had ended up assisting me again.

Barak was last to arrive. He had an air of excitement. 'I called at the office they've set up for the Assize clerks,' he told us. 'The word from London is the rebels in the West Country have refused the Protector's offer of a pardon, and chased away some Reformist preachers he sent to them. Troops are to be sent down there.'

'Any more word of what the West Country rebellion is about?'

'They don't like the religious changes down there; they're calling for the return of the practices of King Henry's time. But they're attack, ing landlords as well. The Protector's been caught on the hop.'

Nicholas shook his head. 'Demands for reform are one thing, but this is rebellion – in time of war, too. They'll smart for this, and rightly.'

Toby was silent, thoughtful. I said, 'Well, that's nothing to do with us. I suggest we look for the lad Scambler first, then visit the address we have for Josephine. Toby, if you want to go back to your farm after we've seen Scambler, please do. Our other visit is a personal matter, and with riding back and forth you cannot have seen much of your parents.'

'Thank you. I should like to do that.'

✝

THE HOT WEATHER returned later in the morning. The air, though, was less sticky, and some of the city stink had been washed away by the rain. As we left the Maid's Head, I saw that the man covered by the blanket was still there. As I looked I heard a groan, and the blanket twitched.

I said, 'That fellow must be ill. We should do something.' I took a step towards him but Toby, surprisingly, put a hand on my arm. 'I wouldn't, sir. If he is sick, you might catch whatever he has. There will be many coming to service at the cathedral this morning; if the name of Christ means anything, someone will show him charity. There are hundreds such as he in the doorways of Norwich,' he added bitterly.

I hesitated, then nodded reluctantly, and we walked down into Tombland. The cobbled square was full of puddles, and water still dripped from the roofs of the fine houses round the square, glinting in the sunshine. Opposite, I saw that the great doors of the cathedral precinct were open, making the body of the great building visible, as well as the ruined buildings of the former monastery attached to it. Most of the walls were down, and carts full of rubble stood by. The cathedral doors were open, too, giving a glimpse of a huge, vaulted space within. Toby led us past, down into the town.

✞

NORWICH WAS QUIET on the Sabbath, save for the ringing of church bells; Toby was right, many destitute figures lay sleeping in the doorways of shops and houses, more noticeable now few others were around. We passed the castle on its great mound, and I wondered whether the rain had penetrated John Boleyn's subterranean cell. I would visit again tomorrow. People were cleaning up the marketplace, which, after yesterday's market, was full of rubbish; rotten fruit, animal entrails, abandoned sacks. Beyond, we passed into a long street with houses and shops on either side, which Toby said was Ber Street. Some houses looked prosperous enough, but others had been divided into tenements. Toby stopped before one which was painted yellow, the paint peeling, exposing the lath and plaster and beams beneath.

'Yellow house, next Hunter's Yard, ground floor. This is it.' He rapped on the door. It was opened by a short, plump woman with a round, wrinkled face, a black coif covering most of her grey hair. Her little mouth was pursed in an expression of disapproval; small grey eyes studied us, widening momentarily at the sight of Barak's hand.

'What is it?' she asked boldly. 'I want no lawyers here.' Then she added, 'Why yew abroad on the Sabbath?'

'We wish to speak to Simon Scambler,' I said. 'Are you his aunt, Goodwife?'

She sighed. 'What's Sooty done *now*? You can't've come to arrest him, else they'd have sent the constable. If he's damaged something, we've no money.' She planted herself more firmly in the doorway.

'He's not in trouble. I represent Master Boleyn; I only wish to ask some questions about the time he worked for him at Brikewell.' My hand went to my purse. 'We will pay for access to him.'

At once she put out a hand, and I put a shilling into it. She closed her fingers on the coin, and I noticed the joints were twisted and swol-len, as Parry had said Edith Boleyn's had been.

'Come in, then,' she said, 'though there's scarce room for four o' you.' She gave us another disapproving look. 'Doing business on the Sabbath, 'tis against God's law.' She waved us into a room furnished only with a table on which a much-thumbed Testament stood, a chest, a couple of stools and a wooden settle against the wall. The open shut-ters, I saw, hung loosely from their hinges. She went to the closed door of a neighbouring room and yelled through it, so loudly I jumped, 'Sooty! Get through here, you grub!' She shook her head. 'That boy, he may be my poor dead sister's child, but he'll drive me sappy with his yammering on, his godless singing –'

I took one of the stools while Toby, Barak and Nicholas crowded uncomfortably onto the settle. A moment later the boy we had seen in the market square appeared, dressed in a dirty nightshirt, skinny legs bare, brown hair untidy. When he saw us, his mouth fell open. He turned to the old woman. 'Who are these people, Aunt Hilda?'

She pointed at me. 'He wants to ask about when you worked for John Boleyn.' She turned to us, laughing mirthlessly. 'I thought I'd got rid of Sooty when he went to Brikewell, but no, he has to find a place where murder gets done.' The boy hung his head.

Toby leaned forward, speaking quietly. 'Shut your clack-box, Goodwife. You've been paid, and we're here to talk to your nephew, not listen to your howen' and mowen'. And I'm not interested in your newdickle religious notions. Leave us alone.'

The old woman reddened, then, with an expression as though she were chewing a wasp, she stomped off into the boy's room. 'Don't keep a' long,' she said. 'We've to get ready for church. I need him to read the words to me.' She slammed the door.

I smiled reassuringly at the boy, who was looking at us apprehensively. 'We've met before, Scambler. Do you remember, two days ago, in the market square? When those boys tripped you up?'

He looked at me, then Nicholas, and his thin face brightened. 'Yes, yew tried to help me,' he said with sudden animation. 'Those boys, I knew them at school, they keep crazing me . . .'

I studied Scambler, more convinced than ever that he was no idiot. After meeting his aunt, I guessed the boys were not the only ones who made his life hard. Still speaking gently, I said, 'I understand from Master Boleyn you were the only one who could handle his horse.'

Scambler brightened further. 'Ay, Midnight was a lovely animal. Never hurt you if you treated him right . . .'

Nicholas said, 'I have seen his stable, heard him kicking. If you could control him, that is some achievement.'

'I've a way with animals. You have to show them you mean to help them.'

'But Midnight could be difficult with others, I believe. Like Master Boleyn's sons.'

Scambler's face darkened. 'I think before I came they tried to hurt him. I heard he gave that Barnabas a good hard kick.'

'Did the twins ever try to hurt you?'

'Whenever they could.' His tone was suddenly weary. 'They punched me, threw things at me – a brick, once. Another time they caught me alone on the road and beat me up, for no reason.'

'I doubt you were the first,' Nicholas said.

'No,' I agreed, remembering the boy they had tormented in London. 'But Master Boleyn trusted you, didn't he? You were the only other person allowed a key to Midnight's stable.'

'Yes. He said I was to keep the key with me always, allow no one else to have it, especially not the twins. I gave the key to the constable after the murder.' He gave me a nervous glance.

'Maybe that was why the twins set on you?' Nicholas said. 'A jealous rage because you had control of the horse and its stable?'

Scambler shook his head. 'People don't need no excuse to set on me. My aunt says it's because I'm on my way to be damned.'

'Do you believe that?' I asked.

'No!' he answered with sudden force. 'I do no wrong. Her

teachings are wicked . . . !' He stopped himself and put a hand to his mouth. 'I'm sorry, I meant no blasphemy –'

'It doesn't matter. We are not the church authorities. Now, Sooty –'

'Please, sir, please, don't use that name. My Christian name is Simon.'

'Very well, Simon. I'm sure you know how important the key to the stable is for the case, given that a pair of muddy boots and the murder weapon were found in there. Can you swear to me you never let the keys out of your possession?'

'I never gave them to no one,' he said, but he looked at me worriedly, shifting uneasily from foot to foot. Scambler had no ability to conceal his feelings, which perhaps was one reason why he had such problems in life. I said, still gently, 'That does not answer my question. Was the key ever out of your possession?'

Suddenly, the boy burst into tears, covering his face with his hands; a desperate, frightened sobbing. Toby said, impatiently, 'Stop blubbering like a great gal, and answer.'

I raised a hand to silence him. 'Here, lad, calm yourself. Tell me the truth. I swear that unless you have committed a crime, you will not suffer for anything you tell me.'

Scambler looked up at me, his dirty face streaked with tears. 'I've done no crime.'

'Then I promise you are safe.'

He looked at me, afraid, then said, more to himself than to me, 'You helped me before. Nobody does.'

'I will again, if I can.'

Simon took a deep, shuddering breath. 'I told you the twins set on me one day. I'd been on an errand to Wymondham, and was on my way back. They were waiting for me in a patch of woodland about a mile from home. They just jumped out at me, set on me and started punching and kicking me, calling me – names, cruel things. Then they disappeared into the woods again.'

'Was there any particular reason for them to set on you that day?'

'No sir. But Gerald and Barnabas, they need no reason.' He took a deep, sobbing breath. 'When I got home, I found the key was gone.

I wore it around my neck, on a chain; it must have broken during the fight. I was frightened, sir. Master Boleyn was not a bad master but he had a temper. So though I was bruised and bleeding, I went right back to where they attacked me, hoping to see the key on the road or the verge. But I didn't.' His voice quickened. 'It was getting dark, so I thought I'd look again next day. I was busy and couldn't get away till the afternoon. I went back to the place and this time I found the key on its chain, in the grass beside the road. The strange thing was' – he frowned – 'I'd looked in just that spot the day before, and I swear it wasn't there then. The chain was broken,' he added.

I glanced at the others. I thought, The twins could have set on him to get the key under cover of the beating, taken it for a day and then returned it, sure that Scambler, even if he guessed what had happened, would say nothing. I could tell from the guilty look on the boy's face that he, too, had hazarded that guess.

'When was this attack, Simon?' I asked.

'The twelfth of May,' he answered at once. 'I remember because it was my mother's birthday, God save her soul.' I drew in my breath. The twelfth, just before Edith's murder on the night of the fourteenth–fifteenth. I looked at the boy. 'You think the twins took the key?'

'They could have, and returned it. But why?'

'Did you not think of telling this to the authorities, after what was discovered in the stables when Mistress Boleyn was found murdered?'

He blushed, and lowered his head. 'I was frightened of what the twins might do. When the constable came, I didn't tell him.'

'They didn't ask you to make a deposition?'

'No. The constable said to his assistant it wasn't worthwhile, everyone knew I was sappy-headed.'

'Were you still working at Brikewell then?'

'No. When poor Master Boleyn was arrested, and not there to protect me from the twins, I left at once and came back to Aunt Hilda's.' He bowed his head again, kneaded his bony hands together. 'I've done wrong, sir, haven't I? But I couldn't work out why the twins would steal the keys just for a day.'

Barak spoke up. 'Do you happen to know whether Master Boleyn ever used a locksmith?'

'Yes. Not long after I came, the barns needed new locks, and a man came from Norwich. I remember I went to watch him work, I've never seen locks fitted before. I asked him questions, but he told me to stop bothering him. Though later I saw him laughing with the twins, drinking beer. He seemed to get on with *them*.'

'Do you know if Master Boleyn had ever used this man before?'

'I think so. Yes, I remember his steward, Master Chawry, told him it was good to see him at Brikewell again.'

'Do you remember his name?'

Scambler frowned. 'It was unusual. It was –' he brightened – 'Snockstobe.' He laughed. 'A silly name –' He broke off, and looked at me with something like horror. 'Oh, sir, do you mean the twins took the key to get a copy made?'

'It is possible.'

His jaw dropped.

'It is just a possibility,' I repeated quietly.

'Then if I'd spoken, Master Boleyn might not be in the castle. Oh Jesu, I've made an awful mess again.' He raised a hand to his mouth and began chewing on his knuckles.

'If that is what the twins did,' Nicholas said, 'we will find out, and put things right.'

'That we will,' Barak agreed firmly.

I took a deep breath. 'I meant what I said, Simon. No trouble will come to you for this. In fact, what you have said may help us. But one important thing: do not tell anyone what you have just told us. Not even your aunt.'

The boy laughed bitterly. 'I know they say I've a loose mouth, sir, but I'll tell nobody. And I never tell *her* anything.' A flash of anger entered his voice.

I took out my purse again. 'Here are two shillings to seal the bargain.'

'Thank you, sir. Since I left Brikewell, we have no money. My aunt used to spin, but her hands are too bad to work now. We're going to have to plead relief from the parish, see if the great rich men will give us any pennies.' He sighed.

'If you remember anything else, I can be contacted at the Maid's Head Inn. Ask for Master Shardlake.'

'Yes, sir.' Scambler attempted a crude bow. 'Thank you.'

We left the wretched tenement. As I closed the door I heard Scambler's aunt calling in her shrieking voice, 'Sooty! Get yourself dressed! We'll be late for service!'

Chapter Nineteen

W E WALKED A little way up Ber Street, then stopped at a corner
to confer. Church bells were still ringing, and people were
hurrying to service in their best clothes, mostly Protestant black.

'So,' Barak said, 'this could put it squarely on the twins. We have
to find this locksmith.'

'The Maid's Head innkeeper will know the Norwich locksmiths,'
Toby said. 'That snivelling little runt,' he added sharply. 'If he'd told
his story weeks ago, Boleyn might never been arrested. I'd swear he was
protecting his skin; he guessed what the twins had done.'

'I don't think so,' I said. 'He didn't think it through. He's only –
what – fifteen or so? And – not normal, though in a way which I do
not understand.'

'Crying like a gal. I'd have given him a good culp, got it out of
him that way.'

'I expect he's well used to that.' I looked at Toby sharply. I was
getting to see more and more that, despite his radicalism, he had a hard,
unsympathetic side.

'There's certainly something amiss with Scambler,' Barak said.
'The tears, the way he speaks so fast. And his aunt says he goes about
singing. He can't seem to – control himself.'

'But he's not a wantwit,' I said. 'Did you notice his voice? He
speaks with less of a local accent than you'd expect. And he talked of
going to school.'

'Maybe they chucked him out,' Toby said.

'Or maybe after his parents died there was no money for the fees,'
Nicholas said, raising an eyebrow at Toby. 'If the twins planned this,'
he went on, 'they must have known their mother's whereabouts when
she returned to Norwich, and killed her despite everyone saying they

were miserable when she left them as children. Killed her, and set up their father.'

'But what would they gain?' I asked. 'If their father is hanged, the lands they would have inherited go to the King's escheator, and they become wards of court till they reach twenty-one.'

'They've got their grandfather's protection.' Barak looked at me.

'We must find that locksmith tomorrow,' I said.

'The twins could have used another one,' Nicholas said.

'We'll try every locksmith in Norwich if we have to. I can say I have an expensive chest that needs mending. Now, Toby, take us to Conisford to find Josephine. Then go back home. Come to the Maid's Head again at seven tomorrow.'

✢

THE DISTRICT OF Conisford lay south of the castle. The main road, Conisford Street, contained some fine buildings as well as a rubbish-strewn open space, surrounding the ruins of a friary. Further south, though, the houses were all poorer, with glimpses into yards behind in which ramshackle wooden dwellings had been erected. Toby led us through an archway leading to one such yard, where the ground was bare earth with a malodorous piss-channel running through the middle. We looked at the dozen or so wooden shacks in what had once been the central courtyard for the large house built around it, its walls cutting off light from the sun. The shacks looked of recent construc-tion; they were unpainted, some with only rags at the windows instead of shutters. Chickens pecked about in the muck, where some filthy children were also playing. One pointed at Barak. 'Lookit yin hand! Yew bin fightin' the Scotch?'

Barak raised his hand. 'No, just naughty little boys!' The children giggled.

Toby said. 'This is the yard. See how the poorest live in Norfolk.'

'It is the same in London,' I replied. I was horrified, however, that Josephine could have ended up here.

'Ask the people which place is hers,' Toby suggested, 'but make clear you're nothing to do with the authorities. They'll be wary of lawyers.'

'I will, Toby. Thank you for bringing us. Now, go see how your mother is.'

He bowed and left us. 'God's death,' Barak said. 'This is a shithole.'

✝

As TOBY PREDICTED, when we knocked at doors to ask for Good-man Brown and his wife, we were met with suspicion. The first was slammed in our face, the second answered by a thin young woman holding a crying baby who was immediately pushed aside by her hus-band. He said loudly, 'If you're come from Master Reynolds looking for rent from the Browns, don't try any of your bullyragging ways here, or we'll throw you out.'

I looked around and saw several doors were open, men in ragged smocks or sleeveless leather jerkins looking at us threateningly.

'Master Reynolds is your landlord?' I asked. Edith Boleyn's father, the twins' grandfather.

'Ay, he built this whole stinking yard, and others like it, to leech off the poor. Yew his men?'

'No. I used to employ Josephine Brown. I am in Norwich on busi-ness, and wished to see her. My companions know her, too.'

'Master Shardlake here gave her away at her wedding,' Barak said, placatingly.

The man's wife nodded. 'That yin's a Lunnoner, like the Browns.'

'Two doors up,' her husband said. 'But be careful, master, we'll be watching.' He slammed the door.

I had last seen Edward Brown two and half years ago, just before he and Josephine left for Norwich. Then he had been a well-set-up, good-natured fellow in his late twenties, with the confidence of an upper servant. When he opened the door, I saw he had lost perhaps a stone in weight; his face and body thin. He wore an old smock tucked into dirty leggings, his face was unwashed and his brown hair and beard were bedraggled. He had several half-healed cuts on his hands, and his right little finger was twisted out of shape. His eyes were angry, but seeing me his expression changed to amazement. 'Master Shard-lake? What are you doing here?' A moment later Josephine appeared, holding a baby at her breast. Once plump-faced, like her husband she

194

too had lost weight. She wore a patched grey dress; a white coif which had seen better days covered her greasy blonde hair. Her mouth fell open for a moment, but then she smiled spontaneously. 'Master Shard-lake. And Master Nicholas and Jack Barak. What are you doing in Norwich?'

'We are here on business,' I said. 'I have been worried about you, Josephine, since I had no reply to my last letter.'

'How did you find us?'

'A legal contact in the city found Master Henning's steward.'

Josephine turned to her husband. 'I told you we should have writ-ten again, I said Master Shardlake would help us.'

'We got no help from Master Henning's children when he and his wife died,' Brown said bitterly. 'They sold his house and threw us on the streets. I say, a pox on lawyers and gentlemen.'

'Edward!' Josephine chided him, almost in tears.

Nicholas said angrily, 'We have taken much time to find you. Your last letter spoke of trouble, you know Master Shardlake will help you if he can. He does not deserve this!'

Edward looked a little ashamed, and put a hand on his wife's shoulder. 'Ay, well, I'm sorry.' He took a deep breath. 'Come in, if you like, though 'tis a sorry place.'

Inside, dim light from the single window showed a room with an earthen floor, with a puddle in the corner from last night's rain, which had entered through a hole in the roof. In one corner was a sagging truckle bed and a home-made crib; some cracked crockery stood on a rickety shelf, and there was a table scored with much use on which a wooden drop-spindle lay beside a little pile of wool. A pair of old chairs and a battered clothes chest made up the rest of the furnishings. Josephine sat on a chair, hugging the sleeping baby – a fair-haired little girl perhaps three months old.

'Ay,' Edward Brown said. 'It's a poorhouse, all right.'

I asked quietly, 'How did this come to be?'

Josephine answered. 'As Edward said, when Master Henning died eighteen months ago, his children put us out on the street. Gave us not so much as a spoon as a keepsake. There's little work in Norwich, and we'd no training except in service. I get a little work spinning, I turn wool on that spindle day in, day out, till I could scream with boredom. Edward has some work as a stonemason's labourer, helping sort stone at the old cathedral monastery.'

'At fourpence a day, and only when unskilled labour is needed,' Edward added bitterly. 'While prices rise by the week. When I began I was good at the job, they hinted they might move me up the ranks to labourer's mate, but then a piece of stone fell on my finger and broke it, so that was that. Since April the city has started collecting money through the parishes for the poor, but as we have work we do not qualify. We only manage by dipping into the rent. Then our landlord sends his men to threaten us. But we are all standing together in this yard, we've seen them off twice.'

'Your neighbour said your landlord was a Master Reynolds. Gawen Reynolds?'

'Ay, whose daughter was murdered a few weeks back. And good riddance, if she was anything like him.' His eyes narrowed. 'Do you know him?'

'I've met him,' I said. 'A nasty old man.'

'That he is.'

I said, 'You should have asked me for some more money. Jack is right, I have been worried.'

Josephine turned to her husband. 'Please, Edward, let go your pride. At least for Mousy's sake.'

I looked at the baby. 'That is her name?'

'It's Mary.' Josephine looked fondly at the sleeping baby. 'But we call her Mousy.'

'Ay,' Edward's tone was more civil now. 'After Mousehold Heath. Jo and I had gone for a little walk there, back in March, to get some air, then suddenly her waters broke. A hard job to get back, wasn't it, my love?'

'It was.' Josephine sighed. 'I always wanted a child, to give it the love my father never gave me. But I cannot grow too fond. Half the children in this yard die before they are two.'

I said emphatically, 'Then let me help Mousy to live.'

Josephine looked at her husband. He bit his lip. Pride was all

Edward had left. There was an awkward silence. Josephine looked at Barak. 'Your poor hand,' she said gently. 'Does it still hurt?'

'I get by.'

'And your hair, Master Shardlake. It is quite white.'

'Ay, I grow older.'

Josephine turned to Nicholas. 'And you?' He was looking around the hovel with horror. He coughed and ran a hand through his untidy red hair. 'I fare well. I hope to be called to the bar, perhaps next year.'

'Then you will need a wife,' Josephine said teasingly.

'Ay, and I may have found one.'

Edward said, 'I fear we have no beer to offer you.'

'No matter. Perhaps we could take you to a tavern?' I offered.

He smiled grimly. 'You would raise eyebrows in the taverns we know. But —' he took a deep breath — 'I thank you for your offer to help us. Josephine is right, we must think of the child. We have three months' rent due. If we could borrow that, it would ease our burdens.'

'I will give it to you.'

Josephine's eye strayed to the pile of wool and the spindle on the table. 'We would ask you to stay. But I must get on with my spinning, Sunday though it is. The woman will be calling for the spun wool tomorrow. But please,' she said eagerly, 'come again.'

Edward said, 'But not wearing those rich clothes. Our neighbours have only just accepted us, Londoners are foreigners to them.'

Nicholas and Barak waited outside, watched by the people of the yard, while I settled the matter of the rent. I said goodbye to the baby, touching her tiny hand. She looked round at me, and smiled. Josephine said, 'She likes you. She's just beginning to take an interest in the world. Some people she likes, some she doesn't.' It moved me strangely.

✙

WE WALKED BACK to the Maid's Head in sober mood, saying little. Nicholas said, 'That honest people should live so. I thought it was only lazy bibbers that came to this.'

'Grow up, Nick lad,' Barak said impatiently. 'How many such yards have you seen in London?'

'Many. But I have never been inside one.'

I said, 'I have arranged for us to meet them on Tuesday evening, at the Blue Boar Inn. They should be acceptable there,' I added bitterly.

'Ay,' Barak agreed. 'But you two should dress down.'

'Edward said we shouldn't come back to the yard after dark. It's not safe.'

'I could have told you that.'

Back in Tombland, the sound of singing was audible from the cathedral. In the alcove by the Maid's Head the man in the ragged blanket still lay unmoving. On impulse I bent down and shook his shoulder. He did not stir. Carefully, I removed the blanket. I almost gagged at the smell. A young man in his early twenties lay there, his cheeks sunken, his hair alive with lice. His eyes were half open, unseeing. He was quite dead.

'Looks as though he starved,' Barak said.

'Ay.' I looked over at the cathedral. 'So much for Christian charity.'

Chapter Twenty

T HE NEXT MORNING, Toby came to the Maid's Head at seven. Barak would be busy with Assizes work all week. It was Monday, the seventeenth of June, three days until Boleyn's trial. The judges would be arriving that evening, and the Maid's Head was busier than ever.

I laid out what we needed to do that day to Toby and Nicholas over breakfast. 'First, we see Boleyn, ask him about this Snockstobe, and whether he used any other locksmiths. And after what Reynolds's steward told me, I need to press him about his relations with his wife. And there is that lack of an alibi. I am sure Boleyn wasn't telling the truth.'

'Maybe the prospect of being hanged on Friday will have made him think again,' Toby said.

'I hope to God it has. We'll see. Afterwards, we'll visit the locksmith, and if he made no copy of the keys, we'll visit every other locksmith in Norwich. Nicholas and I will do that. If we find the twins took the key from Scambler and made a copy, it throws a whole new light on the case.'

'Could the twins have been working for someone else?' Nicholas asked. He turned to Toby. 'Didn't you say they and some other young gentlemen did dirty work for Richard Southwell?'

'So it is said,' Toby replied.

'After we've seen Boleyn, Toby, I want you to try and trace the brother of this Grace Bone.'

'That will not be easy, if he's poor, with no link to a trade guild or someone of rank. There're thousands like your friend Josephine, living in slums around Norwich, with no reason to advertise themselves to the authorities.'

'Do what you can. You found Josephine, after all.' My tone was snappish, for I was conscious how near to trial we were, and the face of the dead man from the night before still haunted my mind. I went on, 'Where *was* Edith during those nine years? If this Grace Bone is still alive and in Norwich, perhaps she could tell us something. If we could find where Edith went, maybe we could solve this case.'

Nicholas said, 'If Edith was not in her wits, she would have needed a protector.'

'Or a guard.'

I bit my lip. 'Then either her protector gave up on her, or she escaped from her guard. And made her way to Elizabeth as a last hope. But we've no idea.'

'And we've still somehow got to get the twins on their own,' Nicholas added.

Just then, a shadow fell over our table. I looked up to find a tall, thin man in his late forties, dressed identically to me in the robe, coif and cap of a serjeant-at-law, smiling down at me tightly. He bowed and doffed his cap. 'God give you good morrow, sir. I did not know any other serjeants were attending the Assizes.'

I rose and bowed in my turn. 'Matthew Shardlake, of Lincoln's Inn.'

'I am John Flowerdew of Hethersett. Most of my work now is local, representing the Norfolk escheator Henry Mynne.' He smiled again, a thin, insincere smile not reflected in the cold, searching brown eyes under heavy black eyebrows. His narrow face with his large Roman nose, no doubt handsome enough once, had deep lines in each cheek.

'Are you staying at the Maid's Head for the Assizes?' I asked him.

'Yes. I need to attend in my official capacity. What case are you here on?'

'I am advising Master John Boleyn in respect of the murder charge against him.'

Flowerdew's gaze intensified. 'Ah, there has been much talk about that matter. It looks as though he will hang. Then I shall be responsible for his lands.'

'I understand you have visited Isabella Boleyn?'

Flowerdew laughed sardonically. 'Does she still call herself Boleyn? Well, she will be out bag and baggage if Boleyn's lands pass to the King. Yes, I made a preliminary visit.'

I raised my eyebrows. Flowerdew asked, 'Will you be attending the ceremony to welcome the judges into the city this evening?'

'Probably.'

'Well,' he said, looking a little put out by the brevity of my responses. 'I have a meeting with the county justices of the peace to attend.'

Nicholas asked, 'Excuse me, sir, is there any more news of the troubles in the West?'

Flowerdew frowned mightily. 'It is said they are besieging Exeter, and an army will be sent against them. They have had the insolence to send petitions to the King, demanding the religious reforms be abolished, the Scottish war ended and God knows what else.'

'It is very serious, then,' I said.

'It could hardly be more so. Worse than the stirs in May, which the county gentlemen managed to squash. Though I hear the disturbances in Hampshire have been put down, and the Protector has sent them a pardon. Pardon! The old king would have had them executed! What example is this to the commons everywhere?'

'I doubt commoners elsewhere will know of it.'

Flowerdew looked at me as though I were stupid. 'Do you not know that deserters from the Scottish war and other stirrers are inciting rebellion across the country?' He shook his head. 'Well, at least the Assizes is well protected; many JPs have brought armed retinues to Norwich. Even if those cowards on the city council think it impolitic to hold the usual feast for the judges. Mayor Codd, there is a wet fish indeed.' With that he bowed briefly and turned away, gown swirling.

'He's a choleric fellow,' Nicholas whispered.

'I wonder what he and the Boleyn twins will make of each other if he tries to take over their father's house,' Toby said with an unpleasant smile. 'Or do to each other.'

✝

IT WAS ANOTHER hot day, and I was already tired by the time we had walked down to the castle. My back nagged painfully, and I was beginning to fear the long ride from London to Norwich might have done some permanent damage. Once more we passed from the sunshine into the cool dank interior of the castle, and again the gaoler led us down the clanging iron steps. Pools of water from the recent rainstorm lay in the space below, already starting to smell. I asked the others to wait outside, for the matters I had to raise with John Boleyn were delicate.

He lay on his pallet bed, staring into space. His hair and beard were more tangled than ever and he seemed to have shrunk a little. He brightened a little, though, as I handed over the parcel of food Isabella had given me. He unwrapped it and ran his hands over one of the earthenware pots. 'Dear Isabella,' he said gently. 'I shall miss her most of all, if –'

'Do not give up hope yet, Master Boleyn, we have a useful new lead.' I was tempted to tell him that if he was found guilty, I had authorization from the Lady Elizabeth to ask for a pardon, but I must keep that news a close secret until after the verdict, and then make my own judgement as to whether the trial and judgement had been fair. It was a heavy responsibility. I told him instead of my visit to Scambler, and the temporary disappearance of the key. He shook his head. 'I can believe the twins beat up Sooty, but never that they would have killed their mother.'

'Nonetheless, sir, we must follow this up.'

'Yes.' He sighed. 'They are my sons. But they have shown me no loyalty. Not even visited me here.'

'So, have you used this locksmith Snockstobe regularly?'

'Yes, for years. Though I hardly knew him; Chawry dealt with such people.'

'You have his address?'

'I think it is in a lane off Tombland.'

'Good. We should soon be able to find it. Have you ever used anyone else?'

'No. Chawry has a list of people he employs for certain jobs.' He frowned. 'Sooty could have missed the key when he first went looking. He was good with the horses but otherwise – well – scatterbrained.'

I took a deep breath. 'There is something else I must ask you, about Edith, and it is personal.'

He smiled sadly. 'Such considerations weigh little given what else is at stake.'

'I went to visit Master Gawen Reynolds. Gerald and Barnabas were there.'

'Ay, they always got on well with their grandfather. They resemble him, you might say.' He looked at me directly. 'Reynolds wants me dead, you know.'

'Yes, I think he does. He was not helpful. Have you ever met his steward, a man called Vowell?'

Boleyn shook his head. 'I do not recall him. But remember, sir, I have not been to his house since I moved Isabella into Brikewell. The twins have often visited, but I have not been welcome.'

'Vowell is discontented in his post –'

Boleyn smiled sardonically. 'With that bad-tempered rogue and his acid-faced wife, I'm not surprised. And now Gerald and Barnabas too –'

I said bluntly, 'According to what Vowell told me privily, Edith came to her father once, years ago, and complained that you had – well, tried to assert your marital rights by force. Her father sent her packing, saying she had made her bed and must lie on it.'

Boleyn looked away. 'Do you believe I would do that?' he said quietly.

'You must tell me.'

He looked me directly in the face. 'Even if I had wished to assert my rights, I would never have forced Edith. But I can believe she went and told her father a pack of lies behind my back.' He shook his head angrily. 'My wife was mad towards the end, Serjeant Shardlake, quite mad.'

'I apologize, sir. But I was told the story, so I had to ask.'

Boleyn nodded, and waved a hand. We sat in silence for a moment, then I said quietly, 'There remains your alibi. Do you still cleave to your story that you were in your study during those two hours, between nine and eleven in the evening?'

He hesitated a moment, then said, 'Yes. I was there, alone.'

'If you were elsewhere, no matter why, you must say. It could make all the difference to you, and to your wife.'

He shook his head. I persisted, 'I will be frank, sir, I do not think you have been truthful with me. Please, if there is any way of saving yourself, tell me now.'

For a second Boleyn hesitated. Then he said, 'I was in my study.'

I sighed. 'Well, if I can find other new evidence, we can present it at the trial. As well as the locksmith, I intend to interview the twins about their attack on Scambler.'

He looked up sharply at that. 'Be careful.'

'We will. We are also trying to trace Grace Bone, as she left your employ just before Edith vanished nine years ago. In case there is something new she can tell us if she is still alive, or her family can. I understand she gave you only a week's notice of her leaving.'

'Yes, notice which she did not even take. Just left the same day.' Boleyn shook his head. 'They could not find her nine years ago; she may be dead by now.' Then he looked at me with sudden sharpness. 'Do you think something might have happened to her as well?'

'It is well worth exploring. Her disappearance just a little before Edith's was strange.'

'I always thought she was just another who had had enough of Edith, even though they had seemed close.' He sighed. 'Well, the twins could not have been responsible for that. They were nine at the time.' He fell silent.

I said, 'I shall see you again tomorrow, or at worst the next day.'

He smiled wanly. 'And then at the trial.'

✝

I REJOINED NICHOLAS and Toby outside. I said, 'I still think he is lying, that he went somewhere on the night of Edith's death, perhaps to meet someone, and has some important reason for hiding it.'

'Or used the time to kill her,' Toby said flatly.

Nicholas said, 'For once, I agree with you. Remember, we are here to investigate the circumstances, not represent Boleyn. He is not our client.'

I thought a moment. 'No, he is not. You are right. But there *are* matters we have discovered that need investigation. The locksmith especially.'

'Witherington seemed to think Boleyn a weak fellow,' Toby said. 'Someone whose lands might be occupied with impunity. Yet he fought back, and hard. And a weak man would not have brought Isabella into his house in defiance of local opinion. And all who know him say he has a temper.'

Nicholas asked, 'How did he react to what Michael Vowell told you?'

'He denied ever trying to force himself on Edith. He thinks she probably lied to her father. Said she was mad. What I do not understand is that, if he still cares so deeply about Isabella – who, as Flowerdew was keen to point out this morning, will be put out on the street if he's hanged – that, surely, would move him to tell the truth about his alibi, if he is lying. Could the truth be something damaging to Isabella?' Then I burst out, 'God's death, every question only leads to another question.'

✞

MASTER THEOBALD AT the Maid's Head was keen to help as usual, and after some brief enquiries among the staff he was able to tell us that Snockstobe's shop was in a little lane running between Tombland and Elm Hill.

We found the shop, which had a sign showing a pair of crossed keys over the narrow door. Inside, it was gloomy, with the sharp tang of metal in the air. Nobody was at the counter, but I could hear tapping from a little room at the back, and called out. A tall, thin lad of about sixteen in the blue smock and cap of an apprentice hurried out.

'Good morrow, lad,' I said civilly. 'We seek Master Snockstobe.'

'He's out delivering some keys; he should be back soon.'

'We will wait.'

He looked at the robes Nicholas and I wore. 'Do you need a key or lock made? Or – is it legal business?'

I did not answer, instead asking, 'I understand your master has been employed for some years by Master John Boleyn, of Brikewell.'

He looked at us apprehensively. 'I believe so,' he answered cautiously. 'Don't he be in the castle gaol, awaiting trial at the Assizes?'

'Yes. We are looking into the case, trying to talk to everyone who knew him. I am Serjeant Shardlake. What is your name?'

'Walter, sir. But you must talk to my master about all that.' The boy looked distinctly nervous now.

'Of course. I understand his sons, Gerald and Barnabas, may have brought you some work recently,' I added non-committally.

The boy shook his head. 'Please, sir, you must speak to Master Snockstobe. It's not fair to threap me with questions. Master'll pash me if I talk about his business.'

'He means beat him,' Toby explained.

Walter shifted anxiously from foot to foot, clearly afraid of Snockstobe.

'All right,' I said. The boy scuttled back to the workshop and we waited a few moments. Behind the counter were rows of keys on rings, hundreds of them. I was studying them when the outer door opened and a skinny little man in an apron, with long greasy hair and the bulbous red nose of a drinker, bustled in. Like Walter, he drew up short at the sight of us.

'Can I help you?' he asked warily.

'Master Snockstobe?'

'Who wants to know?' The response down the ages of a man with something to hide. I repeated what I had told Walter. Snockstobe crossed his arms aggressively. 'Why should I tell you about my customers?'

I decided on a direct approach. 'Because if you don't answer my questions, I will have a subpoena served on you to attend Master Boleyn's trial on Thursday, and you can answer the judge.'

That shook Snockstobe visibly. He said, 'I've worked for John Boleyn for years. Been to Brikewell many times. You know what a farm's like, animals always breaking out, smashing locks.'

'Did you make keys for the stables where he kept his horse, Midnight?'

Snockstobe laughed. 'That creature. Kick you a hefty culp soon as look at you. Ay, I did a lock for the stable a few years back.'

'And other work since, I hear.'

His eyes narrowed. 'Who from?'

'People tell us things,' Toby answered with a smile.

I said, 'I hear you got on well with Master Boleyn's sons. Few do, by all accounts.'

'They're not so bad. They can be a laugh. I go to the bear-baiting when there is one, I've often seen them there, and at the cockfights.'

I remembered them hunting the small boy at their father's house in London. I asked, 'Did they bring you a key to copy, last month perhaps?'

'No, they didn't,' Snockstobe answered flatly. 'Walter!' he shouted. The apprentice scuttled back in. Snockstobe glared at him. 'On your oath, boy, have either of the Boleyn boys been in the shop this last year?'

Walter looked relieved. 'No, sir, I can swear to that. On a Testament, if you wish.'

Snockstobe inclined his head at the apprentice. 'There you are. And Walter's a Bible lad; if he's not on his knees praying, he's off to Preacher Watson's church to hear his endless sermons.'

I looked at him. I felt certain both he and the boy were hiding something. I said, 'We will have the full truth of this, sir. We shall go now, but will be back later. With a subpoena. Perhaps two.' Walter's mouth fell open, while Snockstobe's set in a hard line. I added, 'Though, of course, it would go easier for you if you volunteered any information you have now.'

Snockstobe folded his arms again. 'Nothing to say.'

'Very well. We shall see you later.' I motioned Nicholas and Toby to follow me out.

Outside, Toby said, 'Couldn't you have pressed them further? They're hiding something, even if the twins didn't visit themselves.'

'I know. But under what authority? No, I need a subpoena. Nicholas, go now to the Assize offices, find Barak, and arrange it. A subpoena for Snockstobe to attend the trial, and to provide money to guarantee his attendance. This could be crucial. Toby, would you start looking for Grace Bone's family?'

'I will.' He bowed quickly and walked away. As Nicholas took the road back to the castle, I stood in the middle of Tombland, conscious that we were clutching at frail reeds. But they were something, and one way or the other I would have the full story of the keys.

Chapter Twenty-one

STANDING THERE, I saw that one of the stone gates to the cathedral precinct was open, and I walked towards it. Perhaps if I sat
and reflected inside, some new inspiration would come. And all morning the dead beggar had kept coming into my mind, tweaking at my
conscience. His body, I saw, had been removed.

Within the courtyard was a scene both of magnificence and destruction. Ahead of me was the great cathedral, built of white stone like the
castle, its high narrow windows vaulting to the sky; an enormous tower
topped with its great pointed spire. But to the right, where the former
cathedral monastery had stood, the long cloister wall was ruined. More
carts of stone were being brought through a gate leading to the interior
of the former precinct. Outside, men in sleeveless leather jackets were
working through piles of stone, sorting them by shape and size. I looked
for Josephine's Edward among them, but could not see him.

The main door to the cathedral was open, and I entered one of the
most extraordinary spaces I had ever seen. Westminster Abbey, even
York Minster, paled beside the vast arched space within, the relative
narrowness and enormously high vaulting of the nave somehow
adding to its magnificence. Looking up, I saw, far above, decorations
of extraordinary beauty. Yet here, too, work of destruction was going
on. Workmen were dismantling a chantry in a side chapel, while in
another, men were attacking a richly painted shrine with hammers, the
noise echoing around the cathedral. At the far end of the nave an
ancient rood screen still stood, and stained glass remained in the windows, though, I imagined, not for long. At the far end of the nave an
enormous wall painting was being whitewashed over, men standing
on a rickety arrangement of scaffolding and boards. I remembered the

man removing the wall painting at Whetstone. Only twelve days ago; it seemed much longer.

It was too noisy to sit and think, so I walked quietly out again. I returned to the Maid's Head, my back aching. Feeling suddenly exhausted, I lay down on the comfortable feather bed. At once I fell asleep, and when I was woken by Nicholas knocking at the door, I was surprised to see the sun low in the sky. 'What time is it?' I asked.

'Near six.'

'I have been asleep five hours,' I said wonderingly.

'I think perhaps you needed it, sir.'

'Yes. This case – and the atmosphere in the city –'

He shook his head. 'I know. Somehow one is always – on edge. I have had success,' he said. 'The subpoena ordering Marcus Snockstobe to appear at the trial. It took Barak and I half the afternoon to find a justice of the peace and get him to sign it, but we did.'

'Did you mention the Lady Elizabeth's involvement?'

'No, I said only that I was working for Boleyn.'

'Well done.'

Nicholas produced a folded paper from his knapsack and handed it over. I examined it closely.

'This is what we need,' I said with satisfaction. 'A surety of two pounds for his attendance, plus the threat of contempt of court if he does not. Damn, his shop will be shut now. We'll go first thing tomorrow. Have you seen Toby?'

'He's waiting to take us to the judges' procession into Norwich. They'll be riding up from St Stephen's Gate to the market square; the city fathers will meet them at the Guildhall. They'll be here in an hour.'

'Did he have any luck with tracing Grace Bone's family?'

'I fear not. He says he has been working on it all afternoon, but has found nothing.'

I sighed. 'I'm not surprised, after nine years.'

'He will try again tomorrow morning.'

'Good. If anyone can find them, it is Toby. He is a persistent fellow.'

'Rough in manner, but certainly a good worker. I fear we got into a little argument downstairs.'

'Again?' I asked.

'He said he hoped the peasant risings would force the commissioners to take serious action against the landlords' and officials' abuses. I
told him it was a disgrace to rise against the government while we are
at war. He said the war in Scotland was a barbaric invasion, and everyone knew it had failed.'

I smiled wryly. 'Well, there at least I agree with him.'

'I'm glad the Protector is preparing a new army against them. It is
a matter of England's honour.'

'Honour can sometimes just be another word for prestige and
status. Between, and within, nations.' He opened his mouth to protest,
but I said, 'No antrums, Nick, remember? Now, let us go and see what
these judges look like.'

✝

WE MET TOBY outside. His round face was sunburned now with all
the outside errands he had run, the blueness of his eyes more marked
than ever. We walked to the bottom of the market square. I was grateful
the heat of the day was ebbing, and envied Nicholas's and Toby's
apparent tirelessness. Men with swords, the city badge on their coats,
were positioned around the square. The crowd that had turned out to
watch the processional entry was sparse given the size of the city, no
more than one or two deep. We took places outside the church of St
Peter Mancroft at the side of the square. At the top, outside the Guildhall, stood a group of men in brightly coloured robes. Toby pointed to
a small stout man in robes with white silk sleeves. 'That's this year's
mayor, Thomas Codd.'

'I heard him called a wet fish this morning.'

'He's better than some of them. Organized the parish collection for
the poor earlier this year. That tall fellow by his side is Augustine Steward, one of the wealthiest men in the city. It's just a few merchant
families who run this place, and have for years. They've cornered the
processes of turning wool into cloth. And sometimes selling it abroad
illegally, too.' The bitterness I had heard before had returned to his
voice.

There was a murmur in the crowd, and heads turned towards the approaching sound of hoof beats and jingling of harnesses. A group of armed men came first, followed by the two judges in their bright red robes trimmed with white fur. I studied them, remembering Barak's description. The lean man with a hard, frowning face and a long grey beard must be Judge Gatchet, who, Barak had told me, was a Calvinist. He certainly looked as though he would be stern in his judgements. Plump old Judge Reynberd, in total contrast, sat heavily in his saddle, his red, heavy-featured face impassive. Nonetheless, his sharp grey eyes moved from side to side, weighing up the crowd, whose expressions were mostly hostile. I had appeared before Reynberd in the past, and knew he was fair in most cases, though if there were political implications, he would side with the powers that be. Neither, I guessed, would be easy on Boleyn. Behind the judges rode a retinue of black-robed assistants and clerks. I saw Barak; though, like his fellows, he stared straight ahead, at the judges' backs. Behind followed a group of richly robed gentry, many of whom would be justices of the peace and royal officials, each with an armed and mounted retinue of perhaps half a dozen men. Among them I recognized the hatchet face of John Flowerdew, and, in a particularly resplendent robe, the burly, haughty figure of Sir Richard Southwell. The group, perhaps fifty in all, rode up to the centre of the marketplace, halting outside the Guildhall where the Norwich aldermen descended the steps, bowing deeply. The crowd had watched the display of power in complete silence, and now began drifting away. I turned to thank Toby for all his work, and asked how his mother fared.

'A little better, but it is hard to hear how difficult it is for her to breathe, the rasping sound she makes.' He stroked his beard, his face sad. 'I fear she will not be with us long. And then I think I must return to help with the farm; I doubt my father will be up to supervising our two labourers.'

'Have you no other family who might help?'

'I have a brother who went to Suffolk and has his own small place now. It will be up to me. I should not be sorry to leave Master Copuldyke. And if I can get things settled on the farm, I'm sure I could find a new master in Norwich. Provided I keep my mouth shut.' He smiled ironically.

'Perhaps your mother will recover,' Nicholas said.

Toby shook his head. There was an uncomfortable silence. Then a voice at my shoulder said quietly, 'Master Shardlake?'

I turned to see the burly figure of Michael Vowell, Master Reynolds's steward. He bowed. 'Excuse me for troubling you, sir,' he said. 'But I left Master Reynolds's house yesterday. After Gerald and Barnabas wrecked my room because I argued with them about their treatment of the female servants. I wonder, sir, do you know anyone who may be looking for a steward, or even an upper servant?'

'I am a stranger in Norwich. Might you know anyone, Toby?'

'I fear not.'

I looked at Vowell. 'I should tell you that I visited Master Boleyn earlier today. You should know that he denies trying to force himself on Edith.'

Vowell took a firm stance, his face set. 'That is what I heard said. I will swear it on the Testament.'

'Master Boleyn said Edith was capable of making up the story she told her father, and Reynolds of telling her to get back to her wifely duties.'

Vowell looked relieved. He glanced up at the assembly in front of the Guildhall. Servants were taking mugs of beer to the newcomers. 'Were it not for the murder, Master Reynolds would be up there, getting himself seen, hoping to be the next mayor.' He spoke bitterly; his detestation of his former employer clearly ran deep. It occurred to me that Vowell, if anyone, might know the twins' routine. I said, 'We are keen to ask the twins some questions.'

He looked serious. 'Be careful, sir.'

'We plan to be. There are three of us, and we have another man who will help us. What we need is to get the twins on their own.'

He nodded slowly. 'I understand.' He thought a moment. 'Today is Monday. Every Tuesday and Saturday evening the twins go to the cockfighting over in Cosny, with their young gentlemen friends. That was where they were the Saturday of their mother's murder. Afterwards, they usually get drunk then come back to their grandfather's. I used to hear them come in, sometime between two and three in the morning. If you were to wait in a neighbouring street, around that time, you would likely catch them alone.'

I smiled. 'Thank you. That is very helpful.'

'Watch out. They carry swords, and are good with them, even when drunk.'

'So am I,' said Nicholas. 'And I shall be sober.'

'I can give a decent account of myself with a sword too, if you permit,' Toby said.

'Then tomorrow night it shall be,' I said. 'Thank you, Goodman Vowell, and good luck with your search for another employer.'

'Thank you, sir. I've heard of a prospect in Wymondham, I may go down there.' And with that he bowed, and walked away.

'There you are, sir,' Nicholas said. 'Perhaps our luck is turning. And Barak may help us; we shall see him tomorrow evening, when we meet Josephine and her husband at his inn.'

'You do not mind staying overnight to help us?' I asked Toby.

'No, sir,' he answered determinedly. 'I should not be sorry to settle accounts with those young villains.'

Chapter Twenty-two

THAT NIGHT I slept badly again. It was very hot and, once, I woke in a sweat from a dream of the dead beggar's face. Then I began thinking about the twins. We needed to talk to them, but not in a way in which they could say we had threatened them. At last I fell asleep, only to be jerked awake by the servant knocking on the door, saying it was six o'clock.

He brought in letters on a silver tray, fetched by the post-rider who had accompanied the judges the day before. Both bore the Lady Elizabeth's seal. The first was from Parry; it was brief:

> I thank you for your letter, and hope you have made some further progress and have been able to keep matters as discreet as circumstances allow. Please let me know how things stand, by return. The Lady Elizabeth is anxious; although I have stressed to her that little new may be found at this stage, and justice must take its course. Your loving friend, Thomas Parry.

The second letter, from Elizabeth, was quite different:

> I have received your letter, which in effect says nothing. Kindly reply immediately, telling me exactly what progress you have made in my cousin's case. Time is short, and you are now instructed, should a guilty verdict transpire, to use the request for a pardon which I gave you, whatever your own thoughts about the matter.

And then the large, elaborate signature: *Elizabeth*.

I caught my breath. Not only was she angry that I had not made rapid progress, but she was also now instructing me, should Boleyn be found guilty, to apply for a pardon whether I thought the verdict justified or not. Should I tell Parry? But if that was what Elizabeth had decided, he would be unable to countermand her orders. He and Blanche might argue with her, but her mind was clearly set. I considered whether to wait until we had served the warrant on the locksmith and spoken to the twins. If new evidence emerged then, I could write back more positively tomorrow. But she demanded a reply by return. I therefore wrote identical letters to her and Parry, outlining my progress and saying that I would write again on the morrow. I sealed the letters and took them down to the innkeeper, paying over the exorbitant charge needed to pay the fastest post-rider, who, he assured me, would reach Hatfield the next day.

I was therefore in a worried frame of mind when I descended the broad staircase to the breakfast chamber. To my surprise Toby Lockswood had not yet arrived, but Nicholas was there, also reading a letter, frowning slightly.

'From Beatrice Kenzy?' I asked.

He nodded.

'I have also had one, from the Lady Elizabeth. She is angry at what she considers my lack of progress.'

'I'd like to see her come and tramp the streets of Norwich for days on end.'

I looked at him; such a disrespectful remark was not like Nicholas. 'Bad news from Beatrice?' I ventured.

He put the letter down. 'She talks about the state of things in London, the new security measures and how a drunk beggar called words after her in the street that a lady should not be suffered to hear. As for me —' he smiled wryly — 'she hopes that through the Lady Elizabeth I am making worthwhile contacts in Norfolk society.'

I could not forbear a laugh. 'Write back and tell her about the twins, and the man who knocked you on the head at the tavern.'

'She cannot be expected to understand,' he said more gently. 'What really concerns me is that she says she has met a young barrister at church, and he is paying her court. She said I had better hurry back.'

'Does she give his name?'

'No. But it is obviously someone fully qualified, with money and stature.' He spoke bitterly.

I said, 'She is leading you a dance. She strikes me as one well versed in such womanly arts, no doubt well trained by her mother.'

Nicholas frowned. 'You do not know Beatrice. She is nothing like her mother. If you were not so cynical, about women as much as men –'

'Then I would be married. But not to someone as scheming and superficial as Beatrice strikes me.' I instantly wished I had not spoken, but I was tired and out of sorts.

Nicholas said, with quiet emphasis, 'I say again, you do not know her. Alone, she is gentle and kind.'

To my relief, we were interrupted by Toby's arrival. He looked tired beneath his tan, his black hair and beard uncombed. 'My apologies for being late. My mother was worse again.'

'I'm sorry,' I said. 'Perhaps you should not stay tonight. With Barak we can manage the twins.'

He sighed. 'There is little I can do, at home or on the farm, save cut down the thistles and watch the crops swelk in the heat. It's going to be another stonging day. Let's beard the locksmith in his den before the sun gets too high.'

☦

WE WALKED THE short distance to Snockstobe's shop. I hoped the sight of the warrant would loosen his tongue. The shop was open, but only young Walter stood behind the counter. He looked at us apprehensively.

I held up the warrant. 'Master Snockstobe?' I asked peremptorily.

'He aren't in yet. I don't know what to do, there's a man coming at nine for some keys, and I don't know where they are.' He looked despairingly at the rows of keys behind him, each marked with a number. 'Master hasn't put them in the book.'

'Is he often late?' I asked sharply.

The boy hesitated. 'Please don't tell him I said, but since his wife left him last year he spends most evenings bezzling in the inns. Sometimes he comes in late. But he doesn't miss appointments.'

I nodded and said, 'We will return in an hour. Tell your master we have the warrant, and that if he has anything to tell us about Boleyn's keys he had better do it then.'

'Yes, sir,' Walter said unhappily. We turned and walked out.

'God's death,' I said as we made our way back into Tombland. 'Will nothing go smoothly?'

'Doesn't look like it,' Nicholas said. His tone was frosty; he was still angry over my remarks about Beatrice.

I said, 'If we've got an hour, I suggest we take a look at the Assizes. They'll be opening soon.'

We set off through the morning heat for the castle.

✝

THE SHIRE HALL was a large building with Gothic towers just north-east of the castle, made of the same white stone. A few people stood talking outside the doors, gentlemen by their dress, and I saw Sir Richard Southwell, conferring with a couple of others. He wore his usual haughty, disdainful expression. Catching sight of me, he gave me a brief, unsmiling nod. So he remembered our brief meeting at St Paul's; but then he struck me as a man who would forget nobody. I remembered Toby saying the twins and some of their young gentlemen friends had done dirty work for him on occasion.

Inside, we passed through a small antechamber into a large court-room with a high, vaulted roof, the judges' table on a dais covered with heavy green cloth. I looked at the wooden dock, set on high steps to the left of the courtroom. Black-robed officials had already taken their places at benches before the judges' table, and more were bringing in papers. Soldiers in royal livery stood guard at the doors and round the walls. Many people, mostly gentry, by their fine clothes, were already sitting on the benches facing the judges; others stood talking. A tall figure detached himself from a group and came over to us. 'Serjeant Shardlake? Come to see the opening?'

'Serjeant Flowerdew. God give you good morrow. Yes, indeed.'

Flowerdew seemed in a better mood this morning. 'I imagine they will start with dressing down the JPs and city officials over lack of enforcement of the proclamations. How goes the Boleyn case?'

'There have been some interesting developments,' I answered neutrally.

He looked at me narrowly. 'Have you found something that may help Boleyn?'

'One always hopes for justice.'

'Indeed.'

The bailiff entered and called for silence. Everyone moved quickly to the benches as Judges Reynberd and Gatchet entered the court. Reynberd wore a haughty expression on his plump face, Gatchet looked severe as ever. They sat. Reynberd, the senior judge, nodded to Gatchet. He leaned forward on the bench, bony hands clasped together.

'In the name of our Sovereign Lord King Edward the Sixth, I declare the Norwich Summer Assizes open. We have much business, but I shall begin by telling you of our just anger, on behalf of the King and the Protector, at the lack of proper enforcement of the laws and proclamations. The returns for the sheep tax are late and inadequate. Unauthorized preaching by self-styled prophets and rabble-rousers continues; godless pamphlets are found in the streets and pinned to doors.' He banged a fist hard on the table. 'Though the justices and constables have been lax in finding and punishing the authors of these activities. I remind you, gentlemen, of the words of Master Calvin, who is much favoured by the King, that the common people must be kept on a short bridle. Which brings me to the unrest, the resistance to the law and the right order, which have recently been seen in southern as well as western parts. They must not spread here. Stirrers of trouble must be sought out and dealt with, as they were in the spring commo-tions. Now, though, the Protector is arranging for commissions to look into illegal enclosures to travel the country, and they will see to it that any injustices are remedied. That is enough! So get to your duties, get your informers working. And I tell you we intend the strictest justice to be done on the criminal matters coming before this Assizes. Those found guilty will be publicly hanged in the market square on Saturday, and the executioner has been instructed that all those sentenced will be given the short drop, so their slow strangling may be a lesson to the populace. And nobody will be allowed to approach the guilty and pull their legs to break their necks.'

'When are the commissioners coming?' someone shouted from the well of the court. 'We hear no word of them!'

Gatchet went puce. He pointed to the interrupter, a young man in a fine doublet with a fierce, angry face. 'Arrest that man! He is in con-tempt of court!' Two soldiers hurried across, hauled him from his place, and led him from the room. Gatchet shouted after him, 'Contempt of this court will be severely punished. You'll lose your ears for this!'

Such a penalty could not be imposed for such a minor offence, but nonetheless the court stirred uneasily. Gatchet leaned back, and Reyn-berd sat up. 'I hope you have all taken note of the learned judge's words.' He shifted the papers on the bench with his plump hands. 'And now, we shall proceed to the first civil case. In the matter of the will of the late Gerald Carberry –'

I said to Nicholas, 'A disputed will. I've had enough of those, come on.' We bowed to the court, and went out.

✝

WE WALKED BACK to Snockstobe's shop. 'The short drop,' Nich-olas said. 'The condemned will strangle slowly, rather than breaking their necks.'

'They mean to make a harsh example.'

'The judges in the red robes of blood indeed,' Toby said quietly.

We had come to the top of the marketplace; beside the gallows that already stood next to the Guildhall carpenters were working, digging holes in the cobbles. Newly carved posts of various sizes lay on the ground beside them. They were preparing for a multiple hanging. A little knot of poorly dressed people stood watching. As we passed I heard snatches of conversation.

'– he was in the water right under Bishopsgate Bridge. A boatman coming up the river found him stuck in the waterweed.'

'Must've fallen off. Draahnin', that's a bad way to go –'

'He was always bezzled by nine. Don't know how he kept the shop going –'

'He was a good locksmith though.'

I stopped dead, and turned to the group. 'A locksmith has drowned?' I asked.

They looked at me suspiciously. 'Ay, master. What of it?'

'What was his name?'

'Richard Snockstobe. Found dead in the Wensum this morning.'

'We must go there. Now.' For a moment I felt quite faint, and leaned on Nicholas's arm. The nearest to a key witness we had tracked down, and yet he had been found dead the day we were due to serve the subpoena on him.

'Bishopsgate Bridge. It's quite a walk,' Toby said, looking at me dubiously.

'Now,' I repeated, setting a fast pace.

We returned to Tombland, then again followed Holme Street, past the hospital with the beggars outside and towards the Blue Boar Inn. We passed under the high gatehouse, onto a stone bridge spanning the Wensum. The escarpment of Mousehold Heath loomed up beyond. Several curious people stood on the parapet of the bridge, looking over. We joined them. A couple of men were pulling something from the river, straining against the reeds wrapped around the corpse's feet, while the coroner we had met at the Guildhall stood on the bank looking on. I recognized the thin form of Snockstobe, his red face now white with the pallor of death.

'How do we get down there?' I asked Toby.

He pointed to where, just beyond the gatehouse, a square was sunk in the earth, with steps leading down to it; that way we could get to the riverbank.

'What's that?' Nicholas pointed to the depression.

'The Lollards' Pit,' Toby answered. 'Where heretics were burned. Thomas Bilney was burned there by More.'

We scrambled down the steps, across the pit and down to the bank. The body lay there, the coroner and a couple of constables looking at it.

'Fell off and drowned hisself when he was drunk, I reckon,' a constable said.

'Looks like it,' the coroner agreed. 'Can't see any marks on the body.'

I knelt with some difficulty and examined the head. Edith Boleyn had been killed by a blow to the head, and I remembered what the twins had done to Witherington's man with a club. I brushed Snock- stobe's long hair aside, but could see no sign of any injury.

'Hey, Master Lawyer,' the coroner asked indignantly, 'what are you doing?'

I stood and bowed. 'Forgive me, but I knew this man slightly. I spoke to him only yesterday, about a key. What happened?'

For answer the coroner called over a frightened-looking man in a wool jerkin and white hat. 'This is Sedgley, the first finder. Tell this lawyer what happened.'

The man swallowed. 'I was punting my boat downstream early this morning, with a load of spun wool. As I came to the bridge I spotted something in the water, then saw it was this poor fellow's head and hands. He must've fallen in, and got his feet caught in the water-weed, it's foul thick this year.'

The coroner considered, then turned to me. 'Looks like an accident, gentlemen, the man was a well-known toper.'

I looked back at the gatehouse, then across to the heights of Mousehold, dotted with sheep, the high splendid edifice of Surrey Place at the top. 'Why should he be on the heath at night? I understand that apart from Surrey's mansion there is nothing up there.'

The coroner shrugged. 'Who can tell what notions drunks get into their minds?'

'Will there be an examination of the body?'

He sighed. 'I suppose there will have to be. They'll find his lungs full of water.' He turned to the constable. 'Did you bring a cart?'

'Yes, sir.'

'Then take Snockstobe to the cold-house. You, boatman, come with me, I shall need a deposition.'

The constables lifted up the locksmith, releasing a stink of river-bottom decay. The coroner shouted up at the people on the bridge, 'Get home now, you nosy lubbers! Show's over!'

Chapter Twenty-three

W E RETURNED TO Tombland. The locksmith's death was a bad blow, the subpoena in my pocket now worthless. More than that, I feared I might be indirectly responsible for his death; his plunge from Bishopsgate Bridge coming the day after I told him I would have him in court was too much of a coincidence.

'It could have been an accident,' Nicholas said. 'He wasn't hit on the head, there was no blood on the body.'

'He could have been stabbed, and the blood washed away by the river. They'll find out when they examine the body.'

Toby said, 'There's still the apprentice. He may not yet know of Snockstobe's death. We have to press him now, see what he knows.'

✝

WHEN WE RETURNED to the shop, Walter was still behind the counter. He peered at us, his face falling.

'Master's not back,' he said wearily.

'I'm afraid I have some bad news,' I said, gently. 'Your master was found dead in the Wensum early this morning. It appears he fell from Bishopsgate Bridge last night.'

The boy's mouth fell open. His expression was not one of grief – perhaps unsurprisingly from what I had seen of his master – but fear. I recalled he had looked anxious when we questioned Snockstobe yesterday, gripping the edge of the counter tightly. I said, 'Walter, what did your master do after we visited the shop yesterday?'

He swallowed. 'He said nothing, though he seemed worried. He left the shop, telling me to mind things for an hour. When he came back, he acted afraid, spent the day snapping at me or staring into space. We shut the shop at five as usual. He went back to his house, and I to my room above the shop. I think master was afraid. God save his poor soul.'

'You remember yesterday, we asked about his work for John Boleyn, and whether he'd had a visit from his sons, Gerald and Barnabas, since the spring. You said they had not been here, and he said the same.'

'I did, sir. I told no lie.'

I nodded. 'But there was more to it than that, wasn't there?'

Walter lowered his head and gave a long, shuddering sigh. He was silent a moment – perhaps he was praying – then he looked up again. 'A man came,' he said nervously. 'In May. He brought a key and asked for a copy to be made. He said he came from Master Boleyn. Snock-stobe recognized the key, of course. It had his mark on it, if the man had taken it to another locksmith, he would have sent him back here under the guild rules.'

'Who was this man? Did you recognize him?'

Walter shook his head. 'I had never seen him before.'

'What did he look like?' Toby asked.

'He was quite a big man, not old. He had a beard.'

'That would fit half the men of Norwich,' I said impatiently. 'Come, was his beard fair, or red, or dark?'

'Dark, I think. Maybe red. I don't know.' He blushed suddenly. 'You see, sir, I don't see well. Things close to are all right, or I couldn't do my work, but at any distance I don't see so well. And the man – Master Snockstobe, he was in the other room and he came out at once and took him straight through to the back. But as they went through, Master Snockstobe asked the man which key was it, and I heard him say it was for the horse Midnight's stable, Master Boleyn's key was lost.'

I closed my eyes. How like our cursed luck for the boy to be short-sighted. But he could testify that someone had come in, and asked for a copy of a key to the stable. His evidence could still be crucial. I looked at Walter, who had begun shivering.

'Why are you afraid of this man?' I asked.

'It's not him. It's those sons of Master Boleyn I fear. Sir, Master Snockstobe was sore worried yesterday. Do you think he could have been killed?'

'I don't know. Walter,' I said. 'I want you to come to court on Thursday. But we will protect you until then –'

'No!' the boy shouted. 'Mistress Boleyn was murdered, and now perhaps my master. I won't go to court!'

'Do you have any relatives in Norwich, where you would be safe?'

'No. My family live out in the Sandlings, I've nobody here.'

'The people at your church?'

'No! I'm not safe in Norwich!'

I kept my tone calm. 'Listen, Walter, you can come back with us to the Maid's Head, we can put you in our room, lock you in, if you wish. Then, after the trial, we can arrange safe transport to your family.'

'The Maid's Head?' His eyes widened. 'They won't let the likes of me in there! I've got to get out of Norwich!'

'They will let you stay if I say so. And if you are in danger, do you think you will be any safer on the road?'

Walter groaned and put his head in his hands. 'I must go home.'

'By telling the truth in court you may save an innocent man. You are a Christian, is that not the Christian thing to do?'

Walter bowed his head, rats' tails of hair hiding his eyes.

'Now, this is what I want you to do. Go upstairs, pack all you need, and we will take you to the Maid's Head. You will be protected there, Walter, I promise. Then all you need to do is tell the truth on Thursday, and then we will ensure you get home safely.'

He looked up, a desperate expression on his pale face.

'Go on, lad,' Nicholas said encouragingly.

Walter nodded. He mounted a flight of wooden stairs at the side of the shop. Toby shook his head. 'Another little cringer like Scambler. Once England bred strong, honest farming people, now they're all gone to seed scraping a living in the towns. No wonder we're losing the war in Scotland.'

'You can be harsh, Toby,' I said.

''Tis the truth.'

After a few minutes Nicholas stirred restlessly. 'He should be down by now.'

'Let's go up,' Toby said.

We mounted the steps quickly. Upstairs was a small bedroom,

with a rickety bed and a cheap edition of the new Prayer Book on a table. The shutters of the window were wide open.

'Fuck!' Toby shouted. 'He's gone!' We ran to the window. Outside the sloping roof of an outhouse allowed easy access to a yard. Walter had vanished.

We raced outside. Toby ran up the alley, while Nicholas and I went down to Tombland. We looked at the roads and lanes branching off from the square. Walter could have taken any of them. Nicholas went into the Maid's Head, to see whether any staff had noticed a boy running across the square. He came back shaking his head, and shortly afterwards Toby rejoined us. 'It's hopeless,' he said. 'He could be anywhere.'

'Where are the Sandlings, his home?'

'Down on the Suffolk coast. But there are many roads, and he probably won't take the obvious ones. We've lost him. I said he was a cringer.'

'He was terrified,' Nicholas said.

'There's nothing we can do,' I said bleakly. 'I can give testimony as to what he said, but without Snockstobe or Walter it's all just hearsay.'

'Scambler could testify he lost the key,' Toby suggested.

'I don't think his losing the key for a day would help much. And I doubt he'd make a good impression in court. He seems to be a figure of fun around Norwich generally.'

Nicholas said, 'If Snockstobe was murdered, could Scambler be in danger too? If the twins gave the key to the man who went into the shop?'

I nodded agreement. 'Nicholas, could you go to Scambler's place again, warn him and his aunt to stay indoors until Friday. Perhaps they can get someone from their church to stay with them. Say I will visit them tomorrow, to make sure all is well. Toby, you may as well go back to your parents now. We will see you at the Blue Boar at nine o'clock. Do you know where we might hire a sword for you?'

'How are you going to waylay the twins afterwards?'

'I've thought about that. I'll go to Master Reynolds's house later and say I wish to speak to them. He'll doubtless say they've gone to the cockfight so I'll say I will try and talk to them later. That will cover us accosting them. When we do we say nothing threatening, but knowing those two, I'd rather we had swords. Just in case. I doubt the discussion will go well.'

Toby smiled wryly. 'My carrying a weapon could be seen as suspicious; I'm not a gentleman, the sumptuary rules don't allow me to carry a sword.'

'You can if you're my servant and you're protecting me.'

'You and Master Nicholas would have to buy it. There's a shop over there,' he added, nodding to a small establishment set between the big houses, a display of daggers in the window. 'Plenty of gentlemen in Tombland.' I frowned, for I guessed all this had been simply to make a point about his status.

Nicholas and I went into the shop. We explained that I wished to buy a sword for my servant, given the atmosphere in the city just now. We went outside, the weapon in its scabbard banging against my leg. Toby had left.

'You could have got one for yourself as well,' Nicholas said.

'I'd probably just cut your head off, or Toby's.'

'Toby's might be no loss. Cross-grained radical, unfeeling, too, for all his talk of social reform.'

I sighed. 'It looks like it will be me and Isabella Boleyn alone testifying for her husband on Thursday.'

'Could we not ask Witherington's shepherd to testify how difficult it would be for one man to have carried Edith to the water and put her in?'

'Witherington will probably push him to say nothing that might benefit Boleyn. And having been to the site I can give testimony myself as to how difficult it would be. And now I am going back to the Maid's Head. I slept badly last night, I need to rest to be of use at all tonight.'

Nicholas looked at me with concern. 'Sir, do not let this filthy business tire you out.'

I smiled sadly. 'Yes, this is more than the distraction from routine business we expected, isn't it? A second person, dead now. And, with all this walking and riding, I feel my age and my poor back, but I shall not give in. I shall go to the coroner's office this afternoon, chase up what they found when they opened Snockstobe. If he was murdered, that changes things; we might even ask for a postponement of the trial.' I took a deep breath. 'And then, tonight, the twins.'

✝

As arranged, Nicholas and I called at Gawen Reynolds's house on the way to the Blue Boar. A female servant answered the courtyard door. We were not invited in, but Gawen Reynolds himself hobbled out on his stick. I said we wished to speak to the twins and that we understood they were out at the cockfighting that evening.

His eyes narrowed. 'Who told you that?'

'It's not a secret, is it?'

'What d'you want to speak to them about?' he snapped.

'Their view of the case.' I was not going to say anything about the key.

His expression changed, and he gave a nasty grin. 'Same as mine, that their father killed their mother. Just to let you know, we've decided to give evidence against his character, me and Gerald and Barnabas. You're not talking to them in my house, but if you find them elsewhere, good luck to you. I've told them to get back here after the cockfight — we're going to discuss their evidence tomorrow.' He smiled at me evilly, then slammed the courtyard door in our faces.

Nicholas looked at me. 'Shit,' he said. 'Another three witnesses against Boleyn.'

'We'll interview the twins nonetheless. And we've got that old brute's blessing to talk to them; no one will be able to say we deliberately intimidated them.'

✝

Six of us were due to meet in the garden of the Blue Boar by Bishopsgate Bridge that evening; Nicholas and I, Toby and Barak, and Josephine and Edward Brown. I arrived with Nicholas shortly before nine. Earlier he had been to visit Scambler and his aunt. Both had been terrified at the news of the locksmith's murder, and Nicholas had little doubt that they would stay indoors until Thursday. Until then, the aunt was going to try and get someone from their church to

227

stay with them. She had blamed her nephew, of course, for the whole situation, shouting and yelling at him.

We found Barak sitting at a candlelit table under a tree, frowning over a letter in the failing light. Nicholas and I had both donned grey woollen doublets so that we would not stand out among the clientele, who again were mostly from the artisan classes. I saw no sign of the boatmen who had attacked Nicholas on our last visit. I glanced at the great gatehouse; Snockstobe had walked under it to his death the night before.

Barak raised his eyebrows. 'I've never seen you wear a sword,' he said.

'It's for Toby Lockswood.'

'Don't draw attention to it, we don't want to be singled out as gentlemen again. Mine's in my room.'

We put the swords under the table, then Nicholas went in to get some beer. I looked at Barak enquiringly. 'Who is that from?' I asked.

'Tamasin.'

'Does she say how Guy is?'

'Much the same; no better, no worse. Still gets fevers that come and go. She says she's having to take little Tilda with her as well as George when she visits him; Mistress Marris is complaining about looking after her all the time.' He grunted angrily. 'In fact, the whole letter's naught but a litany of complaints; the price rises, the number of armed men in the city, how she feels lonely at night and wishes I were back. Not that she complains at the money I bring back when I go on Assizes. Oh, and she hopes I'm not drinking too much and mixing with disreputable people. She forgets her background is as common as mine. She can't even write; the letter's in Guy's assistant Francis's hand.'

'It can't be easy being a woman alone with children in London now.'

'No?' He frowned. 'Here's the best bit.' He read aloud, angrily, '"I expect by now you will be in Norwich, with only the Suffolk Assizes to follow. I know Master Shardlake is in Norwich, and I hope you have heeded my entreaty to have no dealings with him. If you should happen to pass each other in court, ensure that you ignore him." Fucking cheeky mare,' Barak said, taking a long swig of beer.

I looked at him. The marriage between these two strong personalities had not always been smooth, and more than once Barak had taken
refuge in drink. 'There's nothing we can do about her feelings towards
me,' I said sadly.

'It's her attitude to me that pisses me off,' he answered darkly.
'Where's Nick? I need another drink.'

'Don't have too much,' I said. 'We've to talk to the twins later.
We'll discuss that after the Browns have gone.'

Nicholas returned with six mugs of beer on a tray. Shortly after,
Toby arrived. Barak greeted him with a smile. 'How go things with
you, Commonwealth man?'

'Well enough.'

'They've got your sword. It's under the table.'

'Good,' he said with satisfaction.

'Can you use one?' Nicholas asked.

'Yes. There are some kept in our church, in case the militia is
raised. When I was young we lads used to pinch them and practise. I
wasn't bad.'

I said, 'Let's hope we don't need to use them tonight.'

'We'll see. I have some news, Master Shardlake. Good and bad.' I
raised my eyebrows. 'I called in on a friend of mine on my way out of
town earlier; he has contacts among the weavers, and has managed to
trace Grace Bone's family.'

'That is good,' Nicholas said enthusiastically.

'Grace lived with her brother and sister in the north of the city. The
brother is a weaver, he's fallen on hard times and only just keeps going.
His sisters helped him and did some spinning. He still lives there. But
the bad news is that Grace Bone and her sister Mercy both died from
congestion of the lungs last spring; they all got it, but only Peter Bone,
the brother, survived. Like so many, they didn't make it through the
hard winter and spring.'

'Well,' I said, 'at least now we know she wasn't killed when
Edith left.'

Toby asked, 'Any news on the examination of Snockstobe's body?'

'It's to take place tomorrow morning. I didn't want to press the coroner too hard. But he said they'd stripped the body, and there were no signs of wounds.'

'Snockstobe is dead?' Barak asked, astonished.

I told him about the locksmith and the apprentice. He considered. 'Someone could have got Snockstobe blind drunk, taken him for a walk and heaved him off the bridge to drown.'

'They could. But there's no evidence.' I turned to Toby. 'Can you take me to see Grace Bone's brother tomorrow?'

'Certainly.'

Barak said, 'I have a piece of news as well, though I fear it's not good. Three new prosecution witnesses for the Boleyn trial have been added.'

'We know. Alderman Gawen Reynolds, and Gerald and Barnabas Boleyn. They'll testify to Boleyn's bad character, no doubt.'

Nicholas said, 'And perhaps Reynolds will recount his daughter telling him Boleyn had tried to force himself on her during their marriage. That's not illegal, but it'd go down badly with the jury.'

Nicholas nudged me, and I saw Josephine and Edward walking towards us across the lawn, hand in hand. A man sitting at one of the tables hailed Edward, and he went over and shook his hand. Then they came over to us. Both looked slightly uneasy, especially Josephine, and I guessed they did not spend much time in company. I introduced them to Toby, and they sat down.

'How is little Mousy?' I asked.

Josephine smiled, a little wanly. 'Grizzly these last couple of days. One of the neighbours is looking after her.' I remembered what she had said about most children in the yard not surviving their second birthday. I had always thought that Josephine would be the best of mothers; she should be enjoying her child, not fearing she might suddenly die.

'It is good to see you both,' I said.

'Ay,' Edward said. 'You and Master Nicholas saw us married, you gave her away.' His manner was much friendlier tonight. He asked Toby, 'Do you work for Master Shardlake as well?'

'For the moment. I am a Norwich man.'

I said, 'Toby is indefatigable in finding people. It was thanks to him that I traced you.'

'And the Bone family,' Nicholas added.

'It's interesting work,' Toby said. I glanced at him; he had spoken with a strange lack of emotion. Was this all the case was to him? Something interesting?

Josephine said, 'Peter Bone and his sisters? We knew them slightly when we lived in Pit Street.'

'You did?' I asked, surprised.

'The world of Norwich weavers is not so large. Peter Bone is a weaver, I did some spinning for him now and again. His sisters were well-known around the area. Grace and Mercy.'

'Ay,' Edward agreed. 'A pair of merry fat wenches, hair black as coal, always ready with a joke, lewd tongues on both of them though neither married. We didn't see them again after we moved to the yard.'

'I fear both sisters died from congestion of the lungs this spring.'

'That's sad,' Josephine said. 'God save their souls.'

'I was just saying,' Toby observed, 'many poor folks died last winter and spring. While the merchants and landlords were snug in their houses with good fires. Let's hope Hales's commissioners and the Protector's Commonwealth friends may bring some justice to the realm.'

Edward Brown snorted. 'The Commonwealth men. They're full of radical talk but they'll do nothing for the likes of us. Too reliant on the gentlemen. All the Protector really cares about is conquering Scotland.'

Barak broke the uneasy silence that followed. 'I hear from talk around the Assizes that the Lady Mary refuses to use the new Prayer Book. Still hears the old Latin service. Her chapel over at Kenninghall is full of images and incense. She'll get herself into trouble.'

'I doubt they'll make too much trouble for her,' I said. 'She's the heir to the throne; the Protector has made efforts to win her friendship. And her cousin is the Holy Roman Emperor, whom the Protector needs to keep friendly, with France helping the Scots.'

'This damned pointless war,' Barak said. 'It all comes back to that.'

'If we could secure Scotland for good,' Nicholas answered, 'it would stop France using the Scotch against us in any future war. And bring our two countries together in religious amity. I hear the

Scotchman John Knox has been sent by the Protector to preach in Ber-wick, close to his countrymen.'

'When did you care for religion?' Barak answered irritably. 'Any-way, the war is lost.' I noticed he had emptied his glass already. 'We've been kicked out of every fort the Protector built.'

'Not Haddington. And the Protector is preparing a new army.'

'More sheep for the slaughter,' Edward muttered.

I stood up. 'I need to go to the jakes,' I said. 'I'll get some more beer for everyone as well.' I looked meaningfully at Barak. 'Make this your last.'

'Want me to come with you?' Nicholas asked. 'After what hap-pened to me last time?'

'No. I've no reason to fear trouble; I'm dressed like a common fellow.'

I made my way between the candlelit tables, the tray in my hands. Dressed as I was, people took no notice, though one or two glanced at my bent back. It took me a minute to find the shed with the lantern outside – more tables had been set out this fine night – but my visit passed without incident. When I came out, I walked back towards the inn to get the drinks, but it was quite dark now and I missed my way – an oak tree which I thought was the one beside our table turned out to be another. I stood still a moment, trying to get my bearings, then heard a familiar voice from a nearby table; Edward Brown's, in a tone of quiet intensity.

'With one army gone to the West Country and another leaving for Scotland they'll be short of forces.' I stood back, sheltering behind the tree. Edward sat at a nearby table, together with the man he had greeted when he and Josephine had arrived, and a third, whom, to my surprise, I recognized as Michael Vowell, Gawen Reynolds's former steward who had told us where we could waylay the twins. The three sat with their heads together, talking animatedly.

Vowell said, 'I've just come back from Attleborough, Miles. They want to rise and destroy all John Greene's fences on the twentieth.'

'That's too soon,' the third man replied angrily. He was tall and well built, in his early forties, with short fair hair and beard and a hard, intelligent face.

Vowell said, 'We can't control people, only guide and try to agree timing, and the Attleborough folk are angry.'

At that moment a girl from the inn came to clear the table and they fell silent. I slipped away and made my way to the inn. As I waited for the drinks, I pondered on what I had heard. Was the man called Miles one of the stirrers roaming the country encouraging rebellion? But such talk was everywhere. I decided, for now at least, to say nothing. I would talk to Barak when I had the chance.

When I returned to our table, the others were quietly discussing the new Prayer Book, agreeing it was good to have it in English, though none were greatly exercised by the religious arguments. Edward Brown's chair was vacant. I smiled at Josephine. 'No Edward?'

'He said something about going to talk to a friend for a moment. He likes to talk when he gets the chance, does Edward.' Her face became sad. 'Usually about how the commons are oppressed. He took our being thrown out of our home by Master Henning's children hard. People can be cruel.' She smiled wanly. 'But you know that, sir, you knew my father.'

'Yes,' I agreed sadly.

'I am sorry Edward was rude to you yesterday. You must under-stand, he feels so bad that he cannot properly provide for us. He's a good man, he cares much for me and Mousy.'

'I see that.' Mousy's name reminded me of the heath, and I stared up at the dark escarpment beyond the river. A light shone at the top, no doubt some caretaker now living in the Earl of Surrey's old mansion.

Josephine said, 'I have been thinking of suggesting to Edward that we return to London. We might have a chance of getting work in ser-vice there. Perhaps – perhaps you could even help us –'

'If that is what you both want, I will—'

At that moment Edward returned, looking round at us cheerfully. 'Ah, more drinks,' he said with a smile that seemed slightly forced. 'Let us have a toast. To Master Shardlake, for bringing old friends together.'

☦

WE LEFT THE Blue Boar at nine, saying we had an appointment. Edward and Josephine accompanied us as far as Tombland, then headed off to the south. We entered the Maid's Head and went up to my room. I asked a servant to lend us a horn-lamp. The innkeeper, Master Theobald, was passing and gave us a strange look, noticing the swords we carried and our lowly costume.

Toby, meticulous as ever, produced a sketch map of northern Nor- wich. 'The cockpit is up at St Martin's Lane, north of the river. To get back to their grandfather's the twins will be coming along Colgate, then down to Blackfriars Bridge. There'll be nobody about at that time, though the watch will be on duty. There are many little yards north of the bridge. I suggest we wait in one for when they pass, then step out after them, follow them a little way, then ask to talk to them. Hopefully, they'll see they're outnumbered, and won't want a fight. And then, Master Shardlake, you can ask them what you want.'

'What if they have friends with them?' Nicholas asked Toby.

'From what I've heard of the gentlemanly young thugs they mix with, if there's a crew of them, we'll have to call it off. But as they're coming back early, it's unlikely.'

Barak smiled, hefting his sword with his good hand. 'It's like the old days, when I worked for Master Cromwell.'

'No it isn't,' I answered seriously. 'We stay strictly on the defensive, unless there's no alternative.'

Chapter Twenty-four

W E SET OUT FOR the district of Coslany, or Cosny, as Toby called it, crossing Blackfriars Bridge. The area beyond was much poorer, with a rotten smell in the air which Toby told us came from tanneries. But it was still light, Midsummer Day only a little way off. Once we were stopped by a pair of patrolling constables, their suspicions aroused by three men with swords, but although the others had kept the clothes they wore at the Blue Boar, I had put on my robe at the inn and was able to get us through by saying I was on a visit to a dying client and needed protection in this poor area. Barak was strolling along confidently but I wondered how well he could use a sword with his left hand.

Toby led us up what he told us was Oak Street. The buildings were mainly old courtyard houses. The courtyards were empty and dim. It was one of these which Toby selected, with a short passage leading into it under an arch. We stood in the yard, which smelled of piss. Toby hid the lamp behind a water-barrel, and I sat uncomfortably on its lip, for my back hurt.

A little group of gentlemanly revellers passed by soon after, but the twins were not among them. But then, shortly after, we heard more footsteps, and a pair of familiar, identical voices.

'That big cock with the spurs was quite a fellow, wasn't he?'

'See the other one? Didn't know there was so much blood in a bird.'

There was laughter, and then a familiar pair of stocky figures, walking shoulder to shoulder, swords at their belts, passed the entrance. After a moment we stepped out quietly behind them.

The twins were, though, sharp as cats. They looked round immediately, putting their hands to their swords. Gerald laughed, 'Fuck me,

Barney, it's the leeching lawyers again. What's that they've got with them, another cripple?' Without hesitation, they drew their swords from their scabbards. An old woman bent under the weight of a pile of faggots quickly crossed to the other side of the road. Toby and Nicholas had put their hands to their swords, but had not drawn them.

'What d'you want, bent-back?' Barnabas asked. 'How did you know we were here?'

'Your grandfather said you'd be at the cockfighting, and coming home early.'

They looked at each other. 'Granfer told you we'd be here?' Barnabas asked, unbelieving.

Gerald laughed. 'He's been taking the piss out of these shitbags.' He looked at me. 'Did he tell you we were going back early because he wants to go over our evidence tomorrow morning? We're all appearing for the prosecution against our father.'

'We know. But we have a couple of questions of our own we thought you might help us with. Particularly concerning a missing key.'

The twins looked at each other. Clearly they knew what we were talking about. Their expressions changed from mocking to threatening. 'Right, then,' Gerald said, 'let's get back into that yard you were hiding in, and hear what you have to say. Go on.' He pointed his sword at my chest. 'You, Lockswood and the carrot-head, and you, one-arm, keep your swords sheathed, or the hunchback gets run straight through.'

We looked at each other, then backed into the darkening courtyard. Our plan had gone badly wrong. Grinning confidently, the twins advanced on us. It was Barak who saved the situation, together with the twins' overconfidence in underestimating him. He suddenly lunged forward and brought the full weight of his metal forearm on Gerald's sword, unbalancing him and causing him to drop it, then he pulled the sheath from the knife on his artificial hand, and put it to the boy's throat. At the same moment, Toby drew his sword and brought it down with a clang on Barnabas's weapon, while Nicholas put his to Barnabas's throat.

'Drop that sword, you ratsbane,' Toby said, 'or we'll have your livers out!' His tone was savage, and I realized the full depth of his hatred for the twins.

The boys' faces twisted with fury, and Barnabas dropped his sword. Nicholas and Toby held their weapons steady to their throats.

'Got you,' Toby said with satisfaction. 'Now, young *masters*, as Master Shardlake here said, he'd like some questions answered. We tried the civil way, but we should have known better with you.'

'We've fuck⁄all to say to you, fen⁄suckled churl,' Gerald answered in a low, furious voice.

'Mammering serf!' Barnabas added. Whatever else, the twins did not lack courage.

'Then we'll kill you here,' Toby answered, 'and chuck you in the Wensum like you did the locksmith!'

I looked at Toby, worried. He sounded as though he meant every word.

'You mean Snockstobe, that fell off Bishopsgate Bridge and drowned last night?' Barnabas asked, with what sounded like genuine puzzlement.

'Like you don't know,' Toby said. 'Answer to our satisfaction and we'll let you go.'

Gerald laughed. 'Why should we believe that?'

'You haven't much choice,' Barak said cheerfully. 'Better get ready to talk.'

'Sure you know how to use that sword, fatty one⁄arm?'

For answer Barak went behind Gerald and put his right arm round his neck, holding his sword to the boy's side as well as the knife to his throat. 'I can use it, matey, and this knife, too.' Gerald winced, and for a single second seemed like a frightened boy, but he gathered himself and looked at me, his cold blue eyes glinting.

'We'll have you all, one way or another, after this,' he said quietly. 'You'll never be safe again, Lockswood. Look out for a quiet knife in the guts from us or our friends one fine afternoon. You three too, so long as you're in Norfolk.'

'Give us a rest, arsehole,' Barak said. 'Are you going to answer our questions, or shall I cut your throat now?' He pressed the knife a little further into Gerald's neck, and a bead of blood glistened. Gerald looked at his brother. Barnabas set his lips, then glared at Toby, who moved his sword a half-inch closer to his chest, smiling coldly. Barak, I knew, was bluffing, but I wondered about Toby.

'What's your fucking questions, then?' Gerald spat out the words.

'That's better,' Barak said, withdrawing the knife. Toby pulled his sword back a little reluctantly. It was getting dark in the yard now, and I fetched the lamp from behind the water barrel. In its glow the square, solid faces of the twins were set, the expression in the two pairs of narrow blue eyes, fixed unflinchingly on mine, still threatening. As he moved his head slightly, the long scar on Barnabas's face seemed to twist like a snake in the lamplight. I looked anxiously up at the blank windows facing us, and said, 'What if some of the tenants hear us and come out? It won't look good for us.'

'That won't happen,' Toby said. 'If some of the quarrelsome Norfolk gentlemen come to town for tomorrow's market are fighting in their yard they'll be happy to let them get on with it.'

'Very well,' I said evenly, looking at the twins. 'Now, I have some things to ask you concerning your father's case.'

'We guessed that, bent-back,' Gerald spat.

'First, about your alibi for the night your mother was killed.'

Gerald frowned, and clenched his hands. 'Are you saying we had something to do with the death of our mother, you bent bag of shit?' he said thickly.

'We just want to know the details. We know you said you were at the cockfighting, and had witnesses.'

Gerald laughed, a harsh, mocking sound. 'There's nothing for you there, crookback. We were at the cockfight, with half a dozen friends, then went drinking at the White Lion Inn afterwards. You want names? John Atkinson, servant to Sir Richard Southwell. William Bailey and Michael Hare, also his servants. Edward White, son of Sir George White. We got pissed and all went back to John's to sleep it off. We had a fight with some turd who tried to get ahead of us at the bar. I hit him over the head with a chair. Knocked him out. The barman will remember, won't he, Barney?'

'Ay.' Barnabas grinned: the boys were getting some of their confidence back.

I said, 'I met the boy you hit with an axe at Brikewell. His wits are gone.'

'We know,' Gerald answered coolly. 'We've seen him, slobbering about the lanes. He shouldn't have come on our land, should he, Barney?'

'No. He's just a serf, anyway.'

'An assault like that could have you hanged.'

'Bogles to frighten children,' Gerald answered contemptuously. 'Witherington hasn't made a fuss because he knows his trespassing would be brought up. So there you are, you cunts, you won't get us on that one.' His mean little eyes narrowed. 'Who are you working for, anyway? Who's set you on us?'

'Lockswood works for Copuldyke, Gerry,' Barnabas said. 'That means the Lady Elizabeth. Thomas Seymour's little whore. She's out to save our father because of the family name.'

I said, 'Don't forget that if your father hangs his lands go to the Crown.'

'We'll get them back,' Gerald said. 'Appeal to the Protector, get our own lawyers. With father's debts, that great barn in London will probably have to go, but we'll get Brikewell. Get the tenants off, turn it over to sheep, and sell it.'

'You won't be able to buy or sell anything. You'll be wards of court, in the power of the Lady Mary and Sir Richard Southwell.'

'Granfer will sort him out,' Barnabas answered. 'He'll buy the wardship.' For the first time, I heard a note of uncertainty in his voice. Gerald caught it and gave him a warning look. I began to realize that Gerald was the leader of the pair.

'Do you feel no sorrow at the prospect that your father will hang?' Nicholas asked, puzzlement in his voice.

'No,' Gerald replied. 'He's a weakling, a lewdster, it's because of his screwing Isabella that mother left. Let the fucker hang.' His voice rose and I heard a new note in it, something strange, and slightly mad.

I said, 'One more question, then we're finished.'

'Provided you continue to be good boys,' Barak added. Gerald clenched his fists, and for a moment I thought he was going to try to throw Barak off, but Barak drew his knife tighter at the boy's throat again.

'I want to know about the key you stole from Simon Scambler,' I said quietly. 'A few days before your mother was killed.'

The twins looked at each other. 'By Mary Magdalen's wet fanny,' Barnabas said. 'They have been digging, haven't they?'

Gerald said, 'That little freak Sooty's been talking. They think we put Snockstobe in the river.' And then the brothers laughed. They had been worried when first they had realized we knew about the key, but seemed not to be now.

Toby moved his sword, pointing it straight into Barnabas's gut. 'You waylaid Scambler, beat him up. The key to Midnight's stable disappeared, but Scambler returned the next day and found the key in a place he had searched the day before.'

'I've fucking had enough of this,' Gerald said.

Barnabas, though, smiled. If Gerald was the leader, Barnabas was the more fluent. 'You want the story, crookback. Here it is. We decided Sooty needed a beating. He was getting above his station, singing away to himself while he worked – I'm surprised the horse put up with the noise – so we caught him on the Wymondham Road and taught him some manners. Took that key as well. You see' – his smile was a cruel slash in his disfigured face – 'we thought it would be fun to let that mad horse out in the yard, set the servants running; then Father would sack Sooty and we wouldn't have to see his crazy face around the place again.'

'But you didn't do that.'

'No. We went into Norwich that evening, it was another cockfight night, and stayed over with granfer. We told him about our plan, we thought he'd see the joke, but he said Scambler would tell Father we'd set on him, and have the bruises to prove it. He didn't want Father to throw us out, he wanted us to keep an eye on the place.'

'So he persuaded us to put the key back in the road the next morn- ing,' Gerald added. 'Pity, we'd told all our friends at the cockpit about the joke the night before. The inn was packed that evening, some champion cocks were fighting.'

The boys' tone had changed. They had been able to answer

everything, and were now cocky, confident. 'Was the key ever out of your possession?' I asked.

'No,' Gerald said, 'I had it in my purse.'

Barnabas said, 'Don't you remember, though, you couldn't find your purse when we were at the inn afterwards, you'd taken your doub' let off because it was hot and left it with your purse on the bench. The key was in it.'

Gerald rounded fiercely on his brother. 'Shut your fucking clack' box, Barney! I found it, there where I had left it.'

'How long was it on the bench?' Nicholas asked.

Gerald hesitated. 'Only half an hour. And the key was there. Nobody had time to take it.'

'So who was at the inn that night?' I asked quietly.

'A load of people. All the friends we mentioned before. Chawry, too, our father's steward, drinking on his own and looking sorry for himself. He's often there nowadays. Anyway, what the hell does it matter? The key was never lost.'

I looked at Barak over Gerald's head. He mouthed the word, 'Wax.' I understood. Barak knew a good deal about locks. The boys had been boasting about their planned prank; everyone knew they had the key. Someone, using a candle, could have made a quick wax impression of it and taken that to the locksmith.

I said, 'All right, I think we're done. But don't threaten us. There will be a full account of our meeting going to the Lady Elizabeth and her Comptroller tomorrow morning. If anything happens to any of us, the authorities will know where to look.'

Barnabas and Gerald glanced at each other. Barnabas laughed. 'Reckon we've wasted your time, fine sirs,' he said. 'That was a clever trick, though, waiting for us in here.'

'Ay, full marks for trying,' Gerald agreed.

Toby lowered his sword. 'Get out, then.' Barak and Nicholas also stepped back. The twins looked down to where their swords lay on the ground. 'Going to let us have our weapons back, then, Master Hunch' back? You wouldn't have two poor lads that will soon be orphans walking through Norwich unarmed at night, would you? What with all the sturdy beggars around?'

'I think you're safer without them,' Barak said.

'Come on,' Barnabas said heatedly, 'they're our only ones. They're expensive, too.'

'Look,' Gerald said, 'we'll put them straight in our scabbards and walk out. You have us well covered.' They did not wait for a reply, but slowly bent and picked up their swords, making to put them back slowly in their scabbards.

We all relaxed slightly, and that was our mistake. Acting as one, the twins pulled out their swords again and lunged at us. Gerald swung at Barak with a fury; he parried, but his left hand was not as strong as his right had been, and his sword fell from his hand. Gerald lifted a foot and kicked him mightily in the gut; Barak fell over. Then he turned on Toby, while Barnabas clashed swords with Nicholas. Both managed to parry a couple of thrusts, but though they were good swordsmen the twins were experts. Gerald's next thrust ran Toby through the right arm and he staggered, dropping his sword and grasp-ing his arm, blood welling through his fingers. Then Gerald turned on me, his face twisted in an expression of ferocious rage. I heard Nich-olas and Barnabas fighting hard, the clash of swords ringing loud in the enclosed yard; Nicholas, at least, seemed to be holding his own.

I expected Gerald Boleyn to run me through, but instead he pinned me against the wall of the yard, then held the sword to my guts, putting his other arm across my throat. He was very strong; I could not move. My heart pounded hard.

Gerald's eyes looked into mine; they were wide now, blazing. 'You bent, crawling lawyer,' he hissed. 'You think Barney and me murdered our mother! Did you ever have a *mother*, or were you hatched out of some fucking egg? We *loved* our mother, do you hear, *loved* her, and we'll see our father hang for what he did to her. I'll kill you for what you said!' He gave a shrill, deranged laugh. 'You know what's inside your guts where my sword is?' He made a little jab to emphasize his point. 'It's where your shit is, it'll all fall out. That's the right death for you! What's left inside will poison you, and you'll die slowly.' The boy smiled widely, showing even white teeth, even as he drew the sword back slightly for the killing blow. I closed my eyes, thinking, I never imagined it would end like this, after all the dangers I had faced, killed by an eighteen-year-old.

And then, suddenly, Gerald fell down like a felled tree, his sword ringing as it hit the ground. By the light of the lamp I stared dazedly at his still form. Nicholas stood facing me, breathing heavily, his shirt gone, his slim athletic frame white in the moonlight. He was holding his sword, but by the blade, wrapped in his shirt. I stared at him foolishly, then over at Barnabas, who was nursing a wound on his shoulder, Toby standing over him.

'What – what did you do?' I asked.

Nicholas took a shuddering breath. 'I managed to wound Barnabas, then saw Gerald about to stick you. If I ran him through, he might still have had time to make a final thrust. So I put my shirt round the blade and hit him over the head with the handle.' He gave a cracked laugh. 'Besides, I thought I'd better not kill him, or we'd be in trouble. Look up.'

At all the windows giving onto the courtyard, I could see faces, and one or two lamps. As Toby had predicted, the tenants were not going to involve themselves in a swordfight, but the clash of weapons had woken everyone.

I grasped Nicholas's hand. 'Thank you, thank you, you saved my life.'

He said, 'I heard what Gerald said. He sounded – mad.' He looked down at the boy's prone form. Gerald groaned and began to stir. Blood oozed from a wound on his head. He hauled himself slowly to his knees. Nicholas reversed his sword and held it ready as Gerald staggered to his feet. The passion of a minute ago was gone, and he gave us a narrow-eyed look of pure hatred as he steadied himself against the water barrel.

Toby was leaning against the wall, blood still dripping from his arm. Barak called across, 'You need to make a tourniquet, matey. Nicholas, help him.' He pointed his sword at Barnabas. 'Get up, you, and help your brother out of here. No swords, they're going in the Wensum. You can swim for them tomorrow.'

Barnabas, blood still pouring from his shoulder, came over and put his arm round his brother in a surprisingly gentle gesture. He looked at us. 'By Christ, we need more practice. An old hunchback, a fat cripple, a common churl without even the right to bear a sword, and that long freak. Yet they beat us. But we'll get you back, you don't do this to us!'

'You don't!' Gerald's savage eyes, glaring through the blood now trickling down his face, made me shiver. Then he groaned again and clutched his head. Barnabas looked at us, spat on the ground, and the pair limped through the arch, trailing spots of blood.

Nicholas crossed to Toby, whose black hair and beard framed a face that had gone white. He tore the sleeve of Toby's shirt from his wounded arm and began to wind a tourniquet. Toby said, 'It's a flesh wound, it'll need sewing, but it'll be all right.' He turned to me. 'Christ, they were fast. Well, young gentlemen get proper training,' he added bitterly.

Barak came over. He looked sad, crestfallen. 'I should never have come,' he said. 'I haven't the strength in my left arm. And like that little bastard Gerald said, I've too much weight on me for a fight against someone young and fit.' He sighed deeply. 'I'm sorry. I should have known my fighting days are over. It could have cost your life.'

I put my hand on his shoulder. 'You did your best in good part.'

A door creaked, and a man appeared in the doorway, holding up a lamp. 'Come on,' Barak said, suddenly brisk. 'Best get out of here.' He picked up the twins' swords. 'Nick, for God's sake put your shirt on.'

'I know the best ways to go to avoid the constables,' Toby said.

I looked at him. 'When we get back to the Maid's Head, we'll get a doctor to you. We'll tell them we were set upon.' I laughed bitterly. 'By God, we must be the subject of plenty of gossip there already. So much for keeping our mission quiet.'

Chapter Twenty-five

As I expected, the staff at the Maid's Head were startled by our appearance. I told Master Theobald that we had been attacked by robbers. From his sharp look I was not sure he entirely believed me, but he organized a physician immediately, a quietly competent elderly man named Belys, who applied lavender oil to Toby's wound and stitched it as well as my old friend Guy could have done.

Afterwards, the four of us sat in my room, recovering from the shock of the fight and considering where it left us. I said, 'If the twins spoke true, there was a whole host of people they told about stealing the key that night. Any of them could have used a candle to take a wax impression when Gerald left his purse on the bench.'

'Assuming we believe the little bastards,' Toby said grimly.

'They gave us several names we could check. Including Boleyn's steward Chawry.'

'So you think the twins weren't involved?' Nicholas asked.

'I doubt it more now. Though it would be foolish to discount them. And it's interesting they are friends with Southwell's men, when he has a potential interest in the Brikewell estate.'

'They're a ruthless crew,' Toby observed. 'John Atkinson abducted that young heiress on Mousehold Heath last year and tried to force her into a marriage. Southwell helped him, and several of his servants.'

'And we can't discount their grandparents or anyone in their household,' I added, leaning wearily back in my chair. 'Any of them could have taken an impression of the key in the night, had a copy made by Snockstobe the next morning, and returned the original to Brikewell.'

'But what motive would anyone, other than possibly Southwell and Witherington, have for murdering Edith and incriminating Boleyn?' Nicholas asked.

'None that I can see. Before we left London I was warned by both Copuldyke and Cecil that Southwell is untouchable, because of his local political power and his links to the Lady Mary. And there is no evidence against him. We have many suspects and no evidence.' I turned to Barak. 'Have you any idea who the jurymen might be the day after tomorrow?'

'Tomorrow, you mean,' he answered, nodding at the window. The early summer dawn was breaking, the birds starting to sing in the tree in the churchyard opposite. 'It's Wednesday already. The jurors are drawn from the yeoman farmers and gentry landlords of the country-side, and the better sort of citizens from the towns. As you know, the local gentry don't like Boleyn.' He raised his eyebrows. 'This time it was mostly countrymen on the grand jury, and the trial jurymen will likely be from the same pot.'

'Let's get some sleep,' I said wearily. 'Toby, you can bunk up with Nicholas. Do you want to share with me, Jack? It's some way back to the Blue Boar.'

He shook his head. 'A walk may clear my head. I've got to go to work in a few hours.'

'All right. We have one more lead to follow; we'll visit Grace Bone's brother later, though it's a frail reed.' I sighed. 'And then I must visit John Boleyn in prison, and brief him for the trial. And Jack, I want you to get subpoenas for Daniel Chawry and Simon Scambler.'

'You said you didn't think Scambler would be any good as a witness,' Toby reminded me. 'And what can Daniel Chawry add?'

'We're at the stage where we need to try everything. It's worth taking the risk to get in the evidence from Scambler that the key was stolen, and Chawry can at least attest that Boleyn was a good master.'

'I wonder why he was spending so much time drinking on his own in an inn away from Brikewell?' Nicholas said thoughtfully.

'Perhaps mooning over Isabella,' Barak suggested.

'Will you be able to get those subpoenas so close to trial?' I asked him.

'I should think so, though eyebrows will be raised in the court offices.'

I rose painfully. 'Come on, I'll see you down.' There were a couple of things I wanted to say to Barak alone.

We descended the broad wooden staircase in the dawn light. Everyone was abed apart from the watchman seated on his chair by the door, who looked at us curiously.

'You'll be the talk of this place,' Barak observed.

We reached the stone-flagged hall. Barak looked at me sadly. 'I realized last night, I'm past being a fighting man. Maybe not much use to anyone any more.'

I laid a hand on his arm. 'That's just not true. You may have overestimated your fighting powers last night, but the help you have given us in this quest has been invaluable. The information about the judges, getting the warrants, and your ideas – they are more helpful than you can imagine, they always have been, and I still miss them at work.' My voice almost broke.

He was silent a moment. 'When we worked at the Court of Requests, I used to feel we were doing something useful, helping the powerless against crooked landlords and the like. And before then – when I worked for Lord Cromwell, I had faith in him. Maybe partly misplaced, but I did. But now –' he shook his head wearily –'my work in London, helping the solicitors gather evidence, it's all like rats fighting in a sack. As for the Assize work, I see every day how the legal system only helps those with power. Three days devoted to civil cases, rich litigants spitting against each other, and one day to hear all the criminal cases before hanging day. I'm sick of it.'

'I understand. But it is work, and you have Tamasin and the children.'

'The children, yes. But Tammy – somehow it's turned out she rules the roost, and she seems to have no respect for me these days.' He met my gaze. 'I don't look forward to going back.'

'Marriages go through stormy passages, Tamasin loves you, and I think you still love her. I'm sure you could mend things.' He inclined his head and made a grimace. 'Jack,' I said quietly, 'there was something I wished to ask your advice on, alone.'

'Oh, yes?'

I told him what I had overheard Edward Brown, Vowell and the man called Miles discussing at the Blue Boar. 'It sounded seditious. By law, I should report them.'

Barak looked at me keenly. 'Probably just rebellious gossip. There's plenty of that about.'

'I think it was more. Those men were talking seriously.'

Barak frowned. 'And if they were? Would you have Josephine's husband, and Vowell, who helped you find the twins, called in for hard questioning?' He shook his head vigorously. 'No, you didn't hear any-thing, and you didn't tell me anything. Besides, if there is a rising among the peasantry in these parts, don't they have every reason?'

'I fear violence, and bloodshed.'

'You don't know what they had in mind.'

'No, that's true.'

'Then say nothing. Not one word.'

I was silent for a moment, then answered, 'All right.'

He clapped me on the shoulder. 'Whatever will be, will be.'

✝

I WAS SO EXHAUSTED I slept deeply until I was called at six. I had promised to write again to Parry and Elizabeth, and I wrote saying that I had uncovered some new evidence – the key – and had another possible lead which I would also follow up before the trial started tomorrow.

At breakfast I told Toby that once he had taken us to where Grace Bone's brother lived, he could go back to his parents' farm, though I would need him at trial tomorrow.

'Thank you,' he said. He still looked pale, and his bandaged arm, concealed under his doublet, no doubt pained him.

I said, 'I am deeply grateful for all the help you have given us, espe-cially last night, and I am sorry you were injured.'

'It was good to get at the little bastards,' he said quietly.

Soon afterwards, the three of us retraced our steps of the previous night, across the river then on up Oak Street, a broad avenue leading to St Martin's Gate, one of the northern entries to the city. In the dis-tance we could see the city wall. It was another hot day; the fine weather seemed to have set in for a long spell. It was Wednesday, market day,

248

and the dusty road was busy with carts. We passed an open area surrounding a large church, then entered a complex of houses near the
gate. To my surprise the house where Peter Bone lived was a moderately
large two-storey dwelling, though the paint was flaking from the exter-
ior and the wooden beams were exposed, not painted over, and looked
afflicted by rot. The door was opened by a tall, lean, beardless man in
his thirties, well-favoured, with dark brown hair. He had intelligent
brown eyes which looked at us very keenly. Unexpectedly he carried a
spindle with wool wound around it.

'Master Peter Bone?' I asked.

He took a deep breath. In a resigned tone he said, 'Ay. I heard a
Lunnon lawyer was looking for me, 'bout when my sister worked for
John Boleyn that's on trial. I suppose you'd best come in.'

We followed him into a chamber which was large and well-lit,
though the furniture was sparse, just a table with a hank of wool on it,
four chairs, and a bed and trunk in a corner. He asked us to sit. 'Can
I get you some beer?'

'No, thank you. We were sorry to hear that Grace and your other
sister have passed away.'

'The bad winter weather went on so long into the spring, many
were taken.' His eyes seemed to go blank for a moment. 'Poor Mercy
caught a fever of the lungs, then Grace right after. I didn't even have
the money for a funeral, they were buried in the common pit like most
others who died around here.' He looked at me, and now there was
anger and, I thought, defiance in his expression. 'Though it be a sin to
say so, I wish I'd gone with them. There's nothing left.'

'The house must seem empty,' Toby said quietly.

Peter sighed. 'I've let out Grace's and Mercy's rooms, and my old
bedroom, to bring in a little money.' He looked at me sharply. 'The
owner doesn't know, it's against the lease.'

'We shall tell nobody. We have not come to add to your troubles, I
promise, we thank you for talking to us.'

He studied us keenly again, then looked down at the table. 'This
used to be my weaving shed. Only two years ago my loom was here,
my sisters helping me. But the masters of the city have concentrated
everything in their own hands, squeezed people like me out. I had to

sell my loom. Grace and Mercy helped us get by with some spinning; but now it's just me, doing this woman's work.' He threw the spindle down on the table with sudden anger.

Toby said, 'I gather one of the big wool men is Gawen Reynolds, father of Grace's former mistress, Edith Boleyn.'

'Ay, he's one a' them. His family have been wool merchants for years, and he's one who's made a pile by taking all the processes, from buying raw wool through to tanning and dyeing, into his hands. Many's the poor man been squeezed out by greedy snudges like Reynolds.' He looked up at me. 'But you didn't come to hear me howen' and mowen', sir. Probably you think me an insolent fellow.'

'No. I am sorry for your troubles.'

He looked at me with eyes which had suddenly narrowed. 'Well, what have you to ask about Grace? God rest her soul.'

'I know she left the employ of Edith Boleyn shortly before Edith disappeared nine years ago. Did she come straight home?'

'Yes. She lived with me and Mercy till she died.'

'Do you know why she left so suddenly? Was she discontented with Mistress Edith, or Master Boleyn?'

'She always said that whole household was full of trouble. She served them five years. She said Edith had a strong dislike of her husband. They slept in separate rooms and she told Grace she could not bear the sight of him, nor of their sons.'

'Did Edith say why?'

He shrugged, though his look was still intent, as though weighing up the effect of his words on me. 'Edith said it was just something inside her, she didn't understand herself. She told Grace once she wondered if she was under a curse. I never met Master Boleyn, but Grace said he was a decent enough man except when he was in a temper. I think maybe Edith was mad, Grace said sometimes she wouldn't eat and would go down from a buxom woman to skin and bone.'

'And she confided in Grace?'

'Ay, Grace allus had a good soft heart.' He looked at us, hard. 'But in the end it got too much for her. Mistress Edith discovered John Boleyn was rutting with a local barmaid, and even though she couldn't bear him, it upset her mightily. And those twins were getting worse, throwing tutors down the stairs and suchlike, and Master Boleyn losing his temper with everyone more and more. She could see a storm coming, and one day she decided she'd had enough, and left and came back here.'

I looked at him closely. 'Edith Boleyn herself disappeared shortly afterwards.'

'Ay, I know.'

'Grace was sought out, as a witness.'

Peter looked at me steadily. 'They never found us, they never knew where I lived, for Mercy and I had moved house a little time before. We talked about it, the three of us, and decided we didn't want any more to do with that family.' He smiled narrowly. 'People of our class stick together; we made sure nobody told the justice our new address, and after a while they got tired of looking and gave up.'

'Grace could have thrown some light on the mystery, at least about her mistress's character,' Nicholas said sternly.

Bone answered, with a sudden sharp anger, 'Don't you read me a morality tale, you boy in your fine lawyer's robe. We didn't want any more to do with that crazed family, especially after Edith disappeared.' He turned on me. 'Are you going to report us now, nine years later, for avoiding the searchers? Well, you've got me, but to get Grace and Mercy they'll have to dig them up.'

Toby raised his hands placatingly. 'Nobody's going to report anyone. It's just my master needs to find anything that might throw light on the case, as Nicholas here said, and time is desperately short. Forgive Master Nicholas there, he's prone to antrums.'

Nicholas blushed. I said quietly, 'I thank you for seeing us. We shall trouble you no longer.'

He nodded. 'I would help if I could, but I know nothing of how Edith Boleyn died.'

I stood, putting five shillings from my purse on the table. 'For your time.'

He looked at the coins, then clutched them in his hand, though he did not look up at us. He picked up the spindle. 'I'd better keep a'doing,' he said.

We left the house. Looking back I saw, through the wide window, that Peter was standing, looking out at us, the spindle moving rapidly up and down in his hand. There was that same narrow, intent look in his eyes.

Chapter Twenty-six

TOBY LEFT US to return to the Maid's Head, assuring us his arm was well enough to ride to his parents' farm. I said to Nicholas, 'I want to see Boleyn alone. I'd like you to go to the coroner's office, find out if they've examined Snockstobe's body yet.'

'I'm sure they have, he'll be starting to stink.' Nicholas's tone was sharp. I looked at him. 'What ails you?' I asked.

'It's that Lockswood, always ready with some remark against me.'

I smiled. 'Your antrums. Well, he had a point. Laying down morality to a man in poor Bone's circumstances was not – sensitive.'

'All right, maybe I was wrong. But Lockswood's the one with antrums, he's no more than a clerk, but talks to us more and more as though he were our equal.'

'Barak is a clerk, too.'

'But you've known him years. Latitude is allowed. And he's not a resentful complainer like Toby.'

I shook my head. 'I hoped you two might get on better, particularly after the experience we shared last night. Nick, you and Toby Lockswood may not like each other, but you're going to have to try and rub along. With luck, we should be away from Norwich in a few days.'

'I'll try. But he doesn't make it easy. You should see the looks he gives me sometimes.'

'A few days,' I repeated. 'Now go to the coroner. I'll meet you outside the main castle entrance later.'

I was sore tired, and feeling last night's lack of sleep by the time I had traversed the steep streets of Norwich and reached the marketplace. The market was in full swing and the huge square was crowded; colourful awnings were everywhere and all the different trades – vegetable-sellers, fishmongers, butchers, ironmongers, wool merchants — were in their different sections, calling their wares. At the lower end of the market was an open space for poor folk bringing in goods from the countryside, their wares set out on cloths — cheese and butter, last season's wrinkled apples and pears. Peddlers displayed a miscellany of small goods — pins, wooden mugs, chapbooks, coloured ribbons. I passed Scambler's former employer at his stall, reminding me that I must visit the boy later.

I reached the castle, glancing over to the Shire Hall where the civil cases would still be going on. Again I was led down the clanging iron staircase. The gaoler followed me into the cell. 'Look at him,' he said derisively. 'Less than two days to live and there he lies, dozing away.' I knew that sometimes people under great strain or fear, unable to do anything about their position, take refuge in sleep. He shook Boleyn roughly by the shoulder and he jumped awake, blinking in the dim light. 'What — what —'

I smiled at him. 'Good morning, John.'

He ran filthy hands through his tangled hair, then sat up. 'I've asked them to let me have a good wash and shave tonight, before I go to court, but they say they can't.'

'I'll make sure they do. It will be a matter of passing money.'

'And Isabella is bringing me some good clothes tonight, so at least I will not look like a stinking beggar. She is staying at an inn in the marketplace, the White Horse, with my steward Chawry. They should arrive about seven this evening. Can you meet them, and talk to them about the trial?'

'Of course.'

'They are allowing her to visit me this evening.'

'Would you like me to attend?'

He smiled sadly. 'No, no thank you. This may be our last chance to be together.' He took a deep breath. 'What news?'

I told him about the sudden death of the locksmith, that Grace Bone was dead too and her brother had no useful information, and, finally, about our confrontation with the twins, though I left out that there had been a swordfight. Boleyn shook his head sadly. 'You know, it is strange, I hope I never see them again. Though I always doubted they were involved in their mother's murder, as I said.'

'If only we knew the identity of the man who brought the key – or a wax impression of it – to Snockstobe's shop. But there is no way of finding out before tomorrow. The apprentice is gone, and even he could not identify the man. He has short sight, or claims he does.' I shook my head.

Boleyn raised a hand. 'You have done everything you can, Master Shardlake. I am grateful.'

Strange that Boleyn should end up comforting me. I had decided, on the way, that I would try once more to question him about where he was the evening Edith died, but also that afterwards I would tell him about the Lady Elizabeth's letter requesting a pardon. In common humanity I could not keep that from him any longer.

He looked at me intently. 'There is one more thing I should tell you, Master Shardlake.' He paused. 'I have a goodly store of money, which I have kept at Brikewell. Just in case things got to the stage where my creditors tried to bankrupt me. Twenty old sovereigns of good gold.'

I raised my eyebrows. 'A goodly sum indeed.'

'I will tell Isabella where it is – if things go badly with me, she will be short of money, and should have it now.' He smiled wryly. 'It is in a hole in the brickwork at the back of Midnight's stable. A good hiding place, hey? With my fierce horse for a guardian. And nobody knowing it is there but me.'

'But Master Boleyn,' I said urgently. 'This could throw a whole new light on the taking of the key. What if someone in your household – the twins, or Chawry, or a servant, had observed you hiding it there, that would give someone a whole separate motive for taking the key.' I dared not say, it could even have been Isabella.

Boleyn answered impatiently. 'Do you think I did not consider that? But my cache of gold has been hidden for a year. Nobody knew of it, and nobody dared go in that stable except me and Scambler. And even if the key was taken so that the money could be stolen, how does that advance my case that I am innocent of my wife's murder? On the contrary, it makes the taking of the key irrelevant.'

I thought hard. 'You are right. But Master Boleyn, if I am to help you I need to know *all* the circumstances. I am the one qualified to decide what is relevant. And there are a couple more things I must ask.'

I took a deep breath, and saw him clench his shoulders. 'First, Wither-ington's raid on Brikewell. Did you know that your sons were bringing a gang of gentlemen roughs associated with Sir Richard Southwell?'

He shook his head. 'I knew they were bringing friends, but not their connection with Southwell.' His voice took on an angry tone. 'I hope you are not going to criticize me again for defending my land.' The sight of the boy with a broken head, reduced to idiocy, came back to my mind, but I said nothing. I spoke, though, in a sharp tone as I said, 'That brings me, again, to the question of your alibi. I have never believed you spent all that night alone in your study. If you went out to meet someone, they could give you an alibi.'

He looked me straight and hard in the eyes. 'I was in my study all night.'

'And you will say that tomorrow at trial?'

'Yes.'

I sighed. 'Then, though I shall do all I can to help you, I have to tell you that you may well be found guilty.'

He bowed his head again and spoke quietly. 'The gaoler says the judge has ordered those sentenced to death to suffer the short drop.'

'So Judge Gatchet said at the opening of the Assizes.'

Boleyn looked up. 'Will he be trying the case?'

'I don't know. Maybe him, or Reynberd, or even both, given its controversial nature.'

He was silent a moment. I thought that now, at last, he would explain where he was that night, but he only said, 'I hear you can hang strangling twenty minutes before you die.'

'Not always so long as that.'

He took a deep breath. 'Very well, then, how should I conduct myself at the trial?'

'Criminal cases are short, it should not last more than half an hour. Answer the judges' questions truthfully and honestly. The coroner will give evidence about finding the body, then the constable who discov-ered the axe and the boots in Midnight's stable.' I took a deep breath. 'Gawen Reynolds and your sons have decided to appear, and no doubt will say that Edith was of good character, while you are not.'

He closed his eyes, then exhaled sharply. It struck me that in an odd way it signified his last breaking of any link with his sons. He said quietly, 'And Isabella will be my only witness.'

'Her evidence that you are a good husband will be important. But I am calling Simon Scambler to give evidence about the stolen key, and your steward, Chawry. Do you think he will also say you were a good master?'

'I'm sure he would. But Chawry never knew Edith; he has only worked for me five years.'

'And I will also give evidence, though I am not allowed to represent you, about the stolen key and the locksmith – though that is, I fear, only hearsay which the judge may not allow. If the coroner's examination of the body uncovers evidence that he was murdered, which I should find out shortly, that will help us. And I will give evidence that I visited the site of Edith's murder and saw how hard it would be for one man to do what was done alone. But the fundamental point which I shall make, and which you should make too, is that to leave the body pub⁄licly displayed would be a mad act for you, placing suspicion on you and ending your marriage to Isabella.'

'That is clear,' Boleyn said, a new strength in his voice. 'I shall do all you say.'

I took a deep breath. 'One more very important thing I must tell you. I did not mention it before, because I was ordered not to.' I looked at him sternly. 'Also because, to be frank, I had hoped that facing trial, you might still change your story about your whereabouts that evening of the murder.'

'There is nothing to change.'

'Very well. It is this. If you should be found guilty, the Lady Eliza⁄beth has instructed me to apply immediately for a pardon. I have a letter signed by her. She will grease the wheels with money.'

He stared at me, his eyes wide while I continued. 'I have no doubt that the Lady Elizabeth's name would be enough to grant a stay of execution if it came to it, but I cannot guarantee a pardon will be granted. Elizabeth is still in bad odour with the Protector after the Seymour affair, her brother the King sees her seldom, while as for her sister Mary –' I did not need to finish the sentence.

I had expected Boleyn to be angry with me for concealing this news, but he only nodded. 'Then perhaps I was wrong,' he said quietly.

'What do you mean?'

'When I was married to Edith, and the twins were growing up, I felt my family was under a curse, perhaps some evil lingering from Anne Boleyn's execution. When I married Isabella, I forgot such notions, but then this happened.' He sighed. 'Perhaps Anne Boleyn's daughter will save me after all.'

'There will certainly be hope.' I remembered that according to Peter Bone, Edith too had talked of a curse.

He smiled sadly. 'I see your reasons for not telling me about the pardon before. Hoping I would confide in you that I was out that night. You are very much the lawyer, Master Shardlake, are you not?'

'Yes. That sometimes lays hard courses upon us.'

He held out his hand for me to shake.

I spent some time going over how he should comport himself in court, and call witnesses – this would be his job as I could not repre-sent him. He seemed attentive and alert. At the end I said quietly, 'I shall see you tomorrow. Have courage.'

'I shall. After what you have told me I may even say prayers tonight. I turned my face from God, you see, thinking him my enemy.'

I left Boleyn, and walked slowly upstairs and out into the sunshine, blinking. Nicholas stood waiting for me, his face grave.

'Well?' I asked.

'They examined the body yesterday. There were no wounds, and his lungs were full of water. Snockstobe drowned.'

'He would, if he was pushed in.'

'The inquest will be next week, and the clerk told me death by misadventure will almost certainly be the verdict.'

'So another door closes on us,' I said quietly. I thought again of Boleyn and Edith, each believing they were under a curse.

☩

THERE WAS A little more to do before tomorrow's trial. Nicholas reminded me that, according to the twins, Boleyn's steward Chawry had been present at the cockfighting on the night they were there with the key. 'He might have seen something.'

'We can ask him at least,' I agreed. 'And we should see Scambler.'

We lunched at an inn crowded with market traders, then walked down to Ber Street and Scambler's house. To my surprise, as we approached the rundown building I heard cheerful singing from within. A group of small boys stood outside, peering through the half-open shutters, giggling. They ran away at our approach.

We looked through the shutters. Scambler, again dressed only in a long nightshirt, was dancing clumsily around the room, waving his arms, singing a song I had never heard:

> God and his angels, they will save,
> Poor souls below who Christ do crave . . .

I was surprised by the purity and melody of his voice, though I could see how strange his antics must have looked to the local children.

'What on earth is he doing?' Nicholas asked.

I shrugged. 'Singing and dancing. He has a good voice, I'll warrant it's had some training.'

We knocked at the door. The singing stopped immediately, then Scambler's aunt Hilda put her sour face cautiously round the door. 'Yew again,' she said, then led us into the main room to see Scambler. Immediately she screeched at him, 'Sooty, I told you to keep those shutters closed. An' stop crazin' me with that singin' and jumping around.'

Scambler stood still, head bowed. His aunt turned to us. 'Well, I've kept him in the house. Not put my nose out of doors, asked my neighbours from the church to guard the house, and had to pay one to fetch some vittles to chaw!' With the same mercenary boldness as before, she extended a palm. I laid a groat in it. She grunted. 'It's not right, people stuck in their houses, old women frightened. An' Sooty keeps crazin' me about wanting to go out.'

Scambler gave us a puzzled look. 'Why be frightened? I've been beaten by the twins before.'

I forbore to say this might be more than a beating, and was again distressed that I had not been able to offer more guardianship. At least if anything untoward appeared, Aunt Hilda would screech the house down. I said, 'Just one more day.' I drew a deep breath and added, 'Simon, I would like you to come to the trial, to give evidence about what happened with the key.'

The boy looked scared. 'Speaking in court, in front of all those people? The judges?'

I said, 'You will be quite safe. I intend to be with you all the time. It is important to get your evidence into court.'

'Will he get paid?' Aunt Hilda looked at me greedily.

'No.'

'Then don't go, Sooty.'

But Scambler took a deep breath, and said, 'I'll go, Master Shard-lake, if you and Master Nicholas will be there with me.'

'Thank you, Simon,' I said quietly.

Aunt Hilda pursed her lips. 'I suppose that means I'll have to go too,' she grumbled, 'to keep an eye on him.'

'As you wish,' I said. 'But Simon, your aunt is right, you should keep the shutters on the windows closed and locked. Just in case.'

'It's hot,' Scambler pleaded.

'I know. But better safe than sorry.'

Scambler's aunt led us back to the door. She said, 'I sometimes think that boy's been sent by the devil himself to torment me.' And with that, the door slammed in our faces.

✟

WE RETURNED TO the Maid's Head and caught up on some much needed sleep for the rest of the afternoon. At seven we had a hasty bite to eat, then set out to walk to the marketplace again, where Isabella's inn was situated. As we crossed Tombland we saw a tall, richly robed man standing in the doorway of one of the prosperous-looking, three-storey houses, enjoying the afternoon sun. He was in his fifties, with a handsome face and grey hair worn long. He had a full-lipped mouth set in a stern expression, and large, watchful eyes. Some of the people passing bowed to him. I remembered Toby pointing him out among the city fathers who had welcomed the judges to the Guildhall on

Tuesday; Augustine Steward, one of the foremost men in Norwich. I remembered what Peter Bone had said about the rich merchants cornering the commerce of the city.

In the marketplace a great clearing-up was going on, men reloading unsold goods onto carts, ragged children ferreting on the ground for scraps amid rotten fruits and bad meat. We entered the inn where Isabella had booked a room. We were jostled by merchants, and lawyers from the Assizes, drinking after the day's work. We asked for Mistress Isabella Boleyn's room. Hearing her name, several people looked at us curiously. We were directed to the first floor.

Isabella answered the door. She wore a green dress with a high collar, of good quality but not ostentatious, just right for the trial, her blonde hair under a matching hood. Her pretty face looked strained, but set. She smiled with relief at the sight of us. 'Thank you for coming, Master Shardlake. We got here half an hour ago. People are looking at us.'

'I'm afraid that will continue until after the trial.'

'Have you seen my husband today?' she asked eagerly. 'Is there any new evidence?'

'I fear not.' Her face fell. I told her about what had happened to Snockstobe.

'Dear God,' she said. 'Someone else dead. Was he pushed off the bridge?'

'I suspect so, but cannot prove it.' I told her of my visit to her husband earlier that day, and that he had money secreted away for her in a hiding place, which he would tell her about. I watched for her reaction, but it seemed one of genuine surprise and delight. 'Thank God John was so careful,' she said. Finally, I told her of the request for a pardon from Elizabeth, because I was sure Boleyn would do so anyway, and stressed it was important to keep it quiet until after the trial. At that she sat down, her whole body shuddering with relief, tears pricking her eyes. 'Thank God,' she said. 'Thank God.'

'I told your husband, the outcome is not a certainty.'

She wiped her eyes with a handkerchief. 'But it gives him hope, even if he is found guilty. Forgive me, I am a weak woman, and thus ever prone to tears.'

Nicholas said, 'I think you have shown rare courage and strength given your terrible trials, madam.'

She smiled at him gratefully. 'Indeed you have,' I agreed. I took a deep breath, then added, 'There is one matter where I have been unable to move your husband. I think he went out on the night of Edith's murder. Have you any idea where he might have gone?'

Nicholas added, 'If you do, you must say so now, or it will be too late.'

She met my gaze. 'I know nothing. If John went out of the house, he left silently, without telling me.' A note of exasperation entered her voice. 'Given what is at stake, do you not think I would tell you if I knew?'

'Very well. Now, before you visit your husband, I must go through what will happen tomorrow. I want to call Goodman Chawry as a witness. Your husband says he would speak in his favour, say he was a good master.'

'Yes, I am sure. Daniel and my husband like each other, he is a good man, the only servant who has stayed loyal to us. I had to travel with him today, as I have no maid to accompany me. He has taken the room next door. No doubt people will gossip about that,' she added bitterly.

'Can you call him in? There is something I wish to ask him.'

Isabella went out, returning a couple of minutes later with Daniel Chawry, also dressed well and soberly in a black doublet, his red hair and beard recently cut. I thought, He would answer the apprentice Walter's description of the man who had come to see Snockstobe, but then, as I had said before, so would half the men in Norwich.

'God give you good evening, Goodman Chawry,' I said.

'Master Shardlake,' he answered in a quiet, respectful voice. 'I am glad you and Master Nicholas are here to help us.'

'We have no new evidence, I fear. Save on one matter. I wonder if you remember being at an inn near the cockpit in Coslany, shortly before Edith Boleyn was murdered, where Gerald and Barnabas were present, and there was a ruffle about Gerald losing his purse.'

'I remember that well enough. They were telling everybody that they had a plan that would cause some fun and games at Brikewell.'

'Those were their words?'

'Indeed. Their friends were laughing.'

I thought, Whatever those fun and games were, they did not mean murder, for that they would have kept a tight secret.

'Do you visit that inn often?' I asked.

'Yes. I attend the cockfights at least once a week. Then I go for a drink afterwards.'

Personally, I could not stomach the baiting of animals, the cruel shouts from the crowd as they bled and died: most people saw it as an eccentric weakness, which perhaps it was. I said, 'I have discovered that in the purse was a key to Midnight's stable, which the twins had stolen from Simon Scambler.'

Chawry shook his head. 'Young Sooty, always getting into trouble.'

'This was not his fault,' I said sharply. 'There is a question as to whether someone may have taken the key to make an impression of it. Did you see anything?'

'I remember the twins saying something about a purse, and then rushing over to a bench. I was watching because I hoped someone had stolen it, but it was still there. That's all I remember. I'm sorry. How does it affect the case?'

I told him the story of the locksmith, and our encounter with the twins. 'So far as the locksmith and the apprentice are concerned it is hearsay evidence, but I shall try to raise it tomorrow.'

Chawry nodded, then looked at Isabella, forcing a smile. 'Perhaps in a few days Master Boleyn will be back, riding Midnight.'

'Yes,' she said. She smiled wryly. 'That horse has been a headache. Missing his master, kicking the doors of his stable. Daniel has managed to feed him, but I fear he takes his life in his hands.'

'He's coming to accept me,' Chawry said.

I took the two of them through what would happen tomorrow; Chawry readily agreed to give evidence for his master, though we both knew it would count for little. Then we left them to cross the market square together to visit Boleyn, Chawry carrying another parcel of food which Isabella had made up. Nicholas and I walked slowly back to Tombland.

'You think she will make a good impression?' he asked.

'Yes, she is no fool. Quite a remarkable woman, considering she was once only a barmaid, and must have no education.'

'How old is she, do you think?'

'A good bit younger than Boleyn, around thirty perhaps.'

'She looks younger than that.'

'Too old for you, Nick lad,' I said, taking refuge in banter – although, in truth, Isabella Boleyn had made an impression on me as well. 'Besides, I thought you preferred demure women like Beatrice Kenzy.'

'Too young for you, also,' Nicholas said, with a smile.

'And,' I added sombrely, 'she is still a possible suspect. As is Chawry.'

'I caught Chawry looking at her,' Nicholas said. 'I think he likes her, too.'

'Recent events will have driven them closer. But she is devoted to John Boleyn, you can see.' I sighed. 'It is strange, we have spent the last week talking about John Boleyn, his sons, his servants and neighbours, and somehow in it all, Edith gets forgotten. Yet she suffered more than anybody, and met that terrible, hideous end.'

'She is somehow – elusive,' Nicholas said thoughtfully.

'Yes. Nobody seems ever to have thought to ask why she behaved as she did. If we could find that out, perhaps we might have the answer to the case.'

He took a deep breath, and said, 'Is Boleyn innocent?'

I looked at him. 'Frankly, I do not know. But from all we have found out so far there has to be reasonable doubt.'

We crossed the marketplace. Behind us, the castle loomed over the city like a gigantic sentinel.

Chapter Twenty-seven

T O MY SURPRISE I slept well that night. I woke, as often on the morning of important cases, with questions buzzing in my head. If John Boleyn had not killed his wife, who had? I had no clear idea of a suspect, certainly none with a rational motive – or indeed, an irrational one. The twins seemed to have a cast-iron alibi, and Gerald's furious rage over the suggestion two nights before that they had killed their mother had seemed genuine.

I descended the staircase to the dining chamber, dressed in my serjeant's robe and coif, without any of the excited animation I often felt on the first morning of a civil case. Here a life was at stake, and our chances not strong. I had the application for a pardon in my pocket, but remembered William Cecil's words to me, back in January: *warn the Lady Elizabeth to be careful no breath of scandal touches her again.* And if it should come out that Edith Boleyn had been at Hatfield ten days before her death –

Nicholas and Toby were waiting for me. Both looked solemn. Nicholas, though, made an attempt at a smile. 'Well, the day has come.'

'Yes. The twentieth of June.' I looked at Toby, the bulge of a bandage visible under his green doublet. His black-bearded face looked tired. 'How is your arm?'

'A bit painful, the stitches stretch when I ride, but it's improving. No sign of poison in the wound.'

'Thank God for that. How fares your mother?'

'A little better. Keeping to her bed.' He grimaced. 'Another hot day, I see. The crops are swelking in the heat, becoming dry. I never thought I would say it after the wet spring, but I wish for some rain. That thunderstorm only batted down the crops. Still, today should be interesting.' I looked at him, noting again his emotional detachment from the case.

The waiter brought bread and cheese. I said, 'I want to get down to court as soon as possible, be ready for the witnesses to arrive – Isabella, Chawry, Scambler and –' I took a deep breath – 'the twins.'

Nicholas said, 'The prosecution witnesses will go first – the Brikewell constable, shepherd Kempsley as first finder, and Gawen Reynolds with his grandsons. The evidence of the constable who found the boots and club in the stable is the biggest hurdle.'

'Yes. And we have the general prejudice against John Boleyn living with Isabella. I dare say there will be some professional pamphleteers in court, ready to scribble down the gruesome details, exaggerate them, and have them printed and sold around the country.'

'As it's a criminal trial,' Toby said, 'the judges will want the case over as soon as possible. In the London Assizes they sometimes try twenty capital cases a day. And if Judge Gatchet is in charge, he'll likely be looking for a conviction, to make a moral example.'

I said, 'Normally, I would agree with you, Toby, but since this is such a notorious case I think the judges will want to take more time and care. And be more active in questioning witnesses than they usually are.' I drained my mug of ale. 'Come, let us go. Sometimes the early bird may surprise a worm.'

☦

However, when we arrived at the Shire Hall and made our way to the anteroom of the court where the criminal trials were being heard, the only worms we found were the escheator's representative John Flowerdew and that of the feodary Lady Mary – Sir Richard Southwell. Flowerdew's tall, thin frame in its black robe reminded me of a perching crow, while Southwell, his stocky figure swathed in a long dark robe with a fur collar, a black cap encrusted with tiny diamonds on his head, wore his usual expression of haughty contempt. They were talking together quietly, but turned as we came in. Beside Southwell was a well-built young man with a narrow face disfigured with two large moles, a hard face and bright, angry-looking eyes. Leaving Nicholas and Toby, I approached them and bowed. Southwell was saying to Flowerdew, 'Are you staying for the whole Assizes?'

'Unfortunately, I must, given my duties as the escheator's agent.

Though I have business back in Wymondham. That wretch Kett may be making trouble for me again.'

'You really ought to deal with him.' Southwell turned at my approach and gave me his cold, intimidating stare. 'Serjeant Shard-lake,' he said in an unfriendly tone.

'God give you good morrow, Sir Richard. And you, Brother Flowerdew.'

'Brother Shardlake,' Flowerdew answered cheerfully. 'The Boleyn case is first on. Judge Reynberd is taking time off from the civil cases to sit with Gatchet on this one.'

'That is unusual.' I wondered whether Reynberd might have chosen to sit in order to soften Gatchet's harshness, if need be.

'Nonetheless,' Flowerdew continued, 'I think Boleyn will lose. The evidence of the items found in his stable is very damning. But we shall see. Sir Richard and I are attending as the feodary and escheator's representatives.' His cheerfulness had a mocking undertone.

Southwell, who had been watching grimly, said, 'I see you have exercised yourself on this case. Your own name is on the witness list.' His eyes narrowed. 'You will remember, of course, that this being a criminal trial, you cannot represent Boleyn. I hope you are not seeking to worm your way into the role of advocate under pretence of being a witness.'

'Certainly not, Sir Richard. I have first-hand evidence to give.'

He leaned closer, looking down on me. 'I see you have not heeded Master Cecil's suggestion to keep a low profile.' He shrugged his big shoulders. 'Well, be it on your own head.'

Beside him, the young man laughed. Southwell turned to him with a smile. 'This is my faithful servant, John Atkinson. He is friendly with the Boleyn twins. They believe their father guilty, don't they, John?'

'That they do.' He smiled unpleasantly, showing yellow teeth. So this was the young man who, the year before, had abducted a teenage heiress and tried to force her into marriage, with Southwell's help.

More footsteps echoed in the high antechamber. Isabella entered, accompanied by Daniel Chawry. I excused myself and went over to where they had joined Toby and Nicholas. Isabella looked pale but composed. I asked, 'How are you, Mistress Boleyn?'

'Don't you mean Goodwife Heath?' It was John Atkinson who had called out. Isabella reddened.

'Neither good, nor wife, from what I hear,' Southwell added with a laugh. Flowerdew turned aside, but I saw him smile first.

Isabella shot back, 'You pair want John's lands, and the twins' wardship, I know!'

Southwell frowned mightily at her insolence, and took a step towards her, but checked himself. I said, urgently, 'Be quiet, mistress, please. You must not respond to any provocation.'

'He's right,' Chawry said gently. Isabella set her lips, but nodded.

Other witnesses arrived, mostly poor folk involved with other crim-inal cases, looking nervously around the stone antechamber with its high, vaulted roof, and at those like Flowerdew and me in legal robes. A familiar trio entered; Boleyn's neighbour and rival, the plump, red-faced Leonard Witherington, and his hefty steward Shuckborough, who held the old shepherd Adrian Kempsley firmly by the arm: the old man looked terrified. I thought, He must lead a lonely life in his shepherd's hut; he would be unused to such crowds and, no doubt, had been told by Witherington exactly what to say. Witherington looked at Isabella, curled his lip, and grunted. She turned away.

Just afterwards Simon Scambler entered with his strange, loping walk. His aunt, her grim face framed by a black coif, accompanied him. Scambler looked less frightened than puzzled by it all, his mouth gaping like a fish. I heard someone in the crowd laugh. Seeing us, Scambler hastened over, his face brightening. 'Master Shardlake. Master Overton.'

'God give you good morrow, Simon. Mistress Scambler.'

Aunt Hilda pursed her lips even more tightly than nature had intended. 'Mistress Marling, if you please. Sooty's mother was my sister.'

'It's good to see you,' Scambler said to me. 'I feel safer now.'

I spoke seriously. 'You must be ready for some strong questioning in court, Simon.'

'They may be harsh with you, Sooty,' his aunt said. 'But you must answer honestly, remembering that God watches all.'

'I am sure you will, Simon,' Nicholas added encouragingly.

The doors opened again to admit the twins, accompanied by their grandfather in his aldermanic robes. Barnabas had one arm in a sling under his fine slashed doublet. All three glared at me like snakes. Old Mistress Jane Reynolds followed her husband and grandchildren, her coifed head held low. Scambler shrank away from the family, Isabella too. Nicholas laid a protective hand on her arm.

The twins and their grandfather jostled their way through the crowd, the old man impatiently shoving aside a young woman who stood in his path. Barnabas looked back at Scambler and called out loudly, making everyone look round, 'Come to tell the court we beat you, have you, you dozzled spunk-stain!'

There was silence. To my surprise, the sharp tones of John Flower-dew broke it. 'Don't you shout out like that, young Boleyn, or you'll be in charge of the court bailiff!'

The twins scowled and took a step towards Flowerdew, but their grandfather said sharply, 'No! He's not one to make an enemy of! He could be in control of your lands.'

The twins halted, still glaring at Flowerdew. Then they spotted John Atkinson next to Southwell, and went over to him. 'Come to see the show, Johnny?' Gerald asked.

'Ay. What you done to your arm, Barney?'

'Just a fight. You given up trying to get that cheeky cow Agnes Randolph to marry you?'

Atkinson frowned. 'We are married.' Gerald nudged him and winked, so that Atkinson smiled wryly.

I looked at the twins. I was sure they would say nothing about attacking us and losing their swords to us. An inner door opened, and a black-robed man bearing a white staff came out. He called, 'Witnesses in the case of the King against John Boleyn, come into court!'

✝

THE PUBLIC BENCHES were already crowded with people of both sexes; some looked like gentry folk, serious-faced at the trial of one of their own. There was a large number of common people too, looking eager to see the game of law played out. Both judges already sat on the raised dais, Gatchet looking serious and Reynberd, as usual, deceptively half-asleep. Below them, at the clerks' table, a row of black-robed men sat, a sea of papers before them. The tipstaff guided us to a bench left vacant for witnesses, showing Nicholas and Witherington, old Mistress Reynolds and Scambler's aunt Hilda to the public benches. The twins and their grandfather sat at one end of the long witness bench, with Kempsley next to them. He cast a worried glance at the twins; he would know what they had done to the boy I met at Witherington's house. Chawry sat at the opposite end, then Isabella, then me, while Scambler rushed to sit next to me. There was a gap in the middle of the bench. Scambler looked round for his aunt; seated a little way off, she stared straight ahead at the judges, her face like a wrinkled white prune. I looked at the jury box next to the dais. Twelve middle-aged men, all soberly but finely dressed. Eight had tanned faces, and I guessed they were rural gentry or respectable yeomen; likely to be prejudiced against Boleyn because of his name, and Isabella. There were also four who looked like prosperous Norfolk merchants.

Two middle-aged men came and took up the vacant space in the middle of the witnesses' bench; I recognized Henry Williams, the coroner, who bowed slightly as he passed me. His neighbour, I guessed, was the constable for the Brikewell area.

A murmur went around the court as John Boleyn was brought in by a gaoler. He had managed to shave and get his hair cut – I had paid the gaoler the previous day – and wore a fresh grey-coloured doublet and white shirt. For the first time he looked like the respectable gentle-man he was, but his feet were chained together, the metal rattling on the wooden floor as he mounted the steps to the dock. He held a little sheet of prepared notes. He stood staring straight ahead at the witnesses and the audience; perhaps my news of the pardon, the prospect that today was not necessarily the end, had given him new confidence.

The clerk of the court read out the indictment, that on the night of 14–15 May 1549, John Boleyn did murder his wife Edith Boleyn. Then Judge Reynberd stirred and spoke in his rich voice. 'I must say, I am surprised by the rash of applications for sureties for defence wit-nesses these last few days. The allowing of defence witness testimony should not be abused.' He looked directly at me. 'I see one is a serjeant-at-law.' He waved a hand, ushering me to my feet.

'Serjeant Matthew Shardlake, my Lord.'

'I must stress you can only give evidence as a witness, not act as counsel for the accused.'

'Indeed, my Lord.'

'You act for John Boleyn?'

'I do.'

He grunted. 'Very well. Then let the accused be sworn in.' Boleyn took the oath in a strong, clear voice. The coroner was asked to give his evidence first, and stepped up to the witness box. He confirmed that he had brought the indictment following the coroner's court's finding that Edith had been murdered by her husband. The constable followed, stating that he had gone to search Boleyn's premises and found a pair of boots and a bloodied club in a stable to which John Boleyn said he had the only keys, and confirmed, too, that there was no possibility that the boots and hammer had been thrown in from the outside. He added, 'Master Boleyn has an alibi from his wife for most of that evening and night, but nothing for the hours between nine and eleven, when, he says, he was in his study working, but nobody else saw him. These are the boots and the hammer.' He placed them on the desk; I could see the dark stains on the hammer. 'I had the devil's job getting them out of the stable,' he said. 'The steward had to help me with the horse.'

Boots and hammer were then taken for the jury to inspect. The entire public gallery turned to look. There was an excited murmuring. Gatchet leaned forward. 'Silence!' he called. 'That hammer is not something to peer at shamelessly; it is the instrument of a foul crime against God and man!'

Next, the shepherd Adrian Kempsley was called, staring fearfully at the judges as he walked to the witness box. Reynberd said, 'Now, Goodman Kempsley, tell us what happened on the morning of the fifteenth of May.'

In a halting voice Kempsley repeated the story about finding the body, glancing occasionally at his master Witherington. He described how the lower half of Edith's naked body stuck up in the air, her thin legs standing out at angles, her private parts visible, and how the top of her head came to pieces when she was pulled from the mud. Her face, he said, remained whole and recognizable, her eyes wide as though with shock. Again there was a murmuring from the public benches, though more subdued after Gatchet's warning. Reynberd released Kempsley and he scuttled back to his seat. John Boleyn stood with his head hanging down. The twins' faces were tight and red, Barnabas's scar standing out a livid white on his cheek. Their grandfather sat expressionless.

Then came the sound of a woman sobbing – a loud, desperate, heartbroken sound. Edith's mother, old Jane Reynolds, sat hunched forward, head in her bandaged hands, weeping as though she might never stop. 'Edith, Edith,' she said, 'God save you, I wanted a boy – I wanted a boy!' The crowd made sympathetic sounds. Reynberd turned to the tipstaff. 'I think Mistress Reynolds should leave the room.' The tipstaff gently ushered her out, unresisting, still sobbing. Her husband Gawen stared at Boleyn. Then the tipstaff returned and called Gawen Reynolds's name.

The old man, his robes swirling round him, walked to the witness box, leaning heavily on his stick.

Reynberd asked quietly, 'You wish to give testimony as to the character of your daughter?'

'Yes, my Lord. I apologize for my wife breaking down just now, but Edith's death has broken her poor heart. And mine,' he added, his own voice catching for a moment. It was an act, I was sure, but a very good one. He continued, 'I was not sure I could bear to come here today, but I decided it was my duty to my daughter and to God.'

A murmur of sympathy rose from the audience. Reynolds took a deep breath, then, in a steady voice, told the court that Edith was his and his wife's only child and that, sadly, since childhood, she had always been prone to melancholy, for reasons he never understood, but John Boleyn had happily taken her in marriage. 'Later, though,' he added, 'my son-in-law took up with a woman of ill virtue, a serving woman at an inn.' He stared at Isabella. 'Word of this – liaison – reached Edith. Perhaps my son-in-law did not care, but in any event, nine years ago, my poor daughter disappeared. When she could not be found I thought perhaps she had been overcome with melancholy, and killed herself. And then she was discovered, murdered in that horrible way, last month. I think her return, after her husband had married the strumpet he had been living with openly for years –' he stared at Boleyn, who looked back defiantly – 'drove him to a mad, devilish rage, and caused him to kill her in that shocking manner.'

At this point I stood up. 'I must object, my Lord. This is specu-lation, not evidence.'

Reynberd glared at me. 'I warned you, Serjeant Shardlake, you are not here as counsel. Nonetheless, I was about to make the same point myself.' He turned to Reynolds. 'Have you no idea where your daugh-ter was during the nine years since she disappeared?'

'None, my Lord. I only wish that she had come to me.' Again his voice broke.

Reynberd dismissed Reynolds. He turned to the accused. 'Master Boleyn, how long were you married to your wife before she dis-appeared?'

'Ten years.'

'Would you call it a happy marriage?'

I drew in my breath sharply. Reynberd was within his rights to raise the issue from the bench, but the revelation of long-term bad rela-tions between the two could only strengthen the case against Boleyn. He hesitated, and looked at me. Reynberd followed his gaze and frowned. I looked down. Boleyn swallowed, then said, 'It was not a happy union, as was well known. Edith showed no affection for me, nor her sons. In truth, my wife did not seem to like anyone; she hated social occasions. Sometimes she would – it is hard to believe – starve herself for no reason, reducing herself to the point where her bones stuck out. She would never answer questions about why she did such things. Nonetheless, I had married her and she was my wife.' He added, in a whisper, 'The cross I was given to bear.'

'Until you turned elsewhere for comfort?'

Suddenly Boleyn's temper flashed. 'What man would not?'

Gatchet cut in, his voice like a file, 'Any good Christian man.'

There was silence. Then Reynberd said, 'I now call your sons, Gerald and Barnabas Boleyn.'

The twins walked, stolidly and expressionlessly, to the witness box, a pair of well-dressed young gentlemen in silken doublets. Boleyn looked at them for a long moment, an unreadable expression in his narrowed eyes. I had warned him the night before to keep steady, not to let them anger him.

Reynberd said, 'You are the sons of John and Edith Boleyn. Gerald and Barnabas?'

'Yes.' They answered politely. So they knew how to behave when they needed to.

'Have you always resided with your father?'

'Till he went to gaol,' Gerald answered coolly.

'Was he a good father?'

'He showed little interest in us,' Barnabas replied.

'And your mother?'

Gerald looked straight back at Reynberd. 'Our poor mother was always unwell. But our father did nothing to help her, he only shouted at her. We loved her, and were brokenhearted when she left because our father had taken up with that tavern-woman.' He pointed at Isabella.

Reynberd turned to Boleyn. 'Have you any questions?'

He looked at his sons, his voice trembling. 'You made your mother's life a misery. And mine. Your indiscipline, your violence even towards the tutors we engaged . . . Was it not your behaviour as much as any-thing that drove my wife away?'

Gerald answered, his voice cold. 'What, when we were nine years old? No, it was your adultery that was the final straw for her. We are glad that now we live with our grandfather, who shows us the affection you never did.'

It was an accomplished performance. I could see sympathy on the faces of many in the audience, even though many in Norwich must know the twins' wild reputation. Boleyn's face darkened, and I feared he might lose his temper again, but instead he set his lips hard and said nothing more.

Reynberd said, 'I believe that completes the prosecution evidence, except for one thing. Master Boleyn, am I correct, the only alibi you have for the evening in question is that of Isabella Heath' – Isabella reddened at the use of her maiden name – 'and that there were two hours, between nine and eleven, when she did not see you, as you were, your deposition says, working in your study?'

'That is correct,' Boleyn answered firmly.

'She did not even bring you a glass of wine, or beer? Or get one of the servants to do so?'

'I asked not to be disturbed while I worked. I was studying estate papers, related to a dispute with my neighbour Master Witherington, who claims some of my land.'

Reynberd inclined his head slightly. I looked at the jury; several were whispering together. This was the most damning evidence against Boleyn.

Reynberd said, 'Very well. I think we will take a short adjournment. There is a document concerning one of the civil cases I must attend to. Return in fifteen minutes.'

The judges rose, and left by their private door. From the corner of my eye, I saw Sir Richard Southwell leave the room. I went across to Nicholas. 'What do you think?' I asked.

'I wish Boleyn hadn't snapped at Gatchet.'

'Yes, though he would make a saint lose his temper. Gawen Reynolds got the jury's sympathy.' I laughed mirthlessly. 'And I got a telling off.'

'Sticks and stones.'

'The lack of an alibi – the unhappy marriage – the twins blaming him for their mother's disappearance . . .' I shook my head. 'Well, we must ensure every bit of evidence casting doubt on Boleyn's guilt is raised, and emphasized. Especially the missing keys. It is up to us now.'

Chapter Twenty-eight

W HEN THE JUDGES returned, John Boleyn was the first to give evidence, from the dock. The room was becoming hot now, with Judge Reynberd mopping his cheeks with a lace handkerchief. Gatchet said to Boleyn, with a wave of the hand, 'The room is yours.' All eyes turned to him.

He looked down at his notes and then, to my relief, began speaking clearly and fluently. 'My Lord, I would submit there is no evidence linking me to this terrible crime. Indeed, my wife's body being left in public view in that hideous way only advertised to the world that she had been alive until the day before, making my second marriage invalid. I submit that I had no motive to leave her body exposed to the world. Further, I have evidence that this crime could not have been committed by one man alone, that mine was not the only key to my horse's stable and that this second key disappeared for a while.' He took a deep breath. While speaking he looked straight ahead, occasionally glancing at the jurors. I had advised him to do this – establishing eye contact would remind them he was a human being whose life was in their hands. There was a murmuring in the court. He had, at least, impressed them.

Judge Gatchet intervened. 'You spoke of your second marriage. But is it not the case that shortly after your wife disappeared, you took Isabella Heath into your home and lived with her for seven years, marrying her only after your wife was declared dead, exposing your servants and young sons' – he cast a glance at the twins who, as if on cue, lowered their heads – 'to ungodly immorality?'

Boleyn looked straight back at Gatchet. 'I never meant Edith to discover my relations with Isabella, it was mean common gossips who told her. After she disappeared, I notified the authorities and made every effort to find her, involving the local constable and assisting the search in every way. I ask the coroner if that is not true.'

The coroner rose in his place and said, 'My predecessor is dead now, but he told me of the efforts to find Edith Boleyn, and I have seen the papers. Master Boleyn is correct.'

'Nonetheless,' Gatchet persisted, 'you lived openly in sin for seven years.'

'I am on trial here for murder.' Boleyn's voice rose; suddenly he was shouting. 'This is not the Church court where gossips and backbiters cast easy judgement on things they know nothing about!'

I took a deep breath. His temper was out. There was a gasp from the well of the court. Gatchet went purple. 'How *dare* you speak to a lord justice like that!' he said furiously. 'You ungodly, shameless wretch —'

Reynberd looked at Boleyn hard. 'Do not speak like that again in court, Master Boleyn. Apart from anything else, it will do you no credit.'

Boleyn swallowed audibly, realizing he had made a serious mistake. 'I apologize, my Lord.'

'That's better. Now, what else have you to say?'

He glanced quickly at his notes. 'I wish to call Isabella Heath, and my steward Daniel Chawry, to give evidence as to my character.'

Reynberd waved a hand. 'Very well.'

Isabella took a deep breath, stepped out and mounted the witness box. Her stance and expression were exactly right — sober and melancholy.

Boleyn coughed, then spoke softly, 'Isabella, how long have we shared our lives together?'

'Nine years, sir. And for the last two, after your poor wife was declared dead, we have been married.' She looked at the judges, her expression one of open honesty.

Gatchet was still in a vile mood. 'Why did you agree to live in sin with this man?'

Isabella looked straight back at him. 'Because I loved him, and his wife was gone.'

Another murmur from the public gallery. It sounded sympathetic; I saw a couple of women nodding.

Boleyn said, 'You would say we have been happy?'

Isabella looked at him and smiled unforcedly. 'I think it a rare thing in the world for two people to feel such natural devotion as we have, despite the difference in our age and status.'

'Do you believe me capable of murder?'

'Never, sir. You are a gentle man, too gentle perhaps, for that has allowed acquisitive neighbours and unruly children to take advantage sometimes.' She looked directly at Leonard Witherington, then the twins, who stared back expressionlessly.

Boleyn said, 'I confess I laid hard courses upon you. Public obloquy because we lived together without being married –'

'Only for legal reasons, sir, since seven years had to pass before Edith, God rest her soul, could be declared dead.'

'You had the burden of becoming mistress of my estate, and bringing up my sons, who were not easy.' Then he asked, 'Did you ever think of leaving me?'

'Never.'

Isabella and Boleyn were both close to tears now. Boleyn swallowed and then suddenly asked, 'If I am found innocent of this terrible crime, now poor Edith is dead, would you marry me again?'

Isabella looked startled. Then she answered, 'Certainly.'

I drew a deep breath. I saw two men scribbling frantically – this was ideal material for a sensational pamphlet; effectively, a proposal from the dock. However, I saw a couple of respectable jurymen frowning at each other, and both judges looked cross. Reynberd called for silence, then leaned forward and said, 'I must ask the jury to discount that last emotional display. Master Boleyn, have you any further questions for this witness?'

'No, sir.'

Isabella stepped down, dabbing her eyes with a handkerchief.

Daniel Chawry leaned across and whispered to me, 'I didn't expect that.' He looked distressed, as well he might if he was attracted to Isabella. Isabella returned to the bench and sat down, wiping her eyes. 'You did well,' I said quietly.

Boleyn called Chawry next. He was still struggling with emotion, but with an effort he gathered himself. He confirmed that he had worked for Boleyn for five years, and had always found him amiable, decent and honest. He did not believe he could have been capable of a savage murder.

'And yet,' Boleyn said, 'I am sure you would not say I was a para-gon of virtue.' This was a point I had asked him to make, in case the jury became bored by paeans of studied praise. 'What faults have I?'

'As your wife said—'

'As *Goodwife Heath* said,' Gatchet snapped.

'I beg pardon, my Lord. As she said, people have taken advantage of you. On property matters, for example.' He, too, looked at Wither-ington. 'And –'

'Go on, Chawry,' Boleyn said.

'You are perhaps a little unworldly over financial matters. In this fiercely acquisitive age.'

A couple of people ventured to give an approving murmur. That point would play well with the poorer classes; but there were none of them on the jury.

Gatchet said, 'We have seen the accused has a temper.' Reynberd nodded sagely. 'You must have seen signs of that.'

'Master Boleyn is not a man of choler,' Chawry answered carefully. 'Sometimes he can become angry, even lose his temper. But only when he is sore vexed, as over a bad harvest or the misbehaviour of his sons.'

'The reappearance of his wife must certainly have vexed him,' Reynberd said pointedly.

Glancing quickly at his notes, Boleyn said, 'To turn to another point. You know the place where my wife's body was found?'

'Naturally I know every foot of your estate, sir.'

'With the court's permission, I should like to pass your lordships and the jury copies of a sketch plan of my estate. I would also ask that a copy be given to the shepherd, Goodman Kempsley, whom I wish to question.' At this poor Kempsley stared at him in horror. Judge Reynberd held out a hand, and Boleyn passed up copies of the plans Toby had drawn – I had got him to make copies. Reynberd looked at them, nodded, and passed them to the tipstaff who handed them round. 'Hurry up,' Gatchet said as a juror dropped his copy. 'Other cases are waiting.'

Boleyn asked Chawry, 'You see that the stream where the body was found is surrounded by boggy ground. What was it like in May?'

'After all the rains? Sore gulshy, lots of mud.'

'And if poor Edith's body was to be carried to the stream and dropped in, even if she were carried only from the nearby bridge, in total darkness, do you think one man could have done it alone?'

'I doubt it. His feet would sink into the mud with the weight of the body. I doubt even one very strong man could have done it.'

Boleyn then recalled Kempsley, who still looked terrified. He asked gently, 'Goodman Kempsley, would you agree with what Master Chawry just said?'

Kempsley looked at Witherington, who turned his head away. 'Remember you are under oath,' Reynberd snapped.

Kempsley took a deep breath. 'Yes, sir, the ground was sodden. One man carrying a body would sink into the mud.'

'One other question,' Boleyn continued. 'In your deposition you said you found boot marks in the mud. Could those marks have been made by more than one pair of boots?'

Kempsley hesitated. 'You must answer, fellow,' Gatchet said sternly.

'There could have been two pairs.' I saw several people look surreptitiously at the twins.

'Yet only one pair was found in my stable. And nobody has identified them as mine. Whoever wished to point to me as the killer did not think to put two sets there.' He paused, to let the point sink in. Boleyn was doing well. If only he had not lost his temper with Gatchet . . .

✝

THEN KEMPSLEY SAID, 'Master Boleyn could have had an accomplice who took his own dirty boots home with him.' He looked at Witherington, who nodded slightly. I set my lips. I knew, of course, that that was indeed a possibility.

'We must press on,' Reynberd said. He looked at his papers, then back at Boleyn. 'I understand there remains some rather convoluted evidence concerning the key to your horse's stable.'

'Yes, your Honour. I would like to call Matthew Shardlake, Serjeant-at-law.'

Reynberd sighed. 'Very well.'

I rose in my place, and stepped out. I had never felt so exposed in court; today, instead of arguing from the advocates' bench, I had to take that lonely walk, under staring eyes, to the witness box.

I faced Boleyn, in the dock, across the judges' bench. For a moment Boleyn looked confused, then he pulled himself together, consulted his notes, and said, 'Serjeant Shardlake, would you please tell the court about the investigations you made on my behalf into the misplaced key to my stable?'

'Certainly.' I looked at the courtroom. 'Master Boleyn has a stable at Brikewell set aside for his horse, Midnight. He is a very unruly animal, and could cause damage if he escaped. As the constable indicated earlier, he can be a danger to people. Therefore Master Boleyn had only two keys made by the Norwich locksmith who worked for him for years, Richard Snockstobe.'

There was a murmur through the court at that; many would have heard about Snockstobe's death. The judges, though, looked puzzled. I said, 'Master Snockstobe was found dead in the Wensum two days ago, under Bishopsgate Bridge. Foul play cannot yet be ruled out.'

Reynberd leaned forward, interested now. 'Has the body been examined by the coroner?'

'Yes, my Lord. It is believed he drowned, but the inquest has not yet been held.'

'Any wounds on the body?'

'I believe not, my Lord.'

The coroner stood. 'The man was a habitual drunk, who may have fallen off the bridge.'

Reynberd grunted. 'Go on.'

'I had visited Master Snockstobe the day before. In order to relate the story in proper order, I must ask Master Boleyn to call another witness.'

Again, Boleyn hesitated. The strain of the trial was beginning to tell. I smiled encouragingly, and he said, 'I would ask to call Sooty Scambler.'

'*What* was that name?' Gatchet asked incredulously.

Boleyn flushed. 'I apologize, my Lord. Simon Scambler, my former stable boy. Everyone calls him Sooty.'

There was a row of blue-robed apprentices on the public benches, and some giggled. Scambler stood, looking confused. I stepped down from the witness box, noting that the twins' grandmother, Jane Reynolds, had still not returned to the room. I expected Scambler to come to the box and take my place but instead he walked with his loping stride straight up to the bench and stood facing the judges. They stared back at him. There was more giggling from the apprentices, and Scambler looked around uncertainly. I went over to him. 'No, Simon, up there. To the witness box. Master Boleyn will ask you some questions.'

'I am sorry, Master Shardlake.' Scambler turned and, tripping on a loose board, almost went flying. The apprentices shrieked with laughter.

Gatchet banged his gavel on the desk. 'Silence! Tipstaff, remove those apprentices!' The boys, still giggling, were led out, the tipstaff whacking one of them on the shoulders with his stick. I went and sat next to Isabella, resisting the urge to bury my head in my hands.

Scambler, in the box, looked expectantly across at John Boleyn, who said, 'Sooty – Simon – do you remember working for me as a stable boy? You looked after my horse, Midnight?'

Scambler's face lit up. 'Yes, Master Boleyn. I got him to like me, didn't I? I handled him well.'

'You did. And do you remember I gave you the second key to Midnight's stable, told you it was the only one apart from mine, and that you were to let no one else take it?'

'Ay, master. An' I never did, except –' He fell silent.

'Except when?' Gatchet snapped. 'Come on, boy!'

'Except when Gerald and Barnabas Boleyn set on me one day, and beat me up. On the road to Wymondham. Afterwards, I found the key, which I kept on a chain round my neck, was gone.' He looked fearfully across at the twins, whose faces remained expressionless. There was a murmur of interest from the court, and I saw two jurors lean forward.

Boleyn asked, 'Do you remember the date of this?'

'May the twelfth, sir. My poor dead mother's birthday.'

'What did you do when you found the key missing?'

'I looked and looked for it. Then I went back to your house. I said nothing, I feared you'd be angry. But next morning, in case I'd missed it, I went back to look again. And there it was.' The boy's voice rose with excitement. 'By the road. But I'd swear by the Holy Cross I'd looked just there the day before.'

There was definite interest in the faces of the jury now, and several looked at the impassive twins. So, for a moment, did Boleyn. Then he asked Scambler, 'Do you think it could have been taken by my sons, perhaps to have a copy made, and returned?'

Scambler nodded. 'It might have been, sir.'

Judge Reynberd coughed. 'Master Boleyn, that is speculation. When Serjeant Shardlake briefed you, did he not tell you about the rule against it?' He interlaced his fingers and looked sternly at Scambler. 'Why did Master Boleyn's sons attack you?'

'They said they were tired of my singing. I used to sing while I worked.'

'That can hardly have been reassuring for a difficult horse.'

Scambler looked back at him. 'Ah no, sir, Midnight liked melo-dies, like this –' Then he began to sing, softly: 'Alas, my lady, lady whom I love so greatly –'

Gatchet snapped, 'What are you *doing*? This is a court!'

Scambler looked downcast. 'I just wanted to show you what I sang,' he mumbled, glancing at his aunt, who looked as if she could have bitten him. Gatchet frowned at Boleyn. 'Is this boy in his wits?'

Boleyn said, 'In truth he has a reputation for – eccentricity. But he was a good, honest worker, and treated my horse well.'

Gatchet sighed. 'Have you any other questions for this witness?'

'No, sir. I would like to recall Serjeant Shardlake.'

Gatchet raised a weary hand. 'Very well.'

Scambler stumbled unhappily back to his bench, and I returned to the dock. Many in the courtroom were smiling openly, including a couple on the jury, although others were frowning. The impact of poor Scambler's evidence had been undermined by his behaviour. Some people, though, were still looking curiously at the twins. I stared at Boleyn, willing him to return to the narrative of the stolen key.

He hesitated, then said, 'Serjeant Shardlake, I understand that after you spoke to Sooty – to Scambler, you visited the locksmith Snockstobe's shop.'

'Yes.' I looked at the judges. 'It is in Tombland. On the seventeenth of June, I spoke to his apprentice, one Walter, to ask whether Gerald or Barnabas Boleyn had visited the shop recently. He said they had not. Snockstobe himself refused to answer any questions. Next day, after the locksmith's body was found, I returned to the shop and Walter told me that someone else, whom he could not identify, had brought a key from Brikewell for copying. He said his master had seemed very concerned by my visit, and had gone out immediately afterwards. He returned looking worried, and that night he died.'

There was a definite murmur in the court now. Reynberd looked at me. 'Where is this apprentice?'

'He has fled. I understand his home is in the Sandlings.'

'Does he have a last name?'

'He ran away before I could get it, my Lord.' I felt myself redden with embarrassment.

'Then any evidence of what he said is hearsay, and inadmissible. Really, Serjeant Shardlake, you should know better.'

'Master Snockstobe is dead, my Lord. When a person is dead, the hearsay rule does not apply, and weight may be given to words he said to a third party.'

'The third party, this Walter, is not present.'

Gatchet asked, 'Did this apprentice describe the man who came to the shop?'

'He could only say that he was a big man, with a beard. Apparently, Walter suffers from shortsightedness.'

'Very convenient,' Gatchet said dryly.

I addressed him directly. 'No, my Lord, it is very *in*convenient. We wish nothing more than to identify this man.' I paused. 'I do not necessarily believe the apprentice's tale of his shortsightedness. There is nothing I would like more than to have him here. Indeed,' I ventured,

'I would ask whether this case might be adjourned, so that efforts to find the apprentice Walter may be made.'

Reynberd leaned forward. 'Serjeant Shardlake, you are acting as an advocate, which I told you *not* to do! You have had over a month to gather evidence –'

'I only came to Norwich last week –'

He waved a hand. 'That is not my problem. This case will be considered today, on the evidence brought before us.'

I took a deep breath. 'Yes, my Lord.' I had expected a refusal, but it had been worth a try. 'If I may proceed with my evidence, I believe I can show the key may have been stolen in turn from Barnabas and Gerald Boleyn during the evening of the day when it was first missing, to an extent that should open the matter to reasonable doubt.' I turned to Boleyn; it was he who must call the next witness. His face set. 'I would like to call my sons, Barnabas and Gerald Boleyn.'

Again the twins returned to the witness box, walking confidently, shoulder to shoulder.

'Why did you attack my stable boy, Scambler?' Boleyn asked them, bluntly. 'I saw his bruises the next day.'

'Because we saw him mistreating your horse, sir,' Gerald answered smoothly. 'Once, through the open door of the stable, we saw him jab Midnight with a pitchfork, and another time he prodded the horse with a nail.'

'Perhaps he was made so ill-tempered because of how the boy handled him,' Barnabas added snidely.

Next to me, Isabella bunched her fists. 'Liars,' she whispered. 'Filthy liars.'

'Quiet,' I said, placing an arm on hers.

Boleyn looked at them incredulously. 'You know Midnight. He would never submit to such treatment.' His voice rose, trembling a little. 'Did you steal Scambler's key?'

'No,' Gerald answered. 'We did not.' They were still, controlled. I wondered if they had been briefed by their grandfather, as Boleyn had been by me, to answer questions as briefly and directly as possible.

'It was never in our hands,' Gerald said. 'Sooty Scambler is not in his wits. It is a matter of common fame in the city. He could have missed the key on his first search.'

Barnabas looked meekly at Gatchet. 'My Lord,' he said, 'may I say something, on behalf of myself and my brother?'

'Very well.'

'Only that we loved our dear mother very much. Nobody can say we did not. On the night of her cruel murder we had an alibi for the whole evening.' He paused. 'Unlike our father.'

Boleyn, who had been staring at the twins, came to himself and asked if he could briefly recall his steward, Chawry. Judge Reynberd assented, and Chawry walked back to the witness box, passing the twins; neither looked at the other.

Boleyn said, 'I understand that you frequently visit the cockpit at Coslany, and afterwards the tavern nearby.'

'I do, sir. Most Saturdays.'

'Were you there on the twelfth of May?' Boleyn was back in his stride now.

'Yes, sir.'

'Do you remember my sons being there that night?'

'I do. I did not speak to them, but they were there with some friends. I remember them talking and joking, and something was said about a trick with a key. Later there was a panic because Gerald had left his doublet with his purse on a bench. The place was crowded and they pushed and shoved to get to it, knocking a couple of people's drinks over. But they said nothing had been taken. They looked relieved.'

'They definitely mentioned a trick with a key?'

'They did. They and their friends, when they get to drinking, they talk loudly.'

'Thank you,' Boleyn said, almost sorrowfully.

'One more thing, if I may,' Chawry said. 'The horse Midnight has always been difficult. Several stable boys have come and gone, but Simon Scambler was the only one who could handle him. Now Midnight is back to the way he was.'

'Thank you, Chawry,' Boleyn said. 'And now —' he took up his notes, which trembled in his hands — 'I would like to recall my sons one final time.' Eyes followed the twins as they returned once more to the witness box, now looking a little put-upon. Boleyn swallowed, and again was silent a moment.

'We must proceed,' Reynberd said, irritated. 'We have been here near forty-five minutes already.'

'I apologize, my Lord.' Collecting himself, Boleyn looked at his sons. 'My steward has shown you lied about Scambler's treatment of my horse.'

'His word against ours,' Gerald said flatly. 'And he is your employee.'

'Do you deny you were at the Coslany cockpit on the twelfth of May, and afterwards in the tavern joked with some friends of yours about a trick with a key?'

'We were staying the night with our grandfather, and we had lost the key to his house. That was all we were talking about.'

Barnabas said, 'And we realized Gerald had left his purse, with his money, on the bench. Like you said, he got it back. And found Grandfather's key there.'

'How long was it missing, out of your sight?'

The boy shrugged. 'Perhaps half an hour or so.'

Boleyn said, 'Is it not true that you stole the stable key because you intended to let out the horse and have Scambler blamed? That you told your friends so, and also your grandfather?'

Gerald turned to Barnabas. 'He's dreaming.'

'And did not your grandfather advise you that your father would realize you had done it if Scambler had marks of injury? He dissuaded you, and you returned the key. But someone could have briefly stolen it, or made a wax impression to take to Snockstobe later, could they not?'

Both twins stared directly at me. I took a deep breath. If they were to tell the court that we had got this information out of them in the course of a fight, Nicholas and I would be in serious trouble with the Bar. But they would look like fools, and their pride would not allow that. Reynberd asked Boleyn, 'How can you possibly know what your sons' grandfather said to them?'

Boleyn took a deep breath. 'I am sorry, your Honour, I may not reveal the source of that information.'

Reynberd raised his eyes to the ceiling. 'Yet more hearsay.'

'My Lord, my sons have not yet answered my question.'

Gerald spoke then, quietly and intently, but with a vicious under-tone. 'None of this is true. It is a story made up by Chawry and our father. Our grandfather will confirm we had no conversation about any key.'

Reynolds rose in his seat. 'Certainly I do,' he said.

'For the rest, our friends will confirm that there was no talk of a jest with a key.'

'Yes,' Boleyn said heavily. 'The same friends who gave you an alibi for the night of your mother's death.'

Barnabas leaned forward and snarled, 'You won't trap us, Father, into being hanged for what you did! Our mother came back and you killed her. You've got Chawry, and that crazy Scambler, to lie for you.' He looked at Scambler. 'Eh, Sooty? I hear you got sacked recently.' Scambler shrank away and Barnabas looked back at his father. 'We'll be there tomorrow, to see you take the short drop.'

'We'll enjoy every minute!' Gerald laughed shrilly.

The twins, as I had hoped, had lost control – but not when con-fronted with the story about the key. The jury and the public nonetheless looked at them with disgust; even the judges were taken aback by their outburst. 'Enough!' Gatchet shouted. 'You are in contempt of this court; were it not for your bereavement, I would have you in the cells! Step down, now!'

Without another word, the twins walked side by side, back to their seats. Their grandfather's eyes followed them; he looked worried. There was a pause, then Judge Reynberd leaned forward, intertwining his fingers. 'That concludes the evidence.' He looked at the jury. 'You have heard the evidence regarding the discovery of the body, and of the boots and hammer found in the stable of the accused, where a horse that could be controlled only by him and the stable boy was kept. The accused had means, opportunity and motive to kill his wife. The sug-gestion from the defence that more than one man was involved is circumstantial, and even if true, would not necessarily mean Boleyn himself was not one of them. As to the question of the stolen key, I have never heard such a mingle-mangle of hearsay and supposition. However, it is for you to decide whether it constitutes reasonable doubt that John Boleyn killed his wife, together with the undoubted fact that while he had a motive for killing her, that motive – to preserve his marriage to Isabella Heath – would also have caused a sensible man to bury the body, not display it. However –' he paused for effect – 'we have seen that Master Boleyn has a temper. Remain in your places while the next criminal cases in this batch are called. Hopefully, they will be shorter and simpler.'

I sat down, and looked at the jury. 'That was a biased summing up,' I said to Isabella.

'Are we then lost, sir?'

I looked at the jurymen. 'All depends on them now.'

Chapter Twenty-nine

REYNBERD LEFT THE courtroom; everyone rose and bowed. Evidently Gatchet was being left to try the other cases alone. The gaoler led Boleyn from the dock to the prisoners' bench, the chains round his ankles clanking, as two more gaolers brought in a ragged procession of half a dozen prisoners – the remainder of this batch of criminal cases – and sat them on the bench. One, a wild-haired woman in her twenties, was coughing incessantly. People on the public benches looked at her apprehensively; attending the criminal Assizes meant the risk of catching 'gaol fever' from the bad humours of the prison. Several poor citizens, relatives of the accused, entered and took places on the public benches. Gatchet lifted a pomander to his nose. The tipstaff announced, 'The King against Fletcher. Theft of six loaves of bread.' A painfully thin old man rose. He was shaking; the bread would be worth more than a shilling; this was a capital offence. Gatchet glared at him. I whispered to Isabella, 'Let's get out of here.'

She followed me, together with Chawry, Scambler and his aunt, and Nicholas and Toby. We stood in the antechamber. I saw the twins' grandmother, old Jane Reynolds, sitting on a bench, hands on her lap, the white bandages standing out against her black clothes. I remembered what Parry had told me about Edith's twisted hands – perhaps the condition was hereditary. Her face under its black hood was like paper in the sunlight, her eyes staring ahead unseeingly. I wondered what she had meant when she said in court, 'Edith, God save you, I wanted a boy.'

We found a bench and sat down. 'It does not look good, sir, does it?' Isabella said, in a small voice.

'Well, the test in criminal cases is that the jury must find the accused guilty *beyond reasonable doubt*. Perhaps we might have done that

with the key at least, although the twins did not break under questioning as I had hoped.'

Chawry looked at Isabella, a strange expression on his face – it
seemed to me part sympathy, part longing. He turned to me. 'I have
heard that in hanging cases juries will find someone innocent if they
can.'

Toby grunted. 'Unless they are prejudiced against the accused.
And there are several fat Norfolk gentry on the jury.'

Isabella looked at him in distress, and I frowned at him. Saying
that now did not help. 'Churl,' Nicholas muttered audibly.

On Nicholas's other side, Scambler looked at me. 'I didn't help,
did I, sir? Made a nonny of myself again.'

'Singing in the witness box.' His aunt shook her head despairingly.

Scambler said, 'Something always happens. I never mean it to.'

His aunt spoke with quiet intensity. 'You don't listen, you don't
think. You're hopeless.'

'No,' I said, 'Simon was clear over what he said about the beating
up and the missing key. It was obvious he was telling the truth.' Yet his
confused behaviour in court would have lent credibility to the twins'
speculation that he had simply missed the key on his first search.

The door swung open and old Gawen Reynolds marched out, followed by the twins. He went to his wife and said, 'Come, Jane, we are
going home. I have arranged to be informed of the verdict.' Jane rose
meekly and followed. As he passed us, Gawen Reynolds glared, but
said nothing. The twins hung back for a moment, looking down at
Scambler. Nicholas moved closer to him, glaring back defiantly. Barnabas smirked, and slowly drew a finger across his throat.

☦

WE SAT UNCOMFORTABLY for nearly an hour. I would have liked
to discuss the case with Nicholas and Toby, but not with Isabella there.
Chawry tried to distract her with news of the farm, how badly rain
was needed. Then an inner doorway opened and Barak appeared. He
looked around quickly, then approached. 'I'll have to be quick, but I
wanted to tell you the jury's gone out. How did it go?'

'We did as well as we could,' I answered neutrally.

Taking my meaning, Chawry gave Isabella a sympathetic glance. She was looking at Barak, puzzled. 'A friend,' I said.

'I thought the jury would take longer,' Isabella said, 'with all the other cases to hear as well as John's.'

'Your husband was given extra time, because it was such a —' I hesitated — 'controversial case.' I meant scandalous, likely to attract publicity. 'The jury won't be out long,' Barak added. 'The judges like to get on with things. No food or water until they come to a verdict.'

She smiled. 'Thank you for coming to tell us.'

Barak nodded and disappeared through the door again.

It was another half-hour before the tipstaff called us into court. When we stood up Isabella faltered. Chawry took her arm.

In the courtroom the jurymen were assembled in their box. Boleyn sat with the other prisoners, looking pale. Many on the public benches were staring at him; the two men I had seen writing earlier sat with poised quills. I saw Southwell and Flowerdew sitting together.

Gatchet banged his gavel and turned to the jury. 'First case, Boleyn. Master foreman, do you find the prisoner innocent or guilty of murder?'

There was a loud, clear answer. 'Guilty.'

I had feared Isabella might faint, but it was her husband who suddenly fell down, hitting the floor with a thud, his chains clanking. The gaoler bent to haul him back to his feet.

Gatchet looked at him implacably. 'John Boleyn, you have been found guilty of one of the most heinous murders I have ever encountered. I sentence you to be hanged by the neck till you are dead, at nine o'clock tomorrow.'

✝

BOLEYN WAS PUT BACK on the bench, the colour beginning to return to his face. He looked at Isabella and managed a little smile. Already Gatchet had proceeded to ask the verdict on another case, a ragged, red-faced man in his forties, known as a drunken beggar, who had stolen a dozen bottles of wine. He, too, was sentenced to death. Nicholas touched me urgently on the arm. 'The pardon. Take it to Barak.'

I came to myself. 'Yes. I must hand it to the judge. Reynberd will be better. I will see if Barak can help me.'

Isabella grasped my arm with both hands, a pleading look in her eyes. I whispered, 'With the Lady Elizabeth's signature, he must postpone the sentence, I'm almost certain.' A third person, a servant girl of fourteen who had run away with some of her employer's clothes, was found not guilty of felony theft, the jury valuing the goods at less than a shilling. Gatchet glared at them, but this was the type of case where juries could be merciful.

We went outside. I told Chawry to take Isabella back to her inn, asking Toby to accompany them lest they were bothered by pamphleteers seeking statements – the two writers had hurried outside once Boleyn's sentence was pronounced. 'Nicholas, come with me.'

Just then the door to the court opened and Southwell and Flowerdew came out. Flowerdew nodded to me. 'My commiserations, Serjeant Shardlake,' he said with a halfdisguised smirk.

'Thank you,' I answered coldly.

'Boleyn's lands are forfeit to the King now, under my management as agent of the escheator, Sir Henry Mynne. That serving woman will have to leave his house.' He looked at me coldly. 'I hope as Boleyn's representative you can facilitate that.'

Southwell added, looking down at me with his steady, unblinking gaze under those halfclosed eyelids, 'And I, as agent of the feodary, am responsible for those boys' wardship.' He smiled threateningly. 'I hope we can arrange things smoothly. I understand their grandfather may want to buy the wardship. I'm sure I can negotiate a price on behalf of the King.'

I took a deep breath. 'Gentlemen,' I said, 'you are, I fear, being a little previous. I shall be applying for a pardon. On behalf of the Lady Elizabeth. Now.'

Flowerdew looked taken aback. Southwell's face darkened and his eyes opened wide. 'She can't do that –'

'She can, and has, Sir Richard.' Remembering that Southwell himself had been pardoned for a murder by the old king, I was happy to add, 'There are precedents. Excuse us, gentlemen.' Southwell looked at me in outrage. I bowed quickly, knocked on the adjacent door which Barak had used, and passed through.

✝

WE FOUND OURSELVES in a large office where half a dozen clerks were working on papers, Barak among them. The others gave me hostile glances, but Barak came across.

'Guilty?' he asked quietly.

'I fear so.'

'I thought that jury didn't look sympathetic. Where's that poor woman?'

'I sent her back to her inn.'

'She's desperate,' Nicholas added sadly. 'Boleyn will go back to his cell now, I suppose?'

'Yes, until the entertainment tomorrow.'

'I have the application for the pardon. I thought it would be better given to Reynberd.'

Barak nodded. 'He's on civil cases now; you'll have to wait till he breaks for lunch. Probably an hour or so.'

I looked at the other clerks, still giving us hostile looks. One in particular, a tall, thin fellow, stared at us fixedly. I bent closer to Barak. 'Should I not have come in here?'

'Can't be helped,' he answered with a shrug. 'Come, I'll show you where to wait.'

He led us into another, windowless corridor which ended at a large door. There was a bench outside. 'That's his chambers. Wait there.'

Nicholas said, 'We were stopped earlier by Southwell and Flowerdew. Came at us like a couple of crows at a corpse.' He smiled. 'You should have seen their faces when Master Shardlake told them about the pardon application.'

'Southwell works for the Lady Mary,' I said. 'She will not be pleased to hear this. The sooner we get the application in to the judge, the better.'

We sat there some time after Barak returned to the clerks' office; the corridor was quiet after the courtroom bustle. We heard the occasional opening and closing of doors, and once a distant, anguished scream, probably from Gatchet's courtroom as someone else was sentenced to death. Nicholas shook his head. 'So these are criminal trials. It's like the anteroom to hell.'

A door opened, some distance up the corridor, and two men came out. From their dress they looked like senior officials rather than court-room staff. They stood talking in low voices. One said, 'Our agent says today's just a local ruffle, the main action's coming elsewhere, and not yet.'

'There's been some familiar faces seen, one or two from Kent. But no firm word of anything.'

'Keep the information coming. Southwell's on my back.'

The other man glanced round and, seeing us, put an arm on the other's shoulder. They walked away down the corridor.

'What was that about?' Nicholas asked.

'I don't know.' But my mind went back to that evening at the Blue Boar: Edward Brown, Michael Vowell and the man called Miles, who seemed like a soldier, talking of something happening on the twentieth of June. Today.

Footsteps sounded from the opposite direction. Judge Reynberd appeared, robe billowing around his plump form, the tall, thin clerk who had glared at us in the office following with a pile of papers. We rose and bowed. Reynberd gave a half-smile. Unexpectedly, he did not look surprised to see us. 'Serjeant Shardlake. The lawyer with all the hearsay.' His tone was jocular, but his eyes were sharp and hard. He looked at Nicholas. 'Who is this?'

'My assistant, Master Overton.'

He turned to the clerk. 'Unlock the door, Arden, put those papers on the table, then go and do what I told you.'

When he was gone, Reynberd ushered us in. He shrugged off his red fur-lined robe, revealing a silk doublet and ruffled collar, then sat behind the desk, kicking off his shoes. 'God's blood, I'm hot.' He smiled, showing grey teeth with several gaps. 'I thought you might be here,' he said.

'You did, my Lord?' Nicholas and I exchanged a puzzled look.

'Oh yes. More of that in a moment. Now, what have you to say to me?'

I took a deep breath. 'The Lady Elizabeth wishes to request a pardon for Master Boleyn.' I pulled the request from my pocket, and handed it over. Reynberd studied the document, raised his eyebrows in surprise, then laid it on his desk.

'Well, well,' he said. 'I did not expect she would go that far. I guessed she was behind your presence – few have the resources to employ a serjeant-at-law and an assistant. You made the best of a poor case, I suppose. Apart from calling that half-witted boy, perhaps.' He laughed throatily, then leaned forward and spoke, in a menacingly quiet voice. 'I take it there will be no argument that this trial was not fairly and properly conducted. We went to great lengths to ensure it was, given the publicity that must follow.'

I hesitated. 'I make no complaint, my Lord.'

Reynberd shrugged. 'Boleyn was arrested over a month ago. If you only got here last week, that's not my fault.' He continued, 'Any word, or hint that this trial was not properly conducted will go ill for you.'

'That is not my intention, my Lord. The Lady Elizabeth asks her brother the King for a pardon under the Royal Prerogative; that is all.'

He gave me his unpleasant smile again. 'Well, I do not know what the Protector will say about the Lady Elizabeth involving herself in scandal. Again. In Mary's country, too. However,' he picked up the request and tapped it on the desk, 'as you will know, all requests for a pardon have to be approved by the judge. Some I do not allow to go forward but, where money and influence are concerned – what can I do?' He smiled again. 'The people will be disappointed when they do not see Boleyn hang tomorrow.'

I did not comment. He asked, 'What about you, will you scurry back to London now?'

'In a few days, probably.'

He nodded. 'Well, I have someone you can take with you.' He shouted suddenly, making us jump. 'Arden!'

The door opened and the clerk entered. Behind him came Barak, his face set and angry. His artificial hand had been removed, and his right sleeve hung empty. Reynberd looked at it and raised his eyebrows. Arden said, 'There was a knife on the end of it. Weapons should not be brought into your Lordship's presence.'

Arden took a position by the door. Reynberd looked at Barak and smiled again, wolfishly. 'So, we have a cuckoo in the nest, a clerk who does favours for particular clients. That is not allowed.'

I stared at him. In every court in England clerks were bribed to move applications along or delay them, to get inside information. Officially prohibited, it was as much part of the system as the tipstaff's stick and the judges' robes. Nonetheless, Reynberd shook his head disapprovingly, while Barak stood wordless, his lips set in a thin line. Reynberd turned to me.

'When Master Barak came to work as an Assize clerk two years ago, he came with an interesting record. Years working in a somewhat vague capacity for Thomas Cromwell, then several more years working for you. Made him a very useful man to chase up reluctant jurors, sound out local opinion in the taverns before the Assizes, as well as the usual shuffling of papers. But his repeated lodging of applications for sureties for witnesses in this case puzzled the chief clerk here, as did the way he brought you here this morning. Serjeant Shardlake, you have been suborning court staff to act in your favour.'

'I have done no more than anyone else, my Lord. Nor has Barak. And no money passed.'

'Nonetheless, it is an infraction of the rules, and cannot be tolerated.' He nodded at Arden. 'A record will be made; I hope it does not become necessary to forward it to the Protector when he considers the pardon application.' He smiled again, raising his eyebrows.

I realized he wanted something to hold over me, in case I did make any criticism of the trial. He turned his gaze to Barak and spoke, briefly and coldly. 'Naturally, you are dismissed from Assize service.'

I feared an outburst from Barak, but he merely smiled at Reynberd. 'All right,' he said casually. 'I've had enough of this nonsense anyway.' He raised his empty sleeve. 'Can I have my hand back before I go? It helps with spearing ugly fat red gobbets of meat on my plate.'

Reynberd gave him a long, hard look. 'Get out,' he snapped.

Barak gave a slight, mocking bow, and left the room. Nicholas, normally respectful, burst out, 'That was not necessary.'

Reynberd raised his eyebrows. 'Not necessary what, boy?' He stared him down.

Nicholas bit his lip. 'My Lord.'

'That's better. Now, I must get on with preparing the order cancelling Boleyn's execution. Come and collect it at eight tomorrow morning. For now, be gone.' When we reached the door he said, 'And Serjeant Shardlake —'

I turned. 'My Lord?'

'I should leave Norwich soon. You have made enemies.'

☦

BARAK WAS WAITING for us outside the Shire Hall, leaning against the wall in the sun, his artificial hand strapped back on, looking down Castle Hill at the spires of Norwich. He gave us a wry smile. 'Well, that's that,' he said.

'I am so sorry. Reynberd wanted something to hold over me.'

'I guessed that. Don't be sorry, I told you I was sick of it.' He looked down over the city again. 'Tamasin won't be pleased, though. My ears will be ringing for months.' He grinned. 'Better not tell her you were involved, eh?'

'Jack, let me make some recompense —'

He shook his head. 'The work I've got with the London solicitors will keep me going.' He sighed. 'Where's Toby?'

'He has taken Isabella back to her inn.'

'Tell you what,' Barak said. He spoke evenly, but he had a slightly wild look in his eyes which I recognized, and which worried me. 'Let's get some lunch, then meet up and go over the case.' He clapped Nicholas on the shoulder. 'Just like old times, eh, lad?'

I ran a hand through my hair, then looked at the great bulk of the castle rising over the Shire Hall. 'I have to see John Boleyn, tell him about the pardon. Then I must write to the Lady Elizabeth and Master Parry immediately, tell them it has come to the worst. Let us meet later, say for dinner at the Maid's Head.'

Barak nodded. 'All right. Just you and me for lunch then, Nick.'

I said, 'Should you not leave Norwich now, get back to London?'

'I'm paid up at the Blue Boar till Sunday. Then I'm supposed to be away another week, at the Suffolk Assizes; I'm not keen to get back to London early to face the music.'

He turned away, began walking down the path. 'I'm sorry,' I called after him. Without turning, he raised his good hand in acknowledgement. I grasped Nicholas's arm, and whispered, 'Watch how much he drinks. I see danger signs.'

Nicholas nodded, then followed Barak down the sunlit path. I began walking to the main door of the castle.

Chapter Thirty

I SABELLA WAS WITH BOLEYN in his cell. She had preferred to go there instead of back to the inn with Chawry. They sat side by side on the bed, holding hands. When the gaoler let me in, they looked up with faces filled with hope and fear.

I smiled. 'The execution is stayed pending the application for the pardon. Reynberd agreed, and the document is being drawn up.' Their faces sagged with relief and they hugged each other.

'Thank you, Master Shardlake,' Boleyn said in heartfelt tones. 'I thought I was done for, especially when I lost my temper with that judge.'

Isabella defended him. 'But it wasn't right, attacking us for living together as he did. It had nothing to do with the case.'

'You are right, but judges on Assize like to read a moral lesson. Especially ones like Gatchet.' I looked at Boleyn. 'It did not help to show such a temper.'

'I was provoked beyond endurance.'

'Well, apart from that, you did well. I'm only sorry the twins could not be shaken about the key, and that Scambler made an exhibition of himself.'

Isabella smiled. 'Poor Simon.' She was the only person apart from me who had referred to him by his true name.

A despairing wail became faintly audible through the thick walls. One of those sentenced to hang on the morrow. Boleyn shook his head. 'It was dreadful, sitting with those other people, listening to their cases. Three were found guilty of theft and will be executed. How Gatchet hurried through their cases, condemned them as sinful though they were poor people without work. I have always taken such things as natural but' – he shook his head – 'how they stank; some have been months in this place. And I was found guilty too, but am saved because of my connection to the Lady Elizabeth.'

Isabella took his arm. 'But you are innocent, my love.'

I looked at him seriously. 'I am afraid you may be here some time. Palms will have to be greased at the royal court, and getting the Protec⁄tor to deal with the pardon may take time. And the outcome is not a certainty. But I have great hope.' I thought, I will ask Parry to write to William Cecil.

Boleyn looked downcast, but Isabella said encouragingly, 'I can visit you, bring food – can I not, Master Shardlake? And Daniel will take care of the farm.'

'Yes, your treatment should be less severe now.'

Boleyn looked at Isabella. 'You will need more money if I am to be here for a very long time. My finances are not – what they were.' He looked into space gloomily for a moment. 'I think it is time for Mid⁄night to be sold. Chawry can handle him now, you said?'

'Just about, if he is careful. But you will want to ride Midnight when you return –'

Boleyn shook his head. 'I shall never return to Brikewell. Even if I am pardoned, the disgrace will remain. And –' he sighed – 'I am not sure I want to. Do you, my dear?'

She considered. 'No, not after all that has been done to us.'

'We could move to London perhaps.'

'But you said the house there was too expensive to keep up.'

'Then we shall sell it, and, yes, the Brikewell estate and my other lands, pay off my debts and buy somewhere smaller in London, or elsewhere, if you prefer. We shall live quietly as modest gentlefolk.'

Isabella sighed. 'Married again, in a place where nobody knows our history. Yes, that I should like.'

Boleyn looked at me. 'I imagine I will not be able to buy or sell any land until the pardon is granted?'

'No. For the moment you are in a sort of legal limbo. Legally, you should not even sell the horse.'

Boleyn laid a hand on Isabella's and smiled gently. 'Have Midnight sold quickly and quietly, for next to nothing if need be. When he is gone, go to the back of the stable. Count four bricks up from the floor and twelve along from the right. Remove the bricks and mortar and you will find the twenty sovereigns. Nobody knows that but Master Shardlake.'

He sighed. 'I shall miss Midnight. I got him as a yearling, Master Shardlake; he was hard to control even then, but by good treatment I managed it. But now he must go.'

Isabella touched his cheek. 'You are good to me.'

'I have brought you naught but trouble.'

I said, 'Well, we have a good chance now. I will fetch the order cancelling the execution tomorrow morning. I shall visit you again then.'

'You will return to London soon?' Isabella asked, sadness in her voice.

'Yes, but I shall keep closely in touch by letter. Now, I must go and prepare a letter to the Lady Elizabeth, ready to send to her with the judge's order tomorrow morning.' I looked at Boleyn. 'I am sorry you lost the case, but it was always going to be difficult.' I paused, then said, 'An alibi for the evening of Edith's murder might well have decided things the other way.' Isabella looked between us, frowning slightly. Boleyn only said, 'That is all done with now.' But I caught the note of tetchiness in his voice.

☩

I WALKED BACK TO the Maid's Head. It was midday, the summer sun hot. I had walked rather than ridden in Norwich; riding around the city would have been difficult in the crowded, narrow streets, and walking was easier on my back, though as I entered Tombland the muscle between my shoulder blades was hurting again. I wondered how Barak was faring; I felt deeply that I had let him down again.

I went to my room, and there prepared letters to the Lady Elizabeth and Parry, writing several drafts. In the end I decided on short, near-identical missives where I explained that Boleyn had been found guilty despite our best efforts, but my application for a pardon had been approved and a stay of execution granted. In the letter to Parry I added that I much regretted the verdict, and the adverse publicity that must follow, but the pardon application was my only option given my instructions. I advised him to get in touch with Cecil. I shook my head as I sanded the letters before going down to order a fast post-rider to Hatfield. Elizabeth would be angry at the verdict, and Parry furious about publicity in the country, and at the royal court, when the pardon request was presented. I had little doubt that both of them would make their displeasure known.

✝

I WAS TIRED – I seemed to tire easily these days – and slept for a couple of hours until a servant arrived to tell me that Nicholas was back, with the two 'goodmen' who assisted us. It was still early for dinner, so I asked him to send them up.

Nicholas looked quite fresh, his pale skin a little sunburned, and he told me he and Barak had taken a walk up on Mousehold Heath after lunch – 'a healthful place, the winds fresh'. I guessed he had taken Barak there to ensure that he did not get drunk. 'Full of tussocky grass that snags your legs though,' Barak added. He looked quite cheerful, but there was still that hard, too-bright look in his eyes. Toby looked tired. I told him the pardon request had gone in. He said quietly, 'Master Shardlake, after dinner I would like to go back to my parents' farm to stay. I am sorry the case was lost, but with the pardon lodged, there is little more I can do. If there is anything you or Master Copuldyke need, perhaps you could write to me.' Given all the work we had done together, his manner remained unemotional, a little distant. But he would be preoccupied with the farm, and his mother's illness.

'Of course, Toby. Thank you for all the help you have given.'

'Stay for dinner, though,' Barak said. He looked at me. 'Meanwhile, I wouldn't mind going over the case again, now it's over.'

Nicholas spoke seriously. 'After all, we still do not know who murdered Edith Boleyn.'

I said, 'A good idea. Will you stay, Toby?'

'I do not think we can penetrate the mystery now. But yes, I will stay.'

I pulled out the table which stood by the window, we brought up chairs, and I fetched out paper and ink to take notes. A spasm went through my back as I sat.

'All right?' Barak asked.

'Yes,' I answered impatiently.

'Well,' Nicholas began, 'it seems pretty much established that the deed was done by two men. Both probably strong, and with knowledge of Brikewell.'

Toby said, 'If only you could find that boy Walter, and identify who came into Snockstobe's shop. I've little doubt he can see as well as any of us. But he is in the wind.' I noticed how 'we' had become 'you'. It saddened me a little.

'Well,' Barak said, 'at least we know who stole the key. The twins. Two strong young men.' He looked at me. 'Are you really sure it isn't them? They're as mad as two rabid dogs.'

'Are they?' Nicholas asked. 'Mad, or just malign?'

'Good point,' I agreed. 'I've seen a fair amount of them now, and I just don't think they'd murder their mother, though of course it can't be ruled out. And think, their relations with their father may have been very bad, but he still got them to lead the resistance to Witherington's attempt to occupy the disputed lands earlier this year. Now they want him dead. I think that means they believe he killed her.'

Toby shook his head. 'Remember the story of how Barnabas got that scar. The twins as children, drawing lots to see who would scar whose face, so that their mother would stop complaining that she could not tell them apart. They're mad.'

'Does that not show they wanted her love?' I answered.

Barak looked at me. 'When they did not get it, love could have turned to hate. And they gain from their father's death. If Southwell agrees to make them wards of their grandfather, and the Protector agrees to return their lands to them, as often happens, they would get the estate. They'll get rid of Isabella, and sell the estate. To Southwell, perhaps, in exchange for his cooperation over the wardship.'

'Reynolds could pay Southwell for the wardship, and though the money goes to the King, he will cream off a good profit. And from what I hear, he is a man who much likes profit.'

Toby said, 'He's already been pardoned for a murder once, and he's a powerful man.'

'I know. Secretary Cecil warned me off him. He could benefit financially from using Brikewell to join his estates together. And from what I've seen of him, I can imagine him capable of anything.'

'And then there's Flowerdew,' Nicholas added. 'He'll have charge of the wardship, and if the twins are to seek to get them back perhaps palms will be greased there too.'

'I wish we could shake the twins' alibi for the night of the murder,' Toby said.

'Who gave them that alibi? Their group of trouble-loving gentlemen friends. Including John Atkinson, whom Richard Southwell aided when he abducted that poor girl from Mousehold Heath last year. Perhaps they were never at the cockfight that night.'

Nicholas said, 'But there would have been dozens there.'

'He only needed enough *respectable* young gentlemen to provide alibis.'

I shook my head. 'If they weren't there, that would lay the twins and their friends open to blackmail from anyone who was.'

Toby's voice became impatient. 'You don't know Norwich, you don't know how scared people are of the Boleyn twins. And of Southwell.'

Barak said thoughtfully, 'Interesting that John Boleyn's steward, Chawry, was there the night the key vanished.'

'It is,' I agreed. 'But the twins answered his allegations about the key well. I expect their grandfather briefed them.' I leaned forward. 'Well, I agree we certainly can't exclude the twins.' I wrote down and circled, *Gerald and Barnabas Boleyn*, then drew a wavy line to *John Atkinson and their friends*. They were not suspects, but could have provided a false alibi. I drew another wavy line connecting them to *Sir Richard South-well*. Then I wrote, *John Flowerdew*. I considered, then said, 'Let us assume, for the moment, that the twins told the truth, and that the key was stolen from them. That could have been done by another of South-well's lads on his behalf — but there is also the possibility that it was stolen overnight, by their grandfather or someone in his household.'

'That old man?' Nicholas asked. 'He's well into his sixties, and has to walk with a stick. I can't see him killing his daughter and putting her into the stream, even with help.'

'He has a motive,' Barak said. 'He hates John Boleyn and Isabella, would love to see John hanged and the estate go to the twins. He could have someone in his household do his dirty business.'

'Yes,' Nicholas agreed. 'It's possible. If only the steward Vowell had not gone; he must know the household inside out.'

I did not answer. I had missed the possibility of speaking to Vowell when I saw him talking with Josephine's husband and the man Miles. Instead I said, 'That whole family is the oddest I have ever encountered, and I've come across a few. The grandfather is a brute, who turned Edith away when she came to him in trouble, the grandmother racked with sorrow for her daughter —'

Nicholas looked at me. 'What were those words she muttered in court?'

'"Edith, God save you, I wanted a boy!"'

Barak laughed uneasily, 'You're not saying *she* killed her daughter?'

I said, 'Perhaps she only meant that a boy would have had an easier life in that household. I saw the old man shove a woman aside in the Shire Hall. And the twins seem to see all women as fair game.'

Nicholas nodded. 'Their grandfather appears to encourage them.'

Toby said, 'But there was malice in Edith as well.' He looked around at us. 'She didn't deserve to be brutally murdered but she treated people badly, too. Perhaps there is something in the family blood.'

I said, 'Certainly there was a strangeness and hostility in her.' I drew more circles, round the names *Gawen Reynolds*, *Jane Reynolds*, *Reynolds household*. Then another connecting line from the key to *Snockstobe* and, separately, the name of the boy who could still throw light on the mystery, *Walter the apprentice*. I pushed the paper to the centre of the table for the others to look at. Nicholas said, 'So much depends on the key being stolen. But the central evidence there comes from Walter.'

'It does. But we're not quite finished.' I drew another circle, round the name *Leonard Witherington*. 'His neighbour, who hated him and wanted part of his land. And, but for the pardon, could now buy it all.'

Nicholas said, 'I doubt he'd stand up to Southwell, if he wanted the land too. And frankly, he struck me as too stupid to get involved in such a plan.'

Toby shook his head. 'We saw how he treated the tenants when they were trying to clear the doves off their crops at Brikewell. And I'm sure he intimidated that shepherd.'

'I agree with Nicholas,' I said. 'He seems too stupid to be involved. But we should add him to the list.'

Nicholas coughed. He had reddened slightly. 'I don't like to complicate things, but –'

'Spit it out, lad,' Barak said encouragingly.

'There is another man who might have an interest in seeing Boleyn dead.' We all looked at him. 'Daniel Chawry, Boleyn's steward.'

Toby looked at him, puzzled. 'But what does he stand to gain?'

Nicholas answered, 'Isabella.'

There was a moment's silence, then Toby burst out laughing. 'Isabella? God's death, boy, I could see she makes you hot, and she's a fine buxom woman, even though she does run her mouth off more than a woman should, but anyone can see she's devoted to her husband. Christ's wounds, he even proposed to her in court and she accepted him!'

I remembered how Chawry had looked upset at that. Nicholas said quietly, 'Even if she does not love him, *he* could be blind with love for her. And they are from the same class.'

Toby laughed again. To prevent yet another argument between the two I said, 'I think Chawry is perhaps in love with Isabella, and possibly she even knows and uses it. But she loves John Boleyn.' I looked at Barak. 'What do you think, Jack?'

'I can't see Chawry as the murderer, but it's possible. It's even possible it was he who took the opportunity to make an impression of the key. I suppose both their names should go on the list.'

I nodded, then said heavily, 'And there is one more who has no alibi.' I wrote down, *John Boleyn.*

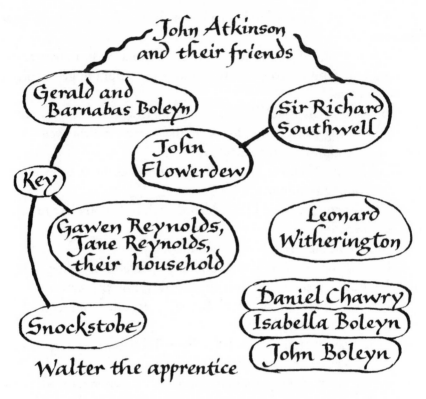

John Atkinson
and their friends

Gerald and
Barnabas Boleyn

Sir Richard
Southwell

John
Flowerdew

Key

Leonard
Witherington

Gawen Reynolds,
Jane Reynolds,
their household

Daniel Chawry

Isabella Boleyn

Snockstobe

John Boleyn

Walter the apprentice

We looked at the list. Gerald and Barnabas Boleyn. Gawen and
Jane Reynolds and members of their household. Leonard Witherington. John Flowerdew. Sir Richard Southwell. Daniel Chawry and
Isabella Boleyn, and finally John Boleyn. Ten names. It seemed a more
hopeless task than ever. I looked at Toby, who was frowning slightly at
Nicholas. I said, 'Toby, you have done a great deal for us, and been
injured in the process. We appreciate it greatly. May I ask one more
thing? When we have left, could you try to trace the apprentice and the
steward Michael Vowell, who could tell us more about the household?
Perhaps you could get Walter's surname from the locksmiths' guild, see
if you could trace him.'

He stroked his beard, and looked at me. 'The apprentice may be
possible, through the locksmiths' guild, as you suggest. As for Vowell,
I can only put the word around.' He sounded reluctant. 'But does it
matter now, with the pardon coming?'

'There is a possibility the application may not succeed. And surely it would be good to find Edith's real murderer, and clear Boleyn's name.'

'The killer may have murdered Snockstobe as well,' Barak added.

Toby looked at me. 'Will Master Copuldyke agree?'

'Whether he does or no, I guarantee to pay you.'

He stroked his dark beard, then looked at me with something like admiration. 'I think, sir, that you are the most persistent lawyer I have met. Yes, I will do as you ask. For now my mother and the coming harvest must take priority, but subject to that I will do what I can.'

'I thank you.' I reached out and shook his hand. 'I will give you a formal letter of engagement. Write to me any time at Lincoln's Inn.'

We sat back, silent. Then Nicholas spoke quietly. 'Where was Edith, those nine years?'

'Not in Norwich, I'm sure,' Toby said. 'Nobody saw her. Unless she was hidden in a cellar somewhere.'

It was an uncomfortable thought. Barak said, 'If she wasn't in Norwich, where was she? And was she a guest, or a prisoner?'

'And how did she end up in—'

I kicked Nicholas under the table, before he could utter the name 'Hatfield'. That was one secret we had kept and must continue to keep, or the pamphleteers would have an even richer tale to tell. I said, 'Come, if Toby is to ride back to his farm, we should go down for dinner.'

We left the room and walked down the broad staircase. Tonight I would try again to persuade Barak to return to London with Nicholas and me, and tomorrow I would tell the Maid's Head innkeeper, doubt-less to his relief, that we would be leaving on Saturday. I looked at my three companions, sad to think that this was probably the last time we should all meet together. As we walked across the stone-flagged hall to the dining room, I heard two merchants talking angrily about rioting at a place called Attleborough, where the local peasantry had thrown down the fences keeping in the sheep of the local landlord.

✝

THE NEXT MORNING, the twenty-first of June, Nicholas and I once more walked down to the castle, to fetch the document approving the cancellation of the execution. The previous evening Barak had reluctantly agreed to come back to London with us, and to face Tamasin with the news that he had lost his lucrative post. Today was Friday; the criminal cases at the Assizes were over but the civil cases would continue today, the judges moving on to Suffolk tomorrow. We were in sombre mood as we walked through Tombland. It was hot again, and we had left off our lawyers' robes; we did not need to impress anyone any more. Nicholas though, as usual, wore his sword at his hip.

'At least you will see Beatrice in a few days,' I said to him. He had written a letter for the post-rider to take, saying he was returning.

'Yes, and this new young man who is courting her.'

'As I said before, she is probably teasing you, to whet your interest.'

'She would not be so cruel.' Yet he sounded less definite than before.

I said, 'You did well last night, saying Chawry belongs on our list of suspects. And agreeing Isabella does too.'

'Why was that doing well?'

I smiled. 'Because you so clearly like her. But your analytical skills as a lawyer prevailed over your emotional attachments. We'll make a serjeant of you yet.'

He smiled, pleased at the compliment.

'I have booked the horses for nine tomorrow. I thought this afternoon we might visit Josephine and Edward again.'

'Yes. Though I hope Edward does not go on this time about the condition of the people; he is almost as fierce as Toby.'

I remembered Edward sitting with Michael Vowell and the man Miles that evening at the Blue Boar, and forbore to say, perhaps he is fiercer.

We made our way through Upper Goat Lane to the marketplace. Passing along the side of the Guildhall, we heard a hum of voices, and saw that those found guilty of felonies during the Assizes were about to be hanged – slowly and agonizingly, on Judge Gatchet's orders. A crowd of about a hundred had assembled in front of the

Guildhall. The wooden structure we had seen being erected a few days before was complete, a wide raised platform with steps leading up, and four gallows from which thick ropes dangled, nooses at the end. The executioner, a powerfully built man in a white shirt with grey hair and a hard, square face, was pulling at the nooses, testing their strength with professional expertise. Half a dozen soldiers with halberds stood in front of the scaffold, facing the crowd, which pressed close. The executioner's assistant, a young man in his twenties, pulled a lever, causing the front section of the boarding, under the nooses, to fall with a crash. He pushed the lever back and the boarding rose into place again. He nodded with satisfaction.

At the bottom of the market square three high-sided carts appeared, drawn by horses. More soldiers from the castle walked alongside. Another walked ahead, beating a drum.

I had seen such carts in London many times, making their way to Tyburn. Nicholas nudged me. 'Look there,' he said. The crowd were mostly poor folk of both sexes, come to see the spectacle, though a number of weeping relatives were being comforted by friends. Two relatives, however, were not weeping. Gerald and Barnabas Boleyn stood with half a dozen other expensively dressed young men, among whom I recognized John Atkinson. They were talking lightly. The rest of the crowd left a space around them. 'Brutes,' Nicholas said in disgust. 'Come to see their father hang. They mustn't know about the pardon.'

'Reynberd can't have made it public.' I looked at them; in court they had threatened to come and see their father hanged, but I confess I was shocked to see them actually do it.

'Short drop,' a man said to his wife. 'Some of them should make a fine dance.'

'I don't want to see this.' Nicholas turned away.

I, though, stood rooted to the spot. For the carts had reached the top of the marketplace, outside the Guildhall, and halted. Four people from the first were being brought down by the soldiers. Their arms were bound tightly to their sides. I recognized them from the day before; the wild-haired girl, a rag doll clutched in one hand, the red-faced man who had stolen wine, and who, from the difficulty the soldiers had in getting him down, had been allowed to get drunk this morning, and the starveling old man who had stolen loaves of bread, shaking with fear. And last, his eyes wide with terror, came one who wore a brightly dyed doublet and shirt instead of the well-worn clothes of the poor: John Boleyn. I clutched Nicholas's arm so tightly he cried out. He followed my gaze. 'Jesus Christ!'

Boleyn shrieked, 'I have a stay of execution!' He struggled against the two soldiers holding him. 'Approved by the judge!'

'And I'm the queen of France!' one answered. 'Come on, the others an't makin' any trouble!'

The other three prisoners were walking quietly to the scaffold, the drunk man swaying slightly, the woman clutching her rag doll tightly in one bound hand, bending her head to look at it. They were almost at the steps now. People laughed at the exchange between the soldier and Boleyn, though the twins' faces wore expressions of contempt. Boleyn, looking frantically over the crowd, saw Nicholas and me and shouted, 'Help me! Help me!'

'Death to all murderers!' someone shouted out. Two voices called as one, 'Die like a man!' I realized it was the twins.

'We have to stop this!' I shouted, and barged through the crowd, Nicholas at my heels. The condemned were mounting the steps. The old man, his shaking now uncontrollable, began to weep. I made to follow them up the steps, but a soldier blocked my path, his halberd pointed at my face. 'What the fuck d'you think you're doing? D'you want hanging, too?'

'John Boleyn does have a stay of execution!' I shouted. 'I'm his lawyer! It was granted by Judge Reynberd yesterday!'

Another soldier pointed his weapon at Nicholas. 'How do I know you're lawyers?'

Two voices from the crowd shouted, 'They ain't lawyers!' The twins.

'Hang them too!' another voice called. 'Death to all gentlemen!' There was a general cheer. The crowd, uncomfortably close, was becoming restive.

I looked up. A soldier set each prisoner in front of a noose. The drunk man, appearing suddenly to realize where he was, tried to step back, shrieking, 'No! No!'

The soldier beside me said threateningly, 'Where's this fucking pardon, then?'

'At the castle! We were on our way to fetch it! A copy should have gone to the castle constable. For pity's sake, let us talk to the executioner!'

'So no paper, then?'

'No, but—'

On the scaffold the executioner had already placed the noose over the head of the old man and tightened it. He watched me expression-lessly, but on hearing there was no paper, he moved the young woman's head into the second noose. Then he did the same to John Boleyn and finally the struggling drunk. Boleyn shouted, 'That's my lawyer, I'm innocent!' The young woman, even with the noose round her neck, bent round to look at her doll. 'Milly, little Milly,' she muttered. The old man shook silently.

'Let us up!' Nicholas shouted. He leaned forward and grabbed the soldier's halberd with one hand, while with the other he began unsheathing his sword, leaving me momentarily free to run to the steps. 'Master Shardlake!' Boleyn yelled. The executioner frowned and nodded urgently to his assistant. He pulled the lever. The board dropped.

There was a roar from the crowd as all four prisoners fell, though only a few inches. The old man was instantly still, but the man next to Boleyn, his protests choked off, jerked wildly with his feet, instinctively trying to find a footing to halt his strangulation, eyes bulging, foam at his lips. The young woman, too, danced frantically on air. The front of her dress darkened as she wet herself, and the doll dropped from her fingers to land on the ground below. Someone instantly grabbed it up as a souvenir. Boleyn, though, did not dance, only jerked convulsively from side to side as his face grew purple, his tongue protruding.

I reached the top of the steps. The executioner stood in front of me, his solid form barring my way. 'There *is* a pardon,' I shouted. 'For pity's sake, before it's too late!'

An elderly woman had struggled to the front of the crowd. She stood at the foot of the steps and raised clasped hands in a begging gesture at the executioner. 'My husband! My husband! Please, please, let me pull at his legs and end his agony!' Looking past the other, swinging, dancing, ghastly forms I saw the old man was not dead after all, he had begun to writhe in silent agony.

I do not know where I got the strength from to push the executioner away. I ran past the woman, whose frantic dancing jerks made her legs rise higher and higher, nearly kicking me on the arm. Then I reached Boleyn, whose eyes were clenched tight shut now, tears pouring from them. His protruding tongue was now blue. I grabbed him round the waist, heaving upwards with all my strength. My back spasmed agonizingly. I heard the crowd booing loudly. Then Nicholas was at my side, also holding Boleyn up to try and stop the strangling. Then I felt strong hands grasp my arms. I stumbled and fell backwards, off the edge of the scaffold, into the midst of the baying crowd. I felt a terrible pain in my back, then darkness.

Part Three

WYMONDHAM

Chapter Thirty-one

I WOKE, A SUDDEN lurch out of darkness. I was lying down, and, for a terrible moment feared I was still beneath the scaffold, amid the baying crowd, Boleyn and the others strangling above me. I gasped and tried to move, but a terrible pain shot across my back, and I cried out. Then I felt a cool cloth on my head and heard a familiar female voice say, gently, 'Do not move, Master Shardlake. The doctor said when you wake you must remain still.' I blinked, and saw I was in my bed at the Maid's Head, Josephine standing above me with an expression of deep concern on her face. 'You are safe,' she said softly.

'Boleyn –' I gasped. My mouth was parched.

'He lives,' she said with a smile. 'Now wait, I must fetch the doctor. I shall be only a few minutes. Please, stay quite still.' She hurried out. The pain of the spasm was fading and, hearing a sound beside me, I dared to turn my neck slightly. Beside the bed I saw, of all things, a light wooden carrying-crib. Lying within was a little fair-haired baby; Josephine's daughter, Mousy. She looked up at me, and suddenly gave a toothless smile and reached out her arms. I smiled back.

Josephine returned with Dr Belys, who had treated Toby after our fight with the twins, his sharp-featured face serious. With a curtsey, Josephine took up Mousy and left the room. Belys raised a hand. 'Do not move your back, or you will hurt yourself.'

Gripped with a sudden terror, I said, 'Will I be able to walk again?'

'Certainly, certainly.' He smiled. 'You were lucky, you could have broken your spine, but God must have you in his view, for you only damaged the soft tissues of your upper back. For now they are stiff as a board. But soon, if you do as I say, you should be up and about again. I examined you thoroughly while you were unconscious. Fortunately for you, I have made a specialism of bone and muscle ailments.'

'You have?'

'I like their — practicality, shall we say, compared to some of my colleagues' weird potions.'

'How long have I been unconscious?'

'Near a day. It is Saturday morning. But you have not fractured your skull, only given it a nasty jolt when you fell. There was much blood, as always with scalp wounds. The crowd thought you dead.' The doctor reached for a pitcher of small beer on the table by my bed, and made me drink slowly. Then he sat, put his hands on his knees and, looking serious, said, 'You have made yourself the talk of Norwich.'

'Josephine said Boleyn lives —'

'Yes, when the executioner pulled you away and you fell off the scaffold, your young colleague held Boleyn up, saved him from strangling. I am told Master Overton was screaming at the executioner that he had killed you, that there was a pardon, and he would end up being hanged himself.' Dr Belys looked at me seriously again. 'Had you landed slightly differently, you could have smashed your spine, and never walked again.' He let that sink in. 'The executioner took Boleyn down, and he has been returned to Norwich Castle. He cannot speak yet, and has nasty compression marks on his throat, but he is safe. His wife asked me to attend him too.'

'And the others hanging? Those still waiting in the carts?'

'All the other executions went ahead, of course.' He raised his eyebrows. 'The commons say the gentleman they had come to see hanged was saved by legal artifice, but the poor folk all died.'

'There is truth in what they say.'

He gave me a sidelong look, then changed the subject. 'You are lucky you have such good friends. Master Overton contacted Goodman Barak and Goodwife Brown, and the three of them have been taking turns to sit with you. Now, the spasms will ease, but only if you move slowly and carefully, and you must stay in bed at least a day. Tomorrow, or the day after, you may get up. I like my patients up and about as soon as possible. Meanwhile, with my approval, Master Overton has written to your doctor in London.'

'Thank you,' I said. 'I think you and Guy might like each other. Have you read Vesalius on anatomy?'

'I have a copy.'

'So does Guy. Thank you, again.'

Dr Belys smiled. 'Wait till you see my bill. Doctors charge even more than lawyers.' He hesitated. 'Two things more. I have a concoction of my own that should ease the pain, but do not take too much. Also, it would help if you were to have your back gently massaged twice a day. Goodwife Brown has offered to do that. A woman's hands are best.'

I drew in a deep breath. I found it distasteful for anyone to see my bent back, and a woman, Josephine –

Belys saw my hesitation. 'She has already agreed. And Goodman Barak or Master Overton will be present as well, to avoid any suggestion of impropriety.'

'It will help?'

'Greatly.'

'Barak, then,' I said. 'He has seen my back before.'

'Good. But for now, lie still.' He looked at me, with my lined face and prematurely white hair. 'I am told you are forty-seven.'

'I am.'

'And with your disability – are you not getting a little old for such escapades?'

✝

AFTER HE LEFT, Barak and Nicholas entered. Nicholas looked pale, troubled. I thanked him for his part in saving Boleyn. 'I don't know how I managed it,' he said seriously. 'I held him up, taking the weight of his body, those poor people kicking and choking all round me, the executioner trying to pull me off, I thought you were dead –' He broke off, shaking his head.

Barak also looked strained, but punched Nicholas lightly on the arm. 'There must be some muscle on the beanpole, after all.'

'And a good thought, Nicholas, to write to Guy.' Then I remembered, 'The letters to Parry and the Lady Elizabeth –' Without thinking, I tried to sit up, and another spasm sent me gasping.

Nicholas said, 'I sent them off as soon as I got the stay of execution

319

from the court office. They swore blind they'd sent a copy of it to the castle constable.'

Barak said, 'The constable says he never got it. I wonder what happened there. But it's too late to find out, the judges move on to Suffolk this afternoon.'

I looked at him. 'You should have been with them. I'm sorry.'

He shrugged. 'Glad to be shot of them all. Anyway, Tamasin doesn't know I'm not with them. I'll stay with you the rest of the week. You can't go back to London yet, can you?'

'Jack's sharing my room here,' Nicholas said. 'I've spoken to the innkeeper. And the doctor spoke to him, too. He's agreed to Josephine visiting – so long as there's a chaperone, and she comes by the servants' entrance. I made free with your purse, I'm afraid.'

I waved a hand gingerly. 'You have done very well.'

'Fortunately, the innkeeper is among those who think you a hero for saving a gentleman from the gallows.'

I smiled ruefully. 'Not all think so, Dr Belys says.'

'It'll be a nine days' wonder, you'll see,' Barak said.

Nicholas looked at me. 'The twins left with their friends when their father was cut down. That pair are –' He shook his head, lost for words.

'What of Isabella? Is she safe?'

'She's just gone back to Brikewell with Chawry, I saw them off this morning. She will be returning to visit her husband.'

I thought, She's gone to get rid of the horse, and to get the gold hidden in the stable. If it is still there. I leaned back with a sigh.

Barak rose. 'I'll fetch Josephine back in, shall I?' he said diffidently. 'To attend your back?'

☩

FOR TWO DAYS I stayed in bed, spending much time looking through the window at the tree and the church outside, too tired to think much due to the medicine Belys had given me to ease the pain. The weather had cooled, there was cloud and a little rain spattered on the diamond-paned windows.

At first it felt shaming to have Barak and Josephine carefully turn me over in bed, then have my nightshirt raised so that Josephine could rub in the ointment Belys had given her, richly scented with lavender. Her hands, though calloused from hard work, were gentle and dextrous. She told me her father had sometimes got her to massage his back, and Edward, too, if he had had a hard day moving stones. She said she had spoken to Edward about returning to London, and he was considering it. I asked whether her husband was happy with her doing this service for me and she replied he was; he trusted her absolutely. Most times she brought Mousy with her.

Lying there, I remembered the evening I had overheard Edward, with Vowell and the stranger called Miles, talking of a rising at Attleborough, which had indeed happened, and of further action to come. Barak told me that the Attleborough landowner, an enclosing farmer named Green, had not dared reinstate his fences and had moved his sheep away. The order for the enclosure commissioners to begin their circuits of the countryside would soon be issued, he told me, while Josephine was working on my back.

'They are needed,' Josephine said. 'Edward is right, the poor commons suffer greatly, this is not the godly Commonwealth it should be. Perhaps when the commissioners come, justice will be done, in the countryside at least.' The Josephine I had known would never have ventured an opinion, let alone a radical one, so forcefully. I wondered if her husband's opinions had become hers – or whether both had been changed by poverty.

Nicholas, who had never seen my bare back, tactfully stayed away from these sessions. I asked him to try and discover what he could about the apprentice Walter. I had given Toby the task, but did not expect him still to be in Norwich. I also dictated a statement to Nicholas, which I signed for him to lodge with the court, stating that the twins had threatened Scambler outside the court. I had a copy sent to their grandfather. That, I hoped, would make them leave the boy alone.

I asked Josephine more about what she remembered of Grace Bone and her siblings from the time she had lived near them. All three, she said, were well liked. Peter was known as a skilled man and a fair employer. While both sisters were jolly, bawdy girls, Peter was more serious, a reader and a Commonwealth man. Grace and Mercy had been in their thirties, and Josephine had wondered why neither had married. Perhaps their loudness and confidence put suitors off.

✝

By Wednesday, I was starting to walk with a stick, Barak and Nicholas at my side. I still had to move carefully to avoid spasms, but I could feel that my back was more relaxed. By Thursday, again with Nicholas or Barak to hand, I was shuffling around the room and managed carefully to straighten my back.

The next day, Nicholas came to my room bearing three letters. Two bore the seal of the Lady Elizabeth; the third was in Guy's writing.

'Those answers have come quick, within the week,' I said.

'There was one for Jack, too, from Tamasin, I think, and I have one from Beatrice. And I have a message from Isabella Boleyn; she would like to come and see you tomorrow morning. She is visiting her husband at the castle.'

'Good.' I smiled. 'By the way, I thought I might go outside later today. I feel – looser. I will take my stick, and you can accompany me. Just out to the street and back.'

Nicholas looked dubious.

'Go and read your letter from Beatrice,' I said.

I first opened the letter from Guy. His writing, once firm and clear, was now an old man's tentative scrawl.

My dear Matthew,

I have had Nicholas's letter, and was sorry to hear of your injury, and the horrible event which precipitated it. I pray for you every night. I fear I am still abed and troubled with fevers. I have had a letter from Dr Belys and have replied. I agree with his suggestions for your treatment. Get moving as soon as you can, whilst taking care. He sounds a good, practical man; I had to tell Tamasin, who still helps Francis and me, of your injury, for she brought me Nicholas's letter and recognized his writing. Please write soon and tell me how you progress.

Your loving friend,
Guy Malton

I felt a pang of conscience. Guy was obviously still sorely ill, yet here was I, again troubling him. I unsealed the letter from Parry. Its tone could not have been more different.

Serjeant Shardlake,

It was with great concern that I learned Boleyn was found guilty and the Lady's command for a pardon request had to be put in motion. I had hoped for a better outcome. There will be much publicity, and it will do the Lady no good. I fear Boleyn will have to wait a goodly time for his answer. I have it from Master Cecil that the Protector and Council are much vexed, for the rebels in the West are now besieging Exeter, and there is fresh trouble in Kent. There has also been trouble in Sussex, and the Protector has issued a pardon to the rebels there — he was ever too soft, and only encourages them. Meanwhile, the senior men of the shires have been called to attend him in London to prepare an army to go to Exeter. On top of that, the Lady Mary still refuses to follow the new service in English, and men sent to Kenninghall to argue with her got nowhere. Protector Somerset will be displeased to hear of this other event in Norfolk, and Cecil believes it politic not to show him the pardon request yet, although on behalf of the Lady I have arranged for a goodly sum to be offered in due time, to whet Somerset's palate, which ever cherished gold. I wish you to return immediately to Hatfield, so I may receive your full explanation.

Thomas Parry

I had not expected a warm response, but this was unusually sharp. And I would have to reply telling him of my injury, that I could not return for a week or more. I turned to Elizabeth's letter:

Master Shardlake,

I am much grieved to learn that despite your finding evidence casting doubt on his guilt my relative was found guilty. Master Parry tells me the pardon request is lodged, though given the current problems in the country it may be some time before it is considered. I have also ordered Master Parry that enquiry now be made around Hatfield to see whether anybody knows of a poor woman answering Edith Boleyn's description being seen around the district. If the true murderer be found, the gossiping pamphleteers Parry so fears may be silenced.

I await seeing you, and I hope again that your evidence indicating Master Boleyn's innocence can be shown to be justified.

I put the letter down. The Lady Elizabeth obviously had the bit firmly between her teeth. She would be making Parry's life difficult — hence perhaps the tone of his letter. Her final sentence also seemed to carry a veiled warning, that if I was wrong about John Boleyn, the blame might be shifted onto me. Elizabeth, I thought, is becoming a politician. I ran my hand vigorously through my white hair, until a spasm from my back made me gasp and lean helplessly back in my chair.

✟

NICHOLAS VISITED ME early in the afternoon. I was again hobbling around the room, pleased to find I could do so now without the stick. 'Come to help me walk downstairs?' I asked. Then I saw his face was troubled. 'What is it?'

'I have just come back from visiting Simon Scambler's aunt, Goodwife Marling.'

'How is Scambler?'

'Gone,' he answered flatly. 'The old crone has thrown him out of her house.'

I sat down carefully. 'Why?'

'Apparently Simon was upset when he heard what had happened at the hanging. Someone from their church told them all the gory details. So far as they knew, you were very badly hurt. Apparently, Simon started shouting that God was cruel to allow such things. It shocked his aunt. She got their vicar to visit and put the fear of God in him, but she told me Scambler gave him the same treatment, telling him how God allowed wickedness and injustice, even said he thought God was cruel himself. So she threw him out, saying she would allow no blasphemy in her own house. She fears her nephew is possessed.'

'Does anyone know where he has gone?'

'No. She said she has washed her hands of him. Went on about how she had only taken him in out of Christian charity when his father died, because he was her dead sister's boy.'

'The old bitch,' I said, gripping the handle of my stick.

'I told her about the statement you had lodged with the court, and she said she was glad at least he was safe from those young Boleyn devils. It was strange, she was sour-faced and sanctimonious as ever, blamed you for indulging him and his ways, yet looking in her eyes I think she felt some shame, too.'

'I wonder what has happened to him.' I sighed. 'Another un-employed beggar in Norwich, probably. Look out for him, and ask Barak to do the same.'

Nicholas was silent a moment, then added, 'I have made some enquiries at the locksmiths' guild too. Gave the clerk some money. He checked the records. Walter's last name was Padbury, and he did come from a district called the Sandlings, on the coast down in Suffolk. He was an orphan, but his father had Norwich connections. And Walter had no problems with his vision that anyone knew of. They wouldn't have taken him as an apprentice if he had.'

'We must send Toby over there. I hope he gets back in touch soon.'

'I could go.'

'No, it should be someone familiar with the country.' I reached for my stick. 'Come, I am going outside. Stay by me.'

Slowly and carefully, I manoeuvred my way down the inn stairs. It was a relief to reach the stone-flagged hallway. A servant opened the main door with a bow and I stepped out into Magdalen Lane. It was good to feel fresh air on my face once more; the sky was blue, the weather warmer again.

'Accompany me down to the Tombland corner,' I told Nicholas. I kept close to the wall, passing the place where the dead beggar had lain. I realized I had not thought of him in days.

I asked Nicholas, 'What did Beatrice say?'

'It was a most gentle letter. She hopes to see me back soon, and at dinner with her parents.'

'Nothing more of this young barrister?'

'No.' He hesitated. 'I think perhaps you were right, her dangling him in front of me was just feminine wiles. Yet I suppose women have but few cards, they must play what they have.'

'Yes, that is true.'

'But after reading the letter, I found myself thinking of Isabella Boleyn, her force of character. Beside her Beatrice seems somehow — pale.' He coloured. 'I do not mean to be disloyal.'

'Isabella is a striking woman.'

'Yet not possessed of Beatrice's social accomplishments.'

I tried not to smile. 'No.'

☩

BARAK JOINED US for dinner. Early as it was, I could tell from his flushed face he had been drinking. His hair and beard were unkempt and he wore an old doublet, unbuttoned, the linen shirt beneath in need of washing. What surprised me most, though, was that he was not wearing his artificial hand. He joined us at the table, throwing himself into a chair. He saw Nicholas and me looking at his empty sleeve. 'I've had enough of the bloody thing. It was aching like fuck this afternoon.'

Nicholas asked, 'Can you manage your food with one hand?'

''Course. I've done it before. You can manage anything if you have to.'

I said carefully, 'Nicholas said you had a letter from Tamasin.'

He looked at me evenly. 'Yes. D'you know what she said? Guy told her what happened to you, and that you were stuck here for now. She said' — he launched into a sarcastic imitation of his wife's voice — '"Maybe now Master Shardlake will know what it feels like to be badly injured; perhaps it is God's justice on him."' He clenched his good hand. 'Maybe all this radical Protestantism is getting to her, I thought she had more sense. Well, I'm going to write back telling her the truth, that I've lost my job, I'm not sorry, and I'm staying here a few days longer to help you. If she doesn't like it, she can lump it.'

I had not heard Barak speak in such terms of Tamasin since the time when they had nearly broken up after the death of their first child. Nicholas said, quietly, 'That is unfair on Master Shardlake. Could you not wait until just before you set out for London, and say you are writing from Suffolk? Otherwise she will vilify Master Shard⁄lake all the more.'

Barak shifted in his chair, looked at me, then nodded. 'All right,

I'll wait till the end of the week, pretend I'm writing from Suffolk. But it's the last damned fib I'll tell her; when I get back I'm not sitting under her thumb any more.'

✝

THE NEXT DAY, SATURDAY, Isabella Boleyn visited us in the morning, accompanied by Daniel Chawry. I had made my way downstairs again, and we met in the parlour. Isabella looked pale and drawn, and Chawry glanced at her with concern, occasionally fingering his red beard.

'I am so glad to see you up,' Isabella said. 'I was shocked to hear what happened.' She looked at Nicholas. 'I thank you both heartily for saving my poor husband's life.'

Chawry said, 'My mistress has been to see Master Boleyn. His neck is sore injured. Dr Belys says it will be another week before he is able to speak. He can only eat soft pottage.'

Isabella said, 'But he wishes you both to visit when you can, that he may in some manner express his gratitude.'

'I am sure I shall be fit to do that soon,' I said. 'I am recovering well.' I hesitated. 'I have had a letter from Master Parry. He says that in view of present political troubles the Protector's secretary, Master Cecil, recommends that he not be troubled with the pardon just yet. He and I both know Master Cecil,' I continued reassuringly, 'and he is a friend to the Lady Elizabeth. But I fear your husband will be in the castle a while yet.'

'Those damned rebels,' Chawry said. 'I hear rumours of some trouble in Kent now.'

I looked at Isabella. She had lowered her head, and I saw tears at the corners of her eyes. But then she looked up again, chin thrust forward. 'Then I must ensure he is kept in good spirits.' She turned to Chawry. 'Daniel has managed to sell that wretched horse Midnight.'

Chawry said, 'I got more for him than I thought. Some men like a difficult horse to train.'

'The stable is empty.' Isabella gave me a quick look. 'I cleared it out myself.' I nodded. That meant she had found Boleyn's money. I wondered if she had told Chawry.

'You will not be able to ride yet?' Isabella said.

'I hope to be able to ride to the castle to see your husband, perhaps by Monday.' I ignored a dubious look from Nicholas. 'And
perhaps leave late next week.'

She looked a little downcast. 'I will be sorry to see you both depart.'

'We will keep in touch,' Nicholas promised.

✝

I WROTE BRIEFLY TO Parry and the Lady Elizabeth, explaining
that I would be delayed because of my injury. I sent a longer letter to
Guy, stressing how much improved I was.

The rest of the weekend I spent walking, with increasing confidence, and exercising my back under Dr Belys's direction. He was
pleased with my progress and agreed I might make a short ride on
Monday, provided I was careful.

On Sunday, from the window of my room, I witnessed a clerical
marriage at the church across the road, the first I had seen since the
clergy were permitted to marry last year. The couple, both in early
middle age, left the church and walked with bright faces to the lychgate. The husband wore his clerical cassock, his wife a modest dress
and coif. A cheering group, perhaps from his congregation, had
gathered outside, together with several onlookers. Someone in the
street called out, 'This is fornication in the eyes of the Lord!' but
the marriage party ignored them. I stood and went over to my table,
where I had been going over the case documents again. I still had
not heard from Toby; it had been over a week and he would surely
have heard about events at the hanging. I thought, Perhaps not, perhaps his mother's health is worse; but still I felt uneasy. After we left
Norwich, our hopes of finding the apprentice Walter would rest on
him.

Chapter Thirty-two

MONDAY CAME, the first of July. I was walking now without my stick, but was nervous at the thought of mounting a horse again. Nicholas, who was to accompany me to the castle, helped me onto the animal's back. We had spent the previous evening visiting Barak at the Blue Boar, and he had seemed less angry, saying little, but still drinking more than he should. I told him that if my riding went well, we might leave Norwich by the end of the week. 'Just as well,' he replied. 'I'm running short of money.'

Nicholas and I rode through the city, dressed in our legal robes. It was early; with few people about there was less risk of getting barged. The weather was hot again, the streets stinking mightily. To my relief riding was not painful. Traders were opening their shops; banging down the shelves on which goods would be displayed, pouring water on the streets, sometimes kicking beggars from their doorways. One such man, dressed in little more than rags, face red and blotchy, staggered into our path. He raised a leather flagon, calling out, 'Good morrow, masters! Off to cheat some clients of their gold? Take a drink to whet your appetite!' Both horses started nervously, and a jolt of pain went through my back.

'Be off, churl!' Nicholas shouted. The man staggered away. 'Are you all right?' Nicholas asked.

'Yes, I think so.'

'He could have had you off, the sot. These people spend what they get from begging on drink.'

'Why do you think they do that?' I asked.

'Because they're good-for-nothings. Why else?'

'Perhaps because otherwise their lives would be unbearable.'

✝

WE ARRIVED AT NORWICH Castle, approached the main gate and asked to visit John Boleyn. The guard looked at us with interest; doubtless he had heard about the hanging. We entered the cold central hall. A new gaoler came to meet us, his manner less surly than his predecessor. He led us along a corridor at ground level to another cell, opening the door for us.

Boleyn's new quarters were more spacious than before, and less damp. A barred window in a deep recess, thick as the castle wall, gave a view down Castle Hill to the spires of Norwich. He had been allowed a table and some stools. He rose from the bed to greet us. A thick red weal ran round his neck, and there was a look of shock in his eyes. I raised a hand. 'I understand you cannot speak yet, Master Boleyn. Do not try.'

To my surprise, he embraced us both warmly, making little grunting sounds. He pointed to the table, where a slate and a piece of chalk lay. He bent and wrote, 'Thank you. You behaved like true heroes. Please, henceforth, call me John.'

'And call us Matthew and Nicholas. Are they treating you better now?'

He nodded, but even that gesture caused him to wince. He turned back to the slate, rubbed out the previous words and wrote, 'Isabella pays them.'

I smiled. 'I believe she found the money,' I said. 'I saw her on Saturday.' I told Boleyn, as Isabella doubtless had already, that delays over the pardon were likely, urging him not to lose heart. I said we would be returning to London soon, but would remain in touch, adding that I had set Toby to try and trace the locksmith's apprentice. At that he turned again to the slate and wrote in large letters, pressing the chalk so hard it almost broke: *I AM INNOCENT.*

✝

WHEN THE GAOLER let us out, I told him Boleyn's wife would pay to ensure Boleyn was well treated, and suggested he be allowed some exercise outside. He nodded. 'Constable Fordhill has agreed he's to be allowed to take the air on the castle roof. The constable would like to see you. About what happened last week.' He looked at us sidelong,

whether out of respect for our courage or amazement at our foolhardi-
ness was hard to tell.

✝

A SOLDIER LED US up two flights of stairs to the constable's quarters. They were comfortable and brightly lit, with tapestries on the
walls. A little boy sat in the hallway, playing with a wooden horse on
wheels – a strange domestic touch in this place. The soldier knocked
on an ancient wooden door and we were called in.

Constable Fordhill was a strongly built, middle-aged man with
black hair and a short beard, dressed in a fashionable high-collared
doublet. He had a military bearing and watchful grey eyes. Bowing
civilly, he invited us to sit on stools before his desk. He sat behind it,
studying us a moment, then spoke quietly. 'So, the pardon request has
now been lodged in London?'

'It has, Master Fordhill.'

He nodded slowly. 'I understand the initiative comes from the
Lady Elizabeth.'

'Yes, sir.' This was common knowledge now.

Fordhill nodded again. 'I take it John Boleyn is related to Anne
Boleyn.'

'Distantly, yes.'

He considered. 'The Protector may not welcome the Lady Elizabeth's involvement in such a scandalous matter. After the Thomas
Seymour business.'

'She wishes only to help a relative.'

'Despite his being found guilty by a jury of his peers?'

'I believe the verdict was wrong. There was reasonable doubt. I still
seek a key witness.'

Fordhill raised his eyebrows. 'And the Lady Elizabeth agrees with
your view? And her Comptroller? Master Parry, is it not?'

I paused, then answered, 'Yes.' Fordhill raised an eyebrow, noting
my hesitation. I continued. 'I am advised it may be some time before the
pardon is considered. Given the problems in the south-west, and elsewhere.'

'Yes.' Fordhill turned and looked out of his window – which like

Boleyn's had a view over Norwich. 'Thank God things are quiet here, though I believe there are a few makebates around the town.' He turned back to us, and said gruffly, 'I am sorry for what happened last week at the hanging. You both seem to have played a brave part. I understand you were injured, Serjeant Shardlake.'

'I am much improved now.'

Fordhill was silent a moment, then he frowned and barked, in sudden anger, 'I am responsible for carrying out the Assize sentences. For a pardon to go missing was a disgrace!'

I asked quietly, 'Do you know how it happened, sir?'

He shook his head. 'I questioned Judge Reynberd. He said that when he signed the stay of execution, he gave it to his chief clerk to make a copy for me, to be brought over urgently.'

'That would be Master Arden.' The chief clerk who had had Barak sacked.

Fordhill raised his eyebrows. 'You are well informed. Well, Arden swears he made the copy and had a junior clerk run across to the castle and pass it to the senior guard on duty, who should have brought it straight to me. But the guard is quite definite he received nothing. I believe him; he served under me in France. The junior clerk whom Arden sent with the message – I questioned him too; he seemed nervous, but stuck to his story. Unfortunately, Reynberd would not allow me to question him alone; Arden was there, and said as bold as brass that the document had been sent, and must have been lost within the castle.' He grunted. 'But I am not letting it go. I have written to Lord Chancellor Rich requesting a full investigation.'

'Did you mention my involvement?'

'Yes. I wanted to stress that, but for you, Boleyn would have been illegally hanged. I mentioned you had been injured.'

'Thank you,' I said, though I knew that when Rich read that news he was more likely to reward Arden than interrogate him. But why had Arden done it in the first place? For whom? I exchanged a glance with Nicholas.

'I will not let the matter rest,' Fordhill went on. 'It impugns my administration, and my honour.'

'Thank you,' I said. I had a momentary flashback of those poor people strangling beside me, knocking against me in their dance of death.

'In the meantime,' Fordhill continued, 'Master Boleyn will be treated well.'

'And if I may suggest, sir,' I said, seriously, 'good care should be taken for his safety. Clearly he has enemies.'

Fordhill nodded. 'You may rest easy. Nothing amiss will happen while he is in my custody.'

✝

WE RODE SLOWLY BACK to the Maid's Head. '*Will* Boleyn be safe?' Nicholas asked.

'I think so. Fordhill's whole reputation is at stake.'

'You think the clerk Arden was responsible for Boleyn being nearly hanged?'

'It looks like it, unless Reynberd was involved. But I doubt that, the possible consequences for him could not be more serious. No, I think somebody paid Arden, and paid well.'

'And he is gone to the Suffolk Assizes. Another person we should question out of reach.'

'Well, we shall be back in London soon, and can look into it ourselves.'

'Your back is really better?'

I smiled with relief. 'Yes, truly. Though I am glad Josephine is coming later to give me another massage. Barak is chaperoning her again.'

We had reached the bottom of Tombland. 'Look there,' Nicholas said, and pointed across the road to where Gawen Reynolds and his wife had just stepped out of their house. The old man, in his red alder-manic robe, leaned heavily on his stick; his wife was dressed, as ever, in black, white bandages on her hands. Reynolds saw us, following our passage with a ferocious glare. Nicholas insolently doffed his cap to him. We rode into Magdalen Street and the Maid's Head stableyard. The ostler brought mounting blocks, and Nicholas helped me down. As I stepped on the ground I heard a harsh voice behind me. 'Can't you even dismount properly, crookback?'

We turned to find Reynolds standing there, hands clenched on his stick. The ostler stared at him. 'Piss off,' the old man said, and the ostler hastened into the inn.

'I was injured, Reynolds,' I answered coldly, 'at the hanging ten days ago. Your grandsons will have told you. They were there, to see their own father hanged.'

'Good. He was lawfully sentenced.'

'Don't pretend you haven't heard of the pardon application,' Nicholas said hotly. 'I'm told it's the talk of Norwich.'

'What do you want, Master Reynolds?' I asked curtly.

'To know how long this pardon will take?'

'I do not know.'

His eyes narrowed. 'I have contacts in London who can find out.'

'I would not cross the Lady Elizabeth,' I said.

'Piss the whore's daughter,' Reynolds snapped. 'It's Mary who counts in Norfolk.'

After a moment's silence, I asked, 'Why do you want your son-in-law dead so much?'

'Because he's a weakling, a lecher, the Boleyn family is tainted, and I want the thorn out of my family's flesh.'

I met his gaze. 'You may be a power in Norwich, Master Reynolds, and your grandsons figures of fear. But there is nothing you can do. The pardon has been lodged, and I have just seen the constable at the castle. He will ensure Master Boleyn is kept safe until the result of the application is known.'

Reynolds looked at me, wrinkling his nose with contempt. 'You are a crookbacked scuttling lawyer, no proper man for all your learning. When are you leaving?'

'Soon enough.'

'Then at least I will not see your ugly face again. The sight of it made my wife cry, I had to send her home.' He looked at Nicholas. 'I will leave you to take your pleasures. I understand from the inn servants that some young woman comes here, and your friend with one arm, and they go to your room. Whatever games you get up to together, they must be worthy of a fairground. Does the lanky boy join in?'

Nicholas took a step towards him, but I laughed, which seemed to

infuriate Reynolds more than anything. 'Have you no honour, sir?'
Reynolds snapped. 'No gentleman would take such remarks for jest.'

'It was the sort of thing your grandsons might say, Master Reynolds. You talk like some malicious boy.' Reynolds gave a disgusted
snarl, but composed himself and hobbled out.

'Old viper,' Nicholas said. 'I'd like to have sent him on his way
with a boot up his arse.'

'You sound just like Barak,' I said, and smiled.

✞

THE NEXT DAY, Tuesday, I went on my own for a longer, unaccompanied ride, through St Stephen's Gate and out into the countryside. I
was gaining confidence now. The hot weather had returned in earnest,
and I noticed how ill-grown the crops were. I passed a large saffron
field. After a mile the road passed a large triangular area enclosed with
a hedge and ditch, the familiar hurdles behind, but cattle, not sheep,
grazed within. I passed a shack, and saw an old man sitting outside
watching the animals.

'God give you good morrow, Goodman,' I said. He stood and
bowed. 'Whose are all these cattle?'

He smiled. 'You be a furriner, master, to ask that. They all belong
to the city folk, who use them for their milk. Some are shared between
two families. The land was enclosed by the city, it stops the beasts a-
wandering; I'm the neatherd, the man who looks after them,' he added
proudly. 'Anyone who pays a ha'penny a week may graze their beasts
here.'

'What of those who cannot afford that?'

He looked at me askance. 'Then they must look to it their beasts
don't stray onto another's land, or pay a fine to get them back. Excuse
me, sir, I must keep a-doin', there's a calf should go back to his mother
over there.' He bowed quickly and hurried off, though I could see no
calf in trouble. I rode down to the river, then back again, reflecting that
nothing in Norfolk was straightforward.

✞

ON WEDNESDAY, I had arranged to take a longer ride, with Barak and Nicholas and also Josephine and Edward Brown. Both had learned to ride in London, but had not done so for some time and were keen to do so again, so we hired a pair of horses for them at the inn. It was partly by way of thanks for what Josephine had done for me. The innkeeper bowed, but I suspected that by now Master Theobald, kindly man though he was, would be glad to be rid of us. I wondered which of his staff had been gossiping to Reynolds's people.

We met Barak at the Blue Boar Inn, for we planned to cross Bishopsgate Bridge and ride south along the riverbank, along the foot of Mousehold Heath. Edward rode his horse easily, though Josephine was a little nervous at first. We clattered over Bishopsgate Bridge and began following the path along the riverside. Barak had his artificial hand in place, and, from the look of him, had not had a drink that day – Nicholas and I had been keeping a careful eye out.

Edward looked up the road leading to the escarpment, which close to was steeper and higher than I had realized, to the palace of the Earl of Surrey at the top, deserted behind its walls. Away to the north two large windmills turned slowly – there must be a breeze up there. 'They say the palace is magnificent inside,' I observed.

'Nobody there now but the escheator's caretakers, same as at the Duke of Norfolk's palace in town.' Edward smiled wryly. 'The late Earl of Surrey built it to be a marvel for the whole city, that's why he put it atop Mousehold Heights.'

'Was not Richard Southwell involved in the fall of the Earl of Surrey and his father?'

'Yes. Gave evidence at the Earl of Surrey's trial, that Surrey quartered his arms with the old king's – though Southwell served his father the Duke for years. He is a man without morals.'

'Sounds like Norfolk's answer to Richard Rich,' Barak observed.

I thanked Edward for agreeing to let his wife minister to my back. 'We were glad to help you,' he answered. 'After your kindness in seeking us out to aid us.'

'Do you still have work carting stone at the cathedral?'

Edward sighed. 'It is almost done.' He looked at me. 'Josephine and I will move back to London, if you can help us.' He looked at me, his thin, handsome face embarrassed at having to ask for charity once more.

'I'm sure I can find you both work.'

Josephine smiled. 'And Mousy can grow up a Londoner, like her father.'

'But not quite yet,' Edward answered, with a quick glance at his wife. 'Perhaps in the autumn.'

'You only have to write,' I said.

As we rode southwards, to our left the ascent to Mousehold gradually became less steep, and we saw thick woods stretching down to flat cultivated land between the river and the heath. We rode into the little hamlet of Thorpe, where we took some beer at an inn overlooking the river.

'It is a beautiful country,' I observed.

'London will be better for Mousy,' Josephine replied.

Edward was looking up at the heath, less wooded here, wide, a gently rising expanse of yellow grass dotted with sheep that he told me belonged to the cathedral. 'Wat Tyler's rebels had a camp up there two hundred years ago,' he said. 'And there's a chapel to St William up in the woods, the boy they said the Jews murdered to drink his blood back in King Stephen's time.'

Barak said, 'My father had Jewish ancestry. We never drank any blood.'

Edward reddened. 'I am sorry, I did not know. Anyway, his shrine in the cathedral was taken down by the old king.'

'Was not Our Saviour himself a Jew?' Josephine asked.

'Yes,' Edward replied. 'And a poor man, a carpenter.'

Barak looked across the river at the spires and towers of the Norwich churches. 'I wonder what He'd make of all those. Not much, probably.'

We rode back the way we had come. By the time Bishopsgate Bridge came into view again, I calculated we had ridden four miles, and I had only a slight ache in my back. I thought that I could make it to London now if we took it in easy stages.

As we approached Bishopsgate Bridge, we saw three men descending the road from the escarpment. They were working men, in grey smocks, one with the rolling walk of a ploughman, the others with the faster pace of city people. One, I noticed, held himself in a soldierly way, firmly upright, pace even, arms swinging. They were almost at the foot of the hill. They halted at the sight of our little party, looking surprised. Edward raised a hand to them. 'I know one of those fellows,' he said. 'Excuse me.' He dismounted, walked over to the men and shook their hands. They were too far away for me to hear more than a murmur. I saw Josephine watching me carefully. I tried to listen, remembering that other meeting between Edward and the soldier at the Blue Boar, but caught only one man saying, 'Apart from lack of water, it's ideal.'

They parted, and Edward rode back to us. There was a sparkle of excitement in his eyes. 'Well,' he said, 'we must get back. Juliet Wingate said she could only keep Mousy till five.'

We left Barak at the Blue Boar, and as we parted from Josephine and Edward outside the Maid's Head, I said we would be leaving in a day or two now. 'You should, sir,' Josephine said. 'You must have business waiting in London.' She sounded surprisingly eager to see me gone, and I felt a little hurt. 'We will write soon,' Edward said.

Nicholas and I rode into the stableyard. To my surprise, Master Theobald himself bustled in, waving a letter with a large red seal. He handed it up to me. 'This came just after you left.'

I reached for it, thinking it some fresh missive from Parry or the Lady Elizabeth, but the seal was strange. I tore it open, then took a deep breath.

'What is it?' Nicholas asked.

I handed it to him and said, speaking low, 'We should go upstairs.'

Chapter Thirty-three

IN MY ROOM I gave the letter to Nicholas. It was from Kenninghall Palace, short and curt:

Serjeant Shardlake,
The Lady Mary requires your presence here at two o'clock in the afternoon of Friday, the fifth day of July.

Richard Southwell,
Steward to the Lady Mary

'What does she want?' he asked.

'Perhaps to discover more about her sister's role in the Boleyn affair.'

Nicholas looked anxious. 'Could she have learned that Edith Boleyn was at Hatfield? Remember, Parry spoke of each sister having spies.'

'I don't know. But our duty as Lady Elizabeth's lawyers is to give nothing away. Even if Mary is heir to the throne.' I looked at him hard.

'I know.'

'Southwell may be there too.' I frowned.

I fetched the map Toby had made for our journey to Norfolk. 'Kenninghall. It's over twenty miles to the south. I couldn't ride that far in one day. We'll have to break the journey at Wymondham or Attleborough. Go and talk to the innkeeper, see which he thinks best.'

Nicholas left, and I crossed to the window. It was market day again, the streets busy. People looked hot and tired. Why had we been summoned by Mary?

Nicholas returned. 'Wymondham is the best place to stop. Going on to Attleborough would be a long ride; it may be better to have the shorter ride the first day.' I nodded agreement. 'The innkeeper said things are a bit uncertain at Attleborough, too, the peasants still in a tickle. Wymondham is a place of goodly size with fine inns, the third largest city in Norfolk, but they have an annual play and a big fair down there this weekend. They call it the Wymondham Game. If we go soon, though, we should be able to find a place to stay. He recom‑ mends an inn called the Green Dragon.'

'Very well. We'll leave first thing tomorrow.' I had intended going to Toby Lockswood's farm, to see why he had not been in touch, but that would have to wait. 'Come, let's go to the Blue Boar and tell Barak. Then we should get a haircut and shave.'

✞

NEXT MORNING, THURSDAY, we rose early, and went down for breakfast wearing our lawyers' robes over our best clothes. Some mer‑ chants who had come to Norwich market from other parts had stayed overnight, and at breakfast there was much talk of peasant rebellions spreading in other parts of the country. Apparently, groups of rebels had set up camps in Essex as well as Kent; the Essex camp allegedly containing a thousand men, and all the camps were sending petitions demanding redress of unlawful enclosures and other grievances to the Protector. There were rumours of serious trouble in Oxfordshire, too. One merchant spoke of a new proclamation from the Protector warn‑ ing that all rioters would suffer extreme punishment as traitors, but he angrily predicted that there would soon be another one saying all were pardoned. 'My customer in Kent says the rebels talk of building a godly Commonwealth,' the man concluded.

'All this talk of Commonwealth will start to be read as meaning all wealth should be held in common. It's no better than Anabaptism,' his friend replied.

I raised my eyebrows at Nicholas, who frowned.

✞

THERE WAS INDEED a new proclamation promising death to rioters posted on the city gate, but beyond, the flat countryside was quiet and still. Nicholas said, 'I wonder how many of those rumours are true.

With the West Country rebels, further trouble is the last thing that's needed. All our efforts should be focused on defeating the Scots.'

'Nicholas, you and the Protector must be the last people in England not to realize that war is lost.'

He was silent for a moment. 'Perhaps you're right. But rebellion in time of war is indeed treason.'

'A lot of it could be hot air.'

'Those merchants sounded serious.' He paused. 'You met the Lady Mary once, didn't you?'

'Yes, three years ago. She's clever, calculating. There's a real hard ness there, too.'

'She refused to accept the old king's supremacy over the Church for years, didn't she?'

'Yes, both that and his divorce from her mother.'

'Catherine of Aragon, wasn't it? There were so many queens when I was growing up, I lost count.'

'Yes. Mary came to accept the Royal Supremacy only after her mother and Anne Boleyn, whom she hated, were both dead. Then she conformed for ten years. But now she won't accept the English Prayer Book.'

'Does she want to go back to Rome?'

'If she does, she hasn't said. But she won't abandon the Latin Mass. And she's shown before how obdurate she can be. And one thing we mustn't forget even for a moment: she hates Elizabeth.'

☩

WE RODE SLOWLY, for I was anxious not to overstrain my back, and allowed others to overtake us. It was Thursday afternoon when we arrived at Wymondham, a market town with substantial buildings in the main street. On a stretch of meadowland to the south tents were being erected for the coming fair, and near the city centre a shallow pit was being dug. I saw a wooden structure with a stage being erected nearby. We passed the market square, where much business was being done around the undercroft of a wooden market hall. To the south I saw a large church of white stone, a tall tower at each end. One tower was a ruin, windows and roof gone, though the other seemed in good repair. Beyond we caught glimpses of that common sight in England, the half-levelled buildings of a monastery.

'That must have been a big place,' Nicholas said.

'It must. Come, the inn is beyond that large chapel over there.'

The doors of the chapel were open, and as we watched, two men dressed as knights of ancient days, with chain mail woven from yarn, went inside.

'I wonder what the play is,' I said.

'The Maid's Head innkeeper said it was originally written about Thomas Becket.'

I looked at him in surprise. 'The archbishop who defied his king. Talk of him has been dangerous for ten years.'

'Apparently they've doctored the play to make it politically accept-able.'

We reached the inn, a large building with shops set into the ground floor. A powerfully built, elderly man with a short white beard was manhandling a pig's carcass into a butcher's shop with the aid of a boy. We left our horses at the inn stables and went inside. We were greeted by a small, plump fellow in an apron, showing us none of the formality of the Maid's Head innkeeper. I asked if he could accommodate us for two nights.

'Yes, sirs. You're just in time, though; hundreds will be coming soon for the play and the fair.' He looked at me curiously. 'Have you legal business in Wymondham?'

'No, far off. We are breaking our journey. I am Serjeant Matthew Shardlake, and this is Master Overton.'

He looked at me narrowly. 'Serjeant? Any connection to Serjeant John Flowerdew?'

'No, though I met him at the Norwich Assizes.'

'Is he a friend?' the innkeeper asked cautiously.

'Certainly not.'

'He's been the plague of Wymondham these last ten years. He lives at Hethersett, north of here, in a fine house. I believe he's there now, probably enclosing more of his land for sheep.'

'Many landowners are doing that in these parts, I believe.'

The innkeeper snorted. 'He's not content with enclosing the lands.

He was the Court of Augmentations' agent here during the dissolution. He resisted the townspeople buying the part of the abbey church
the citizens had always used for their own services, and when we wrote
to Lord Cromwell and he sold it to us, Flowerdew took the lead and
stonework from the south aisle, saying it was part of the monks' dor-
mitory.' He drew a deep breath. 'Excuse me mardlin' on, sirs, but that
man's a thorn in our flesh.'

'Strange for a rich man to go to such lengths over some lead.'

'Flowerdew loves a quarrel, he'd skin a flea for its hide and tallow.
Ask William Kett the butcher in the shop outside.' He shook his head.
'But you must be tired. I'll get a man to show you your rooms and
bring you some water to wash off the dust from the road.'

✞

WE ATE AT THE INN, then decided to walk down to the church: the
air was cooler now. It was still a splendid building, built of the same
white stone as Norwich Cathedral. We could see where the monks'
half of the church had been pulled down. We went inside the townspeople's church, not yet whitewashed though the niches that once
contained saints' images were empty. A patch-up job on the south aisle
gave the otherwise beautiful structure a lopsided look.

Nicholas shook his head. 'Surely it would be in Flowerdew's interests, as a local landlord, to keep the townspeople happy.'

'Some people just enjoy quarrelling. You've worked in the law long
enough to know that.'

We walked past the monastery ruins to a little river, then turned
back to the town. Although it was almost dark now, the streets were
crowded, the taverns full, customers spilling out onto the pavement in
the warm summer evening. As we passed one group, someone called
out, 'Leeching lawyers! Hell has gates for them who prey on the
Commonwealth!'

Ignoring them, we turned into Market Street. Another crowd
stood outside a tavern. One man turned at our approach, then quickly
vanished down an alley. I stopped. 'What is it?' Nicholas asked.

'Did you see that man?'

'No.'

'I thought I recognized him, but perhaps not.' Yet I was sure it was the man Miles, whom I had overheard in Norwich talking to Vowell and Edward Brown. I had still said nothing of that to Nicholas. 'Come,' I said. 'We must be up early tomorrow, to reach Kenninghall by two.'

We went to bed early. I slept well, only to be woken at dawn by the sound of carts trundling into Wymondham, bringing goods for the coming fair.

Chapter Thirty-four

W E SET OUT FOR Kenninghall shortly before six. It was a long, hot ride through the countryside under the wide blue sky, more than twelve miles. We passed through Attleborough, which I remembered from our journey to Norwich. The town seemed quiet, but in the countryside beyond I saw lines of broken earth where fences had been pulled up, and the sheep were gone from the fields.

We turned off the main road past Eccles, following a well-maintained track. The land was fenced, mostly wooded parkland though with fields and sheep pastures too. At length we came in view of an imposing, redbrick palace, fairly new like Hatfield, though considerably larger. The wide entrance had two soldiers on guard. Kenninghall. The palace that had been the old Duke of Norfolk's until Mary bought it. As we approached, stable boys appeared from an outhouse and ran up while a steward, the letter M embossed on his robe, marched towards us with one of the soldiers.

'We have come to see the Lady Mary,' I said. 'Serjeant Matthew Shardlake. My assistant Master Overton. We have an audience at two.'

The man nodded. The stable boys had brought mounting blocks and we dismounted, Nicholas giving me a hand down. The steward led us inside. The interior was very different from Hatfield, richly decorated, with bright tapestries and ornate tables with vases of Venetian glass full of flowers. I caught the scent of incense from a chapel somewhere.

'Did you have a good ride in this fine weather?' the steward asked.

'A little tiring. We stayed at Wymondham overnight.'

'Did you pass Attleborough, where those peasant dogs threw down Green's fences? Are they still down?'

'From what we could see.'

The steward paused before a double door with a guard outside. He knocked. A male voice answered, 'Come in.' The steward inclined his head at Nicholas. 'You stay outside,' he said, then opened the door. I entered. At the far end of a long room Sir Richard Southwell, dressed soberly in a long brown robe with furred collar, looked down at me through those half-closed eyes with his habitual haughtiness, arms clasped behind his back. Next to him was an ornate chair, three steps leading up to it, where, under a crimson canopy of state, sat the King's heir, the Lady Mary. Two ladies-in-waiting were embroidering at the foot of the steps, heads lowered over their work. I took off my cap and bowed, not as low as I should because of my stiff back.

'Rise, sir,' the Lady Mary said in civil tones. She saw the steward still standing by the door and dismissed him with a wave of the hand. She smiled, though her dark eyes were watchful. She was thirty-three now, more than twice Elizabeth's age. She was as I remembered, small and thin yet with an air of iron will, though there were new lines of strain around her small mouth. Her dark auburn hair was covered by a jewelled French hood, and I noticed that her magnificent dress, like the one I had seen her wearing three years before, was embroidered with pomegranates, the emblem of her mother, Catherine of Aragon.

'Thank you for coming, Serjeant Shardlake. I wished to talk to you.'

'How may I help you, my Lady?'

She smiled thinly. 'Do you remember our meeting three years ago? When you were helping Queen Catherine, God pardon her soul, search for a lost jewel?'

'Indeed.'

'You are much changed. Your hair is white, and I think you have lost weight.'

'I grow older, my Lady.'

'The troubles of England today would age anyone, I think. Sir Richard here has just returned from a meeting of senior men of the counties with the Protector. An army is being sent against the rebels in the south-west.'

I looked at her closely, but her expression was flat, unreadable. She looked at Southwell. 'And now there are reports of outbreaks across the country, men setting up camps and wrecking landowners' fences.'

'A new one every day,' Southwell agreed. So the merchants in Norwich had spoken true.

She turned back to me. 'You have been at the Norwich Assizes, I am told. What would you say of the mood in Norfolk?'

'There seems to be discontent in the city,' I answered cautiously. 'I have not been out in the countryside apart from my journey here.' I hesitated, then added, 'I heard some merchants talking yesterday, about risings in Kent and Essex, and Oxfordshire, too.'

'See, the local merchants know more than the Protector about what is happening,' Mary said contemptuously to Southwell.

He nodded agreement. 'These risings are coordinated at some level, they must be. Even if it is only malcontents and runagates going from one place to the next, calling on people to join in. But my spies' information is that Norfolk is quiet, apart from those Attleborough dogs.'

Mary looked at me. 'The discontent in Norwich. What is it about?'

'There is anger about the rising prices, debasement of the coinage, lack of employment.'

'And the religious changes, are they mentioned?' Suddenly her gaze was steely.

'Not that I have heard,' I answered truthfully.

So she wanted to see whether local discontent encompassed the changes in religion; though that could not be the main reason I was called.

Southwell added, 'Outside the south-west, the talk is all of commonwealth. A radical Protestant notion. And I think some believe John Hales's enclosure commissions will bring the changes which those rebels want, and by setting up these camps they can dictate to him.' He still looked at me with that cold expression; and it suddenly occurred to me that he had the wealth, status and formidable reputation to have suborned the clerk Arden over the notice of Boleyn's pardon. But then so did John Flowerdew.

'But the Prayer Book may become an issue,' Mary said quietly. Southwell gave her a quick, warning look, and she turned back to me. 'Of course, all rebellion by common people against the social order is treason against my brother the King, and must be harshly punished.'

I bowed my head in formal acknowledgement.

She turned again to Southwell, her tone suddenly sharp. 'As you suspected, he knows nothing. But it is always worth asking.' She looked at me, her expression quite different now, stern and severe. 'Serjeant Shardlake, my main purpose in calling you was to ask what my sister thinks she is about, sending you here to intervene in the case of her Boleyn relative who has been found guilty of a disgusting murder. I am told you actually went up on the scaffold and prevented the man being hanged.' Her dark eyes were probing and hard now, her thin lips drawn tight.

'The Lady Elizabeth asked only that I investigate the case. When the verdict went against Boleyn my instruction was to lay an application for a pardon, which I did. All that is quite legal,' I said. Then I added, 'The application was accepted by the judge, but the notice cancelling the execution did not reach the castle constable in time. That was why I intervened at the hanging. The execution would have been illegal.'

Mary laughed harshly, and turned to Southwell. 'You see, where a Boleyn is concerned, even the finding of a jury is not enough.'

I glanced at Southwell, remembering that he had once himself obtained a pardon for murder, then said steadily, 'I have done only what is permitted by law.'

The Lady Mary smiled, sourly. 'Certain – discussions – are taking place between myself and Protector Somerset, mainly through Sir Richard here. I will ensure that my discontent over this pardon application is made known to the Protector. Perhaps then he will deny it to please me.' Her voice deepened. 'Anne Boleyn brought ruin to this country and misery to my father. He turned to Jane Seymour – the Protector's sister. Let Elizabeth remember that.'

Southwell addressed me. 'No doubt you will report this conversation to Master Parry. Feel free.' He gave a sudden broad smile, showing white teeth. Mary, I realized, wished to remind Elizabeth of her weakness compared to her own strength. She was, after all, the heir and with the patronage of the Habsburgs, despite her current difficulties.

'I am sorry you are offended, my Lady. Please be sure that I have been concerned only to carry out my duties as a lawyer.'

Mary sat back in her chair. She spoke coldly and harshly. 'As you did for that other patron of the new religion, Catherine Parr. That woman tried to subvert the faith of all the King's children, but she never succeeded with me. I saw her true nature. What was that book she wrote, *Lamentation of a Sinner*? Bewailing how she had fallen to the sins of the flesh before she discovered the Bible? But she fell into sin again, did she not, marrying the Protector's treacherous brother when my father was barely cold in his grave.'

I looked at her. She must have known I had worked for Catherine Parr for years, and of my respect for the late queen. Yet I saw from Mary's eyes, now wide and bright with a furious glint, that her remarks were not mere viciousness. This was what, in her hatred and anger, she truly believed.

Southwell said, 'I think this interview is over, my Lady?'

Mary nodded agreement. 'I think I have made myself clear. Good morrow, Serjeant Shardlake.'

I bowed low again, then walked backwards from the chamber, the doors opening behind me. Outside I stared at the closed door for a moment, overcome with anger. The steward looked at me questioningly. I nodded, and he led me away.

⊕

I MADE SURLY COMPANY for Nicholas on the ride back to Wymondham. I told him only the barest outline of what Mary had said. The encounter had troubled me much. Her threatened intervention in the pardon application could only make matters more difficult. I remembered, too, Southwell's talk of the rebellions being coordinated, and the meeting I had overheard under the oak at the Blue Boar. Southwell had spoken of spies, too. Were some men playing both sides of the fence, pretending to support rebellion but acting for the government? The sooner we left for London the better.

It was dark when we reached Wymondham. I was exhausted and my back ached badly again; Nicholas, too, looked tired, his pale face red with sunburn after the long journey. The streets were more crowded now, the Wymondham play was scheduled for tomorrow. Many doors and windows were brightly lit with lanterns, men with packs on their backs heading for the tents on the meadow. The mood was cheery, with laughter and some singing. We had a quick dinner and went to bed. I gave Nicholas some lavender oil to put on his burned face. Despite the thoughts whirling in my mind, I fell asleep quickly, tired out as I was. In the night, though, I was woken by someone calling out on the streets, 'The enclosure commissioners are coming! There's to be a new proclamation next week!' There was cheering, and I heard the news shouted out again, further away.

☦

IT WAS A LITTLE after noon the next day that we arrived back in Norwich. Saturday, the sixth of July. Even though we would soon be leaving, I needed to write at once to Parry and tell him of my encounter with Mary. It was market day again, the streets busy, and I was glad when at last we rode back into Tombland, the Maid's Head and the cathedral gates coming into view. I said, 'Home again.'

Nicholas sighed, 'I can never see Norwich as home. When can we return to London?'

'Perhaps Monday. Tomorrow I want to ride out to Toby's farm and see what has happened to him. We'll take Jack, he gets on with him.'

Nicholas laughed. 'Unlike me. Don't worry, the feeling's mutual.'

'And I can keep an eye on Jack. See he doesn't drink.'

'I doubt he'll be doing much of that,' Nicholas said seriously. 'I think he's almost out of money.'

Suddenly, Nicholas pointed at the brightly decorated Erpingham gate leading into the cathedral. 'Look there, isn't that Simon Scambler?'

Scambler, dressed in ragged hose and a dirty shirt, stood in the gateway, talking to an elderly surpliced cleric, waving his hands. I saw the cleric shake his head. Scambler groaned loudly, then ran across Tombland into the alleys on the far side. A cart loaded with wool almost hit him, the driver letting loose a string of oaths. Somebody laughed. I turned my horse towards the cleric, who was going back into the precinct. 'Wait, sir,' I called. 'Please.'

He turned and waited for us to ride up. He was small and plump, bald but for a fringe of white hair, kind-faced. 'Can I help you, sirs?' he asked.

'That boy who was talking to you. I know him.'

He looked at us anxiously. 'Sooty Scambler? Not in trouble with the law, is he?'

'No. He was a witness in a case.'

He drew a sharp breath. '*That* case?'

'Yes. I am Serjeant Matthew Shardlake.'

'Canon Charles Stoke. I taught Scambler at the cathedral school.'

'I heard he was homeless now.'

'Homeless and jobless,' Stoke said, wearily. 'He came to ask if there might be a place for him at the cathedral choir. I had to tell him no.'

'He was at the cathedral school, you say?'

'Yes. How much do you know about him?'

'Only a little.'

Canon Stoke took a deep breath. 'His parents were poor, his father a chimney sweep, and his mother died when he was ten. Simon was clever, no question, and had a good singing voice, remarkable after his voice broke. We took him in. But his behaviour —' the old man shook his head vigorously. 'That I could never understand. He picked up some things, like music, with ease, and learned to read well, but other, elementary things he could not grasp at all. Discipline especially.' He looked at me seriously. 'I do not mean he was disobedient, but he could not seem to grasp basic rules of behaviour, with that waving of his arms, speaking and even singing out of turn —'

'A sort of blind unruliness,' I said.

'I see you know him, sir. Well, neither beating nor reasoning put him in order. Other children and even some teachers mocked him. We could not control him. When he was thirteen we had to ask him to leave. And he never seemed interested in the Christian faith.'

'Then he worked for his father?'

Canon Stoke smiled sadly. 'That fared no better. He got stuck up chimneys, or sent down piles of soot before the furniture had been covered.'

'And so he became Sooty.' I smiled sadly.

'Then his father died. I gather Simon's later attempts at employ-ment were not a success. When his father died last year, he went to live with an aunt.' Stoke took a deep breath. 'A lady steeped in radical religion, I believe. Simon told me she has thrown him out.'

'Yes. I feel partly responsible; Simon was much upset by the Boleyn case.'

Canon Stoke bit his lip. 'I wish I could help, but even if I took him into the choir, his indiscipline would soon get him in trouble with Bishop Rugge.'

'Where is he living now?'

'On the streets, I fear. He was much upset when I said I could not help.' The old man turned away. 'I am sorry, but I think there is no more I can do. Except pray.'

He walked away into the precinct. I turned to Nicholas. 'One other thing I will do before we leave. I will find Simon, and help him somehow.'

☦

BACK AT THE INN, I wrote to Parry and arranged for a post-rider to take the letter to Hatfield. Then I lay down, exhausted and sore, to get some sleep. Some hours later, Nicholas knocked on the door. He looked serious.

'You should come downstairs, sir. Isabella Boleyn is there. With Daniel Chawry.'

I made my way down. Isabella was sitting in the parlour, head in her hands. Chawry sat uncomfortably beside her.

'What is it?' I asked, fearing something had happened to Boleyn.

Isabella raised a tear-stained face. She looked at the end of her tether. 'I was thrown out of my house this morning, sir, and Daniel is dismissed. They took my money too, all the money John left for me.'

'Who did?'

'Serjeant Flowerdew's men.'

'What? They can't do that!'

'They said I'd no right to be there, as I am not John's wife. They came on behalf of the twins' grandfather; he has been sold their wardship. The twins came too, they laughed as we were put out. They have taken over the house. Thank God a carter gave us a ride to Norwich. I am penniless, I have nowhere left to go. Please, sir, help me.'

Chapter Thirty-five

I ASKED NICHOLAS TO fetch quill and paper, then sat down and asked Isabella exactly what had happened. Strong woman though she was, she was utterly exhausted, and as Nicholas returned she said, 'You tell him, Daniel.'

'They came early in the morning, as people do when there's an eviction,' Chawry began. 'We were breakfasting in the kitchen – Mistress Boleyn and I. The bag of money the mistress told me the master had left for her was on the table, she was counting out wages for our two labourers. Then came a tremendous battering on the door. When I answered I was shoved in the chest by Gerald Boleyn. He caught me off balance, the devil, and I landed on the floor. Then he and Barnabas pushed their way in, followed by three young thugs, friends of theirs, I think. One was that mole-faced John Atkinson who was at court.'

'Southwell's man,' I said.

'Yes. And John Flowerdew brought up the rear, frowning fiercely. He said that as the King's feodary Southwell had sold the twins' wardship to their grandfather, and that as local agent for the escheator he had agreed with Master Reynolds's instructions to clear out the mistress. Since she is not legally married, she has no right to be there, and the twins had right of occupation. Then he thrust a document in front of the mistress, snatching up her money at the same time, saying that for now, as the escheator's agent, he should have care of it.'

'What did this paper say?' I asked.

Isabella looked up bleakly. 'I can barely read, sir.' She added bitterly, 'As people like to remind me, I was raised a servant.'

Chawry said, 'I tried to pick the paper up, but Flowerdew snatched it back. Then we were both told to leave immediately. The twins were taking up occupation then and there. It looked like their friends were staying too; through the window I could see loaded packhorses.'

'They'll wreck the place,' Isabella said, tears pricking her eyes.

Chawry looked suddenly agitated. 'There were half a dozen of them, sir. I knew the twins wouldn't hesitate to use more violence. I told the mistress we must seek advice from you.'

I wondered whether he feared I might think him a coward, and said, 'You did the right thing. Until the matter of the pardon is decided, John Boleyn's property is frozen – everything should be left as it is. While that situation lasts, Southwell has no right to do anything with the twins' wardship; they have not been made wards of court. Nor can Flowerdew do anything with his property. I would like to see that document of his.' I realized that Southwell, and perhaps Mary, too, would have known this was coming when we spoke yesterday. I wondered if Mary was behind it all, yet doubted it – such a petty move would not make her popular. Could Southwell and Flowerdew have acted together, or was Flowerdew acting on his own?'

'You have no money?' I asked Isabella.

'A few shillings.'

Chawry looked awkward. 'There are my parents, Mistress, we could go to them. I have a little money.' He reached out a hand to her, then withdrew it. Isabella shook her head.

'No, Dan, there is already scandalous talk about us.'

I looked at Nicholas, and said grimly, 'I think we should visit Master Flowerdew. I want to see that paper. I believe he has behaved unlawfully.'

'The Wymondham innkeeper said he was at home, at a place called Hethersett.'

Chawry said, 'It's about five miles from Norwich, off the Wymondham Road.'

I took a deep breath. 'Then we go there first thing tomorrow.' I did not welcome the thought of another ride of several miles, but saw no alternative. 'We'll take Barak as well. The more people the better. Nicholas, spend tonight in my room, Mistress Boleyn can have yours. Could you find an inn, Daniel?'

'I'll find somewhere.'

Nicholas said, 'Perhaps tomorrow we can give Flowerdew a taste of his own medicine.' He smiled reassuringly at Isabella. She gave him a tearful smile in return.

✝

BARAK, STILL AT THE Blue Boar, was only too pleased to be asked to join us; he was, he said, becoming bored and running low on money. 'Can't buy a decent amount of beer,' he said ruefully, scratching his beard with his artificial hand. 'The innkeeper doesn't do credit.'

So we set out early on Sunday morning, taking our horses from the stables. Nicholas and I wore clean shirts and doublets. We had brought our best robes – the others we had left for cleaning – but folded them in our knapsacks, for the weather was even hotter. The roads were quiet. Barak said, 'I wandered around the market yesterday, picked up some gossip. Apparently, the rebel camp outside Colchester has been sent a pardon, and told that the enclosure commissioners will redress their complaints. The commission's to be formally announced in London tomorrow.'

'Does Protector Somerset really intend to have the enclosure com, missioners take dictation from rebel commoners?' Nicholas retorted. 'He should send troops and put them down.'

'With one army trying to hold on to his last forts in Scotland, and another being gathered for the West Country?' Barak answered scoff, ingly. 'The Protector's been caught on the hop. Good thing too, if you ask me. The local landowners will do anything they can to impede the commissioners, so a bevy of armed men ready to enforce their decisions may mean reform is carried out at last. Remember, the com, missioners will have Somerset's authority, in the name of the King.'

Nicholas shook his head vigorously. 'Society is like the human body, those with education and ancestry as the head, and the head directs people like us, the hands. The common people are the foot; they know no more than how to walk behind the plough. They cannot dic, tate policy.'

'So people say,' Barak answered, coldly.

'It's how things have always been. It's what the preachers have always taught.'

'When did you ever take notice of preachers? My old master Cromwell, he was the son of a blacksmith and in his time nobody was more powerful.'

'Except the King. Who executed him.'

'Let's be practical,' I interjected. 'John Hales's enclosure commis, sions are a good thing, I represented poor people at the Court of Requests for years, I know how landlords force people off lands their families have farmed for centuries. But to enforce reform on the scale and at the speed Somerset has in mind, with almost every gentleman in England against him, it's impossible. Furthermore, I can't see him allowing the common people to dictate to him either. And he's not the King; constitutionally, he depends on the Council, and if he goes too far, they'll overthrow him.'

'He's already given way in Essex,' Barak said.

I looked at him. 'Remember the Northern rebellion in 'thirty,six, against the religious changes? The old king promised to meet the rebels' demands, waited till the rebel army went home, then got together an army and massacred them.'

'Somerset isn't Henry,' Barak insisted.

'More's the pity,' Nicholas said. 'I'm sorry, I've seen some grim sights in Norwich, I agree reform is needed – but society has a right order and if it is overturned, there will be anarchy!'

'Enough!' I said with sudden anger. 'We have serious business today, we should concentrate on that. God's blood, this case, the pardon, they're both frozen solid, yet still the matter piles troubles upon us! Jack, have you some ale in your pannier? I'm parched in this heat.'

He passed me a leather pouch, giving me a searching gaze. I had told him, and Nicholas, what had transpired at Kenninghall. I was worried, tired, hot, and had heard enough of these arguments. I did not know then that their consequences would rule my life for the next two months, and reshape it for ever.

Chapter Thirty-six

A S WE TRAVELLED ON, more people appeared on the roads, heading, no doubt, for Wymondham Fair. Towards eleven, we arrived at Hethersett. It was little more than a village, centred on a large open green with cottages and farmland around it. Westwards was a wide area of common land, with many fences and ditches for sheep. We were directed to Flowerdew's house. It lay at the end of a hedged avenue with sheep fields on either side. It was a modern brick building with tall chimneys, clearly the home of a wealthy man. We paused in the lane, and Nicholas and I donned our robes before riding through the gates.

The door was answered by a servant. He said Serjeant Flowerdew was out, riding the boundaries of his lands with his steward and his sons. I gave my name, and he asked us to wait while he fetched Mistress Flowerdew. A thin woman with a severe face appeared. Her expression was surprised, and unfriendly. She gave us the barest curtsey. 'Serjeant Shardlake,' she said coldly. 'My husband has spoken of you.'

'I apologize for calling without an appointment,' I said civilly, 'but I must speak to Serjeant Flowerdew urgently. When will he return?'

'Towards dinner-time. Perhaps five. You may return then, if you wish.' She gave another ghost of a curtsey, then closed the door in our faces.

'She could have offered us refreshment,' Nicholas said. 'Ordinary politeness dictates that.'

I smiled. 'I imagine Flowerdew has given me no good report.'

'What do we do now?' Nicholas wiped his face, which was reddening with sunburn again. 'I'm baking.'

'Return at five. I'm not going back to Norwich without seeing Flowerdew.'

'I saw a tavern in the village,' Barak said. 'We could get something to eat and drink.'

'Didn't look like much of a place.' Nicholas was in a complaining mood. 'I don't fancy sitting in whatever tavern they may have, being stared at by country gruffs all afternoon.'

'It's only three miles to Wymondham,' Barak said. 'They'll probably have the play on today.'

'All right,' I said, 'let's find something to eat at the inn, then go on to Wymondham. Damn Flowerdew, we'll have to ride back to Norwich in the dark. Nicholas, at least let us get these hot robes off.'

We had a surprisingly good pottage and beer at the inn, but were indeed stared at by the locals, and not in a friendly way. I heard someone mutter 'rich furriners'. And so, after the meal, we rode on to Wymondham, though the sun was now at its zenith.

Arriving there, we left the horses at the Green Dragon stables. I was surprised how many people were about now – this festival was bigger than I had thought. We passed the area where the play was being staged but nothing was happening, although the stage had been erected and covered with curtains, and the pit we had seen being dug in front of it earlier was now surrounded by stone flags, with old beams laid over it. The common nearby was now crowded with tents, and buzzing with people. Stalls had been set up along the streets. As we walked along, I marvelled at their variety; some, like those selling clothing and blocks of salt, were substantial, with coloured awnings providing welcome shade, while elsewhere families sold vegetables, cheese, live chickens in cages and the like, from the back of farmers' carts. Craftsmen's stalls sold everything from farm tools to shepherds' crooks with curved cow horns at the end. One sold children's dolls, and I bought a cloth doll with little buttons sewn on for eyes. 'For little Mousy,' I said with a smile. Barak bought another for his daughter. Sarcastically, he asked the goodwife serving us whether she had a doll like a witch to buy for his wife. The woman looked scandalized, stared at his metal hand, and crossed herself. 'Just joking,' he said.

'I didn't know they had such big fairs in the country,' Nicholas observed.

'It's the biggest I've seen,' Barak agreed. 'Though I've seen others when I've been on summer assizes. July's a quiet time for farmers, apart from weeding the crops.'

I saw an old woman arguing with a stallholder who refused to accept one of the old testoon coins. 'They had to be handed in by the end of last month,' he told her.

'There have been so many changes, I didn't realize –' she said, and began to cry.

We walked on through the crowds. I caught a tension in the air, and here and there saw people talking quietly in huddles.

A sudden thunderous bang made us jump. We looked round to where a crowd of over a hundred was now gathered around the stage. Barak and Nicholas began shoving their way towards the front, and I followed. A man in the crowd was handing out printed pamphlets. I took one. Headed, 'A True Sermon of a Faithful Bishop', it was another Commonwealth pamphlet: '. . . sheep fields and the great parks have eaten up whole villages and towns, all for the pleasure and profit of the rich . . .'

The curtains had been pulled back from the front of the stage, revealing a backcloth depicting the interior of a Roman building, copied, perhaps, from a tapestry. At the back of the stage a group of men in black robes, with long, false white beards, sat at a table count-ing metal discs. In the pit in front of the stage a fire had been lit, and from within came another loud bang and a cloud of yellow smoke. Barak murmured, 'Gunpowder; I hope they know what they're doing.'

At the front of the stage a grotesque, horned figure, clothes and face painted red and holding a pitchfork, was laughing dementedly as a man dressed as a cleric knelt before him, a woman wearing angel wings wringing her hands beside him. 'See!' the devil roared in a mighty voice, 'Christ's followers will not survive the blows of the wealthy!' At that four men dressed as knights ran out. They pretended to thrust wooden swords through the body of the cleric, who collapsed groaning on the ground. The crowd shouted and booed. It was a representation of the murder of Thomas Becket by King Henry II, cleverly changed to a Roman setting.

There was another gunpowder bang, and, parting the backcloth curtains, a man dressed all in white, face and hair painted gold, emerged onstage to cheers from the crowd. He went over and lifted up the dead cleric. The four soldiers looked on astonished, the devil shrank away from him, and the angel-woman, who, I realized, was a boy, carried the body of the cleric behind the backcloth.

The golden man addressed the crowd: 'I am the risen Christ, who will see all men of faith receive their reward! See, brethren, how those who rob and harry true Christians receive their due!'

He went to the men at the tables, and, upending the tables, sent the metal discs clinking and rolling across the stage, while the men grovelled on the floor to retrieve them. Then the devil forced them to rise, using his pitchfork to harry them down the steps leading from the stage towards the fiery pit, still issuing smoke. The money-changers, I thought, forced from the Temple. The devil, who was wearing strong boots, stepped onto the metal grille above the fire, which I realized represented the pit of hell. There was another bang, and a huge cloud of thick red smoke. When it dispersed, the devil and his victims had vanished. The Christ figure approached the stage:

See the money-changers tooken away!
So, brethren, should it be today!
Our guild is dissolved, our play is changed,
But still it lasts, its message never feigned!

There was a roar from the crowd. A curtain descended as people cheered and clapped.

'Clever,' said Barak.

'That is very radical stuff,' I said.

'It's the giant next!' someone called out.

Looking round I saw the big white-bearded man I had seen last week outside the butcher's shop, conversing animatedly with a little group of people. I stared, for I recognized another familiar face – not the man Miles, but the muscular form of Gawen Reynolds's old steward, Michael Vowell, who had also been at the meeting at the Blue Boar in Norwich. His brown hair and beard were a little longer, and unkempt now, and he wore a countryman's smock.

'Look,' I said. 'Reynolds's steward. He said he thought he might find work in Wymondham.'

Barak said, 'Some juicy stories about that household could be useful if Reynolds is behind Isabella's eviction.'

We stepped towards the group. They stood just outside the butch-er's shop, black pudding and pigs' heads displayed on the counter outside. A boy was whisking away flies. The white-bearded man, almost as tall as Nicholas, saw us approaching and nodded quickly at his group, who fell silent. 'What do you gentlemen want?' he asked in a deep voice.

'A word with Goodman Vowell, if we may.'

Vowell said, 'It's all right, I know them.' He led us a few yards away.

'God give you good morrow, Goodman Vowell,' I said. 'I remem-ber you said you were coming to Wymondham. Did you find work?'

'No, my contact's household required no more servants. And there is no work in the fields.' He frowned, looking displeased as well as sur-prised to see us.

'You may have heard, Master Boleyn was found guilty, but a request for a pardon has been lodged.'

'Has it?' He laughed. 'That'll annoy Master Reynolds.'

'Boleyn's wife Isabella has been evicted from their home, and the twins put in by their grandfather. Illegally, by John Flowerdew.' I hesi-tated. 'Any information you can give about dark doings in the Reynolds's household may help us. Help poor Mistress Boleyn.'

Vowell bit his lip, considering. Then he shook his head. 'Master Shardlake, if I say too much against my old employer, it could hin-der me in finding new work.' He glanced back to where the elderly butcher and the others were watching us. He bowed. 'I hope you enjoy the Wymondham Fair.' And with that, he returned to his friends.

'Well,' Nicholas said, 'that's that.'

Barak looked at the lengthening shadows. 'Time to get back to Flowerdew's house.'

⊕

WE RETURNED TO HETHERSETT after five. Again Nicholas and I put on our robes, then, with Barak, rode up the avenue, dismounted and knocked at the door. This time John Flowerdew himself answered.

It was strange to see him dressed not in robe, coif and cap but a brown doublet, half-unbuttoned to show the fine linen shirt underneath. His hair was receding from his temples, leaving a triangular widow's peak. His thin, sour face was set in a frown; a worried frown, I thought.

'Serjeant Shardlake. I was told you called this morning. I thought you had left Norfolk by now.' His tone was not welcoming, but neither was it his customary sneering rasp. 'Why do you call on a Sunday?' His eyes widened a little at the sight of Barak's hand.

I answered politely but firmly. 'I come on behalf of Mistress Isabella, who, I understand, was evicted by you from her house this morning.'

He continued in the same even tone, 'That woman is not Boleyn's wife. She has no legal right to be there. His sons, on the other hand, do.'

I looked him in the eye. 'They do not. Mistress Isabella was told the boys' wardship had been granted to their grandfather, though until the pardon is approved or refused no dealings whatever can be made with Master Boleyn's property or his heirs, apart from keeping his affairs in order. Certainly not evicting his fiancée and the estate steward, without notice, appropriating monies Master Boleyn gave to Isabella, and installing Gerald and Barnabas in his house. All that, Serjeant Flowerdew, is illegal. Mistress Boleyn, or Mistress Heath, if you prefer, was presented by you with a document purporting to authorize your actions. I would like to see it. May we come in?' Flowerdew hesitated. I smiled, then added, 'I am sure the Court of Common Pleas would be displeased if I told them a fellow serjeant had refused to discuss any – misunderstanding – in front of witnesses,' I added, glancing at Barak and Nicholas.

Flowerdew hesitated still. He was caught out; clearly, he thought I had already gone back to London and he could act with impunity. What I did not understand was why he had done this. He looked over his shoulder to where his wife stood, looking anxious. Two boys in their early teens appeared from an inner room, along with a short, powerfully built man in his forties. Flowerdew bit his lower lip, then said, 'Come in, to my office.' He looked at Barak. 'He can stay with the horses.'

Nicholas and I followed Flowerdew inside. I noticed that the furniture and tapestries in the house were all of the best quality. He waved
a hand briefly at the onlookers. 'My wife Alice, my sons, Edward and
William, my steward Glapthorne.' Then he led us into a well-
organized office full of documents, estate maps and law books. 'Sit
down,' he said, indicating two stools before his desk. He sat behind it,
and clasped his hands together before speaking. 'If you take this to
court, it is unlikely to come on before the pardon is decided.'

'As I said, I would like to see your authorization for the eviction.'

'I showed it to Goodwife Heath.'

I had had enough of being patient. 'Who, you guessed, probably
could not read; but you kept it from Master Chawry, who, as a steward,
could.'

Flowerdew gave a crooked smile. 'He's bedding her, you can see by
the way he looks at her.'

'The document, Serjeant Flowerdew. Misconduct by a serjeant-at-
law is serious. You may be a man of power here, but in London I work
for the Lady Elizabeth, and count the Protector's Secretary William
Cecil as a friend.'

Flowerdew began to look uncomfortable. He made a poor attempt
at a friendly smile. 'I hear you worked for Cromwell, ten years ago. So
did I. I was responsible for closing Wymondham Abbey for him.' He
frowned, anger showing through. 'You have no idea the trouble that
gave me.'

'With the monks?'

He smiled again. 'Oh no, they fled the coop quickly enough, after
what happened to the abbots of Glastonbury and Fountains. It was the
damned townsmen, saying they were entitled to all sorts of property.
Still, I got some lands myself out of it – and have worked for King
Henry and King Edward in the county ever since in various capacities,
and now, working for the escheator I have brought some good revenues
to the Crown.'

And to yourself, no doubt, I thought. Flowerdew said, trying now
to draw me into a friendly conversation between lawyers, 'I find working in my home county more agreeable than in London.'

'You never aimed to become a judge?'

He flushed, and I realized he had probably been disappointed in that ambition. 'No,' he answered curtly. 'And you?'

'I have never wanted that either. The document, sir,' I repeated quietly.

Flowerdew set his lips, then produced a paper from his desk and handed it over. It was a notice of eviction, granting power of occupation of North Brikewell Manor to Gerald and Barnabas Boleyn on behalf of their grandfather, prospective grantee of their wardship. It was signed by Flowerdew, but there was no seal of authority.

I looked at him. 'This document has no legal validity whatsoever.'

He shifted in his chair, his arrogance gone. 'You know what men like Chawry are like, think they know the law better than you and me and challenge everything. It was easier this way.'

I handed the document to Nicholas. 'This is serious,' I said. 'I shall keep this paper.'

Flowerdew laid his hands on the desk. He looked worried now. 'Sir, we were only anticipating events —'

'We?'

He hesitated. 'Sir Richard Southwell and I. It was he who suggested this after he heard of the pardon application.' He added in a rush, 'You must understand, he is a powerful man, and a dangerous one.'

'So I hear.'

Nicholas asked, 'But why would he be interested in evicting Isabella?'

'Perhaps he wants the estate,' I suggested. 'He has land on both sides.'

'I know nothing of that,' Flowerdew said quickly. 'Listen, sir, tomorrow I will speak to him, tell him it is best we let the woman back in for now.' He ran his tongue along his thin lips, clearly not relishing the prospect.

I smiled. 'See, Brother Flowerdew, it is always good when lawyers talk.'

He gave a tight smile in return.

'Then there is the matter of the sovereigns you took. Those were a gift from John Boleyn to his wife, as I can attest, and therefore belong to her in any event.' I held out a hand.

Flowerdew hesitated a moment, then took a key, unlocked a drawer in his desk, and handed me a black drawstring bag. I looked inside and caught the glint of gold. 'I shall give it back to Isabella,' I said. 'Would you like a receipt?'

'That will not be necessary.' Clearly now realizing the trouble I could make for him, his manner turned ingratiating. 'It is late for you to ride back to Norwich. Would you have dinner with us, and stay the night? You can return tomorrow.'

I looked at Nicholas, who shook his head slightly. I did not relish the prospect of spending a night under Flowerdew's roof, but my back had been aching more and more and the prospect of a night's rest in a good bed was hard to resist. 'Thank you, Serjeant Flowerdew,' I said mildly. 'We should be glad to.'

✞

ALTHOUGH I COULD see it cost him, Flowerdew continued making efforts to be civil at a dinner of well-cooked pork, served by servants under the eye of the burly steward, Glapthorne. Flowerdew did most of the talking, and I got the impression his wife was more used to listening. The two boys struck me as ill-mannered – one put salt in the other's wine when he was not looking – but harmless enough. I said we had visited the Wymondham fair, and been surprised by its size.

'Oh, together with the play it's always made a fortune for the townsmen,' Flowerdew said bitterly. 'They'll be showing scenes till tomorrow morning. That play is nothing but a papist relic, though they've been careful to write out references to Becket.'

'Some of its sentiments sounded quite radical,' Nicholas said.

'Really?' Flowerdew's eyes flashed. 'I must get a copy, see if there is anything which might interest Bishop Rugge. Did you see that chapel in the centre of the city? It used to belong to the abbey, but the townspeople bought it. They wanted every last outbuilding, every piece of church property they could lay claim to as belonging to the parish. They wrote to Lord Cromwell himself, who granted it to them.' His tone grew angry again. 'The arguments I've had with those churls over the years. The Ketts and the like. Men who think that because they've come up a little in the world, butchers and tanners who've acquired some land, they can lead the townsfolk against the King's officials.' He laughed bitterly. 'Robert Kett's still enclosed some of his land though, as I have; sheep are the only way to make money now.'

'I saw a large white-bearded man outside a butcher's shop. I believe that is William Kett?'

'It is.' His voice rose, showing his temper. 'His brother Robert is even worse. But I'll have them both one day, I swear it.' He stabbed viciously at a piece of pork on his plate.

After the meal Flowerdew suggested a game of cards, but we pleaded the need for an early night. Barak, we were told, had been given a place in the servants' quarters. I slept deeply in a comfortable feather bed, and woke late, the sun already high. Breakfast was over but a servant arranged some food for us. We saw no sign of Flowerdew. Afterwards his wife appeared, and I said we should take our leave. She readily agreed, and sent a servant to fetch Barak and our horses. She called to her husband, and Flowerdew came out from his office. I bowed to him. 'I think it time for us to depart, sir.'

'I trust you slept well.' He smiled, though his dark eyes were hard as stones. I was finding his forced amiability wearing, glad to be setting off. But he said quietly, 'Before you leave, may we have a word in my office? Alone,' he added, glancing at Nicholas.

I nodded, hesitantly, for I did not trust Flowerdew an inch, but followed him. He stood behind his desk, laying his hands on it, took a deep breath, then looked at me. 'Master Shardlake, I confess I made a mistake in creating that document to get Isabella Heath out of that house. But' – he shook his head – 'as I said, Sir Richard Southwell is not a man easily refused. Nor, frankly, is Master Gawen Reynolds. If you knew these parts better, you would understand.'

'Nonetheless, I must hold you to the agreement we made.'

Flowerdew forced another smile. 'I have become a rich man, Serjeant Shardlake, all through my own efforts. If you agree to let the eviction stand, and return that paper, I am prepared to give you thirty sovereigns.'

My eyes widened. It was an enormous sum, though no doubt

Flowerdew could afford it. 'In good gold coin, no debased silver,' he added.

'Serjeant Flowerdew,' I began quietly, 'when I entered the law I made two promises to myself. I would never be blackmailed, and I would never be bribed.'

Flowerdew closed his eyes and shook his head, as one confronted by a fool with whom it is impossible to deal. Then he said, 'Twenty sovereigns, then, for the document alone. You know what trouble it could get me into with my Inn.'

'No. It is my guarantee you will do as we agreed.'

He looked at me. No doubt he would have liked to rail and shout, but realized it would do no good. He shook his head wearily. 'I hope neither of us has cause to regret this.'

I made a peremptory bow, turned and walked out. Through the open front door I was glad to see Barak and Nicholas, and a couple of stable boys with the horses. I noticed the sound of church bells ringing wildly from the village and further afield. I frowned, puzzled, as did Flowerdew; it was Monday, not Sunday.

I went down the steps. Flowerdew and his wife remained in the doorway. We had just mounted when there was a clatter of hoof beats and the steward Glapthorne came riding fast up the lane, his face red. He dismounted, breathing hard. 'Master Flowerdew,' he gasped.

His master's face set hard. 'What is it?'

'Men from the Wymondham fair! They're spreading all over the countryside, calling for rebellion. I've been down to the village, half the men are gathered on the green; they've got pitchforks and bows and arrows. They threw insults at me! Listen, they're using the church bells to ring the country awake! Beacons are being lit on the higher ground. There's people on the road, coming to Wymondham from all over. Hundreds! The gruffs from the village said there's some gone to Morley, to throw down all the fences! And, sir, they're coming here next, to destroy yours!'

Chapter Thirty-seven

FOR A MOMENT we all stood looking at Flowerdew. He held himself erect, his thin face hardening. Beside him, his wife clutched her hands together. The two boys appeared from within; she gathered them to her.

Flowerdew snapped at Glapthorne. 'Morley, you say. John Hobart's enclosed part of the village commons there, hasn't he?'

The steward twisted his cap in his hands. 'Yes sir, and they're after your enclosures on Wymondham Commons too.' He hesitated, then added, 'You know what ill feeling there is towards you around the town.'

'John, John,' Mistress Flowerdew called, in sudden desperation, 'how often have I warned your ceaseless quarrelling would end in trouble?'

Her husband rounded on her. 'Quiet, woman! I can deal with these scum!' He thought a moment, looking out over his lands where the sheep grazed behind their hurdles, peaceful in the sunshine. Then he smiled, nastily, and looked at Glapthorne. 'Hasn't Robert Kett recently enclosed a small part of Wymondham Common?'

'Yes sir, but, forgive me, he's popular in the town, while you –'

Flowerdew laughed. 'Are not. Nor ever cared to be. But one thing brings popularity quickly, and that is money. There are few, even doltish plough-joggers, too foolish to decry that. Morley's the other side of Wymondham, they'll take time to get here. How many are there?'

'The villagers didn't say.'

'I'll meet them on the way, and pay them to turn their wrath on Master Robert Kett.' He laughed, and suddenly I realized that he was enjoying this crisis. Behind his back, Barak made a circling motion beside his head, indicating he thought Flowerdew mad.

Possibly he was, but he was clever, too. At once he was barking orders. 'Alice, take the boys inside. Glapthorne, get John and Charles and Peter from the estate, tell them to get long knives and fetch horses. And bring my sword.' He turned to me, frowned, then spoke quietly. 'Master Shardlake, I would ask you and your people to stay here, to protect my wife and sons should anyone come from the village seeking trouble. Will you do that?'

I hesitated, but Mistress Flowerdew was pale and trembling and it was not a request I could honourably refuse. Reluctantly, I nodded agreement. The elder of the boys shrugged off his mother's arm. 'Father, let me come! I am man enough now to face these churls.'

'No, William, you stay here.' Flowerdew looked at me and took a deep breath. 'Thank you, Master Shardlake.' He then ran into the house. He returned shortly, a grim smile on his face. He patted the waist of his doublet, and I heard the chink of coins.

Servants and horses were brought round quickly. Flowerdew buckled on his sword, and mounted a fine grey mare. Then he and his men rode down the lane in a cloud of dust, leaving Barak, Nicholas and me alone with his family.

✝

WE WAITED INSIDE the well-appointed parlour. The older boy said again that he wanted to join his father, though his brother, who was perhaps thirteen, sat quiet, close to his mother. Outside, church bells continued to ring wildly. Mistress Flowerdew suddenly put her hands over her ears and shouted out, 'Can they not stop that noise! It is driving me mad!'

'Go to your room, Mother,' the younger boy said gently. 'You won't hear them so loud from there.'

'Yes,' I agreed. It was bizarre to find myself suddenly in charge of Flowerdew's household. 'You boys go with her.'

They went, leaving me with Barak and Nicholas. Barak said quietly, 'If there's real trouble, and the family have to run, they'd be better off on the ground floor.'

'It can't come to that, surely,' Nicholas said. Barak shrugged. We sat in silence for what seemed an age, then Nicholas stood. 'I'm tired of doing nothing. Come, Jack, let's walk to the end of the drive and see what's happening.'

'Good idea.'

They were gone half an hour or so. When they returned Barak said, 'The road to Wymondham seems quieter, but bells are still ring-ing everywhere, and groups of men are crossing the paths over the fields. We went to the village, but it looked deserted. An old woman leading a donkey told us half the men have gone to Wymondham.'

'I didn't like the smirking look on her face,' Nicholas added.

A servant appeared and asked if we would like lunch; it was long past time. I said we would, and asked him to take some upstairs to the family. Hardly had he gone, though, than hoof beats sounded once more on the drive, and Flowerdew and Glapthorne rode up. Flower-dew wore a satisfied smile, though his steward seemed more dubious. The two boys ran downstairs, followed by their mother. 'What hap-pened?' she asked. 'Are you safe?'

Flowerdew laughed, slapping his thigh. 'Safe as houses. There were no more than a dozen of them. Country clods. I told them Robert Kett was the man they should be after, and gave them money to speed them on their way. I said Kett's enclosures were larger than mine.'

'Are they?' I asked.

'No,' Flowerdew answered happily. 'But they didn't know that. It's always good to win, isn't it, Serjeant Shardlake? One in the eye for Master Kett the tanner and his butcher brother. Now, some lunch.' He rubbed his hands together. 'Then you can get back to Norwich, the road is quiet now. Whatever's going on at Wymondham, the sheriff's deputy will soon put it in order.'

Nicholas said, 'There seem to be hundreds gathering. We walked to the village, and were told the men had gone to Wymondham.'

'They'll soon be back, tails between their legs.'

'Will there be hangings?' young William asked eagerly.

Flowerdew clapped him on the shoulder. 'I hope so; legally this is a riot.' He smiled with real pleasure. 'Now, food.'

'I have already ordered some,' I said.

'Good man!' he answered, so pleased at the outcome of his plan that he seemed to have forgotten I was his enemy.

☩

OVER LUNCH FLOWERDEW, now in expansively cheerful mood, told us more of his encounter. 'They were a mile outside Hethersett, trudging up the roads, carrying pitchforks and spades. They'd walked all the way from Morley, mostly labourers, half-naked in tatty leather jerkins, covered in dust. That leader of theirs, I've seen him before, he's a Wymondham copyholder called Duffield, too big for his boots like all these yeomen who've scratched together a parcel of land.' His mouth twisted with amusement. 'From my horse I could have taken Duffield's head off.'

'Why didn't you, Father?' Edward asked excitedly.

'Leave that to the hangman, lad. Like I said, it's a riot, and I'll be a witness that Duffield led them. He was bold, telling me the commons were gathering all over England to support the commissioners, and to take down illegal enclosures. As though he would know what was or wasn't legal.'

'Was your land enclosed legally?' I asked.

Flowerdew ignored the question. 'Duffield looked me in the eye like he was my equal, and said the hurdles keeping in my sheep would be taken down. He said I had best move them. Then I told them Kett was the man to get after, and I'd pay them if they went there instead. Duffield told the others it was a trick, but the money was real enough and the peasants took it gladly. All men are greedy.'

'Or desperate,' I said.

Flowerdew stared at me. 'And how will destroying the sheepfolds which are all that brings money to this county help? How will common rogues rising up against the King's authority help our country in its war with the Scotch? Though this stir won't last.'

Mistress Flowerdew put her knife on her plate with a clatter. 'Enough, John, enough,' she said. 'Why cannot we all live in peace as God intended?' She stood up and left the room with a swish of skirts. Flowerdew looked at his sons and made a face. They smiled.

'We should return to Norwich now,' I said brusquely. 'Thank you for lunch.'

Suddenly he seemed to remember how I had bested him on the matter of the fake document, and frowned, his good humour suddenly gone. 'Very well, Brother Shardlake. Glapthorne and I will ride down to the village with you, see for ourselves what is going on. Edward, William, you may come too.'

In a short time we made ready, and rode down the drive – Flower-dew and his sons, Glapthorne, Barak, Nicholas and I. The church bells had stopped, and it was a peaceful ride between the sheep fields, under trees planted along the side of the lane to give shade. Then we turned a corner and stopped abruptly. A group of men, twenty or more, were busy with spades and hammers, digging up the hedges enclosing Flowerdew's sheep and throwing them into the ditch on the other side. Another dozen or so stood guard, and I saw they carried not only pitchforks and hammers but also weapons of war, half-pikes and halberds. The sheep, bleating wildly, had fled in a bunch to the centre of their pasture. A couple, though, had been caught by the men, and lay on the ground with their throats cut. Like those Flowerdew had encountered, the men were mostly young, wearing wide-brimmed hats and sleeveless leather jerkins, some shirtless in the heat; but there were older men too, in their thirties and forties, working with the same grim determination.

Flowerdew's face turned instantly to thunder. Someone who seemed to be directing the work of destruction approached us boldly, half a dozen others accompanying him. He was in his fifties, tall and strongly built, with grey hair and a short beard. He had a lined, weather-beaten face, with a straight nose, firm narrow mouth and large brown eyes that fixed on Flowerdew's. He wore a dark green woollen doublet, a black cap set square on his head, and carried a long, sharp-looking cleaver. Flowerdew gazed back at him, his eyes blazing with hatred.

'Well, Master Flowerdew,' the man said, 'your plan did not work.' His voice was unusually deep, the Norfolk accent strong. 'When these men came, I helped them pull down my own enclosures, which, God forgive me, I should never have put up, and I have put myself, my goods and life, at the disposal of them and their fellows. See, I have brought Master Duffield back with me.' He indicated one of the men beside him, a short fellow in his thirties in a cheap wadmol smock, who gave Flowerdew a mock bow. The new leader continued, 'Now we have brought more men from Wymondham to deal with your enclosures, which, God knows, are far larger.'

'Who is this?' Nicholas asked.

The grey-bearded man looked at him. 'I, young gentleman, am Robert Kett of Wymondham.'

✝

I LOOKED BETWEEN Kett and Flowerdew. Our group was heavily outnumbered, and Kett had a solid, commanding air about him. Flowerdew, overcome with rage, reached for his sword, only to find that he had not brought it out with him. 'Fuck,' he hissed. Kett stepped forward and pointed his cleaver at Flowerdew's stomach. 'Steady, master,' he said. 'We want no violence, unless you provoke us to it.'

He turned to his men, inclining his head sharply. At the signal they moved to surround us. The horses shifted nervously. His men, who must have walked miles that day, gave off a powerful stink.

I was beginning to feel real fear, but ventured, 'You say, sir, that you wish no violence. Yet you have killed some of Master Flowerdew's sheep.'

Kett turned that penetrating gaze on me. 'The great gathering at Wymondham will need feeding tonight. We do not wish to shed the blood of men. We took weapons from the manor house at Morley too, and other places, but only lest we need to defend ourselves.' He looked closely at me and Nicholas, and I cursed our well-cut clothes.

There was a sudden burst of laughter from behind Kett. We looked round to the fence, where two lads had dropped their hose and were displaying their backsides at Flowerdew. Once called, 'Come kiss our arses, master, an' maybe we'll let you keep some o' yer sheep! Lucky for you they're shorn, or yew'd ha' lost yer wool too!' Flowerdew exploded in a tirade of abuse. 'Dogs! Leave my sheep, you filth.' He turned to Kett. 'And you, you lead these churls in destroying my property! You are a rioter, a pest to the country, leader of a parcel of vagabonds!'

Some of the men surrounding us looked threatening, and one raised his halberd. I wished we were anywhere but with Flowerdew. 'We are no traitors, Serjeant Flowerdew,' Kett said, his voice deadly serious now. 'It is we who are loyal to the King and you who milk his lands and ours for your profit.' He shook his head. 'You have no idea what is happening, have you? Honest workin' men are setting up camps all over the country, in Suffolk and Essex, Kent and Oxfordshire. We are sending petitions to the Protector, whose commissioners will soon arrive. He has already granted the demands of Essex, where a thousand men sit encamped by Colchester. The Christian Commonwealth is coming!'

Flowerdew laughed scoffingly. 'How can you know all this?'

Kett nodded. 'We have our own riders and messengers. My brother William is in touch with all the butchers' men.'

I thought, So this was indeed planned. Flowerdew laughed again, but with a note of unease in his voice now. 'You think the Protector will take the side of common ruffians like these?'

'I do.' Kett's voice rose. 'You were always a man who used the King's authority to steal every penny from his neighbours. Rich as you are, you are never happy unless you are a-lawyering and a-quarrelling! Like hundreds of so-called gentlemen and lawyers, you will do all you can to hinder the Protector and Commissioner Hales in righting the wrongs of the countryside and fostering the Commonwealth. And so it falls to us to aid their work.' It was a loud, fluent speech, angry but controlled.

Flowerdew said, bitterly, 'You own land yourself, Kett, all around Wymondham. And were once a good supporter of traditional religion, a friend of Abbot Loye. How can you associate yourselves with these stinking radicals?'

A man with a half-pike pointed it threateningly at Flowerdew. 'You shut your clack-box, or you'll get stuck like a pig.'

Kett replied, his voice rising so all around could hear. 'I work with my hands, on my farm, and like all Norfolk men I suffer from the enclosures of the rich gentlemen and the thefts of officials like you. Christ's blood, sir, we'll open the Protector's eyes to the true state of things, God save him, we will!'

Flowerdew looked distinctly worried now. In his meadow some of the men who had taken down the hurdles were chasing the sheep, long knives upraised. Three men brought one down. A knife was raised, the animal jerked, bleating frantically, and blood gushed over its white body. A second sheep was caught and its throat quickly cut too. Flowerdew looked at his steward, who could only shake his head. Then he said, a tremble of fury in his voice now, 'Stop them killing my sheep.'

Kett shook his head.

'My sons are not yet sixteen,' Flowerdew said, his voice suddenly pleading. 'My wife is helpless in my house.'

'We will hurt no women or children. But we don't want you raising people to attack us. You and your sons will come with us to Wymondham.'

Young Edward and William looked at each other. 'You can't command me where to go,' Flowerdew said incredulously.

'We can, and we do.'

Duffield said eagerly, 'We can rough him up a bit, carn't we, Master Robert?'

Kett considered, gave Flowerdew a long, hard look, then said, 'Maybe, but not much, just buffle him about a bit. We'll take the steward as well.'

One of the men surrounding us looked at Barak, Nicholas and I. 'Who be these three beauties?'

I answered, 'We have been visiting Serjeant Flowerdew. On a legal errand.'

Duffield said, 'Show us your hands, all of you.'

'I can only give you one, boys,' Barak said, and a couple of the men laughed. We all opened our palms. Duffield said, 'Just as I thort. Inky fingers, hands soft as women's, all of them.' He held up his own hands, rough and calloused with a lifetime's work. 'Lawyers, friends of Flowerdew.' My heart began to pound; this was looking bad for us. Nicholas looked angry, and I prayed he would keep his mouth shut. I was conscious, too, of the weight of Isabella's gold at my belt.

Then I saw a man approaching from the field. A stocky fellow, with a black beard and large blue eyes. Toby Lockswood, whose family troubles I feared had prevented him getting in touch. But he was here, he was one of the conspirators. I felt a sudden spurt of anger.

'That pignut,' Nicholas breathed.

Toby marched boldly up to us, giving me a cold nod. Nicholas burst out, 'Have you forgotten how to bow, Lockswood?'

'Shut up, you stupid arsehole,' Barak hissed. He could see, as I could, that Toby had some authority here.

'I know these birds,' Toby said to Kett.

'They the people you worked for at Norwich?'

'They are. Master Shardlake, what are you doing as a guest of John Flowerdew?'

'I came to see him about a legal matter.' I looked at Flowerdew, hesitating, but my first loyalty was to Nicholas and Barak, and I continued, 'His illegal eviction of Isabella Boleyn.'

Flowerdew looked at me in fury, as a fresh muttering arose among the men around us and our horses stirred uneasily again. Young William Flowerdew gave me a look of disgust which, I confess, shamed me. Then someone said, 'He's the one that saved that gemmun from the rope in Naarich, while the common folk hanged.'

Kett raised an interrogative eyebrow at Toby. Lockswood studied us, considering. I said quietly, 'I was going to come to your farm today, Toby, to see how you fared. I was worried when you did not get in touch as you promised, especially after all the help you gave us in Norwich.'

His face darkened. 'My life on the farm is over. My mother died a few days ago, and my father fell down and died, too, the next day.' His voice broke for a moment, then he continued, 'The farm was held on a tenancy of three lives, and my father's was the last. I'm out. I knew what was brewing and came to Wymondham to join what was coming.'

'I am sorry about your parents,' I said, quietly. I realized there were new lines on Toby's face, a wildness in those large eyes now. 'I did not know.'

'No,' he replied, his voice distant, 'how could you?' He turned to look at where the last of Flowerdew's hurdles were coming down. Men were dragging the bodies of the slain sheep towards the road, leaving a bloody trail, while the rest of the flock still ran helplessly round the field, other men in pursuit.

'Well, Toby Lockswood,' Kett asked quietly, 'what do we do with these three?'

Toby took a deep breath. 'The long streely lad, he's of gemmun stock, thinks all common folk should keep in their place. He's handy with that sword he's wearing; you should have it off him. If we let him go, he'll stir up trouble. I'd hold him and take him to Wymondham, like Flowerdew. The hunchback – I'm not sure about him. He's a serjeant like Flowerdew, but used to work for the Court of Requests and I think he's got Commonwealth sympathies. But he works for the Lady Elizabeth now, trying to save her gentleman relatives.'

'As have you!' Nicholas shouted. Toby ignored him.

Kett looked at me. 'Why did you leave honourable work helping the poor?'

'Because I made an enemy of Richard Rich. When he became Lord Chancellor I was dismissed.'

Kett nodded reflectively. He said to Toby, 'I think he needs more questioning. What about the one-handed man?'

'He's their servant, and I think his sympathies are with us. Let him go.'

'You're right, Toby, I'm with you,' Barak said in a steady voice. 'Something like this should have happened long ago. But, I won't leave Master Shardlake, nor Nicholas. He's a decent boy for all his antrums.'

Kett nodded firmly. 'Then you all come back to Wymondham with us. We need one more night there, that's where everyone is gath-ering. Get them off their horses, we can use those. Tie their hands, but don't buffle them about. Master Steward, we'll need some of your carts to take those sheep to Wymondham.'

'There're two behind the house,' Glapthorne said. He took a deep breath. 'I'll come with you willing, I'll help you.'

Kett smiled at him cynically, recognizing this was opportunism. He said, 'David, Theo, go with them, watch out for tricks.'

Flowerdew looked at his steward, aghast. I think it was only then he truly realized the extent of what had just happened. I could almost feel a pinch of sympathy for the wretched man, whose world had so suddenly and completely collapsed around him. But so had ours. We, too, were captives. I breathed hard to still my beating heart. Nicholas reluctantly handed over his sword and we all dismounted, till only Flowerdew was left, sitting on his horse, looking dazed. Then suddenly his whole body tightened and he put his spurs to his horse's flank and bolted, his horse throwing three men aside like ninepins.

'Get after him!' Kett snapped. Two men grabbed my horse, and Nicholas's, and mounted them. The animals, though, were already frightened, and Nicholas's horse reared high and almost threw his new rider. By the time the men had gained control of the horses and set off after Flowerdew, he was already a small dot on the road, riding frantically for Norwich.

Chapter Thirty-eight

A ND SO WE FOUND ourselves on the road back to Wymondham. This time, though, Barak, Nicholas and I walked with
arms bound behind us, a position I found painful. To my left, Nicholas's face wore an expression of fury, though on my other side, Barak
was making every effort to gain the confidence of the men walking
beside us, asking where they had come from and laughing when they
told him how they had sent Master Hobart of Morley and his family
fleeing from his fine house. I said nothing; on the one hand, I sympathized with their anger; on the other, I feared the escalation of violence,
and remembered that I too was deemed a 'gentleman'.

A tall fellow of about thirty, carrying a cleaver, had been positioned beside us. Occasionally, he gave Nicholas and me evil looks.
Behind us Flowerdew's sons were similarly pinioned; the elder lad
wore a defiant expression but the younger looked cowed and fearful.

It was late afternoon now, but still hot, and we walked through
clouds of dust that turned our hose and shoes grey. More men, and a
few women, joined us as we walked along, and soon our numbers had
risen to fifty. At the head of the procession rode Robert Kett — he had
taken Nicholas's horse, and beside him, on mine and Barak's, rode
Toby and Duffield, the Wymondham man. The rear was brought up
by two large carts from Flowerdew's house, pulled by donkeys, led by
the steward Glapthorne, who looked uneasy. They held the bodies of
the slaughtered sheep, which left a thin trail of blood on the dusty road.

Halfway to Wymondham another group of about twenty joined
us, labourers or craftsmen, by the look of them, in shirts or leather
jerkins. Several carried bows, with quivers over their shoulders, some
wore sallets, round military helmets, while a couple carried swords or
halberds or half-pikes, no doubt taken from a manor house or church

where weapons were stored for the military musters that had been a regular feature of life since the wars against Scotland and France began. I thought, Wherever the weapons might have been stored, it was these men who would have been expected to wield them if they were sent to war. Behind them a large cart pulled by donkeys contained the bodies of several slain deer.

The leader of the group exchanged greetings with Kett. 'We've been a-raidin' one of the Paston parks! Threw down the fences and went in. Gor, my lads know how to shoot. We took this cart and the dickeys to pull it, too. There'll be venison tonight in Wymondham!'

There was a cheer from our group, and someone called, 'We're heading there too, bor! Jine us!'

The man looked up at Kett. 'It's all right to raid parks, in't it? They count as enclosures.'

'Yes,' Kett agreed firmly. 'Take the cart to the rear!' I began to realize that Kett was already accepted as a leader. As the cart passed, I looked at the rolling heads of the slaughtered deer, which included a couple of young fauns, and suddenly felt sick. The man beside me grinned. 'Too much for yew, Marster Lawyer?' I did not reply, and he leaned close. 'I'm a master carpenter, live in a village near Besthorpe. I grazed a cow and a couple of pigs on the common till last year, for my family, but the manor lord enclosed it. With a bad harvest coming we'll be clammed wi' hunger this winter unless we take our due.' He came closer. 'Some of us would like to deal with you like those lads dealt with the deer.' He nodded emphatically, gripping his cleaver. I made no reply.

✠

WYMONDHAM WAS HEAVING with people, more even than during the fair, well over a thousand, I guessed. The tents still stood on the common, and as we were marched past the marketplace, I saw through the open doors that the chapel was being filled with straw bedding. So was the church, while beyond, people and carts had taken places among the remains of the monastery. The great crowd was orderly, and the town constables seemed to have joined some older men, many with a military bearing, in directing people where to go. A cart filled with barrels of ale passed us. Many of those in the streets greeted Kett's party with cheers, and raised caps and hats. Seeing us bound in the midst of the party, some people booed, and a rotten cabbage came flying at us, almost knocking the elder Flowerdew boy off his feet. Kett raised a hand. 'No!' he shouted sternly. 'We shall give the gentlemen the justice they deserve, but by due process in the King's name!' He looked back over the men who accompanied him, and called out, 'Wait here, all of you!' Such was his authority that everyone stayed in their place.

His brother William appeared, and the two spoke earnestly, Robert leaning down from the horse. Then a figure detached itself from the crowd and approached me. It was Michael Vowell, his mouth open with surprise.

'Master Shardlake? What has happened?'

'My friends and I are prisoners, as you see. We were on a visit to Serjeant Flowerdew when Master Kett and his men called. These boys are Flowerdew's sons. He himself has fled.'

Vowell frowned. 'Why were you visiting him?'

'He evicted Isabella Boleyn illegally from her house. Reynolds was involved.' I smiled wryly. 'I am not surprised to see you here.'

A suspicious expression crossed his face. 'What do you mean?'

'One night at the Blue Boar in Norwich, a few weeks ago, I saw you talking to a man I know, Edward Brown, and a soldier you called Miles. You spoke of Attleborough.'

His eyes widened. 'And you said nothing?'

'It was not my business. And Edward Brown and his wife are my friends. Are they here?'

He gave me a long, searching look. 'No. In Norwich still.' He considered, then said, 'I will speak with the Ketts.' He jogged to the head of the line, and I saw him talk to the brothers. Robert Kett and Toby dismounted, and walked back to us with William Kett. Close to, I saw William was older than his brother, perhaps in his mid-sixties. His square, strong face looked severe. Barak murmured, 'Talk for your lives.'

William faced me. 'Vowell here tells me you overheard a certain conversation in Norwich, yet told nobody.'

'That is true. As I told him, one of the other men involved, and his wife, are my friends.'

'The woman is his old servant, not a friend,' Toby said severely. 'But 'tis true he sought her out to help her,' he added reluctantly.

William looked at me thoughtfully. 'And said nothing about Miles, or Attleborough. He can't have done, or it would have been nipped in the bud.' He looked at his brother. 'We'll need lawyers and scriveners if we're to do what we've talked about.'

Robert nodded. 'I'll take him to Gunville Manor. Let the one-armed man go, he's their servant, he can help get things ready for tonight. But see someone keeps an eye on him. Take the long lad and Flowerdew's boys to the lock-up. Those boys are valuable hostages.'

'Master Kett,' I said, pleadingly, 'let Nicholas stay with me. I will answer for him.' Kett looked at Toby, who said, 'No, he's against us, lock him up.'

'You three, take them,' William said. Strong arms seized Nicholas and the boys. For a second I thought Nicholas might struggle, but he allowed himself to be led away. William turned to Barak. 'Go down to the abbey, ask for Captain Atley, he'll see you make yourself useful.'

There were loud cheers as a fresh column of men appeared; bearing arms ranging from scythes to crossbows and hauling a battered cannon on a wheeled carriage, they entered the already crowded streets. At their head an elderly man in clerical garb carried an ancient banner showing the head of Christ. 'Another village in,' said William. 'I'll send them down to the monastery grounds. They can set the banner up to mark the place and duddle up there tonight.'

'Aye, each village should put up a banner or flag to mark where they're from, or people will get themselves lost in this crowd.'

'I'll see you later, I promise,' Barak said to me, then turned towards the abbey ruins. I felt suddenly alone, and thought of John Boleyn, in his cell at the castle. What would happen to him now? And Isabella, Scambler, Edward and Josephine? Robert Kett turned to me. 'Come with us,' he said abruptly.

✝

MY WRISTS UNTIED, I walked with the brothers and a small escort past the abbey ruins, across the river. Everywhere people hailed and cheered the Ketts, some raising weapons. There was no chance of escape. An old man in a makeshift white robe, with white hair and a straggly little beard, stood on top of the half-demolished wall of the precinct, brandishing a bible as he addressed a small crowd. I heard him say, 'I prophesy that the rule of the saints predicted in Revelation has come, that we are the chosen and shall inaugurate the rule of Christ!'

'Old Gribbin at it again,' William said wryly.

Robert frowned. 'We need people to settle down quietly.'

William nodded agreement. 'There are groups camped outside the town. There'll be more coming in tomorrow. I think we'll have to start moving, Wymondham can't take any more. Miles has had every house with room to spare requisitioned. Thank God the weather's holding.'

'Is there enough to eat?'

'Just about.' William smiled. 'Most have brought food or beer with them. Good Norfik commonsense.'

We walked perhaps a mile, until we reached a two-storeyed house of red brick with a pleasant knot-garden and tall chimneys. We were led up into the house. The hallway was crowded with people, talking animatedly. A young man came over to Robert Kett and threw his arms round him. 'Yer back safe, Father! Thank the Lord! What happened with Flowerdew?'

'He ran, the canker blossom. But his fences are down, and we have his sons! Christ's wounds, Loye, we have a great crowd in Wymondham!'

'Aye. And news has come in from Cambridge and Downham, the commons are risen there too!'

Kett stepped back. For the first time his face showed real emotion. 'This is a mighty work!' he said. 'It has to be God's doing!'

An attractive woman with grey hair, a little girl of six or so at her side, came up, and Robert embraced her. 'Alice, Alice! And little Margaret!'

'Granfer!' The child danced up and down with excitement. 'Did you catch the bad man?'

'No, but we taught him a lesson!'

'Robert,' the woman said, 'if you go tomorrow, I am coming with you. I am decided. Let Loye and the other boys look after things in Wymondham, my place is with you.'

William looked doubtful. 'I think the women should stay at home.'

Kett put his hand on her shoulder and said tenderly, 'We shall see, my dear. Now, I must have a word with this man.' I thought, Where are they planning to go? His family looked at me curiously. Robert said, 'There is a little time before Miles and the others arrive. William, take a turn back up the road again, see how things fare.'

William nodded and left the house. Robert opened a door and motioned me to enter. It was the office of a man of business; tidy, a desk with documents and books of accounts, reminding me Kett was a man of some substance, though in status far below Flowerdew. Or me, for that matter. He drew up a comfortable chair and motioned me to sit, poured us some beer from a flagon, then lit a candle – the light was starting to fade – and sat behind the desk. He laced his fingers together and looked at me. His expression was neutral, but his large eyes narrowed.

'You looked uncomfortable when you were walking here,' he said after a moment.

'I am better now. I have been having trouble with my back. Please, where am I?'

'My home, Gunville Manor. You will remain here tonight.' He considered a moment, then said, 'You fell off the scaffold at Norwich, didn't you? I heard about the hanging.'

'John Boleyn is my client,' I answered quietly. 'A pardon request had been entered, executing him would have been illegal.'

Kett grunted. 'His Boleyn kin in Norfolk came nowhere near him, I believe. Such are the Norfolk gentlemen. But what of you, Master Shardlake? How came you to be involved in that case?'

'I was instructed by the Lady Elizabeth. Then, as I told you, Flowerdew evicted his wife illegally, I came to Hethersett to stop him.'

'He is no friend of yours, then.'

'No. He is a rogue.'

'I believe that, like him, you are a serjeant-at-law. Strong words about one lawyer from another.' He smiled, then said softly, 'You wouldn't be givin' me sweet lawyer's talk, would you, with poison breath beneath?'

'No, Master Kett. I speak the truth.'

He cast an eye to the purse hanging from my belt. 'I heard that a' chinking on the way here. If that's gold, it must be a mighty sum. Did Flowerdew give it you?'

I took a deep breath. 'As well as evicting Isabella Boleyn, he took some money her husband had given her to support herself while he remains in Norwich Castle. I got it back from him, and shall return it when I can.'

'How much?' Kett asked bluntly.

'Twenty gold sovereigns.'

He whistled. 'A very goodly sum. We are going to need money.'

I took a deep breath, then put my hand over my purse. I was Kett's prisoner, but I had to take a stand. 'This is the property of a helpless, innocent woman. If you want it, you will have to take it from me.'

'That would be easy enough.' He made no move, though, to take it. He leaned back, resting his hands on the arms of his chair, trying to gauge what manner of creature I was. At length he said, 'So, you worked at Requests, and call commoners like the Browns friends. Unusual. Have you represented many Norfolk clients?'

'Over the years, a good number. They have always been tenacious, with a sound knowledge of the law.'

Kett leaned forward. 'Are you a Commonwealth man, then, Master Shardlake?'

I spoke carefully. 'Yes. In that I believe the common people of England are subject to great wrongs, which have grown worse these last years.'

'You support the Protector, then, and the enclosure commissions?'

His gaze was one of the most intent I had ever encountered. I sensed he was a man who wanted the truth above all. I answered calmly. 'Yes, entirely. But I fear they may not work. Enclosure commis-sions have been tried before, under Wolsey and Cromwell, but always their findings were overturned in the courts or ignored by the old king. And the task they have been set this year is – impossible. It seems a few commissioners will be asked in each part of the country to overturn illegal enclosures since 1485. I do not think the Protector has begun to think through the practicalities, for him everything comes second to his war against the Scots, which, with the debasement, has caused half the present trouble.'

Kett shook his head. 'No, he is with the godly men, those who wish to build a new and Christian Commonwealth. You make a law-yer's answer.'

'Whatever you might want, the gentleman class will never allow such a reform of landholding to be implemented.'

Kett slapped a hand smartly on his desk, and smiled. 'Exactly! That is why we have risen now. To provide muscle for the commission-ers' decisions, and to ensure our needs are met. That is why camps are being set up across the country, why they are armed, why they are bringing down the gentlemen and sending petitions about our griev-ances to the Protector. We are helping him. God's death, man, he has already agreed to the demands of the Essex men.'

So they would dictate to the commissioners, not support them, I thought, but did not say. Kett raised his eyebrows, waiting for me to speak. I took a deep breath. 'I do not believe the Protector, still less the Council to which he is answerable, will allow the common people a say in government.'

'Do you think they should?'

I sighed. 'Yes. In theory.'

'Yet you do not believe it will happen?'

'No. I fear this will end in violence.'

'We shall kill nobody, unless attacked first. If the men rough up some of the landowners, it's nothing to what they've done to us in the past. We have former soldiers with us, and officials of town and village government. They will ensure everything is orderly. Thus we shall show the Protector we can govern ourselves.'

'Soldiers. You mean deserters from the Scottish wars?'

His voice grew harsh. 'Men who went to serve and went unpaid, starving in rat-holes. They were betrayed, and are angry, but they are soldiers of courage and experience in organizing men.'

'I am no supporter of the Scottish war,' I said. 'It has been a brutal disaster.'

Kett nodded. His look was determined, fierce. 'We shall win. This is God's will.'

I paused. 'What do you intend to do?' I asked eventually.

'As others are doing all over England. Establish a headquarters. Put down the rich gentlemen, capture them to prevent them raising forces against us. Petition the Protector, wait for the commissioners to come. Then we shall have a new rule.'

'And what do you want with me?'

He studied me again. 'You could be of use to us. If you choose to be.'

Before I could ask him what he meant, there came a knock at the door, and Kett's son, Loye, put his head round. 'Excuse me, Father, Miles and William and the others are here.'

Kett stood. 'Stay here, Master Shardlake, I shall return shortly.' As they left the room, I looked at the diamond-paned window behind the desk, and the tidy knot-garden outside, peaceful in the dusk. Yet scarce a mile away a massive rebellion was brewing. I felt suddenly chill, a cold sweat forming on my brow.

☩

I SAT AWHILE, listening to the faint murmur of voices from the hall-way outside. Then I got up and put my ear to the door, which sometimes can be the only way to get information. I heard the voices of the Kett brothers, and several others which were unfamiliar, although one I thought sounded like the soldier, Miles. I heard him say, 'This is Captain Wills, sore brushed in the old king's French wars, as you see, with much experience in victualling.'

'I see people ha' brought in supplies,' another voice replied, 'and killed many sheep, but more vittles must be organized. Ale, too; men must drink in this heat. Don't, they'll collapse. Supplies should be sent from their villages.'

'It's good to organize people by their parish banners,' Miles said. 'But we must move tomorrow — more are coming in from the villages in the north of the county. Those in the south-west are congregating at Downham. But make no mistake, Master Kett, up here hundreds upon hundreds are coming in. We may end up with the biggest camp in the country.'

'Things must be organized fast.' This was Robert speaking.

The voice I thought was Miles's came in again: 'Ay, and we officers are used to organizing things.'

'So are we Norfolk men,' William said brusquely. 'Don't take us as stupid. The villagers are keeping lines open to their homes; they know they'll need more supplies.'

'I don't underestimate you, sir. But in a case of moving possibly thousands of men, we soldiers can help.'

'And now, together, in a great cause,' Robert said, placatingly.

'Can we take Norwich?' another man asked. 'Those walls are low, half broken down in places.'

'The poor there are on our side,' Miles answered, 'but the constables seem to be staying loyal to the city council. They've got arms. It depends what line the council takes.'

'If need be, we can set up camp on Mousehold Heath, outside the city,' Robert said.

Captain Wills replied, 'Then we must indeed organize supplies from the countryside, by force or favour. What are we to do with the gemmun we capture? There are those outside would have their heads off.'

'My brother has an idea,' William said.

'Try them ourselves for their misdeeds, and imprison those we find guilty. Put our findings to the commissioners.' This was Robert.

'We have scriveners among us,' William added.

Miles said, 'I hear we've captured young Thomas Godsalve. He's a lawyer, but he's spitting blood, I doubt he'd help us.'

'We have two lawyers as well,' Robert replied. 'Another young one, who won't help. The other –' he paused – 'might.' I drew a deep breath. Was this what Kett wanted, for me to help with some illegal ad hoc trials?

'There's a bigger problem,' Captain Wills interjected. 'Understand again, we could be talking thousands of men. Who is to lead them? It has to be someone known and trusted locally.'

They must have looked at William Kett, for I heard him say, 'I'm too old. And I get crotchety. Robert's mind is quicker, and he has a rare knack of attracting loyalty.' He must have turned to his brother, for he added, 'And you have great gifts of speech. Can be crafty when it's needed, too.'

They moved away, and I heard no more. I went and sat in the chair, thinking furiously, trying to muster my thoughts on this extraordinary situation. It was near an hour before I heard the sound of men saying farewell, and Robert Kett returned. He sat down and looked at me hard, then spoke, quietly and seriously. 'Tomorrow morning we leave for Norwich. There are hundreds coming in, maybe thousands, and hard tasks ahead. There are those who would have our oppressors, the corrupt officials and rich landowners, done to death. I understand that, but it will not serve our purpose, which is to show loyalty to the Protec-tor and the law. I have in mind to take these men prisoner and subject them to trials. The penalty for unjust oppression of the commons will be imprisonment. Nothing more. An experienced lawyer to advise me would be a good thing. It could help me curb the wilder spirits. Will you aid me?'

I said, 'Just before I left London, I saw a company of soldiers out of control half kill a man who had done no wrong, simply because he had a Scotch accent.'

'Our soldiers are for the Commonwealth,' Kett said stoutly. 'They are men of ideals.' He leaned back and crossed his arms. 'But you are a gentleman, perhaps you fear common people?'

His words struck home. For all my own ideals, my status meant that my whole life I had seen the poor, especially in numbers, as a potential threat, an enemy. As individuals I could advise them, but in the mass, yes, I feared them. I said, 'I am a man of my background, as are we all. Will you let me consider this?' I knew if I refused I would end up their prisoner, like Nicholas. But I needed to think, and think hard.

Kett frowned, then nodded slowly. 'A little time, yes. I see you are an honest man, Serjeant Shardlake; others might agree too quickly, to curry favour, then take the chance to flee later.' He stood. 'And now, I offer you a bed in my house tonight.'

That was an offer, I knew, I would not be allowed to refuse. I said, 'When you get to Norwich, what of the town poor? Their grievances are different. Perhaps some wish not to reform the kingdom, but make all men level?'

He laughed. 'Like the Anabaptists in Germany, fifteen years ago. How often the gentlemen use them as a bogey to frighten their fellows.'

'My point is, Master Kett, the Anabaptists were destroyed by the rulers.'

He studied me with those large, piercing eyes. 'We shall not be destroyed, we shall prove to the Protector that we are loyal.' He stood. 'And now, I must return to town. I will arrange something to eat for you.' He looked at my belt. 'And for now, at least, you may keep that money. But do not advertise you have it.'

Chapter Thirty-nine

THE FOLLOWING MORNING, I was woken at dawn by the sound of voices and trundling cartwheels outside. The smell of cooking fires wafted through the open window. Heavy footsteps sounded within the house. I had shared a bed with Michael Vowell, and Hector John-son, an elderly ex-soldier. He was around sixty, thin and stringy with several scars on his sunburned face. Nonetheless, he moved as swiftly as a younger man, jumping from the bed.

I sat up and rubbed a hand over my stubbly chin. Vowell, already lacing up his hose, said I should rise. 'We shall be on the road soon and must try to snatch some breakfast.'

Downstairs bread and cheese had been set out on the dining-room table, with jugs of ale. A dozen men, including Robert Kett's son, sat eating as quickly as they could, tearing the bread with their hands. I hesitated, then reached out to grab some bread and cheese. I was used to being served my food, eating slowly. Vowell smiled cynically. 'Catch as catch can now, Master Shardlake.'

Afterwards, Vowell and Johnson led me outside – no doubt they had been set to keep a watch on me – and we walked to the centre of town, where perhaps a thousand men, and a few women, had gath-ered, most in workaday clothes and caps or wide-brimmed hats, bags over their shoulders, many carrying weapons. The crowd was quiet; no doubt most were newly awake; many looked tired and some as though they had thick heads after a celebratory night. I looked around for Barak and Nicholas, but saw neither. Hector Johnson walked to the rear of the crowd, where carts were being packed with vittles. Vowell stayed with me. I glanced at him. The well-dressed steward had become a man with tangled beard and hair, dressed in a loose shirt. But his eyes sparkled with enthusiasm.

The crowd's attention was focused on Beckett's Chapel, where the Kett brothers stood on the steps with Miles and several other men. Robert waved his arms for silence, then called out in a loud, deep voice. 'We leave now for Norwich, to erect a great camp at Mousehold Heath! Others will join us by the great oak at Hethersett! Be of good heart and discipline! We are making as great a stir as any in Norfolk's history!' There was a chorus of cheers. Then William and Robert Kett, Robert's wife Alice, and a little group including Toby, the soldier Miles, and some others I did not know, mounted horses, and called for the people to follow. The great concourse – men of all ages, mostly poor but some wearing the richer, deeply dyed fabrics of yeomen, and a few women with their husbands, began marching out of Wymond-ham. Vowell asked, 'Will you be all right walking?'

'I hope so.' I inclined my head. 'Easier with my hands untied.' I looked behind me, where oxen and donkeys drew a long trail of carts, most filled with food, though others contained weapons, helmets and breastplates. At the very back was a cart where five bound men sat; the Flowerdew boys, a pair of gentlemen I did not recognize, fine clothes askew, and Nicholas. His face looked bruised. I drew a deep breath. Somehow I had to get him out of there.

It was yet another hot, dry day, great clouds of dust thrown up from the road. People seemed to be grouped together by locality, for banners taken from local churches were held up by men who often wore the yeoman dress of village leaders; one or two were clerics. As we left Wymondham, people working in the fields stopped and cheered. The crowd called back, 'The commons claim our rights!' and 'God save King Edward!' A few labourers peeled off and joined us.

We marched on. As we passed sheep-runs, men broke off from the crowd and, using hammers and picks, dug up the hedges and hurdles and threw them into the ditches. The shepherds in the pastures fled. One shepherd's dog ran snarling at the men lifting the hurdles, biting one on the leg before he killed it with a hammer blow. I noticed that a few men wore breastplates and walked like soldiers, with an air of command. Some carried trumpets. I stared at the scene; I could hardly take in the import of it all. A rebellion of the common people, which, we were all told, would lead to anarchy. Yet everyone marched in order;

if people strayed too far into the fields a trumpet blast brought them back. Yet was it even right to call them rebels? Had they not called out 'God save the King?' Had they not risen in defence of the commissions? Some of the younger men, though, looked ready for a fight.

Beside me Vowell said, 'We pass the road to Brikewell ere long. You said that Flowerdew and that old rogue Reynolds threw Boleyn's wife out of the manor house?'

'Yes. She and her steward are still in Norwich, so far as I know.'

'Anyone at North Brikewell manor now? We're visiting all the manor houses to get food and arms. Many of the weapons stored in the churches for the village musters are all but useless; some go back to Bosworth.'

'The twins are at Brikewell,' I said. 'And some of their friends.'

He nodded with satisfaction. 'They'll make fine hostages.'

'They'll give you a fight.'

Vowell laughed. 'Against these numbers? We shall prevail, Master Shardlake, there and everywhere else. Those young devils, they're symbols of the oppression that's been brought to Norfolk—'

We were interrupted by blaring trumpets. Ahead, under a large oak spreading wide branches over the road, I saw another huge crowd, almost as large as our own, spilling into the fields behind. They raised a loud cheer as we approached. Word was passed down the line to stop, that Robert Kett was to address us all. Some took the chance to sit on the ground, for we had been walking some time. I eased myself carefully onto a hummock of grass. Robert Kett rode to the oak, his brother William by his side, then he watched as the crowd settled down.

'Where have all these others *come* from?' I asked Vowell, half-incredulous.

'All around Norfolk. You see, Master Shardlake, how we unite!' He laughed, with sheer pleasure.

I looked at him. 'How long have you been involved in planning this?'

'Since the day I left Master Reynolds's house. I decided then to join those who, it was murmured, would bring the doings of men like him to an end.'

I felt a hand on my arm. Barak, now wearing a broad-brimmed

hat, sat down beside me on the hummock. Vowell looked at him questioningly. He smiled back. 'Just wanted a word with my friend. They said at the back I could come up here.'

'Did you see Nick?' I asked.

'Ay, he's taken a bit of a beating. When will he learn to shut his mouth?'

'He would be well advised to,' Vowell said coldly.

'I've tried telling him.' Barak reached into the pack he carried, pulled out another hat, and gave it to me. 'Here, I thought you might need this.'

'Thank you,' I replied gratefully. I looked at him. He seemed quite cheerful. 'Are you all right?'

'Right as rain. They need someone at the carts who can write, to record all the supplies they've got. Even though they do stare at me, writing with my left hand and supporting the papers on this thing.' He waved his artificial hand.

Trumpets sounded again. There was silence, and then, under the oak, Robert Kett began to speak. His brother William stood beside him. We were close enough to hear, but, loud and deep as Kett's voice was, it could not reach all that vast throng, and men passed his words back as he spoke.

'Men of Norfolk! We rise because the oppression of the great men is unbearable, and our condition grows worse each month!

'While they enjoy their pleasures, the commons do nothing but sweat, hunger and thirst. Our misery is a laughing stock to those proud insolent men! We are like slaves, and farm our land only at the pleasure and will of the lords. For as soon as any man offends any of these gentlemen, he is put out! The common pastures which have been our predecessors' time out of mind are taken away; they are ditched and hedged in, the pastures enclosed . . .'

The crowd listened in silence save for the occasional cheer. Barak whispered, 'He's some orator.'

Kett continued, pausing after each sentence to let his words be carried back: ' . . . We can no longer bear such great and cruel injury! We will rather take arms than endure it! Nature has provided for us, as well as them; has given us, too, a body and soul. We have the same form, are born of women like them! Why should they have a life so unlike ours!'

There were loud cheers, and weapons were raised. 'Radical stuff,' I murmured.

'All across the land men rise against the enclosures for sheep, and the other iniquities heaped upon us by the landlords, like the encroachments on common land and the illegal raising of our rents. Soon the Protector's commissioners will arrive, and we shall ensure justice is done. We will ourselves rend down the fences, fill up the ditches, and make a way for men into the common pasture! We will suffer no more to be pressed with such burdens! We shall petition the Protector with our ills, and get good answer, like the people of Essex!'

There were more cheers, ringing to the wide blue sky till Kett raised his hands for silence.

'I promise that the harms done to the public weal by the lords shall be righted.' He paused, surveyed the crowd, then continued, 'Soon, we shall camp and rest. We shall feed ourselves from the countryside, arm ourselves against the gentlemen. As for those we have made captive, we shall try them according to law; there will be no undue violence or murder. That is *their* way! Let *us* show the Protector we can govern ourselves, without the gentlemen!' He took a deep breath, then continued, louder than ever. 'I myself sinned in raising enclosures on my land, but I have with my own hands made them common again.' He paused, then said, 'You shall have me, if you will, not only as a companion, but also as captain; and in doing the great work before us, not only as a fellow, but also for a general, standard-bearer and chief. Not only will I be present at all your councils, but, if you will have it so, henceforth I will preside at them! Before all things else do I put your deliverance, and for this I will spend not only my goods, but my very life, so dear to me is the cause on which we are embarked! Now, do you swear on your oath, before God, to remain and work together until our work is done?'

There was a deafening chorus: 'We do!' I drew a deep breath; nothing was more binding, more powerful, than a man's oath before God. Kett raised a fist. 'And so, my friends, to Norwich!'

Another cheering roar, and Kett took off his cap and waved it.

Beside me Barak said quietly, 'Looks like they've found a leader.'

I nodded. 'Everything was about enclosures, though. What of the hurts of the towns?'

'He's following the Protector's agenda. Hoping to get his support.'

'It may not end there,' I said.

'The start is good enough for me.'

I leaned in closer, speaking intently. 'What are you doing, Jack? You have a wife and children in London!'

'Don't be a fool! I'm being watched, same as you are. I couldn't get away and run to Tamasin, even if I wanted to. Like you, I'm surviving as best I can now we're caught up in this.'

'But you believe in it.'

He looked at me with sudden fierceness. 'It's time something like this happened. Don't you agree?'

'I don't know what to think.'

'Then let it play out.'

The men were settling into line again, amidst a buzz of excited conversation. Barak stood and made his way back down towards the baggage train. Vowell looked at me suspiciously. 'What were you two whispering about?'

'Jack has a wife and children in London.'

'In times like these, ties of the heart are best forgotten.'

'Are they?'

☦

WHEN WE REACHED the turning for Brikewell, two dozen armed men peeled off from the main crowd and disappeared down the lane. Barak was with them, no doubt as a guide. I watched anxiously; if the twins and their friends fought back, blood would be spilt.

Just afterwards the head of the procession reached the bridge across the River Yare. We were more than halfway to Norwich. The crowd, which I estimated now at perhaps two thousand, slowed almost to a halt as men crossed the narrow bridge, though some boys swam across, the cool of the water no doubt a relief, for it was near midday. I was glad to sit again for a while, watching the path to Brikewell. Vowell was called away to some duty, and the old soldier Hector Johnson came and sat beside me, no doubt sent in Vowell's place to watch me. He wore a sallet helmet and a sword at his waist now. 'A hot day,' I said neutrally.

He grunted. 'You get used to marching in the heat when you're a soldier. I was at the battle for Boulogne, then at Portsmouth when the fleets battled in the Solent.'

'I was there too,' I said quietly.

He laughed scoffingly. 'You were never a soldier.'

'I had friends who were. A captain of archers particularly. He went down on the *Mary Rose*.'

'I am sorry,' Johnson said more gently. 'I was a captain of archers too. They dragged me out of retirement for the Scottish war, but God's bones, that campaign is a waste of gold and lives.' He laughed bitterly. 'At Berwick John Knox told us his fellow redshanks would welcome us as good Protestants, but they and their French troops harried us out of those earthen forts the Protector built, one by one. As for the people, they were starved and harried by both sides. When I hadn't been paid for six months I left and came home. Now I'll fight for justice under Master Kett.'

We were silent for a while, watching the slow progress of men crossing the river. Then I saw a party returning from Brikewell. A couple of men wore makeshift bandages, and one walked with a limp, supported by two of his fellows, though, to my relief, Barak was uninjured. The knife at the end of his artificial hand was unsheathed, glinting in the sun. There seemed to be some new recruits from the estates. I asked Johnson if I could go to Barak and he nodded. As I approached, I saw donkeys dragging two carts of provisions and weapons, and at the rear three men with their wrists tied behind them being pushed and shoved along by men with pitchforks. I recognized Leonard Witherington, Lord of South Brikewell. The peppery little man had been stripped of his hose and rolled in the dust. He was shoved along barefoot, the fat white legs beneath his shirt contrasting with his red, terrified face. He stumbled, and a man jabbed him lightly with his fork, making him yell. His captors grinned. 'Git on, you, ter the cart!'

The other two captives were Gerald and Barnabas Boleyn. Like Witherington, they had been stripped to their shirts, and there was blood on Gerald's face, but their captors treated them more warily.

When one prodded Barnabas, he turned and shouted, 'Fuck off, you scum of the earth!'

Barak came up to me, looking excited. 'Their friends have flown the coop, but these two were waiting for us with knives and an axe. Jesu, they put up a fight, despite our numbers. Anyone with sense would have surrendered. God's blood, they've made a mess of that house while they've been there.'

The twins saw me. Gerald shouted out, 'Joined the rebels have you, you hunchbacked ratsbane! It's hanging, drawing and quartering for rebellion. We'll come to Tyburn to watch!'

One of their captors pushed him. 'Git on,' he said. 'Don't, you'll get stuck with this fork.'

The twins, with Witherington, were led down a jeering line of rebels to the carts at the rear. They shouted back; even this gigantic crowd seemed not to intimidate them. I wondered, not for the first time, whether they were quite sane.

Chapter Forty

AFTER CROSSING THE bridge we marched steadily on towards the city. Barak returned to work at the provisioning carts. Pitchers of ale were passed down the line. I had discarded my doublet and walked in my shirt, stinking of sweat. My back was starting to hurt and I struggled a little to keep pace. Even more people joined us along the way. Hector Johnson had left me, to help keep people in line, but Vowell reappeared by my side. I was still being watched.

Soon the great spire of Norwich Cathedral became visible, then we reached the Town Close, where the citizens' cattle grazed. There another astonishing scene greeted me. Numerous men had come out from Norwich, some watching while others tore down the walls of the Close. As our great concourse approached, the Norwich men cheered and waved, calling out that this was common land, which no man should have to pay to use, and a little group ran over to where Robert Kett and his brother sat on their horses. They were carrying little oak boughs, evidently an agreed signal. One young man I recognized immediately: Edward Brown, Josephine's husband. He stood with several others in intent converse with the Ketts. I sat down wearily on the ground again.

A wooden platform was quickly erected from the fences, and Robert Kett dismounted and climbed on top. He called for silence, and again the noisy crowd fell quiet. This time I was too far away to hear his words directly, but, as before, they were passed back. He said the city council had set armed men on the walls, and refused permission for us to travel through the city to Mousehold Heath. We would camp at the village of Bowthorpe nearby for the night. The Norwich men, he added, had brought food, to add to what we had already. He asked the Norwich men to return to the city and gather support. They ran back to their fellows before I had the chance to ask Edward Brown how Josephine fared. 'We have a loyal following in the city,' Vowell said proudly.

'I saw Edward Brown there.'

Vowell nodded. 'He's a good man, for all he's a Lunnoner.'

'Where is this Bowthorpe?'

'A couple of miles to the north.'

Barak had reappeared alongside us. 'I'm tired.' He clutched his artificial hand. 'I could do with taking this off for a bit.'

'You lose the hand in the war?' Vowell asked.

'No, in London.' Barak did not elaborate.

Bread and cheese, and more ale, were passed around and devoured hungrily. Again I marvelled at the level of organization these men had achieved so quickly. Food was unloaded from our carts and more brought from Norwich; these poor men had given what they had. Vowell lay down, to snatch some rest. I said to Barak, 'You still at the back?'

'Ay. Nick is quiet now. They've put the twins and Witherington in another cart, which is just as well for Nick. They kept shouting insults at him until someone smacked them across the mouth.'

'What did the rebels do to Witherington?'

He laughed. 'Just roughed him up a little. They're keeping to Kett's orders.'

I looked at the distant, looming heath.

I said urgently, 'If we make a permanent camp, how do you feed so many? What do they drink? What if the weather breaks? There is no shelter. We saw numbers as great as this on the old king's Progress to the North, and the army at Portsmouth, but that took months of organizing.'

'Much depends on Kett.'

I looked across the crowds, mostly seated now, village banners waving in the slight, welcome breeze that had arisen. I said quietly, 'If there are spies for the rebels in the city, I wonder if the city rulers have spies out here, too.'

Barak inclined his head. 'There's a question.'

✠

THERE FOLLOWED ANOTHER short march across open country to Bowthorpe. The place between my shoulder blades felt as though it was on fire, and my legs were numb, like pieces of wood. But I had no alternative other than to put one foot in front of the other. The dust stung my eyes.

Just outside the village was a wood. Here the march halted, and I headed for the nearest tree, another of the broad Norfolk oaks. Vowell called to me to wait, but I ignored him. The moment I passed under its branches, though, and felt the blessed coolness of the shade, a shiver passed through my body, and my legs buckled under me. In the second before I fainted I seemed to hear again the yells of the crowd at the execution.

✝

I WOKE WITH A START. I was lying on something hard but comfortable, and above me a wide canvas sheet was stretched. I groaned and looked around. Beside me, kneeling on his haunches, was a boy in his late teens, wearing a torn and dirty smock. Young as he was, he was tall and powerfully built, and held a club across his knees. In contrast with his big frame he had small, neat features, curly fair hair white with dust and a scraggy little beard. He looked at me with small, intelligent brown eyes.

'Where am I?' I whispered.

'Bowthorpe Wood, outside the village,' he answered quietly. 'Yew be all right, they rigged this little tent between the trees. Yew fainted.'

My mouth hurt; I tasted blood, and realized my lip was split. 'Yew fell on yer face,' the boy said, holding out a flagon. 'Reckon you'll need some o' this.'

I struggled to raise myself on my elbows. My head swam a little. I heard a crackling sound beneath me, and realized I was lying on a bed of bracken. I took a long swig of ale. 'How long have I been out?' I asked.

''Bout quarter an hour. I've been set to watch you.'

'What's your name?'

'Nathanial. Natty.'

I handed back the flagon. 'Thank you.' I put a hand to the purse containing Isabella's money; it was still at my belt. Natty's eyes had never left mine; as though he were studying me, weighing me up. I felt a spurt of irritation — did he think I was in a state to run away? I lay back on the bracken, and immediately fell asleep.

I was wakened by a hand shaking my shoulder. Barak was leaning over me. The boy still sat on his haunches, looking with interest at Barak's artificial hand. Perhaps an hour had passed, for the sun was lower. I heard the ring of axes against trees, smelt smoke from cooking fires. 'How are you?' Barak asked. 'I heard you'd fainted.'

'Better now,' I said. 'I was — exhausted.'

'You're not the only one. A few of the older men passed out. You're lucky to get this place, Bowthorpe Wood isn't near big enough to shelter everyone. And trees are being chopped down for cooking fires.'

'What happens tomorrow?' I asked.

'There's going to be another go at persuading the city council to allow us to pass through Norwich. So we're going to have to go back to the city. If they won't let us through, we're going to have to march round it to Mousehold Heath. It'll be a long way round.' I suppressed a groan.

A man appeared, bending to get under the canvas, his large eyes red from the dust of the road. Toby Lockswood. 'Master Shardlake,' he said. 'Jack.'

Barak nodded expressionlessly, doubtless remembering, like me, what had happened to Nicholas and how this man, who had worked with us for weeks, now spoke to us as though we were virtual strangers.

'I come from Robert Kett,' he told me. 'He's on his way to see you. You're lucky he could spare five minutes, there's much to organize.'

'There must be,' I agreed quietly. 'How many are there now?'

'Two and a half thousand. They've all to be fed, and latrines dug. But we're set on this. You fit to speak with Captain Kett?'

I sat up carefully. 'Yes.'

'So he's Captain Kett now?' Barak asked.

'Did you not hear him at the oak? He offered to be our leader and captain. And a fine one he is.'

I asked Natty to pass me more ale. As I drank, there was a move-ment at the entrance. Two men took positions outside, then Robert

Kett came under the awning. He looked as tired and dusty as everyone else, but the eyes in his keen face were alive with energy. He nodded to Natty. 'Leave us a moment, lad.'

'Yes, Captain,' Natty said, and went out.

Kett looked at Barak. 'I hear you did well today, noting down the supplies that came in. Despite your – disability.'

'I did my best,' Barak said gruffly.

'Please leave us a little while.'

Barak went out, and Kett looked at me keenly. 'Master Shardlake, I was sorry to hear you fainted. It was a long march. I had hoped it would end in Norwich, but the city council have refused us entry and manned the walls. Tomorrow, if the city refuses us entry again, we will camp at Eaton Wood, then next day march to Drayton Wood, and on Friday to Mousehold Heath, which commands the city. There is enough space there for the many still coming in to us. People in south Norfolk are gathering at their own camp too, at Downham.' I won-dered what that would mean for the Lady Mary.

Kett went on. 'Food and drink will be brought to Mousehold from the villages. The women will stay behind and take charge on the farms. And with the money we are requisitioning, we should be able to buy supplies in Norwich. From Mousehold we overlook the city.'

'We could try an assault, Captain,' Toby said. 'We have hundreds in arms, and support in Norwich.'

'No,' Kett answered firmly. 'We need a secure base first, and our men are tired and untrained. And we need to show the Protector we are men of peace. We shall do well enough on Mousehold.' He looked at me. 'We are a hardy people, and determined. We have become used to living on little these last years.'

'I do not doubt it,' I replied.

'With more men it will be a slower journey tomorrow, and not so long. Do you think you can make it, and perhaps a further journey?'

'If the pace is slower and there are rests, I should be well enough.'

'Good.' He looked at me intently. 'When we get to Mousehold, Master Shardlake, we must have order. To do that, as I told you, we will try our prisoners according to law, so their injustices can be reported to the commissioners and the Protector. We aim to expose their wrongdoings, but not to kill them. If they are not put on trial, some of our people may take matters into their own hands. They are justly angry.' He looked at me narrowly. 'I ask again, will you help us?'

In truth I had been unable to make up my mind. I thought, If I helped them and they lost, what would become of me then? I said, 'I am not quite well, Captain Kett. Please give me a little more time to consider.'

He inclined his head. 'You wouldn't be stringing me along, would you?'

'Just a little more time, please.'

'Only a little, Master Lawyer, or you will join that loudmouthed boy of yours in the cart.'

'My assistant, Nicholas. Sir, I know he is hot-headed and full of — antrums — though, in fact, he is poor. Could you not release him into my care? I worry about him being near those Boleyn twins. They would kill him, if they could. If he gives his word of honour not to run away, it can be trusted.'

Toby shook his head vigorously. 'All the time I worked with young Overton, he did nothing but tell me that gentlemen were the natural rulers. He talked of the poor like dirt.'

I said, 'I remember when he helped a poor boy who was unjustly dismissed, while you stood aside. He has a good heart. A good head too, despite his talk. He owns no land, in Norfolk or anywhere else.' I looked at Toby. 'And he is not the only one with a fierce mouth.'

'He lectured me like I was a fool.' A surly note entered Toby's voice. 'Got so I couldn't bear the sight of him.'

Kett turned on him with unexpected anger. 'Toby Lockswood, I will not have our noble aims used to serve personal dislikes!'

Toby flushed, and lowered his head. Kett turned to me. 'I will consider it,' he said. 'While you consider my offer,' he added pointedly, raising his eyebrows. 'But Overton is in no danger from those boys; they are well tied and quieter since they were beaten. And now, I must see my brother about meat for the camp. Barak may stay with you tonight, along with Natty.' With that he left the makeshift tent, Toby following without another word. Natty returned and settled himself down. My new watcher.

After a while, a man brought bowls of food, and a candle to give light when it got dark. A rich mutton pottage. I wondered how many sheep from the landlords' meadows had gone into its making. Young Natty said appreciatively, 'That's first meat I've had in weeks.'

'Is it?' Barak asked, surprised.

He looked at us. 'All our family's had this spring is bread an' vegetable stuff out the cottage garden. Odd scrap o' bacon at lunch from Marster, till I was put off my job. I was a pigman, but with his rent goin' up, Marster had to lay men off.'

'Have you come far to get here?'

'My family live in a village on the coast, out by the Sandlings. I left last week ter look for work.' He smiled sourly. 'Marsterless man on the road, that's what I'm become. I was near Wymondham, heard about the rising and came to join.'

'You come from the Sandlings?' I asked.

He put down his bowl and looked at me, eyes sharp again. He asked, 'Do yew know anything of an apprentice from there, who lived in Naarwich? Name off Wal Padbury?'

Barak answered, 'Walter was a witness in a case Master Shardlake was involved in. He disappeared before the trial. We thought he might have gone home.'

Natty looked at us narrowly. 'When you fainted, a man from Norwich said you were the lawyer who saved a gentleman from hanging, how everyone was mardling about that case in Norwich, about the gentleman Boleyn, a locksmith who was involved in the case drowning and his apprentice running away. That's why I asked to be put in charge of you. Wal Padbury's name was on all the gossips' lips at home, just before I left home.'

'Then he's back?'

The boy shook his head, 'You're too late, Marster. He's dead. I didn't know him, he came from another village down the coast. 'E'd gone to Norwich long since, but two weeks ago his body was washed up on the beach near his village.'

'He drowned?' Barak asked.

Natty shook his head. 'The coroner said his head was harf stoved in. Reckon whoever did it put him in the sea an' got the tides wrong, he'd not been long in the water when he were washed up. Murder, the verdict was, an' they're looking for who did it. Folks were gossiping about it up an' down the coast.'

I stared at Barak. So Walter, too, had been killed, his head shattered like poor Edith's.

Barak said, quietly, 'So the case follows us here.'

Young Natty's eyes still glinted at us fixedly. I said, 'I am sorry for his death. If he had not run away, perhaps I could have saved him.' The boy looked me in the eyes, then nodded.

'A third person dead,' I said to Barak. 'God help us, what has been going on?'

Chapter Forty-one

NEXT MORNING, WEDNESDAY, after breakfast under the trees of more mutton pottage with bread and cheese, we set off to march the two miles south to Norwich again. Feeding the men and setting them once more on the march had been well organized, local groups chivvied into place by village leaders and former soldiers. There was some grumbling about having to retrace our steps, but the leaders explained that if the Norwich councillors were faced with our entire force at the gates, they might be intimidated into letting us cross through the city to Mousehold Heath, saving the long march round. One village had brought a banner showing the Five Wounds of Christ, symbol of the religious traditionalists, and its people were told to keep it furled; their religion was their own affair, but the Protector must not think this a rebellion against the Prayer Book.

The procession stretched along a good mile, and with the rising of the sun more men came over the fields to join us. Barak went back to the rear, while Natty and I took a place near the head of the march, Kett and the other leaders riding ahead. Far behind, with the baggage train, Nicholas and the twins would be with the other gentlemen prisoners.

The night before, I had said to Barak, 'Who could have killed that poor apprentice? If only he hadn't run from us.'

'Same person that killed Edith and the locksmith. Whoever gave the locksmith Snockstobe the key.'

'The apprentice knew who it was.'

''Course he did.'

'Someone must have followed him all the way to the coast, and caught him just before he got home. It could have been anyone on that list we drew up in Norwich.'

'Yes. I don't think the case can ever be solved now. Boleyn's pardon will go through the bureaucracy eventually and either be granted or not.'

'I can't rest quiet with the killer of three people running free.' I looked in the direction of Norwich. 'Probably in the city.'

✝

THE WEATHER THAT morning was hot as ever. The great proces-sion moved at a slower pace. I had picked up a large branch to use as a stick, and perhaps my muscles were getting accustomed to the exer-cise, for I felt less pain, though I would have welcomed some shade in the open countryside. I wondered how Nicholas, with his pale skin, was coping with the sun in an open cart; at least I had my hat. I wore only my shirt again; my doublet was in the pack Barak carried on his back, my robe still in the panniers of my horse, for all I knew. My growing stubble, like everyone else's, was spotted with dust: I must look now much like any other peasant. Yet sometimes I felt a stab of fear at being surrounded by this mass of poor and angry people bent on overthrowing those of my class. I made myself concentrate on the endless slow marching; tramp, tramp, tramp.

A couple of times the great march stopped, and men stepped aside to pull down hurdles enclosing sheep, killing some of the animals for food. Once, in their panic, a flock of the silly creatures ran straight at us, and men stepped swiftly from the ranks to despatch them.

Someone began singing. A bawdy song was taken up, and then a different one, which sparked loud cheers:

> *Cast hedge and ditch in the lake*
> *Fixed with many a stake*
> *Though it were never so fast*
> *Yet asunder 'tis wraste . . .*

We stopped at the Norwich walls outside St Stephens Gate. Arch-ers on top of the walls had their weapons trained upon us. The Kett brothers and the soldier Miles rapped on the gate; it was opened and Mayor Codd, who looked to be trembling, and a number of other senior aldermen came out. There was a short muttered conversation, which ended with Codd and the others returning to the city, and the gates being closed again.

Afterwards Robert Kett, astride his horse, addressed the crowd. The words were carried back. The city authorities had refused access again, worried about our size and growing numbers. He said that we would have to take the long march round to Mousehold; we would stop the rest of the day and overnight at Eaton Wood, then on the following day march some three miles north to Drayton Wood before turning south-east to reach Mousehold Heath at its most accessible point.

We then marched the half-mile or so to Eaton Wood, and took a rest. Natty was still with me. I stood on a knoll on the fringes of the wood and looked over the sea of heads. How many were there now? Three thousand surely. In the distance a fresh procession of men were approaching, carts rumbling behind, a man with a coloured banner in front; a new village party. Elsewhere, parties of men were setting off to the countryside, no doubt to pull down more fences and find food and weapons. For a second the sheer scale of it all made my head reel.

For the rest of that day I rested under the shade of a tree, sleeping most of the afternoon away. When I woke Natty told me that Barak had been to visit, but had said not to wake me as I was deeply asleep. He left a message that he was fine, helping to organize things, and although Nicholas was still a prisoner, no harm had come to him.

That evening, as before, cooking fires were lit with wood from trees which had been cut down, and good mutton and vegetable pottage distributed. Everyone sounded in good heart, despite the fruitless march back to Norwich. I hoped that Barak would come again, but his duties must have kept him away. I thought of asking Natty if I could go and look for him, but I was simply too tired. I slept the night under a tree with the others.

✝

NEXT MORNING, before we set off, Robert Kett addressed us once more. He reported that while we had a long march ahead, at Mousehold we could build a great camp, collecting others in from all over Norfolk. His speech ended defiantly with the ringing words, 'For you who have already stirred there is no hope but in adventuring boldly.' Nonetheless, someone shouted out, 'We have heard from the city that the Norwich councillors have sent riders to London, to seek authority to put us down! Take them on now!'

Some shouted agreement, but Kett argued back forcefully that time was needed to make camp, take stock and increase our numbers. Messengers from the camp were being sent to the King to proclaim the assembly's loyalty and support for the commissioners. Most cheered him.

✝

THE MARCH RESUMED. Late in the morning we came to the River Wensum, upstream from Norwich. As at the River Yare there was a bridge, but the Wensum was wider and it would have taken even longer to get across than at the Yare. Men were sent to fell some trees which were laid across the river to form another, makeshift bridge. Thus we were able to cross faster than before, though there was time still for the marchers to halt and eat lunch as they waited their turn. Then the march resumed, following the wide flood plain of the Wensum northwards. I had got into a rhythm of walking, trying to copy the military men in keeping erect and swinging my arms, and it helped.

Shortly afterwards a party of around a dozen horsemen approached us from the north, riding slowly, with numerous carts drawn by oxen behind. A command went down the line to halt. Barak had been allowed to join me and we were marching near the front with the old soldier Hector Johnson and young Natty. I stepped aside to see what was happening, Johnson following. The horsemen halted a few yards from Kett. At their head was a man in a bright gown, a cap with a peacock feather on his head. Johnson said, grimly, 'Sir Roger Wodehouse. Landowner from Kimberley. One of the really big gentry. My plot of land was near his place.'

'He can't be hoping to take these marchers on,' I said incredulously.

'No. It's something else.'

Wodehouse rode up to Kett, reaching out a hand. Kett did not take it. Then he and Kett spoke; Sir Roger gesturing back at his carts. Kett abruptly turned his horse round. He shouted down the line, 'Sir Roger

Wodehouse, like Mayor Codd, tells us to disperse and return home! He has brought provisions to make a feast, then says we should depart in good fellowship! I say again, for you who have already stirred there is no hope but in adventuring boldly!'

There was an answering cry of agreement from the crowd, and numbers of men detached themselves from the group and headed to the front, brandishing weapons. Sir Roger and his party attempted to retreat, but the reins of their horses were soon grabbed, men closing round them like a tide. Kett shouted, 'Take him alive! Put him with the other prisoners! Let his servants go, but take the carts!'

I saw Sir Roger and his men unhorsed; Sir Roger struggled and his hat and robe were pulled off before he was thrown into a ditch at the side of the road. Faintly I heard him shout, 'Wolves! Traitors!' Then a man raised an axe, poised to bring it down on his head, but one of Wodehouse's servants grabbed it. There was a tussle, settled by a shout from Kett that there was to be no killing. The man who would have slain him dropped the axe. I could not see clearly from where I stood, but it looked like Toby Lockswood.

'What think you of that, sir?' Johnson asked, satisfaction in his voice. 'There it is, one of the great men dealt with. They try bribing us with ale and promises sometimes, if we get out of hand.' He laughed. 'There, we've taken another step further.'

☩

THE SUN WAS slowly falling to the horizon, and the heat lessening at last, when we saw a large wood ahead and someone called out, 'Drayton!' The weary men picked up their steps now that a destination, and the blessed shade of the large wood, was in sight.

We found a place under the trees. Nearby, a group of people gathered wood to make a cooking fire. Half a sheep was hauled in and men began butchering it. I looked away, to where Natty sat nearby. Barak joined us. He had taken off his artificial hand and was massaging his arm. He looked morose.

'All right?' I asked.

'I was thinking about Tammy and the children. Wondering how things are in London, whether people are rising there, too. I'll try

talking to Toby tomorrow, see what the news is from around the country, and whether they'll let me send a letter telling her I'm stuck in
Norfolk, but safe.'

'I think it was Toby who attacked that man with an axe earlier.'

'I didn't see.' Barak shook his head. 'He's just lost both his parents.
He's consumed with anger.'

'You could leave,' I said softly. 'It wouldn't be that hard to slip
away.'

He shook his head. 'They're setting watches round the perimeter.
Anyway, I'm staying.' He spoke sharply. 'Maybe you didn't see me at
the Hethersett oak, but I took the oath with the others to stand
together.'

I knew he would not be dissuaded. Nothing was more important
in England than a man's oath.

I rose stiffly. 'I'm going to try and see how Nicholas fares.' I turned
to Natty. 'May I?'

'I must accompany you,' he said a little guiltily.

'I understand. Jack, will you come with us?'

'No, I'll stay and talk to these people.' He nodded at the group
round the fire. 'Maybe they'll let us share their dinner. But listen,' he
added, 'something you should do. I get funny looks sometimes because
of my London accent, but your voice is a gentleman's, and that may be
dangerous here. Try to make your accent more like mine.'

'You're right. I'll try.'

I walked off, carefully memorizing the bright green banner marking
the village group, for it would be easy to get lost in this sea of people.
The camp stretched far beyond the wood. Somehow pathways seemed
to have sprung up naturally, allowing passage to men bearing the sheep
and deer carcasses, and sundry messengers. Some men were digging a
latrine. I asked someone where the baggage cart was, trying to make my
voice more like Barak's, and was directed to a patch of higher ground
beyond the wood.

Armed men stood guarding the baggage train, where supplies were
being distributed. I recognized the soldier, Miles, whom I had seen that
night in Norwich. His powerful figure was now encased in half-
armour, a solid breastplate with metal guards for his upper arms, a

sword at his belt, marks of authority, I guessed. He looked at me with the keen, sharp eyes I remembered. 'Can I help you, Granfer?' he asked, and I realized that with my white hair and stubble I did indeed now look like just another old villager.

'My name is Matthew Shardlake. I am a lawyer, advising Master Kett. My assistant, who has a fierce mouth, is a prisoner, though Master Kett said he may consider his release to me.'

To my surprise, Miles laughed, the narrow mouth above his fair beard opening to show many teeth gone. He clapped his thigh.

'God's death, I took you for a commoner. Aye, Captain Kett has spoken of you. Says you could have betrayed us over Attleborough, but didn't.' He reached out a hard, calloused hand. 'John Miles, late captain gunner in the old king's army.'

I shook his hand, glad to have found someone friendly. A captain gunner, I remembered from the *Mary Rose*, meant someone in charge of a whole group of cannon, expert and high-ranking. I said, 'Might I speak with my assistant? His name is Nicholas Overton.'

Miles looked at Natty, who nodded. 'If you wish. They're a sorry lot, I fear, the gentlemen prisoners. They've been getting abuse and catcalls on the march. But they deserve it, the rogues.' His eyes narrowed. 'You know those Boleyn twins? They've been calling your friend rude names.'

'They are our bitter enemies, Captain Miles.'

He called over to another soldier in half-armour. 'Take this man to talk to the prisoner Overton. Just a few minutes, mind.'

I was led past carts full of barrels of ale, bread and vegetables, and slaughtered sheep and deer. Some of the animals were beginning to stink after a day in the heat. At the very back, surrounded by more armoured men, were high-sided carts – six now – where gentlemen in torn and tattered robes, tied or manacled, sat or lay slumped against the sides. I saw Sir Roger Wodehouse, sitting with his mouth gaping open, unable to believe what had happened to him. Many others looked shocked and fearful, and some had cuts and bruises. As I passed one cart the side shook as someone within grasped the rails, letting forth a tide of abuse: 'Fuckin' hunchback, pretending to be a peasant now, are you! Fucking lawyer!' I jumped back. Gerald Boleyn, wearing a torn

and tattered shirt, glared furiously at me from between the slats of the
cart. His face was bruised but still full of savage energy. 'Fawning on
these dogs!' He spat at me, a great gobbet landing on my shirt.

'Leave it, Gerry, we'll just get beaten again!' His twin was slouched
beside him, the scar pale in his bruised face. His look, though, was no
less full of hate, and he shouted, 'When forces are sent to destroy these
peasants, we'll cut your fucking liver out ourselves.'

'Be quiet, for Jesu's sake.' Leonard Witherington was with them in
the cart, the imperious lord of South Brikewell now desperate with
fear. His voice was imploring.

Barnabas said, 'Shut your mouth, you cowardly old fart.'

The guards were grinning, but one jabbed Barnabas lightly with a
spear through the bars. 'That's enough from yew, young muck-spout!'
Barnabas glared at us, but the amusement his antics was causing
seemed to subdue him more than the spear, and he sank back wearily
against his brother. I walked hastily on to the next cart. Again, men
who had once ruled sat or lay, looking shocked, angry, and not a little
frightened. Finally, I saw Nicholas, his long body curled into a ball,
face livid with sunburn, sleeping. His feet were bound. I touched him
gently through the bars and he jumped up, green eyes alert.

''Tis only me,' I said gently.

He looked at me. 'What happened? You look like a peasant.'

'Fine clothes are no good on this march.'

'Are you and Jack safe? I thought something had happened to you
when you weren't put in the carts.'

'I've been asked to help Robert Kett give the gentlemen a fair trial
when we reach our destination.'

'You can't help these rogues!' he said incredulously.

'I haven't decided yet. But I've asked Kett to release you into my
care, and he said he'd think about it.'

Nicholas stumbled to his knees. His shirt and hose were in tatters,
his doublet gone. His face was puffy with bruises as well as sunburn.
He leaned forward.

'You can't work for these brutes,' he repeated.

'Nick, if I get you out of here, you have to control your mouth.'

He looked around the cart, where several men in a similar condition stared at us dully. I recognized Flowerdew's sons, both looking very young and scared. 'Look what has been done to these boys,' Nicholas remonstrated.

'Their captors are angry. But they're not brutes.'

He glanced at the cart, where the twins sat still glaring at us. 'I wish those two would shut up.'

I felt desperately sorry for him. Like the others he had experienced nothing remotely like this before; though I had known worse, sent to the Tower twice in the old king's reign. I said, 'Keep calm, and rest. And in Jesu's name, be quiet.'

He nodded despairingly. 'They say we're headed for Mousehold Heath.'

'Yes. We should get there tomorrow.' I grasped his hand. 'Keep strong.'

He nodded. 'I will.'

Another gentleman in the cart, the embroidered collar of his shirt torn half away, cried despairingly, 'And what then? These mad animals will execute us.'

'Robert Kett will not allow that.' I took a deep breath, and said quietly, 'Nor will I.' In that moment, my decision to help him at the trials was made.

✞

NATTY AND I RETURNED through the camp to where Barak now sat with a group of around twenty villagers round the cauldron. He had made friends with them – he had a silver tongue when he chose. A fire of freshly chopped wood under the cauldron was burning strongly, and there was a rich cooking smell. An older woman was stirring it. I sat beside Barak, nodding and smiling at the others, remembering that I must try to disguise my accent. I accepted a drink from a flagon, which was being passed around, containing strong beer rather than the ale we had had so far. 'Good stuff, bor,' the man who passed it to me said. 'Fresh from our landlord's stores.'

'These folk are from an estate a few miles from a place called Swardeston,' Barak explained.

I nodded. 'What brought you here?'

A middle-aged man answered. 'Our village is dyin'. The lord's been overstocking the commons with his sheep, so there's no room left for our animals. By gor, I'm a churchwarden an' a man of peace, but we've had enough.'

The woman stirring the pot turned to us, smiling. 'So we raided the steward's house, took his money an' weapons, sent his fine wife runnin' to the woods, and turned his sheep off the commons!'

There was laughter round the group. 'Well told, mar!'

Natty was standing at a little distance, looking awkward. The woman called to him. 'On yer lonesome, bor?'

He stepped forward, and was invited to sit with the rest of us. 'No lack o' vittles here, boy.'

'Thank you.' He took a seat next to me. I smiled at him wryly. 'Still keeping an eye on me?'

He nodded. I realized he had been reluctant to impose himself on the villagers. There must be many like him in the camp, single men and boys without a local group. The flagon was passed to Natty, who drank gratefully.

'How was Nick?' Barak asked quietly.

'Tied up in a cart. But he's holding on. Gerald and Barnabas were in the next cart. Gerald spat at me.'

'Nice.'

Food was being passed out now; rich dark venison in a thick pottage of vegetables. Grace was said, for the first time in days, I realized. Everyone set to eagerly. The flagon was passed round again, and Natty took a long swig, then another. There was little talking while we ate, but when we put our bowls down, Natty stood, a little unsteadily. 'Good lady, I thank you,' he said to the cook, who gave a little curtsey. 'I have not eaten such a fine meal in months!'

'Nor have any of us, lad!'

Natty said, 'No, for the rich lords care not if we starve! But now we have them, and their sheep and deer.' His voice broke with emotion. 'At last we are free! Free to eat, and free to speak out!'

'Well said, lad!'

'We shall set all aright! A new world is dawning, the rich will be put down and the common man will have his own land, his own trade, his own life! We shall bring Christ's Commonwealth!' Tears began running down his face, and, I saw, also from the eyes of some who cheered him on.

Chapter Forty-two

NEXT MORNING, we again set off early, heading south-east, slowly, for many were tired now. The weather was cooler, but sticky, the sky covered with a thin milky cloud. At the slower pace I walked more easily.

We tramped on, up the outer slopes of Mousehold Heath, which rose gently here. We stayed with the village group from last night, Natty with me still. We stopped for lunch, and bread and cheese with rabbit stew were passed around. I had only just started eating, though, when a messenger appeared. 'Master Shardlake, Captain Kett would speak with you.' I rose, the villagers looking at me in surprise. They had no idea I was so elevated.

I followed him to the head of the marchers. In one place sheep were being expertly butchered, and I recoiled at the site of a great heap of guts and other offal lying on the ground, flies buzzing over it. The messenger smiled. 'Only the best cuts are suitable for Kett's camp,' he explained proudly.

He led me to where a stool and a small desk had been set out, perhaps taken from one of the manor houses. Robert Kett sat there, surrounded by papers and plans. His brother William was with him, along with Captain Miles in his half-armour, a couple of other men in semi-military attire and a surpliced clergyman. Kett looked tired, but his eyes were keen as ever as he looked up at me. He did not smile.

'How fare you today, Serjeant Shardlake, after all this marching?' Suddenly he laughed. 'Forgive me, but you look like an old peasant. Fear not, though, we have your pack and robe safe.'

'I am better now the march is slower. But my shoes are starting to wear out.'

'We must get you a pair of solid country shoes clouted with nails, such as many of our people have brought. Those that can afford them, at least.'

'I should be grateful, Master Kett.'

William said sharply, '*Captain* Kett henceforth, not Master.'

'Certainly.'

Robert said, 'Soon we shall be at the top of Mousehold Heath, the long journey ends and we make final camp. The bells will ring out across the countryside once more, and beacons will be lit. Word has gone out for men to come, and bring supplies. The lords we have not captured are fled. Tomorrow we shall organize our people by their Hundred districts, the old historic regions of Norfolk, then elect representatives of the Hundreds.' He looked at me hard. 'Our men need to get settled. When the representatives are elected, we shall draw up a list of grievances – demands – for the King and his commissioners. And send out orders for the requisitioning of goods around the county, in the name of the King and the Protector.'

'And soon we must begin the trials of the gentlemen,' the clergy-man added. 'More will be brought in when we send men out to requisition goods, and there are those among us who would kill them. The promise of holding trials, according to law, as well as recording their iniquities, will restrain violence.'

Kett nodded. 'We've some scriveners among us, and the young lawyer Master Godsalve, though he would run if he could, but legal skills such as you have, Master Shardlake – they would be invaluable at the trials. To advise me on points of law and evidence.'

'I see.'

'When we reach Mousehold, the carpenters among us will have great business cutting down trees from Thorpe Wood, making shelters – this dry weather must have been sent us by God, but it surely cannot last forever. And they will build a place of justice, too.' His voice became stern. 'I know you are a man of conscience, Serjeant Shardlake, but it is time for you to decide whether to help us or to become a prisoner yourself.'

I took a deep breath. 'I have decided, and I shall help you at these trials with legal advice. So long as the penalty for wrongdoing is only imprisonment.'

Miles spoke impatiently. 'We can't stop some getting a bit of a buf-feting, not after all our people have suffered.'

'Perhaps you think even imprisonment too harsh,' Kett probed.

I hesitated. 'I understand why you cannot simply let your prisoners go. They might raise men against you.'

'That is true,' William Kett snapped. 'But it is also a matter of justice.'

Robert Kett said, 'When we get to Mousehold, we shall put our prisoners in the Earl of Surrey's old palace. Conditions will not be harsh, not unduly.'

'Will you then take the oath all the men in the camp have taken,' William asked me, 'to stand together come what may?'

I clenched my fists, realizing that my hands were shaking. I looked at Robert and said, 'I cannot do that, at least not yet. But I will take an oath to you to assist honestly in the trials with any questions of law. I understand it will help you to have a serjeant-at-law advising you,' I added boldly, 'so our aims coincide.'

William looked angry. 'Why should we allow this hunchback to dictate terms?'

Robert, however, raised a hand. There was an English New Tes-tament on his desk; he held it up. 'Then take the oath to assist us. An oath to the camp, not to me.' I put my hand on the bible and swore as he asked. I could see from his eyes, though, that he was still not satis-fied. William grunted.

There was a silence. I broke it by asking, 'Do you know when the Protector's commissioners for Norfolk will arrive?'

Kett shook his head. 'We have no word. Soon, I hope. We shall welcome them.'

I thought, But will they welcome you?

I did not wish to try Kett's patience further, but there was one more thing I had to say. 'You told me you would think about releasing my assistant Nicholas Overton, Captain Kett. I beg you again to consider it. He has only spoken foolish words, for which surely a man should not be imprisoned.'

Kett turned enquiringly to Miles, who said, 'I think you could let him go, Captain. He's had some of the nonsense knocked out of him.

420

And he's no friend of those crazy twins from Brikewell. They shout insults at him more than anyone else.'

Kett nodded. 'Very well. Overton will be released when we reach Mousehold Heath.' He looked at me sharply. 'Provided he takes an oath to you that he will not escape.' He raised a finger. 'And I hold you responsible for him, mark that.'

'I understand.'

The cleric coughed. 'We should move on to consider the appoint-ment of a chaplain. There are too many wild prophets preaching the apocalypse –'

'Ay, Master Chaundler. Thank you, Serjeant Shardlake.' Kett nodded his head in dismissal, and I walked slowly back to Barak and the villagers.

✞

WE MARCHED ON, the ground rising more steeply now, Kett at our head, a great train of wagons pulled by oxen and donkeys and horses behind; and in the rear, with a guard of armed men, the carts bearing the prisoners. I realized with surprise that it was Friday, the twelfth of July, less than a week since Isabella's appeal had sent me to Wymond-ham. We passed through the village of Sprowston, where fences enclosing sheep were pulled down and a substantial manor house for-cibly entered. A man in a rich doublet and hose was brought out, shouting in fury and calling his captors dogs and pigs until a smack on the head and a shout to 'stop that dullerin" quieted him. Old Hector Johnson, who had replaced Natty at my side, said, 'That's Master John Corbett.' He looked at me. 'A lawyer on the make like Flowerdew, who bought up old monastic lands.'

'I have never been on the make,' I answered.

'Live in a ditch, do you?'

'I have never been on the make,' I repeated angrily, though I could not but think of my fine London house.

Johnson smiled. 'Just yagging you, sir. 'Tis our Norfolk sense of humour.'

Corbett was being dragged to the carts, while anything useful was carried out of his house. Horses were led round from the stables.

Valuables, including silver plate and coins, were taken to Kett and his senior men at the head of the march, where a treasurer seemed to have been appointed to receive gold and silver, though I could not but wonder cynically how many coins stayed in the purses of the men who brought the valuables out. At least nothing more had been said about Isabella's money that I still kept safe.

A little further on we came to an ancient building with an ecclesiastical aspect, which had been converted into a huge dove house. A party of men with bows and arrows peeled off and took places around the buildings, while others armed with large hammers went inside. In a couple of minutes hundreds of doves flew out, many immediately shot down as they had been at Witherington's field. The men inside set to demolishing the building, pieces of the roof soon crashing down. As the march passed on men stopped to wave and cheer.

'What is that place?' I asked a man walking beside me, who was watching with particular satisfaction.

'Before the dissolution it was a leper hospital. Last year it was sold to Corbett, so his doves could rob our crops for his table.'

'I have seen the destruction they can do,' I said.

'They will do no more,' he replied emphatically.

Some people from Sprowston joined us, and the march resumed. The Earl of Surrey's great mansion came into view, but Kett made for a large chapel, a little nearer. Beside it the escarpment fell steeply to the Wensum, with Norwich beyond. The sky had cleared and the view was the most extraordinary I had seen in my life, the whole city spread out below us, the river, the walls, the many spires, the great square block of the castle, and, dominating everything, the huge spire of the cathedral which on this clear day looked so close I felt I could almost reach out and touch it.

Barak came and whistled. 'That view's something,' he said. 'Really something. And the best vantage point we could have.'

Word was going around for people to form into village or parish groups, and wait until men came to show them where they should pitch up. I asked Barak, 'Where do we go?'

'We could join the Swardeston people. They seem a decent crew.'

'Yes.' As we waited, I looked across at Surrey Place. It was a huge

Italianate palace with decorated columns, large windows and gardens, behind high walls, looking entirely out of place on the heathland. A group of men were hauling out a well-dressed official who, I presumed, was the caretaker, anxious servants standing around. The caretaker was led away, expostulating.

'I'm surprised Kett hasn't taken Surrey Place as his headquarters,' I said quietly.

Barak shook his head. 'Wouldn't look good, setting himself up in an earl's palace.'

'No.'

'And a place that size, it's a big target if the city council got cannon down to the riverside.'

I smiled. 'You're thinking like one of the rebels, Jack.'

'I am, yes. This cause is just, if ever one was.'

'I've noticed you've hardly been drinking since we got here. Though I've heard some rowdiness in the camp round the fires.'

'Need to keep a clear head.'

'And you have something to take your mind off Tamasin. Will they let you write to her?'

'I haven't asked yet. I want to let things settle down for a day or two.' He looked at me intently. 'You recognize the justice in what these men are doing now?'

'I'm not quite sure, not yet.' I sighed. 'I have taken an oath to help with the trials, but no more. I still fear that, one way or another, this could end in terrible violence.'

He smiled. 'Always somewhere in the middle, as usual.' Then his look became serious. 'You'll have to come down off that fence before too long.'

I looked down at the city. 'What do you think of Captain Kett?'

'I think he's the most remarkable man I've met since Lord Cromwell. He has Cromwell's force, his negotiating skills – he's been a local politician and guildsman for years – and his confidence. But none of Cromwell's cruelty, or bullying. Charisma too, practical organizing skills, and from the way he's shaping this camp, a genuine belief in equality.'

It was unusual for Barak to praise someone so unequivocally. I smiled. 'Remember, he is an enterprising businessman and landowner himself. Perhaps angry he has never been allowed gentleman status.'

'Well, it's the commons he wants to help now. And he's no man of violence. And that's not easy in the circumstances. His plans to hold these trials prove that.'

I nodded. 'I wonder what his religious views are?'

Barak shrugged. 'Protestant, I'd guess. Much of Norfolk is.' He looked down at the city. 'The councillors and aldermen must be shit, ting themselves down there.'

'Yes.' Looking down, it struck me that Norwich, bounded by the walls and the river, had the shape of a great teardrop. I thought again of those we knew down there – Josephine and Edward Brown, Isabella and Chawry, Sooty Scambler, John Boleyn in Norwich Castle. What would happen to them all now?

Away to the west, I heard church bells start to ring, then more, out across the countryside. I saw a beacon lit, then another further off, and another. The whole commons of Norfolk were being rung to Mousehold.

Part Four

MOUSEHOLD HEATH

Chapter Forty-three

I T WAS LATE ON Sunday afternoon, two days later. I sat with Nicholas and Barak in the doorway of a lean-to hut built of fresh-smelling
wood planks, roofed with turf and with bracken for bedding. Here, at
night, the three of us had to 'croodle up', in the Norfolk phrase, to
sleep. The hut was only four feet high, too low to stand, but provided
basic shelter. Hundreds of such huts had been erected in the last two
days, stretching across the heath. From Thorpe Wood to the south
came the constant sound of sawing, dozens of carpenters busy cutting
newly felled tree trunks into planks. There were numerous carpenters
among the rebels, and many members of the Norwich carpenters'
guild had come up to help.

The huts were grouped in circles accommodating a village or
hamlet or group of men who had come to Kett's camp, within larger
organizations representing the old divisions of Norfolk, the 'Hundreds'. Ex-soldiers had supervised their physical placing, together with
'governors' elected by members of the camp on the basis of each Hundred, usually people with experience of local politics. Pathways had
been left to allow access. Barak and I, joined the day before by a newly
released Nicholas, had remained with the people from Swardeston,
along with young Natty and the ex-soldier Hector Johnson. Those two
stayed with us, I thought, partly to keep an eye on us, but also because
they were alone, with no local group of their own. The villagers were
friendly with Barak but reserved towards me and even more so towards
Nicholas, who had been uncharacteristically quiet since he had been
passed into my care.

Each group of huts had a central cooking area, flints placed round
it lest fire spread across the tinder-dry yellow grass of Mousehold.
Water had been brought up from the Wensum and even ferried on

horseback from the River Yare some eight miles distant. Our cooking pot had been set to boil and we had learned that this evening our dinner was to be, of all things, swan.

I got up carefully to stretch my legs. Our Swardeston camp was sited near where Barak and I had stood looking out over Norwich two days ago. He rose and joined me, though Nicholas stayed where he was, sulkily pulling the yellow flowers off a stalk of ragwort. We walked a little way towards the escarpment. Behind us, huts continued to go up as far as the eye could see across the flat plateau of the heath, stretching miles to the east. Each evening beacons were lit on the fringes of the camp, to guide new people arriving, and more were coming in, and setting up their camps, all the time. Mousehold was alive with movement, the bright colours of parish banners marking individual encampments, carts bringing in fresh supplies trundling along the sandy tracks. One of the amateur prophets who had come to the camp stood in a cart nearby haranguing a crowd about the imminent coming of the Kingdom of Christ. Peddlers had also been drawn to the camp, some with donkeys, others with trays round their necks, calling, 'What d'ye pick, from my pack!', and passing on news of other camps. Some way off, people were unloading bricks from a cart, together with the implements of a blacksmith's forge. There were cheers as a cart full of barrels of small beer appeared. Mousehold, apparently, was bone-dry, even the old gravel and lime pits dotting the landscape. Rainwater simply soaked into the sandy soil.

There had been a church service that morning, but afterwards, despite it being Sunday, the camp-men worked in the heat as hard as any I had ever seen. I turned and looked over the escarpment, at that extraordinary view down to the river and Norwich. That morning men and boys had descended the steep hill to swim in the river – everybody was filthy, and stank – and some city constables on the Bishopsgate Bridge gatehouse had shot arrows at them, making them move downstream. All the city gates were closed against us.

'How many do they say are in the camp now?' I asked Barak.

'With all the new people arrived from the country, five or six thousand now.' He laughed incredulously. 'Remember the old king's Progress to York? Puts that in the shade, doesn't it?'

'It puts everything I have ever seen in the shade.' I smiled, adjusting the brim of my broad hat. 'Not that there's much shade up here.' Barak and I both now had deep tans and wore wide-brimmed hats and dirty shirts; Barak had removed his artificial hand for comfort today and one sleeve hung empty; physically, at least, we now blended well into the camp. Nicholas, though, stood out with his pale skin, now peeling with sunburn, and his yellowing bruises. Together with the growing number of gentlemen who had been brought in as prisoners, he had been held in the Earl of Surrey's old palace, Surrey Place. It stood on the crest of the hill a little way off, next to the road leading up from Bishopsgate, near a few ruins that remained of the dissolved priory it had replaced. It was guarded by Kett's men now, the Ionic columns of the great house and the temple-like pavilions at each side visible through the open gates, looking more incongruous than ever beside the camp. The Boleyn twins were in there, and Flowerdew's sons. The gardens between the ornamental gateway and the house were occupied by camp-men who had brought out canvas tents from the palace. The great building was being used for storage, too, and as I watched, a large cart trundled up the drive, full of assorted weapons – bills, halberds, swords and crossbows.

'Why so much emphasis on weaponry?' I asked Barak quietly. 'If they think the Protector and the commissioners will grant their demands?' I looked along the escarpment, where groups of armed men had been placed at strategic posts, as well as a couple of cannon.

'Maybe they fear the gentlemen who escaped their clutches will return with armed men. Besides, if you're negotiating, it's good to have steel at your back. Apparently, an area's being set aside for archery practice.'

I frowned. 'Who's running this camp, Kett or the ex-soldiers?' I looked to where, some distance away, another man in half-armour – the mark of the soldiers – was supervising the digging of a latrine pit, the sun glinting on his breastplate. It was necessary work; with all the remains of slaughtered sheep, and the piss and shit of thousands of people, if precautions were not taken disease could spread fast, and I had seen before what dysentery could do to an armed camp.

'Kett, I'm sure,' Barak answered. 'Remember last night, when a bunch of people got pissed? Some soldiers stopped them running wild, but when Kett came over and told them keeping order and discipline was the way to show they could govern themselves, you could see it put them to shame.'

Surrey Place was right on the edge of the escarpment, next to the road leading up from Bishopsgate. A little way along the escarpment stood St Michael's Chapel, survivor of the old Priory, Kett's headquarters. It was there that messengers riding across the country had headed frequently these last two days.

Barak touched my arm. 'Look,' he said. 'Coming up the hill.'

A small party of men was riding up the road from Bishopsgate Bridge. As they approached the escarpment I recognized the short, plump figure of Mayor Codd. Beside him was a thin, white-haired man in aldermanic robes who, for a second, I thought might be Gawen Reynolds come to plead for the twins, until he came closer and I saw that he was more strongly built, his expression one of watchful calm. Behind them rode two surpliced clerics. One was Robert Watson, whom I had seen preaching in the marketplace in favour of social order. They were accompanied by half a dozen men in the uniform of city constables. They looked apprehensive as they reached the crest of the hill, but were obviously expected, for some men from the nearest watch-post approached and, after a word with Codd, led them to St Michael's Chapel. People from the camp turned to look at these brightly robed city fathers, standing out among the camp-men. One called out, 'Leeches on the city poor!' and one of Kett's guards raised a hand to silence him. The little party passed into the chapel. The constables, left outside with the horses and a couple of Kett's men, crouched in the shade of the building looking nervously about them.

'So the city leaders are visiting Kett,' I said. 'Not demanding he come to them.'

'They know the thousands here could come down the hill and take the city if they wanted. And that many in the city support us, too.'

Us, I thought. 'Well, let's see what happens.' I turned back to our group of huts, where a bright green banner showing St Sebastian pierced by swords had been brought from the church at Swardeston, which was dedicated to the saint. Barak had been told he was to start assisting Kett as a scribe the following day: men who could write were at a premium.

A few people sat in the low doorways of the huts, seeking what shade they could. The able-bodied men were absent, most working on chopping down the trees and sawing planks in Thorpe Wood. Only the old woman who had welcomed us at Eaton Wood, a widow called Susan Everneke, who seemed to be the village matriarch, a young woman in the early stages of pregnancy who had accompanied her husband, and a little boy were left. Nicholas sat quietly nearby looking at the ground, near Hector Johnson, who was polishing a rusty sword. We went and sat beside them.

I said, 'The mayor's come, to see Captain Kett. We saw him go into St Michael's Chapel.'

The old soldier grinned. 'One or two are calling it Kett's Castle.'

Mistress Everneke lifted her head from her sewing. 'For shame, bor, to yag like that about Captain Kett that's done all this for us. He wants no castle, only right-doing for all.'

Johnson shifted uncomfortably. ''Twas just in jest, gal.'

'Have some small beer, and stop talking squit.' Goodwife Everneke had a large jar at her side, and she passed it around. Everyone took a drink gratefully.

I lowered myself carefully to the ground, resting my back against the wooden door frame of our hut. 'Are you comfortable, sir?' Good-wife Everneke asked.

I gave her a sharp look; some in the camp, like the little boy, often looked askance at my back, but I saw only kindness in her eyes. 'Yes, thank you. I worried sleeping on bracken might bring discomfort, but it seems to support me well.'

There was the crash of another tree falling in Thorpe Wood. Barak said, 'Those men are labouring mightily.'

'They are,' Goodwife Everneke said proudly. 'They'll keep a'doing till sunset. And more and more are coming in to help.'

'Are many come from Norwich?' I asked.

'A good few skilled men, but I hear Captain Kett wants the poor of the city to stay to support him there.'

The pregnant woman looked up from her sewing. 'I saw some

women yesterday, tiddidolls that looked like city whores.' She sighed. 'Still, it'll keep the men from getting ruffatory with us few women that are here.'

'Your husband will protect you, dear,' Goodwife Everneke said. 'He'll be back come sunset.'

'The amount done in just two days is astonishing,' I said. 'The huts, the provisioning –'

The old woman nodded. 'We country folk can turn our hand to most things. Build our own houses, grow our own crops, tend our animals. Given the chance,' she added meaningfully.

The pregnant woman looked at me. 'Perhaps my child will have a chance to live and grow up healthy. Despite the wiles of lawyers,' she added pointedly.

I smiled ruefully. ''Tis true I was a lawyer, but I worked for people like you, at the Court of Requests. Until my job was taken away by Richard Rich.'

Johnson turned to the women. 'At least your people have some lands left, gals. Mine are gone. I served with old King Henry's army in France two years while my wife and son ran our little piece. I wrote letters, but never got any back. So many of the men's letters were lost. By Christ, I saw some things that made me sick of war. When it ended I came home to find Sarah and John had been evicted. I never found them, though God knows I've tried. I've laboured on farms when I can these three years. Then I started hearing people in taverns murmuring about the common people taking things into their own hands, and I joined 'em.' He clenched his fists. 'And now we've done it. Maybe now I'll get revenge for my suffering.' I saw tears on his wrinkled cheeks. Goodwife Everneke put out her hand to him. Abruptly, Nicholas got up and went into the hut. Wincing a little, I got on my hands and knees and crawled after him, waving to Barak to stay where he was.

Nicholas had wedged himself into a corner of the lean-to, sitting with his hands on his knees. It was dim in there, the only light coming through the door. I sat beside him. He sighed and looked at me. 'These people's stories,' he said. 'I never knew English people endured such things.'

'And now they have reached their limit.'

'The world turned upsy-down. Yes, I saw that in Surrey Place.' It was the first time Nicholas had mentioned his imprisonment. He looked at the doorway, where Johnson and Barak and the two women were still talking quietly. In the distance we could still hear the prophet. 'This is the coming of Christ's kingdom, the masters will be put down and all things held in common, and justice done. Christ's elect will rule, and we shall have true religion!'

'I wish that man would shut his mouth,' Nicholas said wearily. 'He's been ranting on for hours!' He sighed. 'Before, when we were riding around Norfolk and I used to argue with Toby, it was just words, but now it's real. Even so, this is wrong. Society is like a body, and the head must rule – is that not what we have always been taught, is it not what the Bible says?'

'You were never one for the Bible,' I mocked gently. 'What happened at Surrey Place?'

He looked at me. 'We were taken out of the carts, all in chains. Everyone was quiet, afraid we might be killed. Even the Boleyn twins were quiet. Some of the rebels made pretend lunges at us with their bills and pitchforks. Then they opened the doors and took us in, to cheers from the men camped outside. It's a magnificent palace, pillars and decorated ceilings, elaborate carvings on the walls, but just a shell; all the grand furniture must have been taken away when the Earl of Surrey fell. We were split into groups and put into empty rooms, left to sit on the floor with our feet bound. Thank God I wasn't with the twins, but Witherington, Boleyn's neighbour from Brikewell, was with me. When the rebels left us, he started railing and shouting about how the Protector and the council would have all these rogues hanged. I thought he would have a seizure. More gentlemen were brought in later, we had a gaoler who brought in food and said we were lucky to have it, the way we'd starved the commons. Once I heard shouting from another room; I recognized those twins' voices, heard men running and then there was silence, I think they got a beating.' He was silent a moment, then he looked at me and asked, 'Who are these people anyway? They're not all peasants.'

'From what I've seen, there are yeomen, husbandmen with a little land, cottagers and labourers, and a lot of village craftsmen – butchers, carpenters, tailors, thatchers. A cross-section of the villagers. A few have brought their wives, but I think most women have stayed with the children to keep their farms going. And, of course, there are the soldiers.'

'Deserters from the Scottish war. No wonder the redshanks are winning,' Nicholas said bitterly.

'The war is a disastrous mistake. The Protector should never have started it.'

'Yet it is the duty of all to follow and assist the ruler in the waging of war.'

'Even if the war does not meet the criteria of a just war? A sudden and brutal invasion to take over another country? Does the authority of the ruler mean we must abandon all conscience and reason?'

Nicholas shook his head. 'Rebellion in time of war must be wrong.'

I said seriously, 'Nicholas, I had you released on my word of honour that you would not cause trouble.'

He frowned. 'I know, and I won't.'

'Well, keep your mouth closed, and remember your manners. Look, why don't you have a walk around the camp with me and Jack?'

'Among those men who beat me? No.' He looked again towards the doorway. 'Jack seems happy enough.'

'I think it's partly a way of escaping his own troubles, though yes, he sympathizes with Kett.'

'And you?'

'I don't know.'

'What do you think the Lady Elizabeth would say, if she knew you were here?'

I said uneasily, 'I was brought here by force.'

Footsteps sounded outside, and a shadow darkened the entrance to the hut. Toby Lockswood knelt in the doorway, his black beard longer and thicker than ever. He gave Nicholas a cold glance, then turned to me. 'Captain Kett requires you, Master Shardlake,' he said. 'Now.'

Chapter Forty-four

A S W E W A L K E D the short distance to St Michael's Chapel, I asked Toby, 'How long have you known this was going to happen? All the time you were working with us?'

'No,' he answered in a cold, brusque tone. 'I'd heard rumours, but it was only after my parents died and I lost the farm that I decided to seek out those who would rise against the gentlemen, and join them. Captain Kett is glad of literate men.'

'You did much to help us on the Boleyn case. I thought we worked well together.'

He looked at me, his blue suddenly eyes fierce. 'I have always kept a doin' with the work I've been given. Though I didn't much care what happened to Boleyn. But now I labour for the right order of the country.'

The main door of the chapel was closed, guarded by men in half-armour carrying halberds. Toby led me round to a side entrance. As we approached, a door opened and two men came out. My eyes widened in astonishment at the sight of Sir Richard Southwell, whom I had seen last with the Lady Mary, together with his man John Atkinson, the twins' friend. They were dressed only in plain shirts and hose, no doubt to fit in at the camp. When he saw me Southwell's face betrayed a flash of anger before resuming its usual haughty expression. He looked down at me from those heavy-lidded eyes.

'Master Shardlake,' he said. 'So you are become a rebel.'

'I was brought here,' I said. 'You seem to be here of your own will, though, Sir Richard.'

'Things have reached the stage where certain negotiations are needed.' He leaned over me. 'You did not see us here, you understand? Just as I did not see you. Better for both of us once this matter reaches its end.' He nodded at Atkinson, who gave me a surly look, and the two walked down the steep road to the river, Southwell showing some sort of pass to the guard on duty.

I looked incredulously at Toby. 'That man, here? One of the biggest sheep farmers in Norfolk? I would have thought you'd have had him in Surrey Place.'

He gave me a steely look. 'As he said, you didn't see him. And now, Captain Kett awaits you.'

We entered a small anteroom. Toby opened the door to the main chapel and I stepped in. The walls were still brightly decorated and the old stained glass remained. Nothing else, though, of its religious function survived. The steps rising to what had once been the altar now led to an area where a large table had been placed, stacked with papers, a couple of truckle beds beside it. A pair of thick curtains had been erected over the front, which could be drawn to provide a degree of privacy. In the body of the chapel tables had been set around the walls, where men sat writing. By the main door the tall figure of Robert Kett, his grey hair and beard neatly trimmed as always, was talking to Mayor Codd, the old man in aldermanic robes and the two clerics. 'I am sorry I had to leave you just now,' he said, his manner amiable. 'A piece of urgent business.' I thought, Did that mean he had been talking to Southwell in that little office? Kett continued, 'Well, then, it is agreed, the Norwich gates will be opened tomorrow, and there will be an additional market day. And do not fear, our people will keep the peace. This camp, after all, has been set up in the name of the King. And Master Watson, Master Conyers, your preaching in the camp will be welcome.'

'It may help curb some of the wide-eyed prophets we saw,' Codd said.

Kett inclined his head. 'There are a few wilder spirits here.'

Conyers, a young cleric with a thin ascetic face and a preacher's deep voice, said, 'Did you hold services in the camp today?'

'We have ministers of religion among us. They held services, all with the new Prayer Book.'

'No discontent about that?'

'None. All here are happy to follow the new rules in religion.'

The two clerics looked satisfied. Kett shook hands with them, then Mayor Codd and the old man, whom he addressed as Master Aldrich. As the door closed on them, Kett smiled thoughtfully. Then he turned to me, his face suddenly serious, and I was conscious of the power in those penetrating brown eyes. 'Master Shardlake. Welcome to our administrative centre. It is time, I think, we had a serious talk. Come.' He walked up the steps to the altar. As I followed him I cast my eye over the men working, wondering what papers they were transcribing. Kett closed the curtains behind us and stood facing me, his expression calculating, a little intimidating. To break the silence I said, 'You seem to have done a remarkable job of organization, sir.'

He grunted. 'I spent many years organizing my business, the religious guilds, and contesting with corrupt and greedy officials over the abbey church and lands. Most of all I contested with Flowerdew. Once you have dealt with him you can deal with anyone, I think.'

'He is – a strange man.'

'I expect he has fled to London. I may release his sons, they are just frightened boys.'

'I think that true.'

'How is Master Overton? Since I ordered his release he has not been seen around the camp, unlike you and Jack Barak.'

I thought, He does have a good intelligence system. 'I think he felt humiliated by his imprisonment. But he will make no trouble, his word is his bond.'

He gave me a hard look. 'Your client's sons, the Boleyn twins, have been troublesome. They will not be released; they would only join the gentry who will already be gathering against us. They may be transferred to Norwich Castle – yes, Mayor Codd has even agreed to that.'

'I can only agree they are an extremely dangerous pair.'

I found myself glancing at the beds. Kett said, 'Here is where I work and sleep. My wife Alice will not return to Wymondham without me. A good and loyal woman.'

His words brought Isabella Boleyn to mind. Were she and the steward Chawry still in Norwich, or had they returned to a wrecked Brikewell? I looked up, to see Kett staring interrogatively at me. 'I am sorry,' I said. 'I was just thinking of people I know in Norwich.'

'John Boleyn?'

'And his family.'

'Well,' Kett said. 'You may be able to visit the city shortly. As you heard, I have just been talking with the mayor and Alderman Aldrich, the second wealthiest man in Norwich. Shortly I will send word around the camp that Norwich is open to us. The city sent a messenger to London when the rebellion started, and the Protector has asked only that the two clerics you saw, Watson and Conyers, be allowed to preach to the camp twice a day. The market will be reopened, and the men have been given money, wages, from village funds. 'Some money has been appropriated from the gentry, and – other new sources.' He did not elaborate, and I wondered whether Southwell might have paid Kett handsomely to leave the Lady Mary and his own large flocks alone.

Kett continued solemnly. 'And I have intelligence that new camps have also been established at Ipswich and Bury. The Ipswich camp numbers a thousand and is already dispensing justice to the gentry. That news, too, will be passed around the camp. And tomorrow we make our first military endeavour, to take Yarmouth. Then we will have control of a major port, and as many herrings as we want.' He leaned forward, excitement in his voice now. 'Our enterprise is succeeding, Master Shardlake, everywhere. I do not delude myself that the Norwich city fathers are acting in anything but their own self-interest; they know that if we chose, we could descend the hill, cross the Wensum, and take everything from the rich merchants with the aid of the Norwich poor. But we shall do everything lawfully. So, given that assurance, will you confirm that you will assist me at the trials we shall soon hold?'

'I gave my oath that where the law and justice are concerned I will advise you honestly wherever I can.'

'Good. And remember, we act in the name of the King and the Protector, to further their desire for reform.'

I thought of all I had seen done in the camp, and for the first time wondered whether Kett could be right after all, and that the camps here and elsewhere might ensure the commissioners brought a new justice to the countryside – or even brought it without them.

Kett continued enthusiastically, 'Nearby, under a great ancient oak, a place of assembly and justice is being constructed. We shall hold our counsels there, and the camp will gather to pass sentence on the gentlemen we have taken – and on some of our own who have selfishly appropriated monies from the manor houses instead of giving them to the common purse.' He frowned. 'It is a disgrace, that men should cheat their fellows, here of all places.'

I ventured, 'Is that not just people being people, Captain Kett?'

He frowned, and I thought, for all of his extraordinary abilities and stout heart, in some ways he was a naive man. He continued, 'Those who have abused the privileges of the camp will be expelled, gentlemen who, it is decided, have done no wrong will be released, while those who deserve it will have their crimes noted before they are returned to Surrey Place or Norwich Castle.'

'There will be no hangings or mutilations?'

'None. I told you, this camp will be a place of peace and order. And the trials will be conducted in accordance with the rules of evidence, on which you can advise me where necessary. I need you all the more, since the young lawyer Thomas Godsalve has run away.'

'I remember the wretched cottagers and smallholders I represented at the Court of Requests for years, till Richard Rich took my post from me,' I said quietly. 'Even when I won a case – and there were a good many – I knew they were but a drop in the ocean of injustice.'

He nodded approval, then sighed. 'My legs are tired. I have been walking around the camp since dawn, interviewing the newly elected governors. Let us sit down.' I looked at his clever, determined face, his large solid figure, but remembered he was a decade older than me.

We seated ourselves opposite each other at the table. 'What do you hope to achieve, Captain Kett, at the end of it all?'

'A return to the fairer times of the past, but more than that. A share for the common people in the appointment of local officials, and in future enclosure commissions, which should be made permanent.'

'So that authority in the locality is no longer limited to the gentlemen and officials?'

Kett spoke with sudden force. 'Are we not showing here that we do not need the gentlemen to govern ourselves? I know you doubt the great men of the land will accept that, Master Shardlake, but I believe the

Protector is with us, and our camps across England will persuade the Council they must accept. This is no Peasants' Revolt or Cade's Rebellion, desperate military uprisings against the rulers. This is different.'

Again I thought, He is naive, he does not understand that all the Protector truly cares about is the Scottish war. I took a deep breath and said, 'Captain Kett, may I speak frankly?'

He spread his work-roughened hands. 'Everyone in this camp may speak freely. Even those who oppose what we are doing will be allowed their voice at our new place of assembly. We are calling it the Oak of Reformation, is that not a wonderful name?'

I thought, 'Oak of Reformation.' These days that carried a double meaning: reformation of the Church, or the welfare of the State, or both. It was cleverly ambiguous. I framed my reply carefully. 'Most of the King's Council, and all men of status, believe it to be God's law that the head should govern the foot in society, and those who are not gentlemen – who do not need to do manual work for their living – should not govern. I am with you in my heart, but I fear you underestimate the power and hostility of those in power.'

I feared Kett might be angry, but he answered calmly. 'Those rules are not God's law, but men's. They have led to desperate injustice, and must be remedied. We do not wish to overthrow society, but reform it – and the only way to do that is to give the common people some say.' His voice hardened. 'And to let the gentlemen know, when they return, that their powers, which they have abused, are not limitless. The days when a man had to remove his cap and bow and scrape before being even allowed to address his lord are over.'

I ventured a smile. 'Though from my recollections, Norfolk men were less inclined to servility than most.'

'True,' Kett said, 'but that can only help so far when true power lies with the landlords. See there –' he pointed to a little clock set on the table. 'That was taken from one of the manor houses on the way here. Something so simple, so necessary in a camp like this, so we might tell the hour – yet beyond the means of all but a few who are here. And a new hour has struck, Master Shardlake, decreed by God, true Reformation both of religion and of the earthly world. That is why I say the name of our assembly place is a wonderful one.'

I answered. 'Can any of us truly know that such an hour has struck?'

Kett looked at me intently, then said quietly, 'I was a loyal Catholic once, friend to the old Abbot of Wymondham. He was a good man, I named my son after him, but I see now that in religion he was wrong. After the abbey went down a new preacher came to Wymondham, a true Protestant, Henry King. Gradually, I came to see that he was right. I began to study the Bible, and now see that true Christianity lies in faith, and struggle for a true Commonwealth.' He shook his head. 'I have spent too much of my life building up treasures.'

I smiled sadly, and began to quote some lines: ' "I regarded little God's Word, but gave myself to vanities and shadows of the world. I forsook Him, in whom is all truth, and followed the vain, foolish imaginings of my heart." '

Kett looked at me with interest. 'That is exactly right. Who said that?'

'The late Queen Catherine Parr, in her *Lamentation of a Sinner*.'

'Ah, she was a friend to true religion.' He leant forward eagerly. 'You have true Bible faith, like her?'

'Once I did, but now I am uncertain in all things.'

'Do you think Queen Catherine would have supported what we are doing?'

I shook my head sadly. 'No. I think she would have seen you as rebels and rioters, as her brother-in-law Sir William Herbert did when he put down those who rebelled against him in May.'

'Most cruelly, I am told.'

'Yes.'

He looked at me, ran a hand through his grey beard, and said quietly, 'Thank you for speaking honestly, Serjeant Shardlake. But I think you are a man with too much doubt in your soul.'

I thought but did not say, and perhaps you have too little. There was silence for a moment, then Kett squared his shoulders and spoke, suddenly businesslike again, 'All the camps are sending petitions to the Protector, summarizing their grievances. Our governors are drawing up a preliminary petition now. We must get it to London, as the other camps are doing. Perhaps I may ask you to look it over when it is done, to make sure it is not too clumsily written.'

'If you wish.'

'And meanwhile, to ensure that our collections of food and other resources from the gentry have legal status, we are preparing warrants. That is what those men here are doing.' He produced a paper from his desk. 'What think you of this?'

I took the paper and read:

We, the King's friends and deputies, do grant license to all men to provide and bring into the camp at Mousehold all manner of cattle and provision of vittles, in what place soever they may find the same, so that no violence or injury be done to any honest or poor man: commanding all persons, as they tend to the King's honour and Royal Majesty, and the relief of the Commonwealth, to be obedient to us the Governors, and to those whose names ensue.

Signed: Robert Kett.

Two more names which I did not recognize, written like the rest of the document in a neat secretary hand, had been appended but not yet actually signed.

'Whose are the other names?' I asked.

'The camp governors of the particular Hundreds in which the warrants are to be applied. Receipts will be given to those from whom goods are taken.'

'And yet –'

'Yes –'

I took a deep breath. 'Forgive me, but you have no actual authority from the King or the Protector. This, Captain Kett, is not legal.'

His eyes hardened again. 'Everything we do is to further the interests of the King, the Protector, and the commissioners. Does this not show we intend to act legally, in the name of the King?'

'That is an argument,' I said cautiously, though in law it seemed little more than licensed theft – albeit from those who had more than they needed, and to supply the camp. Unintentionally, I laughed. 'Captain Kett, you make my head spin.'

Unexpectedly, he laughed back. 'I make my own head spin, at the labours that have fallen on me, all the things we must do. We are build-ing a smithy to shoe horses and make weapons, and ovens to make bread.'

'How long do you think you will be here?'

'As long as it takes.' He thought for a moment, then smiled. 'You see, we have the whip hand. I know only too well what the Council and the Parliament think of us, though I believe the Protector is our friend. And in any event, the camps have the numbers, the organiza-tion and, in our case' — he raised an eyebrow — 'the gentlemen, as prisoners and hostages.'

'What if they send forces against you, as they have the south-western rebels?'

Kett smiled. 'They call for the return of the Mass. We, though, are loyal to the new order in religion. And with an army sent to the west, and all other forces in Scotland, where is the Council to get an army from?' His face suddenly became serious, his eyes hard.

I said, 'You have thought it all through, sir.'

He clenched a fist. 'Now is the time, now is our chance.'

I did not reply. Kett smiled again. 'I have enjoyed talking to you, Master Shardlake. You speak directly, unlike most lawyers. I am going down to Norwich tomorrow, to visit Codd and Aldrich. Go there too, if you wish, visit your friends, then on Tuesday, help me do justice at the Oak of Reformation. Advise me, make notes of what is said.' He hesitated, then added, 'Your man Barak, I hear he can write tolerably well with his left hand?'

'Yes. He has made great efforts to do so.'

'Good. Then he can be your scribe at the Oak.' He looked at me keenly. 'He is wholly with us.'

I nodded. 'I think he is.' Suddenly I thought of Tamasin, far away in London. And I thought, too, Kett is a clever politician; now he has drawn me even deeper into the work of the camp.

Chapter Forty-five

Next morning, as usual, people rose at dawn. It promised to be yet another hot day. I had slept well last night, though it was stuffy and noisome in the little lean-to, with barely room for the three of us. We all stank to high heaven, but were becoming used to the musty, sweaty smell we shared with everyone in the camp. We all had straggly beards now – mine white, Barak's brown, Nicholas's coppery.

At breakfast bread and cheese were handed around by Goodwife Everneke. As I ate with my fingers, I thought that even a fortnight ago the idea of living in such conditions would have horrified me. The strange thing was that, despite the heat, with the bracken bed and regular movement, I was feeling better than for some time; my body more like a functioning organism than a disjointed collection of aching parts, though after my recent injury I still had to be careful.

There was much laughter among the villagers about Alderman Aldrich's visit to the camp. Apparently, he lived at Swardeston, three miles away, and had been brought into Norwich by a party of rebels. 'E's ours now, bors,' one villager said with pleasure.

Most men had been assigned work for the day, but some, and a number of the women, were going down to Norwich market. The previous evening the leaders of the Hundreds, accompanied by soldiers, had gone around the camp, distributing coins – a shilling for each man, representing wages for their work. New debased shillings, but money nonetheless.

Young Natty, wearing an armless leather jerkin and threadbare upper hose, looked at the coin in his big brown hand. 'First I've had in weeks,' he said.

'Are you going back to tree-felling today?' I asked him.

'Better than that, one of the carpenters is teaching me to saw planks. Perhaps I may become an apprentice, after this is done.'

'Will you go back to the Sandlings?'

'I may stay in Norwich. I never really liked the sea.' He looked at me, and I remembered Walter, washed up on the beach with his head stoved in, like Edith Boleyn's. Evidently he remembered it too, for he leaned forward and said, 'An old pal of mine has come to camp, with some people from the Sandlings. He comes from poor Wal Padbury's village; I thought I might ask him if he remembered anything.'

'If you could, I would be very grateful.'

Old Goodman Johnson rose to his feet. 'I have to go to a meeting of them as fought in the wars. Thanks for the food, Goody Everneke. I'll miss Conyers's sermon, so pray for my soul.'

''Tis early for a gathering, bor.'

'There's much to organize.'

I looked at him. 'So my friends and I may visit Norwich unaccompanied?'

'Ay, those are the orders.' He looked doubtfully at Nicholas, who returned the old man's gaze, a flash of anger in his green eyes.

✝

AFTER BREAKFAST hundreds gathered to hear the sermon by Thomas Conyers. Its tone was evangelical, calling on the assembly to remember they were in God's view and to behave in a sober and peace-able manner, though he also referred to the need for reformation of the greed in the land, as well as giving a long disquisition on the extirpa-tion of sinfulness. It was, I thought, carefully judged. I wondered how many of the camp people were radical Protestants. Some, no doubt, but many, I suspected, were bending with the wind in hope of support from the Protector. Traditionalists – and there must be some – were keeping their heads down.

Afterwards, people, mostly carrying baskets, headed for the road down to Norwich. We walked to the escarpment, past a group of men digging another large pit to bury the remains of some of the slaugh-tered sheep. The stink was terrible.

We watched people descend, cross Bishopsgate Bridge, which had been opened, and enter the city. The mood of those setting off was cheerful in the main, though the peddlers who had come to the camp looked disconsolate, for they could not compete with the city market. I said to Barak and Nicholas, 'Well, let us go down.'

'I wish they'd returned my sword,' Nicholas grumbled. 'Having to go to the city in a ragged shirt like a peasant – it's humiliating.'

'Be glad they released you,' Barak said impatiently, strapping on his artificial hand. He turned to me. 'It's going to be a long day, if we're going to make all the visits you want. Are you feeling up to it?'

'I want to do as much as I can. Go to the Maid's Head to see if there's any new correspondence for me and send my own, give Isabella the money Flowerdew took if she is still at the inn, then go to the castle and see Boleyn. And I would like to visit Josephine and Edward. And perhaps Scambler's aunt – we'll look out for the lad in the city. You have your letter to Tamasin?'

'Yes. It just says I've been delayed by the troubles, but am safe.'

'I have written a like letter to Guy.' I took a deep breath. 'And one to Parry, again saying the same, but also that I will continue to investi gate the Boleyn case where I can.'

Barak looked around at the crowds, the vista of huts. 'That seems pretty small beer now.'

'I still have responsibilities,' I answered stubbornly.

We made our way to the road, just as a party of horsemen in fine but sober clothing appeared – Robert Kett and his brother William, with a group of other men. They included Toby Lockswood, who looked at us with narrowed eyes. Kett waved me to approach.

'Master Shardlake, God give you good morrow.'

'And you, Captain Kett.' He was again in happily enthusiastic mood, his energy returned. William Kett, however, looked at us with sharp eyes. I wondered whether he thought his brother too trusting of me.

'Work on the Oak of Reformation is almost done,' William said brusquely. 'Be ready for tomorrow.'

'I shall.'

'What are you doing in Norwich today?'

'Visiting friends, and Master Boleyn in the castle.'

'I am having further talks with Codd. I hear that a new camp has been set up at Castle Rising, near King's Lynn, which will soon be ours. And we have sent men to occupy Yarmouth. There will be cockles and herrings for everyone!' He smiled, looking around his entourage. Then he nodded to us and set off towards the steep hill, people cheering as he passed. Toby, however, turned aside and approached us. 'You are visiting Boleyn?'

'He remains my client.'

'I heard that last night those twins of his got together with other prisoners in their room at Surrey Place and tried to break out. They are held in chains now. They may be sons of a landowner, but they are vagabonds, savages.'

'You know my views about that pair, Toby,' I answered.

Nicholas looked at him angrily. I feared for a moment he might lash out, but he only said, bitterly, 'Toby, you broke bread with us, even fought with us against the twins. Yet now you look at us as though we are enemies. Did you always think so little of us?'

Barak glanced at Toby curiously. 'Well?'

Toby flushed, looking between the three of us. 'I told Master Shardlake, if I am given work, I make it a point of honour to do it well. But you, young Nicholas, would join those ranged against us if you could. As for John Boleyn, whether his sentence was right or wrong, he is one of the lords. A shame this affair also took the lives of two working people, but no doubt that is just a detail to you.'

'Does not John Boleyn still deserve justice?' I said.

'As do we all. But few of us have the Lady Elizabeth behind us to purchase a pardon.' He leaned down from his horse. 'There are people from Brikewell here, some of those who mistook you for the enclosure commissioners when they were scaring off Witherington's doves. One saw you and asked me what you were doing here without your finery. I told him Captain Kett seemed to favour you. But do not underestimate him, Master Shardlake.'

✣

WE WALKED DOWN the hill. As we passed under Bishopsgate Bridge gatehouse, I noticed yet another proclamation from Protector Somerset.

I hoped it might tell us when the commissioners would arrive, but it only said starkly that a reward was being offered for the naming of renegades and deserters who were stirring up sedition. I frowned. That did not sound like sympathy for the camps.

As we walked along Holme Street, between the high walls of the cathedral precinct and the great hospital, where beggars still sat waving their bowls, I saw a familiar face; a strongly built man with a brown beard, laughing and joking with a group of younger men.

Barak said to me, 'There's Vowell.'

'Yes,' I said. 'Let us have a word.'

We pushed our way through the crowd. 'Master Vowell,' I said, 'good morrow.' I thought he might not recognize me in my changed state but he answered at once, 'Lawyer Shardlake, I see you are free.'

'We are at the camp,' I said.

'Prisoners on parole,' Nicholas added. 'Me, at least.'

'Are you at the camp, too?' I asked him.

'I am.' Vowell raised his chin proudly. 'For a long time the ways of our rulers have sickened me, not least my old master.'

I remembered the night we had seen him at the Blue Boar Inn, and thought, sickened so much you helped plot this rebellion. One of the men with him spoke up, a thin young man with fierce angry eyes. 'Him and all his filthy kind. The rich merchants of Norwich hurt the common people as much as the greedy landowners in the countryside.'

Vowell said, 'Have you ever seen the Sotherton house?'

'No.'

'They are another of the great families of Norwich. It is in St Andrew's Street. The walls are built of flint, knapped and chiselled so they are as even as bricks. It makes a great show. Think of the time and effort so many masons and poor labourers put into making it for a pittance.' I thought for a moment of Edward Brown and his calloused hands. Vowell leaned closer, and spoke quietly. 'Are you planning to visit your client John Boleyn?'

'Yes. And his wife, if she is still in Norwich.'

He shrugged. 'Well, remember what a nest of adders that family is. Old Reynolds, and those twins.'

'Come on, Mikey,' one of his friends said. 'We'll be late for market.' Vowell gave me a serious look, nodded briefly, and turned away.

We arrived at Tombland. The houses of the rich had closed gates, as did the cathedral. No servants bustled about the square now. There were plenty of poor folk around, though, many seeming to walk with a new confidence. I heard a man call at the shuttered windows of one of the great houses, 'We're coming for you, merchants of Norwich!'

Barak fingered his beard. 'You can see why the city fathers are co-operating with Kett. They fear that if they don't, they'll be next.' He looked at me. 'Where do you think the money that was passed about the camp came from?'

'I think plenty came from the villages. But some has been taken from the manor houses.'

'Stolen,' Nicholas said.

I thought of Southwell leaving St Michael's Chapel. I wondered, but said nothing.

✠

WE WENT FIRST TO the Maid's Head. Here too doors were closed, windows shuttered. We knocked, and a servant opened the front door a crack and eyed us suspiciously. I asked for Master Theobald. He came, his eyes widening at our dishevelled state. I told him we had been taken to the camp, but allowed to come into town.

He invited us inside the empty inn. He wrung his hands. 'That you should be reduced to such a state, Serjeant Shardlake, I am so sorry. You should escape the city while you can, by one of the western gates. The constables will not stop you.' He lowered his voice. 'Many of the richest citizens are leaving.'

'I have given my oath not to leave.' I said nothing of my wider agreement with Kett; the fewer the people who knew about that the better.

Master Theobald clenched his hands. 'Oaths to rogues like that mean nothing. These creatures wandering over Mousehold, bathing naked without shame in the river, the whole country is full of these mutinies and commotions, they must be put down.' He leaned close.

'Master Leonard Sotherton rode out to London at first light, to tell the Protector of the size of this camp and to ask for help.'

'Perhaps when the commissioners arrive they may settle things,' I replied neutrally.

He looked at me seriously. 'Things have gone beyond that. I doubt they will ever come now.' He sighed. 'But, Master Shardlake, I have kept your robes for you, will you take them?'

'Keep them for now, if you would. And if you could arrange to post some letters for me?'

'I hear the rebels control most of Norfolk, and are stopping post-riders on the road and examining correspondence.'

'We have been careful.'

'Then I will see they are sent. And I have one for you, it arrived two days back but I did not know where you were.' He passed it over. It was from Parry. I sat down and read it immediately.

Master Shardlake,

I have heard nothing from you since I last wrote. I know much of the country is in chaos with these accursed rebellions, but I understand East Anglia is peaceful, and the Lady Elizabeth and I are anxious about the business we sent you on, and ask you to return as soon as possible. The Lady Elizabeth, as you know, has insisted on making enquiries locally, and it appears that a woman answering our visitor's description lodged with a poor family near Hatfield for a while before visiting us, although she used a different name. Attempts are being made to trace her movements back from there.

The letter had evidently been written before the East Anglian out-breaks were known at Hatfield. 'No news,' I said, 'save that Parry wants us back.'

'We could go,' Nicholas said. 'This is our chance.'

I shook my head. 'I do not give my oath lightly.' This was true, and if I had a chance to help bring law and order to these proposed trials, I had a duty to take it.

'Well said.' Barak smiled. Nicholas bit his lip, but said nothing further.

I put the letter away. 'Master Theobald, have you any idea where Mistress Boleyn and her steward went when they left here?'

'They were going to see if they could find a place at one of the inns at the market square.'

'Thank you. Then let us see if we can find her there.' We took our farewell of Master Theobald, who looked at us with pity. His well-ordered world had vanished.

✝

WE WALKED THROUGH NORWICH, looking out for Simon Scambler, though there was no sign of him. At the top of the marketplace, on the Guildhall steps, Mayor Codd stood with Alderman Aldrich, armed constables behind them. Codd looked frightened, Aldrich sternly watchful. Then, to my surprise, another elderly man stepped out of the Guildhall, leaning heavily on a stick, a sword at his waist, his thin face full of angry contempt. Gawen Reynolds. He exchanged some muttered words with the others, but though Codd put a restraining hand on his arm, Reynolds brushed it off and stepped down to the fringes of the crowd coming to market, glowering at them. Then, from somewhere, a man shouted out, 'They'll hang your Boleyn son-in-law yet, Gawen Reynolds! And Captain Kett will hang your grandsons!'

There was laughter, and Reynolds's face went brick-red. Despite appeals from Codd and Aldrich, he stepped forward and drew his sword. 'Ruffatory makebates! I will see you all hanging on the gallows there!'

He was immediately approached by a number of men, from the camp by the looks of them. One large fellow stepped in front of him, drawing a knife. 'Come on, then, you old rogue, and we'll slay you like a sheep!'

Reynolds hesitated, intimidated by their numbers. Then a cabbage was thrown from somewhere, striking him on his sword arm. He dropped the weapon, and the man facing him kicked it away. There was more laughter from the crowd.

From the Guildhall steps Mayor Codd shouted down, 'Alderman Reynolds, I command you, get back up here! We wish no trouble, for Jesu's sake!'

But Reynolds had lost control, and let out a stream of oaths. The men moved closer, and one smacked him on the face, causing him to stagger back. The soldiers on top of the Guildhall steps made to retaliate but Codd shouted, 'No, we'll have a riot!' He shouted desperately, 'All of you, I command you in the name of sense, step away!'

But it was too late. Another man shoved Reynolds, causing him to stagger again and almost fall. Then, beside me, Nicholas suddenly woke to life. 'Rogue he may be,' he said, 'but he's a helpless old man!' Barak put a hand on his arm, but he shook it off and ran towards those surrounding Reynolds, his face red, shouting, 'Stop it! Have you no shame? Is this the traitor Kett's law?' He pushed the ringleader away from Reynolds. For a second the man was intimidated by Nicholas's size and fury, but then pushed him back. Nicholas grappled with him, the crowd egging the other man on. Mayor Codd looked on in horror, and Alderman Aldrich signalled to the soldiers to descend the steps. At the sight of ten armed men the crowd pulled back. Barak stepped forward, put his arm round Nicholas's throat and dragged him back, while men from the crowd restrained his opponent. Reynolds turned and limped back up the steps to safety, angrily shoving aside a soldier's offer of aid. Aldrich said something to him, and with a final curse he went inside the Guildhall.

Mayor Codd stepped forward, raising his hands, and called out, 'Disperse, please! I deplore Alderman Reynolds's behaviour, and will see him disciplined for it!'

The man who had fought with Nicholas glared back at Codd, but one of his friends said, 'Come, bor, this in't what Captain Kett wants!' The man shrugged angrily and allowed himself to be led away, but he shouted at Nicholas, 'Captain Kett will hear you called him traitor!'

I turned angrily on Nicholas. He was red-faced, breathing heavily. 'God's blood, boy!' I shouted. 'What in Jesu's name did you think you were doing! Reynolds started this ruffle, you should have left the aldermen and soldiers to quiet it!'

'The crowd could have beaten him to death. I would not see that!'

'Why not?' Barak asked starkly. 'Norwich would be better off without him.'

'Have you lost all sense of honour?' Nicholas replied furiously. All his pent-up anger of the past week was spilling out at last.

'And have you lost all sense?' Barak shouted back. 'And Kett is *not* a traitor. He has done what he has in the name of the King and Protector!'

I scanned the crowd. Half the square had been looking up at the Guildhall, and the story of what had happened was being passed around; many glares were thrown at us. 'Let us get to the inn at once,' I said. 'And quietly. Nicholas, this will get back to Kett. Don't be surprised to find yourself locked up again. Perhaps I will be too, as I guaranteed your behaviour.' I strode away angrily, leaving the others to follow.

Chapter Forty-six

To MY GREAT RELIEF, we found Isabella and Chawry were at an inn called the Black Prince. Isabella looked pretty as ever, but tired. Both she and Chawry seemed to have lost weight. Chawry brought a chair for Isabella and stood beside her when she was seated. His manner, as always, was deferential, but the way he looked at her removed any doubt in my mind that he desired her. Isabella would have been a fool not to see it, and she was no fool. But her manner to him throughout our talk remained that of a mistress to a valued servant. Nothing more.

Isabella turned to Nicholas, looking concerned. 'Master Overton, what has happened? Are those not old bruises on your face?'

I said, 'Nicholas has been getting himself into trouble, Mistress Boleyn. But it is a private matter, do not trouble yourself.'

'Master Chawry and I have wondered what had happened to you. We were worried.'

'With this rebellion all around,' Chawry added. 'These filthy dogs in their Mousehold kennel.'

I explained that we had been taken to the Mousehold camp, but allowed freedom under parole. 'We were captured outside Flowerdew's house when I went to get the money he'd taken from you. I got it back.' I felt genuine pleasure at her look of relief as I handed over the bag of coins.

'The rebels did not take it?' Chawry asked in surprise.

'Not when I told Kett it was all that stood between a good woman and poverty.'

Isabella looked at me, blushing slightly. 'I thank you, Master Shardlake, with all my heart. Our money was running out. We have barely enough left to get food to take to John in the castle, and pay for our rooms here. We have not been eating as we should.' She sighed and shook her head. 'I am sorry your quest to help me ended with you all being taken prisoner.'

I smiled. 'We are well. You would be surprised how peaceable a place the camp is.'

'Is it, sir?' Chawry looked again at Nicholas's face.

'Not if you are a gentleman,' Nicholas answered.

I said crossly, 'One who cannot keep his mouth shut, but rants like a muck-spout.'

Chawry looked at me through narrowed eyes. 'You are learning rude Norfolk speech, Serjeant Shardlake.' Clearly he suspected I had at least some sympathy with the rebels. Then he shook his head, remembering his place. 'But I, too, thank you for what you have done.' He spoke a little too smoothly, I thought.

'Can you not escape Norwich now?' Isabella asked.

'No. We have been allowed here today, but must return to the camp tonight. I gave my oath. But I thought I might visit your husband.'

Impulsively, she reached out and took my hand. 'John and I will never forget what you have done.' I noticed that Chawry looked away, his lips set. I thought, If he were seriously in love with Isabella, he had a motive to see John Boleyn hanged. But Chawry could have no connection with Edith – she had been gone for years before he had even taken up his post.

'How is John?' Nicholas asked Isabella.

'Cheerful enough, though still recovering.' She held the bag of money a moment, then passed it over to Chawry. 'Daniel, take charge of this.'

'There may be no progress on the pardon until these troubles are settled,' I said gently. 'The Protector must be much preoccupied. What of you, have you considered returning to Brikewell? I know the twins are gone.'

'I went back three days ago,' Chawry replied. 'The place had been ransacked.'

'That was the twins' doing. They are in Kett's custody now.'

'Thank God,' said Isabella in relief. 'I feared they might come to Norwich.'

'I think the rebels took things as well,' Chawry said bitterly. 'Valuable things.'

'I know, I was on their march from Wymondham.'

'They control nearly all the countryside nearby, I believe. They have patrols on the road, and I had insults on my way to Brikewell. They are raiding the manor houses, and may come to Brikewell again. I think it safer for us both to stay here, now we have the money to do so.'

'So long as Norwich remains peaceful, perhaps that is best.'

'And I will not leave John,' Isabella said.

We talked further, and I surprised them when I told them more about the camp, which they had believed a chaotic den of villains.

'You make them sound like angels,' Chawry said stiffly.

Barak said, 'Of course they're not. There are no angels outside heaven.'

Isabella looked at Nicholas and smiled. 'You must steer clear of trouble, Master Nicholas. I would not see your pretty white skin disfigured again.' I thought, She likes a little flirting; she knows how to use men. Then I reminded myself that she had worked for years in a tavern, where flirting with customers was part of the job.

✞

Standing on the steps of the inn I took a deep breath, then said to Nicholas, 'As I said, I fear you may be in for more trouble. If you want, take the Maid's Head proprietor's advice and leave, try to make your way back to London.'

He looked at me seriously. 'I thank you, sir, sincerely, but I gave you my oath to stay, and I will not break it. I apologize for what I did earlier. If word gets back, I will face the consequences.'

I considered. 'Very well. Say you spoke in temper.' I looked down past the marketplace, to the castle on its high mound. 'Now, let us go and see how Master Boleyn fares.'

✞

There were fewer guards outside the castle, with some gone to keep order elsewhere. Leaving Barak and Nicholas outside, I asked to see John Boleyn and was taken to his cell. He was in surprisingly good spirits, the marks around his neck much fainter. He could speak again, albeit croakily. He was thinner, though, and still had that look of shock in his eyes. His cell now had the comfort of some cushions and a little writing table which Isabella had brought him. He thanked me profusely for returning the money. We spoke of the pardon, and I realized he had convinced himself its granting was just a matter of time. I hoped he was right.

He was still allowed to exercise on the roof of Norwich Castle and, accompanied by a guard, we mounted a long flight of stone steps. My back was hurting by the time we reached the top. The guard stayed in the doorway as we walked along the long, flat roof to the battlements. We stood a moment looking out over the busy marketplace and the spires of Norwich. The long drop to the ground, where men seemed as small as dots, made my head spin. I stepped back.

Boleyn had learned from the guards about the rebellions across the country, and the great camp at Mousehold. Like Chawry and Isabella, he was astonished to find I was now there, and that the camp was not a den of iniquity. I told him Kett hoped that soon the enclosure commissioners would arrive, and radical reform implemented. I went on to tell him that the twins and his neighbour Witherington were in rebel custody. He laughed bitterly. 'I cannot think of a better fate for the three of them.' He sighed. 'Do not think me harsh, Master Shardlake, but I say again, I wash my hands entirely of my sons. To come to their father's hanging and cheer it on . . .'

'I cannot blame you.'

He pondered. 'So, the enclosures set up in recent years are being pulled down. What of the freed sheep?'

'Taken to the camp for food. There has been mighty feasting, but I think now the sheep are being kept penned. I am told there are six or seven thousand people there now, and more coming in.'

Boleyn considered. 'My small enclosures will no doubt be taken with the others. Unfair, when the real sheep-lords are those like the Pastons and Richard Southwell.'

I thought, but forbore to say, Tenants have suffered on Witherington's land, and would have on yours, if his assault had succeeded.

He said, 'You told me Thorpe Wood is being cut down for fuel.

That is Paston land. In all this uproar perhaps my own small debts will be forgotten.' He paused, his expression suddenly calculating. 'My sons are friends with some of Southwell's men. He is dangerous. I hired his boys, through my sons, when I learned Witherington would try to take my land. That was wrong. It would be good to see him fall.' He turned away, looking out over the city. At this height there was a welcome breeze. 'I wonder what will happen to Norwich,' he said. 'I hope Isabella stays safe.' He turned and looked me in the eye. 'You realize, of course, that the Protector, and the King's Council who put him where he is, will never allow common people even the smallest share of rule. That has never happened, and never will, and never should. These camps will be destroyed.'

I inclined my head. 'Kett's camp has considerable forces, trained soldiers. I should think the other camps have, too. The Protector may well feel the pressure to make drastic changes. And Kett stresses his loyalty to the King.'

Boleyn looked at me in surprise. 'Are you become one of them?'

I did not answer.

'By Jesu, Master Shardlake, I owe you my life and what you have done for me and my wife puts me eternally in your debt. But I advise you, be careful of the waters in which you are treading. They may drown you.' He shook his head, then changed the subject abruptly. 'Is Richard Southwell taken by the rebels?'

'No,' I answered. I did not add that I had seen him at St Michael's Chapel.

Boleyn frowned. 'I thought he would have been.'

'Have you met him?' I asked.

'No.'

I hesitated, then deciding to change the subject said, 'Isabella is safe, and in good hands with Chawry to attend on her. But I noticed —'

His eyes were at once as sharp as needles. 'Noticed what?'

'I think Chawry has — feelings — for your wife. I believe both have behaved honourably but — I thought you should know.'

To my surprise, Boleyn laughed, a harsh cynical laugh that set him coughing. When he recovered himself he said, in bitter tones, 'Do you think I did not know that, Master Shardlake? The penalty of an older man being married to a young and pretty wife is that others often desire her. Perhaps Chawry, loyal servant though he is, would take Isabella from me if he could. But he cannot; because, you see, though it may be hard for you to believe, we are as much in love as the day we met. Seeing others' eyes on her is the price I must pay for loving her.' He frowned. 'It is a small penalty compared with those Edith laid on me, in life and now in death.' He fingered the marks on his throat. I thought, Does no one ever pity Edith, think of her terrible and humiliating end? I met Boleyn's angry gaze, and asked quietly, 'Have you had any thoughts about where Edith might have been all those years before she returned to Norfolk and was killed?'

He made a gesture of irritation. 'No. In life and death, Edith was a mystery, and so I think it will remain.'

✞

BY NOW IT WAS midday; we found an inn at the top of Conisford Street, and took some lunch. My back, which had been so improved in the camp, was hurting again after a morning walking the Norwich streets, and I was glad to lean against a settle. After lunch, seeing I was tired, Barak asked if I wished to return to the camp, but I insisted I wanted to visit Josephine and Edward, who were nearby, then Scambler's aunt. I could not help thinking of that poor boy, homeless on the streets.

We made our way to the little courtyard hovel where Edward and Josephine lived; dressed raggedly, we attracted little attention now. I knocked on Josephine's door. She answered, little Mousy on her hip. The child looked better for some good feeding, smiled happily and stretched out her arms to us. Josephine, though, looked tired and anxious. She stared at us in surprise.

'Master Shardlake, I thought you had left. Your clothes, you look like —'

'Camp-men,' Barak answered. 'We fell into Captain Kett's hands. We have a day's parole in Norwich, so are making visits.'

Josephine ushered us inside and laid Mousy in her cradle. The little girl reached out and grasped my finger, trying to pull me down to put it in her mouth. I said gently, 'It would not taste nice, Mousy, it is dirty.'

Josephine looked between the three of us. 'How are you being treated? I have heard from Edward that many gentlemen have been buffled about. Not that a lot of them don't deserve it, but – Master Nicholas, your face –'

'He'd be all right if he could keep his mouth shut,' Barak said. 'As for Master Shardlake and I, we are well treated.'

'Captain Kett has asked me to give him legal advice at his proposed trials of the gentlemen. He has promised there will be no severe punishments. I have promised to assist to see the law is observed, so far as it can be in the strange circumstances. But Josephine, keep that quiet. There are those in London and elsewhere who, if they knew –' I thought of Parry, and Elizabeth. She nodded her understanding.

'Where is Edward?' I asked.

She hesitated, then said, 'Up at the camp. He went at first light. There is a meeting between Captain Kett, his chief soldier Miles and the other experienced soldiers in the camp, with the leaders of their supporters in Norwich.' I remembered the meeting old Hector Johnson had gone to. She went on, a mixture of pride and anxiety in her voice. 'Edward is to help coordinate the poor of south Norwich. In case the city fathers decide to close the gates against the camp once more.' She added, in scarce above a whisper, 'If that happens, the camp will take over the city. Edward says it will be easy.'

Barak nodded agreement. 'Norwich has few soldiers, and now we are up on Mousehold the camp-men could easily get across the Wensum.'

Josephine said, 'I know I can trust you to tell nobody. I support all that Edward and Captain Kett are doing, but – I fear what may happen if there is violence. I remember the past.'

I put my hand on her arm. Josephine was originally a French child taken by English soldiers after her village was burned down during the old king's wars, and left in the care of a brutish man who called himself her father but treated her like a slave. I said gently, 'Captain Kett is a man of peace. If the enclosure commissioners come, a display of force may help them get the reforms they want. That, I think, is all.'

'The old king would have had them all killed.'

'He is dead,' Barak said. 'Protector Somerset is different.'

'Or so we hope,' I added quietly. 'Nicholas, I am sorry to say, keeps getting into trouble. Today he accused Kett of being a traitor in the marketplace. I fear he will be locked up again if word gets back to the camp, which it probably will.' I looked at her. 'Might Edward put in a word for him? Say he knows him and that although he is a gentleman he has never oppressed anyone, and is goodhearted, even though he cannot control his mouth?'

She looked at Nicholas and shook her head affectionately. 'I always thought you a good lad, despite your—'

'Antrums,' Barak finished the sentence for her.

'I will. Edward was not sure if he would be back tonight, but I will speak to him.'

Nicholas took a deep breath. 'Thank you, Josephine. They are right, I must bridle my tongue.'

Beside me, Mousy reached up again for my hand, making little squeaking noises. Josephine smiled and picked her up. 'She likes you. Those noises she makes, Mousy is the right name for her.' She kissed the child. 'When Master Shardlake has clean hands, he may let you play with him.' Her face became serious. 'It is her I fear for, if things become violent. I remember what it is like to be a child caught up in war.'

☩

OUR FINAL VISIT that day was to Scambler's aunt, down in Ber Street. I was tired now, my back hurting again. It was early afternoon, the hottest time of day. It would be another long walk back to Tomb-land, across Bishopsgate Bridge and up to the camp.

As we made our way Barak said, 'So Edward is right in the thick of it.'

'Yes. I suspected so.'

Nicholas shook his head, then laughed. 'So it has come to this, a gentleman needs the word of a stonemason's labourer to keep him from trouble. But I always liked him, and Josephine, and for now at least I must accept my situation.'

'Good,' Barak and I answered in unison.

☩

WE REACHED THE poor little house where Scambler had lived. I knocked on the door, and heard the familiar shuffling and grumbling from within.

'You!' His aunt hesitated then laughed, a scratching sound. 'By heaven, you are come down in the world.'

'We are held at the camp,' I said. 'We have been allowed to visit Norwich, and came to ask after Simon. Have you had any news?'

Her mouth puckered angrily. 'No, Master Lawyer, I haven't. And I don't care where he is, the godless creature. Those who deny the chance of salvation are the most cursed, and Sooty can find his own way to hell. I have enough to worry about, with those rebels up at Mousehold Heath. Some say they are good Protestants, but the Bible tells us to render unto Caesar that which is Caesar's, not destroy the order which God has created. You can tell Robert Kett that from me.'

And she slammed the door in our faces once more.

Chapter Forty-seven

IT WAS A LONG, tiring walk back to the camp. As we crossed Bishopsgate Bridge there were still swimmers in the river, trying to keep cool in the heat.

'I think I'll have a swim,' Barak said, raising his sleeve and unbuckling his artificial hand. 'Haven't washed for a week. Come on, Nick, boy!' He looked at me. 'What about you?'

'I'll watch our packs,' I said. I was not going to display my hunched back before the men of Mousehold camp. Nicholas and Barak disrobed and stepped carefully through the weeds into the muddy water, Nicholas white-skinned, slim but muscular; Barak dark and solid, untroubled by stares at the stump on the end of his right arm. I looked up at the sky, blue and cloudless. Since the thunderstorm several weeks ago there had been no rain; the coming harvest would indeed be bad. I rubbed a painful spot on my hand where I had been stung by one of the burrowing wasps that lived in the sandy Mousehold soil. I had seen adders there, too.

I sat up as a shadow fell over me. The boy Natty had emerged from the river and stood above me, drying himself with his shirt, his strong, heavy body stark naked. Quite unembarrassed, he said, 'You not goin' in, marster?'

'Not today.'

He said, 'You remember the man I told you of, from the Sandlings?'

'I do.'

'I spoke to him. He can tell you something important. I've asked him to come to our huts tonight. He's a bit afraid, but he will. He says it was a wicked thing.'

'Thank you, Natty. I am very grateful.'

He studied me, rubbing his broad shoulders dry. 'You care then, for the death of a poor 'prentice?'

'Yes. And that of his master, and a woman, who I think were murdered by the same people.'

He said quietly, 'Ay, I see you do.' He found the rest of his clothes, dressed, and walked away up the steep hill. The young lad's belief in me moved me strangely.

✝

THAT NIGHT I FELT clammy, and found it hard to sleep. When we rose at dawn, I saw the sky was milky white, not blue, and the air, hotter than ever, was sticky. We breakfasted with the Swardeston vil-lagers as usual – about fifteen of us. Then the men went off to hear Conyers's sermon before starting their day's labour in the woods, dig-ging cesspits, or building huts. A messenger had come round the previous night with the packs from my horse, and I pulled out my robe and put it on. Immediately, there were catcalls from those gathered round the cooking fire: 'He's a-gettin' his lawyer's robe on, hands to yer purses.' The humour was good-natured, though, and no one mocked me for a hunchback; after several days my camp-mates had realized I was harmless.

'I go to help Captain Kett at the Oak of Reformation,' I said with a smile.

'We heard,' one of the men said. I thought, Was there nothing that did not quickly circulate in Kett's camp?

'Will any of you be coming?' I asked.

Goodwife Everneke nodded to a thick-set middle-aged man. 'One or two. Master Dickon there, he goes tomorrow to plead the cause of our village. Our landlord's been brought in by force.'

'A good ding o' the pate's what he needs,' someone said, to approv-ing murmurs.

'I'm only there to advise on the legalities,' I said. I looked at Natty. 'Are you coming?'

'I have no landlord, I will be going with Goodman Johnson to archery practice.'

'Ay, we start today,' the old man said.

I turned to Barak and Nicholas. 'Jack, come along,' I said quietly. 'Nicholas, I think it politic you stay here.'

He nodded and looked down. I wondered whether he was ashamed now of yesterday's performance. Barak and I set off. 'See those rogues are well punished!' someone called after us.

✝

WE WALKED TO St Michael's Chapel. On our way I picked up a pamphlet lying on the ground. It was headed: 'When Adam delved and Eve span, who was then the gentleman?'

At the chapel, guards in breastplates and carrying halberds let us in.

'God give you good morrow, Captain Kett,' I said. He did not look in such good spirits today – the heavy brows under the short grey hair were frowning.

'Good morrow,' he answered curtly. 'Though it could be better. Our assault on Yarmouth has failed, the city people repelled my men. But we shall attack again,' he added fiercely, 'with trained men this time. Training, that is what Captain Miles says we need now.'

'Have the warrants to requisition goods gone around the country-side?' I asked.

'They have.' He waved an arm at the desks. 'More are being writ-ten. And now we labour to produce our demands, to send to the Protector. We must hurry, the camps at Thetford and Ipswich have already sent theirs.' He frowned, fixing me with those large, penetrating brown eyes. 'So, the trials. You are the only qualified lawyer I have left who will assist me. There is young Overton, but I understand he called me traitor in the market square yesterday.'

I sighed. 'Everything gets back to you, Captain Kett.'

'And so it should.' He raised his voice angrily. 'I need informers. Do you not think the city and the landlords have spies in this camp?'

'Nicholas – he just lost his temper. An old man was being attacked.'

Kett frowned. 'Gawen Reynolds, one of the worst men in Nor-wich, and firm against us.'

'Nicholas is sorry for his words.'

Kett answered fiercely, and I quailed a little at the forcefulness in him. 'He called me traitor. We are *not* traitors' – he banged a heavy fist on the desk, causing everyone to look up from their writing – 'this is the King's camp and we serve the Protector in his desire for reform!'

I spoke humbly. 'I entreat you not to imprison Nicholas again, he is but a lad with a loose tongue and an over-strong attachment to his gentleman status – all the more because he has no lands or money; he was disinherited over a matter of the heart.'

'Anyone else who behaved like that would be in Norwich Castle. We're moving some of the prisoners there.' He lowered his voice again. 'But one of my advisers in the town spoke up for him. Someone I trust, Edward Brown.'

'His wife said he was visiting the camp.'

'His assessment of Overton is the same as yours. He says the boy has been kind to him and his wife.'

''Tis true.'

Kett took a deep breath, and gave me a hard look. 'Very well, Master Shardlake, he remains free for now, but he stays quiet in his hut. Any more outbursts and I must lock him up again, or I will be seen by the men as dispensing favours to those who work with me. Is that clear?'

'It is, Captain Kett, and I thank you.'

He grunted, then turned to his desk, and gave me a list of names. 'Those to be tried at the Oak of Reformation today. There will be others later.' I looked at the list. There were fourteen, three I recognized; Leonard Witherington and Gerald and Barnabas Boleyn. Kett said to me, quietly now, 'At the trials there will be calls for violence from some, not surprisingly, given their sufferings. But they have been told their complaints must be presented in an orderly way, and recorded – that is important – to be shown to the commissioners. The men of the camp will decide whether they are to be set free or imprisoned. So, justice will be done.'

'The accused will have a chance to speak?'

'Of course. Everyone does in this camp.'

'What of the jury?'

'Those assembled will decide.'

'No jury of twelve men?'

Kett said, coldly and clearly, 'To satisfy the men's anger we must involve everyone. And move quickly. Come, Master Shardlake, you were at Boleyn's criminal trial and I have seen others – it is all over in minutes, and men are hanged for the theft of a pig. There will be no hangings here, though there may be a beating or two, so be content with that. Just make sure nobody strays too far from specific accusations.'

'I will. But may I ask, what will happen to the men who are imprisoned?'

'They will be handed over to the commissioners, or the Protector's representatives, when our demands are met. Now let us go. They will be gathering at the Oak.'

✞

WE WALKED A QUARTER of a mile eastwards, well into the body of the camp. Caps were doffed and cheers sounded as Kett passed, and he raised his cap in return. We passed a flat area of heath where mounds of turf were being set up as archery butts; a hundred yards off some dozens of young men, mostly strongly built, waited with bows, quivers filled with arrows over their shoulders. Natty was among them.

We halted where a crowd of several hundred was already gathered round a huge oak, alone among the stumps of trees cut down around it. The few women stood close to their menfolk.

The tree was a magnificent specimen, at over sixty feet high one of the largest I had seen, hundreds of years old. The lower branches had been lopped off and a wooden stage thirty feet across erected in front of it, seven feet above ground so all could see. A wooden canopy above the stage provided shelter from the sun. It was a fine piece of carpentry. On the front of the canopy the arms of England had been painted, and the letters E VI R, to stress the camp's loyalty to the King. At the front of the crowd I saw Toby Lockswood, standing with his arms folded, a grim expression on his face.

To one side stood a sorry-looking group of men, dressed either in dirty shirts or the tattered rags of former finery, their legs chained. They were guarded by a dozen men in half-armour, among whom I recognized John Miles, wearing a helmet with feathers attached as a sign of command. Above his fair beard, his sharp, keen eyes watched the crowd, and I guessed part of his job was to deal with any trouble that might arise. I was surprised to see Michael Vowell standing next to him, making notes on a piece of paper. Evidently, his literacy had led him to rise in the camp hierarchy.

I studied the gentlemen; some had bruised faces; many stared about them wild-eyed. Among them was Leonard Witherington of Brikewell. He still wore the same dirty shirt in which I had seen him dragged from Brikewell, and an old pair of upper hose. His jowls hung pendulously, and there was a look of fear on his mottled face. Then I saw the twins, Gerald and Barnabas. They stared back at me with their cold blue eyes. Their shirts and hose were torn and tattered, and both had bruised faces, Barnabas's white scar even more prominent. Each now had a scraggy boy's moustache and beard. Yet they looked totally unintimidated. One of the camp-men carried a rope in his hand, a noose at one end, and he waved it jocularly at the prisoners on the end of a home-made spear, until Miles gestured angrily to him to desist. I noticed many near the front of the crowd carried home-made weapons.

On top of the stage was a wide desk; to my surprise I saw stout little Mayor Codd sitting behind it, and the elderly Alderman Aldrich, both looking anxious. William Kett, whose face was set in a grim smile, sat next to them. He rose to greet his brother. Well, I thought, it is come.

✞

ROBERT KETT MOUNTED the stage. He indicated that Barak and I should take seats behind the desk, then stepped up to address the crowd. Once again I was to be amazed by the power and fluency of his speech.

'We are here to do justice against those landlords who have oppressed their tenants, and to set free those innocent of wrongdoing. These trials will be conducted on the principles of English law, based on evidence, which Serjeant Shardlake here, a lawyer but a good man, will advise me on while his assistant Jack Barak ensures notes are taken for presentation to the King's authorities at a later date. Those found innocent will be set free, those found guilty returned to imprisonment. The city authorities have been invited to join us in seeing justice done.'

Kett paused, then added grimly, 'There have also been some of our men who have taken goods and money from the manor houses and kept hold of them, instead of giving them to the representatives of their Hundreds to be held for the common purse. Tomorrow, we shall deal with those, for every man here is subject to justice under law.' A few in the crowd ceased smiling, and I thought it was a clever move to say that now, to show that all were subject to justice. Kett sat down beside me, and banged a gavel on the desk. 'Now, the first accused, Sir William Jermstone.'

A middle-aged man, stout from good feeding, was led, his chains clanking, by a soldier to stand before the stage; like his fellows he wore hose and a dirty shirt, but his look was defiant. 'Who accuses this man?' Kett asked.

'I do!' A man in his thirties stepped forward. 'Richard Sherman, husbandman of Pullan! I accuse Sir William of passing on feudal charges to his tenants, charges which are due from him personally to the King, and of taking common land!' Others of Sir William's tenants stepped forward, shouting 'Ay'. Everything that he had allegedly done was in breach of the law. Jermstone was asked what he had to say in his defence, but he only blustered loudly that he did not accept trial by an assembly of rude and common people.

By now the crowd was becoming worked up, and there were cries of 'Kill the old swag-belly! Hang him from the Oak!'

William Kett rose and stepped to the front of the stage. 'Shut your clack-boxes!' he roared. 'My brother told you, there will be no hangings! Let the Lord Protector hang those who deserve it! This is a fine display before Mayor Codd!'

'Hang him, too!' someone called out.

Robert Kett pointed at the man. 'Do you want to be locked up too, yag-mouth?' he shouted. He raised his voice to his loudest pitch. 'You appointed me your leader, and I promised justice, not violence!' The man he had identified looked abashed. Kett added, 'Sir William Jermstone is to be committed to prison, his ill-doings recorded.' The soldier led him away. 'Second accused,' Kett said. 'Robert le Grand of West Flegg.'

I was impressed with Kett's restraint in dealing with Jermstone, who had so insulted the assembly. The second trial proceeded much as the first, with similar accusations, and only once did I lean aside to murmur in Kett's ear when le Grand was accused of defaming someone's dead father. Kett spoke up: 'Matters of defamation cannot be raised if the person is dead!'

Again, when the evidence was done, there were cries to hang the wretched prisoner, although he had taken a different tack and admitted to what he had done in a humble voice; he was shaking. Kett let the crowd shout a little before ordering le Grand to be returned to prison. I noticed that those who shouted tended to be the younger men and the most poorly dressed. It was the tenants and craftsmen, with at least a little property to protect, who were quieter. I understood why those who had nothing to lose had cause to be fiercest, but if this descended into a bloodbath, it would be the end of the camp. With Kett in charge, though, I was sure it would not.

Fortunately, the third accused turned out to be something of a model landlord whom several of his tenants asked to be freed. Kett ordered this done; the man looked around him a moment, astonished, then turned and ran off in the direction of the road to Norwich.

The trials proceeded, Kett needing only a few words of advice from me when an accuser went off the point or brought unprovable allegations. A few landowners were released but most were returned to imprisonment, always to cheers from the crowd; sometimes boys would turn round and bare their buttocks.

Eventually, Leonard Witherington was led stumbling to the Oak. He trembled as he stood facing us. 'Who accuses this man?' Kett asked.

Two men stepped forward, both of whom I recognized from my visit to Brikewell – the yeoman Harris, a grey doublet over his shirt, and Melville, the young man who had been fiercest against Witherington. Harris spoke first, reciting the familiar litany of commons encroached upon, rents raised illegally and the passing on of feudal dues. Harris said the feodary's agent himself had come to Witherington to tell the tenants they must pay – John Flowerdew. At mention of his name there was a rumble among the crowd, and someone called out to Witherington, 'How much did you pay him?'

Kett said, 'Well, did you bribe him?'

Witherington shifted uneasily. 'I gave him a sovereign.'

'Note that down, Jack Barak,' Kett said. There were more curses against Flowerdew; he had done well to escape from Hethersett last week.

Young Goodman Melville stepped forward. 'I also accuse Leonard Witherington of spoiling our crops by allowing birds from his great duffus to eat them, so we had no choice but to kill them.' He pointed a finger at me. 'The lawyer who sits there saw it with his own eyes!'

I turned to Kett, and whispered, 'He's right. I was visiting Wither-ington over the Boleyn case. But, Captain Kett, keeping doves is not illegal.'

'What's he saying?' Melville called out. 'He was there, he saw it!' There was more angry murmuring. Neither Codd nor Aldrich had done more than take notes, but now Aldrich leaned in to Kett and said, 'You must answer him, they are getting stirred up.'

Kett was ready for this. He stood and said, 'Master Shardlake was indeed at Brikewell, but he advises me the keeping of great numbers of doves is not illegal.' There were shouts of protest. 'Nonetheless' – he raised his voice – 'it should be made illegal, and it will be! I intend it to be one of the demands to the King and Protector which the Hun-dred representatives are even now preparing. This injustice will be righted!' The shouts turned to cheers. Harris spoke up again. 'There is more against Witherington. Back in the spring his steward recruited us and made us occupy part of his neighbour John Boleyn's land. He told us Witherington had a right to it, and would give part to us as common land. Otherwise we would lose much of our own.'

Aldrich spoke up. 'So you and your neighbours took part in a forceful occupation of his land?'

Melville shouted, 'We'd no fucking choice.'

Yeoman Harris stepped forward. 'That is true, and we hoped to occupy the land peacefully. But someone told Boleyn and a group of young savages came at us, recruited by the Boleyn twins from Sir Rich-ard Southwell's gentlemen thugs. They beat us, and Gerald Boleyn struck a boy from our village on the head so badly he has lost his wits.' He gestured to the crowd, and a man brought forward young Ralph, the boy I had seen at Brikewell. From his looks the man was Ralph's father. Ralph stared vacantly at the Oak, mouth open and dribbling, clearly with no idea where he was. Gently, his father pushed his head down so the scarred bald patch was visible. Men nearby leaned forward to look and a woman stepped forward and shouted, 'For shame, for shame!'

Witherington turned to address Kett, wringing his hands. 'It was not me who did this; it was Gerald Boleyn, acting for his father, John. The attack was led by his steward, Chawry.' I thought, So Chawry was there, then I saw that Witherington was pointing a shaking finger at me. 'And Serjeant Shardlake is Boleyn's lawyer.'

The sight of the boy had infuriated the crowd. 'His lawyer!' someone shouted. 'Boleyn won't get away with this!'

I stood up. 'I represented John Boleyn, but only regarding the charge that he murdered his wife —'

'Ay!' a woman called out. 'He was found guilty, but now sits in Norwich Castle awaiting a pardon, paid for by his kinswoman the Lady Elizabeth!'

'One of the wealthiest landowners in England!' someone shouted. 'Like her sister the Lady Mary, who sits in Kenninghall surrounded by her sheepfolds and priests! Have her out!'

Again Robert Kett stepped forward, and demanded their silence. 'The Lady Mary stays where she is! She is heir to the throne. What do you think interference with her would do for our cause with the Protector? As for Master Shardlake,' he turned to me, 'it is Barnabas and Gerald Boleyn who must face trial on this matter. You have never represented them?'

I stood and looked at the twins, who were grinning at me. I called out, loudly, 'Never!'

The crowd quietened. I stood. 'All I would say, and I know this is not evidence, is that I do not believe John Boleyn would have authorized the wicked thing done to that boy.' My heart was beating fast, as somebody called out, 'Ay, John Boleyn's not one of the worst landlords. It's his sons that are vicious brutes. And his old father-in-law.'

Alderman Aldrich spoke up. 'Gawen Reynolds is a Norwich alderman. It is the country landlords who are to be judged here.'

Kett looked at the twins, who glowered back. 'Leonard Witherington, you are to be returned to prison. Bring forward Gerald and Barnabas Boleyn.' Despite their chains the twins slouched nonchalantly side by side towards the Oak, as though they cared nothing for the assembly.

They came to a halt facing Kett, expressions of amused contempt on their faces. Kett said quietly, 'Gerald and Barnabas Boleyn, you are accused of attacking this boy, of breaking his head and damaging his wits.' Ralph's father held his arm as, seeing the twins, he made feeble attempts to run away. Kett addressed him. 'Did you witness what happened to your son?'

'We were both in the party sent to occupy Master Boleyn's land,' he said, a tremor in his voice. 'We planted banners, but then a crowd rushed us from the trees.' He pointed at the twins. 'Those two were there, and I saw the one without the scar raise his club and smash it down hard as he could on my poor son's head. Ever since he can do nothing on his own, neither eat nor shit.'

A man shouted from the crowd, 'I was there too! I saw it all.' Kett asked his name and Barak wrote it down.

Kett said, 'I have had dealings enough with the law to know that if that happened, Gerald Boleyn is guilty of attempted murder, for which he could hang, and his brother could be indicted for conspiracy.' He looked at me, and I nodded. He turned to the twins. 'Have you aught to say?'

Gerald shrugged his shoulders. 'This ain't a murder trial.'

'No,' Kett's voice deepened with anger, 'but the evidence taken here is, I think, quite enough for an indictment.'

Gerald looked at young Ralph, who shrank away terrified. He said, 'That boy, like his father, is only a serf. Witherington owns him as much as he owns his horse.' Several in the crowd shouted out angrily, waving staves and pitchforks. Barak whispered, 'Are those twins mad? Do they want the crowd to tear them apart?' And indeed there was a surging forward, and cries of 'Kill them!' But the twins were clever enough to realize that if Kett allowed that, in front of Codd and Aldrich, the Norwich gates would be shut against them again.

Kett stood and called out. 'Men! Let it be known the final ending of serfdom in Norfolk will be the strongest of our demands! We shall have bond men made free!'

There were cheers, and the crowd quieted a little, though someone called out, 'Those thugs should be hanged!'

'They will be! Master Shardlake, will you draw up an indictment to be presented to the justices as soon as our demands are met.'

'Certainly. I shall be glad to.' I looked at the twins. Witherington's desire to keep his invasion of Boleyn's land quiet meant that nothing had been done against them before, but now there was ample witness evidence to hang them both. Yet they seemed quite unconcerned. Barnabas said, 'As you wish, Yeoman Kett. Are we going back to Surrey Place, or Norwich Castle with our dear father?'

'Surrey Place for now,' Kett answered.

'Can you get us some prostitutes? I see from the windows there's some in the camp.'

That brought more growls from the crowd. 'Get them out of here,' Kett said to the guard. He addressed the crowd. 'Don't beat them, though I'm tempted to myself. They'll be hanging from Norwich gallows in due time. You have the evidence written down, Jack Barak?'

'I do.'

The twins were led away. Someone thrust a pitchfork at Barnabas, which nearly caught him, but he only laughed. Kett whispered, 'What sort of lads are those? They seem more like devils than people. Surely even they should be frightened at the prospect of hanging; they could have made some defence instead of insulting the victim. Perhaps they are mad.'

I shook my head. 'They are certainly beyond normal understanding.'

Chapter Forty-eight

THE TRIALS CONTINUED all afternoon, with only a short break for lunch. There were none of the rushed sessions of the criminal Assizes; the business was moved through with care for evidence, a substantial minority of the gentlemen were set free, and the crowd was quieter, settling into a routine. At five, the last gentleman was returned to prison and the crowd, having heartily clapped Kett, began to disperse. I heard, though, murmurs of 'A few hangings wouldn't have gone amiss' from a group of young men around Michael Vowell.

During the afternoon the weather had continued close, and most people were sweating. There was a misting round the sun, as there had been before last month's thunderstorm. 'A storm's coming,' William Kett observed.

'Probably tomorrow,' Robert agreed. He turned to me and said civilly, 'You did well today, Master Shardlake. We have gathered a fine set of detailed accusations. I will take them to St Michael's Chapel. Now, tomorrow, I want you to cast an eye over the demands to be sent to the Protector.' He gave me a look that brooked no opposition.

'Very well,' I said. He was driving me deeper into this rebellion every day.

'Meet me at St Michael's Chapel at two. Thank you again for today.'

We returned to our huts, but the others had not yet returned from work. Only Goodwife Everneke sat, mending clothes. 'How went the trials?' she asked.

'Very well,' Barak answered. 'Many justified accusations against the gentlemen were set down.'

She nodded with satisfaction. 'You look like you've had enough of sitting, bors. Why not go for a walk round the camp?' She looked at our hut. 'That long lad has been in there all day. He's mopish. Take him out. He's not a bad young gemmun,' she added.

I smiled at her. 'Good idea.'

Barak crawled into our tent. 'Come on, Nick boy. We've come to winkle you out!'

✣

WE WALKED EASTWARD, into the main body of the camp. The groups of huts, marked by bright village banners lest anyone lose their way, stretched as far as the eye could see, the sandy trails traversing the heath deep with ruts, and a host of new pathways leading through the camp. There was plenty of space, though, so vast was the heath, and there were still places where the long yellow grass remained, dotted with ragwort, thistles and the poppies the locals called copper-roses.

Barak said to Nicholas, 'You'll have been hot stuck in there all day.'

He shrugged. 'How did the trials go?'

We told him, and that Kett had agreed he remain free, at which he visibly cheered. 'I feared men would be hanged. Or that Kett could not control the crowd.' He added quietly, 'And that they might come for me.'

I said, 'Kett is firmly in charge, and took care to follow legal forms. Do not mistake him, Nicholas. He wants no violence if it can be avoided. He is a born leader, and a skilled and experienced polit-ician. But also a man of sincerity, who means what he says.'

Nicholas kicked a flint at his feet. 'Perhaps. But rebellion is no way to achieve it.'

'He's no rebel,' Barak said. 'He's only working to bring justice. Can you say he's wrong?'

Nicholas shook his head. 'I no longer see anything clear. Last night I had a conversation with one of the Swardeston men who served in the Scottish war. It has been so badly run, and so brutal, with killing of civilians, it affected the soldiers, who were told the Scotch would welcome us. Now I do begin to doubt its justice.' He sighed, and looked over the camp. 'This place, who could ever have imagined it?'

We followed his gaze. There was activity everywhere. Shoemakers and tailors had set up stalls. Nearby cuts of butchered sheep had been set out to dry, while not far off, live sheep had been penned in, some cattle too, often with the very hurdles the landowners had used, while some thirty horses were penned into a large paddock with a strong wood fence. A wooden building was being erected nearby, which I guessed might be an abattoir. How these men had laboured these last few days. Most men in the camp would not have eaten so well in a long time, which would help. As ever, peddlers traversed the huts, doing a good trade in pins with the women. Some way off I saw a blacksmith and his assistant working hard in a newly erected brick forge, where they were turning agricultural implements into bladed weapons under the supervision of a soldier. Nicholas watched them. 'Turning plough-shares into swords,' he said quietly. 'It's the other way around in the Bible.'

There were cheers as a cart with a large cannon on a wooden mount passed by, pulled by carthorses taken, no doubt, from a country house. We walked on, to where another large brick structure was being erected, a bakery. Some distance away perhaps fifty young men were practising archery, shooting at earthen butts with longbows, arrows arcing through the air.

'By God,' Barak said, 'how many are there now?'

'Too many to count. Eight thousand?'

Barak nudged Nicholas. 'Hey, look there, the men are getting all their needs met.' He pointed to where two young women, adjusting their skirts, were leaving one of the huts. 'The Norwich whores will be doing a roaring trade.'

'The people don't seem to notice us as different any more,' Nicholas said. 'I suppose because now we wear scruffy clothes, and are dirty and smelly.'

Barak looked at him. 'That should remind you we are all made of the same common clay.'

'And all come to the same end,' I agreed. 'Let's hope it's later rather than sooner.'

We walked on, up slightly rising ground, skirting one of the deep old quarries dotting the heath – there was one near the escarpment where the ground suddenly dropped perhaps a hundred feet; people had to be careful. We took a position from which we could see across the camp; to the western escarpment, where guard posts stood. To the east it stretched further than we could see.

'Come on,' I said, 'people will be finishing work soon. Let's get back.' Barak and Nicholas agreed; in the close weather we were tired and sweaty. Over at Thorpe Wood the sound of sawing had stopped and people started returning to their huts. A man in a white surplice mounted a box and raised a bible. One of the camp prophets, waiting to harangue the workers going home. Yet they seemed popular, few mocked them as they did in London. I drew the pamphlet I had found earlier from my pocket and showed it to Barak and Nicholas. 'What do you make of this?'

Nicholas grimaced. 'Stupid prophetic nonsense.'

I said, 'But this is an age of prophecy – look how the Protestant radicals prophesy about everything – I believe John Knox prophesied that the English and Scotch were God's new chosen people, and together would destroy their popish enemies. That's not come to much. I remember the time of the Pilgrimage of Grace, when people prophesied the king would fall on the basis of prophecies in ancient books about Merlin and the like. Those seem to have got all mixed up with calls from writers like Mors and Crowley for radical change by the rulers such as Kett wants.'

We passed an area where two small groups of men, each holding a village banner, were demanding the other move their huts further away so that an extra cesspit could be built.

'You move instead of yagging us!'

'We were here first, we got further to go to take a shit!'

'Not all stand solidly together,' Nicholas observed wryly.

I smiled. 'That's just people being people.'

Further on, a group of men were digging a pit in the sandy soil, already four feet deep. A man in his forties, probably one of the Hundred representatives, was supervising. 'Sorry, bors,' he said, 'but the cesspit must be deeper.'

I stopped to speak to him. 'You do well to ensure the excrement is well buried. I have seen what the consequences can be in an army camp unless care is taken.'

He looked at me curiously. 'Yew been a soldier, sir?'

'No, but I was at the military camp at Portsmouth four years ago, when the French invasion threatened. The bloody flux came, and killed many.'

He nodded agreement. 'And at Boulogne, where I fought. This place is well sited for a camp, but in this heat and with no water nearer than the Wensum it is truly a breeding ground for the flux: pits are being built everywhere to dispose of ordure and rubbish. There is getting to be a problem with lice as well; the men's beards and hair are to be trimmed.'

We started to move away from the pit, but then I stopped, for I recognized one of the diggers. My attention had been drawn because I had seen him turn his face from me. 'Is that Peter Bone?'

The brother of Edith Boleyn's dead maidservant looked back at me. His hair and beard were longer and unkempt, his keen brown eyes standing out in a face which, pale and drawn when I had last seen him, was now fuller, and tanned. 'Lawyer Shardlake,' he said, with the slight hostility I remembered from before, and laughed. 'And your friends. Where are your fine robes now? Why are you in the camp?'

'I am assisting Captain Kett with legal matters.'

Bone stepped out of the pit. 'Under duress, I'll be bound.' He spoke with a new confidence and with what a few weeks ago would have been called insolence to one of my class. But as Kett had said, the days of doffing caps to gentlemen, and speaking quickly and carefully, were over.

Barak asked, 'What are you doing here, come to that? When last we saw you, you were living in your own house in Norwich.'

Bone rounded on Barak angrily. 'Barely getting by on the poor rents I charged, spinning wool like a woman for pennies. So I came up here, to help right the wrongs done to the Commonwealth.'

I looked back at him. I understood his anger, but why had he turned his face away when he saw me? I remembered, back in Norwich, how I felt he was keeping something back. The other men had stopped digging and were looking at us, perhaps hoping for an argument. The man in charge said, 'Back to work, lads. Perhaps you should move on, sir?'

'No need to "sir" his like now,' Bone said, but he bent to his spade. We walked on. Nicholas shook his head. 'A strange thing, to see what the common people really think of us,' he said.

'There's more to it than that,' I said quietly. 'He's covering some-thing up, I feel it. It's not the only thing I learned today. I hadn't realized Chawry led the party which attacked Witherington's people so savagely.'

'How did you find that out?' Nicholas asked.

'At the trials at the Oak of Reformation. He has at the very least a connection to Richard Southwell's gang of ruffians.' I sighed. 'The case indeed follows us to the camp.'

✠

ON OUR WAY BACK we paused to watch where some men were dig-ging out a rabbit warren – there were several in the heath. Some held dogs by their collars, while others dug down into the ground. A few rabbits ran out, and the man with dogs released them; they caught the animals instantly. Then a man came forward, carrying a large pouch carefully. 'I got this from the stores,' he said. 'Gunpowder!'

'By gor, be careful,' one of his fellows called out.

'They told me what to do.'

The man bent down and carefully let the black powder run out. Fortunately, there was not much. He took a wick, placed one end at the edge of the gunpowder and the other some feet away. Everybody stepped well back. There were a couple of tense minutes until he got a flint to light, then the flame sputtered to the gunpowder and there was a loud explosion, throwing up earth and grass. Dozens of rabbits instantly fled through the holes in the warrens, to be caught by the dogs or speared by the men. A great pile of them was set by the edge of the warren and the men, in pleasure at the result and in relief that they had not been blown sky-high, ran onto the warren. They shook hands and clapped the shoulder of the man whose idea it had been.

Then the portion of the warren where they stood, already honey-combed with burrows under the light soil and now shaken by the impact of the gunpowder and the weight of men, collapsed under their feet. Fortunately, the pit they had created, though broad, was shallow.

The men emerged and stood up, dirty but cheerful, laughing; nobody was hurt. Barak clapped them, and we turned and walked on. At the time we thought the episode a mere diversion; much later, we were to learn differently.

✝

By the time we arrived back at the huts the men had returned from work. Dinner – a haunch of lamb tonight – had been set to cook on a roasting spit, recently taken from a manor house. The constant tang of wood smoke, sometimes drifting into my eyes, was another thing I had got used to this last week. Everyone was sweating, it was hotter and more close than ever, the evening sky milky grey. The villagers nodded to us, and I was pleased to see that Nicholas nodded back, as though to equals. Old Hector Johnson was there, and greeted us, too. So did young Natty, sitting with a fair-haired young man, his face already weather-beaten, who gave me a nervous look. I signed to Barak and Nicholas to stay where they were, and went over to him, extending a hand. 'I am Matthew Shardlake. Are you Natty's friend from the Sand-lings?'

'Ay, sir. Stephen Walker. Come to join the camp with others from my village.'

I sat beside him, carefully, for my back was sore after our long walk. 'I believe Natty has told you I am a lawyer. Before I came to the camp I was investigating three murders.'

The young man frowned. 'Natty said they were poor Wal Padbury, his 'prentice master in Norwich, and some woman, too.'

I thought, Poor Edith, always 'some woman', anonymous, unknown. 'Yes,' I said quietly.

Walker looked at me, anxiety in his sharp blue eyes. 'If I tell what I saw, I won't get into trouble?'

'I promise. At most you may be asked to attend court as a witness.'

He looked at Natty. 'That's what I was feared of.' He turned back to me, took a deep breath, then said, 'I saw Wal Padbury's body put in the sea.'

My eyes widened. 'You saw that?'

Walker seemed to shy away a little. Natty put a hand on his arm. 'Go on, Steve.'

Walker said, 'One of the men I saw do it has a powerful friend, one of the most powerful in Norfolk. I half wish I hadn't told Natty now, but I knew Wal, and he never hurt a fly.'

Natty smiled, showing white teeth in his brown face. 'Powerful friends don't matter like they did, bor. Look around this old camp.'

'I understand your fear, Stephen, but if it helps, I can tell you I, too, have powerful friends. I am lawyer to the Lady Elizabeth.'

Walker looked impressed. He looked at Natty, who nodded. 'Master Shardlake can be trusted. He is advising Captain Kett now.'

'With the Lady Elizabeth's knowledge?'

I coughed. 'No. I – found myself caught up in the rebellion.'

'But this is the King's camp, Steve,' Natty said encouragingly, 'and we serve the Protector's wish for reform; the Protector rules in the King's name and the Lady Elizabeth's his sister. Tell him, Steve, so that Wal and those others may be revenged.'

The young man took a deep breath. 'It was last week. I'd been out' – he looked at Natty – 'collecting oysters.'

Natty nudged him. 'Poaching, bor. Master Shardlake won't report you. Everyone does it round our way – only the land belongs to one of the great men, he don't allow oysters to be taken.'

Walker spoke with sudden passion. 'He's a man who deserves trial at the Oak, if anyone does.'

'Just tell me what you saw.'

'I was coming off the beach at the end of the day when I heard voices. I lay down in the long grass with my catch. Three men walked by, not ten yards from me, and they were carrying a body. I recognized poor Wal, his face all white, blood and brains caked on top of his head. I lay still, I knew if I moved, I'd be dead, too. They took Wal's body across the sand, then right into the water, and dropped it in.' He shuddered. 'I remember the splash it made. They laughed as they did it. They probably thought the tide would carry it out to sea, but they don't know the waters properly. Then they walked back to shore and away across the grass. They probably had horses somewhere nearby.' He looked at me. 'That's it, master, that's all I saw.'

I said quietly, 'You said one of the men has a powerful friend.'

'Yes. He's a terror. The other two I'd never seen before.'

I said, 'Were they by chance a pair of twins, about eighteen, fair-haired?'

Walker shook his head, puzzled. 'No, they were in their twenties, and they weren't twins.'

'And the one you knew?'

'I've seen him before, he visits his master's land sometimes with his friends, makes trouble in the local tavern. You can't miss him, he has a great brown mole on one cheek. There was a scandal last year about him abducting some poor young girl: he's been even wilder since. His name is John Atkinson, and he serves that great lord, Sir Richard Southwell.'

Chapter Forty-nine

I THANKED WALKER and Natty for their help, then motioned Barak and Nicholas to follow me, away from our group of huts. I led them to where an elm tree stood some distance off, within view of St Michael's Chapel. I told them what Walker had said.

Barak whistled. 'Then Southwell could be involved after all? He had a motive for seeing Boleyn hanged – he could buy up Brikewell and connect his two pieces of neighbouring land, run it all to sheep.'

Nicholas looked doubtful. 'But we agreed before that given the scale of Southwell's landownership, committing murder would not be worth it.'

I said, 'Perhaps we were wrong. Southwell is a ruthless man. He has his own gang of thugs, and gained a pardon from murder years ago, from the old king. And now we know one of his men, John Atkinson, who we saw at the trial, was involved in the apprentice's murder – and, it surely follows, that of the locksmith and Edith Boleyn, too.'

'Atkinson and his thugs are friends of the Boleyn twins,' Nicholas persisted. 'They could have been acting for them, not Southwell. They seem to hire themselves out for all sorts of mischief.'

Barak said, 'You're right. It's a possibility. It all comes back to the question of who stole that key – the twins, someone from Southwell's gang who was with them at the tavern that night and was working for Southwell, or someone else. Even someone in Gawen Reynolds's household, where the key was held overnight by the twins.'

'I wonder whether there is any connection between the Reynolds household and Southwell,' I said thoughtfully.

'Where is Southwell?' Barak asked. 'As one of the biggest land-owners in Norfolk I'd have thought he'd have been brought in. Trying *him* at the Oak would be a prize for Kett.'

'Fled to London, I should guess,' Nicholas said.

I took a deep breath, then looked towards the chapel, where another dusty, exhausted messenger was dismounting from a horse. I had prom-ised Kett to say nothing of my encountering Southwell there. But he should know of this.

A familiar sturdy, black-bearded figure exited the main doors of St Michael's Chapel; Toby Lockswood, a leather folder of papers under his arm, an expression of grim authority on his face. Barak nudged me. 'The fount of all Norwich knowledge. He may know whether there are relations between the Southwell and Reynolds households, rather than just an association between his twins and Southwell's thugs.'

'We must keep this matter close. Nonetheless, it's worth asking him that. And Reynolds's old steward Vowell later, perhaps.' I hailed him. 'Toby!'

He frowned, but changed direction towards us. 'Still here?' he asked me brusquely. 'I saw you perform at the Oak. Dancing to Cap-tain Kett's tune now, eh? A lawyer will always dance to whichever tune serves his interests.'

Barak said hotly, 'You danced to Master Shardlake's long enough when we were investigating the Boleyn case.'

Toby fixed him with angry dark eyes. 'As I said, that was before I found a better cause.' And before your parents died, I thought, reading the grief in his face. I said, 'I only wished to ask you a question, which your local knowledge may answer. Do you know whether there is any connection between Gawen Reynolds's household and that of Sir Richard Southwell? Did the two men know each other?'

'Not that I'm aware of.' He laughed. 'Why are you still ferreting around that case? Isn't the Lady Elizabeth arranging a pardon for Boleyn?'

'I do not want the real murderer to remain free. A locksmith and his young apprentice died as well as Edith Boleyn, remember. Common people.'

'Can't help you,' Toby said, and he began to move away. Then Nicholas stepped into his path. 'Lockswood, you are a cold, secretive, vengeful man,' he said with quiet intensity. 'For weeks you worked with us, now you treat us like pieces of shit. And you had me imprisoned unjustly.'

Toby squared his shoulders. 'You are shit,' he said. 'You care for nothing but posing as a gentleman. You should be tried at the Oak.'

'For what?'

'For what you are.'

Nicholas raised a fist. Toby laughed. 'Go on, young gentleman, strike a senior officer of the camp. See what happens to you then.'

Barak laid his hand on Nicholas's arm. 'He's not worth it.'

Toby pointed at Nicholas. 'I'll have you yet, boy.' He turned and walked away into the camp.

We looked after him. 'He's a senior official now?' Nicholas asked.

'He's literate, and has great knowledge of the Norfolk elite. Kett administers the camp through the representatives of the Hundreds, and it's an efficient system. Miles and the soldiers are in charge of military matters, and I think both handle relations with supporters in Norwich. But I think Kett, like all leaders, is developing a circle of expert advisers. And Lockswood, I think, is one of them. We must be wary of him.'

✞

WHEN WE ROSE AT first light the next morning the sky was grey, and growing darker. The heat was oppressive. I felt lice in my hair; I must find a barber. I shared a quick breakfast with the others, then made my way to St Michael's Chapel. At this hour I hoped to catch Kett alone. The guards, who knew me now, let me pass.

The desks around the walls were empty, and the curtain across the altar was drawn. 'Captain Kett,' I called quietly. He pulled the curtain aside. He was dressed in shirt and hose and an unbuttoned doublet. He had been breakfasting; there were plates at one end of the table, and his wife sat there; plump, placid Alice who had loyally followed her husband into the unknown. The rest of the table was covered, as usual, with letters and papers.

'I am sorry to interrupt you so early, Captain Kett, but there is an important matter I must discuss.'

He sighed, then, registering my serious expression, said gently, 'Alice, could you leave us? Perhaps see if Brother William is awake?'

'Yes, Husband.' She passed me with a little curtsey and went outside. Kett sat at the table again, beckoning me to join him. His face was lined and tired, his expression worried. 'I hope you have not brought more bad news,' he said brusquely.

'Some information. I fear it may not be to your liking.'

'Well, I have had a deal of that these last few days. I'm told the enclosure commissioners have accepted the demands of the men in Kent, and more have arrived in Essex. But there's no sign of them getting here. And a whole ten thousand under Lord Russell has been sent to fight the Devon and Cornwall rebels, a thousand soldiers have been sent to put down the Oxfordshire camp, though I hear the camp-men there have got somewhat out of control. There are thousands in Oxfordshire, but not so many as here – we are the biggest camp in the south-east. So why are they not talking to us?' He banged a fist on the table with anger.

'Norfolk is further from London than Kent,' I said.

Kett grunted. 'There is so much contradictory information from outside. I have seen the proclamation against seditious stirrers, but at the same time there comes a new proclamation from the Protector restricting the new sheep tax to the wealthy.' He looked at me with that full, powerful gaze of his. 'All the more important that the camps support his aims.' He shook his head. 'But there will be spies of the great men in this camp, I have no doubt, just as we have our spies in Norwich, and I know the city council would turn on us at a word from London, even though Codd and Aldrich are to sign our demands this afternoon and have been allowed to address the camp, calling for moderation in dealing with the gentlemen. The representatives of the Hundreds gather here this morning to draw them up. As I said, I want you to look them over.' He smiled wryly. 'I ought to pay you a fee.'

I smiled. 'In the circumstances, I think it would be better for me to act informally, with no record.'

Kett laughed, showing his white teeth. 'I like talking to you, Master Shardlake. You have judgement – I have always been a good judge of men. Forgive me, yesterday was not a good day for news.' He shrugged. 'But some of it may be wrong, and everyone is solid here.'

'I think they are.'

He shook his head as though in wonder. 'It seems that I have become a judge of men.' He looked across at one of the wall paintings still adorning the chapel. 'See that, Our Lord expelling the money-changers from the Temple. Reverend Conyers wanted them all whitewashed over, but that one – it inspires me.' He shook his head. 'I ramble. I have only just breakfasted, and already my head is full of a thousand things to be done. Now, what have you to tell me?'

I took a deep breath. 'On our first morning in the camp, when I was summoned to you, I met someone coming out of the side door of the chapel. Someone I recognized from London, and was surprised to see here. Sir Richard Southwell.'

Kett drew a deep breath, and sat up straight in his chair, his expression sharp and alert. 'What did he say to you?' he snapped.

'Only that he was here because certain negotiations were needed, and that I must tell nobody I saw him.'

'Have you told anyone? Barak and that boy?'

'Not even them. I come to you only because I have learned something about Southwell.'

Kett picked up a spoon from the table, began turning it over in his hands. 'Well?'

'Southwell's man, John Atkinson, was involved in concealing a murder. A young locksmith's apprentice. There is evidence connecting that death to that of the locksmith himself, and Edith Boleyn's murder, too. And Southwell would stand to gain from Boleyn's conviction and death, for if he bought Brikewell, he could connect two large sheep farms he owns.'

Kett's gaze bored into me. 'How did you learn this?'

I told him what Walker had told me, without mentioning his name, saying only that it was a man in the camp. He was silent a moment, then said slowly, 'Now that the old Duke of Norfolk is in the Tower, Sir Richard Southwell is one of the greatest landowners in Norfolk, as well as steward to the Lady Mary. He is also an alternate member of the Protector's Council in London, among those nominated in the old king's will to take the place of members who resign or die. I do not need to tell you that he is a great villain, who will stop at nothing to increase his own power and wealth.'

'So I have learned.'

He looked at me fiercely. 'If you repeat what I am about to tell you to anyone, it will go very badly for you.'

I took a deep breath. 'Then I swear to tell nobody.'

Kett inclined his head, his look still dangerous. 'I know you believe in justice, Master Shardlake, but I have thousands of men to supply, and sometimes agreements have to be made with those you dislike, even loathe.'

'I have done the same in my time,' I said, not adding that I had usually regretted it.

Kett said, 'Southwell came to the camp to buy us off, riding fast from London. The Council had given him five hundred pounds for me to pay the men to disperse.'

'That is a huge sum,' I said.

Kett nodded. 'The Council had learned that the camp was very large – from spies, no doubt. But Southwell did not know just how large, and when he saw our size, it shocked him. I met him privately that morning, and refused to be paid off to dissolve the camp.' He leaned forward and stared at me. 'Do you believe me, Master Shardlake?'

'I do.'

'Then I made a separate arrangement with him. I took the five hundred pounds, and agreed in return that his own sheep farms would not be touched, and the Lady Mary and her Kenninghall estate would be left undisturbed. Already men had begun taking down fences round her deer parks, but I said that would stop. I would have ordered it anyway, for as heir to the throne her safety matters to the Protector.'

I looked at him with new admiration. 'So you outsmarted Southwell?'

Kett smiled. 'I have thousands of men behind me. I set him free, to return to London and tell whatever tale he chose. And I have also, shall we say, had a donation from Bishop Rugge, in return for not look⁄ing too closely into the religious views of some in the camp, and leaving cathedral property safe. Had I not, with such numbers we would in time have run out of supplies – shoes, candles, clothes – things my men have been able to buy in Norwich market with the money. And keeping the market open helps me with Codd and Aldrich. Nonetheless, these arrangements are known only to very few. Some among the men would disapprove of my letting Southwell go – but it was the best arrangement for the camp, and that is my concern above all.'

I said, with genuine admiration, 'Captain Kett, your years dealing with Flowerdew and his like in Wymondham have made you a skilled politician indeed.'

'I thank you.' He looked at me seriously again. 'So, you understand that whatever his young thugs, or Southwell himself, may have done, there is nothing I can do. I do not even know where he is. Probably in London, like Flowerdew. He may indeed have been party to murder, nothing would surprise me. But I can do nothing and you, Master Shardlake, must say nothing.'

I sighed, realizing that what he said was true. 'Again, I swear.' I paused. 'But Southwell coming with money is surely more evidence that the Protector wants the camps dispersed.'

Kett frowned. 'As I said, I believe that if the Protector sees the reasonableness of our demands, and, yes, the force we have behind us, he will realize they must settle. Here and elsewhere.' He then reached a long arm across the table and pushed across three sealed letters. 'Mayor Codd agreed to forward letters arriving in Norwich for men in the camp. These came yesterday, one each for you and Barak and young Overton.'

I looked at the seals. All had been broken, either by Codd's men or Kett's. The one addressed to me was in Guy's handwriting, as was a second for Barak, probably written for Tamasin by Guy. I worried what the letters might contain, for they must already have been read, but if there was anything of concern, Kett would have told me. 'Thank you,' I said.

He stood. 'Now I must go to the Oak, meet the representatives of the Hundreds and finalize the demands. After you have gone over them, I would like you to assist me at more trials of the gentlemen this afternoon.'

'There may be a big storm later, the sky is growing dark.'

He smiled. 'Country people are used to working in foul weather.'

His face fell serious again. 'And remember, say nothing of Southwell's visit here.'

'I will not—'

I was interrupted. A young man in a breastplate came into the chapel, hastily doffing his cap. 'I am sorry, Captain Kett, but there is news you must hear. Two prisoners escaped from Surrey Place last night. They were locked firmly in a cell, with a guard on the door, as they had been much trouble, but someone got in, clouted the guard unconscious, and released them.'

'Which prisoners?' Kett snapped.

'Those devilish twins, Gerald and Barnabas Boleyn, who were to be indicted for attempted murder.' He looked at me. I thought, That was why they were so casual at the trial; their escape had already been planned.

'God's bones,' Kett said. 'If prisoners can escape, people will ask what good the trials are.'

'They've probably slipped down through Thorpe Wood, then across the river,' the young man said. 'It was well planned; nobody knew anything until the guard came to and raised the alarm.'

Kett said, 'Whoever did this knew the layout of Surrey Place. Tell the lookouts in the county to keep watch for them.' He turned to me. 'As I said, Master Shardlake, there are spies and enemies here. That is why important matters must be kept secret.'

☦

BACK IN THE HUT with Barak and Nicholas, we were in sombre mood.

'Those rats,' Barak said. 'They are probably fled to London.'

'They might seek refuge with friends in Norwich,' I said. 'They could find it difficult to cross Norfolk. Their looks are distinctive, to say the least.'

Barak looked out at the camp. 'The main work of building is done; fewer are coming in now. There's still much to do, of course, and I've heard more military training is planned, but the men are going to have more time to think, unless these enclosure commissioners turn up. And some may identify the twins with us, as you act for their father, for all we hate them as much as anyone.'

'I fear you could be right,' I said. 'Nicholas, you must be more careful than ever, especially with Lockswood in his spiteful mood. You should not provoke him.'

'I am sorry. I will be.'

Barak fingered the hook on the underside of his artificial hand. 'I wonder who let them out.'

'Someone in their pay, or Southwell's.'

He shook his head. 'Those boys – I know we have a wide field of suspects but we've seen them hunt down a child for sport, and we know they smashed in the head of that boy we saw at the Oak. Why not kill their own mother too?'

I said, 'I still don't think they did that. But I will speak to Michael Vowell about any connections between Gawen Reynolds's household and Southwell's; he will know the relationship between them, if anyone does.' My hand went my pocket. 'Jesu, I forgot, we have letters.'

The leaden sky outside made it hard for us to read in the hut. Guy's letter to me was again written in an old man's scrawl. It was dated a week before and had obviously crossed with the one I had just sent.

Matthew,

I have not heard further from you, and presume you are still in Norfolk. Every night I pray you are recovered from your injuries, and safe from those rebels. Forgive an old man's worry, but it has been near a month since I was in touch with Dr Belys, and if you are able, a line would reassure me. Tamasin, too, is worried about Jack, and I fear how Nicholas might fare amongst those rebels. There is much worry about the commotions in London, and talk of taking down the bridge at Richmond lest the Kent and Surrey rebels get across.

As for me, I fear I slowly grow weaker. If my pilgrimage on earth is coming to its close, I am ready, though I mourn what has become of England, and its terrible troubles. I am grateful to have such good friends here as Tamasin and Francis, but yearn to know that you and Jack and Nicholas are safe.

Your loving friend,
Guy

I hoped my last letter would get through soon. I began to fear that by the time I got home, if ever I did, Guy might have passed away. I turned to Barak. 'How's Tamasin?'

He frowned. 'This one has crossed with the one I sent a few days ago. She says I am cruel and thoughtless not to have written, and wonders where I am. She says the children are pining for me.' His voice shook. 'God's death, is it my fault letters aren't getting through? Hasn't she the wit to realize the whole country is disrupted?'

'Tamasin has plenty of wit, as well you know. It is because of the state of things that she is so worried for you.'

'Well, she'll either get the letter I sent, or she won't,' he answered stubbornly. 'She says she's short of money, as though I could do anything about that, up here. She goes on about the atmosphere in London, with talk of the London Corporation petitioning the Protector for weapons, and a great searching for seditious speakers. But London has always been strong on security; I think any rising there would be crushed.'

I looked at him, wishing he would not interpret everything his wife said in the worst light.

Nicholas said, 'Beatrice has by some miracle received my letter. She says she pines to hear exactly where I am, whether I have seen the rebels, and what they are like. She goes on to say her mother believes they are in league with the devil himself, for they are all heretics, and should I encounter them, I should look for a black figure with horns and hooves stirring them up. Beatrice does not believe that herself, but urges me to take good care, and defy the rebels with my honest sword should I encounter them.' Suddenly he laughed, and put his head in his hands. 'Horns and hooves! Defy them with my honest sword! Once I thought her innocence and pretty ways beguiling, but now – how would she fare here, do you think? No fine clothes or scent for her. And the letters' seals were broken; that letter must have been read, and it will do me no good, as though I were not in bad enough odour already.' He dropped the letter to the earthen floor. 'Oh God, for a woman like Isabella, who sees the world straight.' He reached for the comb he had bought from a peddler the day before, and drew it fiercely through his matted auburn locks. 'God damn these nits!'

Chapter Fifty

LATER THAT MORNING, I found a barber a little distance off. He had set up shop outside his hut, while his neighbour had arranged cobblers' equipment outside his, and called out that he had 'good clouted shoon' for sale. As I traversed the tracks between the huts I had a few hostile looks; news of the twins' escape would be spreading fast and after my appearance yesterday at the Oak I was now a recognized figure, known to represent John Boleyn. A boy turned and bared his arse at me. Once more, in the body of the camp I felt an alien.

The sky was darker than ever, and a cool breeze had sprung up from the west, making the yellow, bone-dry grass rustle. Far off, towards the fens, a silent bolt of lightning split the clouds. A group of men were guiding two large mounted cannon down the lane, the horses straining. 'From Old Paston Hall,' one shouted, and onlookers cheered.

The barber was an amiable fellow, and told me how he had come from Great Massingham with his friend Thomas, a rat-catcher whose services were much in demand. He was just finishing his work when I heard my name called. 'Master Shardlake! I know him! A lawyer, but a good man!' I turned to see, at the centre of half a dozen men, Simon Scambler, thin and dirty but alive. 'Thank the Lord,' I said quietly. I hastily paid the barber and went over to the group. An argument was proceeding and Scambler, on the edge of tears, was at the centre of it. An older man in shirt and doublet watched Scambler curiously as he waved his arms in that frantic manner of his, while the others, mostly younger, laughed. Scambler called out frantically, 'Master Shardlake, you'll vouch fer me, won't you, say I'm fit to join the camp! Don't, they'll send me away!'

'Hush, Simon,' I said quietly. 'How did you get up here? I looked for you in Norwich.'

'I was begging, but got so little I was near clammed to death with hunger.' Indeed, I could see his ribs through his torn shirt. 'Then I heard about the camp, heard that here they were good men, who want to help the poor.'

One of the younger men said, 'I've seen this buffle-head in Norwich. Runs about like a madwag.' He turned to the older man. 'We don't want him here, Master Tuddenham, he'll just be a nuisance. He's probably sozzled.'

I appealed to the older man, who had been pointed out to me as one of the elected representatives of the Hundreds, and who was stroking his beard thoughtfully. 'This boy is not drunk. Smell his breath, if you wish. His behaviour can be – odd – but he is neither mad nor stupid. He has a good heart and would serve the camp loyally.' I had a sudden inspiration. 'There are horses here, are there not? I have seen them penned behind stout fences. Some were taken from the gentry; perhaps they are hard to control?'

The man called Tuddenham nodded. "Tis true. A man got a nasty bite yesterday.'

'Young Simon has a way with horses. Give him a trial helping to look after them, and you will see.'

Scambler shouted out, "Tis right, sir. I love horses, I'm good with them.'

Tuddenham nodded. 'Our Lord said each should follow his talents. Very well. I authorize it as a Hundred representative. I'll take him to the horses.' He looked at me. 'But you, sir, must take responsibility for him. You are Master Shardlake, aren't you?'

'The hunchback lawyer that works for the murdering Boleyns,' someone said.

I turned on the accuser fiercely, 'Never those twins, who, when this is settled, I myself will ensure are tried for attempted murder.'

'All right,' Tuddenham said. 'I'll take this Scambler up to the horses now, and then he can join your group; from Swardeston, isn't it?'

'I thank you, sir.'

He turned to Sooty. 'You understand what we've said, boy?'

'Yes, master. I'm to help work with the horses, and stay with Master Shardlake. I'll do my best, I swear on my oath.'

'You others, haven't you work to do? Get on, keep a-doin'!'

As Tuddenham led Simon away I called out, 'I will see you tonight. Remember, ask for the Swardeston huts!' I watched as the two threaded their way through the paths between the huts. Simon might surprise them with his skills with horses, though finding his way to our huts that evening might be a different matter. Another bolt of lightning split the sky far off, followed shortly by a distant roll of thunder. 'We're in for a drouching soon,' someone observed.

✝

I RETURNED TO the huts, where Nicholas cheered up when I told him of Simon's arrival. I told Goodwife Everneke a new resident would be joining our huts, a poor boy who might seem strange but who would respond well to kindness. 'I'll look after him as best I can,' she said. From a little way off I heard shouting, and she said, 'Some of the younger men are fighting, others betting on them. Now the main work's done, the men'll need entertainment. I hear Captain Kett's asked his men in Norwich to bring up tumblers and jugglers, and storytellers.'

'He thinks of everything.'

'He is a great man. We would have starved come harvest time but for him. I'm an old widow, I hardly have the energy now to keep up my small plot.'

'I am sorry to hear it.'

'My husband, God save his soul, died of fever in the winter.' She closed her eyes for a second, then changed the subject. 'They're having other entertainments too; fighting cocks have been brought up and they're holding a bear-baiting. There's a sort of natural amphitheatre nearby.'

'I think I will avoid that.'

I spent the rest of the morning talking with her. We kept looking up at the dark sky, but the storm was not ready to break just yet. Nicholas was set to go and find some new flints to put round our cooking fire, to which he agreed meekly. After lunch Barak appeared. 'The demands to the Protector are ready,' he said. 'Captain Kett wants you at St Michael's now.'

We walked to the chapel. 'How did it go?' I asked.

'All the representatives of the Hundreds were there, forty-six men. Can you imagine getting so many Norfolk men to agree? All had their own priorities. There have been a few drafts and tearings-up. William Kett threatened to bang their heads together at one point. Robert Kett insisted the demands must be approved at the Oak this afternoon and sent to London, and all was agreed in the end, though it's a bit of a mish-mash.'

We entered the chapel, where a large crowd stood around, while the clerks sat at the tables, which were covered with scribbled papers. All looked a little frayed. Kett beckoned me up to his table on the dais. 'Master Shardlake. Good. Cast your legal eye over our demands.'

I looked at a long roll of neatly inscribed paper on Kett's desk. Although everyone had talked of 'demands', each clause began with 'We pray your Grace'. That would help greatly, for legally this was merely a petition. I read the document through carefully. Many of its twenty-nine articles limited the landowners' powers – in passing feudal duties on to tenants and claiming excessive rights over commons, while the right to keep dove houses was to be limited, and tenant rights over reed ground, marshes and fishing were to be restored. Several articles were concerned with the priests – their amassing of material wealth, the inability of some to preach the Word of God – here it was demanded that such priests or vicars be put out, and the parishioners were to have a say in choosing their successors. This was radical, with a hint of Calvinism.

The King's officials came in for hard censure; one article called for the feodary to be chosen by the commons of the shire, and limited the powers of feodary and escheator both to grant offices and over wardship. While many demands looked to the restoration of rights as they had been in the time of old King Henry VII, much was new. I heartily agreed with all of it. But the most radical demand was a prayer to the King to allow the commons a say in choosing local commissioners to implement laws and proclamations – this read, to me, of an intent to make the enclosure commissions permanent and to give a say in their control to the commons. I thought, The Council will never allow this; but it was not my place to argue the content. And article sixteen prayed for the final ending of serfdom – 'that all bond men may be made free, as God made all men free with his precious blood shedding'. I thought of the boy Ralph who had been clubbed by the twins – a serf, legally the property of his master, no doubt simply commanded with his father to occupy Boleyn's land by Witherington, whom he could not refuse.

'Well?' Kett said, a little impatiently.

'I see nothing contrary to law here. All I would say is that the demands could be better ordered. Why not put all those concerned with rights over land and such things as fisheries together, and follow with those concerning the clergy, then royal officials and, finally, the commissioners?'

Kett shook his head impatiently. 'We haven't time. If we change anything, people will just start arguing again. We are due at the Oak, people will already be gathered there and this should be agreed before the storm breaks.'

✝

THERE WERE THOUSANDS at the Oak of Reformation. Among them I saw a black-faced African, who had perhaps returned with the failed expedition to Yarmouth, which traded with the Spanish Nether-lands. The reading of the demands was to be the main event, followed by the trials of some thieves from the camp, and more gentlemen. All the accused stood in a miserable huddle, soldiers guarding them as before, Captain Miles standing quietly by. Codd, Aldrich and the preacher Watson sat at the table alongside the Ketts; Barak and I were motioned to remain at the foot of the stage for now.

Kett read out the demands slowly, so that his words could be passed to those further back. There were occasional rumbles of thunder, closer now, and people looked up apprehensively at the sky; a heavy storm would flatten what growing crops they still had.

Each article was greeted with cheers, especially those calling for popular participation. At the end, Kett asked if they were accepted. There was a deafening chorus of agreement, though when it died down some younger men called out that landlordship itself should be abolished, and tenants own their own land.

Kett called back, 'These are only preliminary demands; there will be opportunity to discuss further ones later. And now, a rider for London is waiting – are these demands agreed?' There was another chorus of agreement, though some younger men looked a little sour. Kett, surefooted as ever, had side-lined them.

The demands were ceremonially signed by Kett, Codd and Aldrich, then passed to one of the soldiers, who hurried off with them. A good proportion of the assembly departed for the shelter of their huts as the storm approached. Then the trials began, the thieves first. They reminded me of the rumbustiousness of ordinary criminal trials, with angry denials by those accused of appropriating gold, goods or animals taken from the gentry while witnesses shouted that they had seen the items taken. Occasionally, I murmured to Kett that some accusation was hearsay or speculation, and it was disallowed. Most, however, were clearly guilty and found so by the crowd. The penalty was expulsion from the camp. Kett looked at the men as they were led away. 'Many are among the poorest here,' he said. 'It grieves me to have to expel them.' I looked at him; he could be commanding, politically devious, but fundamentally he was a man of compassion, for which I was grate-ful. Few of the leaders of men I had met could be so called.

Trials of more gentry followed. The lord of Swardeston Manor was brought forward and accused by Master Dickon of encroaching on the commons. Dickon, solid and middle-aged, tenant of thirty acres and a churchwarden, contrasted well with his landlord, a thin anxious-looking man, who adopted a wheedling tone and admitted he had perhaps made too great demand upon the common land, but would put things right. His tone made no more impression on the crowd than the blustering of others; they judged him guilty and returned him to custody.

Just as the soldier was leading him away, there was a mighty crack of thunder overhead, and the skies opened. A deluge of hailstones crashed down on us, pounding the crowd and clattering on the wooden canopy above us. Suddenly, it was cold. Mighty claps of thunder sounded, followed by flashes of lightning that momentarily turned everything white. The flat ground was already covered with hail, like grey snow. The hail then turned to rain, which fell in a curtain.

Kett called out, 'We must adjourn the hearings. Back to your huts, men.' Battered, buffeted and soaked, everyone began to disperse. Then everyone turned at the sound of a loud cry. A group of men, and a middle-aged woman, stepped towards the stage. The woman called out, 'We have captured Richard Day, lawyer and sorcerer of Bungay! Let the claims against him be heard!'

Peering through the rain, I was astonished to see a man I knew, his arms tied in front of him, held firmly in the midst of the group. In my days representing poor clients at the Court of Requests I had encountered Richard Day several times, acting for East Anglian landlords. A substantial landowner himself, he was skilled in dragging cases out for months or years. In court, he would angrily denounce poor witnesses, already intimidated by appearing in a London court, as liars and cheats. At that time he had been an impressive man, tall, sturdy and grey-haired, a fiercely aggressive advocate who hated losing, and who more than once had berated me after a trial for representing country clowns. I had heard rumours that he threatened tenants who opposed him with the ills of sorcery, and practised black magic at his manor house.

He was a very different figure now; wearing a torn and stained doublet, soaking wet, his face bruised and, like his hands, covered with scratches. He looked at the people on the stage above him, and when he saw me sitting between Kett and Barak his eyes widened in astonished fury.

The group who had brought him forced Day to his knees before the stage. A young man, blinking water out of his eyes, shouted, 'We've been looking for him all week! He ran from his manor house but Mistress Howell here found him hiding in a briar patch the day before yesterday. We've come all the way from the Suffolk border to get him tried!'

The woman stepped forward and spoke, loudly but with dignity. 'He had my husband and me turned off our land because our copyhold could not be found! He had destroyed the manor record book!'

Another mighty clap of thunder sounded. Day, trembling, shouted out, 'I curse you, Shardlake! All those you care for will die! How can you assist these dogs, these apes and pigs!' As so often among the gentlemen, he referred to the camp-men as animals.

'See, he spoke like a sorcerer! Kill him now!'

The whole scene was like a wild dream – the rain pounding on the canopy, the thunder crashing, the sodden crowd, many with weapons raised threateningly. Codd and Aldrich looked on wide-eyed. Kett called out, 'The villainy of this man is known far and wide! But he will have a trial like everyone else! Not now, this storm will be causing damage in the camp and we must see to that! Take Day to Surrey Place and secure him in chains! We will take him to Norwich Castle tomorrow!' Someone stepped forward and jabbed Day with a spear. He squealed like a pig. A soldier stepped forward and seized the weapon before it could do any real damage. Day collapsed to the ground and began weeping. The crowd laughed. 'Enough!' Kett roared against the hissing rain. 'Captain Miles, take him! He will be tried at the next hearing! Now go, all of you, before we drown on our feet.'

Miles and a couple of soldiers stepped forward and hauled Day off through the curtain of rain. The crowd began to disperse. As the thunder continued rolling, the deluge became even heavier.

William Kett said, 'God's death, Robert, the whole camp will be washed out if we're not careful! I fear for those camped by Long Valley.'

'You're right,' his brother agreed. 'We must get back to St Michael's and organize.'

I looked at them. For a moment I had been shaken by Day's curse, but the common sense of the Ketts brought me back to reality. I, too, should return to my hut. I rose. Mayor Codd looked out at the rain. 'Do we have to return to Norwich in this?' he asked plaintively.

'Stay if you like,' William Kett answered. 'Perhaps you'd like to help clear up,' he said as he descended the steps from the stage with his brother. They walked away, their solid figures instantly drenched.

Chapter Fifty-one

A S BARAK AND I squelched our way back to our hut, the rain mercifully lessened, and the sun appeared from behind the clouds. The camp was a sea of mud, with potholes full of water. People were baling out their huts, shaking water from sodden posses-sions. I saw a man, one of the governors probably, calling people to the Long Valley, where a sudden flood had carried away huts, animals and supplies.

The Swardeston camp had suffered too, turf roofs leaking water into the interior, puddles in the doorways. Nicholas was helping with the baling out. Some of the men had just come back from Thorpe Wood with long branches which they placed in the ground. Lengths of rope were tied between them and wet clothes hung out. Barak and I quickly changed into dry clothes, then joined in, taking everything possible into the sun to dry. Dickon, the man who had given evidence against the Swardeston landlords, joined me in slinging wet clothes over a line. 'Do you think I did well today?' he asked. 'Did your man note down the accusations against that rogue?'

'He did, and I am sure the commissioners and the Protector will follow them up.'

He smiled wryly. 'We've put his sheep off the commons. It's done already, and we won't let it be undone.'

A tall, serious-looking man appeared. I had seen him in St Michael's Chapel; he was another governor. He nodded to us. 'That's right, bors, keep a-doin', get everything dry. Put the top layer of your bedding bracken out as well.' He moved on.

I looked at our hut. Water dripped from the turf, making a puddle on the mud floor. Barak said, 'Far cry from your Chancery Lane house, isn't it?'

I laughed. 'It is indeed.'

'Most of these people are probably used to leaking roofs.'

Nicholas shoved past us and began picking up armfuls of wet bracken. 'Come on, you two,' he said. 'Get this stuff moved.'

✝

I HAD WORRIED about Scambler finding us in the chaos, but shortly afterwards he arrived, together with old Hector Johnson. I was alarmed to see that Scambler was limping, and had a bruise on his chin. John-son said, 'Found him over by the main track, asking for the Swardeston huts, he'd got himself lost. Bit of a hero, this lad.'

'How so?'

'There was a great to-do with the horses. A strong wooden pad-dock's been built to hold them, but many are nervous and the thunder and hail drove them wild. They tried to escape. One big stallion was kicking at the fence to break it down, and the others would have fol-lowed. But this lad went up to it and, God knows how, managed to quiet it, though not before it stood on his foot and butted him with its head. People say he was singing to the animal. If those horses had broken out and gone careering through the camp, you can imagine the damage.' He patted Scambler on the back. Simon looked down, red in the face.

'There!' I said. 'I told them he was good with horses. Well done, Simon.'

Scambler looked up, and for the first time since I had met him, he smiled.

✝

THAT EVENING, as we sat around the cooking fire, damp despite the end of the rain, Scambler told us what had happened to him since his aunt had thrown him out. With nowhere to live, he had joined the ranks of the Norwich beggars. He'd learned how most had once had jobs or families, though some had been beggars from childhood. Most drank strong beer, befuddling themselves to escape their miserable reality, but if Scambler's aunt's church had done one good thing, its condemnation of drink had stuck with Simon and he had refused all offers of it. Begging, however, brought in less than enough to eat and once or twice he was set on by his old tormentors from school. Some of the citizens who had dropped a penny into his cap had said, complacently, 'Knew you'd come to this, Sooty.'

Goodwife Everneke, who seemed to hear everything, passed Scambler an extra plate of mutton, which he quickly devoured. He had been talking quickly, as usual, with wild gestures, but when he had eaten he looked at me and said, slowly, 'One day I was sitting outside the cathedral, so hungry I felt faint. I feared I'd die soon, and my aunt's promises of hell kept coming into my head –'

'She's an evil old bitch,' Barak interjected forcefully.

'I was sitting there, no coins in my cap, when I heard some drop in. I looked and there were three shillings – three shillings, Master Shardlake! And standing over me was old Mistress Jane Reynolds – you remember, from the court?'

'Yes. I would not have thought her one for charity.'

'I was scared, her standing over me, all in black, with that white, lined face. But she just said kindly, "You were at court. Poor boy. I wanted a boy, you know, I needed a boy, not poor Edith." Then she said, "If you see my grandsons, be sure to run." There was such a look of sorrow in her face.' Scambler shook his head. 'Those three shillings saved me, kept me going until I heard about the camp and came up here.'

I looked at Barak and Nicholas, remembering Jane Reynolds's words in court – 'Edith, God save you, I wanted a boy.' I said, 'I think she is in mental agony.' I frowned. 'Why does she keep saying, "I wanted a boy"?'

Nicholas said quietly, 'Perhaps the twins killed their mother after all.'

☦

WE HAD A DAMP night in the hut, but woke to another hot day. As we breakfasted, the Hundred representative arrived and told us there was still work to be done in areas where dry gullies on the heath had flooded as the water ran off. Barak was asked to go and help. Nicholas rose to join him. 'Might improve my reputation if I'm seen doing a bit of work,' he said. Scambler returned to the horses and I went to St

Michael's Chapel. The guard on the door, however, told me Captain
Kett was busy trying to return the camp to normal, and there would
be no hearings today. He added with a grin that Reverend Watson from
Norwich had come up to give a sermon on the flood being a warning
against excess pride, and had had an angry reception.

Free for the day, I wandered across to the nearby vantage point looking down on Norwich. The city spires glistened with damp. The main
road down to Bishopsgate Bridge was churned up with mud, and a
couple of carts had been abandoned. Some way off I saw a gully where
water was still draining from the heath down to the Wensum. Along its
path lay a great mess of clothing, the planks and turf from ruined huts
and people's humble possessions. I shook my head at the destruction.

A voice at my shoulder said, 'People who know the heath gave
warning not to camp in the gullies. But nobody expected a storm like
yesterday's. I've never seen a worse.'

I turned to find myself facing Captain Miles, in a green doublet
and, as usual, a metal breastplate. He was older than I had thought,
perhaps in his late forties, his face seamed with lines. He stroked his fair
beard, looking at me with keen eyes. He extended a hand, which I
shook. 'You've done a good job at the hearings,' he said.

'Thank you. I understand you are in charge of training the men.'

'That's right.' He raised his eyebrows. 'And appointing under-
officers, training people to use all the different cannon without blowing
themselves up, not easy since it's such a specialized trade, and how to
use spears and the longbow. Thank God most of the Norwich lads
have had longbow practice in the villages; some are very good. And
men from the old stonemasons' guild, which they dissolved when its
religious functions were taken away, are making gunballs the right size
for the different cannon.'

'Do you think it will come to fighting?'

He shrugged. 'Best to be ready. And training keeps the men occupied. None of them have been in a situation like this before.'

'But you will have experience of campaigning, of large camps, if
you are a master gunner.'

'I started as a boy back in 'twenty-three, with old Henry's invasion
of France that year. It was a mess and gained nothing, like all his

campaigns.' Bitterness entered his voice. 'But I stayed in the King's army, I was a poor Norwich boy and it paid well enough, especially when I rose to master gunner. I was in the last French war, and in Scotland until last year. By God, some evil things were done there against the people. Every campaign a failure, leaving nothing but thou, sands dead. England has little to be proud of.'

I looked at him keenly. 'A strange view for a soldier.'

'There are more who think like me than you might imagine.'

I nodded, remembering rumours of deserting soldiers moving from area to area, encouraging the setting up of camps. 'Why did you stay so long?' I asked.

He shrugged. 'Money. Why else? I have a wife and two children to support, it is safest if I do not say where they are, given there is at least one spy in the camp, who helped those boys escape.' He looked out over the city. 'Scotland was the end, the filth and lack of pay, the endless fighting and losing. And now I am captain of all the forces in this camp.' He gave me a sudden hard look. 'Captain Kett trusts you. Is he right to?'

'I made an oath to aid him on legal matters. I shall keep it.'

Miles nodded slowly. 'Well, there are some cannon taken from the manor houses to be moved to the crest of the hill. To remind the Nor, wich city fathers what might happen if they change their minds. Excuse me, Master Shardlake. Perhaps we shall talk again.' He nodded, then turned and marched away, back into the camp.

✝

AT LUNCHTIME, I returned to the Swardeston huts. Barak and Nicholas were there with the rest of the men, muddy from their work, having been given an hour's break to eat. Afterwards, I suggested we take a walk along the crest of the escarpment. I had been thinking about Jane Reynolds. As we traversed the path along the crest, a wel, come breeze coming up from Norwich, I said, 'I have seldom seen a more unhappy woman.'

'Hardly surprising,' Barak said, 'given that husband, her daugh, ter's horrible death, and those twins as grandsons.'

'But combining this pity for Edith with the wish she had had a son,' Nicholas said. 'It seems to dominate her mind – to tell it to a beggar boy –'

Barak said, 'Perhaps she thinks that if Edith had been a boy, the twins would never have been born.'

I said, 'Maybe. Yet – I feel there is more to it. I wish I could talk to her.'

'Poor Edith,' Nicholas said sadly. 'Everyone wished her away.'

'And someone put her away,' Barak added grimly.

Our attention was drawn by the sound of shouting and cursing. A crowd of some fifty people were making their way from Surrey Place to the road down to Norwich. Robert Wharton, a lawyer and landowner who had been found guilty at the Oak two days before, whom I remembered seemed to be particularly hated, was at the centre of the group, his arms tied securely in chains, eyes wide with terror as guards in breastplates tried to fend off an angry crowd from the camp, many with pitchforks and spears. Drawn by the commotion, several people had come out of St Michael's Chapel, including Toby Lockswood.

'What the fuck's going on?' Barak asked.

'Kett said yesterday they were taking some prisoners to Norwich Castle.'

I looked at the crowd. The soldiers were trying to reach the road, the camp-men to get at Wharton. A man jabbed at him with a pitchfork, making him yell.

Nicholas said quietly. 'He's had no trial. Even by camp standards, this is no justice.'

Barak said, 'He must have done some vile things to be hated so.'

Another young man made to stab Wharton with a spear. However, the guards, who were carrying halberds, had the advantage, and one used his pole to strike the spear, making its owner drop it. The man shouted angrily, 'Do you act to protect the landlords now you have been made guards? Will you betray the commoners?'

The man leading the guards, a tall strong fellow in his fifties, rounded on him. 'Don't accuse me of betrayal, you fucking runt, or I'll have your balls! I did as much as anyone to spread the word and set up this camp!'

Another shouted, 'Ay, Master Echard, miller with half a dozen employees, like Master Robert Kett with his tannery! But who did you set it up for? The rich yeomen and traders?'

Red with rage, Echard shouldered his way through the guards and grabbed the man by the throat. 'I did it for all the commons of Norfolk. Damn you, did you not hear our demands yesterday, which even now are on their way to the King?' He pushed the man away; he shouted back, 'We should not be camping here, we should be marching on London to enforce our demands!'

A crowd was gathering. Some shouted approval, others called the young man a fool. With an angry gesture Echard indicated the guards should move on. They started walking down the road, still accompanied by some hostile men who tried to make jabs at Wharton.

'Jesu,' Barak said. 'They'll kill him.'

I shook my head. 'Wharton has enough guards.'

Nicholas walked over to the crest of the hill and looked down the road as Wharton was led to Norwich. To my surprise, I saw Toby Lockswood join him. Words were exchanged – it was too far for me to hear but they were not arguing, and Lockswood's manner seemed unthreatening. Then he walked away and suddenly shouted, 'We have a traitor in our midst!' He pointed at Nicholas. 'This fine young gentleman has just said Wharton should be freed, Captain Kett locked up, and that we are a commonwealth of rogues! Are we to allow that?'

Nicholas looked stunned, astounded. Barak and I walked quickly over to him. 'Nick,' Barak said urgently, 'What happened?'

He shook his head. 'Lockswood came up to me and started talking about the clearing-up. I never mentioned Wharton or Kett at all!'

Looking at Nicholas's honest, astonished face, I believed him. He had said some stupid things, but had learned better, and I believed his views were slowly changing. Barak looked at Toby, who was approaching us together with a crowd of camp-men, already fired up by the melee around Wharton. Barak said quietly, 'I believe you, Nick, but Lockswood has put you in the shit.' He unsheathed the knife on his artificial hand. Toby looked me in the eye, a slight smile at one corner of his mouth, and I remembered his last words to Nicholas. 'I'll have you, boy.' This was not about politics, it was personal.

Barak addressed the crowd, several of whom had drawn knives.

'Come on, lads, many of you know me, and Master Shardlake is working with Captain Kett. Nicholas here said nothing of that sort.' He looked at Toby. 'Lockswood worked with us before the rebellion, he has a grudge against Nicholas, and has said bad things about him before, in front of Captain Kett. Let him decide this.'

Toby pointed at Nicholas and shouted, 'That young gentleman is against us!'

I stepped forward. 'Did anyone else hear these alleged words? Did they?'

The crowd looked between us, uncertain who to believe. At length an older man stepped forward. 'Let the boy be taken to Surrey Place till Captain Kett is free to deal with this. The lawyer is right, justice must be seen to be done.'

Two men stepped forward and seized Nicholas by the arms. I looked at Lockswood grimly, then said to Nicholas, 'We'll work this out. Do not fear.'

He was led away, Toby watching with a cold smile.

☦

BARAK AND I waited outside St Michael's Chapel, but Kett was still out in the camp, directing the clearing up. Evening drew on, time for the religious service by Conyers at the Oak of Reformation, and Barak and I decided to go; Kett often attended evening service.

We found an unusual scene. Kett was not present, but there was a large crowd, mostly filthy after a hard day's work. They had been rewarded with several barrels of small beer which had been set out on a table, and some were already a little drunk. Conyers stood by the stage in his white surplice and stole, arguing with another cleric, a stocky man in his forties with a fierce, determined aspect and obstinate chin. I heard him say, ''Tis not the time, Master Parker.'

Barak said quietly, 'I've seen him before; years ago, when I first worked for Lord Cromwell. Matthew Parker, Anne Boleyn's chaplain; he's one of the leading Protestants now.'

'What's he doing here?'

'He's a Norwich man, if I remember right.'

A man in the crowd shouted out, 'Begone, Master Parker, we know the camp in Cambridge is put down and you played your part!'

'Go to Kenninghall and try your arts on the Lady Mary!'

There was a flurry of laughter, although some looked uneasy at this mocking of a senior Protestant preacher. Parker, with an angry gesture, turned and walked away. Someone called, 'Come, Master Conyers, preach to us! You know God's word and our Lord's promises better than him!'

Barak said, 'Come on, let's get back to St Michael's Chapel.'

✟

WHEN WE ARRIVED, the guard told us Kett and his brother were inside, dining after a hard day. I was unsure whether to interrupt, but thought of Nicholas being led away, and went inside with Barak. Several men were poring over makeshift maps of the camp, marking areas damaged by flooding. Kett, his wife and his brother William were eating at their table at the head of the chapel. Kett's face was red with anger, as fierce as I had ever seen him. 'First some try to seize Wharton, then they insult Parker! If things go on like this, we'll lose control!'

'It's not so bad as that,' Alice said. 'The flood was a shock to everyone.'

William snorted. 'Put a few of the malcontents in Norwich Castle, that'll give them something to think about!'

Robert banged his fist on the table. 'No, it'll just make the men angrier!'

'I don't think this is the time,' Barak said quietly. But Kett had seen me. He – the man who I was beginning to consider a friend – glowered at me. 'Master Shardlake! I hear more bad news about that wretched boy Overton!'

I spoke quietly. 'From Toby Lockswood? Captain, remember, he spoke out of malice against Nicholas before. You reprimanded him.'

Kett was in a fierce mood. 'And you remember Master Overton has spoken out before against what we are doing, and is only free at your request. Now I hear he says I should be locked up and that the camp is a commonwealth of rogues!'

'Sir, I was present when Nicholas and Toby spoke privily. It was as Wharton was being led to Norwich. I did not hear their words, but they spoke quietly. Nicholas denies he spoke as Lockswood said. This is a matter of revenge.'

William Kett looked at me. 'Lockswood said two other men heard the words.'

'Then they are liars whom he has suborned,' I replied, angry myself now.

William turned to Robert. 'See, now he calls the camp-men liars!'

Robert took a deep breath to calm himself. 'Lockswood has witnesses to Overton's words. I have ordered the boy is to be taken to Norwich Castle, and there he will stay till I order otherwise.' He looked at me with those fierce, strong eyes. 'And you, Master Shardlake, watch your step.'

Chapter Fifty-two

B ARAK AND I SLEPT little that night, only two of us now in the turf-roofed hut: Scambler was sharing a neighbouring hut with young Natty. When we returned to the Swardeston camp after our disastrous meeting with Kett, Simon asked where Nicholas was. I told him, for the news would soon be around the camp. He looked down-cast, for he liked Nicholas. The others gave us curious looks.

Discussing what had happened at St Michael's, Barak and I agreed we must wait till Kett was in a better humour and appeal to his sense of justice, asking that Toby and his two alleged witnesses be brought before him to repeat the allegations in front of Nicholas.

'Kett may want a hearing at the Oak,' Barak said. 'And Nick hasn't made himself popular.'

'Yes. We must play this carefully.'

'Damn that Toby Lockswood,' Barak said savagely. 'It was just petty revenge. I'd like to beat the bastard to a pulp.'

'Don't you get in trouble too.' I hesitated. 'I see you're keeping sober.'

He looked me in the eye. 'I've found a worthwhile cause. After working at those Assizes, Jesus knows I needed it.'

I went outside for a wash. During the storm the camp-men had laid out barrels and bowls wherever they could and there was a full pail of rainwater outside the hut. For the first time everyone had fresh water. The sun had set, and I looked out over the darkened camp; cooking fires burned, dots of red on the dark heath. A bat, a flittermouse, as they called it here, flew soundlessly past. I walked a little way towards the escarpment; larger fires burned around the guard posts, and in the distance pinpoints of light were visible from Norwich. I thought,

Tomorrow, the nineteenth of July, we shall have been on Mousehold Heath a week.

✝

THE NEXT MORNING, Barak was sent to work cataloguing the large delivery of wood brought in to reinforce the cattle and horses' paddocks. Under Kett and the governors everything was rigorously accounted for. Simon Scambler went to help with the horses. I had a message that there were again to be no trials today, with much work still to be done after the storm. Left alone, I decided to seek out Michael Vowell and ask what he knew of relations between the Reynolds and Southwell families.

I went to the Oak of Reformation, which had become the main gathering point for the camp. I was almost there when, to my astonishment, I saw Reverend Matthew Parker, his surplice stained with earth, face red with anger, limping towards the road back to Norwich together with another cleric and a couple of attendants. I stared at him, and he glowered at me; with my stained shirt, white beard and hair and broad cap, no doubt he took me for an elderly camp-man.

Arriving at the Oak, I found a concourse of men, some hundreds strong. Apart from a few who looked disapproving, they were in merry mood. I saw the stocky figure of Michael Vowell among them, joking with some of the younger men. He was dressed in a leather jerkin and cap, sunburned now. I approached him. 'What has happened?' I asked. 'I saw Reverend Parker just now. He did not look happy.'

This brought further laughter from the young men. Vowell smiled. 'Parker came when Reverend Conyers was giving the morning service, and insisted on taking his place. He stood on the stage and went on at us for having a few drinks last night. Then, damn his cheek, he told us to abandon the camp and trust in the King's emissaries. Wherever they might fucking be,' he added.

Reynolds's former steward was very different now from the rather serious figure I had first met in Norwich. He seemed to have chosen younger men to associate with, the natural radicals within the camp. But, like them, he now had, for the first time, liberty to express his true feelings openly. One of his young friends said, 'Time was we had to bow and tremble to the preachers. Not now! Some of our men went under the stage and pricked Parker's feet with spears.'

There were fresh guffaws of laughter. 'You should've seen him dance! That put an end to his squitty talk!'

'We dinged clods of earth at him!'

'No wonder he looked frampled when you saw him!'

Vowell said, a little regretfully, 'But then Reverend Conyers led this choir of children he had brought from Norwich in singing the *Te Deum* in English; that quieted everybody and gave Parker the chance to run.'

'I noticed he was limping.' I could not forbear a smile, for the story had a humorous aspect and no damage had been done.

One of the men with Vowell looked at me curiously. 'Ain't you the lawyer that's been advising Captain Kett at the trials?'

'That's right.'

'Can tell you're a lawyer by those inky, womanish fingers,' he said. 'How d'you come to be here?'

'That's a long story.'

Several looked at me suspiciously, and I saw that some were among those who had called for hangings at the trials. I said, humbly, 'May I speak privily for a moment with Master Vowell?'

Someone laughed. 'Listen to that! A lawyer asking permission like we were equals!'

'We are, now,' another said forcefully.

I looked at him. This was radical talk indeed. Vowell took my arm and led me away a few feet, still smiling a little. 'What is it?'

'A question that has been going through my mind about Edith Boleyn's murder, and those that followed.'

He looked at me sharply. 'Do you think there's a connection to those damn twins escaping?'

'No. My question was, I know the twins worked with some of Sir Richard Southwell's men. I wondered whether their grandfather and Southwell were associated at all.'

To my surprise, Vowell laughed. 'No, Master Shardlake, you're on the wrong track there. Reynolds and Southwell hate each other. They are both quarrelsome and vicious men. Ten years ago, they had a big

argument over the purchase of a house in Norwich. I heard the shouting and threats when Southwell came to visit my master.' He laughed
again. 'If you think some of the language in the camp is ripe, you
should have heard those two.'

'Who won the argument?'

'Southwell, of course. He had the most power and money, even
then. But Gawen Reynolds never forgot or forgave; he never does. He
was furious when the twins took up with Southwell's band of gentlemen rogues, but' – he shrugged – 'not even their grandfather can
prevent Gerald and Barnabas doing what they want. He had to swal-
low it.'

'I see. I have been thinking too about the twins' grandmother. How
did you find her to deal with, when you were steward?'

'Jane Reynolds was afraid of her own shadow. I sometimes wondered if she was in her right mind.' He looked at me sharply. 'Maybe
her daughter inherited that.'

'She said in court, "Edith, Edith, God save you, I wanted a boy."'

He spoke dismissively. 'Mistress Jane often said things that made no
sense.' Then with sudden intensity, he said, 'Master Shardlake, I want
to forget that family. I have different concerns now. I want to build a
new and fairer England.'

I nodded. 'I notice you seem to mix with the younger men, the
more radical element.'

'Yes. Those who have nothing, and should have their fair share.'

'Yes, they should. But young men are excitable, and we do not
want bloodshed.'

He smiled bitterly. 'So Matthew Parker said. I think you are a good
man, Master Shardlake, but you remind me that you are, like him, a
man of the gentleman class.'

☫

EARLY THAT EVENING, after work, there were entertainments in the
camp, in the wide natural amphitheatre Goodwife Everneke had
spoken of, beyond St Michael's Chapel. Barak and I went to watch.
We arrived to see a stage occupied by jugglers, tossing coloured balls to
and fro with astonishing skill. Afterwards a tightrope walker crossed a

rope between two trees, balancing himself with a long pole held in his arms. The crowd stood silent, fearful of seeing him fall, but he made it and descended the opposite tree to loud cheers and claps. Pennies were thrown to him.

A cockfight followed, which I did not wish to see, and I persuaded Barak to walk a little. I asked, 'Did you notice a change in the attitude of the villagers towards us at dinner? They did not invite us to come here with their party.'

'The news about Nicholas is out. People asked me about it, but I said there was a mistake. Perhaps we could sound out Kett again tomorrow.'

'Yes. Ask the guards at St Michael's Chapel first if he's in a better mood.'

Barak answered, a little sharply, 'Kett is anxious that nothing has been heard from the commissioners. And he has huge responsibilities. You can't expect him to make Nicholas a priority.'

'I know.'

'Look, there's young Natty, with Sooty Scambler.'

'Don't call him that! His name is Simon. Perhaps now he is among people from the villages that nickname can be forgotten.'

We approached the two boys. They were an oddly assorted pair; the quiet, powerfully built Natty and the thin, forever gesturing Simon.

'God give you both good evening,' I said.

'And you,' Natty answered cheerfully.

'How is your friend young Stephen Walker?'

'Diddlin' along well enough. He's with some other villagers from the Sandlings.'

'Did you not feel like joining them?'

Natty shook his head. 'He has family there. I like the Swardeston camp. They're happy to take in waifs and strays, eh, Simon?' He clapped Scambler lightly on the arm.

Scambler nodded. 'Ay, waifs and strays though we be, we are not treated like grubs any more.' He smiled at me, tremulously, as though unsure of his new happiness. It struck me that these two boys, abandoned by their country, were perhaps not such unlikely friends after all.

'There's a puppet show about to begin,' Simon said to Natty. 'Shall we watch?'

'Ay, I've never seen such a thing.'

'The puppeteers are Norwich men,' Simon said excitedly. 'I saw them once before. They're wonderful.' He clapped his hands and turned to us. 'Will you come?'

'Yes. So long as the cockfighting is over.'

Barak said, 'He doesn't like the sight of blood.'

'No,' I agreed emphatically. 'I do not.'

✝

WE MADE OUR WAY back to the Oak, where a large, brightly coloured stage had been erected, a curtain before it. The large crowd was noisily good-humoured, passing flagons of beer around. It was small beer, weak, and I heard someone complain that Captain Kett should allow more strong beer.

The curtains parted, to reveal a scene representing the interior of a wealthy house, with beautifully constructed miniature tables and chairs and even a buffet displaying tiny plates and flagons. Two puppets, held by puppeteers kneeling below behind a cloth, shuffled onto the stage. Their clothes were those of a rich lady and gentleman, and their painted faces were both severe. There were cheerful boos from the crowd.

The lady said in a haughty, scratching voice, 'The rents from our land no longer keep me in fine dresses. What is to be done, Husband? I can afford no fine hood to cover my tresses.'

Her husband answered in a deep, ogre-like voice, 'Fear not, good wife, I have a plan. I'll turn my land to sheep, evict each and every man!'

The woman clapped. The play continued with the introduction of a villainous steward, who suggested they conspire with a lawyer to say the tenants' leases were ended. The lawyer then appeared, a dark-haired man in black robe and cap.

Simon began hopping with excitement as the play continued. It introduced a yeoman farmer with his own land, obviously intended to represent Robert Kett, accompanied by a group of tenants, who said they would take over the land. A fight followed in the house, with much knockabout humour as the puppet figures beat each other with sticks. People shouted, even the phlegmatic Natty calling on the tenants to 'Culp the landlords proper!'

In the end the tenants won the fight and took the furniture from the house. The landowners and their lawyer, much buffeted about, were left alone on stage.

Clever as the performance was, I became a little tired with the stock characters and turned to ask Natty what people were saying about Nicholas. He looked at me seriously. 'Most villagers have been suspicious of him, he's known to have said things against the camp, but Goody Everneke says there's no harm in him, it's just that being here he's like a fish out of water.' He smiled. 'And what she says counts.'

'He has said stupid things in the past, but not this time. He was betrayed by Toby Lockswood, who worked with us before the rebellion, and who hates him.'

'Are you sure?' Natty's honest face registered surprise.

'I would swear it.'

'So would I,' added Barak.

Natty raised his eyebrows. 'Toby Lockswood is become a powerful figure here. He is one of those who can read and write, and has thought much on the Commonwealth. But Captain Kett will find the truth of it.'

'I hope so.' I turned back to the puppet play, which was almost at an end. Left alone in their empty house, the landowner and his wife argued about what they would do. The man said, 'Wife, the days of your fine clothes are over. You must sell them all, dress like the wife of a poor drover.' The wife shrieked, and then the puppeteer did an amazing thing. He upended the puppet, pulling her clothes over her head to reveal that underneath was another set, woven to represent poor, torn rags. But the biggest surprise was that under her dress was a second head, exactly the same, so that in an instant the fine lady was transformed into a ragged woman. The crowd roared and cheered. Something stirred at the back of my mind, some thought I could not quite formulate connected to the Boleyn case. But then I was distracted by Simon nudging me hard in the ribs again with a bony elbow. 'Master Shardlake, how did they do that? It was wonderful, wonderful!'

'Yes, Simon, it was,' I answered. The thought was gone.

The play was ended, all the puppets bowed. The puppeteers rose up and bowed too. Roars of applause greeted them.

The cheers were dying down when I noticed a disturbance to one side of the crowd. People were gathering round a young man who was talking animatedly. I recognized Edward Brown. Barak and I hastened over. Fearing something might have happened to Josephine, I stepped forward and grasped his arm. 'Edward, what goes on?'

He paused to take a breath. 'Our scouts in the countryside have reported a royal Herald from London riding fast for Norwich with his attendants. They are almost at Wymondham. His coming is known to the city council, who are making preparations to receive him. We have informants among the servants.'

'Does Captain Kett know?'

'I just told him.'

Someone asked, 'A Herald, not the commissioners?'

'Yes. And he's headed for Norwich, not the camp. But,' he added excitedly, 'this may be an answer to our demands. I had heard that Heralds have been sent to other camps.'

Barak's eyes narrowed. He fingered his artificial hand nervously. 'But what sort of answer?'

Chapter Fifty-three

HAVING DELIVERED HIS MESSAGE, Edward was due to return to Norwich immediately. I detained him a moment to ask how things were in the city. 'There's a bit of trouble sometimes, but nothing serious.' He grinned. 'Gentlemen getting pushed and shoved in the streets, their caps knocked off, lads baring their arses at them.'

'And how is Josephine? And little Mousy?'

'Mousy is thriving, thanks to the money you gave us.' His face fell. 'But Josephine – the troubles in the city, mild as they are, and seeing the camp here, on what the gentlemen call the frowning brow of Mousehold – they worry her. She fears any threat of violence; it brings back her childhood. I have to be away from home a lot, and she gets frightened. I do my best to take care of her.'

'I know,' I said gently.

'You look surprisingly well, sir, after what happened at the hanging.'

I laughed. 'It's strange, sleeping on bracken and moving around all day instead of sitting at a desk has improved my back. I just wish it were not so hot.'

'So do we all.' He bowed, our conversation at an end, and began running back down to Norwich.

✝

LATER THAT EVENING, men gravitated to the escarpment above Norwich, looking down at the city. But Norwich retained its usual aspect, the setting sun turning the white spire of the cathedral pink. At the guard posts reinforcements arrived, spearmen and archers. Captain Miles hastened to and fro, checking the cannon, gunpowder and gun-balls taken from the manor houses. Few slept that night, knowing that the following morning the Protector's response would be known. The general mood was optimistic, but nobody knew for certain. From our hut, Barak and I frequently heard hoof beats as messengers arrived at St Michael's Chapel.

Next day, nothing happened, though the mood in the camp was tense and messengers from the city reported the Herald was expected by the council to arrive soon. The following morning, the twenty-first of July, there was still no word of his arrival. Although we did not usually attend, Barak and I went to the Oak of Reformation with the Swardeston villagers to hear the morning sermon. Birds sang in the yellow, rustling grass and the few remaining trees.

There was a large congregation present. Conyers began the service by saying that the King's Herald was expected imminently in Norwich. Then he began his sermon. I looked at him; he was a tall, thin, serious man known for commitment both to the Commonwealth and to peace, and he had a gentleness about him, a quiet sincerity. He chose as his text the passage from St Matthew: *Behold, I am sending you out as sheep in the midst of wolves; therefore be as wise as serpents and as innocent as doves.* He said that whatever news the Herald brought, it was probable he would criticize the camp, even call us rebels, as Heralds had done in other camps and in letters; but concessions had also been made and we should consider them carefully, with calm thought. The congregation listened quietly, and at the start of this crucial day I felt a moment of calm I had not felt for years, almost as though it came from outside me. I sighed deeply, drawing a couple of curious glances.

Conyers concluded by saying that peace and reconciliation must be accompanied by justice, then led us in singing the *Te Deum* in English, followed by psalms. Simon showed again what a beautiful singing voice he had, and several in the congregation looked at him. Barak murmured, 'Shows me up.' He had the singing voice of a cat.

Then came an interruption. A young man, sweating and breathless, mounted the stage, bowed to Conyers, and whispered to him. Conyers nodded and addressed the crowd. 'The King's Herald has arrived; he is in Norwich and we have a message that after refreshment he is coming here.'

A large number of people, including Barak and me and the two boys, Natty and Simon, went to the top of the escarpment, some men walking part of the way down the hill to get a better view. But for an hour, then another, nothing happened except the church bells in Nor' wich ringing for morning service. Across at St Michael's Chapel, people kept coming in and out. Then one of the guards came over and told me Captain Kett wished to see me.

When I entered the chapel I found several men seated round the table on the old altar. William and Robert Kett and Captain Miles faced me. The others were familiar, too, though I was surprised to see them together – Michael Vowell, Toby Lockswood, old Hector John' son, Edward Brown, who must have come up again from Norwich, and, to my surprise, Peter Bone. Kett extended an arm and waved me to the table. His expression was more troubled and anxious than I had ever seen it.

'Serjeant Shardlake,' he said, 'I want your counsel.' He took a deep breath. 'As you know, the King's Herald is coming today. I have been convening meetings of people to advise me since before dawn, mostly people who know each other and can speak freely between themselves and with me; ordinary camp'men like good Peter Bone here, soldiers, administrators and men from Norwich. I realize you and Goodman Lockswood have your differences, but please forget them during this meeting and advise me honestly. The question I ask is this, how do we respond to the imminence of the Herald's visit?' He took a deep breath. I thought with a flash of anger, this was asking me to go far beyond my agreement to advise at the trials, but I could scarcely turn and walk out.

'First, though, I must tell you that yesterday evening a messenger from the Herald brought a letter from the Protector.' Kett held up a paper. 'Several East Anglian camps have also received letters. They all start as this one does, berating us for setting ourselves up in rebellion, but they have concluded with concessions – the one to Thetford seems to promise future commissioners will be appointed by local men.' There was a murmur of approval, but Kett raised a hand. 'The letter to us contains the usual strictures; the King takes it for a great indignity that we offer to deal with him as enemies holding the field – as though I had not done enough to show our loyalty to his Majesty and the Prot' estant cause.' For a moment his voice almost broke. 'But the concessions are vague, saying the commissioners will deal with enclosures, but we will have to wait until a new Parliament in October before landlords who refuse to cooperate will be forced to do so. Yet those of you with knowledge of politics'— he looked at me — 'know that Parliament consists of lords and gentlemen, who would never approve such measures. Meanwhile, he tells us to return home, and not drive him' — he looked at the letter and quoted — '"to sharper means".'

Toby Lockswood stroked his black beard. 'I've been helping coordinate information from the countryside, and there's no sign of any commissioners beyond Kent and Essex. Promises are being made there, but only on condition the campmen disperse. And in Canterbury there are rumours that a leader called Latimer is in government pay, handing out money to make the camp disperse.' Then, with fire in those blue eyes, he added, 'And we know a thousand soldiers were sent to put down the men of Oxfordshire. There are reports of a great battle, with many killed, at a place called Chipping Norton. There are to be trials, and executions.'

Miles nodded. 'The Oxfordshire rebels seem to have run amok amongst the villages. We have not; we have proclaimed our loyalty, kept the peace, and killed nobody.'

'But we have put down the landlords,' Hector Johnson interjected, 'taken their sheep and other property. How will the Protector look on that?'

'We needed to feed ourselves. And we are doing the commissioners' work for them in removing the enclosures.'

'Will the twentynine articles have reached London yet?' I asked. 'They were only sent on Wednesday.'

William Kett scratched his grey, leonine head. 'Yes, the letter refers to them. We have also sent emissaries, though have had no word from them.'

Vowell said, 'Maybe the harsh tone of the letter is meant to scare us, and the Herald will offer more.'

I took a deep breath. 'Captain Kett, as I have said before, my fear all along has been that demands for any sort of representation in organs of central government by people not of the gentleman class will be unacceptable to the Protector, and certainly the Council.'

Toby Lockswood snorted. 'There speaks a gentleman lawyer.'

Robert Kett banged a fist on the desk. 'Let Serjeant Shardlake speak his mind, without insults.'

'Thank you, Captain. That was all I had to say, save that this is the largest camp in England, and will be seen as a threat.'

Kett replied, 'Whatever the Herald says we must maintain the camp. We, too, can make a show of power.' I looked at him. Like all good leaders, he had an alternative strategy in reserve.

William Kett added, 'And if no serious concessions are made, what have people to look forward to? We've known for months it would be a poor harvest, the storm will have blown down what grow-ing crops there are. And of one thing I am certain, the great majority of people in the camp will not disperse.'

There were murmurs of agreement. Hector Johnson asked, 'If we stay, how much money have we in our treasury to buy goods in Nor-wich market?'

Kett smiled. 'Enough to keep us going for a good time.'

Johnson added, 'What if the Herald orders Codd and Aldrich to close Norwich against us? They would doubtless be happy to obey him. And we cannot rely on the countryside to feed – what is it now? – nine thousand of us for ever.'

Captain Miles sat up straight in his chair. 'The answer to that is clear, and I speak as a soldier. The Norwich walls are but parchment defences, with sections falling down. And we can easily get across the river to Bishopsgate. We could take the city in a day.'

Edward Brown added, 'Many of the watch and constables are coming over to us. As for cannon, they have only a few old pieces at the castle. And the poor of the city are with us.'

Robert Kett said, 'Nonetheless, if the city fathers are ordered to resist us, there will be bloodshed.' He hesitated. 'It may not be needed, the Herald may grant our demands – but otherwise, I agree, we must be ready to take the city. I think it is what our men will want.'

'Our bowmen will be our principal weapon,' Miles declared.

'We have some good ones already,' Johnson added.

I said, 'Remember, a Herald is a very senior man. Though the commissioners would have been better –'

'Let's face it,' Edward Brown interrupted, 'they've all vanished like smoke.'

I continued, 'His stopping first in Norwich makes sense; he would need to rest and eat. Gain intelligence on the size and mood of the camp.'

William Kett replied, 'They know that already, I am sure, from the spies they will have among us.'

I said, 'I was going to say, all hope is not yet gone.'

Miles said, 'I pray to God this can be done without blood, and that I can return to my wife and children in London. I have had word that they are being searched for, questions are being asked every-where, including the London Bishopsgate.' Then suddenly he closed his eyes, and said bitterly, 'I am a fool, I have just told you where they are. I beg you all, say not a single word of this to anyone.' For the first time, he looked distressed.

Robert Kett looked around us, 'No word of anything in today's consultations is to be repeated outside this building. Anyone who does so will be imprisoned. I thank you all for speaking freely. Do not fear, Captain Miles. All here are loyal.'

'Thank you.' He clenched his fists on the desk. 'God's death, I swore to them I would never reveal their whereabouts. Forgive me, I must be losing my senses.'

'No one will speak, sir,' Peter Bone said gently. Then, at Kett's request, everyone took an oath on the Bible to say nothing.

'Thank you,' Miles said. I could see the strain he was under. Within a day he might have to lead an invasion of Norwich.

There was a loud knock at the door. A soldier entered, his face excited. 'He's coming,' he said. 'Riding up the hill in gorgeous robes, accompanied by Codd and Aldrich and other city leaders.'

Kett rose, his face set. 'Then it is time.' He turned to the soldier. 'Tell the camp to gather at the Oak.' He looked at us. 'Captain Miles, fetch some well-armed men and take them to the crest of the hill. The rest, come with me.'

✠

We walked the short distance to the crest of the escarpment. A crowd had already gathered, and I saw Barak standing with Simon, Natty and others from Swardeston. Goodwife Everneke was there, her lips moving quietly in prayer. I joined the party. Barak said quietly, 'Now we'll know.'

A party of perhaps two dozen men on horseback were nearing the top of the steep hill. A man walked before them, in a robe embossed with the castle and lion emblem of the city, carrying a sword. Somebody laughed. 'Old Pettibone, the city sword-bearer. He'll be pissing his hose.'

Behind him rode a man in what I recognized as the uniform of a royal Herald, a brightly coloured robe of gold, red and blue, and a black cap with a peacock feather. Behind him, as they approached, I recognized Codd, Aldrich and the preacher Watson, together with others in aldermanic robes. Simon was entranced by the Herald's robe. 'It's beautiful! The colours, the gold!'

'It's the man that matters,' Natty said, ever practical.

A group of soldiers in helmets and half-armour, carrying bows and spears, came up, led by Miles. The crowd cheered. They stood a little back from the crest, but near enough for the Herald to see. Robert and William Kett moved to the front.

The party reached the top of the hill and halted before the Ketts. The Herald, a strongly built middle-aged man with a sharp, shrewd face, stood for a moment looking over the immense crowd. For almost a minute there was silence. His eyes lingered on Miles's men. Then Robert Kett stepped forward and bowed. 'Master Herald, I pray you to accompany us to the Oak of Reformation, our gathering-place, so your tidings may be read to the camp.'

The Herald hesitated a moment, then nodded imperiously. Preceded by the sword-bearer, the Ketts leading the way, we all headed for the Oak. The crowd parted to let them through, then followed behind.

At the Oak almost the whole camp seemed to have gathered, with more men in armour carrying weapons strategically placed near the front, the Hundred representatives drawn up on either side of them. 'I would dismount,' the Herald announced in a haughty tone, and one of his party brought a mounting block. He stepped onto the stage. The Norwich councillors stood below him, the sword-bearer Pettibone standing with his sword raised. The Herald's eyes roved over the crowd, then he pulled a rolled parchment from a bag on his shoulder. He declared in a mighty voice, his tone severe, 'This is the proclamation from his Majesty King Edward.' He began reading:

'Hearken all of you that be here, and you, Kett, captain of mischief' – there was a murmur of anger at that, and Robert Kett's face went first white, then an angry red – 'and as many of you as are present, give ear. Although the manner of our ancestors, and the dignity of this empire, and the majesty of the name of the King, seem to require that you, which have wickedly taken upon you arms against your country, and cast yourself into open conspiracy and rebellion, should be put to flight by sword and fire, should receive due punishment for the wickedness which you have committed – yet notwithstanding, so great is the kindness and clemency of the King's Majesty, that those whose heinous offence craves punishment, of his singular and incredible favour, he will have you preserved with safety. And therefore he commands the camp and this den of thieves, and every one of you to depart to his own house. And if you have done this wicked thing, being deceived, you have your pardon, and warrant of impunity, of all the evils you have done: but if you shall remain in your former mind, and purpose of wickedness, He will surely revenge all the hurts and the villainies that you have done, as is meet, with all severity of punishment.'

He rolled up the parchment; evidently there was nothing more; no word at all of commissioners or reforms. Some of the men fell on their knees, calling out, 'Thank God and the King's Majesty for his Grace's clemency and pity!' But the main body of the camp looked shocked and angry. There came shouts: 'What of our demands!' 'Is he a real Herald, to insult us so, or an agent of the gentlemen?'

Hundreds of eyes turned to Robert Kett. Slowly he stepped forward, until he was directly in front of the Herald, looked up at him, then turned to face the camp. He shouted, in a voice as mighty as the Herald's own: 'Kings are wont to pardon wicked persons, not innocent and just men; we for our part deserve nothing in the way of punishment, and are guilty of no crime, and therefore despise such speeches as idle and unprofitable to our business!' He turned to the crowd. 'Do not forsake me, or be fainthearted, but remember my promise that I would, if needs require, lay down my life for your sake.'

There was a chorus of cheers, all but those on their knees joining in. The Herald, evidently not expecting this response, shouted out, 'I charge you, Robert Kett, with high treason. You are a traitor, and all who take your part.' There was an angry rustling and murmuring, the men of the camp moving a step or two closer. The Herald called out, 'Master Pettibone, arrest the traitor Kett for treason.'

Pettibone looked at the Herald, aghast. He took a step towards Kett, who turned and glared at him, and immediately hundreds of men moved closer. Bows were raised. Mayor Codd spoke urgently to the Herald, 'We should leave. Now.'

'God's blood,' the Herald replied, his face purple with rage. However, he descended from the stage and joined the group from Norwich. Some of the camp-men picked up clods of earth, but Kett waved his hands to indicate they should drop them. The humiliated party remounted their horses, accompanied by cries of, 'Fuck off back to Lunnon!' 'Where are the commissioners we were promised?' Some would have pursued them, but Kett nodded at Miles, and his soldiers drew up in a line, protecting the way down to Norwich.

Then a number of camp-men stepped forward, mostly those who had bowed at the King's name, and, with guilty or defiant looks, began to follow the Herald. More followed, I think over two hundred in all. The great majority, though, remained where they were, save some who stepped forward and looked likely to attack the deserters, but Miles and his men blocked their way. William Kett shouted, 'Let them go! If they will break their oath to serve our cause, we are better without them!'

I turned to Barak. 'What will you do now?'

He looked back at me, furious. 'After that arsehole insulting Kett and this camp, refusing even to mention our requests' – his voice rose – 'after this I stay, even if it means death!' He looked at me, and added, in a sorrowful tone, 'Now's your chance, if you want to get away. I've never truly known where you stand.'

I looked at him, at Simon and Natty standing nearby, at the Ketts conferring with Captain Miles. I said, 'In truth, neither have I. But after this monstrous injustice, now I do. Kett must be devastated, but he has chosen to remain. And I stay here, in the camp, to help him.'

Barak gripped my arm and nodded. 'I knew it,' he said, and turned away, though not before I saw tears in his eyes.

Part Five

BOND MEN MADE FREE

Chapter Fifty-four

T HE VAST CONCOURSE at the Oak was ordered to disperse and return two hours later, when full plans to take Norwich on the morrow would be discussed. The mood after the Herald's proclamation was shocked, angry, simmering with violence and, at the call to action, there were loud cries of approval. 'Go back to your huts,' Kett concluded, 'and make your weapons ready.'

Barak and I walked slowly back to the Swardeston huts. Barak said, 'How could Protector Somerset be so stupid? If he had set out on purpose to enrage the camp, the arsehole couldn't have done better.'

'I know. I don't think he realized the strength of feeling in the camp, or the confidence our numbers gives.'

'If we occupy Norwich tomorrow, he may think again, and come to terms. All his forces are dispersed in putting down the western rebellion, and in Scotland.'

'By Jesu, Jack, I hope you're right.'

✝

WHEN THE CAMP MET again at the Oak, thousands were present, many now bearing bows and other weapons. The Kett brothers and Captain Miles stood on the stage, Miles in half-armour, sword at his waist. Next to him stood a serious-looking older man in a cheap doublet. Kett began to address the crowd, pausing as usual for his words to be passed back.

'This man is Master Colson, tailor of Norwich, who has been coordinating our supporters there. The poor sections of the population – perhaps a quarter, especially in the north – are with us, and will help us. The city authorities – Codd, Aldrich and the rest – are obeying the Herald's orders; they have come out in their true colours!' There was a chorus of boos and calls for their execution, which Kett allowed to proceed for a minute before raising his hands for silence and waving Colson forward. The tailor looked nervous facing the huge crowd, but Kett nodded encouragingly, and he found his voice.

'The city authorities have closed the gates, and are ramparting Bishopsgate Bridge with earth to reinforce it. They have perhaps a couple of hundred men under their orders – city constables, soldiers from the castle, servants of the great men – and are placing them to defend the walls, mainly with longbows. They have released the gentlemen prisoners from Norwich Castle, and some of their number are helping them, though many have chosen to stay where they are for fear of the common people.' This brought a chorus of boos and jeers, and I wondered what had happened to Nicholas. Colson continued, 'If you make a determined charge downhill to Bishopsgate Bridge tomorrow, we can call out that you have entered another part of the city to create a diversion. Help us end our poverty and subjection as well as your own!'

There were cheers, then Captain Miles stepped forward, looking more serious than I had ever seen him. 'Men of Mousehold!' he called. 'I wish we had had more time for training, especially with the cannon, but events have fallen out as they have, and we must act now like men and take the city lest the government send forces against us! Many of you have training in the longbow, we have spears and halberds and a few cannon, and outnumber the city forces by thousands.' He paused and looked over the crowd. 'But there will be casualties, I cannot hide that. We shall now move all the cannon to the edge of the escarpment. Tomorrow at dawn we meet there, under my command, and that of the officers appointed by the Hundreds, and' – his voice rose – 'we – take – Norwich!'

There was more cheering, louder than ever – the prospect that some would die seemed to have discouraged very few. The assembly dispersed quickly, those whom Captain Miles had been training in the use of cannon following him.

Natty and Simon approached us. Natty, his face serious, said, 'I shall fight tomorrow, I am good with the longbow. Now is the time to bring the rule of the gentlemen to an end.'

'Remember what Captain Miles told you,' I said. 'Lives will be lost.'

The boy looked at me, frowning. 'Are you saying I should not fight when I can?'

'No. Only that – a good soldier must be aware of what he might face.'

'I am. And if we lose – what have I left anyway?' He turned away.

Simon looked downcast. 'I am not to fight. I have been ordered to help bring the draught horses forward.'

'Just as well,' Natty said with amiable roughness. 'You'd only trip over your own feet.'

'That I would,' Simon agreed sadly.

I looked at Barak. He had removed the leather cover from the knife on his artificial hand and was testing its sharpness. I said, 'You're not thinking of fighting, are you?'

'No, I don't think I'd be of much use.'

I sighed. 'Did you see the sadness in Captain Kett's face earlier? He hoped this could be resolved peacefully.'

'He offered to serve as the camp's leader at Wymondham, and stay with them to the end. I think he knew it might come to this.'

'Well,' I said. 'An old hunchback like me would be of no use.' Feeling sad and ashamed, I walked away.

✟

AS SO OFTEN, I found myself drawn to the escarpment, looking down on Norwich. It was as though a part of me longed to be down there. Perhaps it was even an inner wish to be with others of my own class. I fancied I saw movement around Bishopsgate Bridge gatehouse, but it was hard to see clearly from this distance. Many others had gathered at the escarpment, looking down on the city. The remaining cannon arrived, drawn by big draught horses, and were put in place at the watching-posts. Captain Miles ran between them, ensuring that the right shot and powder was available for each gun, and the men there competent to use the great weapons.

Suddenly, I saw a flash and heard a loud boom. A moment later a waterspout erupted in the river below. I remembered the cannon I had seen at the castle. There was another boom, and a small tree fell over at the bottom of the hill. Captain Miles, nearby, laughed. 'They haven't sighted properly. Come on, let's show we can answer them! Give them a fright.'

A moment later there came a mighty roar, and smoke billowed over me as the nearest cannon fired down towards the city. The earth shook under my feet and for a second I was back four years, on the warship *Mary Rose* as it fired its mighty barrage at the French fleet just before it sank. I thought I had got over the terrible memory of that day, but at the firing of the cannon I let out an involuntary cry and crouched down, holding my hands over my head. I heard some of the men crew-ing the cannon laugh, and someone call, 'The hunchback lawyer hasn't even stomach for our own weapons!' After a few moments I got up, though I was shaking still.

For a while there was quiet, no firing from the crest or from the city, only a murmuring from the men around our cannon as soldiers guided them in their better use, while Miles darted to and fro. I did not move. From their talk, their shots had gone right over the defenders into the city. I felt a hand on my shoulder, and, looking up, saw Miles regarding me curiously. 'Are you ill, Master Shardlake?'

'No, Captain,' I replied humbly. 'I am sorry, you will think me a great coward.'

'No, sir, I am a fair judge of men and while I have seen you were in two minds about our cause, I thought you a man of good courage.'

I let out a long sigh. 'The firing of that cannon so close brought back something from my past.' I took a deep breath. 'I was on the *Mary Rose* when it sank four years ago. I survived, but many good men I knew died that day.'

Miles looked at me, astonished. 'I was at Portsmouth myself then, half the trained soldiers in England were.' His seamed face was full of curiosity. 'What on earth were you doing on the *Mary Rose*?'

'It is a long story, too long for now. Suffice to say it involved Lord Richard Rich, and that he was up to no good.'

'Rich?' He frowned. 'Word came today from Essex that the camp there has been put down, and executions have begun. Promises to the camp-men there were betrayed. The man sent to take charge there is Rich.'

'He will cut a mighty swathe,' I said bitterly.

'But not here,' Miles said determinedly. 'Here we shall turn the tide against the Council.'

'And the Protector? I fear he is behind all this.'

Miles gave me a concentrated stare. 'If he is, we shall bring him to terms. Tomorrow we take the second largest city in England.'

'How many deserted after the Herald's visit?'

'Near four hundred, I believe, mostly of the yeoman class.' He spat on the ground. 'We are better off without them.'

We looked up as another roar sounded from the city. The gun ball crashed harmlessly into the hillside. Miles laughed. 'They've little chance of reaching us from Norwich castle. And we've little chance of reaching them. But we'll show them what we're made of. I should return to your hut for now, Master Shardlake. Be of good cheer; tomorrow we shall win easily. We shall send men down at dawn to ask them to open the city to us peacefully. I doubt they will agree, but we can only try.'

✠

DURING THE NIGHT there was intermittent firing from both sides, but none from the city came anywhere near the camp. In our hut, Barak fell asleep despite the noise. I lay awake, tossing restlessly, relieved when the first birdsong signalled the approaching dawn. We rose and breakfasted quietly. Goodwife Everneke constantly fiddled with something under her dress. I realized it was a forbidden rosary. She was a Catholic.

The time came for Natty to join the forces to which he had been assigned, and for Simon to go to the horses. Barak and I shook their hands. 'Go well, all of you.' I turned away abruptly, and walked back to the escarpment, where great rows of armed men now waited. A light breeze came up from the river. Two riders passed me, carrying a large white flag, and rode downhill to Bishopsgate Bridge. The men were seeking a peaceful entry to the city.

Behind me, one of the self-appointed preachers of the camp was addressing a group of soldiers. 'Remember, men,' he called, 'that what you do is the work of the Lord, and death matters little, for He will receive you in Heaven. The evil rulers must be destroyed before His

Second Coming, which is soon now, as the Book of Revelation tells us!' He held up a Testament. 'First the end of the great men, then the end of the world, when men who did His will shall sit at His right hand, as all others roast in agony in hell for ever!'

'What about our wives and children?' someone shouted out.

'If you are of the Elect, they are of the Elect!'

I knew my Bible; he was making that up. I looked at him, wondering why – although for a time I had come to have some sympathy with the Anabaptist belief in a society no longer divided between rich and poor – something about the camp prophets repelled me. They were so-called prophets who had picked up smatterings of Anabaptist ideas, but their belief in holding goods in common was a secondary thing – what mattered was that it brought closer the Second Coming, and the Last Judgement.

I turned away, looking down towards Norwich. Our cannon were being taken down the hill by the large horses – no easy task – and I saw Simon among those cajoling the animals. On the opposite side of the river I just made out what looked like men setting up cannon on the city side of the river. Not long after, I saw the two men bearing the white flag ride up the hill again. Word was passed along that they had failed.

✝

THE HORSEMEN CONFERRED with Miles and Kett. Then Miles addressed the assembled forces. 'The city cannon have been moved to the Great Hospital fields, and trained on the approach to Bishopsgate Bridge. But we have our own cannon placed to face them. Now, let us take Norwich!'

There were cheers, and men descended the Hill in hundreds. Most were longbowmen, many in half-armour, quivers of arrows over their shoulders. Some of these were half empty, and I realized our supplies of arrows were limited. They were followed by others with halberds and spears. Old Hector Johnson, once set to watch me, gave me a wave as he passed. I felt helpless; there was nothing for me to do now but observe. Barak joined me. 'Come on,' he said. 'Let's walk down nearer the city, we can get a better view.'

'That might be dangerous.'

He shrugged, and I followed him down, stopping not far from the river to sit down on a tussock. I turned to see someone sit beside me; Goodwife Everneke, still fingering the rosary under her dress. Seeing me looking, she laid her hand over it guiltily.

'Your faith does not matter to me, goodwife,' I said gently. 'I have almost none left myself.'

'Sometimes I feel the same,' she said unexpectedly. 'You know one of our Swardeston men left in the night.'

'No.'

'Goodman Jackson, the carpenter. He did so much good work in the early days, helped build the platform at the Oak of Reformation, but to fight was too much for him.' She looked at the ranks of men still proceeding downhill. 'I thought better of him. But he has a family.'

We watched in silence. I saw our cannon set up on the riverside, firing crews forming under Miles's direction. Our bowmen faced the gatehouse, the key to the city, on the top of which I could make out the figures of the city's own bowmen. There were more standing on mounds of earth which had been built during the night on either side of Bishopsgate Bridge. Before our guns could be fully set up there was a roar from within the city, a cloud of smoke rose up, and I saw some of our men run, leaving bodies on the ground. I heard shouts from the officers, no doubt ordering the remaining men to keep their places – these were inexperienced fighters, and if they scattered, all would be lost. But the ranks held, even though a second and then a third cannon shot was fired from within the city, both mercifully landing in the river. Then our cannon fired back, aiming at the gatehouse, but the guns must have been set to aim too high, for the gunballs went over it, bring-ing a chorus of mocking cheers from the men stationed there.

The cannon fire went on for perhaps half an hour, but with untrained men on both sides little damage was done. Then, at orders from the officers, our bowmen surged onto the bridge, shooting arrows at the gatehouse defenders. Fire was also exchanged between the bowmen standing on either side of the river. I could not help but think, is Nicholas among those on the other side? Men fell from the bridge into the Wensum. Goodwife Everneke clutched my hand.

After a few minutes it was obvious we were losing. The gatehouse was too strong and well defended to be stormed. Our men fell back. A runner came panting up the hill and passed us, his face glistening with sweat. We waited and watched.

Suddenly, there was a great shout from the top of the hill. Perhaps a thousand men rushed past us down the hill, sending up clouds of dust. I realized Miles and Kett had kept back a large reserve, and were now bringing it into play. As they passed I saw there were relatively few bowmen, and many were armed only with bills and halberds; others had only pitchforks with sharpened tines and other weapons adapted from farm implements. And many, especially those at the head of the crowd, carrying banners and cheering, were achingly young, some still in their teens.

Beside me Goodwife Everneke said, 'What have we done? Will God forgive us?'

'It's what the camp wanted,' Barak answered.

The great crowd joined the men at the foot of the hill and again Bishopsgate Bridge was stormed. Then, many of the young newcomers cast off their clothes and, clutching their weapons, swam across the river, protected by a volley of arrows from our side.

This assault by overwhelming numbers was too much for the defenders. As our men reached the other side of the river they grappled with them on either side of the gatehouse, and, faced with their numbers, many defenders turned and fled. I saw others leave the gate-house, apparently at orders which I heard shouted from behind them. It puzzled me at the time. Our men were now in a position to move behind the gatehouse, and in a few minutes I saw the gates opened. There was a mighty cheer, and our men surged through. In a moment the whole mighty force was inside Norwich. They left behind perhaps fifty bodies on the ground, or floating in the river. Cheers sounded from those on the hillside, many of whom began running down to the city. I sat on the tussock a good while, then said, 'Jack, we should go down, see what has happened to Nicholas and the others.'

'I will go back to the camp,' Goodwife Everneke said wearily. 'That is my place. God knows, I have seen enough.'

Chapter Fifty-five

I WALKED SLOWLY DOWN the hill, towards Bishopsgate Bridge. The bodies in the river were floating downstream now. I looked at those on the riverbank, and on the bridge, some dozens of them; the pools of blood on the cobbles took me back to the day before I left London, when vicious Captain Drury's men had assaulted the Scotch-man. My heart was in my mouth, for I dreaded seeing Natty's among those dead white faces, or even Edward Brown's, but I did not. Most of the dead had fallen to arrow shots, though some had been literally blown apart by the cannon. I averted my eyes.

Already the upper floor of the gatehouse and the earthworks thrown up round the sides the night before had been occupied by camp-men who stood on guard, bows at the ready. The gatehouse itself was guarded by three men with halberds. We were asked our names and when I gave them, one said, 'Let them through, they were with Captain Kett at the trials.' We passed under the gatehouse and into Holme Street. More victims of the fighting, from both sides, lay dead on the street. Again all were strangers. The inn where Barak had stayed during the Assizes was open, and beer was being served to the victori-ous camp-men. 'I could do with a good drink,' Barak said feelingly.

'Not now, Jack, there are things to do.' He shrugged, but fol-lowed me.

Some wounded men were being helped in the direction of Tomb-land, and many from the camp seemed to be headed there, too, so we followed them. I wanted to discover what had happened to Nicholas most of all, but I wanted to check on Isabella Boleyn and Edward Brown and then, if I could gain permission, to visit John Boleyn and, if he was still there, Nicholas in Norwich Castle.

There was a shout of, 'Make way! Make way!' We moved quickly aside as half a dozen cannon, drawn by heavy horses, trundled along the street; the city cannon, no doubt, being taken to the heath to bolster our defences. The rear was brought up by a cart loaded with barrels, moving slowly, the driver and the men accompanying it shouting, 'Out the way, it's the city's gunpowder supply.'

'Our friends in the city must have been waiting with information about where all this was stored,' Barak said.

As we passed St Martin's Plain with its houses and gardens I saw that some men from the gentleman classes had come out to the street to find out what was happening. The camp-men moving towards Tomb-land subjected them to abuse such as none of them would have ever heard from commoners before, calling them traitors to Reformation, gilded peacocks and other, coarser names, while some of the younger camp-men bared their arses. A teenage boy ran over to a severe-looking old man in a feathered cap and snatched it, placing it on his own head, to laughter and cheers. The gentlefolk hurried back to their houses. 'We'll be coming for you later!' the boy called after them. 'We'll have you all hackled in chains!' I pulled my cheap felt hat over my head and walked on.

✝

THE GREAT SQUARE of Tombland was crowded with men, though all the houses, including the Maid's Head and Reynolds's house, had their courtyard doors firmly closed and windows shuttered, while the gates to the cathedral were also shut. Beside the cathedral gates a couple of dozen men were being treated for wounds by barber-surgeons from the city. I recognized the dark-robed figure of Dr Belys, who had looked after me so well when I had fallen from the gallows. The focus of attention, though, was on the opposite side of Tombland, where Robert Kett stood at the bottom of the steps of the house two doors up from Reynolds. I recognized, too, Alderman Augustine Steward, with his tall figure and curly white hair, standing at his door. At the foot of the steps were several well-dressed gentlemen, probably city council-lors, guarded by some men from the camp carrying halberds. As I watched, another gentleman was dragged along the cobbles and shoved into the group. There were cries from the crowd: 'Traitors!' 'Kill them as they killed our men!'

'No!' Kett shouted back. 'The gentlemen of Norwich shall stand trial at the Oak as did those from the countryside, and if found guilty they will be imprisoned!'

One of the amateur preachers shouted from the crowd, 'The Bible says, an eye for an eye and a tooth for a tooth!'

'No!' Kett roared back again. 'Christ himself said that passage from the Old Testament should not be followed! To the camp with them, we can hold them at Surrey Place till we bring them to the Oak! Not Master Steward, he is to stay behind.' Kett nodded to the armed men, who began leading the prisoners away. There was angry murmuring from some in the crowd. Kett's powers of leadership – and his knowledge of the Bible – had prevailed, but not without difficulty.

I heard my name called and turned to where the wounded men were being treated. Natty sat leaning up against the Erpingham Gate, Hector Johnson beside him; Hector was unhurt, but Natty had a nasty wound on his forearm, a piece of cloth forming a makeshift tourniquet. Both were trying to control a shuddering, weeping Simon Scambler. We crossed to them. 'Thank God,' I said. 'You are all alive. Simon, what happened? Are you injured?'

'He's gone sappy,' Hector Johnson said. 'He was only asked to help lead our horses into the city, to fetch the enemy cannon. But at the sight of the bodies he hulluped up his stomach and now he's all quavery.' He shook his head.

'I was near sick at the sight myself,' Natty said. 'But everything – everything comes to the surface with Simon.'

I bent and looked the boy in the eye. My presence seemed to calm him a little. I asked, 'What was it, Simon?'

He said, 'I never realized – people could just – come apart, like the sheep being cut up at the camp!'

I said, 'You must know it is so, that in our bodies, if not in our souls, we are built as the animals.'

He whispered, 'Always I have feared I might suddenly fall apart.'

'Good men died out there today, brave fighters,' Hector Johnson admonished him, though his tone was pitying rather than angry.

Meanwhile a group of Norwich men had come to join the crowd around Kett. He gestured to them and called on the camp-men to go with them and find all the stores of weapons in the city. As they dispersed with cheers, one young man nudged another and said, 'Look! It's Sooty Scambler. They said he'd gone to Mousehold. He's the same nonny as ever he was!'

Hector Johnson turned on them with unexpected fierceness. 'Why don't you go fuck your mothers, brats!'

I jumped slightly at a hand on my shoulder; looking up, I saw Dr Belys, staring at me with astonishment. 'Serjeant Shardlake,' he said. 'I would not have recognized you. I thought you long gone.'

I hesitated. 'I have been at the Mousehold camp.'

He looked at me, then at Barak and Hector Johnson and Natty, and fell silent.

'You are treating the wounded?' I asked.

'I have been brought here to do so,' he said, his tone indicating that he had not come willingly. He looked at Simon. 'What ails this lad?'

'The sight of the dead unmanned him,' Hector replied.

'Shock,' Dr Belys said in his matter-of-fact way. 'I can give him something to drink which will quiet him, if you wait a little.' He looked at me. 'Your bodily movements seem much changed, Serjeant Shardlake. More fluid.'

I smiled. 'Rough living seems to suit me.'

He leaned in close. 'You should be careful, sir, there is talk in Norwich of a hunchback lawyer helping Kett at the trials at the Oak of Reformation.'

'Mayor Codd and Alderman Aldrich themselves helped at the Oak.'

'No more, now the Protector has made his intentions plain through the Herald. You should leave, sir. There is your future to consider.' He turned to Natty, looking at the ugly wound in his forearm. 'You need that stitched, boy. I'll do it.' He had a little bag with him, from which he produced needle, thread and some oil. Natty clenched his jaw. I looked away, towards Kett. Most of the crowd had dispersed at Kett's behest, to look for arms. Weapons were something the camp needed, and it would be a way of focusing some of that potentially dangerous energy among the men. One group walking away from the steps was, I saw, led by Michael Vowell. He paused to speak to me. He was in high spirits. I stood up, my knees creaking.

'Master Shardlake. You have come to the city!'

'Yes. To find my friends. I saw the bodies on my way in.'

'The camp has the city poor to thank that more were not killed. At the height of the fighting they got some men to shout out, "To your weapons, the enemies are entered the city!" and half the defenders of Bishopsgate ran towards the other side of the city. That'll teach them to treat us as doddipolls, eh, lads?'

'I see some gentlemen have been taken prisoner. Do you know aught of your old master?'

Vowell lowered his voice. 'The first thing I did after entering the city was lead some men to his house. He answered the door himself — he hasn't got a new steward, and his other servants are all women, you understand. But the old bastard paid them off with gold. Not all our men are incorruptible.'

I looked over at the Maid's Head. 'I wonder whether any correspondence might have arrived for me there.'

He shrugged his broad shoulders. 'The royal Herald is shut up in there, they won't open the door, and Captain Kett's orders are he's not to be touched. But I don't think there's been any correspondence in or out of Norwich this last week. And now, we must go.' He waved an arm, and led his group away.

I looked at Simon, quieter now. Natty was enduring the stitching of his arm in silence; beads of sweat standing out on his forehead. I said, 'Goodman Johnson, when Dr Belys is finished, will you and Natty take Simon back to the camp; I think that the best place for him. Barak and I have some friends to find.'

Barak said, 'We don't know the state of affairs at the castle; maybe we should go to Edward and Josephine's first. Hopefully now he will be back at home.'

'It is further, but you're right.'

'I did well with the horses,' Simon said with a sudden, unexpected smile.

'You did, lad,' Hector Johnson said roughly. 'Never seen someone with such a gift for calming them.'

'One thing you should know,' Natty said. 'The people who hit me with an arrow were a couple of yellow-haired twins. It was those Boleyn lads, fighting with the defenders. Fortunately, the arrow that struck me, like most of the defenders', was a practice arrow for the butts, with no backward-pointing spikes to tear the flesh. I was able to pull it out. Some other of our wounded lads pulled arrows out, too, and passed them back to our archers. No one will ever say the men of Mousehold weren't brave.' His voice shook.

'No,' I agreed. 'They won't.' I took a long breath. 'I thought the twins would have made for London. So,' I said grimly, 'they are still here. They must be found.'

Chapter Fifty-six

WE WALKED DOWN past the castle. Groups of men had already broken in the doors of some gentlemen's houses, and were carrying out weapons, money and plate. Down in the poorer southern areas of Conisford Street things were quieter, the streets much as normal. I made my way into the dusty courtyard where Edward and Josephine lived; all was quiet apart from some chickens pecking at a dog-turd. I knocked on Edward and Josephine's door. Josephine opened it a crack, looking nervously out. When she saw it was us her eyes widened. 'Master Shardlake!' she said with relief.

'How are you, Josephine?' She looked tired and strained. She had been changing Mousy's cloth; the child, lying on the table, smiled at us and Josephine held her and wiped her bottom, making sure she was clean. As she did so she said, 'I have had a message Edward is coming soon. And that Captain Kett has taken Norwich.'

'He has. I saw the battle from the road down to Bishopsgate.'

'Was there much fighting?'

'Some, round the river. But all is over now. The city is taken.'

Josephine looked relieved. She sat on a chair and held Mousy on her knee. The child reached out a hand to me, and I smiled and waved at her. Josephine said, 'At least there has been no firing of the city. I remember my village in France being set on fire when I was little —' Tears rolled down her face, which she brushed away angrily. 'I know this cause is just, but I so fear blood and fire.' We were silent for a moment; I did not want to talk of the things we had seen, and after a few moments she held the baby out to me. 'Take Mousy, she wants to see you.' I took her, and she settled happily on my knee. Josephine said quietly, 'I tell Edward, I fear what may happen to her.'

I was silent, for I had no answer.

There were footsteps outside, and Edward entered. In contrast to the downtrodden figure I had first visited in June he now had a firm footstep and his stringy frame an air of strength and authority. While recent events had tested Josephine, bringing back bitter memories, they had strengthened Edward. He smiled when he saw us. 'Master Shard-lake, Jack, you are down from the camp?'

I answered, 'We came to visit the castle. Nicholas was put there and is maybe there still, and I want to see John Boleyn.'

Josephine cried out, 'Master Nicholas? Why?'

'Lies were told about him,' I replied grimly. I explained what had happened. 'I tried to speak to Captain Kett but – he had other things on his mind. Edward, might you be able to speak to him?' Mousy was tugging at the buttons on my shirt. I made a mock frown, and she gig-gled at me. 'Also, and I am sorry to ask this when you have just come home, but I wondered whether you could help me get into Norwich Castle.'

Edward nodded. 'I can get you in. Captain Kett has given me a pass that will get me anywhere in the city. Our men are guarding the castle now, but Constable Fordhill has been cooperating with us, allowing us to use his cells and some of his men as guards. We shall keep him on for now. I think he fears the gentlemen prisoners may be murdered if one of us replaces him. But Nicholas' – he looked me hard in the eye – 'if he has done wrong, he should face trial at the Oak.'

'He has not,' I said firmly.

Edward sighed. 'Well, I will see what I can do. And I will take you to the castle. Things are – unsettled – in the centre of the city. Gentlemen are fleeing with their families, and we're letting them go provided we've nothing against them and they don't take much with them.' He laughed. 'Some have fled in their undergarments so they are not recognizable as gentlemen by their rich clothes. Others – well, they need locking up, and we need supplies.' He laughed. 'I don't think they realized how the poor of Norwich hate them. We townsmen played our part today, and will do so in future. Norwich is now an extension of the camp. The Norwich gentlemen will be tried at the Oak.' He frowned. 'After this betrayal by the Protector, feelings are running high.'

Josephine said, 'Are you staying tonight, Husband?'

Edward went over to her, his face filled with genuine concern. 'Yes. But I must return to Mousehold for a meeting tomorrow morning. My love, come up to the camp with me, they are good people, I would rather you were there.'

She looked at him. 'Why? Do you feel the Protector will send an army against the city?'

He took a deep breath. 'He may, though I think it as likely, now we have taken Norwich, that the Council will change tack and meet our demands, perhaps even send the commissioners at last.'

'The commissioners!' Josephine said in sudden anger. 'They'll never come.'

Edward replied, 'Our strength – taking the second city in England so easily – means the Protector may now realize he must consider our demands. Perhaps the King will even intervene with the Protector now.'

'Do not be a fool!' Josephine said, angry again. 'King Edward is eleven, how can he make decisions on anything?'

Edward shook his head despairingly, and Mousy, who was now playing with the white hairs of my beard, looked up at her parents and began to cry. Josephine took her and soothed her, Mousy's cries turning to unhappy sobs. Josephine said quietly, reaching out an arm to her husband, 'I am sorry, I know you are working for a great cause, but I cannot face going to an armed camp when I spent my early years in one.'

I said, 'I think Edward is right, Josephine. At least until things settle down in Norwich. We have already made friends in the camp.'

'We have,' Barak agreed. 'Good people.'

Josephine put her face in her hands. 'I am sorry, Edward, but I cannot.'

He sighed, and turned to me. 'Then let us go to the castle now.' He added quietly, 'Things may get rough in the city later, with the taverns full of our men celebrating. Perhaps you should go back to the camp when we return.'

'I need to visit Boleyn's wife first. Then we will go back.'

✝

WE SET OUT FOR the castle, walking up Conisford Street to the richer houses at the top. The afternoon was well on now, the heat of the day starting to fade. The mansion of the wealthy Paston family had been broken into and a store of swords and pikes was being carried out, watched by a crowd – some cheered, others looked disapproving. A red-faced man with a bandaged arm who, like many we had passed, had already been drinking, called out, 'Come to the camp tomorrow and buy a cod's head for a penny! A cod's head for a penny!' Edward laughed.

'What does he mean?' Barak asked.

'Mayor Codd has been taken prisoner to Surrey Place!'

'Surely they won't execute him –'

'Of course not,' Edward answered impatiently. 'He'll likely be tried at the Oak. That fellow's just a totty-head – it's a joke going round.'

We turned left towards the castle. As we did so I saw a familiar figure, a large pack on his back, approaching. Peter Bone, brother of Edith Boleyn's late maid. His nut-brown hair and beard had been cut short like that of most camp-men, and his thin, handsome face wore a tired expression. I had never seen him walking before and I saw now that he did so with some difficulty, taking slow steps. Seeing me he halted, and I think would have turned away, but Edward hailed him. 'Peter! So you have come down into town.'

'I have. My poor feet made me unfit to fight.' He nodded to me. 'Master Shardlake.'

'What have you there?' Edward asked.

'My belongings,' he answered grimly. 'When I left my house the landlord kept my things, so this afternoon I went there with some friends and got them back.' He laughed. 'By God, things have changed now. The landlord huddled himself up in a corner, begging us not to kill him. We just gave him a good loud yagging, then I took all my clothes, shoes, and some family possessions. I hear the town centre is a bit wild, so I'm taking the long way round to Bishopsgate.' He hesitated. 'I am sorry if I have been uncivil, Master Shardlake. Only – when you first came to see me it brought back memories of my poor dead sisters.' Tears pricked the corners of his eyes.

'I am sorry,' I said.

He nodded, and hitched the pack on his back. 'Well, I walk slow, I must keep a-doin' if I'm to get back to the camp. Fare ye well.'

'And you,' Edward said. 'What was that about?' he asked me as Peter trudged away.

'When I came here last month, to help John Boleyn in the murder case, I asked Peter Bone about his sister who worked for Edith. I did not know both his sisters had died in the spring.'

'Ay, and without them his business failed. And years of working the treadle have given him problems with his feet, walking far pains him. But he is one who has found a new spirit of hope in the camp. And, like me, as a city man he has local knowledge which will help us with what may come. He is a decent man, honest and hard-working.'

'What may come – you mean a force sent by the government?'

'It's possible, though I believe negotiation just as likely now, as I told Josephine.' He sighed. 'Well, whatever happens, we must face it.'

'Yes. After hearing that proclamation I can do no other than sup-port Captain Kett.'

'He took his time in deciding, though,' Barak said. But he was smiling as he looked at me.

We passed a prosperous-looking house, and could hear prayers said in cultivated voices through an open window. 'Lord, deliver us from the forces of evil and darkness, from murderers and men of war . . .' Edward smiled wryly. 'The rich are pissing themselves.' I thought, but did not say, they are frightened, like Josephine. To change the subject, I asked, 'What do you think of Captain Miles? He seems a good sol-dier, but things today could have been better ordered.'

'He and the other ex-soldiers he has appointed as officers are able, but we lack weapons, which is why we are taking all we can find from the city. And training –'

'Yes. Sometimes it is easy to forget the camp has only been in exist-ence ten days.'

'Miles and Captain Kett have plans for more training. To make sure everyone who is fit learns military discipline. And to involve the city poor, in case there is street fighting next time.' He looked at me.

'Captain Kett is no fool. He believed, perhaps too much, in the sup-port of the Protector, but he had an alternative plan ready.'

'Some men may be hard to discipline. Michael Vowell, for example, do you know him?'

'He can be rowdy and seems to like the company of the more rad-ical, younger people. But, like Peter Bone and me, he has excellent knowledge of the city. He is a useful man.'

I hesitated, then asked, 'Do you know Toby Lockswood well?'

He looked at me. 'The one who accused young Nicholas?'

'Falsely. Lockswood worked with us on the Boleyn case and used his local knowledge industriously. I did all I could to accommodate him when his family fell ill; I thought he respected me, and he and Jack got on well.'

'My mistake,' Barak said darkly.

'He and Nicholas, though, were always arguing over social matters and detested each other. But – to do this to Nicholas, it is simply vicious.'

'Maybe Nicholas really did say what Lockswood reported.'

'Never! I was nearby, and can swear there were no angry words between them. Nicholas told me the accusation was false and – yes, he has too high an estimation of his gentleman status, but the one thing Nicholas has never been, ever, is a liar.'

Edward looked at me closely. 'Toby Lockswood is becoming an important man in the camp. He works tirelessly, he is literate, and his local knowledge is unsurpassed. Yes, he seems a hard and angry man. But he has just lost both parents, so perhaps it is no surprise.'

'That is no reason to take it out on Nicholas,' Barak countered.

'Yet the lad did say bad things about the camp-men before.'

'I know, but not since.'

'Yet Toby Lockswood has witnesses.'

'I was there, and I saw none. Witnesses can be perjured. As a lawyer I know that better than anyone. You have influence, Edward, I ask you to think on what I have said.'

Edward pursed his lips, considering my plea. We walked on in silence for a few minutes. Then I said, 'I understand what the camp-men hope to get out of this, reform of the abuses in the countryside. But what will Norwich gain?'

He smiled. 'Same as the country folk, teach the great ones of the city a lesson they will never forget. You know they started a poor rate at the beginning of the year, but a tiny amount? Well, I'm sure we will see that increased, for a start. And we have other grievances, about wages for example, which they will be afraid to resist now. And remember those demands Kett sent to London were drawn up before the city became really involved. Others can be sent. Do you not think the townspeople suffer as much from the rise in prices and lack of work as the country folk? And look at how we were charged money to use the Town Close. Well, we have brought down the fences.'

'Yes. Remember, like you I have seen what conditions are in London, and in Norwich they seem worse.'

We had reached the foot of the Castle Mound. Already I was tired, it had been one of the most tumultuous days in my life. I took a deep breath as we began the long ascent to the huge, square building, stand/ing stark against the cloudless blue sky.

Chapter Fifty-seven

OUTSIDE THE CASTLE I noticed the soldiers who had stood guard previously had been replaced by men from the camp, wearing the steel breastplates and round sallet helmets that served as military uniform there. The cannon which had stood outside the entrance had gone, tracks along the castle mound showing where they had been dragged down to the river. Now they were in the hands of the camp, to help resist any further attack.

Edward approached one of the guards. 'I have a pass from Captain Kett,' he said. 'This is Lawyer Shardlake from the camp and his assistant. He wishes to visit two of the prisoners. Nicholas Overton and John Boleyn.'

At the sight of the pass the man looked at him with respect. He consulted a list. 'They both be here.'

'Where are the castle soldiers?' Barak asked.

'Most fled after losing against us at Bishopsgate. Our men are in charge now. The mayor and senior aldermen are taken to Surrey Place, but some servants of the city authorities who fought against us are being held here.'

I asked, 'What about Constable Fordhill?'

'Captain Kett's made an arrangement with him. He'll stay in charge, but under his orders. We're keeping on the gaolers.'

I said, 'May I talk to the constable?' The guard looked at Edward, who nodded.

'You've gained much respect for a Lunnoner,' Barak said to him as we walked under the castle barbican.

'I've done a lot to help the camp.' Edward laughed. 'Who'd have thought that three years ago I was just steward to old Lawyer Henning?'

'Talent will out,' I said.

'If people get a chance, but precious few do. The camp has given me one.'

I looked at him seriously. 'It has. But do consider Josephine.'

He shook his head. 'I worry about her all the time. I wish I could get her and Mousy to the camp. But she won't go.'

We entered the castle. The afternoon sun was fading, and the great cavernous hall was dim, but I saw more people than before, gaolers supplemented by men with spears and halberds from the camp. Edward spoke to one of the men from the camp, and we were led up to Constable Fordhill's quarters. I remembered the previous occasion I had visited him, before the rebellion. His little son had been playing in the hallway then.

Fordhill was in his office. He exuded the same air of authority, his grey hair and beard were neatly trimmed, but he could not quite hide his anxiety. Edward bowed briefly and showed him the pass from Captain Kett. Fordhill looked at me wryly. 'So you ended up at the camp, Serjeant Shardlake?'

'I am assisting at the trials at the Oak of Reformation, ensuring legal rules are observed. This is my assistant, Jack Barak.'

'I imagine you are doing the same as me – trying to ensure some order and justice. I think the London authorities have forgotten me, I have had no orders from them so I have placed myself under the authority of Captain Kett – where, as is my duty' – he glanced at Edward – 'I try to see the prisoners are held securely and not mistreated.'

Edward answered, 'That is what we want too, Constable.'

Fordhill nodded in acknowledgement. 'So, Serjeant Shardlake, I imagine you have come to see John Boleyn.' He gave me a sharp look. 'Was anything ever discovered about how that stay of execution was mislaid?'

'No. But I think someone paid for it to be lost.'

His face became serious. 'I imagine you have come because of the attempt to poison him?'

I stared at him, taken aback. '*What?*'

Fordhill looked surprised in his turn. 'You did not know?'

'No. I came only to visit him – and also my assistant Nicholas Overton, who was held here, too. What in God's name happened?'

Fordhill sat back heavily in his chair. 'Boleyn is safe, but the man who ate the chicken delivered to him last night is dead. There is some shortage of space here now, and we put one of the senior city constables who fought against the camp to share his cell. A bullying fellow, according to Boleyn; when his food was delivered he took it from him and set about the chicken. There must have been some powerful poison in it; within two hours he was emptying his guts all over the floor, within three he was dead. His body has gone to the coroner.'

'So it was intended for Boleyn.'

'No doubt of that. Like all the parcels his wife has sent to him it was wrapped in cloth, tied with string, with a label attached in his steward Chawry's handwriting.'

'Could the parcel have been interfered with at the castle?'

'It was well tied, as most food parcels are lest the guards take their pickings.' He leaned forward. 'Boleyn denies his wife or steward could have intended him harm, and certainly Mistress Isabella has been the most conscientious of visitors. But whether any accusations are laid now rests with the coroner and, I suppose, the camp authorities.'

'Can I see him?'

'Yes, but I warn you he is much shaken.'

I took a deep breath. 'And Nicholas Overton? Where is he?'

'In a cell with some other gentlemen. Conditions there are less – comfortable – than Boleyn's new cell, but then' – he raised his eyebrows – 'young Master Overton has no application pending for a royal pardon.'

I looked at Edward. 'May Barak and I speak to Boleyn alone?'

He considered, but shook his head. 'A man has died from poisoning. I think I should be present, and this should be reported to whatever authorities Captain Kett establishes for Norwich.'

Fordhill stood, went to the door, and called in a loud military bark, 'Parker! Visitors for John Boleyn! Escort them at once!' Footsteps hurried towards us. Fordhill still had some authority – for now.

☦

JOHN BOLEYN was still in the well-appointed cell to which he had been moved after the trial. It stank to high heaven, though, with shit and vomit all over the floor, the remains of a chicken and other foodstuffs in a corner. Boleyn sat behind his desk, head in his hands. He looked up as we were shown in. He looked pale and drained of energy, and had a large purple bruise on his cheek, but there was fury in his eyes.

'Matthew.' His tone was cold. 'So, you are still with those rebel clowns? I'm told they've taken Norwich now, many unfortunate gentle-men are being brought in as prisoners.' He gestured at Edward Brown. 'Who is this?'

'The man who got me in to see you,' I answered sharply.

'And I think it best you keep a civil tongue in your head,' Edward added.

Boleyn sighed and shook his head. 'You will have heard what hap-pened yesterday?'

'Yes.' I looked at the stinking mess on the floor. 'Has nobody been to clear this up?'

Boleyn laughed bitterly. 'What do you think this is, the Maid's Head? They'll come when they feel like it.'

'What happened?' I asked.

He said in softer tones, 'Isabella is still at the inn, God bless her, and she brings me a parcel of food each day. Well tied and labelled in Chawry's hand, for she cannot write. It arrived as usual yesterday after-noon, but by then I had a fellow-prisoner, a constable. He was captured but took his fists to the camp-men, and ended up here.' His voice rose angrily. 'He was nothing more than a thug, and when my parcel arrived he grabbed it. I fought the swine, big as he was. He gave me this.' He touched his bruised cheek. Then he laughed bitterly. 'He tore open the parcel and started tearing at the chicken, telling me I could suck on the bones. But within half an hour he was screaming at the pain in his guts, then he spilled out that lot –' he inclined his head to the mess on the floor – 'and by the time I got a guard to come by shout-ing and knocking, he was dead. Whatever was in that chicken, it was powerful. And meant for me.'

'Did the parcel look as though it might have been interfered with?'

'I didn't get the chance to look at it, it was being stolen in front of my fucking eyes!' Boleyn shouted, reminding me of his temper. 'But it must have been – you're not suggesting that my wife or Chawry, the most loyal servant I ever had, did this, are you?'

I raised my hands. 'I am only trying to discover how this happened.'

'Then look to those who would like to see me dead. My neighbour, Witherington, who tried to steal my land. I hear he has been a prisoner some time, but who knows what he could have arranged through bribes and intermediaries. Or those damned sons of mine and their friends, if they are still in Norwich.'

'They are,' Barak said. 'They were seen fighting against Captain Kett's forces this morning.'

I added, 'And there is reason to believe one of their friends, John Atkinson, was involved in the murder of the locksmith's apprentice.'

'They wanted to see me hang,' Boleyn said, savagely. 'I will see them hang if they did this.'

I said, 'I will ask Constable Fordhill to arrange for your food parcels to be checked by someone in authority.' I turned to Edward. 'Will you support me in that?'

He shrugged. 'Why do you care so much about this man? He's just another landowner who thinks us brutes. I don't like his insults.'

'He is my client. Please, as a favour to me, and in the interests of justice.'

Edward sighed. 'All right, though it's not as though I haven't enough to do.'

Boleyn said angrily, 'Fordhill can't stop someone coming in and murdering me in my bed. It's chaos out there, didn't you see?'

'I have an idea there,' I said. 'John, I will leave you now, but will return soon. Edward, could you take me to visit Nicholas? Please?'

As Edward knocked on the cell door for the guard, Boleyn said pleadingly, 'Will you visit Isabella, see if she is all right?'

'Of course.'

☧

NICHOLAS WAS IN a basement cell, similar to the one John Boleyn had first occupied. The gaoler, whom I recognized from my first days visiting the castle, gave us a nasty smile as he turned the key in the lock.

'Hold your breath,' he said, 'it stinks. We haven't had time to clear the pisspots.'

He led us into a damp, smelly chamber. A guard from the camp with a club at his waist and holding a sharp-looking half-pike stood by the door, a cold look on his face. All round the walls gentlemen sat in torn finery. A few, who, I guessed, had just been brought in from the city, were talking quietly but angrily in a corner, calling the rebels the refuse of the people, ruffellers and seditioners. Others were silent, staring into space or trying to sleep, and I guessed they had been here longer. I looked for Nicholas and saw him, sitting against the wall with his hands on his knees. A fat middle-aged man leaned against him. He was very pale, his breathing laboured. To my surprise I recognized Leonard Witherington, Boleyn's feuding neighbour.

Nicholas looked up at us with surprise. 'Master Shardlake, Jack, Edward.' His voice was croaky, his hair and beard unkempt, his green eyes sunken.

'How long have I been here?' he asked. 'I lose track of time – I think I've been here a week.'

'Four days,' Barak replied.

I said, 'I am sorry I have not been to visit you before.'

Nicholas shook his head. 'Being in the camp, I thought that was strange, but this – this is truly another world.' He looked at me with sudden sharpness, lowering his voice. 'I hear Norwich has been taken, the men being brought in now are city constables and officials.'

'Yes, it was taken this morning.'

He laughed bitterly. 'When the Herald ordered the city closed the gentlemen were ordered to be released, but many were afraid of what the city poor would do to them and chose to stay here. Last night the authorities asked if I would fight with them but I pretended I was ill. I knew the numbers in the camp, and that they would win.'

'You were right,' Barak said. 'The Herald ordered the camp to disperse, but we took Norwich easily, though not without some blood-shed.'

Nicholas swallowed, then said, 'And I didn't want to be fighting the Swardeston people. Are they safe?'

'Yes, all of them.' I saw tears prick Nicholas's eyes, and he turned away. I looked at Witherington. The fat little martinet of South Brikewell who had invaded Boleyn's land was a pitiful figure now. Nicholas said, 'Don't wake him. He doesn't know where he is half the time. Keeps asking for his wife, though she died last year. Remember I feared he might have some sort of seizure? Well, he did, in the middle of shouting at the guards, just after he was brought in.' He sighed. 'I can't help feeling sorry for the old devil. Remember that day at Brikewell when he was so full of himself?'

'Yes.'

'I think he'll die soon. The prisoners aren't used to this. They're gentlemen, after all.' Nicholas gave a cracked, humourless laugh. I realized that everything he believed, everything he had based his life on, had turned to the darkest irony. Next to him, Witherington stirred and saliva drooled from the corner of his mouth.

'Have you been here all the time?' I asked Nicholas.

'Yes, I just sit on the floor, trying to sleep, but sleeping is hard, rats climb over you constantly. But awake I just – thoughts whirl around in my head, in no order.' He gave me a sudden sharp look. 'You know Toby Lockswood lied about me.'

'Of course. I have been trying to get Captain Kett's ear. But with the Herald coming, and then the attack – I am sorry, Nicholas.'

He gave that cracked laugh again. 'The world turned upsy-down.'

'I have thought of you all the time.' I pressed his hand. 'I have an idea. It may get you more comfortable quarters, and help John Boleyn. Did you know that someone tried to poison him?'

For the first time his face showed interest. 'No. Will that man never be left alone?'

'It was in the food brought to him by Isabella –'

'She would never –'

'Either it was poisoned before it got here, or at the gaol.'

'Do other prisoners get their own food brought in?' Barak asked.

'Some. We others get a horrible pottage, last year's beans mixed up with sheep entrails. Witherington hardly eats at all, I've tried spooning food into his mouth but half of it goes down his chin.' Nicholas saw Edward looking at Witherington and suddenly burst out, 'Is he not still a human being? Are we not all of one common flesh, as the Commonwealth men say?' He gave that cracked laugh again.

The mention of Commonwealth men caught the ear of the little group of newcomers in the corner. One turned and started railing at Edward. 'You dogs, you apes, you think you can lock us up here and humiliate us? The Protector and the Council will send an army now.'

One of his fellows grabbed his arm and said 'Be quiet!' but the man ranted on. 'We are the true leaders of Norwich. When we get out, we'll have you hanged from your fucking Oak, every one of you! We know your names, we know your faces!' He looked at Edward. 'And we remember your voice, London foreigner!'

Edward laughed. 'Yes, you look like you're in charge, don't you?'

The man lost all control, shouting 'Churls! Peasants! Serfs! Dogs! Thieves!' The guard came over and gave him a clout on the head with the blunt end of his pike. He cried out. 'Keep your mouth shut,' the guard said.

One of the other Norwich gentlemen said, his voice pleading, 'How long are you going to keep us here? Where are our wives and families? What are you going to do to us?'

Edward said, 'You'll all get a fair trial at the Oak of Reformation, once Captain Kett has made provision for organizing the city you closed against us with your treachery. Now shut your fucking mouth.'

The man sat back wearily.

Edward said to Nicholas, 'I am sorry, but I believe you, too, will be tried at the Oak, for what Toby Lockswood and his so-called witnesses reported you said. If you are found guilty, you'll be sent back here indefinitely.'

Nicholas looked at him. 'The rumour here is that you're going to execute people.'

'No. That we do not do.'

Nicholas said, suddenly animated, 'Then yes, take me to the Oak, let me question Lockswood and his witnesses in open session. I never said a word of what he reported, and I will show him up for the liar he is!'

'Well said,' Barak agreed. 'Edward, you remember Nicholas from before. You know he is a good man.'

I took my chance. 'Edward, I want to ask a favour. I want to get your permission, and Fordhill's, to move Nicholas in with John Boleyn. I am going to see Boleyn's wife, and ensure the parcels are properly sealed and secured before they leave her. If Nicholas can share his cell, it will give Boleyn some security against attack.' I grasped Nicholas's shoulder. 'His quarters are much better, you'll eat Isabella's food; you'll have the chance to build yourself up again.'

Edward shook his head, irritated. 'This Boleyn matter is not Captain Kett's business.'

'I am concerned for my client – you know Gerald and Barnabas Boleyn were seen among the city defenders this morning.'

'Yes, and we will find them. Our men have already closed the city gates.'

'Will you help me?'

Edward sighed. 'I will, on one condition. That, in turn, you help persuade Josephine to come to the camp with Mousy.'

I answered readily. 'Agreed.'

Chapter Fifty-eight

W E RETURNED TO Constable Fordhill, who quickly agreed to my suggestion – he did not want a prisoner for whom the Lady Elizabeth had put in a request for a pardon dead on his hands. Edward left us outside the castle, saying he had business connected with the reorganization of Norwich. I thanked him for all he had done, and promised I would visit Josephine and try to persuade her to return to the camp with us. I watched his rangy figure walk quickly away. The long summer afternoon was waning, bringing a welcoming breeze from the river, and I thought of Nicholas, trapped in that filthy place. I said to Barak, 'Poor Witherington can be dismissed as a suspect where Boleyn's poisoning is concerned.' I frowned. 'There are others.'

'Are you thinking of Daniel Chawry?'

'I think he loves Isabella, and that gives him a motive to kill John Boleyn. I wonder if I might somehow separate them, perhaps suggest Chawry goes back to Brikewell.'

'Let's see if we can find out a bit more first.'

We made our way down to the marketplace. After a day of constant activity my back was hurting and I was tired, jowered out as the Norfolk people said. A large crowd had gathered round the city cross. We walked over to see what was happening.

It was the Herald. Accompanied by a number of city councillors who, evidently, had not been arrested, he was again calling out his proclamation to a crowd of weavers, traders, masons and some camp-men. This time, however, he got only insults and mocking catcalls as he read, concluding that if the rebels did not lay down their arms and go home, they might expect 'grievous torments, bitter death, and all extremity!' Someone shouted, 'Be off! Plague take you with these idle promises of pardon!' Another called, 'Long live Robin Hood!' The audience were as angry as the Mousehold men had been, and no doubt feared the offer of pardon was a trap. Many would remember how pardons had been promised after the Northern rebellion against old King Henry's religious changes in 1536, but the end of that had been mass executions.

Despite the rowdy atmosphere, nobody actually dared touch the Herald. He turned and walked down the steps of the Town Cross, the councillors following.

I crossed the marketplace to Isabella and Chawry's inn. I was shown into the reception room. They soon appeared, both looking tired and anxious. I saw that Chawry had a long, deep cut, newly stitched, running across his forehead and into the roots of his red hair.

'Master Shardlake,' he said coldly, 'you look more like one of the rebels every day.' There was contempt in his expression; like Miles, the faithful steward had turned into someone much more assertive, though on the other side of the political divide.

'You have been injured, Goodman Chawry,' I answered civilly.

'I fought this morning against the rebels when they took the city.'

'Would you have not been better employed looking after your mistress?' I said sharply.

He met my eye. 'I did not know what the rebels might do to women of gentle class if they took Norwich.'

'So far as I know, no women have been hurt.'

'But what will happen now your friends have taken control? I hear men are being dragged off to gaol, the houses of the rich are spoiled.'

'I know only that Captain Kett intends to restore proper order to Norwich.'

Isabella turned to him. 'Daniel, cannot you see how tired Master Shardlake and poor Goodman Barak are?' She smiled, waving us to sit. 'I have been worried about you, and young Nicholas.'

I took a deep breath. 'Nicholas, I fear, is a prisoner in Norwich Castle.'

Isabella's hand flew to her mouth. 'Oh, no, the poor boy.'

Chawry said, 'Of course, he is a gentleman.'

I ignored the remark, and turning back to Isabella, told her as gently as I could about the attempt to poison her husband, adding that

I had arranged for Nicholas to be lodged with him. I watched Chawry as I spoke; he seemed as shocked by the news as Isabella.

When she recovered a little, I asked Isabella to explain, step by step, how she got food to her husband. She told me Chawry bought supplies in the market or from shops and she prepared the meal at the inn, parcelling it in linen cloth, then tying it securely before Chawry addressed it for her. A guard cut the thin rope securing it in front of him. The day before had been as usual, except that with Norwich closed against the rebels and an imminent attack expected, Chawry had been accosted while shopping by a city constable on the way back to the prison and asked to join the defence of the city, to which he had agreed. I realized, then, that he had been absent for much longer than usual.

I said, 'I think from now on you should shop together and make sure you keep the parcel close until the time comes to deliver it. Do you go to the prison together?'

'Of course,' Isabella answered. 'Do you think I would go there alone? Daniel is my rock and staff in all this terrible trouble.' She touched his arm.

He frowned at me; clearly guessing that I suspected him. He said softly to Isabella, 'I am sorry I left you to fight this morning, but I felt it my duty.'

'I know. You were only trying to protect me, as usual.' She smiled at him.

I looked between them. These two were certainly becoming close, perhaps inevitably, given the situation in which they had found themselves. But all Isabella's concern after hearing about the poisoning had been for her husband. She turned back to me. 'What will happen now? Some say the King will send an army to take back Norwich.'

'The sooner the better,' Chawry said. 'Hang them from their own front doors.'

'I do not know,' I replied, 'but I strongly recommend you both stay quiet and unnoticed, and make sure your money is well hidden. And Daniel, I warn you not to go around insulting Kett and his men; that is what started Nicholas on his path to prison.'

Chawry said to Isabella gently, 'If there is another battle, I won't fight. I promise.' She smiled and nodded. I thought, Is it possible he is the one who has been out to kill Boleyn from the start, to gain Isabella? But he would have needed accomplices, and money, to kill the lock, smith and his apprentice. And why leave Edith's body grotesquely displayed like that? Furthermore he knew nothing of the missing key. Or perhaps he had nothing to do with the earlier killings, but had decided to poison Boleyn? I remained convinced he was better away from Norwich. I asked, 'Have you heard any news from Brikewell?'

Isabella sighed. 'None.'

Chawry said, 'I imagine the house is still the wreck the twins left it in, and with everything valuable stolen by the rebels.'

Isabella had been holding back tears since she had heard of her husband's attempted poisoning, but now a couple trickled down her face. 'Everything John built up.'

Chawry laid a hand on hers. 'The land is still there; when this is over, we will return and rebuild.'

I said, 'Goodman Chawry, might it be an idea for you to go there now, so that at least someone is in charge? Begin to sort out the house?'

He looked at me, eyes narrowing. 'The estate is in the midst of rebel territory. They don't like the stewards of rich landlords. I might be taken prisoner myself.'

'With respect, it is men of the gentleman class they are targeting.'

'I should stay here. Isabella needs my protection more than ever now.'

Looking at me with her clear blue eyes, she said, 'Yes, I do. Master Shardlake, you forget that otherwise I am a woman alone. I will not consider it.'

I comforted myself with the thought that she was no fool either; if Chawry had been acting suspiciously, she would surely have noticed. Unless they were lovers, which I doubted. 'Very well,' I said. 'I will come and visit you again, and your husband, I hope soon. I will do all I can to ensure the safety of you both.'

Isabella said, 'I suppose there is no word of the pardon, in the middle of this — what are they calling it now? — this commotion time.'

'No, and I do not think we can expect any news yet.'

Chawry rose and said, 'We thank you for your help, Master Shard, lake. Let me show you out.'

Barak and I bowed farewell to Isabella and followed Chawry to the street door. I guessed he had something to say. There he looked at us and said, 'You know the idea of me going to Brikewell is nonsense, sir. Are you trying to separate me from Isabella? Do you think I tried to poison the employer I have served loyally for years?' His voice rose angrily.

'Careful, matey,' Barak said warningly.

I said, 'I have to consider all the options.'

'Then consider this,' Chawry said savagely. 'Isabella is a beautiful woman. She attracts men. I see your own interest in her. But she is devoted to John Boleyn and always has been. I desire only to protect and help her.'

I looked at him. His lips were set hard, eyes narrowed. They were hard to read, always had been. I said, 'Then she is in good hands. I will see you again soon.'

I saw contempt in his eyes. 'How much gold are the rebels paying you for your legal advice?' he asked unpleasantly.

'None.' I bowed to him and walked away, sensing his hostile eyes on my back.

✞

EVENING WAS FALLING, though candles were not yet lit in the windows. As well as visiting Josephine again, there was something else I wanted to accomplish before returning to Mousehold Heath – to speak with Jane Reynolds. Her coldness had broken in court, and again when she had given Scambler the money which probably saved his life. As we walked along Barak observed, 'Everything Chawry said sounded plausible.'

'He was away from the inn longer than usual on the day Boleyn was poisoned.'

'Isabella herself could have been involved.'

'I cannot believe she wants her husband dead.'

Barak shrugged. 'Aren't you a little moonstruck with her? Don't forget, she worked at an inn for years, and will have gained the flirting habit there. She has Chawry wrapped around her little finger.'

'I'm not moonstruck,' I answered sharply. 'Certainly not enough to suspend rational judgement, and I do believe she loves her husband.'

Barak hesitated. 'Isn't Edward right? Aren't you spending too much time and energy on the Boleyn case, given what is happening all around us?'

'I can't forget that an innocent man was poisoned to death yesterday; with Edith Boleyn, the locksmith and his apprentice, that makes four people killed.'

Our attention was drawn by shouting and cheering from the Guildhall at the top of the Market Square. I saw a crowd of men come out, carrying weapons – swords, spears, pikes and halberds – and placing them in carts. Michael Vowell was there, and he came over as I approached. He seemed a little drunk, but in good spirits.

'Master Shardlake! See what we have! A little bird told me that above the Common Council's meeting room is a false roof, hiding a store of weapons should the men of Norwich cause trouble! A fine addition to our stock, is it not?'

I looked at the weapons. 'It certainly is.'

'And another little bird told me about a stock of weapons at the City Chamberlain's house. Not just arms but gunpowder, lots of it! It is ours now!'

I smiled. 'You know a lot of little birds, Goodman Vowell.'

'Good Norwich fellows.' His chest expanded with pride. 'I have been getting to know them.'

Two well-dressed women hurried by, and one of the men loading weapons called after them, 'Come, feel some rebel's meat inside you! Show us those soft ladies' titties that have never seen the sun!'

Vowell laughed, but a soldier in charge of the work called out, in a sharp voice, 'Shut you up! No women to be molested!' The man turned back to his work, and the women hurried away. It was interesting to see that a chain of military command was clearly established now, and obeyed.

'There were some barrels of wine in the Guildhall,' Vowell said, half-apologetically. 'Some of the men have been bezzling. Have you heard? The Herald has gone.'

'I saw earlier that he got a rough reception at the Market Cross.'

His eyes narrowed as he looked east, towards the slowly setting sun. 'And now he will ride back to London, to report to the Protector. And then we shall see. Fare ye well,' he said abruptly, and walked back to the carts. A man with a bell was walking round the marketplace now, calling out loudly, 'The market reopens tomorrow for an extra day's trade, and will be open on each regular market day from now, and some extra days besides. Bring your goods, from town and country! Remember, you will have customers from the camp again!'

Chapter Fifty-nine

WE WALKED UP TO Tombland. Barak complained that we had already had one of the most testing days of our lives, and suggested we just visit Josephine and go home. But I was in obstinate mood, perhaps because he had said I was moonstruck with Isabella. Plenty of people from Mousehold and the poorer parts of Norwich were abroad, in celebratory mood, but we attracted no attention, apart from a call from someone to 'Join us fer a drink, old granfer!'

The Reynolds house was shuttered and bolted. A terrified-looking maid answered my knock, opening the door just a crack. I asked, 'Is your mistress at home? My name is Overton.' I gave Nicholas's name rather than mine, which might be known to her, and spoke in my most cultivated tones to impress her.

I knew I was taking a chance, that Gawen Reynolds might appear and make us go. But the girl said, 'She in't here. She and the master have gone to visit the Sotherton house. It's been raided, sir, those black-hearted rebels were looking for Master Leonard Sotherton, he that rode to London and came back with the Herald.' The maidservant added, 'It's not far, in St Benedict's Street off Pottergate.' Then she closed the door.

I knew the Sothertons were another of the wealthy, long-established merchant families in Norwich. I was not surprised the rebels were after Leonard. Gawen Reynolds and his wife did not strike me as the sort to visit neighbours in distress, but doubtless the rich men of the city were sticking together now.

The Sotherton house was magnificent even by the standards of the Norwich merchants; I remembered Edward Brown telling me about the vast amount of work that had gone into building the flint walls. The outer courtyard wall, flush to the street, was indeed built of flint bricks, that hardest of materials knapped with such care and detail that the whole wall was smooth as actual brick.

The courtyard door was open, the lock smashed. We crossed the courtyard and climbed the steps to the main door. This time a steward answered. He had a black eye and looked as though he had been in a fight. He seemed relieved it was only a white-haired hunchback and a one-handed man who had come. 'Yes?' he asked warily.

'I was told Mistress Gawen Reynolds is here. Might I speak with her privily? I am a lawyer, Master Overton.' Again I gave Nicholas's name.

The man looked at the suspicious contrast between my dress and accent, then sighed and opened the door. 'The rebels have been here,' he said. 'They were after master's brother. They buffeted me about.'

He told Barak to wait in the courtyard and led me along a corridor, to one of the most magnificent dining halls I had ever seen, with a high hammer-beam ceiling of beautiful proportions. Portraits and a tapestry covered the walls, and the room looked over a carefully tended knot garden. Some of the pictures hung at an odd angle, however, and several chairs had been broken. A large, decorated porcelain vase had been knocked from the long polished table and smashed. Leaning over it, trying to pick up the pieces with her bandaged hands, was Jane Reynolds, as ever wearing a black dress, and a black French hood beneath which wisps of white hair showed. The steward said, 'Master Reynolds is with Master Nicholas Sotherton. I cannot interrupt them.' From a neighbouring room I could hear raised, angry voices. I said, scarcely daring to believe my luck, 'It was Mistress Reynolds I wished to see.'

Jane Reynolds had stood up as the steward entered, introducing me as Master Overton. She stared at me with those cold, still blue eyes as I removed my cap and bowed. Her thin body held its usual rigid stiffness. She nodded to the steward to depart. She did not approach me, or ask me to sit, but put the shards of broken porcelain carefully on the table and stood beside them. 'Master Shardlake?' she asked in surprise.

'Yes, madam. I am sorry to disturb you.'

'Why did you pretend to be your young assistant?'

'I thought otherwise you might not speak to me.'

I had expected her to be angry at my deception – most gentle-women would have been furious – but she said only, 'It would be better if you left.' She cast a nervous glance at the door, behind which the argument seemed to be continuing.

'It is about your poor daughter.'

She stared at me for a long moment, then something in her stance seemed to soften a little. 'You care about what happened to her.'

'I do.'

'My husband is come to visit the Sothertons, to see what has hap-pened to them. The city is falling apart around our ears, he says.' She spoke evenly, as though she did not care. 'He brought me to visit Mis-tress Sotherton, my relative, but, as with most people, a few minutes of my silent company were enough.' For the first time I saw her smile, a bitter, crooked rictus. She continued, in the same cold, even tone. 'It is said you have joined the rebels.'

'I was taken prisoner on the road, and made to help Captain Kett with his trials. I have sought to ensure justice and mercy.'

She gave a bitter little laugh. 'Mercy? In this world? You ask too much.'

I said, 'You showed mercy to a poor boy I know, he told me the money you gave him saved him from starving. Simon Scambler.'

She nodded, though her face was expressionless again. 'Ah yes, Sooty Scambler, the boys call him; they mock him around the town.'

'Madam, Simon told me you said something to him, that echoed words you spoke in court. I remember them. "Edith, Edith, God save you, I wanted a boy – I wanted a boy!" I remember you running out of court in tears.'

She flinched slightly, and I thought she might break down, but she only stood more rigidly again, one hand playing with the broken por-celain on the table so that I feared she might cut herself. She said quietly, 'My husband wanted a boy as his heir. If that had happened, or if I had had more children, none of the evils that have followed would have happened.'

'You did not cause them, madam.'

She went on in the same monotone. 'When Edith grew up, and John Boleyn showed interest in her, my husband saw a new focus for his ambitions. It was the talk of the country then that King Henry wanted to set aside Catherine of Aragon and marry Anne Boleyn. John Boleyn's kinship was distant, but even remote kinship counts at the royal court.'

'I know, madam. I well remember the crowds of distant relatives of the great men who thronged the public spaces of Whitehall Palace in the old King's time.'

'How do you know that?' she asked, showing genuine interest for the first time.

'I worked on the Learned Council of Queen Catherine Parr, God save her soul.'

'Then you will know that to make your way at court you have to be clever, quick, know who to befriend and who to bribe. But John Boleyn was a child in that world – he never even got to meet Queen Anne, as she became. Oh, the fact that he had a connection to the Boleyns helped my husband's rise in Norwich.' She gave that bitter smile again. 'But then suddenly Queen Anne was gone, executed, and King Edward's mother Jane Seymour was Queen. My husband was much angered with John Boleyn and poor Edith.' Venom suddenly infused her voice. 'As though it were Edith's fault the King tired of Anne Boleyn and cut her head off, or that young John Boleyn was a clumsy innocent.'

'You are right, madam.'

She sighed. 'It has been said since then that the Boleyn name is cursed, and I think perhaps it is.' She fell silent, retreating inside herself again.

I took a deep breath. 'Madam, I have to ask, have you any idea who killed your daughter?'

She shook her head wearily. 'No.'

'Or know where she could have been during those nine years after she left her husband?'

'I know only that she was right to leave John Boleyn and my pestilential grandsons. Where she went – who knows, perhaps far away.' She sighed. 'It does not matter now. None of it matters.'

'Not the identity of your daughter's murderer, or John Boleyn's fate?'

'England is crumbling all around us, Master Shardlake. Well, let it.' She fell silent. Next door, the argument between Sotherton and Gawen Reynolds was getting louder. I heard Reynolds shout, 'It's only for a few more days, Nicholas! Our information from London is that an army is to be made ready in case the Herald failed, as he did.'

'Those brutes almost found my brother in his hiding place and took him! What do you think they would do to me if they found —'

There was a knock at the door and it opened, making both Jane and me jump. But it was only a servant lad, bearing candles. He bowed. 'Mistress Sotherton said to light the rooms.'

'Are all the outer doors locked?' Jane asked.

'All except the courtyard doors, those dogs smashed the lock when they broke in. I will secure it.' He went round the room, lighting candles, righting several sconces which had been knocked over. When he left, Jane asked me, 'Were many killed when the rebels attacked Norwich this morning?'

'Some dozens, I think.'

She looked out onto the garden. 'Perhaps the prophets are right, and the end of the world is nigh. Then we shall be judged. I wonder whether it will be heaven or hell for me. I remember the story of Job in the Bible; God granted him peace at last after all his trials. I hope it is the same for Edith and me.' For the first time her voice shook, and she turned her head away.

Then the door opened, and Gawen Reynolds limped in with his stick, the thin face beneath his black cap thunderous. He was followed by an expensively dressed man in his forties, with a bad cut on his cheekbone. Reynolds glared at his wife; at first he did not see me. 'Mistress Sotherton had enough of your company, Jane?' He laughed. 'This frightened rabbit won't help us any more, he's sent the steward—' He broke off, eyes widening as he finally noticed me. 'Christ's bloody nails!' he shouted. 'What in the name of the Virgin's tits are you doing here with my wife?'

'I wanted to ask a few more questions about your daughter's murder.'

Reynolds turned angrily to his wife. 'What have you been saying?'

She shrank back a step. 'Nothing, Husband. I know nothing.'

Reynolds turned back to me. 'I heard there was a hunchback

lawyer in the camp. So, it was you. I'll see you hang before this is done.'
Overcome with anger, he raised his stick and crossed the room, clearly
with the intention of striking me. Nicholas Sotherton dashed forward
and grabbed it, wresting it from the old man's hand. 'In Christ's name,
Gawen, if this man is one of Kett's people, leave him alone! You seem
to want to bring ever more trouble down on me!'

Reynolds took back the stick. He leaned on it, breathing heavily,
looking at me with hatred. But Nicholas Sotherton's reaction to Reynolds's attempt to assault me made me realize I held some power here. I
said, 'It is you that must take care, Master Reynolds. I am at Mousehold,
my task to ensure judgements are arrived at in a proper legal manner. As
for your grandsons, they will be indicted for the attempted murder of the
boy they struck at Brikewell, whose mind is gone. By me.'

Reynolds almost snarled at me, showing a set of yellow teeth.
'When the Protector sends his army to deal with you and those dogs
on Mousehold, none of you will be left to indict anybody. My friends
and I will ensure the leaders are hung from that Oak of yours, and I
shall see that includes you.'

'Fine words,' I replied, 'but who controls Norwich now? I could
soon arrange for more "visitors" to come to this house, yours, too,
though I hear you bought your way out of trouble this morning.'

At that Reynolds fell silent. Sotherton said to me, 'Sir, please leave
my house now, unless you have business with me.'

'No, I came only to speak to Mistress Reynolds, though she had
naught to tell me. I will leave gladly,' I said.

Then everyone turned at the sound of thunderous footsteps on the
staircase outside. Gerald and Barnabas Boleyn banged open the door
and strode angrily into the room. They wore rough leather jerkins, their
muscular arms bare, and each carried a long knife. They were dirty,
their yellow hair and straggly boys' beards full of grey dust, Barnabas's
scar standing out.

Sotherton closed his eyes. Gawen Reynolds set his mouth hard.
Jane retreated to the darkest corner of the room. Instinctively, I followed her.

The twins looked at Reynolds. 'What the fuck's going on, Granfer?' Gerald asked loudly. 'That fucking steward came and lifted the

floorboards in the attic, told us we had to go. Why? We're well enough hidden! They didn't find us when they came for Leonard Sotherton!'

Reynolds said in biting tones, 'Master Nicholas Sotherton has had an attack of nerves since his house has been buffeted about.'

Gerald turned to Sotherton and shouted, 'You'll get your house properly broken about, you cowardly pissing-woman, unless you give us the refuge you promised!'

'Yes,' Barnabas agreed. 'There's a few vases outside, and Venetian glassware hidden in the kitchen, I'm told – what the fuck?' He broke off, for he had seen me standing near his grandmother. The twins ignored her, but approached me, shoulder to shoulder, knives lifted. 'You!' Gerald shouted. 'You've been trying to fuck up our lives since London.' He turned to his grandfather. 'How did he find out we were here?'

'He wouldn't have done if you'd stayed quiet instead of rampaging down the stairs like wild bulls!'

Gerald asked quietly, 'Is he alone?'

'His one-armed friend is outside. The insolent dog came to talk to your grandmother, more nonsense about your father's case.'

Gerald smiled nastily. 'Then nobody will know if we kill him. Deal with the other freak outside, then cut this one up nice and slow with our knives.'

'Yes,' Barnabas agreed. 'We've a big score to settle with you, hunchback. Lend us your kitchen, Master Sotherton, the blood can be mopped up easier there. Just give us half an hour.'

'Say an hour,' Gerald said, in a quiet, considering tone that chilled me to the bone. 'We'll start with his nose, go on to the fingers and then his cock and balls, if he's got any.'

'I want to do the eyes,' Barnabas said.

'No, no, no,' Jane Reynolds said pitifully, then buried her face in her hands.

'What's matter, Grannykins?' Gerald asked in a tone of mock solicitude. 'Don't you want us to rip up the nice old hunchback?' I looked at his knife, glinting in the candlelight.

Jane collapsed slowly to her knees, burying her face in her hands. Her husband and grandsons ignored her. It was Nicholas Sotherton who stepped forward, suddenly authoritative. 'No! If you kill him, he'll be missed at the camp and those dogs will come searching for him.'

'They will,' I said, trying to keep my voice even. 'I was with a senior man from the camp earlier this afternoon, and I told him I was coming to visit Master Reynolds.' In fact, I had not told Edward, but the twins did not know that. 'And the serving woman at your grandfather's house directed me here.'

I knew Gerald and Barnabas dearly wanted to kill me, but their grandfather stepped forward, pushing Gerald's knife-hand away with his stick. I thought, Nobody else could get away with doing that. He said, regretfully, 'The hunchback's right, lads.'

'He'll say he's seen us,' Barnabas said. 'Then the rebels will be after us.'

'That won't matter if you're on the road out of Norwich, which you should have taken earlier.'

Sotherton said, 'You can hide in one of my carts of wool, the driver can get out by Ber Street Gate, say he's taking it to be finished by weavers at Wymondham.'

'It's a bit late for that,' Gerald said, looking out at the gathering dusk.

'He can say we were delayed because of the fighting. They'll let him out of the city, they are keen trade should continue in Norfolk.'

'Go on, now,' Reynolds said. 'You said you wanted to be in on the fighting – there will be an army coming soon, you can join it; once you're out of Norwich leave the cart, find some horses and head for London. And for God's sake, Barnabas, rub some ashes into that scar, it gives you away.'

'Shit!' shouted Gerald, always the less controllable one. He glared at me. 'I want to kill this cunt.'

'You'll get your chance. But now, go. At once.'

'I'll take you to the yard at the back,' Sotherton said.

Reluctantly, the boys followed him. In the doorway Barnabas turned, 'We'll get you when the army comes, have no doubt.'

I asked quietly, 'Tell me, where is John Atkinson? He helped you kill the apprentice boy Walter out at the Sandlings, didn't he?'

The twins looked at each other, then at me, in what seemed like genuine surprise. 'What the fuck are you talking about now?' Gerald asked impatiently.

'Come on,' their grandfather said, waving a hand. 'Leave. Now!'

The twins left with Reynolds and Sotherton. There were voices from the yard behind the house, then creaking, heavy wheels. I swallowed hard, remembering the cold, vicious eyes of the twins as they said what they would do to me, and realized I was shaking. I heard Jane move and saw that she was painfully rising to her feet, one bandaged hand on the table, tears streaming down her face, spots of red in her white cheeks. I moved to help her, but she waved me away with her free hand, casting her head down.

The two men returned, Sotherton mopping his brow with a handkerchief. 'There, they're gone.'

Reynolds looked at me. 'You'll forgive me if we lock you in here for an hour, just so Gerald and Barnabas have time to get away.' He smiled nastily. 'It will be an easier hour than they would have given you.' He turned to Jane. 'Come on, you. Stop snivelling, we're going home.'

The three left the room, and there was the sound of a lock turning in the door. I picked up one of the broken shards of vase from the floor. Then I sat down. I found myself shaking, for I knew that the twins would have done exactly as they said. I jumped when the door was thrown open again. The steward and two servants manhandled a cursing, struggling Barak into the room, shoved him to the floor and locked the door again.

Barak said heavily, 'So those twins got away again. They have the luck of the devil.'

'Not luck,' I said. 'Just rich contacts in the right places.'

He smiled. 'Every day you sound a little more like a camp-man.'

⚓

AN HOUR LATER, our anger ebbing only slightly, Sotherton's steward unlocked the door and showed us out of the house, suddenly as polite as though we were ordinary visitors. It was dark as we made our way to Edward and Josephine's house. Edward was there, and I told them of my visit to the Sotherton house, and stressed that they expected an army from London.

Josephine said, 'But surely now the Protector sees our strength he will negotiate with us.'

'We do not know that, Josephine. And if forces do come against us, as I heard today, it will likely be Norwich they'll aim for first. I must report everything I have learned to Captain Kett.'

She looked at Mousy, asleep in her cradle, then at her husband, who nodded. She looked at me. 'You truly think we would be safer at the camp.'

'I do.'

Her shoulders slumped wearily. 'Then we will come.'

Chapter Sixty

THE NEXT MORNING, I was wakened, as usual, by birdsong. Remembering that Edward had said Captain Kett would likely wish to speak to me about what Sotherton and Reynolds had said about an army, I rose wearily from my bed of bracken and dressed. Beside me in the hut Barak was still fast asleep.

I stepped out into yet another warm morning. In this weather it was a great relief to wear only my shirt, hose and wide hat; sometimes in court in summer, in cap, coif and robe, I felt as though I were being boiled alive.

Everyone else in the Swardeston group of huts was still asleep. I looked into Simon and Natty's hut; Simon had been given a potion by Dr Belys and had almost immediately fallen into a stupor. Between their hut and Hector Johnson's, another had been hastily erected for Josephine and Mousy. She had been very quiet travelling to the camp, holding Mousy tightly to her, but the friendly welcome given her by Goody Everneke, who seemed always happy to have someone new to mother, had relaxed her. Goody Everneke had cuddled Mousy, and given Josephine an extra helping of that evening's meal – stewed dove, no less. We owed much to that kind woman.

I washed hastily and took some bread and cheese from the hut where food was kept, eating it as I walked to St Michael's Chapel. I glanced across at the great Italianate palace of Surrey Place, where Mayor Codd and the other senior Norwich councillors were being held. The guard opened the door to me. Kett was already up and about, his wife clearing away dishes from the big table while he, his brother William, John Miles and a couple of others in half-armour stood poring over a diagram at the other end of the table. Kett smiled and waved me forward; he was in a better mood after taking Norwich. I wondered again at the relentless energy of this extraordinary man.

'Master Shardlake! God give you good morrow! I hear you were in Norwich yesterday.'

'Yes. I met old friends, and some old enemies, too.' I told him of my terrifying encounter with the twins at the Sotherton house.

'I have ordered our guards on the road to watch for them. Their friends, John Atkinson and the others, have fled the city, too.'

'Michael Vowell told me he sent some men to find his old employer Gawen Reynolds, but the men were paid off.'

William Kett frowned. 'Too much of that is happening. It is bad for discipline.'

'I know,' Miles said. 'And discipline's what we need now.' The two men with him, officers appointed by him, I guessed, murmured agreement.

Kett said, 'Indeed. Norwich must be properly organized. Yester-day I appointed Alderman Augustine Steward as acting mayor. He is aged and respected, and has agreed to act under my orders. Our supporters in the town, like Edward Brown, will be watching him carefully, as he knows. I dare say he would betray us like Mayor Codd, given the chance, but for now he will organize the city effi-ciently.' He turned to me and asked, 'Did you visit young Overton at the castle?'

'Yes. He is to be moved in with John Boleyn; an attempt was made to poison Boleyn recently.'

'I am sorry I did not have the time to discuss the boy with you earlier. I am happy to have him tried at the Oak, and allow the serious questioning of Lockswood and his witnesses, to establish the truth of what was said.' From his look I sensed he, too, had doubts about Lockswood. I would rather Nicholas had been freed, but realized Kett could not give him special treatment, so the chance to question Locks-wood and his witnesses closely was the best option available.

'Thank you, Captain Kett. I would be grateful for that in due time – but for the moment I would rather he stayed at the castle to help protect Boleyn.'

Kett inclined his head. 'As you wish.' He had no interest in John Boleyn one way or the other. He studied me. 'You look tired.'

I said, 'I found it hard going into Norwich, and seeing – well, the bodies of those killed in battle.'

'This is war now,' William Kett said soberly.

His brother added, 'Which brings me to the main thing I wished to speak to you about. I understand Gawen Reynolds and Nicholas Sotherton boasted that an army is being prepared in London.'

'They did. They seemed very confident of it.'

Miles nodded. 'Our spies say that is the gossip among the gentlemen in London. But we do not yet know the army's size, or who will lead it.'

One of the other men present said, 'I'd stake my life it will consist of the Norwich landowners who escaped, and those loyal to them. It will be organized by our enemies on the Council. Perhaps the Protector does not even know.'

William Kett nodded. 'Many in the camp are saying that. It is possible.'

'It is,' Robert agreed. 'But it was a royal Herald who came, and his message was in the King's name.'

The other man who had spoken earlier said, 'Or maybe someone in borrowed robes, impersonating the Herald, a servant of the gentle-man who read us a false message.'

'That was the dress of a royal Herald,' I said firmly. 'I have seen it on State occasions. Richly dyed, with gold thread. I should say it would be near impossible to create an exact copy in little more than a week. And to masquerade as a royal Herald would be treason.'

'The great lords of Norfolk have plenty of money, and care nothing for the law.'

Robert Kett looked at his brother. 'That is being said in the camp?'

'By some. There is disagreement.'

Robert sighed. 'Well, we must wait and watch, and do what we can to fortify Norwich. And parties are being sent out to the country-side again today to bring back more resources – we need all we can get. We expect to find more gentlemen, who will be tried at the Oak tomor-row. I shall need your help there, Master Shardlake, and Barak's. I will be too busy to preside, as will my brother, but I have appointed one of the Hundred delegates, William Doughty of North Erpingham, to preside in my place.' He sighed. 'Some of our men have been caught thieving, too, and will be tried later in the week.'

'We shall be there.' I paused, then asked, 'What is to happen to Mayor Codd and the others taken to Surrey Place?'

'They will be held there, as hostages to ensure Augustine Steward's good behaviour.'

William said, 'Mayor Codd was in a bad state, weeping and shaking and saying he was forced to obey the Herald's orders. I think it has all been too much for him.' He laughed gruffly.

Robert looked at me closely. 'Do I still have your loyalty?'

'I gave you my oath to help, Captain Kett, and after what the Herald said, have no doubt now that I am on your side.'

'Thank you.' In one of his spontaneous gestures he reached across the table and shook my hand. 'I had to ask; I know that bloodshed such as happened yesterday is not part of your familiar work.'

I sighed heavily. 'I have seen bloodshed before.'

'William and I must tell the men to concentrate fully now on military training. I am going to address them at the Oak after Master Conyers's sermon.'

'All who can fight must be trained, and fast,' Miles added.

'We should get on,' William said, 'if we are to plan the taking of Great Yarmouth and set up men along the road to Norwich to harry the coming army.'

'Of course.' Kett smiled at me again. 'Thank you, Master Shardlake.'

✝

RATHER THAN ATTEND KETT'S address, I returned to the huts in the hope of getting some more sleep. Josephine sat beside Goody Everneke, helping with her sewing, Mousy in a little basket at her feet. She rose to greet me. 'Master Shardlake, you look tired.'

'I am all right. And you?'

She smiled. 'You and Edward were right. I feel safer here. Jack is awake,' she added. 'He has had a letter from Tamasin.'

'Has he?' I went over and entered the hut. Barak was sitting there, staring gloomily into space. He looked up at me. 'What news from St Michael's Chapel?'

'Codd and the Norwich gentlemen are to be held in Surrey Place. Kett is to address the men on preparations for training. They hope to set up diversionary forces on the road to Norwich, and take Great Yarmouth.'

Barak nodded, picking at a loose thread on his shirt. 'I've had a letter from Tammy. Jesu knows how it got here from London, sheer chance, according to the man who brought it up from the Blue Boar Inn. She never got my last letter. I'll show it to you; come, let's get out of this fug.'

We left the hut and walked a little way off. He pulled a letter from his shirt, handing it to me. It was dated 19 July, four days before, and its tone was desperate.

Husband,

It is over a month since I heard from you last; I do not know if you are even alive. I have made enquiries everywhere. I even went to Master Shardlake's house, but his steward has heard nothing of him since he went to Norfolk. I went to the house of Mistress Beatrice Kenzy, whose daughter you told me Nicholas was courting. Mistress Kenzy's mother treated me with great haughtiness, but said they had heard nothing from Nicholas. All in London know of the rebellions across the country, and that the trouble in Norfolk is bad. I pray you are not a prisoner of the rebels. Goodwife Marris and I have had a hard time, vittles grow ever more expensive. The city is under martial law, and full of soldiers — people say an army is to be prepared to march against Norfolk now, as well as those sent to Devon and Oxfordshire. There are Italian mercenaries here, dressed like peacocks. They cry obscenities after women, and the constables do naught to stop them. Four rebel leaders from Essex and Kent are to be executed as traitors in three days, and the King is to ride through London. There are rumours of the very end of the world.

I beg you, Husband, if you are alive, please write. I want nothing in the world but to see you again. The children constantly ask where you are, and I cannot comfort them.

Guy has written this for me again since you know my lettering is not good. He himself is a little better, and sends his wishes and prayers.

Your loving wife,
Tamasin

Barak sat on a little knoll, his head down. 'I am ashamed,' he said. 'So much of what brought me here was my resentment against her. Now I realize I have left her alone and desperate.' He shook his head. 'But I have given my oath to Captain Kett.'

I sat beside him. 'You can write back. I can ask Captain Kett if he can do his best to ensure your letter gets through.'

'Thank you. But in this chaos there is no certainty.'

I laid a hand on his. 'It is hard for you, yet I am glad in a way. I always knew you still loved Tamasin, that there was a way back for you both.'

He looked me, his eyes narrowing suddenly. He said slowly, 'I cannot leave, but you could. It's easy, the eastern side of the camp is too large to be policed.'

I shook my head. 'I, too, have given my oath. Besides, I realize now how little I have to return to.' I smiled. 'Well, at least my steward Goodcole and his family have not run off with the silver.'

'If you got home, you could tell Tamasin I am safe,' he pressed.

'Is that all you are thinking of?' I asked, suddenly angry.

He looked at me. 'No. I have been thinking about what might happen to you if the rebels lose. Consider your future. You are widely known to have helped Captain Kett.'

'Only to dispense justice, and it is also known that I have been responsible for some gentlemen being set free for lack of evidence. I have done less to help the camp than Codd or Aldrich.'

'They turned their coats when the Herald arrived.'

I smiled and spread my hands. 'They were in Norwich. I was in the camp, I had no such option. Or so I can argue.'

Barak looked at me seriously. 'A good lawyer's argument. But imagine what Lord Chancellor Rich may make of it. And do you think the Lady Elizabeth would protect you then? You have heard nothing more from her or Master Parry, though if any letters got through, it would be from them. They will be keeping quiet.'

'You may be right. But I have made my stand. I shall not move.'

'Then you are even more stubborn than I.'

'Perhaps. But consider Tamasin's letter. She talks of leaders of the Kent and Essex Rebellion being executed —'

'Which means the camps there have been put down —'

'It shows the Protector's strategy is what one would expect with a rebellion — execute the leaders but give the small fry pardons. There are hundreds of small fry. Mayor Codd is small fry. So am I. So are you.'

He looked at me seriously. 'That may be the strategy elsewhere, but it could be a lot rougher here. Remember the Herald's message and promise of vengeance. Think what has been done to the rulers of the countryside and of Norwich these last two weeks. Imagine what they will do to everyone here if they find themselves in charge once again.'

'And if I leave, what becomes of Nicholas, and John Boleyn?'

'I'm tired of hearing about Boleyn — but Nick, yes, you must see him safe.' Barak rubbed his hand across his forehead. 'I'm sorry, I don't know what I was thinking. That arsehole Toby Lockswood — how about I have a private ten minutes with him?'

I smiled. 'Better not.'

We sat in silence for a while. Then I said, 'What happened at the Sotherton house yesterday while you were outside has set me wondering again about who murdered Edith Boleyn, and the locksmith and his apprentice.'

He grunted. 'My money is still on the twins. They're insane. And that John Atkinson, who Natty's friend recognized at the beach, he's a friend of theirs.'

I shook my head. 'I haven't forgotten the expression on their faces when we had that fight in Norwich. Their absolute denial that they would kill their mother. I believed them. And when I accused them again yesterday they honestly seemed not to know what I was talking about. And they are not born actors. I think their hatred for their father stems partly from their belief that he killed their mother. And Atkinson — he and his friends are just swords for hire.'

'Do you think Boleyn's neighbour old Witherington is off the list?'

'Yes. I saw him in the prison. Someone who fell apart as easily as he has would not have the strength of body or mind to organize three murders. I always thought so. But then there are Sir Richard Southwell and John Flowerdew, who both seem to have a strange interest in Boleyn's land. But they are far away.'

'And Boleyn's estate – it's not that big – the stakes have always seemed too low to commit such a very public murder. Then follow it with others.'

'Yes. One with all the marks of a passionate hatred.'

'What about old Gawen Reynolds?' Barak asked. 'He seems to encourage the twins in their outrages. He could have paid someone to kill his daughter.'

'But why?'

'Hatred? He's full of it.'

I shook my head. 'He couldn't have involved Southwell's young thugs. According to Michael Vowell, Reynolds and Southwell had a quarrel years ago and hate each other. Reynolds also tried to stop the twins mixing with Sotherton's people, but he couldn't control them. And he himself is old, and frail, and with Vowell gone there are only women left in the household.' I frowned. 'And Jane Reynolds, poor creature, had nothing new to tell me yesterday. Though I still think Peter Bone knows something, perhaps something his late sister told him – but he won't tell.'

Barak said, 'There are still Isabella and Daniel Chawry to con-sider. If they are lovers they have a motive for trying to kill Boleyn – and the opportunity. Or if Chawry is in love with her and she still loves her husband, which seems more likely, he has a motive to get Boleyn executed for murder. And as that didn't work, to murder him instead.'

'I don't see him having the money to pay for help in organizing four killings. And whoever did it certainly had help.'

'He had the money to pay for someone to provide the poison, given the money Isabella got from Boleyn. Maybe we're looking at two sep-arate crimes.'

'Chawry has denied any designs on Isabella.'

Barak laughed scoffingly. 'For what that's worth. And even with-out Chawry, Isabella had one powerful motive to kill Edith if she came back – with Edith alive her marriage was invalid.' He looked at me steadily. 'And she has a strong spirit.'

I shook my head. 'I cannot believe it of her. But, you're right, she has to be a suspect.' Barak's eyes had sparked with interest again; I had managed to distract him. 'Well,' I said, 'the twins are gone now, as are Southwell and Flowerdew. But we can keep an eye on the Reynolds household, Chawry and Isabella, too. And it will be interesting to see how Nicholas gets on with John Boleyn.'

Barak raised his eyebrows. 'John Boleyn could still be guilty of Edith's murder himself, of course. And could even have directed the murder of the locksmith and his apprentice from prison.'

'I know. The trail starts with her disappearance nine years ago. Someone held her prisoner, or hid her, probably far from Norwich.' I frowned, for the memory of the puppet play came back – the landlord's wife, the puppet woman turned upside down. There was some connec⁄tion to all this, but it eluded me still.

'What is it?' Barak asked.

'Nothing – I don't know – I am still so tired.'

In the distance, rows of armed men were being led away by officers and Hundred representatives, probably to the less populous parts of the camp to train. Many of the men had metal sallet caps and body armour, no doubt brought up from the town. Barak said, 'Captain Kett should see Tammy's letter, he may not know Italian mercenaries have been employed. If I write back now, will you ask him to try and make sure my letter reaches Tamasin?'

I put a hand on his shoulder. 'Yes.'

He returned to the hut. In the distance more men marched away in order, bearing bows and pikes. An army was forming.

Chapter Sixty-one

T HE ATMOSPHERE IN the camp that week was very different from the one before; then there had been games and shows, gorg-ing of food, the celebration of freedom. But now, despite the victory in Norwich, there was the threat of an army to be sent against the rebels, and the need to train, fast. That afternoon I went to St Michael's Chapel again and asked to see Captain Kett, but the guard said he was unlikely to return till evening. I left Tamasin's letter with him, saying there was a reference to Italian mercenaries gathering in London. Then I returned to my hut and slept awhile before returning to the chapel as the sun was going down. The longest days of summer were over, dusk coming a little earlier each day. There was a line of people outside the chapel, waiting to see Kett. I joined the queue, and in due course my turn came.

Kett was in a serious mood, and looked careworn. 'Master Shard-lake!' he said. 'Thank you for passing on that letter.'

'I thought I should.'

He nodded, studying me. 'We shall not be holding any trials tomor-row. They can wait a day or two.' He unfolded Tamasin's letter. 'This confirms word we have had that mercenaries are to be sent against us.'

I handed over the reply Barak had written. 'Barak asks if this might be sent to his wife somehow. It says only that he is alive and well.'

'I will do what I can, but it is hard to get anything through now. And meanwhile' – he riffled among the documents on his desk and gave me a signed paper – 'a pass, giving you access to the castle and anywhere you wish in Norwich.'

'Thank you, Captain Kett.'

'It will make it easier to see John Boleyn and young Overton.'

'I saw many heading down to the town this afternoon.'

'Yes. Norwich market will be open again tomorrow. The men are still paid regularly from the money we have under close guard at Surrey Place. Talking of that, have you any money left yourself?'

I shrugged. 'A half-sovereign. I can get by.'

As I returned to the Swardeston huts, I thought – Kett's Treasury, Kett's Court, it was becoming like a state within a state. I remembered what Barak had said about the risks to my future. They were real enough; but I had made my stand, and I shrugged off my worries. After all, who on Mousehold knew what their future might be?

✤

THERE WAS LESS paperwork now, and the next day Barak was sent to where most of the captured cannons were kept. Both the cannons themselves and the gunballs they fired needed to be checked over closely, to ensure the gunballs for each were exactly the right size. New gunballs were also being made by members of the former Norwich stonemasons' guild, who had come to the camp in some numbers, and Barak's job was to check their working hours for payment, and itemize the different sizes of gunballs for Captain Miles and his gunners, mostly other ex-soldiers, to check. Left alone, I decided to seek out Toby Lockswood and try to reason with him. Edward had said he was becoming an important man, and indeed, for most of the day I was told he was closeted in St Michael's Chapel, but late in the afternoon I found him in his hut – an ordinary dwelling like the others, attached to another village group. He was washing himself, using a pail half full of water. He had a solid body, thick dark hair covering his chest. Like most of us his hair and beard had been cut short because of the risk of lice, making his round face look severe. He narrowed his eyes as I approached. 'Master Shardlake.'

'Toby. Might we have a word?'

He towelled himself with his shirt, then put it on. 'What have we to discuss?'

'It grieves me still to recall how we all worked so closely last month, and now Nicholas is in prison, because of you. His views are far from yours, far from mine, come to that. But that's no reason to punish him.'

Toby nodded. 'That's exactly why you and Barak have joined the camp, while Overton is in prison.'

'There is more to it than politics; you took a personal dislike to him.'

'I hate him and all his type.'

'But is it fair to use the power you have now to pursue a personal vendetta? Is not your judgement perhaps warped by the grief you feel for your poor parents? That is something I can understand, I have lost my parents, and others close to me as well. But one must separate grief from judgement.'

'Must one?' He mocked my accent. 'Is not judgement about revenge, as can be seen on any hanging-day?' He leaned forward. 'Do you remember my master in London, Aymeric Copuldyke?'

'I do. My own employer, Thomas Parry, told me at the start of all this that your abilities greatly exceeded his.'

'Remember how he mocked me at our first meeting, my social status and Norfolk accent? I worked for that lazy fat slug for ten years. Jack Sauce, I called him behind his back. He knows far less law than I do.'

'That I believe.'

'So I have no love for those who rule the common people, nor any belief in their ability to rule at all. Look how well this camp is organ-ized by ordinary people.'

'I agree with you,' I said impatiently. 'But that does not justify bear-ing false witness against Nicholas Overton out of spite, which I believe is what you have done.'

His full mouth narrowed unpleasantly. 'Master Shardlake, you cannot expect me to discuss a legal matter in which you have an inter-est. By the way, I understand you are keeping Overton in Norwich Castle, rather than bringing him to open trial.'

'I have my own reasons for that, which Captain Kett knows. But there will be a hearing at the Oak, when you and your witnesses will be questioned. Be careful you do not make yourself look like a man motivated by vengeance before Robert Kett a second time.'

Lockswood's face reddened with fury. I turned on my heel and walked away. I hoped that whatever position he held in the camp did not involve command of men, for he was the type who would have favourites – and victims.

☩

OVER THE NEXT FEW days, serious training was carried out under Captain Miles and the officers – mostly ex-soldiers – whom he appointed. Men went willingly, from what I could see, to the training grounds. The booming of cannon firing practice shots often resounded over the camp.

Bad news, though, soon reached us. A camp at Hingham, fifteen miles away, intended to harry the flanks of an approaching army, was attacked by forces under Sir Edmund Knyvett of Buckenham Castle, a bulwark which had held out against the rebels. The castle was too strong for the small force to counter-attack, and they returned to Mouse-hold. A few days later, on Sunday, 28 July, we learned that the camp at Downham, near King's Lynn, had been taken by the local gentry. The sight of defeated men from Downham drifting in to the camp lowered the general mood, which was already anxious now. The army was expected, though many still disputed it had been sent by Protector Somerset at all and it was rumoured to be composed merely of Norfolk gentry and their retainers.

☩

ON THE FOLLOWING DAY, Monday, there were more trials at the Oak. I had been assisting Representative William Doughty to pass judgement on some gentlemen brought in from the countryside, and a dozen thieves who were, save one, found guilty and expelled from the camp. They were few, given the numbers here, but I found it depress-ing. I suspected many would make their way down to Norwich and become beggars there. By the time the proceedings were over the morn-ing was advancing.

At that moment a messenger arrived and summoned me to see Captain Kett. I followed him to St Michael's, walking past the rows of clerks – fewer now – and up to his large table. Captain Miles sat with him. Both gave me penetrating looks.

'Master Shardlake,' Kett said, 'I understand that during the old king's reign you worked for Queen Catherine Parr.'

'I did.'

'Did you ever meet her brother, Sir William Parr, now Marquess of Northampton?'

'Once.'

Miles asked, 'Could you describe him?'

'A thin man, average height, with pointed features and auburn hair and beard. He would be in his late thirties now.'

Miles and Kett exchanged glances. 'Then it's him,' Kett said, 'not someone from the Norfolk gentry using his name.' He turned back to me. 'The army is on its way, and the man you describe is its com-mander. The deputy commander is young Lord Sheffield, a local man of no good reputation.'

Miles asked, 'What would you say of Parr's ability to command men?'

I took a deep breath. 'He rose to the Council only because he was the late queen's brother. He is not stupid, but – not greatly intelligent either: his skills were as a courtier. I do not think he has military experience.'

Miles turned to Kett. 'By God, they must be short of experienced commanders.' He looked at me sharply. 'Would you call him your friend?'

'No. As I said, I met him just once. My only loyalty was to Queen Catherine, and she is dead.'

Kett steepled his fingers. 'Northampton's army is approaching Norfolk, we expect it in perhaps three days. Fortune may have smiled on us. There are indeed Italian mercenaries among them, but no more than three hundred in an army of one thousand five hundred, and they are not as feared as their Swiss and German counterparts. We have over five thousand men ready for battle, as well as the poor citizens of Norwich, who are well organized now, and ready for street fighting. Your friends Edward Brown, as well as Michael Vowell and Toby Lockswood, have done fine work preparing them.'

Miles continued soberly. 'There will be bloodshed, no doubt of that, but I believe we can win. There are many Norfolk gentlemen returning with the army – Sir Richard Southwell, Sir Thomas Paston and others, as well as men of the court, all with their own retainers. Few experienced soldiers.' He gave a bark of laughter. 'I've seen it before, in France and Scotland; they assume that just because you're an aristocrat you can fight.'

I thought, So Southwell is returning. That probably meant his associates as well, like John Atkinson. And I had little doubt the twins would return too, for the fight. Flowerdew, on the other hand, I suspected would remain safe in London or whatever other bolthole he had found.

Miles asked Kett, 'Any news of the Lady Mary?'

'She remains closeted at Kenninghall. Food is allowed to reach her, in accordance with our agreement with Southwell.' He smiled wryly. 'I very much doubt the Protector knows of that arrangement.'

Miles said, 'Southwell maybe dead in a few days, along with many others.'

Kett turned to me. 'You and Barak are to remain in the camp.'

'I fear I would be of little use, but Barak would fight if he could.'

Kett looked round at his officers. 'Do what you can to encourage morale. A good fighting spirit must be fostered. If we defeat this army, the news will resound through the country like a tocsin!'

✟

THAT AFTERNOON I RETURNED to Norwich. Men from the city and the camp were shoring up the walls and reinforcing the gates. At the castle I found Nicholas and Boleyn playing chess. Like everyone else, they knew of the coming army. Nicholas looked better now he had decent food – the two always checked Isabella's food packages carefully to make sure that they had not been interfered with. Then I visited Chawry and Isabella – I told her that in view of the coming battle it might be safer to leave the city, but Isabella refused steadfastly to leave her husband, and Chawry said that in that case he, too, would stay.

In the early evening, Barak and I went for a walk through the camp. We needed something to take our minds off the fact that, according to Kett's scouts, Northampton's army was expected to reach Norwich on the morrow or the following day. At breakfast that morning the Swardeston villagers had greeted us warmly; we were accepted now, and Nicholas diplomatically forgotten. Josephine was there with Edward. She looked cast down again, no doubt worried about the approaching battle. Edward would probably be in the fighting. Mousy let me pick her up. Josephine smiled, and Simon clapped his hands.

'Off with the horses again today?' I asked him.

Hector Johnson replied. 'Ay, they'll be putting him in charge of them before we know where we are,' The old man was clad in half-armour and sallet helmet; appointed an officer, he was involved in the training. I looked at Natty, who had arrows slung over his shoulder and his longbow at his feet. 'I can shoot five arrows a minute now,' he said proudly. Goody Everneke looked at him, and I wondered whether, like me, she was wondering how many would survive the coming battle.

☫

BARAK AND I WALKED east, to the further reaches of the camp. Horses and cattle were penned in now by wooden fencing – how much work the carpenters had done! – while sheep were contained by the landowners' old hurdles, although now they were kept for meat, not wool, as were the chickens and ducks, geese and doves we also passed. In the horses' paddock men were improving their riding skills, Simon Scambler among them. Among the groups of huts, each with its parish banner, pigs rooted. Yet the smell of the camp was not as bad as it might have been, for cleanliness was still rigorously enforced, especially where cesspits were concerned. There had been no signs of disease. We passed a bakery – and the foundry, turning out spears and halberds. Carts were still coming in from the villages with supplies, but fewer now – we were in the weeks before harvest, the leanest time of the year. Kett had done well to ensure the reopening of the Norwich market so goods could be bought.

We must have walked three miles, reaching the fringes of the populated area. Here, where there was more space, military training was still going on, for all that the sun was setting. We saw a line of fifty bowmen, who, at a shouted order from an officer, sent a rain of arrows hissing through the air. Elsewhere men were charging with half-pikes at straw figures set in the ground, yelling ferociously. Others followed, hacking at them with home-made spears and halberds.

'They're doing well,' Barak said. 'Miles and the experienced gunners under him are also doing a fine job of ensuring our cannon will work.'

'They have still had so little time for training.'

A little way off an officer was addressing a group of longbowmen. To one side Hector Johnson stood, leaning on a halberd. We approached him. 'How're ye diddlin'?' he asked. I remembered how he had been set to guard me on the march from Wymondham. But he trusted me now, and was always friendly.

The officer was telling the bowmen that the coming army was full of their old enemies the landlords, aided by Italian mercenaries. 'Foreigners who kill for money, with loyalty to none, but they will be unable to resist stout Englishmen fighting for their homes!' he shouted. The men cheered, but Johnson smiled cynically. 'There are English mercenaries, too,' he said. 'Veterans of the French campaign. Stayed in Europe and fought for whoever would pay them – and for much higher wages than the old king paid.'

'People are the same everywhere,' I observed.

'That they are.'

We bade him farewell and returned the way we had come. I saw a group of about forty, mostly older folk who could not fight and some women, gathered around one of the bearded prophets. He stood on a box, Testament in one hand, waving the other fervently at his audience.

'This time was prophesied in the Book of Kings, where Josiah, King of the Jews, a most righteous ruler, came to the throne aged eight and put down idols, removed pagan images, and saw God truly worshipped. Now in King Edward we have a second Josiah, who is removing the last vestiges of popery and who seeks true equality among men to establish the righteous kingdom the Bible says will be with us before Christ's second coming.' He paused, beating his fist on his chest in a dramatic gesture, while most of the audience cheered wildly.

✞

THAT NIGHT THERE WAS an argument around the cooking fire amidst the Swardeston huts. We had dined well, and had drunk well, too, for although Kett did everything to discourage heavy drinking, a barrel of strong beer had been obtained and by the time night fell on the company most men, including Barak, were the worse for wear. The only exceptions were myself – my father had been a tippler and I had sworn as a youth only ever to drink moderately – and Simon Scambler, who still cleaved to his church's belief that drink was sinful. We had been joined by Michael Vowell, whom I had met walking from the meeting at Kett's Castle, looking tired, and invited to join us. Master Dickon, who had argued for the prosecution of the Swardeston landlord and who was the leader of the village group, was half asleep, head on his chest. Edward Brown was in Norwich, but Josephine sat next to Barak and me. Mousy was asleep in her hut. The other young woman in our camp sat leaning against her husband, and next to them sat three other men who would be fighting when the army came; a blacksmith, a tanner and a labourer, all drinking from mugs which periodically they refreshed from the barrel. Goody Everneke had gone to bed.

Talk turned to the Herald. One of the men said firmly that he had not been a real Herald, but an agent of the landlords, and it was they who had created this army. The Protector, in his opinion, knew nothing about it.

Dickon raised his head. 'That must be true. Captain Kett has sought to support the Protector from the beginning.'

The blacksmith, a strongly built, square-faced man in his thirties named Milford, shook his head. 'Master Shardlake, did you not say the man wore a real Herald's uniform?'

'Yes. And from his description the leader of the army is undoubtedly the Marquess of Northampton.'

Milford, the blacksmith, looked at me suspiciously. 'You *know* the enemy leader?'

'I met him once, as I told Captain Kett. It is no secret I used to work for his sister, the late Queen Catherine. I thought you trusted me by now,' I concluded sadly.

Milford was in an aggressive mood. 'I see you don't keep up with us drink for drink.'

'They say lawyers can't hold their drink,' another said.

Barak pointed to the knife on his artificial hand. 'Watch your mouth,' he said.

Michael Vowell stepped in. 'Leave Master Shardlake alone! Surely he's done enough to show himself our friend. And you've all had too much beer. You've lost the point. Which is that the Protector has betrayed us, and we must force the great ones of the realm into submis-sion, not rely on him to do it for us. Defeat this army, then secure all Norfolk and spread out across England, bring those defeated camps back into existence.'

'That's right,' Natty agreed emphatically.

'And start killing some of the gentlemen we have in custody, as a warning!' Milford said.

'I didn't say that,' Vowell answered quickly.

Hector Johnson spoke firmly. 'Captain Kett is against killing them.'

Milford stood up. 'Kett – Kett – Kett – it's all we ever hear! Don't you see, his notion of working with the Protector has failed! The com-missions have gone, the other camps are being bribed or threatened or pulled down by force!'

Master Dickon, who was not as drunk as he seemed, stood up. 'Don't you criticize Captain Kett, bor! Look at what he's done – led us here, brought justice to all, taken Norwich itself. He didn't have to, he could have stayed at home with his family!'

Josephine said, 'Please stop this, it does no good.' Nobody paid any attention and she went to her hut where Mousy, disturbed by the noise, had begun crying.

One of the other men stood, swaying slightly on his feet. 'We will win the battle to come! We have the men, we have the resolution, and behind us, if not the Protector, we have the King, as I heard a prophet say today! Captain Kett is too soft, Milford is right – we should have some executions as a warning!'

Hector Johnson approached him, his hand on the knife at his belt. 'Shut your clack-box! You forget you're part of an army, and under orders. Perhaps you need reminding!'

'I'll give you fucking orders,' Milford said, his hand going swiftly to his own belt.

Simon Scambler stood up, wringing his hands. 'Please! We should all be friends! We should all work together!'

Milford turned on him. 'Shut up, freak! I heard a story about your antics from one of the Norwich lads.' Like many men, too much drink had put him in a vicious mood. He went on, 'Sooty they call you, you wander about singing. Well, go on then, give us a song!'

Simon looked at him a moment, and I thought he would burst into tears. But then he stood up, walked a little away from the fire, and slowly began to sing. It was a song I had heard before, an old German one, 'Jerusalem'. It should have been accompanied by a lute, but Simon's clear, beautiful voice was enough to stop the argument in its tracks. I see him singing now, his head outlined against the stars and the half-moon, sparks from the campfires twirling up to the dark sky:

My life will change utterly
since my sinful eyes saw
this noble land so much admired
so that I live in a noble way.
What I most wanted has come to pass,
I have come to that land
where God walked in the form of man.

Beautiful, rich and noble land
such as I have never yet seen,
Are you, above all the lands I have known.
What wonders have occurred here!
A maid bore a child,
Lord over all the host of angels,
Was that not a wonder indeed?

As the song ended there was silence, then Hector Johnson began to clap, and others followed. Simon stood blinking, surprised and delighted.

'I'm going to bed,' Milford said grumpily. One after another, everyone went to their huts.

Natty came and clapped Simon's shoulder. 'You saved the day, bor.'

'So you did,' I agreed.

Simon smiled, a smile of wonder, as though he had indeed seen Jerusalem. Barak shook his head. 'The sooner this army comes, the better, there's nothing worse than waiting.'

'I don't think we'll have to wait long,' I answered quietly.

Chapter Sixty-two

I T WAS TUESDAY, 30 July. Scouts reported that Northampton's forces would arrive at Norwich the next morning. The weather had turned close again, thick and humid, as Barak and I joined the crowd assembled under the Oak to hear the Kett brothers and Captain Miles address the camp. Those who would fight tomorrow were drawn up in ranks under their officers, bowmen and spearmen and cannoneers – the cannon were to be dragged down the hill today and set to face Bishopsgate Bridge.

William Kett spoke first, of the mighty blow they would strike. 'Think how far we have come since Wymondham only three weeks ago! Those sent against us include our old enemies, the gentry, men like Paston and Southwell –' At this name, there was a chorus of boos, and someone shouted out that his papist mistress the Lady Mary should be dragged from her lair at Kenninghall. William ignored this and called out, 'Where is that other great crooked official, John Flowerdew? Hiding in London! He is wiser than his fellows, and realizes this force can never, never beat us!'

He was followed by Robert, at his most persuasive and charismatic, gesturing with his arms, his face and short grey beard soon bathed with sweat he did not trouble to wipe away. 'They called us traitors! But *they* are the traitors, for we have always been loyal to King Edward!' He paused for cheers. 'Once our enemies are defeated, our wrongs will be righted. Never forget those wrongs! We shall have, by his Majesty's grace, permanent commissions to remedy abuses, in which we will have a say!'

There were more cheers and clapping, although I noticed that some men, again mostly the poorer and younger ones, responded half-heartedly. Kett wiped his brow and gestured to John Miles. 'Now our good Captain Miles will speak of our strategy.'

Miles stepped to the front of the platform. His face under a crested morion helmet was set and determined, his words clear and sharp. 'Men of Mousehold, our spies in Northampton's camp tell us he plans to occupy Norwich first before assaulting us. That is good, we can trap him there, harry him and then attack across the river at Bishopsgate Bridge! He has made a blunder, he would have been more sensible to attack the heath first, even though we have the advantage of high ground. I will not hide from you that he has some skilled commanders with him as well as the dross of the Norfolk gentry, and Italian mercenaries who dress like popinjays but are good fighters. But we have the men, over five thousand of you ready, and the weapons and cannon in which some of you are now trained. We outnumber them over three to one. Above all we have our cause! So go you, train again today, for tomorrow we fight!'

Loud cheers rose from the ranks, Natty and Hector Johnson among them. The speeches over, Barak and I turned to leave but Kett called to me in a sharp voice. 'Serjeant Shardlake! Please, follow me to my headquarters.' I exchanged a puzzled look with Barak, then headed to the chapel. Others were making their way there, too — Michael Vowell, Hector Johnson, Edward Brown, Peter Bone — and Toby Lockswood, who studiously avoided my gaze, as well as the Kett brothers themselves and John Miles. Everyone, I remembered, who had been in that consultation with Kett before Norwich was taken.

When Kett arrived at the old chapel, he bade us all follow him to his table. He drew the thick curtain separating it from the clerks at work in the body of the hall, and told everyone to sit.

Kett studied our faces, then said, 'Captain Miles's wife and children have been captured, at their refuge with friends in the London Bishopsgate district, and taken to prison. A rider from the Council brought the news yesterday, giving details of where they had been found. He offered Captain Miles amnesty on condition he surrender himself immediately.'

Miles raised his head. His expression was drawn now, pale under his tan. He said, 'I refused. When first I left London, my dear wife said that that is what I must do if they were found.'

Kett banged his fist on the table. 'And the only mention of their whereabouts was accidentally made by Captain Miles at one of the meetings I held before the Herald came, when you' – he raked us with his gaze, one by one – 'were the only ones present!'

There was a moment's silence, then Toby Lockswood said, 'It could have been spies in London who found them. Did the rider say otherwise?'

'No. But some suspicion must naturally fall on all of you. Did anyone tell any other person about John Miles's wife?' He looked at me. 'Your friend Barak?'

'I have spoken no word to him, nor anyone else.'

'Nor I,' Michael Vowell said. 'What would I gain by it?'

Hector Johnson said, his voice shaking slightly, 'I, too, have said nothing. I have been loyal from the start. I risked my life in the taking of Norwich. You know that, Captain Kett.'

Toby Lockswood looked at me. 'Master Shardlake is the only one present from the gentleman classes, who might have a stake in our defeat.'

Kett banged the table again. 'As my brother and I are the only one of the yeoman class sitting here, you might as well say! But you're right, Lockswood, the betrayal could have come from London.' He looked at us all again. 'But be aware that until that question is resolved you are all under suspicion.' Nobody stirred. Kett said, 'Get about your duties. Master Shardlake, there are some trials of thieves to be held. Please join Master Doughty at the Oak of Reformation. I want these out of the way before the battle.'

We left St Michael's Chapel in silence, tears flowing down Hector Johnson's face at the thought he was under suspicion.

✝

I WALKED TO THE OAK, eyes cast down, deeply troubled that I should be suspected. It was typical of Toby Lockswood to take the chance to dig at me, and I was glad Kett had put him in his place. If it was one of us, then who? Not the Kett brothers, and surely not old Hector Johnson. And all the others – Edward Brown, Michael

Vowell, and, to do him credit, Toby Lockswood, had been devoted to our cause from the beginning. I knew less of Peter Bone, but from the first time I met him he had been a strong Commonwealth sympathizer. It occurred to me, as it had before, that after his double bereavement Toby Lockswood might not be fully in his right mind. But his devotion to the cause had only intensified since then – I could not see him selling out for money. I thought, I will probably be watched again, but I still had naught to hide.

I found that morning's work under the Oak depressing, not helped by having to wear my robe in the heat and humidity. The sky was a uniform grey; another storm coming. More thieves where found guilty, others had their cases dismissed for lack of evidence. There were some brawlers, too, nearly all younger men, who were sentenced to expulsion from the camp. Afterwards, as we walked away from the Oak, Doughty told me he had been made captain of a company for tomorrow's battle; like many of the Hundred representatives he had had a share in organizing the regular official musters in his area, which were organized by Hundreds. 'I shall send a few fine gentleman to their reward in hell,' he said. I was surprised by his fierceness, but he continued, 'They decided to attack us, when all we want is peace and justice. Let them pay the price.'

✝

I walked back to the huts for lunch. All the Swardeston men had gone for training, and only Mistress Everneke, Barak, Josephine and Mousy sat outside their huts, fanning themselves with pieces of bark. Josephine told me Edward had gone into Norwich; to prepare their allies in the city, no doubt. She said she needed to go to the jakes, and asked me to hold Mousy. The little girl was fractious in the sweaty heat, and struggled against me. She began to grizzle, but stopped as I held her close. Josephine returned and took her back. She looked weary. 'Are you all right?' I asked.

'Yes.' She smiled sadly. 'It looks as though I was right to leave Norwich, doesn't it?'

'We thought so.'

'Yes.' She looked me in the eye. 'But what if we lose, and they come here from the city afterwards?'

✝

To try and settle my troubled spirits, after lunch I went for a walk, despite the heat. I went to where Simon and several others were training the horses, trying to settle the more fractious of them. So awk-ward otherwise, he rode a horse, as he sang, as though born to it. I stood leaning on the heavy wooden fence surrounding the paddock. He rode up and brought his mount to a halt. 'You are doing well, Simon,' I said. 'Will you be taking the horses down to Norwich?'

'Yes, we will be using them to take more cannon downhill this afternoon, and I will be helping with them later as required.' He swal-lowed, and I saw deep anxiety in his eyes.

'You will be all right, I am sure.'

'I fear –' he began, then stopped.

'More bloodshed?'

'If I am killed – I cannot help thinking, what if all my aunt's church said is true, and I am sent to hell for my denial of true religion?'

I said quietly, 'When I was growing up, we still had the old Catholic faith, and believe it or not, for a little while I believed I had a vocation. Then all the changes came, and under King Henry we were ordered to believe one thing one year, another the next. And now we have the Protestant radicals. Why should your aunt's church have the truth of it any more than any of the others?' I smiled. 'And you have led a charitable life. That still counts for something, I believe.' I reached up and laid a hand on his arm. 'No one is less deserving of hell than you, if hell there is.'

'Thank you, Master Shardlake,' he said quietly. 'I will try to remember that.'

✝

I walked slowly back to the huts. On my way I passed men dig-ging a fresh cesspit, and to my surprise I saw that, once again, Peter Bone was among them.

He looked up. His eyes narrowed for a moment. 'God give you

good afternoon, Serjeant Shardlake. As you see, I am on digging duty again.' His tone was friendly enough but with, I sensed again, a certain reserve: he was, like me, now a suspect of Miles's betrayal, so perhaps that was unsurprising.

'I would have thought you would be training, either here or in Norwich.'

'I have bad feet,' he said. 'So I stay here and dig.' He wiped his brow.

'You will be safer, at least,' I said. 'And the digging is useful; we have had none of the flux in the camp.'

He looked at me. 'Perhaps, but I would rather fight. I would not mind dying. With my sisters gone, and my trade, I have little to live for.' He looked at me with sudden anger. 'Perhaps if we win, the Protector will agree to the changes we all want. Then there will be hope.'

'Yes, perhaps.'

He turned away and resumed his digging.

Chapter Sixty-three

NEXT MORNING, the last day of July, the weather had still not broken, though the sky remained grey, and the damp heat even greater. I stayed in camp with Barak, who said part of him wished he had been allowed to fight, throughout that day and the next, and hence – with one gruesome exception – my knowledge of the battle that followed came at second hand. That first morning, at the Oak of Reformation and elsewhere in the camp, Holy Communion was administered under the new English rite to those due to fight that day, by Reverend Conyers and the scattering of other clergymen in the camp. I had been drawn to Conyers before; I little doubted the trouble he would face when his superiors knew he was giving Communion before battle to the Mousehold men. And as he now gave Communion to a long line of men who knew they might not survive the day, it was his gentleness, his quiet sincerity, which struck me. Among those waiting in line I saw Natty and Hector Johnson. Barak had stayed away, for he had always wanted as little as possible to do with religion.

It was a long time since I had taken Communion myself, and never under the new rite. When I had done so in the last years of the old king's reign, it had been through political expediency, to show good conformity. Yet now my mind went back, past the days when I had been a Lutheran radical, to when I was a child, a firm believer like everyone then in the old Catholic religion. I remembered the time, which then had felt so special and pure, when I received the wafer, the body of Christ, and, for a moment, felt a mystical union with God. I surprised myself at these memories; I thought such feelings long gone after the terrible things I had seen done since in the name of God, both by Protestants and Catholics. And then I crossed the ground, beaten flat by many feet, and joined the line. Having done so, I felt for a moment ashamed, that I did not belong here among these men facing death, but I stayed.

My turn came, and Reverend Conyers gave me the bread and wine, saying as I took it, 'The body of our Lord Jesus Christ which was given for thee, preserve thy body and soul to everlasting life. The blood of our Lord Jesus Christ which was shed for thee, preserve thy body and soul to everlasting life.' Once again, I felt something strange, mystical, a unity with something beyond. I looked into Conyers's face; he nodded and gave me an unexpectedly sweet smile. Then I moved away. What I had felt momentarily was gone, though something, like an aftertaste, remained.

☦

I WALKED TO THE crest of the hill, where a number of older men and women, together with the wounded from the taking of Norwich, had also gathered. Barak was there, but not Josephine; he told me she was in her hut with Mousy, trying to distract herself from thoughts of what might happen to Edward. Hundreds of men armed with spears, halberds and bows appeared and began descending the steep hill. I saw one group led by Hector Johnson. Then came the mounted cannon, the horses steadying the gun carriages from behind while in front men eased the guns across the iron-hard ruts. Simon was among those guiding the horses. A group of horsemen with pikes followed. Then, with set, serious faces, rode Robert and William Kett, to loud cheers, and John Miles. More and more men followed, near a thousand. At the bottom of the hill everyone gathered in formation on our side of the river, waiting.

We stayed there all day. Still nothing happened, and for a while I even dozed off. Josephine came, carrying Mousy, and woke me up, but when I told her I had seen nothing she went away again. A little later Barak nudged me awake and we saw a strange thing – Mayor Codd on horseback, accompanied by some of our men, riding downhill as fast as they could, then crossing Bishopsgate Bridge and entering the city.

☦

I LEARNED WHAT had happened in Norwich from Edward Brown, that evening – he came back quickly to see Josephine before returning to the city. He told us the story outside his hut, his arm around his wife, Mousy asleep in Josephine's arms.

'I slipped back into Norwich last night where the northern wall is crumbling. All our men were gathered in the abandoned gentry houses. We waited all night and all morning. Then at noon, from a church tower, we saw the army approaching. Fifteen hundred armed men, a fearsome sight, I must admit. I believe it was about that number they sent to fight the Oxfordshire rebels. They stopped about a mile outside Norwich, then sent a man dressed in golden robes, a few others accompanying him, forward to St Stephen's Gate.'

'Another Herald?' I asked.

'It was. Then there was a to-ing and fro-ing that went on till mid-afternoon. Apparently the Herald demanded that the city surrender, but Augustine Steward, who came to meet him, said the surrender agreement would have to come from Mayor Codd.'

'I thought he was locked up in Surrey Place, poor half-silly man,' Josephine said.

'So he was, but he was taken down to Norwich to agree the surrender.' Edward smiled. 'They were playing into our hands, that's just what we wanted, Northampton's army shut up in the city as the light began to fail.'

'We saw Codd go down the hill,' Barak said. 'We wondered what was happening.'

'He agreed to surrender, then Augustine Steward went out and delivered the city sword of state to Northampton – a skinny little red-headed man, the young Earl of Sheffield beside him with his nose in the air, though I heard he disfigured a woman once, a relative's lover, so he'd have no more to do with her. Anyway, the whole army rode in. I saw several hundred of those Italians, dressed more for a festival than a battle, brightly coloured doublets slashed to show the lining, big morion helmets with peacock feathers. But their horsemanship, in close formation, was impressive.' His voice became contemptuous. 'And then all the great landowners of Norwich followed; Sir John Clere, Sir Henry Bedingfeld, Sir Richard Southwell.'

'Southwell?' I asked. So he had indeed come.

'Well, he's close to the Council, isn't he, and just about the biggest man in Norfolk now the old duke's gone. He carried the sword of state into the city before Northampton.'

I remembered Southwell that day at St Michael's Chapel, being told by Kett of the deal Southwell had done to protect the Lady Mary and his own estates. Southwell would not want that story to get out. Yet he had the cold courage to return with the army.

'There was no resistance from the citizens?' Barak asked.

'No. Northampton and the other leaders went to Augustine Stew- ard's house to dine, they and their horses were jowered out, riding from London in this heat. As for the resistance – that's coming soon.' He hugged Mousy, whom he had taken from Josephine, and turned to his wife. 'I must return now, my love. But do not worry, all is well planned.'

He left after dining with us round the fire. Josephine took Mousy back to their hut, saying heavily that she would put her to bed and try to sleep herself. Barak, too, was tired, and I returned alone to my watching-post in the early dusk. There, half an hour later, I witnessed the only episode of savage violence which, so far as I know, ever took place in the Mousehold camp. Hearing a scrimmage behind me, and a voice shouting angrily in a foreign language, I turned to see a burly young man in exactly the apparel Edward Brown had described – a brightly coloured doublet and a helmet decorated with peacock feathers – being dragged along by half a dozen camp-men in breast- plates and helmets, armed with spears. One was bleeding from the face, another from his arm, which was bound with a cloth tourniquet. Their expressions were savage. I joined a crowd drawn by the noise.

'Look at this fucker we found,' a young, fair-haired fellow called out.

A woman asked, puzzled, 'Who is he? A juggler or something?'

'Is he shit!' the young man replied contemptuously. 'A dozen of us were scouting along the north side of the city, when we found a little group of these Italian bastards. We saw them off and took this one. They're not the great fighters they're said to be.' The prisoner let out an angry stream of Italian, for which he received a sharp prick from a spear. 'Stop winnicking!' The spearman pulled off the Italian's helmet, pulling out the feathers. 'This'll do me, gives more protection than that old sallet helmet.'

'Strip him bare!' the yellow-haired man said. 'Their leader's called Malatesta, they say that means bad balls. Let's see what his are like!' There was laughter from his friends, and from some in the crowd, as the Italian's rich clothes were torn off and thrown to the ground, his sweat-stained linen undergarments following until he stood there stark naked, his powerful body heavily marked with scars from past engage-ments. He put his hands over his private parts but two men forced his arms away and looked between his legs. 'Just an ordinary old cock'n' danglers,' one said, disappointed.

Mistress Everneke had joined the crowd and cried out, 'For shame!'

'Shut your mouth, old beldame, or you'll get a culp you won't forget,' the man with the bleeding arm shouted at her. He pointed to his wound. 'See what he did to me!' I looked round anxiously, hoping some figure of authority would be drawn to the scene.

'What are you going to do with him?' someone asked. 'Put him in Surrey Place?'

The straw-haired man grinned nastily. 'No, we're going to hang him from the walls!' Grinning at the Italian, he drew the shape of a noose with his hands. The mercenary's eyes widened.

One of the man's comrades looked doubtful. 'We'll get in trouble!'

The yellow-haired man turned on him. 'How many good Norfik men have these bastards killed? Don't go quavery-mavery on us, young Jimmur!'

An old man shouted from the crowd, 'Captain Kett will be angry. We lock enemies up, not kill them.'

I was reluctant to interfere, afraid of the boiling violence of the Italian's captors. Nonetheless, I forced myself to step forward. 'That man was right. Captain Kett has instructed captives should be held prisoner, not killed.'

The man with the bleeding arm shouted, 'I know who you are, you're the fucking hunchback lawyer that got my friend Silas kicked out of camp for theft, you're another gemmun for all you're dressed no better than us now. So you favour him, do you, this fucking foreigner come here to kill us for money?'

'Captain Kett will be angry.'

'Captain Kett's not here,' one of the men answered brutally. 'Hang the bastard!'

They led their prisoner away. A man darted out and stole the Italian's shoes, another his torn doublet and hose, while a soldier took his steel breastplate. I could do nothing but follow and watch as the man was led, struggling, to Surrey Place. He and his captors disappeared behind the high walls. Some minutes passed and then the men reappeared, standing on top of the wall. The Italian now had a rope round his neck. The other end was tied to one of the decorative stone figures on the wall, and the naked man was thrown from the top, the noose tightening and breaking his neck at once. It all happened very fast. There were cheers from those who had come to watch. Mistress Everneke said to me, 'Is this what war does to men?'

'Some men,' I answered. I looked downhill, where our men were lighting campfires now. Far in the distance, there was a faint roll of thunder.

Chapter Sixty-four

A FTER WHAT I HAD seen I could not sleep that night. I sat on a little grassy mound some way down the hill, looking down on Norwich. It was a dark night, cloud covering the half-moon and the stars. Occasionally, one of our guns fired into the city, with a flash and boom. I felt far now from the moment's peace I had known at Communion that morning. I could just make out a huge bonfire which was lit, so far as I could judge, in the marketplace. And then I heard, rather than saw, the fighting that followed. There was a sudden loud bombardment of Bishopsgate Bridge from our cannon, making me jump, then distant yells as, I later learned, our men stormed across the bridge. I understood what had been planned; in the pitch-dark the men of Norwich would know the streets intimately, unlike Northampton's forces. I put my head in my hands, thinking of Simon and Natty, Hector Johnson and Edward Brown.

After a while the distant noise ceased. I waited for the summer dawn, which seemed an eternity in coming, as did the threatened storm, for I heard only other, more distant, rolls of thunder. Perhaps it would pass us by this time.

When dawn finally broke, and I looked down the hill, my heart sank. I saw our charge had failed. There was a crowd of our men at the bottom of the hill. Many of us walked down almost to them, to get a proper view. We saw wounded men being tended, and the white faces of the dead laid out on the grass. But I realized that, as with the taking of Norwich, much of our army had been kept in reserve. To the north of the city, at Pockthorpe Gate, I heard a trumpet sound, and a stream of our men descended the hill; suddenly a new bombardment came from our men, mightier than before, aimed from what I could see at the walls of the Great Hospital, which I was near enough to see col-lapse. Several thousand men then crossed the bridge and ran into the city. I was puzzled at first but then understood the purpose of the bombardment – Holme Street was hemmed in by the Norman walls of the cathedral on one side, the hospital walls on the other. It would have been easy for Northampton's army to trap us in Holme Street, but with the hospital walls down we had access to the fields beyond. People in the buildings near the hospital walls, though, would not have stood a chance unless they had been warned in advance.

I saw perhaps three thousand men – our reserve – charge down the hill and across the bridge, to be met by Northampton's forces. Many houses along Holme Street were ablaze, whether fired deliberately or accidentally I did not know. Our men advanced, and I saw the crowd move west, into St Martin's Plain, where the melee continued a long time. Around midday Northampton's forces must have given way, for suddenly I saw a great rush of men run to Tombland, then down towards the castle.

✟

LATE IN THE AFTERNOON, men began trudging back up the hill, weary and limping, faces and clothes covered in blood and dirt, drag-ging their weapons. They were fewer than I had watched descend yesterday, and at first I feared casualties were huge, but later Natty told me many men had stayed behind in Norwich with the Ketts, to secure the city and arrange for the wounded to be tended. It was from him I learned that around four hundred of our men had died, and perhaps half that number from Northampton's army, which, after losing the Battle of Palace Plain, had fled wholesale. As evening fell we sat, with many others, looking down on Norwich. Holme Street was still on fire, and I could see smaller fires elsewhere in the city. I remembered that much of Norwich had burned down thirty years before, and feared the same might happen now. Josephine had joined us with Mousy, and for the first time in days wore a contented expression, for Natty had reported that he had seen Edward, quite safe, together with Michael Vowell and Toby Lockswood, who all seemed unharmed, in a group around Robert Kett outside the cathedral. Edward had called to Natty to tell Josephine he was well, the city secured and Northampton's army fled.

Mousy had fallen asleep on my lap as Natty told us his story quietly. 'I wasn't in the first attack, the night one, that was mostly men with knowledge of the city who could go more easily through the darkened streets. Much of Northampton's army was camped in the marketplace, with a huge bonfire lit so they could at least see the entrances to the surrounding streets, the rest of his men on patrol.'

I remembered that Isabella Boleyn's and Chawry's inn gave on to the marketplace. 'What of the people in the buildings round the square?'

'They did what you'd expect – locked their doors and shuttered their windows. From what I heard, nobody there was hurt, Northampton's army was just yagged by our people in the city crying out, "To arms, to arms!" to scare them, but when we attacked them, despite the darkness in the streets favouring us, we lost many, while they had but few killed.'

While he spoke, Natty kept glancing round at Surrey Place, where the naked body of the Italian still hung. I told him what had happened to the mercenary. He shrugged. 'They killed plenty of ours.'

Josephine sighed. 'Fighting changes men, I saw it as a child in France. They become brutal.' She looked down at the fires in Norwich. 'And they burn homes, as they did my parents' village.' For a moment we were silent. Then Natty resumed his story.

'This morning we launched the main attack. First, though, friends of ours in the city told Northampton a large group of rebels was gathered at Pockthorpe Gate. We hoped he'd be fooled into sending part of his force there. He only sent a few men, though, with the Herald and his trumpeter. The sound of the trumpeter brought some of our men down from the hill – the Herald offered a pardon again if we'd disperse, but was told we weren't rebels, we were loyal to the King, they were the ones holding the laws of the realm in contempt.'

'As they are,' Josephine said.

Natty grinned. 'He got a right old telling! Then just afterwards we set off the bombardment to put down the hospital walls, and charged across Bishopsgate Bridge. That was the real battle.' His voice quiet-ened. 'Something like I've never seen. By God our men were brave; they never flagged. I heard Master Fulke killed the Earl of Sheffield in Holme Street. We battled our way to Palace Plain, the open space by St Martin's Church. Their main force was waiting there. They fired off half a dozen cannon at us, then it was a pitched battle. The Italians did better than Northampton's English troops, a lot of those had been mustered by the local landlords, they didn't have our fierceness.' He closed his fist tightly. 'It was that which won the battle for us, that and our numbers and skills with the bow – thank God we spent last week training together.'

He stopped suddenly and took a deep breath. Josephine put her hand on his shoulder, encouraging him to continue. 'It seemed to go on for hours, the slashing and striking and parrying, I saw a man's head slashed off with a sword, another got a leg cut off below the knee and went down in a heap.' He closed his eyes. 'Then Northampton's army broke and we were pursuing them through the streets. We chased them back to the marketplace, then down to the castle, and then they all ran through the gates in a mighty huddle, together with some of the rich Norwich people.' He paused. 'I killed four men today, and wounded more.'

'Do you know what happened to Simon?'

He shook his head. 'I saw him with the horses this morning, not since.'

'What of Hector Johnson, he led your troop?'

Natty closed his eyes for a moment. 'He did, and bravely, from the front. Each side aimed first for the other's officers. I saw a group of men charge Hector. They were some of Southwell's thugs, I saw the one with the big maul on his face, Atkinson, that my friend said helped dispose of that apprentice's body.' He paused. 'And I saw those twins a few times this afternoon, always together, fighting mightily, always smiling.' He took a deep breath. 'Atkinson and some others surrounded Hector Johnson. He slashed at them mightily with his sword but they got him on the ground, and – and – they hacked him to death.' He swallowed. 'That brave old man is gone. He was a real dymox.'

I looked in puzzlement at Josephine. 'A mighty fighter,' she explained, then lowered her head.

Natty put his face in his hands and began to cry. Josephine held him to her. I remembered when I had first met Hector, when he had been set to watch me on the march from Wymondham. The years of battle he had told me about, the loss of his family, the way that, in his own rough manner, he had cared for Simon in the camp. I hoped he would be buried with dignity.

✝

As we sat and watched the fires burn in the city, Josephine said, 'After this defeat, the Council will have to settle matters with us, won't they?'

'I think perhaps they will,' Barak replied. 'Unless the Protector abandons this new assault on Scotland he's got planned.'

I said, in a voice too low for Josephine to hear, 'He may do just that, and come to deal with us.'

We had paid little attention to the darkening sky. Suddenly there was a bright flash of lightning which brought several screams from the camp, followed by a mighty roll of thunder directly overhead. Then a mighty downpour, even worse than the one a fortnight before, crashed down on us: it was impossible to see more than a yard ahead. Josephine grabbed Mousy and, holding her tight, fled with Natty and Barak and I, splashing through what was already half an inch of water to the shelter of our huts. Fortunately, the ferocious downpour lasted less than an hour, though it was enough to cause much damage in the camp.

When I stepped out of my hut afterwards, the skies were clear again, a half-moon illuming the scene. The air was clear and, suddenly, cold. I splashed through puddles to the crest of the hill again. The downpour had been so heavy it had even doused the fires in Norwich, which those loyal to established authority would later take as a sign that God was on their side.

As I stood there I heard the sound of hoofbeats, voices, and heavy wheels approaching. A group of filthy, weary men were guiding heavy horses made nervous by the storm, pulling half a dozen cannon.

Among the men I saw Simon Scambler, stroking a horse though his hands trembled and tears rolled down his face. One of the men accompanying him turned to me and called triumphantly, 'The Marquess of Northampton's cannon, bor! They're ours now!'

Chapter Sixty-five

THE DEFEAT OF NORTHAMPTON'S army was the high-water mark of the rebellion. Although we had outnumbered them greatly, it was still an extraordinary feat of arms for men who, a month before, had for the most part little or no military training, to send a government army backed by foreign mercenaries fleeing from Norwich. Truly, the men of Norfolk had made themselves free.

But from that day onwards, things turned slowly against us. On the way to Norwich Northampton's army had successfully put down the camp at Thetford, and refugees from there, some wounded, trailed up to Mousehold Heath. Even the weather changed; after the great thunderstorm of 1 August, it became much colder, with cool winds from the north-west, few sunny days but much cloud and drizzle. As is the way, having complained about the heat people now grumbled about the cold and wet, but it was hard, living in those lean-to huts and working and training outside in such weather.

That first evening after the battle, and the following day, when our exhausted men needed rest more than anything else, they had once again had to clear up after a mighty thunderstorm. Fortunately, the water soaked quickly into the sandy soil. Nonetheless, many huts were flooded, and everything was soaked. Word went around that Norwich market would reopen tomorrow, Saturday, and people hoped they would be able to find dry clothes. The mood in the camp was a strange mixture of triumph and grief – around three hundred and fifty had died, over one in thirty of the camp numbers, which totalled some eight thousand now, and many people were mourning the loss of friends and relations.

For myself, I wanted above all to return to Norwich; I needed to know what had happened to Isabella and Chawry, Nicholas, and John

Boleyn. But Edward Brown, who had arrived in camp late on the evening of the battle, advised me strongly to leave it at least another day. He had come from the cathedral, where Robert Kett had set up a temporary headquarters, to spend the night with his wife. He told Barak and me that Kett was making sure that from now on his own men would hold the key positions in the city, although Augustine Steward, who had cleverly passed responsibility for Norwich's surrender to poor Mayor Codd, was to be allowed to stay in charge under Kett. Edward said many horses were also being stabled in the cathedral, and the wounded, who numbered another three hundred, were being cared for there. Bishop Rugge, apparently, was keeping quietly to his palace. Edward also told me that despite Kett's orders that only the goods of those who had actively collaborated with Northampton were to be confiscated, people were taking things into their own hands and a good deal of looting was taking place. Kett had sent men down to try and keep order. Meanwhile, there were hundreds of bodies – men and horses – to gather up and bury.

I was sitting by the campfire when Simon Scambler emerged from his hut. He wandered aimlessly around, waving his arms and singing snatches of song. A cry of 'Shut your fucking clack-box!' came from another hut. Edward said quietly, 'He saw too much again, and worse this time. I think when you go down to Norwich you should take him with you; he can help with the horses in the cathedral. Best if he keeps a-doin'.'

Josephine left her hut, drawn by the noise. She had stayed inside, guessing perhaps that Edward and I had been speaking of things she would prefer not to hear. Now, however, she came over to us, rubbing her hands on a damp apron. 'What ails Simon?' she asked.

'He was in Norwich these last two days,' Edward said. 'He saw too much fighting.' His tone was impatient. He could sympathize with Josephine's fear of blood and battle, she was a mere woman, but Simon was, after all, nearly a man.

Josephine frowned at her husband and went over to Simon. 'Here, lad,' she said. 'Sit you down. What's the matter?'

He looked at her tearfully. 'I saw such things again yesterday, men coming all apart again, the blood. And poor Hector Johnson.' Another burst of sobbing shook him.

Josephine took him in her arms. He seemed a little surprised – perhaps no one had ever hugged him before – but, after a moment, he hugged her back. 'There, lad,' she said softly. 'It's naught to be ashamed of. I saw the same in France, when I was a girl. But it's all over now.' He sobbed at her breast.

Barak's face set. He rubbed the place above his artificial hand which often hurt him. 'Over?' he said quietly. 'Is it?'

✟

FOR THE NEXT TWO DAYS I remained on Mousehold as Edward had suggested, though he himself returned to Norwich. There was no training – the soldiers realized their men needed time to rest. The sky remained grey, and the weather distinctly colder. I went for one of my walks, trying to gauge the mood. I saw the body of the Italian soldier had been taken down. People sat in their doorways, looking out at the cool, cloudy day. I stopped by a group of men sitting round a campfire. A man in his thirties was saying that he wondered how his family would fare, news from the countryside was that this would be the worst harvest for years; the battering the thunderstorms had given the crops had been the final blow. Another man observed gloomily that the government might send a big force now, like the ten thousand reported to have been sent to Devon. He did not know whether we could beat such a force. A third man, a young fellow, was more optimistic. 'Don't be so downy! We're jowered out after the battle, and drouched with the rain. But we had a great victory, and Captain Kett's sending forces to spread rebellion further. Yarmouth will be ours soon.'

It was quite customary in the camp for strangers to join in others' conversations; and I ventured to say it was indeed peculiar that the one item of food we had lacked in the camp was the famous Yarmouth herring.

'We'll have a great feast of those ere long,' the young man replied. I noticed spots of blood on his torn, damp shirt; he had been in yesterday's battle.

The man who had spoken first stirred the campfire with a stick.

'Whatever happens now, we'll fight to the end. We've come this far, and even if we go down, which I don't believe we will, this will be remembered forever! What say you, Master hunchback?'

I answered, 'I don't know. If they do send another army, it'll take weeks to organize, and they'll need to withdraw men from Scotland.'

'You're right, bor,' the young fellow agreed, nodding vigorously.

The older man said, 'I'm sorry I called you a hunchback.'

I smiled wryly. 'It's what I am.'

A SMALL NUMBER of desertions began about this time – men who feared what might come, others, perhaps, who wanted to help their womenfolk at home with the harvest, such as it would be. Among the vast majority who stayed, though, reinforced by men from the camps which had been put down, many doubted the Protector would abandon his plans for a new Scottish campaign, which he surely must do if he decided to send a large army to Norwich under a strong leader. They hoped for some sort of settlement. Others believed they could defeat a larger army as they had Northampton's by again luring their opponents into Norwich and using their knowledge of the city's narrow streets and difficult topography to win another victory. Then, indeed, they could once more spread rebellion.

The prophets were out in increasing force, preaching that Northampton's defeat was part of God's plan for the victory of the common people, that the Lord's hand would ensure our victory against the largest army, even as David had destroyed Goliath. From then on, too, I noticed a new type of prophecy. For some time doggerel lines had been circulating, including some that went so far as to predict the overthrow of King Edward, saying such things had been predicted long ago, quoting Merlin and the ancient kings Gog and Magog. Copies of these prophecies were brought by the peddlers who frequented the camp; they were passed around, read out to the illiterate by the prophets, and seized upon by many who feared what might come. I remembered similar stuff from the Pilgrimage of Grace in 1536, predicting the overthrow of King Henry. Possession of such documents had been dealt with particularly harshly.

One in particular I showed to Edward Brown when he came up again that evening:

The country gruffs
Hob, Dick and Hick,
with clubs and clouted shoon,
Shall fill the Vale
of Dussindale
With slaughtered bodies soon

The heedless men within the Dale
Shall there be slain both great and small . . .

He laughed. 'I suppose it keeps men's spirits up.'

'I would prefer good hard strategy to such stuff.'

'You are an educated man.'

'Where is this Vale of Dussindale?'

Edward shrugged. 'Dussin's not an uncommon name in Norfolk. Could be a number of places. Don't worry, few take real notice of these things.'

'If a government army does come, it might influence where we choose to fight.'

Now he frowned. 'Do you think Miles and his officers such fools? No, if it comes to it, Kett and Miles will indeed look to good hard strategy.' He went to Josephine's hut.

✠

ON SUNDAY, I walked about the camp, watching the military training, and the representatives from the Hundreds who walked around the camp discussing matters with village groups. I stopped now and then to engage in conversation with people. Despite the general anxiety as to what the Protector's next step might be, the mood of the people was, as ever, in the main open and friendly. There was a cheerfulness, a sense of something released, about the Mousehold people. Their contentedness in the leanto huts brought home to me how hard their life must have been before. I heard, as I had before, many stories of lands enclosed and rents increased, often to the detriment of the very poorest, like the small craftsmen who supplemented a meagre income with a cow, a horse, or a few sheep on common land which the landowners had crowded out or appropriated. A constant, and happy, topic on Mousehold was food; how with sheep, pigs, every sort of fowl and even deer held in pens in the camp, few had eaten so well in years.

I remember passing a group of huts where men from Withering, ton's estate at South Brikewell had set up a group of huts under their village banner. I remembered the boy whose head had been staved in, whom the twins had referred to as 'just a serf'. Well, there were no distinctions now between serfs tied to the land and others here. I thought of Kett's request to the Protector, that bond men be made free. Here on Mousehold, they had been.

✞

THE FOLLOWING DAY, 5 August, I finally went down to Norwich with Barak and Simon. I insisted that Natty come, too, for the wound in his arm which he had received during the battle to take Norwich had become itchy and sore, and when, reluctantly, he let me examine it, I saw it was red and swollen. 'You must get that looked at again,' I said firmly.

'It'll be all right,' he said. 'No need to make a tutter of it,' but I saw anxiety in his large brown eyes and when I insisted, he agreed. We walked down the road, part of a large crowd making their way down into the city. Wages had been distributed around the camp the previous evening, so the men would have money to spend on warmer clothes in the special Monday market. Simon was concerned about Natty – the first time I had seen him worried about someone else, which was a good sign, but he was still nervous. 'There won't be more fighting?' he asked loudly. Nearby, I saw Toby Lockswood in the crowd; he turned and gave Simon a contemptuous look.

'Of course not. People are just going to market.' Though I, too, was squeamish by nature, I began myself to feel a little irritated with him. I reminded myself of the life he had led before coming to the camp, isolated and afraid.

Bishopsgate Bridge still stood, though the once-magnificent gate, house was a wreck; great lumps of stone had been shot out of the central portion by cannon, widening the entrance to Norwich. It was blackened with smoke, where the wooden beams of the interior had caught light, and the lead on the gatehouse roof had partly melted, little gobbets of it lying on the ground. Someone picked up a piece, looked at it curiously, then threw it in the river. What was left of the gatehouse was closely guarded by our soldiers. We followed the stream of people through; I was glad the whole thing did not collapse on our heads.

Beyond, Holme Street was a scene of devastation. The cathedral wall still stood, but the houses along both sides of the street were black- ened and burned, the Blue Boar Inn where Barak had stayed was little more than a pile of rubble, while on the other side the Great Hospital wall, and the buildings bordering it, had indeed been knocked to pieces by our cannon. I could not but admire the accuracy of our cannoneers. A crowd had gathered; some looked on the scene appalled; others gloated at the destruction of the houses of the rich on Holme Street. There were red stains on the road, which caused Simon to look away, and more as we passed Palace Plain, as well as the bloated bodies of horses. When we arrived at Tombland, we found the Maid's Head shuttered and padlocked. The gates giving onto the yard of Augustine Steward's house had been burned down; beside it several men stood round a cartload of property, likely stolen, examining the contents. For the first time I began to wonder whether Kett was in full control. Near to it Gawen Reynolds's house was untouched; bribery still spoke loudly.

Barak, Simon, Natty and I crossed Tombland and went through the Erpingham Gate, which was open, into the cathedral grounds. The cathedral door was open, too, with more of Kett's guards on the door. I showed them my pass and we were allowed through, stepping into the splendid, vaulted space of the cathedral. The floor space was full; to the right of the door four dozen or so horses had been stabled, wooden partitions erected to separate them, most happily munching hay. To the left, dozens of wounded men lay on straw mattresses; some coughing or groaning in pain, others playing cards cheerfully as though they were at home. One mattress had been surrounded by a makeshift screen of sheets and poles and from behind it muffled screams, together with the sound of sawing, could be heard. In this vast echoing place every sound was magnified. Heavily coifed women took jugs of small beer round to the patients, and some men whom I took to be barber-surgeons tended to them. I saw the thin figure of Dr Belys, and two other men in the dark robes of doctors. Any lingering smell of incense was gone, displaced by those of horse-manure and blood. A side chapel halfway up the cathedral guarded by two soldiers seemed to be a focus of attention, men waiting to go in, or coming out and walking purposefully to the doors, footsteps echoing loudly. I guessed Kett was working in there.

'Simon,' I said, 'why not present yourself to the man in charge of the horses? They're keeping some here, it seems, perhaps to help keep order in Norwich. See if you can assist him.' Keeping his eyes averted from the wounded men, Simon loped off while Barak, Natty and I stepped carefully between the mattresses, heading for where Dr Belys was rewinding a bandage round the head of a wounded man. The doctor stood up and turned to look at me. The expression on his face was utterly different from when he had taken care of me; worn, tired, frightened, his lips set and eyes angry.

'So,' he said bitterly. 'You are still with Kett and his kitlings.'

I replied quietly, 'God give you good morning, Dr Belys. My young friend here has a wound in his arm which I fear may be going bad. I wondered if you might examine it.' I pointed to Natty, but Dr Belys did not look at him, only continued staring at me.

'By God,' he said, 'you dogs have no end of insolence. This time you have not just taken over Norwich, you have fought the King's army, bombarded and burned part of the city to ruin and robbed many of our best people. Do you seriously think you have anything to look forward to now but the revenge you deserve?' His voice trembled. 'I have been forced to help treat these men, they threatened to burn my house round my ears if I didn't, but why should I do anything at your command?'

I stared at him. If the experience of rebellion had changed some of the camp-men, it had clearly done the same to the wealthier citizens, even one as well disposed to me as Belys had been just six weeks before. I answered quietly. 'Only because he is a wounded man who needs medical care, and I would not think you would deny him that.'

Belys's lips set even harder. He shook his head, and I thought he would refuse me, but he waved Natty forward peremptorily. The boy exposed a muscular arm and Belys ran his fingers over the wound, making Natty wince. Belys grunted. 'Yes,' he said. 'Poisoned. All you can do is try and keep it clean.' He indicated an old woman sitting at a trestle table, a large basket full of bottles beside her, doing a good trade. 'She's a basket of wayside cures there, some of them are useful — vinegar, for example. Have you barber-surgeons in the camp?'

'A few.'

'Look to them, then. Unless you'd like me to stop the risk of infection spreading by taking his arm off, like they're doing with that fellow behind the sheets.' He looked at Barak. 'Then you'll have two one-armed rebels to follow you around.'

Natty blenched. I said angrily, 'I thought better of you, Doctor,' then turned and led Natty and Barak to where the old woman sat. I told Barak, 'See if you can buy something useful from her. Vinegar. And lavender,' I added, remembering my doctor friend Guy's favourite remedy. 'I'm going to see if I can talk to Kett.'

I was in luck. Robert Kett indeed sat in the side chapel, talking to Michael Vowell, at a table thick with papers. Despite our victory his face was thoughtful, worried. 'Captain Kett?' I asked quietly.

He looked up. 'Serjeant Shardlake,' he said abruptly. 'Good, I wanted to talk to you. There are to be more trials at the Oak tomorrow, I shall preside and I want you with me. Not trials of gentlemen this time, but thieves and looters.' He shook his grey head. 'They're robbing the houses of the richer citizens. And not just them. Augustine Steward, who I need to help me, has had his house stripped. A further example has to be made.'

'I saw, on the way here.'

He ran a hand through his grey hair. 'I didn't expect this.'

'It is a consequence of war, sir,' Vowell said.

'Master Fulke the butcher has been brawling with others who claim that they, not him, killed Lord Sheffield. The killing itself — well, as you say, this was war. We were forced into it, they attacked us, but our community should still be apostles of peace.' He sighed. 'In any event, I want the looters we can catch expelled from the camp. And there are more thieves, too, I fear, to be tried.'

'I shall attend.' I hesitated, then added, 'What of the gentlemen captured in the fighting?'

'In Norwich Castle and Guildhall prison for now. We shall see.'

I hesitated again, but knew I might not have another chance. 'Captain Kett, I wondered if I might bring Nicholas Overton back to the camp, for the hearing you promised.'

He gave me a puzzled look. 'Who?' I reminded him and Kett thought a moment, then said, 'I agree to his being tried at the Oak.' He looked at me sharply. 'If he's freed he won't take the chance to run from the city, will he?'

'Not if he gives me his oath not to.'

Kett nodded at Michael Vowell. 'Go with him, I don't need you for a couple of hours. Make sure Overton returns to the camp. He'll get his hearing tomorrow.'

I felt a stab of disappointment that Kett seemed not to trust me as before. I wondered whether it was because, like Peter Bone, Edward Brown and Toby Lockswood, I was still under suspicion of the possible betrayal of Captain Miles's wife and children. But Michael Vowell had been at that meeting, too. As had poor Hector Johnson, who had died in battle for the cause. Nonetheless, I ventured, 'With the mood in the camp, I hope Nicholas will be fairly heard.'

Kett said sharply, 'Master Shardlake, there must be no suspicion I am favouring you. My authority has been defied by some. You heard about the Italian hanged from Surrey Place?'

'I saw it.'

'By the way, the men who took the money from Gawen Reynolds to leave his house alone paid it into our exchequer. Michael here saw to that. Oh,' he added, 'a letter came for you yesterday. It was addressed to the Maid's Head, but in view of the seal it was intercepted and read, then passed on.' He pulled a paper from his pile, and handed it to me. He said, 'If you write back, be careful what you say, in your own interest. Others will read it first.'

The letter was grubby, the seal broken, but I saw it was from Hatfield Palace.

A man appeared in the doorway. He looked like a messenger, still sweating from a long ride. 'News from Suffolk, Captain!'

'Dear God, not another camp gone down,' Kett said quietly. He motioned me to leave, and I returned to the nave, Vowell now accompanying me. Barak and Natty were putting a selection of bottles into the bags they had brought. 'Well,' Barak said, 'that's most of our money gone.' Natty smiled weakly.

We walked back into Tombland. There was more trouble round Augustine Steward's house, where men were carrying out fardels of wool. This time, however, they were approached by an older man with an air of authority, who told them, 'Enough of this robbing and spoiling, you dausey-heads!'

A man carrying a heavy bundle said, 'Don't get frampled, Goodman Doo! We need wool, ain't you noticed it's got colder?'

Michael Vowell shouted, 'You want me to fetch Captain Kett and the soldiers from the cathedral? If you want wool, go to the market!'

Sulkily, the men threw their booty back into the house and walked off towards the market. I said, 'Jack, take Natty back to camp and help him treat that arm. I'm going to see how Isabella is, then I'm going to the castle gaol.' I told him what Kett and I had agreed about Nicholas. He whistled. 'Nick had better use his tongue wisely.'

'He had,' Vowell agreed.

'Have you done what we discussed?' I asked. Barak winked. I said to Natty, 'I'm sorry Dr Belys would not help you more.'

'I'll be all right with these potions.'

'Stop scratching that arm,' Barak told him crossly. 'You'll make it worse. Now come on.' They walked away. I looked at Michael Vowell. 'Were you in the battle?'

'Yes; guiding men through the Norwich streets. Fortunately, I was unhurt.'

'You will come to the castle with me?'

'Yes.' He looked at me, and said with that superior air he had adopted lately, 'We'll be all right in Norwich. People know me.'

Chapter Sixty-six

OUTSIDE THE CATHEDRAL, I asked Michael Vowell if he would wait while I read my letter. It was strange how relationships had changed; once he had been just a servant, Gawen Reynolds's steward, now he was here to ensure I brought Nicholas safely back. He nodded agreement, and stood looking at the people heading for market as I read the letter. It was from Thomas Parry, dated 22 July, fourteen days ago. Its tone was milder than his last.

Serjeant Shardlake,

I have received your letter of 15 July, which, it seems, crossed with mine. In these whirling days one should not be surprised. But I was concerned you gave so little detail about what has happened to you. I pray you have not fallen into the hands of those rebels whose pranks threaten to tear all asunder.

I thought, How often, when the gentlemen spoke of the rebels, it was as either unruly children or animals. He continued:

The Lady Elizabeth and I are most concerned for you, and all at Hatfield pray you are safe. I know a royal Herald is to be sent to order the Norwich rebels to disband, and that force will be used if they should dare defy him.

Well, I thought, both those ships had sailed.

Master Secretary Cecil reports that until this dreadful stirring time is over, he dare not trouble the Protector about John Boleyn's pardon — the Protector is constantly engaged in dealing with the camps, and in no good state of mind, from what I hear.

As for attempts to follow the movements of the woman we discussed, on which the Lady Elizabeth still insists, we know now she lodged at a poor tavern in Knebworth briefly, under another name, before moving to the house nearby of which I wrote previously. Where she came from before that we cannot trace. Her story was that she was from Leicester, travelling to her family in London following recent widowhood, slowly, due to poor health. The Knebworth innkeeper said she was indeed thin, pale, and sick-looking. But there for now the trail ends. May you have had better luck tracing her in Norwich.

I hope I may hear from you more fully soon.

Your loving friend,
Thomas Parry

He had been careful not to name Edith Boleyn, trying as ever to keep a distance between Elizabeth and the murdered woman; but apart from the tone in which he discussed the rebels there was nothing in the letter to worry Kett or whoever had intercepted it. I put it in my purse; I must write back, though I could hardly say I was in the camp working for Kett. Well, I thought, at least the Lady Elizabeth seems concerned for me.

Michael Vowell looked at me curiously. I said, 'Nothing urgent. Thank you for waiting. Let us go on.'

We walked through Tombland, turning up Pottergate Street to the castle mound. There were more signs of looting in the central, richer parts of Norwich, with the courtyard doors of some houses smashed down. Bands of men still roamed about, but so did groups of Kett's soldiers, keeping an eye on them. I was glad to have Vowell beside me. I took the opportunity to tell him of my recent encounter with Gawen Reynolds's family, and asked him if he thought Reynolds ever beat his wife.

'I don't think so, he yagged at her all the time but she is such a frail creature, even a little culp might kill her. The bandages on her hands are because of a swelling and twisting of the knuckles. It runs in her family. Apparently, her mother had it from late middle age, and so did Edith. The twins will probably get it, too,' he added with satisfaction.

'I hear they were in the Norwich battle.'

'I heard so too. They probably fought better than the Italian mer-cenaries, they didn't put up quite the fight I think Northampton expected of them. If it had been the German and Swiss landsknechts –' he shook his head. 'Those people are the terror of Europe.'

'You were lucky to escape uninjured.'

'Ay, I was. I was leading men from the countryside through the streets of Norwich, I escaped the main battle and after that it was just a matter of chasing Northampton's people out.'

We took the turning into the marketplace. I was relieved to see the buildings around it were undamaged, though blackened with soot from where Northampton's army had camped. Otherwise it was like a normal market day, stalls crowded, people bickering over prices. The camp-men had been given enough from Kett's treasury to buy new heavy shoes, horn-lamps for the slowly lengthening evenings, and woollen clothes and caps for the colder weather. I was a familiar figure at the inn now and we were readily admitted to the parlour, told Mis-tress Boleyn would be informed of my presence, and invited to sit.

We rose and bowed when Isabella and Chawry entered. Isabella had an unusual expression on her face; cold and set. Daniel Chawry, meanwhile, looked angry yet somehow hangdog at the same time. Three long, parallel scratches ran down the right side of his face.

I introduced Vowell, saying only that he was an official from the camp. Chawry gave him a glare.

'How fares your husband?' I asked Isabella.

'Well enough. It appears the castle gaol, and the one beneath the Guildhall, are fuller still of gentleman prisoners since the battle five days ago. One of Kett's men has been placed to work with Constable Fordhill; Robert Isod, a tanner, who seems a decent enough man. John is safe in the room he was given, and pleased to have Nicholas for company. They spend much time talking, and playing chess.' She smiled, then looked downcast. 'Nicholas learned that one of those held prisoner in the castle, my husband's neighbour Leonard Witherington, died yesterday. He and my husband were enemies, but it is still sad. Gentlemen are not used to such treatment.' She gave Vowell a challen-ging look, which he returned.

'I wish my old master Gawen Reynolds would be taken into custody,' he said boldly. 'Your husband's father-in-law. He is a great villain, as you will know.'

Isabella said, 'My concern is with my husband, who was imprisoned before the rebellion, and played no part in it.'

'True,' Vowell said more peaceably.

I said to Isabella, 'Were you safe when Northampton's forces took up their position in the market square?' I took another look at the scratches on Chawry's face.

She took a deep breath. 'Everyone was ordered to close their shutters. Though the great noise the soldiers made, and the glow from that mighty bonfire, was frightening.'

'There have been no more attempts at poisoning, or violence, against your husband?'

'None. We buy the food and tie it tight. Constable Fordhill says he has placed a guard permanently outside the door of the cell.'

'You have been to see him?'

'Yes, today, I saw both Fordhill and Isod. I suggested a new arrangement, which they agreed. I will join my husband in his cell. Fordhill will arrange for a trusted man to buy our food in the marketplace. I've given Fordhill some money for that already. And, of course, they will want no trouble with the Lady Elizabeth.'

I said, 'I am glad to hear that, Mistress Boleyn, for it bears on something I must tell you. Captain Kett has ordered a trial of Nicholas's case, and he is to be released into my company today.'

She smiled. 'That is good. I was worried about him, lest he was moved to rougher quarters again. Daniel' – she gave Chawry a forbidding look – 'will return to Brikewell today. It is time the house was set in order, and things made ready for the harvest, such as it will be.'

Chawry, reddening, said, 'I don't know what conditions will be like there. And for a woman to join her husband in prison, it is unsafe and – immodest.'

'You would know all about modesty,' she answered sharply. She turned to me. 'Does it not sometimes happen, in cases where the final outcome is not yet known, for wives to stay with their husbands in prison?'

'Yes. With the authorities' agreement.'

She took a deep breath. 'So, it seems all has worked out for the best.'

'For the best?' Suddenly Chawry lost his temper. 'A woman alone in a prison groaning with men? Leaving responsibility for gathering food and preparing it to the castle constable and his rebel deputy! What if someone came up to whoever they appoint, in the market, and offered ten marks to poison the food? You know the rebels are rich with the money they have stolen!' He took a step towards Isabella, and, to my surprise, she flinched. Michael Vowell stepped between them. 'Hold hard, bor,' he said quietly. 'Keep your tongue behind your teeth when talking of my people, and don't threaten the lady.'

Chawry shouted, 'Why? I suppose because, despite her antrums, she's just a servant like you, rebel dog.'

Vowell replied, 'A rebel who'll give you such a ding o' the head it'll be singing for a week.' He was bigger and stronger than Chawry, and the steward paused, then stepped away. Isabella stood, breathing hard. I said to Vowell, 'Michael, may I speak with Isabella alone for a few minutes?'

He sighed, looking suddenly tired of the whole business. 'Very well. Do you want me to see this – steward out of the room?'

'Yes please.'

He stepped towards Chawry, who, after a second, turned and made for the door. Vowell followed him through, and there was a moment's silence.

'What happened, Isabella?' I asked gently.

She took a deep breath. 'I have known for some time that Daniel has – feelings for me. He told me so, back at Brikewell, some time before Edith died. I said all my love was for my husband, and as his servant he should not say such things. I know I have a habit of jesting with men, it comes from my years as a serving woman at an inn, but I made things plain as I could with Daniel.' She looked at me fiercely. 'And I can be very plain when I need to be; again, I'm used to it from my time at the inn.'

I smiled. 'I do not doubt that,' I said gently, encouraging her with her story.

'I thought that was the end of it, and even felt sorry for him, and was grateful for the way he helped me after we were thrown out of the house.' Isabella fell silent a moment, angrily brushing a wisp of blonde hair from her face, then took a deep breath. 'The night Northampton's army occupied the market and lit that great bonfire I was terrified, I feared the fire might spread to the buildings, while all around I heard rebel shouts of "To arms!" from the streets. I confess I broke down and cried like a weak woman, for all I have tried to be strong.' She lowered her eyes, then looked up again fiercely. 'Then, suddenly, Daniel grabbed at me. He took me in his arms, though I resisted, and said he would protect me, make me forget what was happening, in the way a man should; a strong, young man, unlike my husband.' Her voice shook. 'He began pulling at my clothing, fiddling with the ties on his upper hose. I scratched his face – you saw the marks – and told him if he tried to force me I would scream till the whole of Northampton's army came in.' Her voice steadied. 'I told him I had relied on him for so long, and now he had betrayed me. But he just went on saying he loved me, we were meant to be together.'

'Will you tell your husband?'

She hesitated. 'Not yet, at least. He has enough to trouble him.' Tears showed at the corners of her eyes, and suddenly Isabella reached for my hand. 'I thank God I still have you, Master Shardlake.'

'You can rely on me.'

'I know.' She sighed. 'I thought for so long that I could trust Daniel.' She blinked back her tears, and said stonily, 'If I had not scratched him and threatened to yell the place down, I believe he would have raped me.'

I said, 'Is it safe to allow him back to Brikewell? If I told Michael Vowell he tried to rape you, he may take him back to the camp as a prisoner. Perhaps that is the best place for him.'

She hesitated, then said, 'I do not want this known publicly.'

'But Isabella, is it safe to let him back to Brikewell?' I asked again.

'I shall not return there without John. And I do not think Daniel will go back, he will run away. Once he is gone I shall tell the innkeeper he is not to be allowed back in here.'

I hesitated, then said, 'If he would rape you, perhaps he would have killed Edith.'

She set her lips hard, then said, 'I do not believe he did that. And I would rather he simply left.'

'Are you sure?'

'Yes,' she said, suddenly angry. 'I just want him gone. And tomorrow I shall be with John.'

There was one more question I had to ask. 'Isabella, after this – is it not possible that Daniel Chawry might have been the one who tried to poison your husband?'

Isabella shook her head wearily. 'I think not. Daniel has a good regard for his safety, he would not risk a charge of murder.' She fell silent, then gathered herself and looked at the table. 'There is a parcel of food there for John and Nicholas. Would you take it to them?' She smiled. 'I hope I see Nicholas again, to thank him for what he has done, and keeping my husband safe.'

☩

VOWELL AND I LEFT the inn. Vowell told me Chawry had walked off immediately after our encounter, disappearing into the crowds in the marketplace. As we walked uphill to the prison I could not help thinking, if Chawry had had these fantasies for years, it would have suited him to kill Edith and make it public, to seem as though John Boleyn had done it, and then to try and kill Boleyn, too. I was surprised by Isabella's readiness to let him go.

As we trudged up the Castle Mound, my pace slowed, and I realized how tired I was, physically but mentally, too. My life this last month had been a whirl such as I had never known. And for most of the time I had been little more than an onlooker. I glanced at Michael Vowell. He had been at the heart of all that had happened, culminating in the battle, but his face had settled into its usual calm expression, showing nothing of what he had been through. But he was many years younger than I, and full of commitment to the cause. He looked up at the grey sky. 'We'd best keep a-doin', it looks like more rain.'

☩

THE INTERIOR OF the gaol was even more crowded than before, and the space, huge as it was, had the prison smell of unwashed bodies, badly cooked food, and fear. A small group of gentlemen were being led upstairs. One said furiously, 'I'm a former mayor of Norwich!'

'Don't get it yet, do you?' the man leading them said wearily.

Vowell secured us a gaoler to take us to Boleyn's cell. To my relief, he and Nicholas both seemed well enough, and were playing chess at the table. They looked up at me in surprise. I introduced Vowell as an official of the camp, and Boleyn gave him a steely look. Then he turned to me and smiled. 'Isabella is coming to stay with me from tomorrow. God bless her stout heart. Chawry is going back to look after Brikewell.'

'Yes, so I understand.' He obviously suspected nothing of what had happened, though I guessed that Vowell, who raised his eyebrows slightly, did.

'What of me?' Nicholas asked ruefully. 'Will I go back to the other cells, or the ones under the Guildhall? I hear they are bad.'

I felt a pang of conscience. I had left him here, his future uncertain, for two weeks. 'No, Nicholas, I have managed to take care of that at last. You are returning with us to the camp. You are to have a public trial at the Oak tomorrow. But truth is on your side, you are a lawyer, and I have every hope you will be freed.'

Nicholas looked at Vowell. 'If there is justice at these trials, I shall be.'

To my surprise, Vowell said, 'I've sometimes thought Toby Lockswood's gone a bit funny in the head. He's always so ferocious against the gentlemen, never stops – people get tired of it.'

'He lost both his parents just before the rebellion,' I said. 'And the family farm.'

Vowell inclined his head. 'Well, that would unsettle anyone.' He looked at Nicholas, 'Boy, you must give an oath to Master Shardlake to stay with him, and not try to escape before your trial.'

Nicholas looked me in the eye. 'I swear it.'

Boleyn asked, 'What will happen to the Norwich gentlemen taken prisoner? Are they to have trials before that Oak of yours, too?'

'That remains to be decided,' Vowell said, his voice suddenly authoritative. 'You and your wife should sit safely here, and ask no questions.'

'It's a long time since I dared ask anything,' Boleyn said, with an edge to his voice and a savage glance at Vowell that reminded me again he had a temper.

Quickly changing the subject, Nicholas said, 'We saw Northampton's defeat from the window. We couldn't see the fighting in Palace Plain, but late in the afternoon we saw Northampton's forces running away, past the castle and through the gates.' His brow clouded. 'I never thought I'd see anything like it, a royal army, men trained to fight honourably to the last, pushing to get through the gates, shoving aside some of the richer citizens who were trying to get out – old people, women, children, many dressed only in their under-clothes, their fine dress thrown aside to try to hide their status.' He shook his head. 'It is not what I was brought up to believe warfare should be.'

Boleyn said, 'I thought I saw the twins among those fleeing, but I couldn't be certain. My devilish sons,' he added with a sigh. He rose and embraced Nicholas. 'Thank you, lad, for your company and friendship.'

'And may you get your pardon.'

'So I pray,' Boleyn said. He looked at me. 'Matthew, have you discovered any more about who killed Edith?'

'It is hard to make enquiries in the present circumstances. But I will not give up.'

Boleyn embraced me too, though pointedly he ignored Vowell. We left him sitting on his bed, his face thoughtful.

✞

AS WE WALKED DOWN the hill, I told Nicholas the news from the camp: first, that old Hector Johnson was dead.

'I am sorry, he was a good man.'

'And a brave soldier. He died honourably.' I went on to tell him that Barak, Scambler and Natty were all safe, though Natty's arm wound was giving him some trouble. 'I spoke to Dr Belys, but he was little help. He is no friend to the rebellion. But if Natty fails to improve, I may contact him again, try to appeal to his better nature.'

Vowell raised his eyebrows. 'Special treatment for one you have befriended?'

638

I sighed, too tired to argue. Nicholas shook his head again. 'I cannot believe a royal army could flee so dishonourably.'

'Against a pack of commoners?' Vowell asked. 'Is that it?'

'No,' Nicholas answered seriously. 'The camp-men had greater numbers, but were not fully trained. Northampton's army were the trained soldiers.' He added quietly, 'I wonder if our armies' defeats in Scotland were like that.'

I asked Vowell, 'What will happen to these new captives? Is Boleyn right, will they go for trial at the Oak?'

'Captain Kett and his advisers have yet to decide. The mood in the camp after the battle – there may be demands for executions, they're probably safer locked up.' He looked at me. 'I know you think me a dangerous radical, Master Shardlake, but I do not want them killed. Captain Kett was much angered by what was done to that Italian.' It had started to rain. Vowell looked up at the sky. 'We'd best get back quick as we can, or we'll get drouched again.'

I thought, If that was the mood in the camp, then how would Nicholas fare on Tuesday?

Chapter Sixty-seven

THE ATMOSPHERE IN camp that evening remained euphoric after the victory over Northampton's army, and, after the afternoon drizzle petered out, there was much drinking around the campfires, with music and singing. I remember one song I heard over and again; a jesting letter which a rebel had left at a manor house set to music:

> *Mr Pratt, your sheep are very fat,*
> *And we thank you for that;*
> *We have left you the skins*
> *To pay for your wife's pins,*
> *And you must thank us for that.*

Some groups of huts though, were quiet, not joining the celebrations, and I guessed people there had lost friends or relatives in the battle. It struck me, too, that there was something forced about the cheerfulness, and I heard the occasional fight erupt; for all their bravery, many who had had their first experience in battle would be in shock.

On returning from Norwich, Michael Vowell had said Nicholas must remain in our hut, so he and I and Barak — reunited at last — stayed there that evening. I told Barak what had passed between Isabella and Chawry. He looked serious. 'That's a surprise.'

'This has been brewing a long time. Up to now he certainly kept himself under control, but to try and rape her — Daniel Chawry is not the man I thought.'

Nicholas said, 'And if Isabella Boleyn had not been of such strong character, and prepared to fight, he would have done it. And to go to the castle and arrange things by herself – what a woman,' he added admiringly.

'I thought you liked them quiet and courtly, like that Beatrice Kenzy.' Barak spoke jestingly, but from the sadness in his eyes I guessed he was thinking of Tamasin. He had heard nothing yet in reply to his letter.

I said, 'This makes Chawry a more likely candidate for Boleyn's poisoner, and maybe Edith's killer. His feelings towards Isabella have been there for years. I do not think she realized the depths of his – passion. I think he might have attacked her today had not Michael Vowell intervened. It puzzles me that she should have let him go free so readily.'

'She wants to be rid of him,' Nicholas suggested.

Barak nodded. 'Most men told they had no chance would surely have given up long ago, perhaps gone away. There's something wrong with Chawry.'

I said, 'And if I remember correctly, he had no alibi for the night Edith was killed.'

Nicholas said, 'And yet I remember how upset he was when we visited the site of Edith's death.'

'Guilt, perhaps,' Barak observed.

I answered, 'But if he did kill Edith, and was responsible for the theft of the key and the killings of Snockstobe and his apprentice, he *must* have had accomplices. By God, I wish we could have detained him. Why did she let him go free? Though I doubt Vowell would have agreed to take him to the camp. Kett's people are not interested in the case.'

'They've bigger concerns,' Barak said.

Nicholas asked me, 'Do you think Chawry will return to Brikewell?'

'I doubt it. Isabella isn't going to tell John Boleyn what happened, at least for now. But she will, I am sure, so he has probably fled. In which case we've lost him.'

I looked out at the campfires and horn-lamps dotting the dark heath. A song carried on the night air:

When Adam delved and Eve span,
Who was then the gentleman —

✟

AT BREAKFAST THE next day, Goodwife Everneke said that a preliminary expedition of a hundred men was to be sent to Yarmouth, to
see if the city could be persuaded to join us — otherwise it might be
attacked with a large force. Religious services went on as usual under
the Oak and elsewhere in the camp, and for a moment I considered
taking Communion again, but I had slept badly; with three of us the
hut was crowded again. It was hard to get my back comfortable, and
I could not get what Chawry had done out of my mind.

I went to visit Josephine — she was alone with Mousy, Edward
being once more in Norwich, and in a low mood. I stayed with her a
while and played with Mousy, then went to see Natty and Simon.
Natty said his arm was better; I looked at it and was pleased to see there
was less redness now around the wound. Simon, still affected by the
battle and the news of Hector Johnson's death, sat in a corner of the
hut, singing quietly to himself, arms round his knees, rocking to and
fro. Both were still shocked after the battle, and after a little while I left
them.

✟

THEN I DISCUSSED Nicholas's forthcoming trial with him. 'I won't
be able to take any part,' I said. 'I have an interest.'

Nicholas looked at me, his green eyes sharp. 'I had much time to
think while I was in the gaol. I have thought of a strategy.'

I smiled. 'I'm sorry, I forget you are experienced in court proceedings now. But remember, this will be different, the jury will be
camp-men and they may be hostile.'

'I think I can win,' he said. He looked at Barak, who smiled and
nodded. 'I've been making some enquiries about the so-called witnesses,' he said, and winked.

'Good. I——' I felt suddenly faint, and leaned forward with a groan.
Nicholas grasped me. 'Are you all right?' he asked urgently.

'I – I think so. There is so much on my mind, for a second my head spun. The air in here –'

'Yes, it stinks.'

'It's more than that,' Barak said. 'He's taken the troubles of the whole world on his shoulders again. John and Isabella Boleyn, you, Simon and Natty, Josephine, everybody.'

I said quietly, 'Perhaps you're right. And I worry what will become of the rebellion.' I put a hand to my brow. 'I am not myself – things go through my mind and I cannot catch hold of them. Something that happened at the puppet show, and something too that Michael Vowell said yesterday that struck me – but I have forgotten.' I pounded my brow with my fist.

'That's right,' Barak said wearily. 'Punish yourself.'

✝

THERE WAS A CROWD of several hundred at the Oak of Reformation, talking about the small force that had left for Yarmouth. That day Robert Kett himself was presiding over the trials, and I watched as he mounted the platform and stood a moment looking over the crowd, gauging the mood of the people after the battle. Despite the troubles of the last few days, his air of authority was as strong as ever, and he was greeted by loud cheers. Nicholas's was to be the first case to be heard, and I stood with him and Barak a little way from the platform. We had discussed our strategy earlier, and I thought it could work – if Nicholas got a fair hearing. Toby Lockswood stood at the front of the crowd, arms folded, his blackbearded face fierce. He looked at us, this man who had once worked with us so closely, with savage contempt.

Kett called out, 'First, we have the case of Nicholas Overton, accused of defaming the camp.' There were a few catcalls and boos, and Kett shouted for silence. He went on, 'Afterwards, there will be trials of those who took property from Norwich households without authority, which is simple looting, and there is also another man who has allegedly stolen property from his fellow campmen. This thieving angers me, which is why I am presiding today. To succeed we must work together like brothers!'

Someone called out, 'What of the Norwich gentlemen who helped

Northampton kill our men? My cousin died! Why have they not been brought here?'

'Ay!' another agreed. 'They should be hanged!' There were murmurs of agreement from many, and Toby Lockswood nodded vigorously.

Kett stepped to the edge of the platform, hands on hips, his expression fierce. 'The leaders of the Hundreds and I are considering what is to be done with those gentlemen. For now they are secure in custody. I shall place the issue before you to decide, but not today!' His voice rose. 'Today we take Yarmouth!' There were cheers at that. Kett looked at the man beside him who served as an usher. 'The Overton case. Have the parties and witnesses been sworn?'

'They have, Captain.'

Kett nodded. 'Nicholas Overton, come before the platform. Toby Lockswood, you are the accuser. Speak.'

I took a deep breath, and looked at Barak. His left hand was supporting his artificial one, his fingers crossed.

Chapter Sixty-eight

TOBY OPENED CONFIDENTLY, 'My evidence, Captain Kett, is simple. On the eighteenth of July, I was at the crest of the escarpment the day that crooked lawyer, Robert Wharton, was taken down to Norwich. Overton, whom I knew as a great enemy of the Commonwealth, said, at the top of the road going down to Norwich, that Robert Wharton should be freed, Captain Kett imprisoned, and the camp is a commonwealth of rogues.'

There were angry murmurs from the crowd. Kett called for silence, and turned to Nicholas. 'What say you?'

Nicholas faced the hostile crowd directly. I admired his courage. 'I never said any of those words. When we worked together, Toby Lockswood formed a fierce dislike of me, and this is his revenge.'

Kett intervened sharply, 'The issue here is not whether you and Lockswood disliked each other, but whether you used the words you are accused of.'

'Again, I swear I did not.'

Toby bowed briefly, then said, 'May I bring forward my witnesses?' Kett nodded, and I exchanged a glance with Barak. He winked; while Nicholas was imprisoned he had been making his own enquiries around the camp.

The first witness, who had been standing nearby, was an elderly peddler, Goodman Hodge. He often visited the camp with his donkey, and, like many peddlers, was a source of information and gossip about events beyond Norwich. He stepped forward and looked at Kett, then Nicholas, a little uneasily. Then he said, 'I was standing near the accused when he used those words. I heard him clear.'

Nicholas asked, civilly, 'Goodman Hodge, you say you heard me say what Goodman Lockswood reported.'

Hodge glanced at Kett. His demeanour was shifty now, which Kett could not fail to notice. 'Yes,' Hodge answered. 'As wicked words as ever I heard.'

'You remember what was happening in the camp that day?'

'Yes. That man, Wharton, was being led down the hill. There was great anger towards him. You and Toby Lockswood were standing at the top of the road. I remember it well.'

'Where were you, when you heard the words?'

'Under a tree, for the shade – it was a powerful hot day.'

Nicholas said, still in a pleasant tone, 'As is common knowledge, nearly all the trees on the escarpment have been cut down, to provide wood and give a clear view of Norwich. There is only one large one left. I have sheltered under it myself.'

'Yes,' Hodge agreed.

'The distance between the tree and the path to Norwich is at least a hundred feet. I will be happy to measure it out before Captain Kett. At that distance you could not possibly hear anything I said to Toby Lockswood.'

'You were shouting!'

Nicholas laughed. 'To hear me from that distance, amid the commotion that was going on, I should have had to have used a trumpet!'

Some in the crowd laughed; they liked humour.

Hodge made no reply. Nicholas waited a minute, then asked for the witness to be dismissed. Hodge gratefully disappeared into the crowd. Toby glared at us.

Wallace, the second witness, was very different, a large, solid middle-aged man. He took a confident stance, arms folded, and in answer to a question from Toby said he had been standing near them and heard the words Nicholas was reported as saying. Nicholas then asked, 'What exactly did you hear?'

'What you said, gemmun, at the crest of the hill as Wharton was being led down. I was not ten feet away. You said, clear as day, that Robert Wharton should be freed, Captain Kett imprisoned, and that we are a commonwealth of rogues!'

There were boos from the crowd. Nicholas turned to Kett, and asked quietly, 'May I ask, Captain Kett, that Goodman Wallace remain where he is while I call my witnesses, Edward Bishop and Thomas Smith, of Tunstead?'

Kett nodded, and Nicholas waved to two men. As they stepped forward, Wallace looked uneasy. Nicholas said, 'I am told you come from the same parish as Goodman Wallace.'

'I do.'

'You remember the eighteenth of July?'

'Yes,' Goodman Bishop replied. 'We was working over towards Thorpe Wood, building a new pen for some of the pigs. I remember the day because that evening there was much talk about what had happened to Wharton in the afternoon.'

Smith nodded agreement, then turned and pointed a finger at Wallace. 'He was with us all day, the job took that long. Not least since Biller Wallace is the laziest man in our parish, and did not half the work we did. We was jowered out by the end of the day, but not him.'

There was laughter from the crowd. The fact that two others had been present with Wallace at the pig-pen a mile away clearly showed him to be a liar. Wallace clenched his fists and shifted angrily. 'Those fools have the day wrong, it was the day before that we worked with the pigs.'

Nicholas said, an edge to his voice now, 'If it was the day before, why would Goodmen Bishop and Smith remember the talk about Robert Wharton that day?'

'I don't know,' Wallace answered belligerently. 'Ted Bishop's always had no more sense than a May gosling, and Tom Smith's not much better!'

Bishop snapped at him, 'At least I tell God's truth under oath, as a good Christian should, and do a fair job of work without making a tutter of it!'

At this there was more laughter; the mood of the crowd had clearly swung in Nicholas's favour. The fact that he had spoken to the commoner witnesses civilly probably also helped. Toby Lockswood looked round, furious. I guessed he was a man who would hate being laughed at above all else.

Nicholas turned and bowed to Kett. 'That is all my evidence, Captain. I submit myself to the judgement of the camp.'

Then Toby Lockswood lost his temper. He pointed a finger at Nicholas and shouted, 'Overton spoke against the Commonwealth and the rebellion many times in the early days. He is only allowed in the camp because of his connection to Serjeant Shardlake. I say that being a gentleman is itself enough to send him back to prison!' There were a few cheers and claps, but most remained silent.

Nicholas's face first paled, then turned as red as his hair. He stepped forward and spoke to the crowd, raising an arm. 'Yes! I was born a gentleman, but I was disinherited. I have no lands, no tenants, I am but a junior lawyer. It is true I came to Norfolk believing gentlemen were born to rule and be obeyed, but now – having seen how this camp has been organized, and witnessed a royal army, which I was brought up to believe would be skilled and honourable, run like so many sheep, I no longer know what I think. But I swore to Master Shardlake I would cause no trouble in the camp, and nor have I. Imprison me for having the birth and education of a gentleman, if you like. I cannot help that.' He paused for breath, then, in his turn, pointed a long finger at Toby Lockswood. 'One thing I am not is a liar, nor a man who garners his hatreds as a squirrel hoards nuts! Is that to be Toby Lockswood's Commonwealth, where men abuse their power to hurt others? Is that not what you are all trying to change?'

For a moment the crowd was silent. Then Toby shouted back, 'We will have an end of all such men as you!'

Robert Kett banged on his desk, making everyone jump. He stood up and shouted at Toby, in a voice far louder than either Lockswood or Nicholas could have managed, 'I trusted you, Lockswood, as a man who would help our fight for justice. But the boy is right, we will not win a better world with lies, and lies you have told! You are no fit man to help build a just Commonwealth! I revoke your authority as a liaison officer.' Toby took a step back, shocked. Kett turned to the crowd. 'Well, is Nicholas Overton guilty or innocent of the charges brought against him?'

A few called 'Guilty' but far more shouted 'Innocent!' And then, 'Set him free!' My biggest worry had been that Nicholas might have been unable to win over the crowd, but he had done it, and beautifully. Kett turned to him. 'Master Overton, you are found innocent. I give you the choice of staying in the camp, or leaving it in peace if you prefer.'

Nicholas looked at Barak and me. Then he said, 'If you permit, Captain Kett, I will stay with my friends.'

Toby pointed at Nicholas again, and yelled, 'This is not over. None of it is over.' I was reminded of Michael Vowell saying he wondered whether Toby was entirely in his right mind. Then Toby turned and pushed his way through the crowd. Most edged away from him. Nicholas walked, a little shakily, to where Barak and I stood. Kett took a deep breath, then waved to me. 'Come up here, Master Shardlake, and be my guide on the law as we try the next cases. The looters and the thief,' he added distastefully.

✝

AFTER THE DRAMA of Nicholas's trial, those that followed were an anti-climax, at least for me. Half a dozen alleged looters, denounced by their fellow-men, were brought forward. There was anger against them, not for stealing from the Norwich gentlemen, but for defrauding the common treasury in Surrey Place. Goods found in their huts were brought forward in evidence, gold and silver plates and vases, expensive jewellery, gold coins. All but two were found guilty by their fellows.

There remained only the thief who had stolen from his fellow camp-men. He was a pathetic figure, a thin, ragged middle-aged fellow with the red, broken-veined face of a drinker. His accuser, one of the Hundred representatives, said he was one of those who had come up from Norwich and attached himself to the camp, and that since his arrival ten days ago, several items had gone missing from neighbouring huts. A search of his hut had revealed stolen goods buried under the earthen floor. The evidence was brought up to the table, in a large leather bag which the accuser emptied. I looked at a little pile of goods of small value – a battered New Testament, a few silver coins, a necklace of cheap stones, rings and little brooches of poor gold. Those objects, though, would have great sentimental value for those who had brought them to Mousehold.

The man, whose name was Dorton, spoke in a voice which

cracked slightly. 'I'm guilty, Captain Kett, there's no use pretending. I'm a bezzler and a sinner. But I'm a poor man with nobody in the world, and Christ our Lord forgave even the worst of men, did he not?'

Kett said to me quietly, 'I think this confession settles matters, Master Shardlake?' I nodded. He turned to Dorton. 'I hope Christ may forgive you, but a poor man should not rob other poor men. The law of the country would have you hanged, but we are more merciful. You will leave the camp at once, and never return.'

I hardly heard Kett administer the sentence for, poking through the little collection of stolen goods, my eye was suddenly caught by the bright glint of pure gold. It was a woman's wedding band, and an expensive one. I picked it up and looked at the inner side, screwing up my eyes to make out the inscription running round the ring. Then I froze. The tiny letters read: *John Boleyn, 1530, Edith Reynolds*. I was hold-ing Edith's wedding ring, that had been missing from her arthritic finger when she had visited the Lady Elizabeth. And now here it was, amidst a collection of cheap goods stolen in the Mousehold camp.

Chapter Sixty-nine

HOLDING EDITH'S wedding band, for a moment I felt faint, as I had in the hut, and shook my head. I heard Kett order Dorton to tell us from where he had stolen each item, so that the owners could claim them. I clutched the wedding ring in my hand. Some men came to the bench to claim their property, while the thief stood by, guarded by a soldier, head cast down. When the last item had been claimed, I opened my hand, showing Kett what lay within.

He gave me a curious look. 'Whose is that?'

'It belonged to the woman whose murder I am investigating. Her name and that of her husband are engraved inside the ring.'

He shook his head, briskly gathering up his papers. 'Not that again. Well, keep it, if you wish. I must ride down to the cathedral now. Thank you for your help, I hope today taught people that thievery will not be tolerated. By the way, put that Overton boy to some useful work.'

'I will, but first may I question the thief about where he found this ring?'

'Very well, but he is to be put out straight afterwards.' Kett shouted to the soldiers, who were leading away those found guilty, 'Keep Dorton back. Serjeant Shardlake has something to ask him.'

I waved to Barak and Nicholas to join me, and we walked across to Dorton. He cringed as we approached. I opened my hand. 'Where did you find this ring?'

He looked at it. 'Everything else I stole from the huts, sir, but that ring – that was a gift from God.'

A soldier cuffed his greasy head. 'Talk sense, you bezzled puttock, or you'll get the shit beaten out of you at the camp boundary.'

'What do you mean, Dorton?' I asked quietly.

'Only that I didn't take it from the huts, I swear. I was walking along the path to my own hut and I saw it lying on the earth, glimsing in the sun – it was about ten days ago, before the weather changed. Someone must have dropped it.'

The soldier snorted. 'A wedding ring of good gold?'

'It's true, I swear it!' Dorton said, frantically. 'Why would I lie about this when I've admitted everything else?'

I nodded. 'True. The ring, by the way, belonged to a woman with whom I have a connection. Did you find anything else with it?'

Dorton reached into his tattered clothes and produced a double-sided nit-comb, tiny black bodies between the tines. 'This was next to it, I kept it for myself.'

'Nothing else?'

'No, I swear. I was going to sell the ring in Norwich market, but then the battle came, and afterwards –' the beery smell of his breath was enough to finish the sentence.

I looked at him. He had indeed nothing to gain by lying. I said, 'Take my friends and me to where you found the ring and comb. By your leave,' I added to the soldier. He shrugged, and followed as Dorton led us into the body of the camp. He came to a place where two paths intersected, and pointed to the ground. 'Just there, sir. My little hut is –' he swallowed – 'was a quarter-mile up that path.'

I bent down. The path was muddy now, but a fortnight ago it would have been dry and rutted. If anyone had dropped a gold ring, it would soon have been spotted. I looked around the crossroads. Toby Lockswood's hut was nearby. I nodded. 'Thank you, Dorton.'

He gave me a smile, showing a few discoloured teeth. 'Won't you help me, Master? Give me a little money to help me on my way?'

'Help you to the nearest inn, more like,' Barak said. I shook my head, though I pitied the man, and the soldier led him roughly away.

✟

BARAK, NICHOLAS AND I returned to our hut. I was pleased when Goody Everneke, Simon, Natty and Goodman Dickon, who had brought the accusations against the Swardeston landlord, came and congratulated us on Nicholas's victory. 'Are you going to help us now, boy, earn your keep?' Dickon asked.

Simon spoke up. 'You can help with the horses, Master Nicholas, can't you?' He jigged up and down. 'You've had training as a horseman.'

Nicholas smiled. 'A good idea. Yes, I can do that.'

Simon waved his hands with pleasure. I asked Natty, 'How are you?'

Goodwife Everneke said, 'The swelling on his arm has gone, thanks be to God. I made him use the stuff you bought from the cathedral.'

'It stings like hell,' Natty said, though with a smile for Mistress Everneke, who had done so much to help those in need in the camp.

'Thank you,' I said to her. 'Now, we three have something to discuss, and must go to our hut.'

Sitting in the gloomy interior, leaning against the walls, I passed the gold ring to Barak and Nicholas. Barak whistled. 'This is it, all right.'

'How in God's name did it get to the camp?' Nicholas asked.

I pulled out the scurfy nit-comb. 'It was with this. Sounds to me like both fell from a hole in someone's purse or bag.'

'And near two weeks ago. Dorton must have found it just after it was dropped, before someone else did.'

'But who in God's name dropped it?' Barak asked.

'Whoever it was must have had it for years,' Nicholas said slowly. 'Remember what Master Parry told us, Edith's knuckles were too swollen to get a wedding ring off. And this was pulled off, not cut.'

I said, 'We need to question people in the huts leading off that crossroads. It may be a long job. We can say we found a gold ring nearby and ask people if it's theirs.'

Barak laughed. 'Everyone will claim it.'

'We'll ask them first to say what's engraved inside. Come, we'll start with Toby Lockswood. Nick, you'd better stay down on the road. Whoever had the ring could have been harbouring Edith Boleyn, or holding her prisoner, for years. It could even be her killer. We should take our knives.'

✝

We arrived at Toby's hut half an hour later. For once, the sun had come out. Toby was outside, this time sharpening a large sword with a whetstone. Barak quietly slipped off the cover on the knife on his artificial hand. Lockswood looked up at us, eyes full of hatred – and something more. Madness? The thought came to me, if his reason was going, could he have been the one who betrayed the whereabouts of Miles's wife? But no, surely, his devotion to the cause of the camp was wholehearted. He rubbed a hand through his curly black hair.

'What do you two want?' he snapped. 'Where's your boy gentle-man? On a horse to London, I expect.'

'He's at the end of this road,' Barak said. 'Got a sword now, have you?'

'Yes. Commoners are allowed them in the camp. To gut any gen-tlemen and courtiers who dare come here.'

I made an effort to be civil. 'We have not come to fight, Toby.' I pulled the nit-comb from my pocket. 'Is this yours? I found it.'

He shook his head, pulling another comb from his pocket. 'No, I have one.' He frowned. 'You haven't come to see if I've lost my comb.'

'No. Perhaps you remember the days when you helped us try to discover who killed Edith Boleyn and those others. You might be inter-ested to see this.' I held the wedding ring out to him.

Toby looked at it, and could not hide his curiosity. 'Good gold, engraved with their names. Where did you get it?'

'There was a petty thief tried at the Oak this morning for stealing things from people's huts. This was among them. He confessed to his mitchery, but said he found the ring on the ground near the crossroads. He showed us the spot. He had no reason to lie.'

Toby said incredulously, 'Just lying in the road?'

'Yes. Someone must have dropped it.'

Lockswood tossed it back to me. 'Better find them, then.' He frowned. 'That comb was with it, wasn't it?'

I hesitated. 'Yes.'

'And if I had claimed it as mine, you'd have taken that as evidence I had the ring, too.'

'Any lawyer would try such a tactic.'

He lifted the sword and said, with deadly quiet, 'Fuck off, the pair of you. And don't come back.'

☦

THE THREE OF US each took a lane and spent the next hour and a half calling at huts. I had in mind what I had said about the possibility of danger, but we were armed, and the likelihood of someone attacking us in this thickly populated area was, I hoped, small. Most people said they had not lost a ring, and those who did claim it could not tell us what was engraved inside. Although the possibility of finding more about Edith and where she had been these last nine years had galvan-ized me, I was tired by the time the three of us met again back at the crossroads. Barak said gloomily, 'Whoever dropped it could have taken any of the four lanes, then walked miles, for all we know.'

'Let's take the last lane together,' I said. 'And then – perhaps tomorrow – we can persuade others to join the search; pay some of the men –'

'There are eight or nine thousand on Mousehold by my reckoning,' Barak said. 'This could be a long job.'

But the answer came sooner than we had expected. At the third circle of huts, its parish banner hanging limp in the still afternoon, several men were re-laying bracken on the roof of a hut, which had been torn down in the storm. One of them, a slim man in his thirties standing on a short ladder, I recognized at once; Peter Bone. And I remembered with a jolt that I had met him coming from Norwich to the camp with a bag of his possessions, near two weeks ago, just when Dorton said he had found the ring. I called out, 'Peter, may we have a private word?'

Once more he looked as though he would rather avoid a conversa-tion, but stepped down. 'Excuse me, bors,' he said to his fellows, who looked at us curiously. He led us into one of the small huts occupied by single people. Everything inside was neat and tidy. The pack I had seen him carrying lay in a corner. We all sat down, Barak and Nicholas on either side of the door.

Nicholas nodded at the pack. 'I see the seam is coming away there. You should sew it up, or you will lose things.'

'Like this perhaps.' I opened my hand, showing him the comb and ring. He looked at us for a moment, eyes wide, then bowed his head and stared down at the mud floor. I said, 'You know what is engraved on the inside of this ring?'

He spoke in a monotone. 'Yes. It is Edith Boleyn's wedding ring.' He looked up, his narrow face suddenly etched with sorrow. 'I spent hours searching for it; it must have slipped through that tear in the seam the day I brought my things to the camp.' He made a sound between a sigh and a groan. 'Where was it?'

'A thief found it on the path by the crossroads, probably the day you dropped it. He was tried at the Oak today. I examined the ring and saw the engraving.'

Bone looked at it. He was silent a long moment, then said, 'Edith was wearing it when she came to us. She took it off soon after – her hands did not get bad till much later – but kept it in a drawer.' He paused, then gave a bitter laugh. 'I see I must tell the whole story. Before, I was frightened of being dragged before the court, accused of kidnapping by her father. But the gentlemen of Norwich can hardly do that now.'

'Did you kidnap her?' I asked sharply.

He looked at me, his eyes prominent in his thin, lined face. 'No.'

'Did you kill her?'

He spoke angrily. 'If I knew who did, then I would kill them with this.' He produced a knife from his belt and held it up.

'Give that to me,' Barak said quietly. Reluctantly, Bone passed it over.

I said, 'If what you say is true, I promise there will be no trouble. Now please, for Edith's sake, tell me what you know.'

Peter Bone leaned back against the wooden wall. I thought at first he was not going to speak, but then he said, 'My father was a weaver, and farmed a small plot of land towards Wymondham. He had three children, first me, then my sisters Mercy and Grace. Some weavers are wealthy, others just small men, like my father. He died, God save his soul, in 1531, the year after our mother. The lease on his house and bit of farmland ended with his death, and my two sisters and I were left only with his equipment and a little money. I had learned the weaving trade from him and the three of us, who were young then, agreed that I should come to Norwich and try to make my way in the trade, while Mercy and Grace, who had been trained in the skills of serving women by our mother, would try to find employment as ladies' maids in gentry houses. So, I came to Norwich, rented a house, and for a while I was successful, employing my own spinners and cloth finishers. I moved to the house where you first met me. I married a good Norwich girl.' He shook his head sadly. 'That was a happy time, but it didn't last. She died of the smallpox. Trade became more difficult – the great men of Norwich were taking more and more of the cloth-making processes into their own hands, limiting what small men could do.' He closed his eyes, and sighed. 'But I worked on, I kept a-doing. Everyone knew that I had two sisters away in service. Serving the gentry families, Grace and Mercy had to behave, though by nature both were noisy, friendly, sometimes a little provoking.' He smiled sadly.

'Would you like some beer, Goodman Bone?' I asked gently.

He shook his head. 'No, thank you. What you want me to do is get on with my story, isn't it? Well, my sisters served in various houses. Grace, as you know, eventually went to serve Edith Boleyn. That was in 'thirty-eight. But it was Mercy who had the sadder story.' He wrung his thin hands together. 'I told you my sisters were alike in their ways, and both had lovely dark hair and large blue eyes. But in one way they were different – Grace seemed to have no interest in men, while Mercy – well, she liked them. She was working for a family on an estate over near Cromer, and in 'thirty-three, only two years after our father died, I was summoned there by the owner. He told me his son had got Mercy pregnant – oh, I don't doubt she'd encouraged him – and she had had a baby son. She died in childbirth.' He was quiet again for a moment, then said, in little more than a whisper, 'I saw my nephew just once, a little newborn, in the hands of his wet-nurse. I saw his father, too, a good-looking young man. I could see he, too, was grieving. For the boy's father, though, it was all about business.' His tone darkened. 'He said he had already had Mercy quietly buried. His son would look after the boy and see to his education; it's a common enough arrangement. But what I can never forgive is him saying I must never come near his family, nor mention what happened, or he would cut the child off. Mercy, after all, had shown herself a wanton and a sinner.'

Then suddenly he was crying, sobbing like a child. I asked him gently again if he would like something to drink, but he shook his head, wiping his face angrily, and continued, 'I agreed, for the child's sake. He will be in his teens now. I don't even know his name. And when people asked where Mercy was, I said she now worked up in Yorkshire, so far away she could not visit. After a few years, hardly anyone remembered her. Grace was a comfort to me, living nearer she came and visited often. Then, in 'thirty-eight, she went to work for the Boleyns. The pay was good, and needed to be for the family was known to be very difficult. But Grace became attached to Edith Boleyn, more, I think, than she had been to anyone save Mercy and me, despite her strange ways. Edith confided in Grace that she could not give her husband affection, nor any man.' He looked up at me. 'She told Grace her own father had interfered with her as a child.' Nicholas made a sound of disgust, but Peter said, 'You'd be surprised how often such things happen, in rich houses as well as poor.'

'Yes,' I agreed grimly, remembering Thomas Seymour and the Lady Elizabeth.

'In any case, Grace stayed with the family, despite all the mutual hatreds. Edith said her husband could never understand why his wife would not sleep with him.'

'Did Edith tell him what her father had done?'

'No. She was ashamed. She told only Grace. Grace felt sorry for John Boleyn, even if he was liable to outbreaks of temper, and savage over his quarrel with his neighbour. And those twins were already violent and unmanageable, though not yet ten. Perhaps it was partly because Edith felt nothing for them, not since their birth. You've probably heard the story of Gerald scarring Barnabas to try and get their mother's attention. Grace saw that happen. Afterwards, Edith felt guilty and, as she did sometimes, refused to eat. The trouble Grace had then, trying to persuade Edith to take just enough to stay alive.' He shook his head wearily.

'Was she mad?' Nicholas asked.

'She was punishing herself,' Peter said in sudden anger. 'If that is madness, so be it.'

I said, 'And then came the affair between John Boleyn and Isabella.'

'Yes. When Edith learned of it through local gossip, she stopped eating again. Grace told me she thought that, too, was from guilt, because her husband had been driven to another woman.'

Peter sighed wearily. 'Between Edith learning about her husband's affair with Isabella and starving herself, Grace felt things could not go on. What happened next was her idea. Grace proposed she and Edith leave Brikewell, and come to me in Norwich, where Edith would pass herself off as Mercy come home. Remember, nobody knew she was dead. Grace put the idea to me. I took some persuading, I may tell you, but Grace was –' he smiled ruefully – 'forceful.'

I was about to ask whether Edith and Grace were the type of woman attracted not to men, but other women. But such matters did not affect the case, and were not my business.

Peter continued, 'Edith got what she had never had before, peace and security. And she and Grace were as close as any two people I have seen. And I liked Edith; when she was freed from the bonds of the Boleyn family she blossomed, put on weight, even showed a sense of humour. She worked hard, too.'

I said quietly, trying to keep the tremble from my voice, 'So Edith did, after all, have people who loved and valued her. I always feared that she never did.'

Peter Bone nodded, his face working.

Nicholas said, 'Our friend Josephine Brown told us both sisters were alike, dark and buxom. But was not Grace blonde?'

For the first time, Peter smiled openly. 'When Edith came to us, the first thing Grace did was dye her hair black, as Grace's was and Mercy's had been. Then we made her eat – Grace made it a condition that Edith must never starve herself again. She readily cooperated, and soon regained a buxom figure.'

'And what did you get out of all this, Goodman Bone?' Barak said quietly.

Peter looked at him steadily. 'Helping my sister rescue a poor woman who otherwise would probably have died. And with two women in the house again – sometimes it felt almost as though Mercy had returned to life. And, yes, getting one over on the rich masters.' He laughed. 'You know what Edith found the most difficult part of her – disguise – even though it was the most necessary one? Wearing the apron and wadmol dress of a poor woman, letting her face get dirty. Wearing cheap shoes. Disguising her accent, that mark of those who rule.' He looked at me. 'You have tried to do the same thing here.'

'Yes, I have. It makes life easier.' And I thought, That is what the puppet show had brought to my mind, the possibility that in our society a woman might turn into someone different just by changing her clothes. But I had been too tired to think it through, then.

Peter went on, 'Edith knew she must do it, to survive. And she got used to our ways, quite quickly. Oh, the three of us had some merry times together. Edith tended to stay in the house on market days, and avoid the richer parts of town, but occasionally people of her own class she had known before passed her in the street. And none ever gave her a second glance. She was just another poor woman, you see.'

Nicholas shook his head. 'So. That is where Edith was all those years.'

There was silence in the hut, as we tried to take it all in. Peter Bone gave a wry smile. 'There's a newdickle for you, eh, Master Shardlake. Someone giving up being rich and turning themselves into someone poor.'

'Yes. I would never have guessed that.' I smiled sadly. 'How did Edith come to leave you?'

Peter's face sagged. 'By the turn of last year, times were getting hard. I had to let my workers go. Edith and Grace helped me with spinning and weaving, but Edith had developed pains in her hands, and her knuckles had become swollen.' He sighed. 'She was often in pain, couldn't work. Then last spring the influenza came, and carried off poor Grace. It was a terrible shock to Edith and me. By that time we could no longer afford the rent on the house, and Edith still could not work. Then she said there was one thing left she might try, a distant but very rich relative of her husband's, who she could appeal to for help. I didn't know then it was the Lady Elizabeth. She left in March, with a little money for the journey. She promised to return within a few weeks, but never came back. Then I heard her body had been found at Brikewell.'

'You lied, then, saying both your sisters had died of influenza.'

His expression became clouded. 'I told you Boleyn's people sought out Grace after she and Edith disappeared from the Boleyns' estate. When I heard of Edith's murder I was bereft; I wasn't going to say where she had been. It wouldn't have helped; I had no idea who could have murdered her.' He looked at me. 'It would not have helped your friend Master Boleyn's case to discover that Edith hated living at his house so much that she fled and changed her very identity. Besides, Edith and Grace were both now dead, nothing I could do would bring them back.'

I asked quietly, 'Have you no idea who might have killed her?'

He shook his head. 'None. Except that it was done with an unbelievable hatred.'

I added, 'But she kept her wedding ring.'

'Yes, in a drawer, as I said. Then I brought it here, it was the only keepsake I had of her. I don't know why she kept it — but with that inscription she could hardly sell it in Norwich Market, could she?'

I said, 'We hope to find out who killed her, but there are many suspects.'

Peter sighed again, and tears began trickling down his face. 'Let me know if you find out, but otherwise, please, leave me alone. Every day I try to put it all behind me, and work to build a new and better Commonwealth, perhaps even one where such things may no longer happen.'

Chapter Seventy

I SAT ON MY favourite grassy hummock, on the crest overlooking
Norwich. It was a rare sunny day — with the frequent showers of
rain, Kett's forces stationed in the city had occupied some of the
churches as well as the cathedral, to the ire of the more pious citizens.
It was the sixteenth of August, nearly ten days since Peter Bone had
told me where Edith had been all those missing years.

In the camp, I was largely at leisure. Kett had decided there would
be no trials of the Norwich gentlemen at the Oak; some who had
agreed to cooperate had been freed, others were still held in the castle
and Guildhall prisons. Apart from the occasional thief or brawler,
there were no more cases to try. As my life became quieter, I realized
how much strain I had been under, and for how long; in recent days I
had spent a good deal of time asleep. As for my friends, Nicholas was
helping with the horses along with Simon; Natty's arm was better;
Barak, though, I was concerned about. Although he still had clerical
work, dealing mainly now with materials brought up from Norwich —
everything was still meticulously recorded — like me, he had less to do
and spent much of his free time wandering around the camp, watching
the ceaseless military training, stopping to gossip but also, I noticed, to
drink. I knew he felt anxious and guilty about Tamasin, from whom
nothing more had been heard.

Looking over the city, I sat mulling over the issue of Edith yet
again. Logically, after her rejection at Hatfield, she would have returned
to Norwich and Peter Bone. But before she reached him, someone had
murdered her and I was no closer to finding who that might be. The
twins, Chawry, Boleyn himself — his lack of an alibi still preyed on
me — or Isabella — all were possible candidates, and there was also the

whole murky issue of Southwell and Flowerdew's interest in the Brikewell estate to consider.

I reflected on the other mystery in which I had become involved — who had betrayed the whereabouts of Captain Miles's wife to the authorities in London? Was it someone from the capital? I began to think it was. I did not think I was seriously suspected, and had no sense of being watched. That left as suspects the increasingly unstable Toby Lockswood, Edward Brown, Michael Vowell, Peter Bone and the old soldier, poor dead Hector Johnson. But I could not think it was any of them. Lockswood I had not seen since the day I had showed him Edith's ring, which I now kept in my purse. I heard he had been given a job felling trees over at Thorpe Wood. His demotion would have hurt him and I imagined him taking his rage out on the trees with his axe.

I had promised Peter Bone I would tell only those who needed to know about Edith. I was duty bound to tell Parry; apart from anything else, it would choke off further enquiries around Hatfield by the Lady Elizabeth. I wrote to him, telling him about Edith. Regarding my present whereabouts, I said I was detained in the rebel camp but under comfortable conditions. And then, of course, I had to tell Robert Kett. Unless he agreed the letter could be sent with a covering note from him saying the seal was not to be broken, Edith's visit to Elizabeth would become common gossip throughout Norfolk, the very thing I had been asked to avoid.

He read the letter, which I took to him at St Michael's Chapel, shaking his head in amazement over the story. His face seemed more lined these days, more worried. He frowned, though, at one word on the letter. 'Surely,' he said indignantly, 'it is untrue you are "detained" in the camp. You gave your oath to serve me.'

I had expected this. 'It is only that I do not think Master Parry or the Lady Elizabeth would be pleased to learn I was here voluntarily.'

He looked at me with those large brown eyes that seemed to pierce the soul. 'Insurance, then, for future employment with the Lady?'

'Yes. And her protection.'

He smiled wryly. 'But if we achieve our goals, you could return to working in the Court of Requests, aiding the poor against the landlords. There will be more cases, and life will be easier for the defendants.'

'In truth I would prefer that, but I will never be allowed to return there while Richard Rich is Lord Chancellor.' I remembered that terrifying January day when I had found him waiting for me in Parry's office. 'Indeed, it is from him that I need the Lady Elizabeth's protection.'

Kett said, 'Perhaps we may be able to get rid of Rich, when our cause wins.'

'Amen to that. But – if you agree, I would like my – insurance.'

Kett said, 'Cross through the word *detained*. Just say you are in the camp.'

I hesitated, then took the quill Kett offered me and crossed out the word, so thickly it could not be read at all. He nodded, and sanded the letter. 'I will ensure it gets to Hatfield unread. Through one of my couriers who brings information from London.'

☩

FINALLY, JOHN AND ISABELLA Boleyn had had to be told. I had visited them the day after Peter Bone told me his story, Nicholas accompanying me on the now familiar walk down the escarpment, through the remains of Bishopsgate Bridge gatehouse, along the streets where so much blood had been spilt, and down to the castle. In Norwich those going about their business looked nervous if they were of gentleman status, more confident and sometimes cocky if they were poor. The walls, I knew, were now patrolled by men loyal to Kett.

Norwich Castle was quieter today, though the prison stink was strong as ever with so many held there. John Boleyn's cell, with its space, furniture, and now with Isabella in residence, was like an island in a sea of gloom. The two seemed happy enough. I told them of my discovery of where Edith had been those nine years. I watched them closely as I recounted the story; both seemed genuinely shocked. Boleyn said bitterly, 'And she never thought to send even a note that she was alive.'

Isabella said gently, 'Perhaps she thought in time her silence would give you freedom to marry again.'

'You did not know her as I did, my love. God save her soul, but the only person Edith ever thought of was herself.'

I said, 'Would you like her ring, John?'

His eyes flashed with anger for a moment. He shook his head vigorously.

Nicholas said, 'Have you heard any more from Chawry?' Isabella gave me a quick look, and I saw from Boleyn's face that she had not yet told him of the attempted rape. Perhaps she thought he already had too much to bear. 'Nothing,' Boleyn said. 'But it has not been long, I hope for some news soon. Jesu knows what state Brikewell is in.' So he believed Chawry had gone there.

We left after taking a glass of wine and began the walk back to camp. As we passed through Tombland, I saw a familiar couple walking past the cathedral – Gawen Reynolds and his wife, Jane. He walked slowly, bent over his stick, she with an arm through his, white bandages on her hands. I hesitated; surely if anyone had a right to know what had happened to Edith it was her parents.

'Leave them,' Nicholas said warningly.

'That poor woman at least should know.'

'Then try and get her on her own again, as you did before.'

'That was a piece of uncommon luck, unlikely to be repeated.'

As we stood there a boy in his teens, in a tattered wadmol jacket and cheap hose, came up to within a yard of Reynolds, and called out, 'Greedy old snudge, you should be in Guildhall prison!' then bent and bared his arse at the old man. Reynolds, crying 'Rebel filth!', raised his stick to bring it down on the boy's head. The lad was too quick, though, jumping away, causing Reynolds to overbalance and fall to the ground, the stick rolling away. The boy yelled with laughter, and the men guarding the cathedral gates smiled. Reynolds, his thin face red with fury, tried to rise but could not. 'Help me, you stupid old bitch!' he shouted at his wife. The moment the boy bared his arse she had done something I had never seen before – smiled, just for a moment. Now she looked down at her furious husband. 'I can't, Gawen, my hands –'

'Bugger your hands, help me up!'

With a sigh, I crossed the street to them, Nicholas following. Reynolds did not at first see who we were, and as we helped him to his feet and returned his stick he gasped, 'Thank you!' Then he recognized us and his face darkened again. 'You!' he snarled. 'I need your help no more than that time in the Market Square. Why do you haunt me like a pair of devils!' He lashed out at us with his stick, catching me a blow on the shoulder. Nicholas wrenched it from his hands.

'Have you no gratitude, sir?' he asked hotly.

'Give me my stick, you carrot-haired cunt!' Reynolds shrieked. 'You pair of traitors! Do you know where I have just been? To the Guildhall prison, to visit a supplier of mine shut up in there, a vile, dark, underground place stinking of damp. He can no longer run his business, and I have contracts with him! You rebel filth will destroy this city! You two gentlemen are in league with these scabby renegade apes! We'll hang you in the end – hang you, hunchback!' His tirade ended in a fit of coughing, which was just as well as a grinning crowd was gathering. Jane Reynolds leaned against the wall of Augustine Stew-ard's courtyard, now looking at her husband with disgust. I motioned Nicholas to step back. As we walked away, though, I still wished I had been able to tell old Jane her daughter had enjoyed at least some years of happiness before her terrible death.

Chapter Seventy-one

During those middle days of August, it seemed that only
bad news arrived from the messengers who came to St Michael's
Chapel. Everywhere in the south-east the smaller camps were going
down; there were threats of force combined with promises of pardon
to all except the leaders, and offers of money – £67 in Suffolk, more
than £100 to the camp outside Canterbury. Those sums were big,
though dwarfed by the £500 given Kett by Southwell – but Mousehold was by far the biggest camp. From the West Country came news
of a major military defeat of the rebels there. And on the seventeenth
of August, the first essay having been rebuffed, a large expedition sent
from Mousehold to take Great Yarmouth failed, with thirty rebels and
six cannon captured. It seemed all hope of taking Yarmouth was lost,
for afterwards a number of poorer Yarmouth citizens, some with their
wives, arrived in camp, adding to the refugees from the Suffolk and
Essex camps.

There was, though, news of a small uprising in Lincolnshire, and
another in Warwickshire. But already, on the eighth of August, France
had declared war on England. This had long been in prospect, for
French assistance to the Scots was growing, and it was said that, hopefully, the Protector's forces would now be gathered for yet another
attack on Scotland. But, two days later, it was announced publicly in
London that a new army was to be sent against us. First it was said the
Protector himself would lead it, then it was confirmed that the commander would be the Earl of Warwick, an experienced soldier on land
and sea. And for all the size of the camp, and its control of Norwich,
it began increasingly to seem like an island in a hostile sea.

Kett, honest as ever, shared all this news from the Oak. In the camp,
divisions of opinion began to appear. Some said that perhaps, after all,

a pardon should be sought; yet another proclamation from the Protector had pardoned all those guilty of 'riotous assembly' who made 'humble submission'. Others said the size of our camp, the possibility of new risings, and the Protector's obsession with the Scottish war, meant that if we held on, our demands would be met. A third faction, the largest, said we should await the new army and fight it, despite word that it would be far larger. After all, Northampton's army had been easily defeated, by men with little intensive training but who now had several weeks' more. And if we won, we could then sweep on, gathering men from the disbanded south-eastern camps, perhaps move on London. This faction was encouraged by the prophets, both those who spoke of ancient prophecies and those who claimed inspiration from the Bible, claiming to hear the very voice of God. Meanwhile, some in the camp still said this army was not sent from the Protector at all, but by treach-erous members of his Council supported by the Norfolk gentry. In reality, all depended on the size and scale of the army the Protector sent.

Another, more practical consideration also weighed with those who wished to fight to the end – after all the humiliations inflicted on the Norfolk gentry, what would they do to the common people if they won? And now, sadly, there was no mention of enclosure commissions or reform in the Protector's proclamations. With this faction, I had to say, I had some sympathy, causing Barak to say that I was becoming more radical every day.

Arguments about what should be done took place quietly, around the campfires. Robert and William Kett, representatives of the Hun-dreds and clerics who supported the rebellion, still addressed the camp-men from the Oak and spoke of holding out until our aims were achieved. Meanwhile, military training redoubled. But the atmosphere in the camp was one of deepening anxiety, a far cry from the exuber-ance of the early days.

✝

AS NEWS OF THE Yarmouth defeat filtered through the camp, Barak returned to our hut in a sombre mood. 'I was approached by one of the Hundred leaders earlier on,' he said. 'If we're to defeat this new army, we need every man who can fight.' He paused. 'He said the government army could be here in as little as ten days. He asked me to join in training.'

Nicholas said, 'But with –'

Barak lifted his artificial hand. He winced a little, it was paining him as it often did in the evenings. 'Yes,' he answered quietly. 'But it's known I've been something of a fighter in the past.'

I looked at him through the gloom of the hut. 'Do you want to?' I spoke quietly, for the Swardeston villagers were firmly for holding out.

He shook his head. 'No. I realize more and more the duty I have to Tammy and the children. I want to see them again.'

'Is that why you've been drinking more?'

He nodded. Then he said softly, 'There's another reason I don't want to fight. I've been talking to a lot of people around the camp, watching the training. It's going well, but this time they're not sending a ragtag army under a useless commander; they'll bring together every professional they can find, and there's word more foreign mercenaries will be used. Swiss landsknechts. From what I hear our strategy is to try and beat them in the Norwich streets like before, but if that fails, we'll assemble all our forces on the Mousehold escarpment and fight them there.'

'That sounds like military sense.'

'I'll train, and keep my ear to the ground, but' – he shook his head – 'this isn't going to be like last time.'

We were silent a moment. Then Barak said, 'Kett's planning a fair, with jugglers and the like, for next Tuesday, to cheer people up. They're going to have the camping game.' He laughed grimly. 'Good preparation for a battle. The northern Hundred against the southern. It'll be worth watching.'

'I've heard of the camping game in London.' I smiled. 'A mixture of football, wrestling and general mayhem.'

'Goody Everneke says mayhem's the word in East Anglia. Still, it'll let the younger men work off some energy.'

✝

IT RAINED FOR the rest of the weekend, but Tuesday, the twentieth of August, dawned fine and sunny. I made my way to the fair with the rest of the Swardeston villagers, Barak and Nicholas and Edward Brown, who had come up with many from Norwich. Josephine walked with him, cradling Mousy in her arms. The little girl, five months old now, looked round her, examining the crowds intently with her thumb in her mouth. I glanced at Nicholas. He had been quiet these last few days. He was still working with the horses and had not yet been asked to join in training for the battle; I feared that if he was, he might refuse. Natty walked with Simon, who was waving his arms and chattering about what there might be to see. 'He's over-excited,' Natty said to me, a little wearily. Goodwife Everneke told Simon to quiet himself, lest people think him a nonny.

The fair was held on open heathland a mile from the crest; it was used for military training and the yellow grass had been cut down. Tents had been brought from Surrey Place, trestle tables erected and a stage built. As ever, I was amazed by the ability of the camp-men to organize so much in so short a time. Stewards guided the thousands gathering for the various events to the viewing places. Michael Vowell, standing with a group of his young friends, gave me a wave.

The fair began with a military display. A hundred archers shot their bows at earthen butts. Most of the arrows whistling through the air reached the circular targets in the centre. People clapped. This was followed by a mock battle between a hundred men in half-armour and helmets, using swords, halberds, spears and half-pikes. The choreography, by men with only the briefest practice, was remarkable.

The final part of the military display was the shooting of a currier, a type of small arquebus, captured from Northampton's army. Few had ever seen such a weapon, and there were many curious stares at the gun, half as long as the man who held it was tall, with its long barrel and heavy stock. A second man lit a little fire. People peered in puzzlement as a lead ball was dropped into the barrel and the man aimed the arquebus at a heavy piece of armour captured from one of Northampton's soldiers, set up fifteen feet away. Those standing close enough saw a little pan of gunpowder on the side of the arquebus uncovered, and a lit match attached by the assistant to a fuse. The trigger was pulled; there was a flash, a bang, and a round hole appeared in the armour. Natty turned to me, puzzled. 'Seems a lot of effort for one shot,' he said, scratching his head. His hair needed cutting again; I hoped he did not have nits.

'Imagine a hundred of those facing you,' Barak said grimly.

Grumbling among the crowd, most of whom had been able to see little, turned to excitement as Robert Kett mounted the nearby stage, with his brother William and Captain Miles. There was cheering and clapping. He raised a hand for silence, then began to speak, his great voice carrying far, his words, as usual, repeated back to those beyond hearing distance. It was a short speech, but every word counted.

'My friends! You have followed me loyally for six weeks now, you have worked and trained as hard and successfully as any assembly in history! You have built this camp, and lived here in comradeship! You have put down the gentry and the rulers of Norfolk and of Norwich itself — we have taken the second-largest city in England and sent an army of lords and noblemen fleeing!' There were loud cheers, which, again, he stilled with a raised hand. 'I have always been open with you, never hidden anything, and you will know we failed to take Yarmouth, and that though some camps remain and there are new stirrings, most camps to the south are put down! Nor do I hide the fact that a great army, with many thousand men, led by the Earl of Warwick, has, according to one report, set out from London today. My friends, we face another, greater battle, but I know the stout hearts and strong arms of the Norfolk people, and in the end we shall win!' He took a deep breath. 'Think what will happen then! The end of forced enclosures and the unchecked oppression of the landlords and the great merchants! The end of the corrupt officialdom that has aided them, whose deeds would shame His Majesty if he knew. We shall win, and this time we shall lead the people to London, and present our demands to the King himself, with no earls or landlords to stand in our way!' The audience cheered louder than ever, some throwing their caps in the air. All the time he spoke, Kett's face had worked with emotion. Now he cried, 'God save King Edward!' and with that, amidst more clapping and cheering, he stepped down. I caught a glimpse of his face as he did so; it was, suddenly, desperately serious.

'He's right,' Natty said quietly. 'We can win, and bring a new Commonwealth to England!'

671

'I hope so,' I said. Like everyone, I was moved by Kett's speech, but the image of streets red with blood came into my head.

✝

WE SPENT THE NEXT few hours at the various entertainments. There were tumblers, juggling boys and a bear-baiting which Barak, Natty and Nicholas went to see, but which I avoided. I walked away a little with Josephine. 'What did you think of Captain Kett's speech?' I asked.

'A great speech by a great man. Edward believes we can win. And I feel stronger now, the path is set and we must go down it.' She gave me a direct look with her clear blue eyes; how far she had come from the timid Josephine I had once known.

'Yes, it seems we must,' I agreed.

She smiled. 'You said, "we". Does that mean you count yourself fully amongst us now?'

'Yes, I think it does.' I answered seriously. 'Though I do not know what will happen.'

'Who does?' She smiled. 'Sir, you ever foresaw the worst.'

'Perhaps.'

'Will you hold Mousy a little? I would like to look at the stalls.'

As always, I was happy to hold the child, who smiled at me, said something that sounded like 'Ellow', though it was probably just a gurgling, then nestled into my chest and fell asleep. I walked with Josephine among the trestle tables, where pies and beer were for sale, together with objects taken from the manor houses but not valuable enough for Kett's treasury – a porcelain bowl set with holes, smelling of the lavender within, a tin stork painted gold, once a doorstop, a toy wooden dog which I bought for Mousy.

We walked on. We passed Michael Vowell and his friends again. 'That was the greatest speech Captain Kett has ever made,' he said enthusiastically. 'That will end talk of seeking some sort of pardon.' His young friends agreed loudly.

Josephine and I began walking back to rejoin the others, making our way through the good-natured crowds. But we had only gone a few yards when a man stepped into our path. Toby Lockswood, looking unkempt and smelling of drink. 'Master Shardlake,' he said sneeringly. 'Taking another man's wife and child for a walk?'

I made to push past him, but he grabbed my arm. 'Have a care for the child!' I shouted. Mousy began to cry, and Josephine stared at Lockswood with horrified anger.

He leaned in to me. 'I hear you had a letter from the Lady Eliza beth's Comptroller a while back, insulting our camp.'

'How could you know that?'

He smiled, a flash of white teeth amid his thick, tangled beard. 'I heard a lot before that boy of yours lost me my post. I've been spreading the news. Telling my fellows you serve one of the richest people in the land. And that you nurse our enemy, that viper Overton, to your bosom as closely as that baby. Watch out, Master Shardlake, word about you is spreading.' He turned and walked away.

Josephine looked at me. 'Was that the man who used to work for you?'

'Yes. I think he is a little mad now.' I heard a trembling in my voice, for the idea of someone with Toby Lockswood's connections spreading poison about me around the camp was troubling indeed.

✞

THE HIGHLIGHT OF THE afternoon, just before the camping game, was a mock joust. Two lines of hurdles had been set up, small tents at each end. Two competitors on horseback emerged from the tents carry ing lances. One was dressed in armour of painted linen, with the arms of the Marquess of Northampton on the front. He looked over the crowd with a haughty expression. His lance was of cloth painted black. In contrast to the great horses of a real joust, his horse, too, was made of cloth, its painted wooden head sporting a ridiculous grin. Inside would be two men, one the front legs, the other the back. No doubt these things had been brought from village plays. From the opposite tent a young man from the camp dressed in an ordinary shirt and sleeveless leather jacket held up his own painted lance. He sat on a real horse, though, a small placid looking animal. The crowd laughed loudly, especially at the 'knight's' horse.

'Mock me not, country blockheads!' the knight shouted in a put on aristocratic accent: 'I am a warrior knight, and shall have this seditious stirrer's head from his shoulders!' There were boos and shouts from the crowd, and the painted horse shook its head in disapproval.

We were standing with the Swardeston people just by the pretend 'knight'. Everyone was laughing, even Nicholas, while Simon laughed so uncontrollably that Barak warned him not to piss himself.

Then Simon did a stupid thing. He leaned over the hurdle and gave the knight's 'horse' a resounding smack on the rear. There was a cry of 'Hey!' from inside and it staggered, so that the knight and his mount nearly fell over. The knight turned his head and said, in broad Norfolk, 'What the fuck are you doing, girtle-head?' I heard someone nearby say, 'Sooty Scambler, might've known.' Nicholas took his arm. 'Oh, Simon,' he said. 'You're so good with horses, why do you always make these mistakes with people?'

Simon lowered his head, and did not see the hilarity that followed as the knight charged the peasant lad, shouting, 'For lordship, land and money!' The boy replied, 'For the common people!' and urged his horse on. As he approached the knight's horse, it turned round and ran clumsily back to its tent, finally urged inside by a thrust at its bottom from the boy's cloth lance. He got off his horse and bowed to resound-ing cheers. I laughed as loudly as the rest. Simon slowly raised his head. 'Are people still looking at me?' he asked.

'No, lad, it's forgotten. You know, when this is over, I'm going to get you a job working with horses somewhere.' He gave me a watery smile of thanks.

☨

THE FINAL EVENT OF the afternoon was the 'camping game'. Where the 'joust' had been comic, this was seriously, brutally competi-tive. Natty left us, for he had been selected to play. Goody Everneke shook her head. 'This'll be rough,' she said.

'I'll warrant no more than in London,' Barak said.

She looked at him. 'I saw Norfolk play Suffolk last year; the Nor-folk lads asked the Suffolk ones if they'd brought their coffins.'

A large area was cleared, ropes secured, and about thirty competi-tors from each side, all strong lads or young men, stripped to the waist and, wearing coloured sashes to identify their side, began fighting – it was the only word – over a ball made from a pig's bladder. There was wrestling and kicking to get hold of it. There was a referee, but few if any rules. It was surprising to see Natty, the quiet, thoughtful lad I had come to know, charge as fiercely as any of them. I saw Toby Lockswood was on the other side. He looked at Natty, and I guessed he knew the boy was associated with me.

Late in the game, with the ball a good way off and Natty running towards it, Toby suddenly charged straight at him, shouldering him in the face and bringing him down. He followed this up with a mighty kick to the balls which made Natty scream and double up. Toby glanced at me, grinned, then turned to run at the ball. The referee, who was watching the wild scrum of bodies fighting over it, had seen nothing, and the crowd's attention too was focused on the scrum. Groaning, Natty limped painfully towards us. Nicholas and Barak helped him sit down; he put his head between his knees and vomited. Barak raised his head and examined his face. 'You'll have a mighty bruise, lad,' he said. 'It's lucky he didn't smash your cheekbone.'

'That mad dog,' Nicholas said.

'Why did he do it?' Natty gasped.

'Because he knows you're friendly with us,' I answered tightly. 'How are you – down there?'

Natty, one side of his face pale with pain and the other red and swelling, ran a hand across his broad bare chest and ventured a rueful laugh. 'I'll be all right. A horse did something like that to me once. I hear some Norwich girls are coming up this evening, I was planning to see them, but I shan't now.'

✞

ONE MEMBER OF THE audience, however, had seen what Toby Lockswood had done to Natty. The game over, with a narrow victory for North Norfolk, the crowd dispersed in the late afternoon sunshine. I felt a touch on my arm and turned to see Michael Vowell looking at me seriously. He said quietly, 'That was a vicious thing done to your young friend.'

'You saw it?'

He nodded seriously. 'I have an eye out for Lockswood. I always thought him a loyal camp-man, but now I wonder. Remember, he is one of those who could have betrayed Captain Miles's wife and family.'

'Yes; along with you and me and Edward Brown.'

'It's not me, and I don't believe it was you or Brown.'

I shook my head. 'Lockswood always had a nasty streak, and it's got far worse since he lost his case against Nicholas. But the one thing he has always been is loyal to the cause.'

Vowell raised his eyebrows. 'Are you sure? He worked for that London lawyer Copuldyke for years, and he's represented many Norfolk gentry as well as your patron the Lady Elizabeth.'

I frowned. 'How do you know?'

'It's common knowledge. And Lockswood came to visit my old master, Gawen Reynolds, more than once. He tried to make a deal between him and Sir Richard Southwell, after the two quarrelled. My master wasn't having it, of course. Toby Lockswood has many connections, and his master Copuldyke many clients.'

I smiled at him wryly. 'More gossip heard at keyholes?'

He shrugged. 'I've said before, it's what servants do, so they know what's going on. And I begin to wonder whether Toby Lockswood is quite what he seems. He's certainly mixed with gentry, and got hard cash out of it. I hear he acted for his master Copuldyke when he represented John Flowerdew in one of his many cases; Captain Kett's sworn enemy.'

I shook my head. 'But when we were together he was constantly arguing with Nicholas over Commonwealth issues.'

'Have you ever heard the phrase, "A man may wear two faces under one hood"?' Perhaps he protested the cause a little too loudly. Perhaps he's the one who betrayed Miles, and perhaps it's that rather than losing his parents that's driving him mazed. It's just a thought, Master Shardlake.' Vowell looked over the now empty camping ground and continued quietly. 'Strange, isn't it, how easy it can be to change people's loyalties. Take young men who've lived and fought together for weeks, then set up a game with no prize other than a pig's bladder, and there they are kicking and beating the shit out of each other.'

He had given me much to think on as I returned to our huts with the others. I had never considered that Toby Lockswood must have had acquaintance with those who governed Norfolk; it seemed they included Richard Southwell and John Flowerdew. He had never spoken of any other cases when he worked for me. And I thought, If he had business connections to Richard Southwell and John Flower' dew, could that even be a link to the death of Edith?

✝

I HAD HOPED TO discuss this with Barak and Nicholas in the even' ing, but after a merry dinner around the campfire, with people still laughing over the mock joust, and Natty red with embarrassment as people asked if his balls were still in working order, a messenger arrived from St Michael's Chapel with a letter for Barak. He took a horn'lamp and disappeared into our hut. After a while I went to join him. In the dim light of the lamp his face was serious. He held a letter in his hand.

'Are you all right?' I asked.

For answer he passed me the letter. It was from Tamasin, written for her in Guy's shaky hand. At least, I thought, my old friend still lived. The letter was short, and desperate; it was addressed to the only place Tamasin knew, the Blue Boar in Norwich, now blown to pieces:

Husband,

Still I hear nothing from you, and begin to fear you are dead. I hear many of the camps have gone down now, and there has been much violence in the Western counties. Everywhere in London the atmosphere is fearful, men have been arrested for speaking in favour of the rebellion, and a constable came to ask me if I knew your whereabouts, since it is known around the law courts that you went to the Norfolk Assizes and never returned. All our money is gone now, and I have had to ask Guy, who remains ill, for a loan, or the children and I would starve. Little George constantly asks when you will be returning, and his voice becomes more anxious every day. I hear a great army is being gathered to put down the Norfolk rebels.

I do not know if you will get this letter, but if so I beg you, on my knees, knowing my pride and forwardness in the past have offended you, return to me, return to me.

Barak said quietly, 'Kett's set up a proper organization in Norwich now to deal with incoming letters. One of his men brought it. He said getting a letter back would be another matter, there are indeed watchers everywhere in London, and if the letter were found and it became known I was here, Tamasin could be arrested.' He looked at me, his eyes desperate. 'I have to get back to her.'

Chapter Seventy-two

I CALLED NICHOLAS inside. Barak handed him Tamasin's letter, then unstrapped his artificial hand and threw it across the hut, lift-ing his sleeve and rubbing the ugly stump. 'This is killing me,' he said. 'Tammy would rub oil into it every night, never a word of complaint though she had the children to see to.' He shook his head. 'I can't abandon her. Yet I gave my oath. I'm bound to Kett, even if I'm not much use as a fighting man with one fucking hand. Can I leave just as this army is coming? Word is that Warwick's already on his way to Cambridge, to meet what's left of Northampton's army.'

I asked, 'What would happen if you were caught trying to flee?'

'A beating; but they'd let me go. They don't want unwilling troops. And the patrols on the eastern and northern edges of the camp can't cover the whole area – it's too big. But –' he looked at us – 'there's the question of what might happen to you two. Nicholas has never been exactly popular, for all he won his case at the Oak.' He looked at me. 'And there are rumours about your loyalty going around as well.'

I pursed my lips. 'Toby Lockswood.'

'Yes. But I'm seen as loyal. If I vanished, it could come back on you.' Barak took a deep breath, then looked at Nicholas. He said quietly, 'They'd be less surprised if you left. In fact, Captain Kett gave you the choice.'

Nicholas returned Barak's gaze, his green eyes glinting. 'And I said I would stay.'

'But you've no true loyalty to the cause.'

'You want me to leave, just so I can return to London and tell Tamasin you are safe?'

'I can't think of any other way, unless I go.' Barak slammed his fist on the earthen floor. 'How is it none of my letters got through?' He looked at me. 'You and Parry have been able to exchange letters, why not us?'

I sighed. 'Kett doesn't want to make trouble with the Lady Elizabeth. He made those letters a priority.'

Barak looked at Nicholas again. 'Would you do it?' he asked, pleading now. 'You'd have to be careful going through Norfolk, but it sounds like the other camps are down. You don't belong here. And in London you could see Beatrice again.'

Nicholas ran a hand through his untidy red hair, then turned to Barak angrily. 'I belong nowhere. Did you not hear what I said at the Oak? That I may have been brought up a gentleman, but have nothing? That I have seen such things done by the rulers of Norfolk that I have come to question what a gentleman truly is? You're right, I don't belong here, I can't fit in with people I was trained from childhood to think of as stupid, dangerous creatures. I feel like a straw in the wind. And Beatrice Kenzy and her world interest me no more. I told Kett I would stay, and I will not break my word. It's the last thing I have left!'

I said to Barak, 'What if I were to ask Captain Kett if one of his couriers to London could take a letter to Tamasin?'

Barak waved his good hand in the air. 'There must be hundreds here would like to get a message to their families.'

'Few with a desperate wife in London.'

He looked at me hard. 'You think you could do it?'

'I don't know. I can only try. Tomorrow. Though it may be difficult to reach him now, with Warwick's army on its way.'

'Then thank you.'

Nicholas left the hut and walked off into the night. Barak made to follow, but I restrained him. I said, 'I felt something like Nicholas does when I was young, and lost my faith in the old Church. Uprooted, like a straw in the wind, as he said, the beliefs that sustained me gone.' I sighed. 'It is hard, but he must find his own way.'

✞

NEXT MORNING, WEDNESDAY the twenty-first of August, news reached the camp that Warwick's army had reached Cambridge and joined the remnants of Northampton's forces. They were now marching fast on Norwich, and expected in two or three days. A large number of men had been sent to the northern edge of the camp to prepare a site for a possible battle. I walked in that direction in search of Kett, but was stopped by a soldier standing guard. 'Only those selected for work here are allowed through.'

'I wished merely to ask whether Captain Kett is here.'

'He's at Surrey Place.'

I thanked him and walked back towards the palace. I stopped to listen to two men discussing the advancing army. 'Our spies say there's over a thousand Switzer mercenaries coming.'

'We set those Italians a-runnen last time, bor.'

'These are Switzer landsknechts, apparently they're fierce dymoxes.' The man broke off and gave me a suspicious look. 'Lawyer Shardlake, isn'it?'

'That's right.'

'Why you listenin' to our talk?'

'Is not everyone interested in the coming army?'

'Ay, though not all on the same side.'

I said angrily. 'I know rumours about me are being put round by Toby Lockswood. They are false!'

'So you say.' The two men stood, arms folded, the picture of Norfolk obduracy. I turned away.

✝

I WALKED THROUGH the ornate gate of Surrey Place, remembering the Italian mercenary hanged there three weeks before, past the tents in the grounds and up to the men standing guard on the wide doors. I gave my name, asked whether Captain Kett was within and whether I might see him. One guard went in and shortly after returned and escorted me inside. He led me up the main staircase to a large room guarded by two more men. All the other rooms were closed. I could hear sounds from within, though, and remembered that some of the captured gentlemen were imprisoned here. The soldier knocked, and Kett's voice called us to enter.

The room was full of wooden chests, mostly strong and with locks. Several were open, the contents spread out on tables where a dozen men were carefully examining them, before making entries in makeshift ledgers. There were coins, jewellery, gold and silver plate. Michael Vowell was there; he smiled. I also recognized a man working on the contents of another chest in a corner of the room; Toby Lockswood. He glared at me.

Captain Kett was studying a sheaf of papers. His face had changed in the few days since his great speech. It was more lined, the mouth tighter, the eyes which could blaze so fiercely somehow withdrawn. He said, rather wearily, 'What can I do for you, Master Shardlake? I imag-ined you would be at leisure these days.'

'If you have a moment, I wish to make a request.'

He sighed. 'If it is quick.'

I told him of the letter Barak had received, his desperation to let his wife know he was alive, and asked whether one of his couriers might take a letter to her.

'My couriers see only their contacts,' he said, impatience in his voice. 'It would be dangerous for both the courier and Barak's wife were he to be caught. I am sorry, Master Shardlake, but the answer must be no.' He turned on me in sudden anger. 'You demand too much! Forever asking for letters to be sent. Have you no idea of the danger my couriers face?'

I sighed. 'I am sorry.'

He grunted, a sort of half-apology for his loss of temper. I was tempted to tell him Lockswood was passing rumours around the camp, but this was not the time. I bowed to him, and went over to where Michael Vowell was recording items carefully on a sheet of paper. 'What is happening here?' I asked.

'We men who can write and have at least some knowledge of valu-ables are making an inventory of goods taken from the gentry. Tomorrow we take them to an extra Norwich market, and sell them to buy up all the supplies we can.' I looked down at his table. There was a beautiful gold necklace, with a locket from which three fine quality pearls hung.

I smiled sadly. 'That reminds me of a necklace I saw Queen Catherine Parr wear sometimes, though this is far less magnificent.'

'They won't fetch a fraction of their worth. The Norwich traders know we're running short of food from the countryside with harvest approaching – the leanest time of the year. And there's not much money left.' He looked at me. 'Perhaps you could come to Norwich tomorrow, help us beat down the traders.'

'Certainly.'

I left him. I was conscious that I was qualified, better than Vowell, to do work like this. Why had I not been asked? Had Lockswood's tales made Kett suspicious of me? But he knew Lockswood for what he was now, surely Kett would not listen to base rumour.

The soldier, still waiting outside the room, accompanied me down the stairs. As I reached the door it opened and several more soldiers led in a sorry-looking procession of about twenty men, wearing the remnants of fine clothes. I stared at them as they were led up the stairs. The soldier said, 'We're bringing prisoners up from Norwich Castle.'

'Why?' I asked.

'Orders.' From his smile, I guessed he knew more than he was saying.

I walked back to the Swardeston huts to tell Barak my mission had failed. He took the news quietly, shrugged and said, 'I wasn't hopeful.' He was strapping on his artificial hand. 'I've been asked to help record deliveries up to the north-west of the camp. Natty's coming too.'

'Where's Nicholas?'

He shrugged again. 'Wandering about somewhere feeling sorry for himself.'

✝

NICHOLAS RETURNED in the early evening; he had been down to Norwich, which he reported was being fortified, the gates reinforced with earth and wood. 'Apparently the rebels' – for so he still spoke of them – 'are now going to try to bar the army's entry this time. To begin with, wearying them by beseiging us.'

Barak, who had returned from his work, snorted. 'It'll be a short siege. I doubt those gates will hold an army of nine or ten thousand, however they're shored up; perhaps they're going to put up what defence they can to weaken them, then fight on the streets. It'll be a bloody business.'

At the meal round the campfire that evening, the mood was thoughtful, though the food was, as ever, good; mutton in a vegetable pottage, well cooked under Goodwife Everneke's supervision. Nich- olas had returned with a load of stones from the heath, to replace those surrounding the campfire, which had grown blackened and cracked. Dusk was beginning to fall; the evenings were drawing in. Some way off a rowan tree, one of the few to survive the general felling, was red with berries.

'I've never eaten better than here,' Natty said.

'My aunt didn't give me much,' Simon said, slurping his food down noisily as usual.

'I wonder if we'll ever eat so well again.'

'Or be alive to eat at all, after what's coming,' said Ralph Wil- liams, a blacksmith in his thirties.

'Come on, bor,' the Swardeston leader Dickon said reprovingly. 'Don't talk so downy. A fierce battle there will be, but we beat them once and can do it again. God and justice are on our side, and our men are well trained as any could be. I've seen the bowmen – gor, how those arrows fly.'

'Who's the "them" we're fighting?' Nicholas asked suddenly.

Dickon frowned, and all heads turned to him. Dickon said, 'The lords and gentlemen, and their money-grubbing soldiers and mercenaries.'

'And Protector Somerset? Who made so many promises and kept none? He rules the land in the King's name, so this must be his army.'

Josephine was there, sitting with Mousy on her lap. Usually, she was quiet, especially when Edward was down in Norwich preparing the town for battle, as he had been for the last several nights, but now she spoke up: ''Tis a fair question, Master Nicholas' – out of habit, she still used the old deferential term – 'and none know the true answer. Perhaps others on the Council forced him to send the army, perhaps he decided himself, but either way, if we win, we may take all England.'

There was a general murmur of approval. Nicholas said no more while Barak, usually full of opinions, remained silent. After the meal there was drinking round the fire, but Barak went early to our hut. Nicholas and I joined him not long after. I slept soundly that night, but when I woke shortly after dawn, to the sound of spearmen walking past, weapons clattering, I saw that although Nicholas was in his usual place, Barak was gone.

✝

NICHOLAS AND I KNEW at once what had happened, but dared say nothing. An official came during breakfast, saying Barak was due at the north of the camp. I answered hastily that he had been asked to do other work, down in Norwich. The man looked at me suspiciously and went away.

Soon after I was sent for, to accompany the trade goods to be taken to Norwich market. Although everyone was still paid a small daily wage, I imagined coinage was running out. Two covered wagons were waiting, with heavy horses to take them down into the town. As usual, Simon had been selected as one of those to lead them. Accompanied by a large guard of soldiers in helmets and breastplates, we made our way slowly to the market. On the way through Norwich we saw that every gate and breach in the walls was being shored up with earth and timber.

It was a day of hard, rough bargaining. The Norwich traders knew the food they had brought in large quantities could command whatever price they asked, and in the way of traders did not hesitate to ask for pieces of jewellery, and gold and silver plate, at prices far above the value of the food they bartered. Only a few, through sympathy for the camp, traded for an honest price, and they quickly sold out.

In the late afternoon, we made our way wearily back to the camp. I had looked for the pearl pendant I saw the day before among the goods offered, but had not seen it. I was too weary, and worried about Barak and what people would say when his desertion was discovered, to visit Boleyn and Isabella at Norwich Castle. With luck there would be time tomorrow.

We reached the camp, the horses taking the unsold valuables back to Surrey Place. I walked back to our hut. And there, sitting outside with Nicholas, was Barak, looking shamefaced. With an angry jerk of the head I indicated they should follow me inside.

Barak said, 'When it came to it, I just couldn't do it. It was easy enough, the eastern boundary is only marked with stones, patrols few and far between. I could have got out easily. But' – he shook his head and looked down – 'I couldn't, not when I'd given my oath to Kett and you both stayed. Poor Tammy,' he added.

'You'll see her soon,' Nicholas said consolingly. Barak did not answer. I stepped outside again. Smoke was rising from campfires as preparations for dinner began. I thought, So we are together again. To await the great confrontation.

Part Six

DUSSINDALE

Chapter Seventy-three

E ARLY THE NEXT MORNING, a cool day of scudding clouds, we were called to a meeting at the Oak of Reformation. Everyone from the Swardeston camp attended, including Nicholas, Barak and I, Edward and Josephine, Mousy in her arms, Simon, Natty and Goody Everneke.

The mood was serious in the massed ranks facing the Oak. William Kett and several of the Hundred representatives stood on the platform as Robert Kett stepped to the front and addressed the crowd. His face was stern, but full of resolve.

'My friends, the hour of reckoning is at hand. My informants within the Earl of Warwick's camp say he has just reached Intwood, three miles from Norwich – he is staying at one of the houses owned by the Gresham family, the richest merchants in London!' There were boos and catcalls. Kett smiled.

'Warwick has his two sons with him, Ambrose and Robert, boys in their teens – I think we shall give a good account of ourselves against them! He has also, God help him, appointed the Marquess of North-ampton, who has been skulking in Cambridge with the Norfolk gentry since we defeated him, as his second-in-command! Moreover, the grand officials of Norfolk have pleaded with Warwick that they cooperated with us only under pressure, and have been forgiven and allowed to accompany the army – though made to wear laces round their necks as symbols of their perfidy!' Everyone laughed at this, though Kett's tone became more serious. 'I must not hide from you that we face our greatest trial. This new army is as near as numerous our own. One thousand four hundred Switzer landsknechts, far more ferocious fighters than the Italians we faced last month, are also on their way from London to join them. Warwick has with him not merely gentry popinjays, but professional soldiers, including a contingent from the Scottish wars led by one of his most experienced commanders, Captain Drury. They may arrive as early as tomorrow!' He was silent a moment, looking over the crowd, gauging its mood. But nearly all the faces I could see, especially those of the younger men, were firm and set. Voices shouted out, 'We are prepared, we are ready!' 'Ready to die, for they will leave us nothing to live for!'

Kett pressed on. 'Norwich is being fortified, and should the army penetrate the city our men are trained to fight them street by street, as we did the Marquess of Northampton! And if, at the end, we must fight in the open field, we are ready for that, too, with weapons, skilled leaders and the advantage of high ground! By the grace and mercy of God, whose cause we have served from the start, may we win – and our aims prevail – at last!' Yet a shadow crossed his face, and I could not help wondering whether, having received full report of the strength of Warwick's army, he was beginning to doubt the outcome.

But there were cheers and clapping; Kett waited a moment before resuming: 'And now, one last thing. I believe the time has come for the womenfolk who have accompanied their men here to return home, to bring in the harvest and await their victorious menfolk. With what may happen in the coming days, I think Mousehold Heath no longer a place for women.' He took a deep breath. 'Also, those men wounded in past battles, or who are sick or aged, should now go home. But I thank you all for the help you have given us. And now, men, to your tasks!' He raised his hands and nodded thanks as fresh cheers rang out, then left the stage with the others. As he passed me, William Kett said, 'Master Shardlake, there is to be another additional market today, and you are to come to it; be at the crest of the hill in an hour.'

☩

WE RETURNED TO the Swardeston camp, sombre yet determined faces surrounding us. One of the prophets walked through the crowd waving his Testament, crying out that the hour of the Apocalypse was come, and the men of the camp were God's chosen. Some cheered him on, others ignored him. 'Kett made a brave speech,' Nicholas said. 'He promises victory, but does not hide the strength of Warwick's army.'

'He has been honest with us all since the first day.'

'That he has,' a voice behind me agreed, and I turned to see Michael Vowell. He said, 'I go down to Norwich shortly, to help with military preparations there.' He clapped me on the shoulder. 'A great victory is coming, Master Shardlake. Many of my friends doubt, as I do, whether this army is even sent by the Protector. He may rescue us yet.' He nodded and walked away.

Nicholas looked after him thoughtfully. 'I hope he's right. I hear there have been some desertions, and there may be some more now Captain Kett has made it clear what we face.'

'You will fight?' Simon asked him.

'I don't know. And you?'

Simon looked him in the eye. 'I shall do as I am told, take the horses wherever they are needed.' He added quietly, 'I have never been happier than here.'

'And you are as good a man as any of them,' Nicholas said.

Goody Everneke squeezed Simon's arm. 'I pray God bring you all safe through this trial.' There were tears in her eyes. 'Since my poor husband died I, too, have never been happier than at Mousehold. But it seems I must go.'

'But you are a widow,' I said. 'Captain Kett spoke only of women-folk who had accompanied their men.'

Goody Everneke smiled. 'No, he said the camp is no longer a place for women. And' – she looked at me shrewdly – 'I have seen for myself that supplies are running low. The villages have little enough left to live on themselves till the harvest is brought in, they can send no more.' She took a deep breath. 'A couple of the older men are coming back to Swardeston with me, we should start snudging along.' She hugged us in turn, Josephine the longest. 'Let me go on ahead. No long goodbyes. Fare ye all well.' She walked quickly away.

Josephine looked at me. 'I, too, am returning to Norwich.'

'But Josephine, if there is fighting, it will likely start in the city.' I turned to Edward. 'Surely it is safer if she stays here.'

He shook his head. 'If we keep the city, Josephine is safe. Should we lose there, she will be just another Norwich woman at home with a small child. But if there is a battle up here, God knows what may happen to any helpless women and children left if, God forbid, they win. No, Josephine should now be with me, at home in Norwich. We go down this morning.'

Josephine's face was set. 'Do not argue, please, Master Shardlake. Edward is right. We will accompany you down to Norwich when you go with the supplies.'

'Very well.' I would miss her, and Mousy too. We walked on. Nicholas put a restraining hand on my arm, letting the others walk ahead. He said seriously, 'What will you do now?'

'Whatever Captain Kett wishes.'

He smiled wryly. 'Forgive me, but you could be deemed old and unfit to fight. You could go.'

'No. Not while I can be of use.' I looked at him. 'What of you?'

He bit his lip. 'I don't know. Fight for a cause I'm still not sure I believe in?'

I said, 'It's likely to be bloody. That Captain Drury, I encountered him in London, just before we came here. Some of his men were beating up a Scotchman, and Drury encouraged them. They looked fearsome brutes, and they've experience in the Scottish war.'

'Will Sir Richard Southwell be with the army? He came up with Northampton's army.'

'I don't know whether he stayed with them at Cambridge. With his sheep farms and his duties to the Lady Mary, I'd think he'd keep as close as he could.'

Nicholas smiled crookedly. 'Well, he's worth fighting, at least.'

✞

THAT WAS THE MOST I could get from Nicholas about his intentions. We made our way to the road at the crest of the hill to await the carts going down to the city. I saw Captain Miles there, who, I guessed, like Edward Brown, was going down to make the final preparations for a siege, and probably a fight. A company of archers joined us. Josephine approached me, Mousy in her arms. 'Do not be angry with me, Master Shardlake,' she said. 'I believe I will be safer in Norwich.'

'I am not angry, Josephine, just sad that you and Mousy are leaving the camp.'

She turned to look back at the endless circles of lean-to huts, their parish banners flying. 'I am sorry to leave, too.' Then she added quietly, 'Nobody will ever again say the commoners of England cannot rule themselves.'

I tickled Mousy under the chin, and she gurgled happily. 'Look after this little one,' I said quietly, then smiled. 'Do you remember when you came to work for me with your father? Only five years ago, but it seems an age.'

'Sometimes I have felt that time has moved differently in the camp, as though it was such an unheard-of, special place it affected the movements of the very planets.' She laughed self-consciously. 'You will think me foolish.'

'No, I understand.'

My attention was drawn by the sound of mocking voices. Simon was surrounded nearby by a little group of boys, Norwich apprentices, I guessed, who had taken part in the habitual mockery of him there. One said, 'You nearly fucked up the joust, didn't you, Sooty? The way you slapped that horse – did you think it was real?' Simon reddened and looked down. One of the men waiting to handle the horses stepped across. 'You leave him be! If any of you dwainy weaklings could handle a horse half as well as Simon, you'd be worth having here!' The boys dispersed sheepishly.

✝

ON THE WAY DOWN to Norwich market Simon, like his fellows, was fully occupied with getting the horses and carts down the steep hill, but when we had safely reached the bottom, I approached him. 'I saw you had a little trouble, Simon.'

He shrugged wearily. 'I've had a rest from it in the camp, but those lads were up from Norwich.'

I looked at him. The man had called the boys who had taunted him dwainy weaklings. But Simon, after several weeks of good food and hard work, had filled out. I thought, then said, 'When this is over—'

'When we've won,' he interjected emphatically.

'Yes, when we've won, I have been wondering whether it might be good for you to come back with me to London. I could find you work with horses, and your natural skills would serve you well.'

He looked at me in surprise. 'You would take me to London?'

'If you wish. After all, what is left for you in Norwich? Your aunt?'

A flash of anger crossed his face. 'She left me to beg. I never want to see her again.'

'In London, you would not have the reputation of someone to be mocked.'

He looked at me, his face suddenly bright. 'To get away from Nor/wich, start anew —' Then his face clouded. 'Yet the thought of Lunnon frightens me. I hear 'tis very big.'

'I will make sure you are looked after. As will Barak and Nicholas.'

His eyes filled with tears. 'Then I thank you, Master Shardlake. I will come. And I will — try to control what I do.'

I smiled. 'You should see what some London folk get up to.'

✝

NORWICH WAS FULL OF Kett's soldiers. As we walked to Tomb/land, I saw over a hundred men at archery practice on St Martin's Plain. Spearmen were being guided through the narrow lanes leading down to the Market Square by Norwich men, who pointed out col/oured posts set in the ground to mark the way, while everywhere the city walls were being reinforced, men patrolling the top. Among those piling up stones I saw Toby Lockswood; at least he had never been afraid of hard work. At Tombland we said farewell to Josephine and Edward, who disappeared with Mousy. I wondered when I would see them again.

The market was again full of traders. Our carts were unloaded and bargaining began, though the traders haggled less intensely today — perhaps, with Warwick's army almost at their door, they felt a sense of duty. Nonetheless, several times I had to point out the true value of a Venetian crystal vase or piece of gold jewellery. Again I looked for the pendant which reminded me of Catherine Parr's, but did not see it.

Robert Kett was not present today; his brother William had taken his place. By early afternoon the carts were empty of valuables but, together with others we had brought down, full of food. William Kett approached me. He looked contemptuously at the gold plate and jewellery the traders were stuffing into their bags. 'Stuff,' he barked. 'What use are such things to us now?'

'None, sir, I agree. It was a good idea to sell everything.'

He looked at me. 'I imagine you have some valuables at your home in London.'

'Nothing I could not do without. I wondered, sir, whether before returning to camp I might visit Master Boleyn in Norwich Castle, with Master Overton. I doubt I will get the chance to see him again before –'

'Before things get rough.' He nodded. 'Ay, go, but be back at camp tonight.'

'I will.' I signalled to Nicholas, who was assisting Simon in quieting a restless horse. 'Would you like to see Isabella Boleyn again?' I asked him.

✝

AS USUAL I FOUND the long walk up the Castle Mound tiring; although the bracken bedding in the hut had been strangely good for my back, recently it had become painful again, and my joints ached. The wetter, cooler weather of August had probably played its part.

Once more we were admitted to the castle. In the Central Hall something was happening; a large table had been set up and several gentlemen, their feet chained, were being questioned by one of Kett's men. It reminded me of the odd scene at Surrey Place a few days before. I asked the guard accompanying us what was happening.

'Nothing,' he replied evasively. 'Just some stuff to be recorded.'

He led us to Boleyn's cell. When he knocked at the door, Boleyn's voice called hastily, 'A moment,' and I heard a loud creaking from the bed. The guard smiled. 'Nice way to pass the time, eh?'

He waited a minute, then opened the door. John Boleyn was hastily buttoning his doublet. Behind him, Isabella was smoothing down her dress. Boleyn said, 'Master Shardlake, Master Overton, I had not expected to see you. Word is the Earl of Warwick's army may be here tomorrow. I hope we will be safe enough here, but you should return to London while you can.' He looked at me seriously, and Isabella nodded agreement.

I answered evasively. 'Certainly this may be the last chance we have to meet for some time. How are you?'

'We are both well enough.' He looked at Isabella and smiled. She smiled back, reddening slightly. He continued, 'Something is going on in the castle, we don't know what, but some gentlemen are being moved. They have been put in chains again.'

'We saw something down in the Castle Hall, but nobody would tell us what is happening,' I replied.

Boleyn put a hand in Isabella's. 'We will be safe, my dear, we were put here by the authorities, not Kett's men.' He turned to me. 'Have you any more news about Edith?' He shook his head. 'That was an extraordinary story you told us.'

'None, I fear. We know she visited a – distant relation – seeking money early in May, but then nothing, till she was found murdered.'

Isabella said, 'I have been thinking about that poor creature. It seems her parents treated her harshly.'

John Boleyn said nothing, still resolutely unforgiving of his late wife. I asked, 'Have you heard aught from Daniel Chawry?'

'Nothing,' Boleyn replied angrily. 'I think he has fled.' He took a deep breath. 'Isabella told me what he tried to do to her. Thank God for her strong spirit which prevented it.' He held his wife's hand tightly, then his face darkened. 'God's death, could he be the killer? If I ever get my hands on him –' He clenched his fists.

'He is probably far away,' Nicholas said.

Boleyn asked, 'Will Sir Richard Southwell be coming with Warwick's army?'

I said, 'It is possible Southwell will be at Norwich with the army. We think he will have stayed with the Marquess of Northampton in Cambridge, looking after the Lady Mary's interests.'

He looked at me sharply. 'And his young confederates? Like that rogue Atkinson, and my wretched sons?'

'Possibly.'

Boleyn paced the room. 'When Warwick's army wins, which it

will, do you think Southwell and the Lady Mary may get into trouble? After all, she has sat at Kenninghall throughout the rebellion, when she could have fled.'

'I doubt it. Her political importance as heir is only increased now by France declaring war on us – the Protector needs the support of the Holy Roman Emperor all the more, and he is Mary's relative.'

Boleyn looked at me. 'And you – you have been in the camp since the beginning, could you be in difficulty if the rebels lose?'

I sighed. 'I have tried to be a moderating force. If there is trouble, I must rely on the Lady Elizabeth.' I looked at him directly. 'It would help me even now if I could discover who killed Edith that night. It is a pity you did not have a full alibi.'

Anger flashed in Boleyn's eyes. 'I have said a thousand times, I never left my study.'

There was silence for a moment. Then Isabella laughed nervously and said, 'John, let us tell them our news.'

His face lightened instantly, and he grasped her hand. 'Isabella tells me that, at last, she is pregnant. Three months gone. Now perhaps I may have a son who is not a monster. She has known for several weeks, but did not wish to tell me till we were together again.'

I calculated quickly. Three months ago was May, so she could have conceived just before her husband's arrest, but if she had conceived after John Boleyn had been imprisoned, he could not be the father. Had she had some relationship with Chawry after all? Yet everything she had said and done indicated otherwise. I looked at her; she smiled at me tentatively. I said, 'My sincerest congratulations to you both.' Then she came forward and took my hand. 'Go to London today, Master Shardlake, while you can. We thank you most heartily for all you have done.'

'Yes,' John Boleyn agreed gruffly. 'May we meet again in happier times.'

Isabella took Nicholas's hand in turn. 'And you, young Master Overton, take care of yourself. Find a pretty young woman with a strong and honest spirit, I think that is what you need.'

'If I can find one as beautiful as you, madam, I shall be well pleased,' Nicholas said chivalrously. Isabella curtsied to us. We both bowed to her, then shook John Boleyn's hand and knocked for the guard. He let us out, then shut and locked the door behind us. I thought, It will be a long time before I see John Boleyn again. I could not have been more wrong.

Chapter Seventy-four

WHEN I RETURNED TO camp late that afternoon the mood seemed to have hardened; men went about their duties with grim determination. When Barak returned for dinner he told us about the defensive fortifications being set up at the northern edge of the camp, at the place called Dussindale. 'There's tons of equipment gone up there. Captain Gunner Miles is supervising; by Jesu, he knows what he's doing.' He added in a lower voice, 'If it comes, we could win after all, especially if we soften them up first in the city.' He turned to Nicholas. 'I'm sorry, lad, for trying to make you leave in my place when I thought of deserting. I'd no right, not when I couldn't do it myself.'

Nicholas smiled and nodded. 'I know you were in a hard place.'

'And you're staying?'

'I'm going to wait and see what happens next.'

Natty, who had heard the exchange, turned his face – one side now a mass of bruises, thanks to Lockswood – to look at him. 'Victory,' he said firmly, 'that's what happens next.'

'Ay, we'll show them,' Simon agreed.

I looked around the little Swardeston camp, empty of its women now. We had gristly beef for dinner, undercooked by the men. I thought of Goody Everneke and the other women, now trailing home, and hoped fervently they would be safe. I did not pray, for that part of me which had briefly opened up when I had taken Communion had closed again – like most here I could only focus now on our survival.

✝

NEXT MORNING, THE twenty-fourth of August – another of the rare warm days that month – I had taken up my favourite position on the crest of the hill, looking down on Norwich, along with several others. There was, however, nothing to see – if Warwick's army was approaching from Intwood, there was no sign of it yet. A messenger rode up the hill, spurring his horse to make speed. He dismounted and ran straight to St Michael's Chapel. A quarter of an hour later Kett himself emerged, his face set and anxious. He stood looking down on Norwich a moment then, seeing me, beckoned me over. He gave me a searching look.

'Master Shardlake. Tell me what you think of this. That man was my spy in Warwick's camp.' He was silent a moment. 'He tells me Warwick's army is well armed and commanded. They are only waiting for the Switzer mercenaries to arrive.'

'And they will try to take Norwich?'

'I think so. But there is another royal Herald with the army, and apparently he is to be sent to Norwich this morning to talk to the city, no doubt to try and obtain its peaceful surrender. I am going down to Norwich now.' Kett studied me keenly. 'And you are staying, whatever comes next?'

'Yes. Barak and Nicholas, too.'

'There are rumours going around the camp that you and young Overton are spies.'

'Set by Toby Lockswood, no doubt,' I said grimly.

'The story is you met with gentlemen in Norwich, passed information about our strength to Warwick.'

'It is evil nonsense, Captain Kett.'

He continued looking at me steadily, then said, 'Yes, I think it is.' He turned his face to the city. 'I shall ride down to Norwich. I will allow Augustine Steward to meet with this Herald, see what he wants. If it is to talk to the men, let them decide.' He shook his grey head. 'Though the odds now –' He broke off.

At that moment three soldiers on horseback drew up, leading a horse for Kett. He mounted, and together they rode down to Norwich.

☘

SEVERAL TENSE HOURS passed. I learned only later that day of events in the city. Kett persuaded Augustine Steward and another senior city official to meet the Herald outside the walls. They in turn suggested to the Herald that the camp be offered a pardon on condition of surrender. I never knew whether or not Kett was party to that. In any event, the Herald rode back to Intwood to consult the Earl of Warwick, then returned to confirm he would offer a pardon to all save Kett. He was readmitted to the city, together with a trumpeter and a small party of Warwick's soldiers, including several men carry- ing curriers – small arquebuses – while a man behind brought a container holding the live coals to light them. Some forty of Kett's men, on horseback, accompanied them across Bishopsgate Bridge. I heard Kett had returned to camp separately.

In the camp we heard the loud blast of a trumpet. This brought a huge number of camp-men, many armed, running downhill to where the Herald's party stood by the riverside. Barak and Nicholas and I were among those who went down, together with Natty. I saw Simon Scambler some way off, with a group of young men. I recognized those who had tormented him the other day, but they all seemed on friendly terms now.

Most of the camp had assembled in a massive show of force, some on horseback; I saw the Herald, gorgeously robed, ride across the bridge, accompanied by Augustine Steward and the little retinue of soldiers. I recognized the commander of the arquebusiers; it was Cap- tain Drury, whom I had encountered in London; a senior officer in Warwick's party, he had doubtless come to weigh up the opposition.

At sight of the Herald, many in the vast crowd shouted out, 'God save the King!' As ever, I thought, both sides claim loyalty to the eleven-year-old boy in London.

Augustine Steward asked the camp-men to separate into two groups to allow the Herald through, so that his words could be heard by as many as possible. They did so, and accompanied by his soldiers the Herald rode a little way up the hill, then stopped, right in the middle of the sea of rebels. Like his predecessor, he did not lack courage. A large, solid man in his fifties, he had a commanding, haughty expression. He began by commending the men for their declarations of loyalty to the King. Then, with an extravagant gesture, he unrolled a sealed and decorated paper, and began to read, in a loud, resonant voice.

I listened, horrified. The tone of his address was even more savagely insulting than the one inflicted on us by the previous Herald the month before. I saw the expressions on the faces of some camp-men turn from hope to fierce anger, though a small minority also looked scared. The Herald accused them of being a violent, horrible company, guilty of *cruelty and despoliation and condemning to prison many worthy and excellent persons* — at this there was a discernible murmur of fury. He called his audience *men of detestable madness, disloyalty, and mischievous treason.* At the end he said the King's mercy was such that despite all this, a pardon would be offered to those who surrendered now, all bar Kett himself, but if they did not accept, the King had commanded the Earl of Warwick *to pursue them with fire and sword.*

No sooner had he finished than a chorus of angry shouts rose from the crowd. Men called out, accusing the Herald of being himself a traitor, sent not by the King but by the gentlemen; the offer of pardon was called a lie, and one man shouted that in reality it offered nothing more than the ropes and halters of imprisonment and hanging. 'He is no real Herald, his robes are sewed together out of old popish vestments,' another shouted out. It made me think, some still cling to the belief that the Protector is not behind this. Weapons were brandished, and the Herald's face hardened. I saw Robert Kett ride up; if the tactic had been for the Herald to intimidate the camp-men without their leader present, it had failed spectacularly. Kett joined him, and called to the camp-men to make a space so the Herald could declaim his message to others who had not heard. Reluctantly, the crowd parted to allow the Herald's party to ride some way further, though angry insults against him and his message followed. Barak said quietly, 'He's fucked up any hope of a settlement. If he'd offered some remedy of grievances, spoken to the men like they were adults, he might have got somewhere.'

'You're right,' Nicholas said. 'You can see from their faces that some at least might have accepted a pardon and redress of wrongs, but now most are enraged.' He added angrily, 'Who wrote that damned proclamation?'

I said bitterly, 'The Protector, of course, just as he wrote the last one. The fool, he hasn't the political skills of a rabbit.'

Nicholas said, his voice shaking, 'Whatever they've done, these are men with just grievances. How could anyone think talking to them like this would help?'

Barak said, 'You might have done so yourself two months ago.'

'Not now,' Nicholas answered grimly, 'not now.' He looked over to where the Herald was still reading his proclamation. He was being heard in silence, but again I saw far more angry faces than frightened ones.

Then it happened, the terrible thing that still haunts my dreams, and which finally ended any remaining chance of a negotiated settlement. My eye had been drawn by movement and, unexpectedly, the sound of laughter. I saw Simon Scambler standing, with some of the boys he had been speaking to, only a few yards from the Herald, who had just finished reading. In the silence I distinctly heard one of the boys say, 'Go on, Sooty, do it. We'll throw you a party afterwards.'

Simon looked uncertain, pleased by the apparent friendship of his old tormentors but also afraid. 'Go on,' one of the boys urged. 'Show the cunt what we think of him.'

Simon stepped forward from the crowd, facing the Herald from only a few yards' distance. Then he turned round, lowered his stocks, and presented his rear to the Herald, who stared in utter outrage as roars of laughter erupted from the crowd. Simon waved his backside slowly from left to right, adding to the insult. Then Captain Drury snapped his fingers at the man holding the container of live coals, who instantly opened it. Drury bent and lit the rope fuse, put the stock of the long weapon against his shoulder, then pressed the trigger. The fuse hit the gunpowder pan, there was a loud bang and a puff of grey smoke, and Simon's backside exploded in a mess of blood and shit. He screamed, tried unsuccessfully to stand up, then staggered. The bullet had gone right through his body and as he turned I saw blood gushing from his stomach too, and his intestines slowly falling out. He crouched, swaying, for a moment; then fell onto his face. I saw the boys who had encouraged him melt away as I shouted, 'No!' and, followed by Nicholas and Barak, elbowed my way through the crowd.

The campmen, momentarily silenced by the crash of the gun and Simon's collapse in a welter of blood, now roared their anger and fury. Weapons were pointed towards the Herald's party. A voice yelled, 'See, they come not to pardon but to murder us!' A party of our horsemen rode up to the crest of the hill, shouting as they went, 'The Herald has come to have us destroyed! Our men are killed by the waterside!' The Herald stared after them, stupefied by what had happened, though Captain Drury, looking at Simon, had a slight smile on his face.

I reached Simon, lying in the middle of a slowly spreading pool of blood, and bent down, gently turning him over. His face held that expression of puzzled surprise he had worn so often in life, but his eyes were now still and dead. Groaning, on the verge of tears, I gently closed his lids. Barak knelt beside me and said urgently, 'Get up, it's not safe here.' He and Nicholas, their faces stricken as mine, had to pull me to my feet; my clothes were covered in blood.

I looked round me, dazed. The camp-men had closed in around the Herald and his troops, and would probably have pulled him from his horse had Kett not said to him urgently, 'You must go, I will return with you to the earl.' He added grimly, 'Perhaps after what you have seen of our anger, you will advise him to proclaim a remedy for our grievances.' The Herald and his troop rode away down the hill, the crowd parting reluctantly before them; but they had gone only a little way when a group of Kett's horsemen rode up, surrounding them again. I heard one of them cry, 'Whither away, whither away, Captain Kett? If you go, we will go with you, and with you will live and die.' The man's tone was angry, suspicious; it was the first time I had heard Kett addressed in tones other than respect. 'Go back and stay the tumult,' the Herald told Kett urgently, and at his signal the men began moving back uphill, towards the camp, allowing the Herald and his party, including Simon's killer, to flee downhill, across Bishopsgate Bridge and into Norwich.

Barak, Nicholas and I were left standing by Simon's body. A group of men, Natty among them, approached us. Natty said, through tears, 'Let's take him, at least give him a decent burial.'

'Come, bor,' one of the men with him said to me gently. 'Leave him to us.'

'No,' I said. 'I will come with you.'

'We must give him a proper farewell,' Nicholas said, blinking back tears.

Barak said bitterly, 'Simon never wanted to be the centre of attention, did he, just to live his life, not harming a soul, but he was never
allowed that. He always got the attention, and it was always bad. Shit!'
He kicked a large flint through the air.

I looked at the camp-men walking back up the hill, talking animatedly. I asked angrily, 'Where are those boys who were with him?
They put him up to it, they were too afraid to do it themselves. By God,
they're near as guilty of his murder as that soldier. For murder it was.'

'There's nothing to be done there,' Barak said. 'Though I'd like to
root them out and beat them to a pulp myself.'

I looked down at the city. 'And what now?'

'War,' he answered. 'Without question, war.'

Chapter Seventy-five

W E CARRIED SIMON'S BODY down to what was left of Thorpe Wood, and buried him in a little clearing where the leaves were already starting to yellow. We had only two fallen branches tied together to make a cross. None of us could think of any words, until Natty said quietly, 'May you find peace at last.' Then we walked silently back to the camp.

There was much activity there, and approaching the crest I could see why: even from this distance the coiling black snake of Warwick's army was visible, approaching the western side of the city, and everywhere on the heath men were being ordered to their weapons. A sergeant in half-armour approached us and ordered Natty and Barak to fall in with his company of spearmen. Nicholas waited uncertainly; the serjeant said brusquely, 'Not you, lad, I know who you are.'

We looked on as men ran to and fro with orders from St Michael's Chapel, and companies of bowmen, spearmen and crossbowmen, some in half-armour and round sallet helmets, descended the hill under their captains' leadership. Barak gave me a salute as his company passed. Cannon, too, were being dragged down by horses. A roll of artillery fire reached me from the city, I saw clouds of smoke and then Warwick's army, marching like some huge and monstrous insect, passed through the gates. Somehow, the enemy was already in.

☩

ALL NICHOLAS AND I could do that afternoon was stand watching Norwich, though we could see very little. Others unable to fight for whatever reason where also strung along the road, waiting.

'Warwick's army got in easily,' Nicholas said. 'Looks like they had assistance.' He leaned forward, screwing up his eyes. 'Seems like a lot of smoke around Tombland. At least I think it's there.'

Then, late in the afternoon, our men came wearily back up the hill. That was a bad sign. They brought, however, a whole new train of cannon, which they must have taken from the enemy. Rather than torment ourselves by watching to see whether Barak and Natty had returned, we went back to the Swardeston huts and began preparing dinner. The soldiers straggled in, dirty, clothes torn, some nursing wounds. To our great relief Barak and Natty were among them. Natty was unharmed, but Barak had a long graze on his calf, which had been crudely stitched.

'An arrow grazed me,' he said. 'It's nothing.'

Master Dickon, the leader of the Swardeston group, was absent. I asked where he was. 'Slain,' the man Milford, a blacksmith, answered dully. It was he, I remembered, who had started the argument which Simon ended by singing a beautiful song. 'Along with Fletcher and Harmon.' Exhausted, the men collapsed on the ground.

☥

As NICHOLAS AND I served food to the men, Barak and Natty told us what had happened. They had reached the city to find the Earl of Warwick already in occupation of the centre of Norwich. He had immediately hanged no less than forty-nine captured rebels. It was believed Augustine Steward had told Warwick that he could enter through one of the weaker city gates; two other gates had been brought down by artillery. Our men had fought mightily, gathering in Tombland and dividing into attack parties, and at first a great rain of arrows looked as though it might drive Warwick's forces back; but Captain Drury had brought up a company of arquebusiers and a mighty volley of bullets had dispersed our forces. Faced by these new and terrifying weapons and Warwick's numbers, the order to retreat had been given, though not before a large part of Warwick's supply train and artillery, which had got lost in the narrow streets, had been captured.

'Hundreds are killed,' Barak said grimly. 'We've lost the city, except the northern part. We would have joined up with the men there, but Warwick's forces have control of the bridges over the river, so most of us have come back up.' He looked at me. 'I saw Toby Lockswood in the midst of it, leading a company of Norwich spearmen straight at an armoured company of Warwick's men. Whatever else, he doesn't lack courage.'

Natty said, 'Captain Miles says there's a new plan of attack, we're going to take Norwich back tomorrow.'

'You're going down again?'

'Yes.' Barak began to remove his artificial hand, which I could see was paining him. He said quietly, 'Warwick's is some army. I half wish we'd taken the fucking pardon.'

'I don't,' Natty said, his bruised face firmly set. 'We must defeat them, or they will destroy us all. They think of us as hardly more than animals. Look what they did to Simon.'

♱

THE FOLLOWING MORNING was clear and sunny again, though cool. It was Sunday, but no church bells sounded in Norwich, and there were no calls to sermons on the heath; everyone was preparing to march downhill to battle. I heard Barak get up and leave the hut. I must have been exhausted, for I fell asleep again at once, and was woken only by the sound of tremendous gunfire from Norwich. I thought with a sudden, terrible guilt, 'I may never see him again.' I hastily rose and walked to the crest, shrugging my shoulders to ease my back. Nicholas was already there.

Looking down, I saw the fresh assault on Norwich had begun. The smoke and noise of cannon fire came from Bishopsgate, and from the area to the north of the city. Our men were attacking on multiple fronts; to the south, I saw a pall of smoke over the southern part of Norwich, and from the staithes by the river where grain was stored.

'Good God,' I said. 'That's Conisford, Josephine's down there. Why is it afire?'

'Perhaps the rebels have set the fire as a diversionary tactic.'

We continued watching in horrified silence, as the roar of cannon continued. Then a familiar figure approached us, limping along the crest; Peter Bone, the problems with his feet more apparent now. He bowed to us.

'Master Shardlake. Master Overton.'

'Goodman Bone.' I took his hand. 'It seems we are near the climax.'

'I wanted to fight, but again they wouldn't let me, said I'd be more trouble than I was worth with my dwainy feet. What have you seen?'

'It looks like our forces have fired the south of the city, and they seem to be firing at the north walls as well, from the position of the smoke. But can they retake the centre?'

Bone said fiercely, 'If it comes to a last battle on the heath, I'll join in, even if it is only handing gunpowder to the cannoneers.' He shifted from one foot to the other, and I realized how much walking hurt him. He sighed. 'They are all gone now; Grace, Mercy, my wife, Edith – so if I die in battle, I care little.'

I looked at him. 'At least poor Edith had those years of happiness with you and your sister.' I fumbled in my purse. 'Here, I still have her wedding ring. Her husband refused it. Would you like to take it back?'

'I thank you,' he said quietly. He took the ring back and placed it gently in his own little purse. Then he asked quietly, 'Have you any more notion of who killed her?'

I shook my head. 'No more than before. Possibly the Brikewell steward, Chawry, who has fled; perhaps Boleyn himself; even his wife Isabella is a suspect. And the twins.' I sighed. 'I think I have failed.'

'At least you tried,' Peter said. 'At least you cared.'

We turned to look back at the city, but could see little save that the fires in Conisford still burned. Again I thought about Josephine and Mousy.

Peter said, 'But it seems our men are inside and fighting. Come,' he added, 'let me show you the preparations made to fight on the heath. Even if Warwick keeps Norwich, we have a good chance up here. Captain Miles and the other soldiers have made great plans.'

With his awkward limping gait, he led us along a freshly cleared trackway for about a mile, until we reached a point a little north of the city, where the escarpment was less steep and gave onto Magdalen Road, leading north out of Norwich.

'There it is. The place called Dussindale.'

What I saw impressed me anew. All along the lower slope of the crest, men were digging in large, heavy wooden stakes with sharply

pointed tips, close together and pointed outwards, so they posed a formidable obstacle to any attacker. In front, trenches were being dug.
Other men were piling up earthworks at an angle, presumably to prevent a flanking action. Some way behind, earth had been dug up to
make a wide, level platform; cannon, including, no doubt, those taken
from Warwick in the previous day's battle, had been set in position.
And already some were firing, aiming at the gates in the north wall of
the city, only a few hundred yards southward, making the ground tremble under us. I could see now that the tactic was to bring the whole of
Norwich, north of the Wensum, under our control. Among those
digging I saw the tall muscular form of Michael Vowell. This surprised
me, for I thought, as a Norwich man, he would be working with our
people in the city today. He saw us and came over.

'Well, Master Shardlake,' he said cheerfully, 'you see we are making
ready for what may come.' He had recently had his hair and beard cut
short, to discourage nits and lice.

'Impressive preparations,' I said.

'And we face away from the rising sun,' Peter Bone said approvingly. 'But it will shine right in the eyes of the enemy.'

'So it will,' Vowell agreed. He looked at us. 'Any news?'

'Only what little we can see from the crest,' I answered. 'The south
is on fire, I think, and there seems a great melee around the centre.'

Vowell bit his lip. 'It may be touch and go.'

Peter Bone said, 'If it comes to it tomorrow, I'm ready to give any
help I can up here, despite my problems walking.' Vowell looked at him
enquiringly, and Bone explained. 'I was born with my feet splayed
inward, and years working the treadle on the spinning machine made it
worse, just as spinning contributed to my – my sister's swollen hands.'

'Your sister?'

'Yes. She died last winter.'

Vowell looked at him strangely. And then it hit me, like a lightning
bolt, there among all the battle preparations at Dussindale. Something
Michael Vowell had said once, which had struck me as inconsistent at
the time but which I had forgotten, lost in the mass of detail surrounding
Edith Boleyn, and subsequent events at the camp. Yet Peter Bone's mention of his disability, and of being a weaver, suddenly brought it back.

Three weeks ago, the day I visited Norwich under Vowell's guard, fol/
lowing the defeat of Northampton, we had spoken of Gawen Reynolds
and his family, and the bandages which Jane Reynolds wore. I remem/
bered his words quite clearly: . . . *a swelling and twisting of the knuckles. It
runs in her family. Apparently, her mother had it from late middle age, and so did
Edith. The twins will probably get it, too.* And it struck me forcibly now:
how could he have known that Edith had developed this disability in
later life if he had last seen her, at the latest, nine years before? I looked
at Michael Vowell, and in my brain cogs turned, connections fell into
place, and I realized that I could be looking at one of Edith Boleyn's
killers. And then I realized who the second man must be, who had been
with him that night. I had thought there was more than one. And who
had killed the locksmith and his apprentice. Something may have
showed in my face, for Vowell gave me a long, hard look, before saying,
'Perhaps you should return to your hut, Master Shardlake. After all,
you would not want to find yourself hit by a stray gunball.'

✝

I SAID LITTLE AS we walked back to the escarpment. The fires in
Conisford seemed to have lessened, but there was still smoke over the
south of the city. Then I saw a long line of gentlemen, chained by the
wrists to each other, being brought up the hill by soldiers. They
reached the top and turned towards Surrey Place. There were about
twenty of them, and to my horror I recognized John Boleyn, better fed
and clothed than the others, but chained, nonetheless. Nicholas and I
walked rapidly over to one of the soldiers, whom I remembered as a
man who had kept guard at the trials at the Oak, and who might,
therefore, remember me.

'Excuse me, what is happening here?'

'Serjeant Shardlake, isn't it? We're bringing up the last gemmun
from Norwich Castle. It'll be in the Earl of Warwick's hands soon; he's
pushing us out of the city centre. We're taking them to Surrey Place.'

'But why? Why do they matter now?'

He smiled grimly. 'You'll see, if it comes to a battle. They're all
going to be chained together before the front rank of soldiers. That will
give Warwick's men pause.' I must have looked at him in horror, for

he frowned. 'This is war, Master Shardlake. Things are going badly in the city, we may have to fight outside and we need every possible resource.' I looked at the gentlemen prisoners, whose dull or frightened eyes told me they knew their coming fate. John Boleyn stared at me pleadingly. I pointed to him and said, 'That man is not one of the captured gentlemen. He is in prison after a murder trial – a pardon has been lodged on his behalf by the Lady Elizabeth. This is a mistake.'

The soldier looked at Boleyn. 'He's a gemmun, isn't he?' he snapped. 'His name's enough to tell us that. We were told to bring all their sort from the prison, and that's what we've done. If you've a complaint, make it to Captain Kett.'

I said, 'All this time, Captain Kett has refused to allow the gentlemen to be killed. Is that to change now?'

The soldier became angry. '*We* won't kill them, it's a question of whether Warwick will. It's all-out war now, bor. Our men are dying in the city by the hour. Come on, let's move.'

As the wretched column clanked on, I fell into step with Boleyn. 'How is Isabella?' I asked.

He looked at me desperately. 'They threw her out of the castle. She's down there, somewhere, in the city. The fighting, Matthew, it's terrible. Please, try to help us.'

✝

THAT EVENING ONLY wounded men returned from Norwich; the fighting had stopped for the night, and we learned that Warwick was now in charge of most of the city, only the districts north of the river still under rebel control. The blacksmith Milford arrived with a heavy, bloodstained bandage across his side which, he told us, came from a spear thrust. He said grimly, 'They've got control of the marketplace, we can't get any more supplies. And these Switzer mercenaries arrive tomorrow. Unless we can make an assault from the north of the city, it's going to be a battle on the heath.'

Nicholas asked, 'Did you see any sign of Jack Barak, or young Natty?'

He shook his head. 'In a battle you just see what happens around you. I'm sorry, I must lie down.'

Again, Nicholas and I cooked the evening meal. Then we went to our hut. 'It's not looking good,' he said quietly. 'What will happen to Boleyn now, and Isabella, and Josephine?'

I shook my head. 'I don't know.' I sighed. 'But I do think I know who killed Edith Boleyn, for all the good that may do now. Michael Vowell, and his old employer Gawen Reynolds.'

He looked at me aghast. 'Her own father? But he's ancient, he walks with a stick.'

'He does now. He said he hurt his leg some months ago, remember? I think it was while he and Vowell were doing what they did to Edith.'

'But Vowell hates Reynolds.'

'He says he does. I think he is lying. I think he has been lying all along.' I told Nicholas what I remembered Vowell saying about Edith's hands. 'Tomorrow, will you help me get him alone somehow, and confront him? I need the whole story, there are more involved than just those two.'

'Of course.'

I sighed. 'Then there's nothing to do now but try to get some sleep. And await what happens tomorrow. Dear God, I hope Barak and Natty are safe.'

Chapter Seventy-six

THAT NIGHT I SLEPT badly again. Someone – Nicholas perhaps – had rearranged our bracken bedding, and made a poor job, and twigs and branches dug into my body. It rained before dawn, and I heard the drip of water through the turf roof, but the morning was clear, though cloudy. With a sense of foreboding, Nicholas and I went again to the crest.

Wounded men, a good number, were trailing back up the hill to Mousehold. Barrels of small beer had been fetched, and Nicholas and I assisted in passing out mugs to the parched soldiers, who helped each other along, while those with major wounds were carried up on stretchers. We learned that Warwick still held the central area of the city, though further attacks would be made against him that day. He had erected his coat of arms, the bear and ragged staff, on Augustine Steward's house in Tombland. The one thousand four hundred Switzer landsknechts were expected that day, and we had to try to beat Warwick's army before they arrived. We asked after Natty and Barak, and a man from their company of spearmen, who had an arm nearly severed, said he had seen Natty resting during a break in the fighting that morning, but had not seen Barak yesterday. Another soldier told us Toby Lockswood was dead, killed in close sword fighting in Tombland the day before. The man had obviously heard the rumours about me, for he said pointedly, 'He was willing to give his life for the Commons, while the gemmun sit up here.'

'I never doubted his courage,' I said.

'He was a good man.'

'That's another matter.'

714

The man spat on the ground in disgust at my words, then walked away, limping badly from a wound in his leg.

✝

LUNCHTIME ARRIVED. Nicholas and I, depressed by the sights of the morning, returned to the Swardeston camp to eat a meagre meal – there was only stale bread and beer left. We were sitting round the ashes of the campfire when we heard footsteps approaching. Four soldiers carrying halberds appeared. At their head, looking grim, was Michael Vowell.

'What is it?' Nicholas asked coldly.

Vowell spoke in a formal tone. 'Serjeant Matthew Shardlake, Master Nicholas Overton, we have reason to believe you are spies for the enemy, and thieves, too.'

I rose to my feet, a cold feeling in my stomach. 'What are you talking about? We are neither.'

Vowell, his eyes still on me, waved to his men. 'Search that hut. Turn it inside out.'

'You can't do that,' Nicholas protested. 'Where is your authority?' For answer one of Vowell's men levelled the point of his halberd at his chest.

We had to stand outside while the hut was searched; we heard our bracken bedding pulled apart. Then one of the soldiers reappeared, holding a letter in his hand, as well as the pendant I had admired that day at Surrey Place; I remembered Vowell had been present then. The man handed both to Vowell, who waved the pendant at me. 'I remember you coveting this. You said it reminded you of a similar one worn by your former employer, the late Queen Catherine Parr – whose brother the Marquess of Northampton led the first attack on us last month.'

'Traitors,' one of the soldiers said. 'Kett should never have allowed them here.'

I looked at Michael Vowell. 'Take us, then, to Captain Kett.'

For answer Vowell opened the letter and read it aloud: '"Urgent and secret; to the noble Earl of Warwick; 25 August 1549: My Lord, today we managed to study carefully the defences which the rebels have erected against an assault on Mousehold Heath. I have prepared a dia-gram, which is enclosed. Your Grace's loyal servants, Matthew Shardlake and Nicholas Overton".' The signatures were crude imper-sonations. The diagram, which Vowell held up, was a rough but accurate representation of the defences we had seen yesterday.

Vowell turned to his men. 'I myself saw Shardlake and Overton inspecting the defences yesterday. Toby Lockswood, God save his soul, who died yesterday fighting for the Commonwealth, knew they were traitors but Kett was too soft, he trusted them.'

I said, 'That letter is a crude forgery, and I did not steal the pen-dant.' I remembered the disturbed bracken. 'You planted both in our hut yesterday. I say again, take us to Captain Kett.'

Vowell laughed. 'Do you think he has time to waste on you? Now? But he will be shown the letter and diagram.'

I looked at the soldiers. 'None of what Michael Vowell says is true. He is doing this because he knows I have discovered he is a murderer.'

'Kiss my arse,' one of them replied flatly. 'Master Vowell is a trusted aide to Captain Kett. As for you pair, you're going to Surrey Place, to be chained in front of our forces with the other gemmun.'

I looked at Nicholas. Stupidly, given the information I had about him, I had not thought Vowell an immediate danger. But he had pre-pared everything carefully.

He looked at me coldly. 'Take Overton to Surrey Place now. Tie Shardlake's hands, but leave him with me. I think I will give him a lesson about telling lies to a captain of the Commonwealth; I shall fetch him to Surrey Place shortly.'

My hands were bound behind me, then Nicholas, resisting fiercely, was taken away. Vowell, smiling openly now, gestured me to enter the hut.

He pushed me roughly to the floor, and sat down comfortably in the opposite corner, giving me a concentrated stare as he pulled a knife from his belt, and began gently picking at his fingernails.

'I need to know,' he said quietly, 'how you guessed I was one of those who murdered Edith Boleyn. I realized you knew from the way you looked at me yesterday – a spy like me learns to read faces quickly –

and yes, I have been a spy for the government myself since the beginning, that letter and diagram are copies of the ones I took to Warwick's camp myself. You can either tell me, or I can torture it out of you with this knife. I told the lads I was going to teach you a lesson.'

Realizing there was nothing I could do, I took a deep breath. 'When you came with me to Norwich three weeks ago, you said Jane Reynolds's swollen hands were a family trait, and Edith had it in later life. But how could you have known that unless you had seen her recently? It was being with Peter Bone, and his talking of his sister, that reminded me. One of his sisters was actually Edith Boleyn in disguise. She ran from Brikewell with Grace Bone nine years ago, taking the identity of their other sister, who had died.'

Vowell laughed out loud. 'So that was what happened to her. I have wondered over the years. The lady of Brikewell Manor, husband of Anne Boleyn's relative, working as a spinner. Oh, that is funny.'

'It was a family tragedy.'

In a change of mood, he frowned slightly. 'That was a stupid mis-take I made, effectively letting out that I had seen Edith. It just goes to show, one little error can bring all your secrets tumbling out' – suddenly he grinned again – 'unless you take quick preventive measures.' He looked at me sharply. 'Did you tell Overton? Anyone else?' He pointed the knife at me. 'I can easily shove this under your fingernails and rip them out. It is very painful.'

'Only Nicholas,' I said. 'Barak is – somewhere in Norwich.'

Vowell nodded, his expression thoughtful. I asked, 'Why did you not just have us killed last night?'

'Because I needed to be sure how much you knew. And because there might have been some enquiry – Kett seems to see you as some sort of pet. The old fool, does he really think he can take on the rulers of England?'

'He has done well so far. Won two battles. And who knows, may yet win a third.'

He looked at me askance. 'You, a gentleman and lawyer, hope Kett and his kitlings will win?'

'England has long needed reform, and he is the man to bring it.'

'He will bring chaos. Have you heard the prophets preaching the end of the world?'

'They do not rule this camp. Captain Kett does.'

'Control is starting to slip to the radicals, as you may have noticed. I have been helping shift it along, to divide the camp.' Vowell shook his head and laughed again. 'Christ's bones, you are indeed a traitor. To King and Protector.'

'Better traitor than spy.'

He looked offended. 'Spying can be an honourable profession, as well as a pleasurable one, if one believes in what one is doing.'

'Like helping Gawen Reynolds murder his daughter?'

He looked me in the eyes. 'You worked out Reynolds's involvement, too?'

'Yes. If you were lying about having seen Edith recently, that could only connect you to Reynolds. She came to see him, didn't she, to ask for money as a last, desperate resort after the Lady Elizabeth's Comptroller turned her down?'

Vowell smiled again. 'Yes. Gawen Reynolds and I have worked closely together for many years. I have been more than a steward, I have acted for him on many matters, including joint affairs with Sir Richard Southwell.'

'You said they hated each other.'

'On the contrary, they are the best of friends. Like attracts like.' He spread his hands. 'It was part of my job.' Then he shook his head. 'But things went wrong the night Edith was killed. Reynolds, like his grandsons, can let his temper get out of control. He made a mess of Edith's murder.'

'Were Gerald and Barnabas involved?'

'Good God, no. Mad as they are, they always loved their mother. But you guessed right about Edith contacting her father as a last hope. She did not dare turn up at the house, but sent a note, saying she was alive and in desperate need of money, and asking him to help. When Gawen Reynolds read it —' Vowell laughed — 'he nearly had a seizure. He showed it to me. He said Edith may have hidden away safely somewhere all these years, but now she was alone and he was going to exact his revenge on her.'

'Why did he hate her so?'

Vowell shrugged. 'Reynolds can't keep his hands off women. I was around the house when Edith was young, and I believe he tried it on with his own daughter. My guess is she fought him, at least to begin with. Gawen Reynolds does not tolerate any woman who resists him. I remember once or twice hearing the sound of screams from her chamber.'

Now I realized exactly why Jane Reynolds had so wished Edith had been a boy. I imagined her standing, helpless, in the shadows all those years.

Vowell spoke of this horror with no more emotion than if he had been discussing the weather; his tone had become conversational; he was enjoying telling the tale. I had encountered spies before, and knew the pleasure they could get from removing their masks – when they were safe. I wondered, would he kill me before leaving the hut?

But for the moment, he continued his boasting. 'Gawen Reynolds planned it all out. He would kill Edith and make it look as though John Boleyn had done it. He always hated his son-in-law, and his setting up home with that Isabella. So he would kill two birds with one stone. In fact, three.' He laughed. 'Sir Richard Southwell wanted Boleyn's land, so he could join his two neighbouring plots together. It would make running the sheep cheaper, if it was all one site. Given his wealth, it was a relatively small matter, but you know how Norfolk gentlemen can become – obsessive – if their wishes are not met.'

'Like his man John Atkinson. Still pursuing that helpless girl he abducted, I hear.'

Vowell frowned, looking annoyed at my interruption. He continued: 'The plan was that Boleyn would be executed for the murder and the land put in the hands of the escheator, and Southwell would work with Flowerdew to make sure he got it. The twins would get some compensation.'

'Yes,' I said grimly. 'The corruption of the King's local officials. Part of what Kett wants to end.'

'Better corruption than disorder. I may be only a lowly steward by origin, but I believe the social order of the realm must be maintained by any means. I always have. I am a spy, Master Shardlake, by conviction. I have not only helped Master Reynolds and Sir Richard Southwell, I have spied for the city authorities on makebates who would stir up discontent here – Norwich is full of wily troublemakers. I left Gawen Reynolds's employ because it was obvious that trouble was coming among the commoners and I could join the rebels – even present myself as a radical, work with the naive younger element, encourage them and perhaps split the camp against Kett.' He smiled again. 'That request came from Southwell himself; the Protector and his counsel were looking for spies.'

'I imagine it pays well.'

He shrugged. 'I have never had much interest in money.' His cold eyes lit up for the first time. 'When I was a child I wanted more than anything to be an actor. I took part in all the guild mystery plays, in the old days. But actors lead a precarious life, and I wanted security, too.'

'You are certainly a good actor.'

Vowell nodded to acknowledge the compliment, then fell silent. I decided to lead him on. 'So it was you who stole the key to the stable, and planted the muddy boots and hammer to incriminate John Boleyn.'

'That's right,' he boasted. 'I have always cultivated friendly relations with the twins. One day they were at their grandfather's and waxing fierce about that Sooty Scambler who was killed before the Herald. It was me who suggested they give him a beating, steal the key to the stable and let that dangerous horse run wild. I knew they were going to the cockfighting that evening, and arranged to have the key taken briefly, so an impression could be made. The locksmith Snockstobe, who would do anything for money to spend on drink, would make a copy. So far as the twins knew, it was never stolen, so they believed the evidence against their own father of the muddy boots and the bloody hammer in the stable. A good plan, was it not?'

'You thought it up while talking to the twins about – about Simon?'

'Yes, though it was the pure luck of Gerald leaving his purse on the bench that night which gave me the chance. But I would have found another opportunity.' His voice turned sharp. 'It is not only lawyers that have quick minds, hunchback.'

'No,' I said. 'It was clever indeed.' I spoke quietly, preening his actor's vanity. 'But something went wrong with Snockstobe?'

'He knew when he was asked to make a key from a wax impression that it was likely stolen. When you threatened him with a subpoena, he came running to me and Master Reynolds. If he'd had the balls to lie in court there wouldn't have been a problem. But he'd likely have turned up drunk and spilled out everything. So we arranged for him to be disposed of. The apprentice, too, who I was sure had been listening to our conversation earlier at the shop. Master Reynolds brought in some of Sir Richard Southwell's men for that, with John Atkinson in charge. So all was well again. But earlier, the night of Edith Boleyn's killing – well, men can be such fools. Even a Norwich alderman like Gawen Reynolds.'

'So it was his fault she was left in the condition she was?' I tried not to let my disgust show.

Vowell frowned, fingered his knife again. 'I had planned the whole thing out.' He tossed his head angrily; the man's vanity was indeed limitless. 'Master Reynolds and I agreed he would reply to her note, which came from a cheap lodging house in Norwich, and arrange to meet her at the bridge separating Boleyn's land from Witherington's – I hear he's dead, too, now; when this is over Sir Richard Southwell will no doubt have his land too.' He raised his eyebrows. 'It was all settled, she replied agreeing to meet her father at the bridge. Master Reynolds and I rode down there, with a heavy hammer and a spade in my horse's knapsack. I was going to clout her on the head, and then we would bury her in a shallow grave on the South Brikewell side, without bothering to replace the grass properly so the old shepherd would notice the next day. But when we arrived at the bridge, and Reynolds saw her standing there in the dusk, white bandages on her hands like her mother's, he lost control. He shouted and shrieked at her, demanding to know where she had been these nine years, and when she refused to answer it made him worse. He called her a slut and a whore who had abandoned her poor sons. She was afraid, she backed away from him, and that gave me the chance to step behind her and hit her a fine culp on the head with the hammer.' He smiled. 'She went down on the

bridge like a sack of wood.' He slapped his free hand on the floor, start-
ling me. 'Just like that.'

'I thought seeing her dead might cool old Reynolds's anger, but
it seemed only to fire it up more. He had somehow convinced himself Edith had spent the last nine years as a whore. He said if her
hands were bad, it was probably through pulling off customers. He
said he wasn't going to bury her, he wanted her put head first in the
river with her worn-out old cunt displayed to the world. I warned him
that could take suspicion off Boleyn, if people were to believe the husband murdered Edith so his new marriage would not be declared
invalid, he would not display her body to the world. But old Reynolds
was beyond reason. Silly old fool, he's never learned that to truly succeed in this world you must control yourself.'

I thought, Like you, and others like you whom I have met, cold as
ice, thinking of killing people as if they were flies.

Vowell was frowning; angry, I guessed, not with me but with
Reynolds. 'I told him I was going to bury her, and went back to the
horses to fetch the spade. On my way back I heard a splash and then
saw Reynolds standing in the mud, with Edith's body sticking up out
of the water, pulling her drawers off to expose everything she had. He
shouted at me to help him out, he had wrenched his leg badly – I was
surprised someone his age managed to do that alone, but it is amazing
what a man may do when overcome with fury. I got him back to the
bridge, and told him I was going to take Edith out and bury her as
planned, but he said if I did, he would tell all Norwich that I was no
secret radical as I pretended, but an agent of Norwich council and of
Southwell.' Vowell shrugged. 'Well, Reynolds was too powerful a man
for me to kill, it did not matter that much to me whether Boleyn was
hanged or not, and if he wanted to let his anger get the better of his
judgement, that was up to him. So I helped him back to the horses – he
really had hurt his leg, I don't think it's ever got better – and we rode
home. It was after that I decided to offer my services to Sir Richard
Southwell as a full-time spy. I had had enough of Reynolds, and
trouble was already stirring among the people. Though I agreed to do
him a last favour in freeing the twins from Surrey Place when they were
taken prisoner. Southwell wanted it done too; he wants Gerald and

Barnabas working for him full time. He had a final go at killing Boleyn through poison at the Castle, but it didn't work.' Vowell smiled nastily. 'And that, Master Lawyer, is the end of my story.'

'What of Boleyn's lack of an alibi for the hours between nine and eleven that night?'

He shrugged. 'I heard Gawen Reynolds talked about that to Sir Richard Southwell; I think he arranged something.' He smiled again. 'There, you have learned more from me than I from you. But it doesn't matter. I shall take you to Surrey Place as I promised, and you will doubtless die in the battle tomorrow.'

I stared at him, my head spinning with astonishment. I said, 'I thought you would kill me here.'

He shook his head. 'Your murder might raise enquiries, and I do not want my cover blown all over the camp. You and Overton can repeat our conversation to anyone you like in the hours you have left, sing like birds, for all I care. Nobody will believe you, and I do not care whether Reynolds or Boleyn hangs. Most important, I shall be gone. It has been decided my usefulness in Norwich is at an end now. Every-thing now will be decided in battle. I have orders from Captain Kett to take a message to some people who were in the Suffolk camp, asking if any could support him tomorrow. But I shall not deliver it, or go anywhere near Suffolk. I shall slip away. I have other orders, a new commission, abroad.'

'From whom?'

He smiled. 'The King's Council. I have received my orders from Southwell. I am glad I shall not be in London. I have a feeling Pro-tector Somerset's days are numbered. He has made a great mess in Scotland, and the Council say he was too soft with the rebels at the beginning.' Vowell stood up, patted himself complacently on the chest, and smiled at me. 'I know so much; it is great entertainment. Now, come on.' He put his knife away, then stepped over and reached behind me, hauling me roughly to my feet and pushing me outside. The sun was lower in the sky now. From the direction of Norwich I heard the sound of loud, repeated gunfire. Vowell smiled again. 'Ah, the lands-knechts have arrived. Firing their guns in the air, no doubt. I hear they love to make a show before the killing starts.'

Chapter Seventy-seven

VOWELL HAULED ME roughly along to Surrey Place. As I stumbled uncomfortably across the rough ground, he said not another word, and when I ventured to speak told me to shut my mouth. His face had resumed its customary hard, slightly blank expression. What an actor he indeed was. My back hurt as he shoved me along. He delivered me to one of the soldiers standing guard at the courtyard gates, whispering an explanation to him, then turned away and walked towards the road down the hill, without even a backward glance. I endured more rough handling as two guards bundled me into the building and up the stairs. A door was opened and I was dragged inside.

I found myself in a room with a large window looking out over the camp, from which perhaps, in his brief glory days, the Earl of Surrey had shown his visitors the heath. It held some twenty prisoners, tied together with a long chain stretching from wall to wall, both ends padlocked firmly to heavy brackets nailed to the wall. All had the chain pulled round their wrists and secured with a padlock. They looked up at me with hollow eyes, these gentlemen who, two months ago, had ruled the county. Nicholas was at the very end of the line, John Boleyn next to him. I was forced between them, the rope binding my hands was cut and my wrists were pulled in front of me and padlocked to the chain like the others. Then the guards went out and closed the door. I looked at Nicholas and Boleyn. Nicholas's face was set, but Boleyn was white-faced and haggard as the others.

'What did Vowell do to you?' Nicholas said.

I told them of how my earlier talk with Peter Bone had made me deduce that Vowell, with Gawen Reynolds, was responsible for Edith's murder, and that Vowell had realized I knew. As I recounted our conversation in the hut, Nicholas and John Boleyn listened, wide-eyed and horrified, while the nearest men in the line of chained prisoners bent sideways to eavesdrop; even in the face of imminent death, human curiosity persists. At the end Boleyn lowered his head with a sigh. 'Gawen Reynolds, I always knew he was a villain, but never guessed he could be capable of that. Poor Edith. If only she had turned to me, I would have given her money to resume her imposture.' Two tears rolled down his thin, dirty cheeks. At last, he had shown some pity for his dead wife. He said quietly, 'So Barnabas and Gerald had nothing to do with her death?'

'Nothing. They were used by Vowell and your father-in-law to get the key, that is all.'

He closed his eyes. I waited, then said, 'Vowell indicated your lack of an alibi was connected to Sir Richard Southwell,' I said quietly. 'You might as well tell us the truth about that now, John; likely we will all be dead tomorrow.'

Boleyn leaned back, resting his head against the wall, his face utterly miserable. 'You know I have been in debt. I bought my London house with a loan, and have been unable to service it from the rents and produce from Brikewell and my other manors. Even back in May the signs were this would be a bad harvest, less money would come in than ever before. But with the way my Isabella was treated by the local gentry, to say nothing of the twins' behaviour to her, I wanted to move to London, though I wanted to keep Brikewell, and I took a mortgage on my land from Southwell. It was stupid, stupid, I know he has coveted my estate, among others, to run his sheep.' He sighed. 'The rate of interest was high; I think he had been into my affairs and knew things would reach the point where I could no longer pay.' Boleyn laughed. 'Yet I was reluctant to have him call in the mortgage and take my estate. What an obstinate fool I was. As I fell behind, Southwell put greater pressure on me. He told me to meet him on the road just outside Brikewell at half past nine on the fourteenth of May. He warned me to tell no one. It was an odd request, but Southwell is not a man to be refused.

'When we met, he told me he wanted the estate, now. I asked for more time, but he insisted, and added that if I did not do as he asked,

something bad would happen to Isabella. That was why I said nothing, and persisted in my pretence that I was at home that evening.' He
sighed. 'No doubt he had cooked this all up with Gawen Reynolds to
ensure I had no proper alibi. The day I was imprisoned I got a message
from him to say that if I ever spoke of our meeting, Isabella would be
made to disappear. Given my arrest, nobody would question her van-
ishing suddenly from Brikewell. I am sorry, Master Shardlake, that I
did not tell you the truth. But Isabella means more to me than life itself.'
He lifted his head and laughed bitterly again. 'And she was the only
one who believed my alibi. Dear Isabella.' He looked at me with a
sudden wildness. 'What will happen to her now, alone out there in that
city?'

'I wish I knew. But few women are more resourceful.'

Nicholas clenched his hands, making the chain rattle. 'The three
of us are guilty of nothing against Kett. We have been checkmated
by Reynolds and Vowell and made to face death. If only Barak were
here. If only we could get the truth to him.'

I said quietly, 'We do not know whether Jack is even still alive.
And as Vowell knew, there is no point appealing to the guards here.
They seem keen to take us all to our deaths, I think they have been
chosen for that reason.'

We fell silent. Hours passed. Along the line of chained men some
began praying together, while another group – they must have been
Catholics – produced rosaries and prayed over them, again and again,
in Latin. Dusk came, and the blue sky outside the big window turned
dark. A thin crescent moon rose. From the camp we began to hear
voices, thuds and the sound of creaking wheels. Although we were all
tied closely together, Nicholas, at the end of the line, had a little more
space to move and with difficulty he got to his feet and looked through
the window. He said, 'There are lots of torches lit. It looks like men,
equipment and weapons too, are being moved from the camp.'

Just then the door opened with a crash, making everyone jump so
that the long chain clanked heavily. A young soldier in helmet and
breastplate entered, accompanied by guards. He looked at us with
contempt.

'Well, gentlemen of Norfolk,' he said, 'I have come to tell you our final attack on the city has failed. We have been driven out of the north' ern parts. All Norwich is now under Warwick's control, we are cut off from the market. We cannot survive long without supplies, so we are evacuating the camp where' – his voice broke for a second – 'where we have lived these seven weeks. But we are not defeated. We are moving everything to the site where, tomorrow, we shall give battle to Warwick, his mercenaries and gentlemen, and we are about to send them a signal that we are ready to fight. You will all be taken to Mousehold Heath and tomorrow, chained together, you will be in the front line facing the enemy. It will be a nice dilemma for Warwick, whether to fire on you or not.'

One man put his head in his hands and began to howl. He was told brusquely to 'stop winnicking!' Another gentleman shouted out, 'You promised us justice under the Oak of Reformation. Robert Kett said nobody would be killed. He's broken his word!'

The man next to him asked, 'Does he even know of this?'

The soldier did not answer directly. 'Hundreds of our men have died in Norwich. It is the King's Council, and Warwick, who have forced us into this. Now shut up, aren't you supposed to be gentlemen, ready to face your end with dignity? You will be called for later.' And with that he left the room, the guards locking the door behind him.

More time passed. Some men wept, others resumed their prayers, but most sat in shocked silence. It was quite dark in the room now. But presently we saw a faint red glow outside. It grew brighter, and we heard the crackling of flames. Even though the window was closed, a faint smell of smoke came into the room. Someone said in horror, 'They're setting Surrey Place on fire.'

Again, Nicholas got carefully to his feet and looked out of the window. 'Holy Jesus Christ,' he said in an awestruck tone.

'What are they doing?' someone asked frantically. 'Is the house afire?'

'No. They've fired the camp, that must be the signal they are ready to fight or die.'

I staggered to my feet, Boleyn leaning into me to make it easier. Through the window I saw a sight I shall never forget. The whole camp was ablaze, as far as the eye could see. All the little huts where we had lived were now fiercely burning circles of turf and bracken. Smoke billowed up, blown towards Norwich by an easterly breeze. I said quietly, 'The end of the Mousehold camp.'

Nicholas said, 'But if they win tomorrow, where will the rebels go?'

'Into Norwich, I should think, through the northern gates they have been firing on. And then – try to spread the rebellion again.' I groaned, for my back had been wrenched as I stood up, and Nicholas and Boleyn helped me back to a sitting position. Someone shouted out, 'Will you stop moving up there? The chain's pulling our arms.'

We sat in silence again, the room now lit by a bright, flickering redness. I saw Nicholas lean forward, looking towards the far end of the room. He said quietly, 'Can you see who the man is at the other end of the chain? By the opposite wall?'

I screwed up my eyes and looked down. 'A small man, old, I think, yes, with white hair.'

'Damn,' he said. 'All may depend on the strength of the man at each end of the chain.'

I looked at him. My eyes were stinging now, for the room was full of smoke. 'What do you mean?'

He muttered, 'Maybe nothing. I doubt it will be possible.'

✟

MORE HOURS PASSED. At one point, through sheer exhaustion, I fell asleep. Then the door crashed open again and the same officer entered, this time accompanied by a dozen soldiers, all young and strong, swords at their waists. 'On your feet!' he shouted. 'Time to go!' He nodded, and one of his men unlocked the padlock securing the chain to the wall beside Nicholas, wrapping the chain firmly round his wrist. Another soldier did the same at the other end of the room where the old man was. The soldiers took positions along the line. Their captain said, 'You go to Dussindale now.' As I stood up painfully I looked from the window; the fire seemed to be dying now. The sky was a little less dark; soon it would be dawn. The captain said, 'Mind your feet outside. Anyone tries to escape, they'll be gutted on the spot. Now, out.' The guard at the opposite end of the room pulled on the chain. The old man swayed slightly, then found his feet and staggered out of the room, the rest of us following in a macabre procession behind him.

Outside in the Great Hall another twenty or so ragged, chained gentlemen prisoners had been taken from other rooms. A further group of a dozen was being led down the stairs, slowly lest they slip. At the bottom their chain was secured to the end of the one holding the other group, then to ours, with heavy padlocks. Nicholas deliberately hung back so that he, Boleyn and I were right at the end of the long line of about fifty haggard, frightened men. Another young captain walked along the line, checking each man's padlock was secure. One gentleman began pleading frantically for his life, saying he had money hidden. He was ignored. The doors of Surrey Place were thrown open, grey smoke billowing in.

'Now, gentlemen,' the captain said, 'make a line and start walking outside. Slowly, don't anyone dare trip.' We began to move, the long chain rattling and clanking as the first men shuffled outside.

The courtyard was empty, the tents and other supplies stored there gone. The gates were open, and we were led outside. There, the smoke was thicker, and through it I could see countless huts glowing red. One collapsed, then another, sending showers of fiery sparks into the slowly lightening sky. Patches of grass had caught and sent their own billows of smoke skyward. I thought of our hut, the Swardeston people who had welcomed us, poor dead Hector Johnson and Simon, and of Natty and Barak. Had they survived the fighting in Norwich? It suddenly occurred to me that I had never asked Natty what his last name was.

It was a long, slow, horrible march. The guards on each side of us carried horn-lamps, but the light which they and the burning camp provided was obscured by the smoke. We were led past St Michael's Chapel, which was deserted but had not been set alight, then some way uphill and along trackways between the dying fires of the huts. We looked down at our feet as we walked, but even so some men stumbled and fell, risking the balance of the whole line; the fallen prisoners were hauled roughly to their feet.

Oddly, the man next to Boleyn, a middle-aged fellow with greying hair, took to treating our terrible situation with humour. He said his name was Dale, and he owned a couple of manors in the south of the

county. 'All I did was put one of them to sheep, I would have compen‑
sated the tenants, but I don't live there and my bailiff got together with
a local lawyer and turned the tenants out, saying their leases were at the
landlord's will. I remember you were at my trial, sir, you said the stew‑
ard should be brought as a witness, without him everything he was
supposed to have said was hearsay. You tried to get the trial postponed
till he was found, and I am grateful for that, but my tenants said he had
fled, which I imagine he has, so it fell back on me. Now he'll be living
somewhere quiet, on my money, while you and I face being killed by
our own side. What a jest and confusion life is, hardly worth the
trouble in the end.'

'Keep quiet,' Boleyn said roughly. 'Concentrate on keeping your
balance.'

We turned northward, walking roughly parallel to the bend of the
river, then west, now in a line close to the city's northern walls. We
were moving slowly downhill. Many campfires burned on the open
ground in the northern part of the city; Warwick's army.

At length we passed the northern perimeter of the camp, beyond
the smoke from the huts. We began to encounter groups of camp‑men,
walking purposefully westward, all carrying weapons; halberds and
spears, twelve‑foot‑long pikes, sharpened pitchforks, scythes fixed to the
end of long poles, and a great number of archers carrying longbows.
All looked at us with contempt, some spitting on the ground as we
passed. We heard snatches of conversation:

'They say an adder jumped out of a rotten tree into Mistress Kett's
bosom; some take it as a bad omen, but it didn't bite her –'

'There's some deserted in the night –'

'Good riddance, there's over six thousand of us fit and trained men
left, and we'll fight to the end –'

'Wait – I have to hulp –' A man stepped aside and was violently
sick.

'Don't shit your pants like young Hunter –'

And then, as the sky began to lighten properly, we reached the
crest of the spur of land projecting from Mousehold Heath named
Dussindale, which I had visited with Peter Bone two days before. The
gun‑platform was complete, a flattened area onto which a couple of

dozen cannon had been pulled. Below, being drawn up in battle array by their officers, were the thousands of men from Mousehold camp, horsemen, foot soldiers with pole weapons raised, parish banners flying alongside the red banners of war. Halfway down the hill supply wagons had been turned on their sides, and behind them thousands of archers were taking up positions. Some had armour, others quilted jackets, but many had only their ordinary clothes.

At the bottom of the hill, facing a flat area, the last of the wooden stakes were being hammered into the ground, sharp points facing outward towards the enemy. In front of them the long trench was complete, the excavated earth thrown up in front to form a low barrier, while to the north the new earthworks stood high. A little way to the south stood the city walls, many of the towers bombarded into ruins by cannon over the last few days. If the rebels won, that was how they would re-enter Norwich.

Forced to descend, we came parallel to the gun platform. I saw Captain Miles there, walking to and fro, shouting orders to the gun-crews. I thought of his wife and children in detention in London, and realized it must have been Michael Vowell who betrayed him, too. I saw Peter Bone, standing behind a cannon, and I thought he looked at me, but he was too far off for me to be sure. Some way to the left I saw a group of men in helmets and bright clothes standing together, looking down the slope of the hill. The commanders, awaiting the start of the battle. Robert Kett was there with his brother; he glanced at our pathetic line being dragged along, then quickly looked away again.

We continued slowly downhill, past the main body of soldiers. Boos and catcalls sounded as we passed, from these men among whom I had lived peaceably all these weeks. We were brought to a halt just behind the stakes and ordered to stand in a line parallel with them. 'Merciful Christ,' someone muttered, 'they're going to do it.' Some of the men who were hammering in the last of the wooden stakes brought two exceptionally large ones across to us. Boleyn and Nicholas and I were at the southern end of the line, and we watched as, next to us, our end of the chain was looped and padlocked tightly to a stake, then the stake hammered into the sandy soil. At the other end of the line another stake was being dug in. We stood, shackled and helpless, facing the coming enemy.

And they were coming; Warwick's army, slowly, in a seemingly endless line through Coslany Gate, first horsemen in armour, a great many of them, the white cross of England emblazoned on their chests, then seemingly endless lines of men, foot soldiers and more horsemen, this time big men in battle armour, but with brightly coloured hose and huge feathers fixed to their helmets. The landsknechts. Many carried heavy arquebuses with apparent ease. Warwick's army began slowly to move into position, only a few hundred feet from where we stood, as more soldiers continued marching through the gate behind them; English soldiers now, I recognized Captain Drury at their head. There seemed to be nearly as many of them as there were of the rebel forces, and they had many more horsemen, our only advantage being that of height and a greater number of cannon. As more and more came and took their places dust rose in clouds.

And now we were alone, standing chained together in a line, between the two armies. I felt the chain start to rattle and shake, slowly but steadily, all along its length, and realized many of the prisoners were trembling, as I had begun to do myself.

Chapter Seventy-eight

N O MORE THAN six hundred feet before us, Warwick's army
formed into battle array, men called to take their places by shouts
from their captains. Cannon — fewer than ours — were rolled into place
flanking the main body of troops. Landsknecht arquebusiers, enormous, bull-like men, stood right at the front, hundreds spread out in
two lines, one behind the other. Little fires were lit at various points
beside them, reminding me of Simon's terrible end, and then of the
demonstration at Mousehold where a bullet had pierced armour as
though it were butter. The big men stood there waiting, faces set but
eyes constantly roving, big guns by their sides, the gaudy feathers in
their helmets stirring in the light breeze. I glanced up at the sky; it was
cloudless, the start of a perfect late summer day. As Vowell had noted,
the rebels had the advantage that Warwick's army were facing the rising
sun. Some landsknechts raised their hands to shade their eyes.

Behind the arquebusiers more landsknechts formed up, holding up
their twelve-foot pikes. And behind them horsemen, then foot soldiers.
Apart from the shouting of orders from the captains of each army all
was extraordinarily silent. Although even Warwick's foot soldiers wore
breastplates and helmets, many of the rebels — I realized I was suddenly
no longer thinking of them as 'our men' — lacked armour.

A man on horseback rode up the side of Warwick's men and
halted beside the landsknechts. He carried a standard, the emblem of
a bear chained to a tree-trunk; the bear and ragged staff, Warwick's
emblem. And then I saw the earl himself, riding through the lines, in
glittering armour and helmet; I had seen him briefly four years before
in Portsmouth, and recognized the hard sallow face and pointed black
beard. Then, he had played a crucial part in preventing the invasion of
Hampshire by the French fleet; he was known as a great commander

both on land and sea. He halted near the front of his lines, looked at the ditch, the stakes, and at us standing chained behind, all with the same hard, calculating gaze. Then he looked up the slope at our army, before turning and riding back. I thought, When the warship *Mary Rose* sank it had all happened in a matter of minutes, while this slow forming up seemed endless. I tried to control my shaking legs. Next to me, Nicholas grasped my arm. 'Courage,' he whispered.

I said, my voice breaking with emotion and fear, 'If this is the end, know I have never had better friends than you and Barak.'

'And I could have had no better teacher or friend. But hold fast, this may not yet be the finish.'

A little way up the line of chained gentlemen, Dale, who had reacted during the march to Dussindale by making a jest of it all, laughed. 'A bear chained to a staff. Like us, really. What might that symbolize?'

His neighbour turned on him viciously. 'It means we have been captured and humiliated, and are about to be killed, by a crew of peas-ant dogs that would have all men to be such common beasts as they. By God, if we escape with our lives – I am a magistrate – I will see them all hanged.' He shouted out across the ditch at the landsknechts, 'Help us, damn you! We are on your side, we're prisoners!'

None of them reacted. 'They're foreign mercenaries,' Dale said, impatiently. 'I doubt they even understand English!' He laughed again, but with a frantic edge now.

Four more horsemen rode through Warwick's ranks, fully armoured with plumed helmets. One carried a white flag of truce. Two soldiers marched before them, carrying a broad wooden plank which they laid across the ditch. The riders made their way with difficulty up the earthen mound, then across the plank, between the stakes. They passed us without a look, and continued uphill to where Kett and the other leaders stood. Dale said hopefully, 'Maybe they're offering a pardon.' But as they rode up alongside the rebel ranks, the chorus of boos and insults hurled at them told me what the result of that would be.

There was another wait while Kett and Warwick's men held a parley. The last of Warwick's troops were still riding up from Coslany gate, and I drew a sharp breath as I recognized two unmistakable blond heads among a body of men, armoured and with swords at their waists, surrounding their captain, a horseman. They were ordered into position near the front of the line.

I said, 'I'm not sure, but I think that's Southwell.'

Boleyn said in a dull voice, 'And I would recognize my sons any' where. I think that's my steward Chawry with them. So that's where he ended up.'

'No Flowerdew, though,' Nicholas said.

'He'll be back for the pickings afterwards,' I answered bitterly.

Warwick's emissaries rode back down the hill; the frowns on their faces and the fresh chorus of insults from the rebel army showed that whatever offer they had made had been rejected. I felt a new tension in the men beside me as they rode past us again, and back along the ranks of Warwick's soldiers.

Then came the sudden boom of a cannon firing from the rebel gun platform. We did not see the cannonball but heard a whistling and saw the standard-bearer's leg, and the shoulder of his horse, explode in a fountain of blood. Both dropped, instantly dead; the standard drop' ping to the dusty ground.

Behind us came a shout from the back, passed up the line, 'To battle!'

With booms and crashes, both sides fired their artillery, the rebels' superior height and quantity of cannon wreaking havoc among War' wick's forces, men and horses screaming and falling, gunballs hitting the ground and bouncing into the men. More orders were shouted from behind us, and a hail of arrows whistled through the air, over us, and fell among Warwick's men, bringing more terrible screams.

Then the arquebusiers lit their gunpowder pans. It was Nicholas who shouted, 'Crouch down!' – the stakes pinning us at either end made it impossible to lie – and everyone fell to their knees. The arque' buses fired, with a great crashing sound that nearly deafened me, and a volley of iron such as I could never have imagined crashed into the rebels behind us. I believe the mercenaries tried to avoid hitting us where they could, though I saw several men at the other end of the line judder and fall, most shot through the body, blood and intestines gushing forth. Some bullets hit the chains, breaking them, sparks flashing. Many of the rebel horsemen behind us were hit by the hail of bullets and crashed to the ground, their horses, too. I looked at Nicholas, and saw that he was, with great courage, kneeling and trying with all his strength to pull the stake beside him from the ground. 'Help me!' he shouted. Boleyn and I pushed forward, drawing the chain taut, and helped him pull. We felt the stake move in the sandy soil and then suddenly it was up and out.

'The other end,' I said breathlessly, but Nicholas pulled us down again as a fresh volley, from the second rank of the arquebusiers, hit the rebel lines behind us, mowing down another line of horsemen attempting to advance through the remains of their dead comrades.

'I think the chain at the other end's broken,' Boleyn said breathlessly, and looking along the line I saw that where the prisoners hit by the arquebusiers lay dead, bullets had also broken the chain in several places, separating it from the other stake. Perhaps the arquebusiers had fired thus deliberately.

'Go!' Nicholas shouted, just as a fresh volley of arrows thudded into Warwick's men, several hitting the landsknechts, who let out mighty cries as they fell.

I am certain we would all have died that morning had not Nicholas begun to scuttle, crouched on all fours, to the right, between the two armies, separated now only by the ditch and stakes. From the other end of the chain everyone except those who had been hit followed Nicholas in the same crouching scuttle, until at last — it seemed like hours — we were beyond the ranks of the armies and stumbling downhill. We crawled up a knoll and down the other side, staggering into one of the many exposed rabbit warrens dotting the heath, the rabbits having been dug out for food weeks ago. Then someone near the front caught his foot in a rabbit hole and crashed to the ground, bringing everyone else down with him. Under the weight of all the men, the hollowedout earth gave way beneath us, as it had the time gunpowder had been used on the warren on Mousehold, and we all found ourselves lying in a shallow earthen depression. Only just behind and above, we could hear the unbelievable din of battle, yells and crashes and gunfire that almost deafened us. We pressed ourselves into the ground, waiting for some of Kett's men to follow and kill us, but after a few minutes I realized we had been forgotten.

Panting, I looked around me. Ahead, the ground sloped down to the city walls, closer than I would have thought, with the gates broken by cannon fire in the days before. Some of Warwick's men stood on top of the walls. They could easily have shot us down, but must have known who we were. For the moment at least, we were safe.

'Thank you,' I said to Nicholas. 'You saved us.'

'So much for your rebel friends,' Boleyn said angrily. 'They betrayed you in the end.'

'No,' I answered. 'That was Michael Vowell.' I sighed. 'These men are fighting because they can no longer believe in promises. Who can blame them?'

'I can,' said one man beside me. 'Beasts, dogs, serfs and traitors, death to all of them!'

Dale laughed again – the sound was a little more high-pitched and shaky this time. He said, 'Do you know what you look like, lying there with earth on your faces, arguing away?' His laugh changed to a bloody splutter as a volley of half a dozen arrows came whistling from the sky, and one hit him in the heart, killing him instantly. Another pin-ioned a man to the ground by an arm. He lay screaming helplessly as blood welled out over the ground.

'We have to get back to the city,' Nicholas gasped. 'If only we could get this damned chain off!' He had become the natural leader, and many gentlemen at once turned on their backs, trying frantically to push the chain through the hasps of their padlocks, but in most cases the chain links were too wide. Soon men's wrists were covered in blood as they frantically pushed and pulled. Nicholas, though, managed to pass the chain through his padlock, and I also got mine through, though Boleyn, next to us, could not.

'We should try to run for the city wall,' I shouted.

'No,' Nicholas answered. 'The knoll above us and this low pit give some cover, but if we run, we'll be visible to the rebel side and the next volley of arrows will be heavier.'

He was right. We lay there, waiting, the battle only a few yards away from us, a fact brought closer when a horse from Warwick's side, maddened by the arrows sticking from its flanks, charged over the top of the knoll and crashed to the ground only a few feet away, screaming in pain. Its rider was dead, a spear in his side, blood oozing out in a red stream. Nicholas, crawling on hands and knees, took the rider's knife and cut the horse's throat lest its screaming draw attention to us. One of the still-chained gentlemen also crawled over, grabbed the dead soldier's helmet and put it on his head.

'What's happening out there?' someone shouted in panic.

Finding new courage, I crawled slowly from the shallow pit and up the knoll. I held out a hand to the man who had taken the dead soldier's helmet, who was once again lying flat on the ground, in the hope he might give it to me, but he only looked at me defiantly.

Glancing over the top of the knoll, glad my white hair and my face were covered with earth, I saw the most terrible sight I have ever witnessed. Warwick's men had breached both the ditch and stakes, though several bodies were impaled there, and on the battlefield thousands were engaged in close-quarter fighting, moving so fast it was hard to follow with the eye. I was almost deafened by the screaming and shouting, the firing of guns, the clash of weapons and the wild neighing of horses. The landsknechts were now charging the rebel forces with their long pikes in close formation, and the rebel soldiers, unable to reach them with their swords or halberds, were being run through in their dozens. Volleys of arrows, however, still arced through the air from the rebel side, and cannon pounded volleys from the gun platform, aiming at Warwick's artillery; I saw one soldier explode into pieces as a cannonball hit. On other parts of the battlefield men on both sides, in smaller groups, were slashing and stabbing at each other with swords and pole weapons – I saw a rebel soldier cut the head clean off one of Warwick's men with a scythe on the end of a pole, before he was run through with a sword. Groups of three or four soldiers from each side were engaged in individual combat at the centre of it all, swords against halberds and spears, cutting and slashing, the lack of armour on the rebel side a disadvantage in such hand-to-hand fighting. I realized that many of those fighting now stood on the bodies of dead soldiers and horses. Blood oozed across the ground everywhere, I could smell its sharp salty tang from where I lay, mixed with the smell of shit as men's bowels were torn out. I crawled slowly back down.

'Who's winning?' one of the gentlemen asked.

'No one,' I answered grimly.

✝

WE LAY THERE for hours as the battle swirled and crashed above us. The sun rose high and soon we were parched with thirst, though that would be nothing to what the men on the battlefield would be suffer-ing. Once a rebel soldier staggered over the top of the knoll, scrabbling frantically at his face; his lower jaw had been shot away. He tripped on a rabbit hole, rolled down the little hill and lay on his stomach, making horrible gurgling noises which slowly ceased. Soon after, a thin stream of red began to trickle over the knoll at its lowest point. People looked at it in puzzlement before realizing it was blood from the battlefield.

From the sounds above I sensed the battle was moving, first away from us as Warwick's army advanced, then back towards us as the rebels counter-attacked. At length the sound of battle seemed to move away decisively, uphill. The man who had taken the dead soldier's helmet was lying in a sort of stupor. I crawled over and lifted the helmet from his head, ignoring his angry cry. I put it on and, brushing earth over my hair and face, began crawling to the top of the knoll once more.

'Let me go,' Nicholas said.

'No, I must see what is happening.' Again, I crawled to the top and looked over.

The battle had indeed moved away from where we lay, halfway up to the baggage train where the archers had taken position – I saw sev-eral lying dead behind the overturned carts, though the majority were still firing. Below, the close-quarter fighting continued, captains shout-ing at their men to keep formation. Between the fighting and where I lay I saw a huge pile of dead horses and men, many in pieces like slabs of meat. A group of several hundred men was being gathered together by one of Warwick's officers, Captain Drury, I think, including lands-knechts with arquebuses and pikes, while elsewhere on the field a few men staggered around among the bodies, wounded or shocked out of

their wits. A group of rebels had surrounded a smaller group of Warwick's foot soldiers, who fought them desperately, standing back to
back. I crawled down again.

'The rebels are retreating, but still fighting,' I said to Nicholas and
Boleyn, who was still chained to the other men.

'You sound sorry,' Boleyn said.

'I am,' I replied quietly. 'Even now.'

Then every man in the earthen pit jumped and looked up as a voice
shouted down at us from the top of the knoll. Looking up, I saw to
my horror that Gerald and Barnabas Boleyn were standing there,
shoulder to shoulder, in helmets and breastplates, carrying swords,
filthy and covered in blood. They smiled, their faces happy as though
after a day's hunting. They were disobeying orders by leaving their
company to find us – but when had orders ever mattered to the Boleyn
twins?

'Well, Gerry,' Barnabas said, his scarred face opening into a wide
grin. 'You were right. It was them at the end of the chain.'

Gerald looked at us wolfishly. 'I recognized the bent shape of the
hunchback when we got near the front of the line. And there they are
next to him, our dear father and the long stringy lad. Where's the one-
handed freak?'

John Boleyn answered angrily, 'Down in Norwich, dead, for all we
know.'

'Fighting for the fucking rebels, no doubt.'

'Yes,' I answered.

'We're all gentlemen here,' one of the chained men said piteously.
'Please, free us somehow, help us back to Norwich.'

Gerald gave him a careless glance. 'We've a battle to get back to,
my brother and I. But now the fighting's moved away, we thought we'd
come and see where you rats had taken cover.' He looked at his brother.
'Now's the chance to kill them, our father that murdered our mother
and his damned lawyers.' He looked threateningly at the chained men.
'None of you will say anything, will you? We're just killing a murderer
and a pair of rebel sympathizers.'

'You wouldn't want to incur the anger of Sir Richard Southwell,'

Barnabas added. Many of the gentlemen shook their heads, causing the chain to rattle, which made the twins laugh.

The two began descending the knoll, pulling their swords from their scabbards. We had survived the battle by a miracle, only for it to end at the hands of this wretched pair.

'Start with our father,' Gerald ordered, in charge as usual. He covered Nicholas and me with his sword while his brother moved towards Boleyn.

'I didn't kill your mother!' Boleyn shouted frantically. 'We know who it was now.'

Gerald had raised his sword for the killing blow, but hesitated at his father's words, frowning. That moment killed him for, as he stood, an arrow, aimed from the Norwich walls, hit him in the middle of the forehead. He dropped like a felled log, the sword falling from his hand.

Barnabas stared at him, wide-eyed, seemingly unable to believe what had just happened. Then he let out a yell of misery and despair. He took a step towards his brother's body, then turned towards the Norwich walls. The soldiers there had seen two men come down and make to attack the chained prisoners; thinking they were rebels, they had shot Gerald. Standing there with raised sword, he had made a clear target. With a scream, Barnabas threw himself on Gerald's body; there was a clang as his breastplate hit his brother's. He held Gerald's face between his hands, not weeping, but letting out cries and gasps of despair. I looked at Gerald's face – the arrow stuck grotesquely from his forehead: there was almost no blood.

Nicholas lunged forward and picked up Gerald's sword. As he stepped back another arrow from the Norwich walls thudded into the ground beside Barnabas, who stood up, stared round wildly, then, with a last look of devastated horror at his brother's body, clambered up the side of the knoll and disappeared onto the battlefield.

Boleyn, lying on the ground, reached out a hand towards his dead son, but stayed it. Then his head sank onto his breast.

'Who *were* they?' one of the gentlemen asked. None of us answered.

'Rebels, of course,' another said impatiently. 'At least now we know we're safely covered from the Norwich walls.'

'Unless the battle swings this way again,' said a third.

But it never did. As we lay there, and the sun passed its zenith and afternoon came, the sounds of battle grew more distant. Thousands of flies had been drawn to the scene and settled on the bodies of Gerald, the dead soldiers, and the horse. At length I again dared, this time accompanied by Nicholas, to climb the knoll and look over. The scene beyond was, in its way, more terrible than ever. The rebel lines had all been broken, and men were fleeing wildly from the battlefield, past the now silent gun platform, towards the wide spaces of the heath. They were being pursued by landsknechts and horsemen from Warwick's army, who cut them down mercilessly with their swords. Hundreds were killed as they fled; the battle was turning into a massacre. Only at one place, the baggage train the archers had used for shelter and where the carts had now been drawn into a semicircle to give more cover, a large body of rebels still fought on, shooting arrows and cutting down those of Warwick's men who tried to climb over the carts.

'They're killing those running like so many beasts,' Nicholas said. 'Beasts they are, to them.'

We slithered back down the hill and passed the news on to the gentlemen, some of whom let out a ragged cheer. More had managed to free themselves from the chain, and now they dared to get to their feet. One said, 'Head for Norwich. We're safe at last.' They began running unsteadily towards the city walls, making for a gap blown out by the rebels in the previous days' fighting. It was protected by Warwick's soldiers now. Nicholas and I could have gone, too, but somehow we had to see the end.

☩

THOSE OF US LEFT – perhaps twenty now – lay exhausted where we were. Eventually, Nicholas and I climbed up to look over the lip of the knoll again. The battle between the men defending the baggage train, a thousand or more, and Warwick's army, had ceased. Several officers from each side stood together, and some sort of parley seemed to be taking place. Everywhere else the battle was over; I saw rebel prisoners being herded into lines.

A horseman rode off towards the rebel gun platform. Glancing over to where Kett and his commanders had stood, I saw no one. Again we lowered ourselves slowly down. My back hurt terribly now. At least the afternoon sun was lower in the sky, the heat beginning to abate. Boleyn still sat crouched over, looking at Gerald's body as at some strange unknown creature, a dragon or a unicorn, making no effort to wave away the flies that crowded over his dead son's face. I remembered the brothers baying for their father's death at the hanging.

Everyone was exhausted from fear and thirst; we lay in a dull-eyed row. I wondered what these men would do to their tenants and servants when they recovered. I remembered someone in the camp saying that the pardon offered to them by the first Herald was nothing more than a barrel of ropes and halters for hanging them.

We all jerked at the sound of jangling harness and voices above us and looked up, dreading what we might see. A group of mounted soldiers, the red cross of England emblazoned on their armour, gazed down at us.

'So there they are,' one man said. He laughed. 'Hiding in a rabbit warren. As sorry a crew as ever I saw.'

Another man rode up and looked down at us. Captain Drury, whom I had first seen tormenting the Scotchman in London near three months ago. He smiled.

'You are safe, gentlemen of Norfolk,' he said. 'The battle is over, the accursed rebels scattered or dead. The earl himself has negotiated a pardon with the last rebel archers. Come, climb up, it is time to reclaim what is yours.'

Chapter Seventy-nine

THE SOLDIERS HAD to help us up. Reaching the top of the knoll and looking over the thousands of dead on the battlefield, many of the gentlemen vomited, to the soldiers' amusement. Tools were sent for, and the remaining padlocks removed. I looked over at the supply train; rebels from there were being led away by Warwick's soldiers.

'They've been pardoned, worse luck,' a soldier said as he removed Boleyn's padlock. 'It was their condition for surrender. The Earl of Warwick came and granted it himself.' On the battlefield the victorious soldiers were searching the bodies of the dead, looking for valuables and removing armour and helmets. I looked for Barnabas Boleyn, but there was no sign of him.

'What of Robert Kett?' I asked Captain Drury.

'He and his brother fled the battlefield when they saw that all was lost.'

'I witnessed what happened to those who fled,' I said quietly. 'How they were cut down.'

It was an unfortunate comment, for one of the gentlemen who had railed against the rebels before the battle pointed at me. 'That man is not one of us, he is a lawyer, a serjeant-at-law no less, who worked for Kett, helped him at the trials at that accursed Oak of Reformation.'

Drury looked at me with narrowed eyes. 'You worked for Kett?'

'I was made to,' I answered. It was a lie, but I realized that many lies would have to be told in the days and weeks to come if I were to survive. 'I came to Norfolk on a legal case, under instruction from the Lady Elizabeth, to represent Master Boleyn here. I was caught up in the rebellion.'

Another gentleman said, 'If it wasn't for the quick thinking of that red-headed lad, his friend, in lifting up the stake that held us between the battle lines, we'd all be dead.'

Drury still looked at me suspiciously. 'This matter must be for the Earl of Warwick to decide. You' — he waved at Boleyn, Nicholas and me — 'come. The rest of you, get yourselves down to Norwich.'

He and two of his soldiers led us away, round the side of the battle-field, past the unbearable stench and the endless buzz of flies. The blood covering the innumerable bodies was drying now, turning black. I saw, too, the quick brown shapes of rats, slipping in among the mounds of dead.

✞

DRURY TOOK US to the gun platform, which was guarded now by landsknechts. Rebel cannon were being hauled away. The bodies of some who had manned the guns were being removed as well, and briefly I saw the pale dead face of Peter Bone on a wooden stretcher, before his corpse was dumped with the others on the hill below the gun platform. The last of his family apart from the nephew he had never been allowed to know, the only man who had shown poor Edith Boleyn true kindness.

Breathing hard, I looked to where a trestle table had been set on the flat area of the gun platform. There, seemingly oblivious to the carnage all around, a group of senior officers studied a sketch map. They looked up as we approached; among them I recognized the lithe frame and dark-complexioned face of John Dudley, Earl of Warwick; and another — the strong square body and haughty features of Sir Richard Southwell. He stared down at me from under those hooded eyes. With him was John Atkinson, who looked out with a fierce expression. I realized Atkinson's reminded me of John Flowerdew's; there was the same determination to possess all he desired, the same conviction he was entitled to it.

Drury and his soldiers bowed to Warwick, as did we. 'You did mightily today,' the earl told them in his deep voice. 'I thought this battle might be over quickly, but those rebels fought hard.' He turned to one of his officers. 'We'll have to start clearing the battlefield at once, or the bodies will bring disease to the city.'

I looked downhill, where soldiers were still busily scavenging the innumerable corpses. I heard a shriek and, turning in the other direction, saw a rebel straggler on the heath, running for his life, pursued by a landsknecht horseman who leaned down and thrust a sword through his bowels. Warwick looked at the scene with cold disinterest; Southwell smiled. Then Warwick looked at Nicholas, Boleyn and me. 'Who are these three?' His eyes narrowed. 'Are they rebel leaders?'

'No, sir,' Drury answered. 'All three were among the chained gentlemen. The red-haired lad apparently saved them by pulling the stake which held the chain out of the ground; this one is John Boleyn, in prison at Norwich Castle for the murder of his wife, awaiting the result of a pardon application from the Lady Elizabeth. Apparently, it was great gossip in Norwich before the rebellion. The hunchback' – he looked at me – 'is a serjeant-at-law who apparently acted as Kett's adviser at those childish trials of his, but says he was forced to work at the camp. The hunchback and the boy are Boleyn's lawyers.'

'Boleyn returns to the castle,' Warwick said firmly.

Boleyn protested, 'My lord, it has been discovered who really killed my wife.'

I said quietly, 'We have no proof yet.' As indeed we did not, for Michael Vowell was long gone.

'Speak when you're spoken to, both of you!' Warwick snapped. He looked at me. 'Name,' he asked sharply.

'Matthew Shardlake, Serjeant-at-Law.'

'You were at the camp under duress?'

I took a deep breath. 'My assistant and I were taken at Wymondham, at the start of the rebellion. We were on a visit to John Flowerdew, the feodary, about some money taken improperly from Master Boleyn's wife.'

Southwell snorted. 'His concubine, you mean. This Shardlake is a pestiferous poor man's lawyer, well known for his radical views. When you hang the leading rebels tomorrow, he should be there.' His gaze on me was cold and intent. I thought, Boleyn should not have said Edith's killer had been discovered, for Southwell was implicated, and would want him – and Nicholas and me – dead more than ever. And he would remember, I am sure, that morning I encountered him at St Michael's Chapel.

I said to Warwick, in humble tones, 'I was taken by the rebels, as I said. Robert Kett made me act as an adviser at those trials. I had no choice; I did all I could to mitigate the sentences. My assistant Master Overton vocally opposed the rebellion, and was himself tried at the Oak.'

'Did you try to escape? Kett's first lawyer did, Thomas Godsalve.'

'My Lord, you will see I am not young, nor built for escape.'

Warwick smiled coldly at Southwell. 'Then he's no more guilty than men like Mayor Codd, who was forced to help the rebels at the start. And these three ended up chained with the rest of the gentlemen. I think we must forget Shardlake's cowardice in aiding the rebels, as we must that of officials all over the country faced with rebellion, to ensure government continues in the localities.'

Southwell spoke again, more forcefully. 'I think he should be exe, cuted as a rebel. There is much hanging to be done tomorrow, he should be included.'

'Damned rebel, he is,' Atkinson repeated.

'My Lord,' I said, 'the Protector's secretary, Master William Cecil, knows me, and of my past services to the State. And I lodged the pardon on behalf of Master Boleyn's distant relative, the Lady Eliza, beth. Before the rebellion started.'

Warwick inclined his head, but did not look as impressed as I had hoped. He turned to Southwell. 'You have met this man?'

'Once.'

I said quickly, 'In company with Master Cecil.' Then I dared to say, 'I think we met a second time, too, though I cannot remember where. I would give five hundred pounds to recall it.' I forced myself to look at Southwell directly. For the first time, his eyes opened fully and he took a deep breath. Even if Warwick sentenced me to execution as a rebel, I had time to tell Warwick the truth about him. Warwick, who seemed to miss nothing, looked between us, clearly divining something personal was involved here. And hopefully he was not going to arbitrarily hang people connected to Cecil and the Lady Elizabeth. He considered, then said decisively, 'There are no grounds for trying this man, Sir Richard.

He and the boy may go. Now come, we have much to do.' He looked at Drury. 'Any word of Robert or William Kett?'

'None yet, my Lord, but I am sure they will be captured soon.'

Warwick turned back to his papers, though Southwell stared relentlessly at me. I ventured to address Warwick again. 'My Lord, pardon my interruption, but may I ask that when Master Boleyn is returned to the castle a special guard is put on him, as was done before? There have been attempts to poison his food.' I looked directly at Southwell and Atkinson. Atkinson's face twitched, the moles on his face moving up and down each time. Warwick followed my gaze.

He said, 'It seems indeed there is more to this business than meets the eye. Very well. Sir Richard, now the battle is over should you not go to your mistress the Lady Mary, and put your own estates in order? Shardlake, you and the boy go back to London, but be ready to give evidence about your involvement if called upon. Understood?'

'Yes, my Lord. But may I stay in Norwich a day or two longer? I have friends there, and I do not know what has become of them.'

Warwick shrugged, clearly tired of us. 'Very well. But be careful in the city.'

'Things are quiet enough there now,' Drury said. 'It's as well we quartered the soldiers raised by muster in Norwich. They'll keep order, and I've begun the search for the leaders of the Norwich men who aided the rebels, as you commanded. If the rebels had won this battle, they planned to go straight to the north of the city through the breaches in the walls. Those we have captured already told us that.' I drew a deep breath, thinking of Josephine and Edward Brown.

Warwick smiled. 'Yes. Our mustered men are not from Norfolk, and should be willing to keep order here. Though many of them are common rabble raised from the villages. If we had brought them to the battlefield some might have changed sides. Who knows, in these whirl-ing days?' He smiled again, secretively. 'Which, I suspect, are not yet quite over.' He wrinkled his nose. 'By God, the stench from the field down there. It's getting worse.'

Chapter Eighty

A ND SO, TOWARDS EVENING, Nicholas and I, stunned and exhausted, trailed back to Norwich. Nicholas carried Gerald Boleyn's sword. We walked downhill to the city gates, avoiding the battlefield. Every bone in my body hurt, my back was sore, and Nicholas had to help me down the hill. I could not get the image of Peter Bone's white corpse out of my head.

I felt unable to clamber up the rubble and through the breach in the city walls blasted by the rebels, now manned by Warwick's soldiers. Although they waved us in, we waved back in thanks but walked along to Magdalen Gate, aiming to follow the road into the city from there. I wish we had not. A great gallows was being erected outside, big enough for hanging five men at a time. Even worse, the naked bodies of defeated rebels from the city were being brought on carts and dumped outside the gate in a heap. Already there were over a hundred. Looking back up the road, I could see other carts coming from Dussindale, the bloodied bare arms and legs of dead rebels hanging over the sides. Nearby, dozens of labourers fetched from the city were starting to dig a great pit under the supervision of soldiers – no doubt a mass grave.

I looked at the bodies, white flesh and great red wounds.

'Come away,' Nicholas said.

'I was looking – looking to see if Barak was in amongst them. Dear God, do you remember three years ago when I had to tell Tam-asin her husband had been maimed? Am I now going to have to tell her he is dead? We may not even discover it, how can we find him among all these dead?' My voice broke.

'Come on. We can't stay here. We must make enquiries in Nor-wich.'

749

The attention of one of the soldiers standing guard by the piles of dead had been drawn by my staring. 'What's your problem, hunch-back?' he asked in an unfamiliar accent, Lincolnshire perhaps. 'They're rebels, every one.' He looked at me suspiciously, lowering his halberd to point it towards me. 'You're not rebels escaped from the battle, are you?' His suspicion was understandable, for two more dirty, smelly, ragged creatures than Nicholas and me would have been hard to imag-ine. I said, in my most cultivated accent, 'We are lawyers. We were in the line of prisoners chained before the rebel forces. Look, here!' I held up my chafed, bloody wrists.

'I'm sorry, sir,' the soldier said, his voice immediately deferential.

'We are making our way back into the city.' I took a deep breath. 'I see they are building a gallows.'

The man smiled broadly. 'That's right. The Earl of Warwick's presiding over trials under military law in the castle tomorrow, and the leaders will be hanged. Drawn and quartered too, some of them, here, in the town and at that cursed Oak of Reformation.'

'I see. Thank you.'

He nodded at the sword Nicholas carried. 'But I must take that. Only soldiers may carry weapons into the city.'

✝

WE MADE OUR WAY down Magdalen Street, towards the centre of the town. 'Where are we going?' Nicholas asked.

'I thought we'd try the Maid's Head first.'

He looked dubious. 'We caused them some trouble when we were there before.'

'We can show them we were chained up, just as we did that soldier. Remember, we've both got spare robes there. They may let us clean ourselves up, even take a room while we discover what has happened to Barak, and Josephine and Edward.' I smiled bitterly. 'We must become gentlemen again to survive now.'

'What if we come across someone who was sentenced at the Oak while you were advising Kett?'

'We say what I said to Warwick, I was there by force and tried to mitigate the judgements, and Warwick himself let me go. Nicholas, we're going to have to bend the truth a good bit from now on. Come,' I added impatiently, 'my back pains me. I would give anything for a bed.'

✟

WE CONTINUED DOWN Magdalen Street, across the river, and towards Tombland. Everywhere there were signs of the intense fighting that had taken place in the city; some houses had been set on fire, others hit by cannon. The smell of smoke mingled with the stink from the bodies which Warwick's soldiers, aided by poorer citizens, no doubt requisitioned for the task, were loading onto carts. Each body was stripped, if they were rebel troops. Dead horses were being dragged away in butchers' carts, although one had already been set on by a pack of dogs and was being ripped to pieces. I looked up at Mousehold Heath – smoke still rose in places from the burned and blackened camp. Few citizens were abroad, but soldiers stood about in groups, some drunk. We crossed Fye Bridge and walked down towards the Maid's Head. There we saw even more signs of the three days' fighting for the city – overturned carts, one pierced with arrows, destroyed equipment, shreds of clothing and yet more bodies. In Tombland numerous soldiers guarded the square, the closed cathedral gates, and Augustine Steward's house, to which the banner of the bear and ragged staff had been fixed. From the many people going in and out I guessed this was Warwick's headquarters in the city now. A few houses away, Gawen Reynolds's courtyard was shut and locked.

We turned into the Maid's Head entrance. The doors were open and the place was busy, officers from Warwick's army talking in the hallway, servants scurrying around. Master Theobald, supervising, saw two dirty, ragged creatures enter, and hurried over with a grim look. As he came close, though, his eyes widened in recognition. 'Master Shardlake?'

'Yes.'

'I thought you were at the camp.'

Again, I displayed my wrists. 'We were among those chained facing the earl's army this morning.'

'Dear God, I heard about that, but doubted it was true. Those filthy animals, to do such a thing to gentlemen, thank God it is over. There will be much hanging done now, and a good thing.'

I said, 'I have some belongings here; I also wondered if we might clean ourselves up, even take a bed, if one is available. We need to stay in Norwich a day or two before returning to London.'

'I have kept your belongings, sir, and you may have your old room tonight, though the two of you must share it – most have been taken by the earl's officers, though they are out now, attending to matters at Dussindale and in the town. You will have seen the horrible state the city is in, it is even worse down by the Market Square. Rubbish and filth and terrible sights everywhere.' He leaned in close. 'Tomorrow, though, you must leave, for the earl is making the Maid's Head his permanent headquarters while he deals with matters in the city. Be careful in town after dark – some of the soldiers have been set to search out the leaders of the Norwich men who supported the rebels, and they have not been gentle with the populace.' Again I thought of Edward and Josephine – those searching would have the names and descriptions of those they sought, perhaps supplied to Warwick by Michael Vowell.

I asked Master Theobald if there had been any letters, but he told me there had been no post for a fortnight. We went up to our old room – it was strange to see it again – and bowls of hot water were brought, enabling us to wash away the worst of the filth that caked us, and to don our old clothes. Food was also brought, and we ate ravenously. Afterwards, I lay back on the bed, sighing at the relief it brought my poor back. 'What did you think of the Earl of Warwick?' I asked Nicholas.

'A strong man. A born commander, mightily clever. Probably more skilled politically than the Protector, though that's not difficult.'

'A classic hard man from the old king's days,' I mused. 'I wondered what he meant by saying these whirling times may not yet be over. With the rebellions, the disasters in Scotland, the French declaring war – perhaps the King's Council will be looking for a new Protector soon.' I sighed. 'Give me half an hour and then we will go out and try to find Barak and the others. And before we leave Norwich,' I added grimly, 'we are going to visit Master Gawen Reynolds again.'

Nicholas looked from the window at the churchyard on the corner of Elm Street opposite. It was already getting dark. He said, 'I don't think you should go anywhere, sir, you need rest. I will beg a horn-lamp and go to see what I can discover.'

I wanted him to go, I was desperate to find out what had happened to Josephine and Edward, to Isabella, above all to Barak, but warned him, 'The innkeeper said it could be dangerous after dark.'

'Not for a gentleman, I think, not now. I will wear my robe. If I encounter soldiers, to show my wrists should be enough – it seems to be becoming a badge of honour.'

✝

IT WAS QUITE DARK when Nicholas shook me awake; he had lit a candle by my bed. I sat up painfully. 'What time is it?' I turned towards the window; I could hear drunken yells and shouts. A woman's desperate cry of fear sounded from outside, very near.

'Past midnight. Master Theobald was right, things are rough in the city. Soldiers coming back from Dussindale think all the poor of Norwich are rebel sympathizers. I saw many prisoners from Dussindale, too, being led to the Guildhall prison and the castle. Barak was not among them.'

'Are you all right?'

'My clothes and accent saved me trouble, I got as far as the Market Square.' He smiled, and beckoned someone forward. To my amazement, Isabella Boleyn stepped into the candlelight. She looked tired and drawn, her clothes were dirty, but she was unhurt. She reached out a hand and took mine.

'You are safe,' I said.

'Yes, when they took my husband to Mousehold, they put me out of the prison, but thanks be to God the innkeeper at the place I stayed before let me return. Nicholas says my husband is safe, and to be returned to the castle.'

'Yes. On Warwick's orders, and they will be obeyed. And we have discovered much.' I told Isabella what Peter Bone and Michael Vowell had revealed, though not about her husband's false alibi. I would leave Boleyn himself to tell her about that.

'So Chawry was innocent. I had begun to think him responsible for everything.' She smiled sadly.

'So had I.' I did not mention that she, too, had been among my suspects. 'Your husband saw him briefly, at Dussindale. I do not know whether he survived. I should tell you, the twins were there. They tried to kill us where we were hiding, but it was your stepson Gerald who died, shot by an arrow from the city walls. It seemed to unman Barna-bas, he ran back to the battle. I do not know what happened to him.'

She lowered her head. After a moment she said, 'I can feel no grief for Gerald, only relief. Is that a sin?'

Nicholas took her hand. He was hollow-eyed and exhausted. 'No, Isabella, not after what he put you through.'

She looked at his wrist, then touched it with her other hand. 'Poor boy, what they did to you. And your wounds are the same, Master Shardlake. I owe you both so much.' She sat down on a chair and began to weep. I got up painfully. 'It is over now, Isabella, or nearly so.'

She sighed, then stood. 'Nicholas has arranged a room for me next door for tonight. I should go there, try to tidy myself up, then return to my husband in the castle tomorrow.' She curtsied, and left the room.

I asked Nicholas, 'Is there news of Barak or the Browns?'

'None yet, I fear. Before I looked for Isabella I went down to Con-isford. Josephine's yard, like so many places there, was burned down yesterday. No sign of Edward or Josephine, nor the child.'

'They will be looking for Edward, as a rebel.'

'Perhaps they escaped the city. Many must have fled after the fighting.'

'I hope so.'

'And nothing of Jack?'

'I asked several people of the poorer sort if they knew anything of a one-armed man who took part in the fighting in Norwich, offering a little money, but nobody did. I learned that the injured from both sides are being treated at the cathedral; we can go there tomorrow morning and see if he, or Edward and Josephine, are there.' He added quietly, 'It's dreadful in the town. Soldiers celebrating in the streets, telling tales of things they did this afternoon, often given drinks by the wealthier citizens. The mess in the Market Square is terrible – dead horses, piles of shit everywhere, the bodies of the fifty rebels Warwick hung when he took the square still there on the gallows.' He sighed. 'Apparently, there will be mass executions tomorrow, but there's also to be a great service of thanksgiving at St Peter Mancroft, and the city are planning a masque in Warwick's honour.'

'He's probably just allowing his men to let off steam tonight. It's tradition, after a battle. Like rifling the bodies of the losing side.'

Nicholas sat on the bed. His hands were shaking. 'One thing I do know. Natty is dead, I saw his body being carried away naked on a cart.'

I put my head in my hands. 'Oh, no. God save his soul.'

'They're going to sell everything taken from the bodies of the rebels in the market.' Then Nicholas put his head in his hands and burst into tears. 'This terrible day, and out there – it's like the city has become a part of hell itself.'

I said quietly. 'I long feared it might end like this.'

'By God, though, the rebels put up a good fight, didn't they?'

'For commoners?' I asked, half-jestingly.

'No.' He looked up. 'For men.'

✝

THE NEXT MORNING, we breakfasted at the Maid's Head for the first time in near two months. Isabella had gone, leaving us a note thanking us again for all we had done, saying she was going straight to the castle. Her courage and constancy were truly remarkable. My back still hurt, and before we went down, I performed my exercises, long neglected. As we ate I thought of the breakfasts Barak had shared with us back in June, and Toby Lockswood, too, whom Nicholas confirmed had also perished in the fighting round Tombland. He had cruelly persecuted Nicholas, but had been loyal to his cause to the last. I thought of Natty, too, one of so many lost lads come to Mousehold, brave and loyal and kind.

From talk at the tables around us – it was mostly senior army officers staying at the inn now – I learned the Earl of Warwick was already at the castle, passing speedy judgement on the senior rebels. Many officers, apparently, had been detailed to attend executions later in the day in the

Market Square, Magdalen Gate, and the Oak of Reformation. Mass graves were still being dug for the dead of Dussindale. I heard, too, though, one officer say that the rebels of Norwich had fought valiantly, and a volley of arrows had nearly killed Ambrose Dudley, Warwick's elder son. And at one point, I learned, with the rebels still in control of much of Norwich, that because of the destruction the city elite had asked Warwick to give up the city to the rebels; he had refused. Had he agreed, the outcome yesterday could easily have been very different.

A captain entered the room, waved his helmet, and shouted out, 'Robert Kett and his brother are captured! Robert fled to Swanning/ton, and was taken at a farm!'

There were loud hurrahs. One captain asked when they would be executed, and the man who brought the news said they were to be taken for trial in London.

'Pity,' a man at the next table said, 'I'd like to have seen them die.'

✝

CLAD IN OUR lawyers' robes, Nicholas and I crossed to the cathedral, explaining to the soldiers at the gates that we were looking for friends who might be among the injured. They were reluctant to admit us, until we explained we had been among the chained men at Dussindale, and showed them our wrists. This seemed indeed to have become a badge of honour, for they promptly let us through.

As we walked towards the cathedral doors, Nicholas said, 'If we do find them among the injured rebels, how do we explain they are our friends?'

'Quick talking. We're lawyers, after all.'

Inside the cathedral, as after the battle with the Marquess of North/ampton a month before, the whole great building had been turned into an infirmary, only this time with far more injured lying on the floor, or on rough straw mattresses behind the great pillars supporting the nave. Coughs and cries of pain again echoed around the vast space. On the left/hand side the beds were guarded by soldiers patrolling up and down; presumably the injured were rebels. On the right the injured were unguarded, and seemed to be receiving more attention from the barber-surgeons going to and fro. I also saw the robed form of Dr Belys tending to them, and steered Nicholas away from him.

A captain sat at a desk near the altar, and I walked towards him, pushing up the sleeves of my shirt so my wrists showed, having ges-tured to Nicholas to do the same. The captain looked up, then stood. 'Gentlemen, how can I help?' he asked in a Midlands accent. 'Were you among the chained gentlemen yesterday? We saw you run, and thanked God for your escape.'

'We were. We are looking for three friends, two men and a woman, who were in Norwich. We have had no luck, and wondered whether they may have been brought here, perhaps even put among the rebels by mistake. I believe there was much confusion here during the fighting.'

'There was.'

'Are you a Midlands man?' I asked. 'I am from Lichfield myself.'

It is wonderful what a local connection may do, I thought. The soldier said, 'I'm from Aldridge, quite near you. A yeoman farmer, head of the local muster; we were conscripted by the Earl of Warwick.' He added more quietly, 'The troubles were spreading up there last month; he put them down before organizing this army.'

'I met the earl yesterday. A strong leader, I think.'

The captain looked at me with new respect. 'Ay, hard as stone but with good judgement.'

'I came here in June for the Assizes, then suffered an injury and had to stay. Then my assistant and I were caught up in the rebellion.'

'Well, look for your friends, if you wish. There's a separate section for women over there.' He pointed to an area sealed off by curtains. 'If you find them, you must bring them to me for identification, and authority to be released.' He lowered his voice again. 'It's rebel leaders we're looking for, I've a list.'

'Thank you.' I thought, Barak and Josephine would not be on that list, but Edward Brown surely was.

I led Nicholas along the rows of beds. We had scarce begun our task when a familiar figure, sitting up on a straw mattress on the rebel side of the nave, waved a hand made of metal, a hook and sheathed knife on the end, and called out, 'You two! About fucking time, I thought you were dead!'

'Jack!' I ran over and embraced him, as he had embraced me when he found me after the *Mary Rose* sank. He grasped Nicholas's hand, and said, 'You look like shit, lad. Jesus, your wrists. Were you with the chained gentlemen? That story's all over the infirmary. How did that happen?'

'We were betrayed, by Michael Vowell. Listen, there is much to tell you, but we must get you out of here first. Are you hurt?' I looked at him anxiously. He was very pale.

'When we went back down into Norwich I took a blow on the leg from one of Warwick's soldiers. It's not bad, only a flesh wound, but I bled like a pig. Would you believe, I bloody fainted, collapsed into the doorway of a shop. I was found afterwards; I've lost a lot of blood, but they stitched me up.'

I spoke quietly. 'So there's no actual evidence you were fighting with the rebels.'

'I had no uniform but my sword was beside me. That was enough to make the soldiers bring me this side of the aisle.' He pushed aside the rough blanket covering him and showed me his right calf, covered with a bandage. 'I'll need a stick to walk for a bit.'

I considered. 'Perhaps you could say you are a citizen who picked up a sword to protect himself.'

'With my London accent?'

'Then you are my assistant, accidentally left behind in the town.' I smiled. 'I think I can persuade the captain here it was all a mistake.' I looked at him closely. 'But if asked, you must say you're no supporter of the rebels. Understood?'

Barak set his lips, but nodded quietly in agreement.

'We're back at the Maid's Head, at least for this morning. You can get some food there.' I took a deep breath. 'Have you heard anything of Edward or Josephine? Could either of them be here, too?'

'I don't think Edward's here. Nor Natty. But you could look. I don't know who's in the women's section.'

I nodded, and gave Nicholas a look to stop him telling Barak that Natty was dead. I continued walking along the ranks of the injured men, some with horrible wounds, but Edward Brown was not there. When I went to the women's section the pretty, plump young woman in charge, kindly in tone, said nobody named Josephine Brown, nor answering her description, was there, with or without a child. She said herself she was a midwife drafted in to help the women, some of whom had been injured in the fighting or had had – she gave me a steely look as she said this – bad things done to them by Warwick's soldiers. I thanked her and returned to Barak. We got him up and took him, supported by Nicholas, to the captain, where my explanation was accepted. I felt a little guilty lying to the man, but it had to be done.

✝

WE RETURNED TO the Maid's Head. As we approached the entrance I saw the door of the church opposite was half-open.

'There's something squealing in there,' Nicholas said. 'Can you hear it? Too loud for rats.'

'It sounds like a child,' Barak said.

I remembered the woman's scream I had heard the night before. I said to Nicholas, 'Take Jack inside. I'm going to look at the church.' When he looked set to argue I snapped, 'Just do it!'

I walked slowly in through the half-open door. The sound we had heard was louder now, and it was indeed a child crying, over in the far corner where a dark and bloody heap lay.

Edward Brown was sprawled on his back. His face had been battered to a pulp, and he had been finished off with a knife to the chest. Half on top of him, as though she had died trying to protect him, lay Josephine. She, too, had been beaten and stabbed, but almost worse was to see where her dress had been torn away and her underdrawers pulled off. The bloody mess between her legs showed she had been raped, not once but several times, before she too had been killed, her throat cut. In one dead arm she clutched Mousy, filthy with blood and her own excrement, bawling in terror.

I heard Nicholas's voice behind me. 'Oh, dear Jesus.'

I bent, gently pulling away Josephine's cold arm, and picked up Mousy, holding her to me. I said quietly, 'This happened last night. Josephine must have taken Mousy to escape the fire, and found Edward.

Then some soldiers searching for the leaders must have chased them in here.' I turned on him, my voice sharp again. 'Where's Jack?'

'Lying down in our room. I came back to see what was happening. Oh, dear God, poor Josephine, poor Edward.' Tears came to his eyes, as they already had to mine.

Mousy was still bawling mightily. Nicholas stroked her fair hair, so like her mother's. I turned my eyes from the bodies. 'We have to get her cleaned and fed somehow, poor creature.'

'Jack will know what to do. He has two children.'

'Yes. And we must find a wet-nurse, immediately. Even I know that. Nicholas, tell Barak what has happened then go across to the infirmary and ask the woman in charge of the female patients if she knows a wet-nurse, tell her it's an emergency. Later we can find one willing to travel with us to London; I'll pay her well.'

'You're bringing Mousy back with us?'

'Where the hell else has she to go?' I shouted, then shook my head. 'I'm sorry, this has – unmanned me.'

'And me.' He stood looking at the dreadful scene again for a second, then roused himself. 'Yes, we must save Mousy.' He left the church.

I held the child; she clutched at me frantically. Thank God she was too young to understand the horror that had taken place here. I took a last look at my murdered friends, but averted my eyes from what had been done to Josephine. Poor Edith Boleyn came to mind, stuck in a ditch with her bare legs up in the air. Before we left Norwich, I would deal with the man who had done that to her, her own father.

Chapter Eighty-one

I CROSSED THE road and entered the inn, heads turning in amazement at the sight of a white-haired lawyer carrying a filthy, bloody,
wailing baby. Mousy was pushing at me now, screaming and wrig-
gling, trying to escape. I shouted at a servant to bring warm water to
our room before mounting the stairs; I knew little about babies, but
Barak must know what to do.

He was sitting in the middle of our room. He stared at Mousy,
looking shocked. 'God's death,' he said. 'So it's true, they are dead.'

The child, though becoming exhausted, was slippery in my
arms. I said to Barak in panic. 'Help me, how do we quiet her?'

A servant appeared, carrying a ewer of water. Barak said decisively, 'Give me Mousy, I'll clean her up. Put the bowl on the table.'

I watched as he limped across and washed Mousy thoroughly. She
screamed and bawled all the time, a far cry from the gentle, biddable
child I had known. Then he took off his shirt, swaddled her in it and
walked up and down, making soft cooing noises. 'She needs milk more
than anything,' he said. 'And soon.'

I sat and looked at them, still numb from this latest, terrible shock.
Barak looked at me incredulously. 'Nick says you want to take her back
to London with us.'

'She has nobody else. I'm going to adopt her.' I had not even
thought of it till then, but the moment the words were out of my mouth
I knew it was what I wanted to do.

✟

IT WAS ANOTHER HOUR before Nicholas returned. With him was a
woman in her thirties, an apron over her cheap wadmol dress. She was
short and buxom, with a round, kindly face and, beneath her white

coif, large, intelligent blue eyes which softened immediately at the sight of Mousy. Nicholas said breathlessly, 'The woman at the cathedral directed me to this goodwife. She's her cousin. Her name is Liz Part/ lett, she is a wet/nurse and has just left her employer.'

'Can you help us?' I asked. 'I will pay well.'

'Yes,' she said in a quiet Norfolk accent. 'My own baby died last spring, poor lallen thing, but I just keep producing milk.' She gently took the baby from Barak. 'Come, you're not holding the poor grub right, give her to me. Don't, you'll drop her.'

I said, 'We have the key to the room next door, you can go there.'

'Very well, sir,' she said obediently, smiling down at Mousy who had quietened at once and was already pawing instinctively at her breasts. 'How old is the poor child?'

'Six months now.'

'Your boy told me both her parents had just died.' She looked at me keenly, her eyes lingering on the marks still visible on my wrists, though she said nothing.

'Yes. One of the many Norfolk tragedies,' I added bitterly. 'Her name is Mary, but her parents called her Mousy.'

'Come, then, Mousy.' She left the room.

Barak said, 'I think you found a gem there, Nick boy.'

'Yes,' I agreed. 'I think you did.'

✝

LIZ HAD BEEN GONE only a short time when Master Theobald appeared. He looked at us, taking a deep breath. 'My servant says you have brought a baby and a wet/nurse here.'

'We had no option. We found her in the church over the road; her parents had been killed. We knew her mother.'

Master Theobald's eyes widened. 'Well,' he said, 'I am afraid you must still leave within the hour. The Earl of Warwick is making the Maid's Head his headquarters, everyone other than his men must leave. I am sorry. There may be room at other inns, perhaps in the market/ place. Most of the soldiers have been quartered on the citizens.'

I said, 'We shall need fresh horses to return to London. But we have next to no money left. Might you help us?' He looked doubtful,

and I added, 'If you let me know what is owed, I will give you a prom-
issory letter now, and will pay as soon as I get back to London.' I
paused. 'I am a serjeant of Lincoln's Inn, I may be trusted. For myself,
I have no money left here, like many in the city.'

He looked at me for a moment, then nodded. 'Very well. I trust
you, Serjeant Shardlake, despite the strange goings-on your stay has
sometimes brought. And you suffered with the other chained gentleman at Norwich. I will arrange horses. But please despatch the money
and horses promptly when you return to London. You will understand
our trade has been much disrupted.' Despite himself, he smiled. 'A
baby now.' He shook his head, bowed, and left.

☦

THE THREE OF US, left alone, were silent a moment. Then Nicholas
said, 'Josephine's and Edward's murders must be reported.'

'There's no point,' I answered wearily. 'There can be little doubt
Edward was sought out and killed as a senior rebel on Warwick's
orders, and Josephine was killed for – for sport. If we report it, nothing
will be done, and we could find ourselves questioned about our relationship with Edward. No, if anybody asks, we heard the sound of a
crying baby in the church, and found it was the child of my former
servant. That is all.'

'At least we could arrange a Christian burial,' Nicholas said, his
voice breaking.

Barak answered impatiently, 'Can you imagine how many burials
there will be in Norwich this week? No, we should leave as soon as
possible.'

'There is one thing left to do,' I said grimly. I was still determined
to deal with Gawen Reynolds.

☦

THE FIVE OF US made our way to the marketplace; Barak, Nicholas
and Liz Partlett carrying Mousy. Fed and comforted, the poor child
had mercifully fallen asleep. I looked at her, amazed by the sudden
decision I had made, wondering whether I could love this child

enough to adopt her. A clutch at my heart told me that perhaps I could.

On the way we saw more grim sights; a cart containing bloodied bodies and severed heads, probably of those executed at the Oak of Reformation. The Earl of Warwick had indeed worked fast. His popularity among the wealthier citizens was clear; the emblem of the bear and ragged staff was nailed to many doors. I wondered bitterly whether he had brought a supply with him.

The marketplace was still the filthy mess Nicholas had described, men from the poorer classes set to clean the debris left by Warwick's soldiers. The gallows by the Guildhall had half a dozen bodies dan/gling from it. There was a little crowd; more men would probably soon be brought to share their fate. I remembered the day when I had saved Boleyn, the woman with the doll writhing in her death agonies. I looked away, feeling faint for a moment. Nicholas pressed my arm.

We made for Isabella's old inn, where, to our relief, we were offered two rooms. I made it clear that although Isabella had had money, the rest of us did not, but my serjeant's robe, and the marks on my wrists which I was careful to let the innkeeper see, sufficed. 'I have many offi/cers here,' he said ruefully, 'and only the earl's treasurer's promise that I will be paid. I'm sure your word is as good as his. And there has been no Wednesday market this week, of course, so none of the wealthier traders have come to stay. Damn those rebels. But hopefully the traders will return on Saturday.' He grimaced. 'I'm told the soldiers will be selling things taken from the bodies at Dussindale.'

✠

I WANTED TO GO to Gawen Reynolds's house immediately, but Barak and Nicholas said we were all exhausted, it could wait until tomorrow.

'God's death,' I said impatiently, 'he's the last witness to all that happened to Edith – Peter Bone is dead and Michael Vowell beyond reach, wherever the Protector sent him. We need a living witness.' But even as I spoke I felt my head swim again and said wearily, 'All right, tomorrow morning.'

'There's Southwell, too,' Nicholas said. 'He was intimately involved in the whole thing.'

'You saw him at Dussindale, he's at Warwick's right hand now. We can't deal with him ourselves, but we can inform Parry and the Lady Elizabeth about his involvement, and about the money he gave Robert Kett, and ask them to inform William Cecil.' My voice hardened. 'But Reynolds is a different matter. I say we should take him now.'

'He's not going anywhere,' Barak said impatiently. 'Not even outside, I shouldn't think. Tomorrow is soon enough.'

I nodded and sank down on the bed. I could not help reflecting that, though younger, Barak and Nicholas looked as exhausted as me. We were at the back of the inn, with only a view of the stableyard. I was glad, for I had no doubt more hangings would be taking place in the marketplace.

I slept most of the day, waking only to take dinner. Afterwards, I went next door to visit Liz Partlett, tapping carefully before I was called to enter lest she was feeding Mousy. The baby, though, was fast asleep on the bed, little bubbles of milk at the corners of her mouth, while Liz sat sewing.

'Is all well?' I asked.

She stood and curtsied. 'Yes, sir, I have cleaned the child thoroughly and she fed like a bezzler.' She smiled. 'I think she's beginning to teethe.'

I looked at the wet-nurse gratefully. She had asked nothing about the details of Mousy's parents' death; but there had been so many deaths in Norfolk this last week. I turned to the sleeping child, her tiny, plump, yet perfect little fingers. I hesitated a moment, then came to a decision. 'We plan to leave Norwich and ride to London by way of Hatfield, tomorrow or the next day at the latest. Would you come with us?' Liz looked doubtful, so I quickly added, 'Once we are back in London I will engage a wet-nurse there, and pay for you to be accompanied safely back here.'

She returned my look, and I was surprised to see anger flare in her blue eyes, though her voice remained low. 'I will not return to Norwich, sir,' she said. 'My husband is dead, my child is dead, and

Norwich is become a city of death.' She took a deep breath. 'I should tell you now, sir, if you plan on taking me to London, my husband was Kett's man. Our child died in the plagues this spring, as much of hunger as sickness, as my David had no work. When the rebellion started, he went to Mousehold, with my blessing. He died a month ago, fighting the Earl of Northampton's forces. I had a job as a wet-nurse with a merchant family, but they knew who my husband was and after the Marquess of Warwick's victory they cast me out.' She took a deep breath. 'I have seen the marks on your and Master Overton's wrists and I guess you were among the gentlemen prisoners set before the earl's forces. So I should tell you my background before some gossip whispers it.' She lifted her small, shapely chin.

'I thank you for your honesty.' I smiled sadly. 'Things are, though, not always quite what they seem. Yes, we were with the chained gentle-men, but we were made prisoners only because of lies told about us by a man who wanted us dead. There is much more I could tell you, and perhaps one day I shall, but not now. Will you take my word that we are not necessarily on different sides?'

She went on staring at me with that penetrating gaze. A servant would not have dared look at a new employer in such a fashion before the rebellion, but many had learned new ways. Then she said, simply, 'Yes, sir, I take your word.'

'Thank you. Then you will come to London with us? Perhaps,' I added tentatively, 'if you do not wish to return to Norwich and things go well, you might stay to look after Mousy there. But you must decide.'

She nodded then, and smiled. 'Thank you, sir. I will come, and we shall see.'

Afterwards I should have liked to return to bed, but there was a document I had to prepare, a long deposition to the court giving an account of the story told me by Peter Bone, and then by Michael Vowell after he had betrayed us. Bone was dead, but hearsay evidence of what a dead person had said might – just about – be admissible in court. Michael Vowell, I guessed, would be protected from any pro-ceedings. I got Barak and Nicholas to help me with the drafting, for it had to be worded tactfully, more than stretching the truth in saying we had been held under force in the camp, and avoiding any mention that

Vowell had worked as a spy. At length it was done, and I went to bed, leaving poor Nicholas to draw up a second copy for me to sign tomor-row and take to London. Now we had only the second murderer, Gawen Reynolds, to deal with, and I believed I had a way to draw him out, given that crucial factor in his personality, his lack of self-control.

Chapter Eighty-two

ARLY THE NEXT morning, to my surprise, we were wakened by
the sound of church bells. Nicholas, Barak and I were all crowded
in the same bed, and I looked at them in sleepy astonishment.

'Why are the bells ringing? It is only Friday, surely?'

Barak sat up and rubbed the stump of his arm. 'It'll be for the great
thanksgiving service at St Peter's Church at the marketplace. The service is at ten, it's eight now. We should get to Reynolds's house; he may
be going there.'

We breakfasted hastily. The inn was full of officers, but I went to
look at Mousy before we left. Liz was changing the absorbent rag for
her bottom. I was surprised at the lack of any smell. Liz smiled. 'Breast
milk doesn't stink, sir.'

I smiled. 'I did not know that; but I know so little of children. We
have to go out, to Tombland.'

'Shall we leave today, sir?' she asked.

'I hope so, but it depends how this morning's – business – goes.'

I returned to Barak and Nicholas. We all carried knives. I would
rather Nicholas still had the sword which had been confiscated the day
before, and Barak, still limping, needed my stick. Nonetheless, we
could expect only Reynolds, his wife and female servants at his house.

✙

IT WAS A CLEAR, sunny day. Averting our eyes from the fresh bodies
hanging from the gallows and the heads which had been set up outside
the Guildhall, we made our way to Tombland. Here, unlike in the
marketplace, the clearing-up was nearly finished, the square looked
almost normal. Magdalen Street, however, that led to the Maid's Head
entrance, had been closed off by a line of soldiers. I saw a massive

shield with Warwick's coat of arms nailed above the front door of the inn. I could not bear to look at the church where Josephine and Edward had been slain.

'All these signs of the bear and ragged staff all over the city,' Barak said, perhaps to distract me. 'Warwick is showing his power.'

Nicholas said, 'I remember it first being rumoured that the Protector would lead the government forces, but then he ordered Warwick to do it.'

I grunted, 'Perhaps Somerset knew that leading the army would be the final nail in the coffin of his presenting himself as a friend of the poor. But he should have seen how this victory would strengthen Warwick.'

We had arrived outside the doors of Reynolds's yard, which were firmly closed. I took a deep breath. 'Now, in we go. Unfortunately, we must force the women servants to let us in.' I drew my knife, as did Nicholas, while Barak took the sheath from the knife on his artificial hand. I banged loudly on the door.

There was no reply. We all three banged again, louder. We heard footsteps, and a female voice said tremulously, 'What is it?'

I put on my most commanding voice. 'We demand to be admitted at once, we are officers of the law!' There was silence from within. Barak shouted, 'Do you want us to break down this door?'

There was the sound of a key turning, and the courtyard door creaked open. A middleaged woman, eyes wide with fear, stared at Nicholas and me in our dark robes, and Barak with his grotesque handknife. 'What is your name?' I asked brusquely.

She curtsied. 'Laura Jordan, sir, mistress of the female servants. We have no steward now.'

'We demand to see Master Gawen Reynolds immediately.'

The woman's shoulders sagged. 'He is on the top floor, with the mistress, watching for the body parts of executed rebels to be brought through the city.'

How like Reynolds. 'Take us to him.'

The woman led us across the yard to the house, then up three flights of stairs to the top floor. All the doors we passed were shut. There were two more doors on the top floor, one small, one larger. The smaller one was closed but the larger stood open. It gave on to what looked like a study, a spacious room with a desk, racks of papers and comfortable chairs. Gawen Reynolds was looking through the large, mullioned window at the street below, resting his hands on his stick. Jane, as ever, stood in the shadows at the back of the room, dressed in black except for the white bandages on her hands. Her husband was giving her a running commentary. 'Soldiers coming, on horseback, with halberds. They're not risking any trouble from the mob.' I heard the sound of horses passing, then the squeak of wheels. Reynolds's voice rose. 'Here comes the cart, they've cut them into quarters, the heads in a pile on top. Mouths wide open in their death agonies, most of them!' He barked a grotesque laugh. 'Come here, woman, look at the men responsible for the death of your grandson!' He turned, and saw us in the doorway. His face turned puce.

'By God,' he said, his voice unexpectedly quiet. 'I had hoped you were all dead.' His voice rose. 'Laura Jordan, why in the devil's name did you allow them in?'

Goodwife Jordan took a step backwards. 'They said they came in the name of the law. They threatened to break in the yard door.'

'I'll break in your fucking door before the day's done. Get out!'

She retreated, terrified. Jane Reynolds remained still and silent in the corner. Her husband rasped at us, 'What do you want? I hear my son-in-law is to be returned to the castle.'

I looked at him directly. 'Master Reynolds, we are here to arrest you for the murder of your daughter, Edith.'

'Are you mad?' Reynolds shouted, but I caught the tremor in his voice. Jane suddenly looked up, staring wide-eyed at her husband.

'We have the whole story. How your daughter left her husband and took on the identity of her servant Grace Bone's dead sister, and lived with Grace and her brother peacefully for nine years. The brother, Peter, gave me his testimony, up to the point this spring when poverty drove Edith first to seek succour from the Lady Elizabeth, and when that failed, this last May, from you.'

'Oh!' The loud exhalation of breath from Jane Reynolds made us all turn. She stared at her husband with an expression of horror and disgust, then said quietly, 'That letter that came, in the spring. Vowell took it, but I was sure I recognized my daughter's handwriting, though you denied it.'

Reynolds took a step towards her, leaning heavily on his stick, and now, as I had anticipated, he lost control. 'So, your precious daughter lived with another woman for nine years,' he shouted, 'and we can guess what they got up to in private, probably with the brother looking on! She deserved what she got, she was no natural woman, she could not bear the normal attentions of a man.'

Jane backed away, against the wall, causing a small portrait of some Reynolds ancestor from a hundred years ago to drop from the wall, the frame shattering on the floor. 'Now see what you've done!' Reynolds snapped angrily. I think it was then I realized he was insane.

I continued, calmly. 'The testimony as to Edith's visit to your house seeking help, and what happened next – your decision to murder her and seek to blame John Boleyn, and the involvement of Sir Richard Southwell – all this came from your steward and confederate, Michael Vowell.'

Reynolds may have been mad, but he was sharp as ever. 'Vowell would never give such testimony, it would send him to the gallows.'

'Not given that he is in the service of the government,' I answered. Reynolds, of course, did not know that Vowell had been a spy, so would never be allowed to give evidence. The old man changed colour again, going pale. I pressed on. 'Vowell told me you were going to bury your daughter in a shallow grave on your neighbour's land, where she would be discovered quickly, but then you insisted on leaving her in that ditch, her body exposed in that vile way. You damaged your leg doing it.' I shook my head. 'Your plan might have worked but for your mad action, which cast doubt on John Boleyn's guilt.'

I thought the old man might begin ranting again, but instead the eyes in his pale face narrowed. Then he inclined his head towards the wall connecting to the next room, and shouted, 'You must have heard all that, Barney! If Shardlake succeeds, I will be executed, and the family fortune will go to the King. It's up to you now, boy! You came back here after your brother was killed, now strike in his memory!'

I heard the door of the next room open, the tread of slow footsteps. Barnabas Boleyn entered the room. His short fair hair stood on end, his face was haggard and unshaven, his scar standing out amid his blond fuzz; he wore only a shirt and hose. But he carried the weapon he had had at Dussindale, a razor-sharp sword, held high in his short, muscular arm. The blue eyes in his pale face were alive with fury. As he entered the room, I noticed he staggered slightly to the left, then corrected himself. I remembered how the twins had always stood shoulder to shoulder; instinctively he had sought to lean against his dead brother.

Reynolds smiled, his expression triumphant again. 'Kill them, Barney.' He raised his stick. 'I'll deal with the hunchback, you get the other two. Look, the one-handed one's been hurt, he's leaning on a stick.'

Barnabas had been staring between the three of us, ignoring Jane as usual, but now he turned to his grandfather. He said, quietly, 'Gerald was the only one I let call me Barney.'

His grandfather glared back at him. 'What?'

'Only Gerald.' Then he said, 'You – you killed our mother. Our mother, who we only wanted to love us!'

From the corner, Jane spoke quietly. 'He did more than that. He interfered with your mother when she was a child.'

Barnabas's eyes widened. His grandfather yelled, 'It's what women are for, you blockhead, I thought I'd brought you up to see that! You and your brother have been fucking women since you were fourteen.' He waved his stick at us, his voice shaking a little now.

'Deal with them, do you want me executed and the family fortune lost?'

'I don't care!' Barnabas shouted suddenly. And then, the sword held out before him, he ran straight at his grandfather. The old man raised his stick helplessly, but Barnabas thrust his sword with the full might of his short, strong body, straight through his grandfather's heart. The force of his charge sent the old man back against the window, and then, with a crash of breaking glass, right through it. Barnabas could have withdrawn the sword, but he did not – alone, I think he no longer wished to live. He, too, crashed through the window, and the two fell together to the street three floors below. Nicholas and Barak and I rushed over. Grandfather and grandson lay dead on the flagstones of Tombland, blood spreading from their shattered bodies as people gathered round, looking down at them, then up at us.

I turned to Jane. She had not moved from her corner, and her white face wore the same stone-cold expression as when I had first seen her in June.

'God's bones,' Nicholas said.

Barak said, 'There goes our last living testimony.'

'No.' We all turned as Jane spoke from the corner. She stepped forward a couple of paces. 'I heard it all, his confession,' she said quietly. 'And I know the things he did to my daughter, God rest her. My marriage has been hell on earth, I have no wish to hold anything back. I shall prepare a deposition in support of my son-in-law's freedom.' She raised her bandaged hands and gave a grim smile. 'Someone will have to write it for me, but I can sign, just about.'

Chapter Eighty-three

THE DEATHS OF Gawen Reynolds and Barnabas Boleyn meant there was business with the coroner in the following days, and we did not manage to leave Norwich until the third of September, nearly three months since we had first arrived. Post-runners were back at work, and Barak wrote a letter to Tamasin saying he was safe and had been held at the rebel camp with Nicholas and me, while I wrote a very long but carefully worded letter to Thomas Parry, telling the story of what had happened but leaving out the role of Richard Southwell – that was something for private discussion when we met. I hoped the letter arrived before we did; I knew the Lady Elizabeth would be sixteen on the seventh of September, and Hatfield busy with celebrations.

I spent a good deal of time with little Mousy. She was thriving under the care of Liz Partlett, who combined efficiency with a natural kindness. It was a strange thing, at my age, to find myself playing with a little child, running my fingers along the floor as she chased them on all fours. Occasionally, I looked up at Liz with embarrassment, but she offered only smiles of encouragement. Once or twice Mousy became fretful, and once she wept and called for ma-ma. It cut me to the heart.

I went into the city as seldom as possible, but got all the news from Barak and Nicholas, as well as gossip at the inn. The Earl of Warwick was staying in Norwich another week, to preside over more trials, set others in train, and put Norfolk back in order. There had been, I heard, an argument between him and some of the gentlemen, who called for a huge swathe of rebel executions such as was taking place in the West Country, where the rebellion was finally over. War- wick had called, though, for a policy of killing the leadership but

leaving the rank-and-file alone. Apparently, he had asked them sarcastically whether, if they would kill so many, they would end up walking
behind their own ploughs, which settled the matter; though the daily
hangings continued.

There had been, it was said, three thousand rebels killed at Dussindale, in the battle and the pursuit of those who fled afterwards – almost
half those who had fought. It was given out that the number of dead
on Warwick's side was under two hundred, but having seen the savage
close-quarter fighting myself I knew the number must be far greater.
On the Saturday, the last day of August, I stayed in all day, avoiding
the market, where all manner of goods taken from the rebels' bodies
were up for sale – piles of clothing, shoes and even, according to Barak,
wedding-rings pulled from the fingers of the dead. I realized that
Edith's wedding ring might well be among the articles for sale.

I had taken a full deposition from Jane Reynolds in the presence of
a notary. She gave some account of her life with her husband, his pursuit and sometimes rape of the women servants, as well as his own
daughter. She gave her account in the house in Tombland, in a tone-
less, unemotional manner, even when relating how her grandson had
thrown himself and her husband from the window. Her thin face was
always white as a tallow candle. Later, the notary before whom she
painfully signed the document told me her miserable life with Gawen
Reynolds had been common gossip in Norwich for years, and she was
generally pitied. Nothing could be done, of course, he said, to interfere
in relations between man and wife.

I said farewell to Jane, telling her I would see her again, as later I
must return for the inquests on Reynolds and Barnabas, but there was
so much official business to be done in the city that might not be for
months. I asked whether she was going to stay in the house. She
answered bleakly, 'Where else would I go?' Her eyes filled with tears
and she turned her head away, dismissing me with a wave of a bandaged hand.

The day before we left, on a mellow early autumn morning, I went
to lodge the depositions of myself, Barak, Nicholas and Jane with the
court at Norwich Castle. I had to brace myself on the way in, for I
knew the heads of several rebels had been placed on stakes along the

path to the entrance, as at the Guildhall and the city gates. But what almost unmanned me was that I saw one head was that of John Miles. The crows had taken his eyes, but there was enough left of his face to recognize it, his jaw slack and open, a stinking ooze running from his severed neck. I closed my eyes, wondering what had happened to his wife and children in London. Inside, my hands shook as I deposited the documents with the senior clerk who had had Barak sacked. He acted as though he had never met me. I believed he had a part in the disappearance of the document cancelling Boleyn's hanging back in June, but I knew that question would never be resolved, though I suspected Southwell was behind that manoeuvre, too.

After leaving the papers I went to say farewell to John and Isabella Boleyn. They were in his cell, Boleyn looking stronger, the marks on his wrists faded to light bruises as they had on me. Once again he thanked me profusely for all I had done. Isabella, ever practical, asked me when I thought the pardon might come.

'Soon, I would think, when copies of our depositions reach the Protector.' My smile was a little forced after what I had seen at the gates. 'What will you do when John is released?'

'Sell Brikewell and my other estates, and move to London,' Boleyn answered. 'That house I bought in London is too large, I shall sell it and buy something smaller.'

'Will you sell your estate to Southwell?'

Boleyn shrugged helplessly. 'He has the mortgage. If he wants to connect his other parcels of land together and run sheep, I cannot pay the mortgage off other than by selling him the land.'

'He will have the tenants out.'

'It is the way of things.' He looked away.

There was a moment's silence. Isabella broke it, asking, 'Do you still plan to adopt the little girl?'

'Yes. The wet-nurse is coming with us to London.'

She patted her stomach. 'Perhaps when my baby is born you can bring the child to visit us in London. In more peaceful times.'

'Yes, indeed.' I exchanged a glance with John Boleyn, and some-how knew that visit would never happen, he would wish only to forget all that had happened in Norfolk. Besides, we had nothing in common.

We conversed a little more; he did not mention the twins, and I had a feeling he never would again. Shortly after I took my farewell.

☦

I WAS LEAVING the castle, preparing to pass that dreadful row of heads again, when I heard my name called. I turned to see John Flower⁄dew, like me in his black serjeant's robe, a thick folder under his arm. His thin face wore a hard, triumphant smile. He walked towards me.

'Well, Serjeant Flowerdew,' I said. 'So you have returned to Nor⁄wich now it is safe. I hope your wife and sons that you ran off and left are well.'

His expression hardened. 'No thanks to you. I only got back two days ago, but already I have heard much news. I gather you surren⁄dered yourself to the rebels, and made yourself of service to Robert Kett. Be thankful the behaviour of some gentlemen is not to be inves⁄tigated too closely.'

'Be grateful you escaped from Wymondham,' I said.

'I remember that day, when you told Kett you had come to get Boleyn's money from me.'

'As I had. It has kept him and his wife fed and well in the castle, and soon his pardon will be granted.'

Flowerdew smiled and tapped his folder. 'Well, I have other fish to fry now. I am on my way to the courthouse. The gentlemen of Norfolk seek compensation for the livestock and other goods stolen by those wretched rebels; they are drowning the Earl of Warwick with peti⁄tions. Well, they will be compensated, one way or another. There will be good profit in it for me.'

'You are a monster,' I said, my voice shaking.

He laughed. 'You call me that, you hunchbacked enemy of the right order of society ordained by God? Oh, by the way, Robert Kett and his brother are to be taken from the castle to the Guildhall prison tomorrow, then to London for trial. Afterwards there will be an inqui⁄sition post⁄mortem, and I shall be present, to give evidence as to the value of Robert Kett's land and goods. They will go to the King, and, who knows, some of them may be used to remit the losses of the gentle⁄men.' He smiled. 'I look forward to that day.'

I turned in disgust and walked away, hearing his creaky laughter as again I passed that row of severed heads.

☩

THE FOLLOWING DAY, another mellow autumn morning, we pre-pared to leave Norwich at last. But there was one more grim sight to endure. The horses that Master Theobald had duly supplied for us had been brought round from the stables and as we were about to mount I noticed an unusual number of soldiers in the marketplace. Then I saw a horse-drawn cart, surrounded by more soldiers with halberds, making its way up to the Guildhall. Standing in it, hands tied behind his back, was Robert Kett. He wore a cheap smock, and his face was bruised and filthy, but he stared defiantly ahead, chin lifted, his bearing still proud. He was taken to the Guildhall, past the gallows and the heads staked outside, then the tail of the cart was lowered and he was roughly taken down and led inside. Beside me I heard Liz mutter, 'God save you, Captain Kett.'

☩

AND SO WE RODE out of Norwich, Mousy secured to Liz's front with tight swaddling. Her late father had been a blacksmith's assistant, and she knew how to ride. None of us spoke as we rode down St Ste-phen's Street and through the gate. On the outside the emblem of the bear and ragged staff were nailed, together with the arm and upper body of another rebel, where black crows fluttered and pecked. We lowered our heads. Once out on the road, though, I took a last look back at Mousehold Heath in the distance, black from the burning of the camp, bare and empty now. For a moment I seemed to hear poor Simon Scambler again, and the song he had sung round the campfire, as sparks flew up to the night sky:

> *my life will change utterly*
> *since my sinful eyes saw*
> *this noble land so much admired*

Gone, I thought, all gone.

Chapter Eighty-four

WE ARRIVED AT HATFIELD on the afternoon of the sixth. There, all was quiet and peaceful, yellow leaves beginning to drift down from the trees in the gardens, peacocks calling, the red-brick mansion beautiful in the mellow autumn sunshine. When I had told Liz Partlett during the journey that I was to visit the Lady Elizabeth's Comptroller, who was my client, her eyes had widened in surprise, as they did again at the sight of Hatfield Palace. I gave my name, and the guards at the gate sent for the big Welshman, Fowberry, who had accompanied us on our journey from London that rainy June day, which now felt like years ago. I was admitted, but Nicholas and Barak and Liz were told to stay at the gatehouse with Mousy. Fowberry looked in surprise at Liz and the baby, and Barak's artificial hand. Barak gave him a cold stare in return. A mounting-block was fetched and I dismounted, stiffly after the long ride, brushing the dust of the road from my robe as I accompanied Fowberry to the house.

Thomas Parry was in his office. He invited me to sit and gave me some beer, then sat and stared across the desk at me for almost a minute, as though I was some strange animal arrived from the Indies. At last he said, 'I had your letter. A remarkable story.'

'I never expected events to turn out as they did.'

He raised his eyebrows. 'That I can imagine.'

'Has the Lady Elizabeth seen it?'

'Oh, yes.'

'I hope she is well.'

'She is. Though vexed that she has not yet received her birthday gift from her brother, the King. I have told her it will arrive later today. It galls her all the more since she has had her present from the Lady Mary.' He raised his bushy eyebrows again. 'Can you imagine what

Mary sent her? A book of prayers in Latin!' He shook his head and laughed, then turned to me, eyes suddenly hard and sharp. 'You said you were called to Mary at Kenninghall, just before the rebellions reached Norwich.'

'I was. She tried to sound me out as to whether the rebels might be sympathetic to traditionalist religion. I knew nothing of that then, and told her so.' I took a deep breath. 'Sir Richard Southwell was there; there are things I should tell you about him, that I thought better not to commit to paper.' Parry inclined his head, and I related the story of Southwell's involvement in the murder of Edith Boleyn, the locksmith and his apprentice. I said also that I was sure he had given money to Robert Kett, I suspected in return for a promise to leave Mary's, and his, estates alone.

Parry was silent, digesting this new information, rubbing a hand across his plump chin. He sighed, then said, looking me hard in the eye again, 'I must discuss this with the Lady Elizabeth. Now. Whether any of this should be revealed.'

'But surely – when he was one of those who conspired to kill her relative –'

Parry interrupted. 'Matthew, much is happening on the Council now. We are all but thrown out of Scotland, and after these terrible rebellions and now the war with France, there are those who say the Duke of Somerset should be removed as Protector. You can imagine the main candidate to take his place.'

'The Earl of Warwick?'

'Yes; but Somerset still has his supporters. I do not know how this will fall out, but I suspect trouble to come. And the Lady Elizabeth's policy is, and must always be, to stay out of high politics.' He leaned back in his chair. 'Remember, Southwell was nominated by the late king as an alternate member of the Council, should any member die. And do not forget that after two months in the rebel camp consorting with Robert Kett, your own continued safety is largely a matter of luck, because it is the Council's policy to forgive gentlemen who were forced to aid the rebels under threat, not just in Norfolk but all across the coun-try. Otherwise local government would be stripped bare.' He eyed me narrowly. 'Though I have a suspicion your work with Kett, however you may have sought to moderate his policy, was not wholly involuntary. No, do not answer, I do not wish to hear. But if I have suspicions, so will others. Richard Rich, for example, who is currently busy executing rebel leaders in Essex.' He frowned slightly. 'By the way, I am told you brought a one-armed man and a woman, both commoners from what Fowberry said, back with you from Norwich – together with, of all things, a baby. Who are they?'

'The man is my old employee, Barak, who, I told you in June, was working at the Norwich Assizes. The baby is the daughter of an old servant who went with her husband to live in Norwich. They were both killed during the rebellion. The woman is a wet-nurse I have employed. I intend to adopt the child.'

'Killed? Rebel supporters, then, I take it.'

'They were murdered,' I said, returning Parry's hard look.

'If you are going to adopt the child, you must invent a less incriminating story for her background.' He rose abruptly from the table. 'I am going to tell the Lady Elizabeth about Southwell. Stay here.'

☩

IT WAS AN HOUR before he returned. I sat there, thinking of all those I had known that summer who had died in the rebel cause, poor Simon Scambler most of all. I would have brought him back to London and found him work, young Natty, too. I thought, How could Parry, or anyone I knew in London, understand the things I had seen? But he was right, I must invent some new story about Josephine and Edward's death.

When he returned, Parry's mood had softened. 'Well,' he said, 'the King's birthday present has arrived. The Lady Elizabeth is much relieved.' He folded his hands across his broad stomach and studied me. 'As for Southwell, she may confide the matter to William Cecil, and leave things to his judgement. She will think on it.'

I sighed. If the matter went before Cecil, whatever he did would be a political decision. Parry added, 'And I am to send him the depositions you brought, which should make the pardon a formality.' He looked at me sharply again. 'The Lady wishes to see you, Blanche

Parry will come in a moment to take you. Be careful what you say, Mat⁄
thew. Do not mention this proposed adoption.'

There was a knock at the door and Mistress Parry entered. She
curtsied briefly, her face expressionless. 'Serjeant Shardlake, please
come with me.'

✝

ELIZABETH WAS AGAIN in her study, writing at her desk. Probably
in anticipation of her birthday celebrations, her black clothes had been
replaced by a bright red dress with sleeves slashed to show a yellow
lining. She looked healthier than in June, and had gained some weight.
Mistress Parry announced me and went to stand behind her mistress,
but Elizabeth, without looking up, said, 'You may go, Blanche. I wish
a private converse with Serjeant Shardlake.'

Blanche's mouth tightened a little, but she said quietly, 'As you
wish, my Lady,' and left the room with a swish of skirts. Elizabeth put
down her quill and carefully sanded the document she had been writ⁄
ing; only then did she look up, smiling slightly. I bowed deeply.

'A translation of Virgil, Latin to French. I ever enjoyed study.' She
indicated a chair. 'Sit,' she said. Her gaze was keen, questing. 'You
look thin, sir.'

'I have had a – difficult time, my Lady.'

'I have read your letter, and heard the story. So, John Boleyn is likely
to be freed. At last.' There was a bite in her voice at the last words.

'I would think so, my Lady.'

'What did you think of him?'

I considered. 'An ordinary country gentleman, caught in the toils
of a conspiracy to gain his land.'

Elizabeth inclined her head. 'Did I catch a note of contempt in
your voice when you called him ordinary? But then, of course, you have
been consorting with rebels for two months, have you not?' Her voice
sharpened.

'My Lady, I was captured by them. Yes, I helped Captain Kett,
but I did all I could to ensure his judgements were based on law.'

Her voice rose. 'His *judgements*. And who was he to make himself a judge of his betters?' Impatiently she brushed aside a strand of long auburn hair.

I ventured to say, 'That is all over now.'

'Over! You say it is *over!*' She was shouting now. 'No, Serjeant Shardlake, it is not! You have brought me accusations against Sir Richard Southwell. I *may* decide those should be passed to William Cecil.' She leaned forward, her brown eyes boring into mine. 'I can trust *him* to make a decision that will not jeopardize me in any way. He may well consider it best to keep the whole thing quiet.'

'Three people were murdered, my Lady,' I dared to say. 'Surely it is a question of justice. Justice is something we have discussed before, and I thought we agreed that all deserve it.'

Elizabeth banged her fist on the desk, making me jump. 'God's blood,' she shouted, 'your time consorting with those rebel dogs has made you insolent, sir! You, of all people, should know that justice is often the servant of politics. It is your duty, it was always your duty, to protect *me!* But instead you spend half the summer in that camp of seditioners, the spittle and filth of our society! Did you ever think of the repercussions that might have for me, when you sat helping Robert Kett dole out his monstrous perversions of justice?'

And now my own temper flared. 'And why did they rebel, those men? Because they had no alternative after the injustices wreaked by greedy landlords and crooked royal officials!' Realizing that I had gone too far, much too far, I added quietly, 'And I was always careful to say and do nothing that could harm you.'

Elizabeth's eyes were blazing now, her normally pale face red, her hands tightened into fists. She shouted, 'God's blood, do you dare support those men of mischief to my face? I thought you were one of the few I could trust in the pack of wolves that surrounds me, and God knows I have paid you well these last two years!' She stood up, face blazing, and yelled, 'No more! You ingrate, you consorter with traitors! God's death, get out! You are dismissed from my service! Go!' And with that she picked up the inkpot from her desk and threw it at me. It landed on my chest, splattering my robe and face with ink. 'Get out!' she shrieked again. I scrambled to the door, almost tripping as I made a hasty bow, grasped the handle and ran out.

On the other side I stood in the anteroom, breathing heavily. I rubbed my face, which succeeded only in transferring some of the ink to my hands. Thomas Parry stood there with Blanche; no doubt she had called him when the shouting began. From the other side of the closed door I heard an unexpected sound – Elizabeth weeping, a loud, desperate sound. Blanche gave me a chilling look and went in to tend to her mistress.

To my surprise, Parry smiled. 'The inkpot, was it?'

'Yes. I – I misspoke. Badly. She has dismissed me.'

Parry smiled again. 'You're lucky it was not the paperweight. If it is only the inkpot, she will regret her words later. Wait a few months, she will recall you again. I know her.'

I said, 'Perhaps I may not wish to serve the Lady Elizabeth again. She did not even thank me for saving her relative.'

Parry smiled ruefully. 'She did not like having to apply for the pardon. It made waves, you see.'

'I doubt I shall return.'

Parry shook his head. 'Do not be pettish, Serjeant Shardlake. After your questionable part in the rebellion, you need a powerful patron. And though she may say she no longer trusts you, I believe she does, and there are very few who command her trust. Reflect on that. Now come, let us see if we can get some of that ink off you. I have had the inkpot a few times myself, you know.'

Chapter Eighty-five

A ND SO, AT LAST, we returned to London, arriving early in the afternoon of the eighth of September. I was morose throughout the journey, still angry with the Lady Elizabeth, and brusquely dismissed questions from Nicholas and Barak about what had happened. Despite Master Parry's help, my robe and fingers were still inky. Liz Partlett had withdrawn into herself, avoiding conversation; nervous, perhaps, as we approached London.

There were grim sights there, too, heads and body parts spiked on poles on the gates. Rebel leaders from the lesser camps, no doubt, from Essex or Sussex or Kent, God knew where.

We were all tired, me most of all, and my back hurt badly. As we rode down Cornhill towards Cheapside, Nicholas said to Liz, 'We will soon be home now. Master Shardlake has a fine house in Chancery Lane, and you will meet his servants; I am sure you will like them.'

I looked fondly at Mousy, asleep in her pannier, a thumb in her mouth. I said to Liz, 'She will be going to the house where her mother lived. But first there is one visit I must make. It is on our way. I want to go to my friend Guy's house; I do not even know whether that good old man is still alive.'

And so we turned off Cheapside and rode through the narrow lanes into the apothecaries' district. We caught glimpses of the Thames, Liz staring in awe at its size. Guy's house was quiet. With Nicholas's help, I dismounted and knocked at the door. There was a slow shuffle of feet and Francis Sybrant opened the door, his eyes widening at the sight of us. 'Master Shardlake! Master Overton! Jack Barak! Oh, thank God, we did not know what had become of you, we thought you might be dead at the hands of those rebels until Jack's letter to

Tamasin arrived two days ago.' Then he looked at Liz and Mousy with a puzzled expression, and raised his eyebrows questioningly at Barak. Liz reddened.

I said hastily, 'The child is Josephine's, my old servant. I fear she and her husband are dead. This is Goodwife Partlett, her wet-nurse. Now tell me, Francis, quick, how is Dr Malton?'

'A little better, but still weak.' He sighed. 'He sees no patients, and I doubt he will again.'

'Thank God, though, he is alive.'

'Thank God indeed.' He looked back into the house, then came outside and said in a low voice, 'Tamasin is here. She has spent much time with us over the summer. Oh, she has been so worried –'

'Where is she?' Barak asked, dismounting quickly.

'In the kitchen –'

Barak limped past us into the house. I saw the open kitchen door, and Tamasin's face as she turned round, her expression turning to astonishment and delight. Barak took her in his arms, then closed the kitchen door.

Nicholas helped Liz to dismount. Francis said, 'You have been in Norfolk all this time?'

'Yes, Francis.' I smiled tiredly. 'It is a long story.'

'Come through to Dr Malton, he is in his bedroom, he spends much of his time in his chair reading now, but he can walk with his stick, sometimes he even walks up and down the street, though it tires him.'

Nicholas and I followed Francis down the hallway. Liz stood uncertainly, and Francis suggested she and Mousy wait in the parlour.

My old friend was, indeed, reading in his chair. His face was still pale, but he looked somewhat better than three months ago. He, too, stared, amazed, for a moment, then, with a cry, rose and embraced me. 'Matthew, thank heaven, where have you been? I know you were injured, I corresponded with Dr Belys, but then the rebellion came and for weeks, until Jack's letter to Tamasin arrived – nothing.' His voice quavered.

I got him to sit down again and told him the bare bones of what had happened to us. He listened intently, then leaned back and sighed.

'We knew in London that there were risings everywhere, the whole country seemed under threat. We were told the rebels intended to over- throw the King and hold all goods in common, like the German peasant rebels twenty years ago.'

'No, Guy. Most wanted only to keep their villages safe from greedy sheep farmers and officials. They trusted Somerset's promises of reform, you see. They were waiting for the commissioners. But the commissioners never came; Somerset sent two armies instead.'

'They said as well that the rebels wanted to end the English Mass, go back to Rome.'

'Not in Norfolk. Elsewhere, I cannot say. There were Catholics among the rebels, but most were Protestants – and everyone stressed their support for the religious changes, playing to Somerset's gallery. Much good it did them.'

He sighed. 'I know there have been many executions at Tyburn, and hear there are rebels' heads on all the gates. It makes me glad I cannot walk far; I have never liked to see such things.'

'Then it is well you were not in Norwich in the days before I left, Guy. Rebel heads everywhere. And many thousand dead at the Battle of Dussindale.'

'Poor souls.' After a moment he added quietly, 'You sympathized with them, didn't you?'

'Yes, and have just had the benefit of the Lady Elizabeth's temper for it.'

He fell silent. 'And how are you?' I asked at length.

'A little better.' He smiled. 'I think my time is not quite up yet, though I doubt I shall recover fully. It galls me that I cannot even iden- tify what is wrong with me. I shall not practise medicine again.'

I said, 'That is a pity. I have Josephine's baby with me.' I explained what had happened to her parents, and my plans to adopt Mousy. I added diffidently, 'Perhaps you might just look her over, to ensure everything is all right. If you feel up to it.'

He smiled. 'Very well, as it is Josephine's baby. Have her nurse bring her in.'

I sent Liz in with Mousy, then took her place in the parlour with Nicholas. He said, 'How is Guy?'

'Somewhat better, but I think perhaps he spends too much time sitting in his room.'

He said, hesitantly, 'It is awkward for you, with Tamasin here.'

'Yes, but I think things are going well with her and Jack.' The kitchen door was still closed. I looked at him. 'And you, how are you?'

He scratched his head. 'I still cannot quite take it all in.'

'Nor I. But I shall return to work. Will you come, too?'

He smiled. 'Yes.'

'And Mistress Kenzy?'

'I shall let her down gently.' He smiled sadly. 'I do not think she will be too upset. She is not for me. I know that now.'

I nodded, then ventured to open the door and peep out. The kitchen door was still shut, though I could hear soft voices. I wondered what Barak had told Tamasin — not the whole truth about his participation in the rebellion, I guessed, and that would be wise. But I hoped he and Tamasin now realized how much they needed each other. I closed the door quietly again.

A few moments later, Francis called me back to Guy. Nicholas accompanied me. Guy was holding Mousy gently in his frail hands. I was touched when she reached out to me and smiled. Guy said, 'This is a fine, healthy child, and I give the credit to your wet-nurse. Perhaps she should be promoted to full nurse.'

'Yes,' I said. 'I think she should.' I smiled at Liz, who said quietly, 'Thank you, sir.'

There were footsteps in the hall. I turned. Barak and Tamasin stood in the doorway, hand in hand. Tamasin had new lines on her pretty face, but looked happy. At the sight of Liz and Mousy, her face softened. Under her coif Tamasin's blonde hair was just the colour of Mousy's. Tamasin said, 'So this is poor Josephine's child. How lovely she is.' She went over and stroked Mousy's head.

Guy ventured, 'And in good health, thanks to Master Shardlake's rescue of her and the care of Goodwife Partlett here.'

Tamasin turned to me. For the first time in three years, she addressed me civilly. 'Jack says you are going to adopt her?'

'Yes.'

She took a deep breath. 'We have some of George's and Matty's old baby clothes, I will send them on to you. Jack has told me how all of you were captured by the rebels and made to work for them. He says he owes much to you.' Behind her back, Barak winked at me. I felt guilty, for if he had not accompanied me to Wymondham that day he would not have been taken. And yet, I realized, given his mood when the uprising happened, he would almost certainly have joined the rebels anyway.

'Tamasin,' I said gently, 'I have always understood why you did not wish to speak to me, after I was responsible for Jack losing his hand. But if you could forgive me, if we could be friends again, I should be the happiest man in London.'

She looked at me directly with her cornflower-blue eyes. 'I do.' She swallowed. 'It is when you fear you might have lost people that you realize how much they mean to you.' And then she came forward and embraced me. I saw the happiness on Guy's face.

Liz, who naturally did not understand any of this, said quietly, 'Well, if you will excuse me, it is time for Mousy's feed.'

Chapter Eighty-six

THE SILVER TABLEWARE glinted in the light of the beeswax candles set in their sconces on the table. A fine dinner was again in progress at my friend Philip Coleswyn's house, a seasonal platter of grouse in the centre, and fresh fruit and vegetables, the best of the poor harvest. Unlike my last dinner there, in June, the shutters were closed against the night, and a fire blazed in the grate. It was late October, a month and a half since our return from Norwich.

Those present, however, were the same people as before; myself, Philip, his wife Ethelreda and his crotchety old mother; our fellow barrister Edward Kenzy and his snobbish wife Laura; their daughter Beatrice, and Nicholas.

It was to bring these two young people together that the dinner had been organized. A week before, Philip had come to visit me in chambers, where I was trying to catch up with my cases, at the same time pondering where to find new work, for the regular flow of conveyancing from Elizabeth had, after that last encounter with her, abruptly dried up. I resolved to ask Barak to try, in his work as a jobbing solicitor, to drum up some work for me in London. Now that Tamasin and I were reconciled, I could do so openly.

Philip looked worried when he visited, as many did that month. The power struggle between Protector Somerset and the Earl of Warwick had threatened for a while to turn into another full-scale military conflict; but in the end Somerset had surrendered his office. However, it was not that which he had come to discuss, but Nicholas and Beatrice.

He sat down in my office, stroking his long, silky beard. 'I am sorry to trouble you, Matthew,' he said with some embarrassment. 'But I have been asked by Edward Kenzy to speak with you. He said his wife is snapping at his heels like a terrier since your return. Have you seen him?'

'No, I have spent most of my time here since I got back from Nor-wich, trying to catch up with everything.' I did not add, and trying to forget.

Philip sighed. 'Well, Kenzy's wife and daughter are most con-cerned that Nicholas has not been in touch. Beatrice Kenzy wrote him a letter asking for news in the summer, but he never replied.' He looked embarrassed. 'Kenzy feels, and I have to agree, that given how things were developing between the two of them, Nicholas is being discour-teous. He suggests I arrange another dinner, where they can at least be brought together.'

I rubbed my chin. 'You are right. But Nicholas – I have been keep-ing him busy, although he was much affected by what happened in Norfolk. And I thought before we left that he was more interested in Beatrice than she in him.'

Philip smiled. 'Perhaps absence makes the heart grow fonder. And the mother, I think, still has hopes. She is one for the proper proprieties.'

I sighed. 'I should warn you, Nicholas is much changed. He is – melancholy.'

Philip looked at me. 'As are you. People remark on how you have lost weight, have a haunted look about you now.'

'We saw terrible things. It affected me, but Nicholas even more. To be frank, I think he has pretty much forgotten Beatrice. But you are right. She deserves to know where she stands. What date had you in mind?'

'The twenty-first would be convenient for us.'

'I shall speak to Nicholas.'

'Thank you.'

'No. Thank you, Philip. If I remember aright, there was too much dissension over religion for the last occasion to go well. It is good of you to bring that mix together again.'

'I think conversation this time will be more about the struggle between the Protector and the Earl of Warwick. I am sure everyone will agree the Protector had to go, for the peace of the realm.'

'What is the latest news?'

'Somerset goes to the Tower today. Warwick has won.' Philip shook his head. 'He is a hard man; the poor will not fare well under him. But better than a civil war, which many predicted.'

'And the poor hardly fared well by trusting Somerset. It is said eleven thousand died across the country in the suppression of the rebellions.'

Philip sighed. 'Was there ever such a year as this?'

'I cannot remember one.'

He left soon after. I sat staring from my window, where the cobbles of Lincoln's Inn courtyard were now covered in autumn leaves. I remembered the Earl of Warwick hinting to me after Dussindale that these whirling days might not yet be quite over. And indeed, throughout September, there had been rumours that most of the Council wanted a change of government. In early October Somerset had issued a proclamation asking his subjects to repair to Hampton Court, where he had taken the young King, ready for battle. Some six thousand, mostly poor Londoners, had gone to support him – incredibly, even after Dussindale, some still saw him as the friend of the poor. They had, though, only the most basic arms and no training, whilst Lords Russell and Herbert, leaders of the military forces against the rebels in the West, declared for Warwick on the way back to London with their armies. Somerset moved Edward to Windsor, but on the ninth of October he had surrendered, realizing he could not win. The Protectorate was abolished, and authority returned to the whole Council, though there was little doubt that Warwick would be its leader. A few days later, I saw the young King ride through London, cheered by the crowds, waving in acknowledgement. The poor boy had been moved around like a chess piece by his uncle, and though I noticed he was growing taller, his thin face filling out, his features were marked by the fear he must have experienced that month.

After my talk with Philip I went through to see Nicholas. He had his own room now, and was reading a deposition. But he looked bad, his red hair uncombed, his face thinner, emphasizing his long nose, and dark bags under his eyes. I told him of Philip's visit.

He put down the deposition and looked at me. 'He is right, I have been discourteous. Though as I have said, Beatrice is not for me.' He sighed deeply. 'But who is?'

'There will be someone.'

He shook his head. 'I have been thinking about my family, how they disowned me when I refused to marry a girl I did not love, and who did not love me.'

'That was cruel. But Nicholas, it was three years ago.'

He stood up. 'All I had left was my status as a gentleman, one without a penny to his name but with proper education and manners. It was all I had left,' he repeated sadly. 'But if I am not a real gentle-man, nor a commoner, then what am I?'

I crossed the room and took him by the shoulders. 'A lawyer, Nicholas, and a good one. Let that be enough for now. Memories of Norfolk are still raw, I know, and they will never leave us, but they will fade with time if you let them. And cut the knot with Beatrice as kindly as possible.'

He grasped my arm. 'Thank you.'

I smiled. 'And in heaven's name tidy yourself up, get a shave and a haircut.'

☩

PHILIP HAD PLANNED the seating so that Beatrice and Nicholas were opposite each other. Philip sat at the head of the table, his wife Ethelreda at the opposite end, while I sat next to Beatrice with her mother Laura on my other side. That left me once more opposite old Margaret Coleswyn, with Edward Kenzy on her other side.

The dinner began quietly, with comments confined to compliment-ing the food. Beatrice and Nicholas spoke little, Beatrice asking nothing about his time in Norwich. At length he said, 'I regret I was unable to write when I was away. Circumstances were very difficult.'

'You have been back over a month.'

'I am sorry.'

Old Margaret Coleswyn, in her sober black dress and old-fashioned square hood, who did not seem to have grasped the purpose of the dinner, turned on Beatrice and said, 'You should not pester Master Nicholas, girl. What he must have endured, a prisoner of those godless rebels all these weeks. Look at him, you can see he is but a shadow of himself.'

Beatrice bent her head to her plate.

I looked at old Margaret. Despite their difference in class, she reminded me of Simon Scambler's aunt. After Dussindale I had made no effort to find her and tell her what had become of her nephew. She would only have been outraged, I was sure, by his baring of his bottom at the Herald. When I thought of Simon I found it hard to keep my tongue bridled, and now I said, 'The Norfolk rebels were not godless. There was constant preaching in the camp.'

She looked at me, outraged. 'Then they were not true godly preach-ers, for did not our Saviour say, "Render unto Caesar that which is Caesar's"? Do you speak up for the rebels, Master Shardlake?'

With a warning glance at me, Edward Kenzy bent towards her. 'Do you know how many words there are in the Bible, good Mistress Coleswyn?'

She looked at him, puzzled. 'What has that to do with anything?'

'Over seven hundred and eighty thousand. And so many phrases contradict each other, or need scholarly interpretation. Unfortunately, people these days just pick and choose the passages that suit them.'

'Good Master Calvin is a great scholar,' she snapped back, 'and he has said that where the poor are concerned the bridle should be kept tight.'

Kenzy sighed. 'Ah yes, Master Calvin. We hear more and more of him these days.'

'A better scholar than your popish priests, sir,' she snapped back.

'Mother, that is enough,' Philip said, 'Let us eat in amity.' The old woman pursed her lips, but returned to her plate, mumbling some-thing about burnings needing to be brought back.

Laura Kenzy said, brightly, 'I hear the Earl of Warwick's younger son, Robert Dudley, is to marry a Norfolk lady, Mistress Amy Robsart. Apparently, they met at the Robsart estate after Robert fought in that great battle against the rebels.'

'Marry young and rue later,' her husband said.

'We married young.'

'There are exceptions, of course,' Edward replied, straight-faced.

He turned to me. 'Did you know, Master Shardlake, that Sir Richard Southwell is in trouble?'

I looked at him with interest. 'I had not heard. Only that he had been promoted to the full Council now Protector Somerset is gone.'

'Apparently, he has been accused of giving an enormous sum – five hundred pounds of government money – to the rebels. Did you hear anything of that when you were prisoner in the Norfolk camp, Matthew?'

'No,' I lied, though my heart leaped in my chest. So Elizabeth had informed Cecil after all, and he had acted.

Philip looked at me. 'And what of the man accused of murder, whom you and Nicholas went to defend?'

'He got his pardon at the end of September.'

Beatrice looked at Nicholas. 'So at least some good came of it all,' she said.

'I suppose so,' he replied, then fell silent again.

Philip asked, 'How is the little girl you brought back from Norwich, Matthew?'

I smiled. 'She thrives under the care of her good nurse. My application for adoption is with the courts.'

'Is she not the daughter of your former servant?' Laura Kenzy asked disapprovingly.

I looked back at her. 'She is a child, mistress, left alone and friendless in the world.'

'At least she will have a gentle upbringing. Who knows, in time she may marry a gentleman.' She looked at Beatrice and Nicholas, still eating in silence.

And so it went on, the second dinner party as awkward as the first. The conversation turned to the inflation, even worse after the bad harvest, and whether Warwick would emerge as leader of the Council. Edward Kenzy hoped he would, he would rule the country with a firm hand and hopefully end the wars with France and Scotland. With the last, at least, I could agree.

✝

795

ONCE AGAIN THE DINNER broke up early. Servants brought our coats. As we rose from the table Nicholas said to Beatrice, 'May we have a private word, mistress?' She nodded, and they left the room. The rest of us went and stood awkwardly in the hallway. Edward Kenzy came across to me. He said quietly, 'I think that will be the end of their – relationship.'

'I agree. I am sorry.'

'My wife is furious, I fear. She thinks young Overton has treated Beatrice badly, and has been working the poor child up.' He looked at me with sudden shrewdness. 'The boy looks like death, and you little better. What happened up there in Norfolk?'

I met his gaze. 'Dussindale. Bloodshed such as I have never seen, and countless executions afterwards.'

Kenzy sighed. 'What else could they expect, Matthew?'

'The Protector offered the people much, with his radical talk and enclosure commissions. The rebels intended to help – all right, give muscle to – the commissioners in enforcing what was, after all, the law.'

Kenzy shook his head. 'By setting themselves as judges over gentle-men, beating and imprisoning them? Did they truly think the Protector and the Council would allow them a say in the rule of the country? It would be like allowing the foot to rule the head.'

'I think they did. At first.'

'Then they forgot that such a thing could, and must, never be allowed.' He sighed. 'But perhaps, after all, if they were truly loyal to Crown and Protector, the whole thing was no more than a terrible misunderstanding, by people too backward to see the social order could not be changed.'

'No,' I said. 'The Protector offered them much, while Cranmer and the reforming bishops spoke of England as a diseased body that needed treatment. Even after the rebellions began, it is true the Protector ordered the camps to disperse, but he offered reform and changes to the government of the countryside.' I looked at him fiercely. 'Until he sent a Herald to Mousehold Heath who ordered them to disperse, used savage terms, and offered nothing. That was no misunderstanding, it was a betrayal. As people said in the camp later, they were promised much at first but in the end got only a barrel of ropes and halters to hang them.'

Kenzy inclined his head. 'Be careful who you say that to, Matthew.' 'I will.'

I excused myself. The smoke from all the candles was making the house stuffy. I stepped outside for a breath of air. I looked up at the stars. Then, from nearby, I heard the sound of a woman crying. There was a gate beside the house, leading to the garden behind, and I opened it quietly. In the garden Beatrice Kenzy was sitting on a bench, her form dimly illuminated by the light from the windows.

'Beatrice,' I said.

She wiped her face angrily. 'What do you want?'

'Only to help, if I can.'

She glared at me. 'You never liked me, did you?'

I sat beside her. 'I felt you were dangling Nicholas on a string, at your mother's instigation, no doubt, perhaps because of the exaggerated idea she had about my contacts in high places.'

I thought she might fly at me, but instead she gave a brittle laugh. 'You are right. Since I was a little girl she has been training me in the womanly arts, that I might ensnare a wealthy husband. I did not love Nicholas, though I liked him much and thought he might prove a kind husband. When he told me tonight that his feelings for me had changed, although I had guessed that already, it upset me: I felt as though I had been defeated. Is that not foolish?'

'I do not know.'

She spoke with a force and fluency I would never have expected. 'No, men never know what it is like to be a gentlewoman, brought up to think of nothing but styles for clothes and hair, how to simper and tease, approach and retreat. I am good at it, I have been taught well. My mother thinks it all there is in the world.'

'But you know it is not.'

'It is all – artificial.'

I said, 'I am sorry I misjudged you.'

She shook her head. 'Mother will soon be planning further introductions for me. And I will go along with her plans, for you have seen how she rules this family. My father cares little, all he wants is a quiet life.'

'You could stand up to her.'

'She would shriek and rail at me.'

'Perhaps you could shriek and rail back, insist on making your own choice, in your own way. Then your father would have no peace, and perhaps he might even step in on your side.'

She smiled through her tears. 'It would not be so easy. But thank you.'

There was the sound of a window opening, and Laura Kenzy's voice called out in fluting tones, 'Beatrice, are you there? It is time to go!'

She rose, sighed, and walked heavily along the pathway to the rear door of the house, her shoulders sagging. She turned at the door and said to me, 'You are adopting a little girl. I beg you, do not bring her up as I have been.'

'I can promise you that.'

Epilogue

7 December 1549

I STOOD AT THE window of my study, watching the snow whirl down. It had begun early that afternoon, driven by a strong wind. Now it lay thick on my path, and on Chancery Lane beyond. I looked out, and thought of Robert Kett. He had been executed in Norwich that morning, his body tied in chains and then hauled from the ground up to the top of Norwich Castle, where he had been hanged. His corpse had been left dangling from the top of the castle in its chains, and would stay there till it rotted away. His brother William had been executed in the same manner from the tower of Wymondham church.

After lunch, Barak and Tamasin had brought their two children, four-year-old George and two-year-old Tilda, to visit Mousy, who, at nine months old, was turning into a lively, cheerful child, busily crawling around, investigating everything she could reach and trying to put unsuitable things into her mouth, though Liz Partlett kept a constant, careful eye on her.

Barak took me aside at one point, and said, 'I thought it would be good for us to come round. I know what day this is.'

'Thank you,' I answered quietly. On the surface Barak seemed far less marked than Nicholas or me by what had happened in Norfolk, but looking into his eyes sometimes I could see a burning, intense anger.

I changed the subject. 'Have you grubbed up any more cases for Nick and I? We have enough to keep us going – that disputed will we got through you involves a dozen family claimants, and Edward Kenzy referred a big property case to us last week. It surprised me, it was decent of him. But without the Lady Elizabeth's work, we could do with more.'

He grinned wickedly. 'A nice juicy murder, perhaps?'

'That I think we can do without.'

'How is our carrot-head doing?'

'Still brooding. That's why I want more work for him. But a little better since he separated from Beatrice Kenzy.'

'I'll see what I can do. With Warwick firmly in charge now, people talk of setting new commercial schemes afoot, and some will need lawyers.'

'Good.'

Shortly after, as the snow began to come down thickly, they left for home. I went to my study, to brood.

I had not attended the great show trial to which Robert and William Kett had been subjected at the end of November; it would have been impolitic. I heard both men had pleaded guilty to the long list of charges read against them. They were first sentenced to be hanged, drawn and quartered at Tyburn but shortly after it was decided they should die in Norfolk, no doubt as a deterrent to further rebellion. I thought of Robert Kett, a man not far off sixty, being slowly raised from the ground to the dizzying heights of the castle roof in the bitter cold. With disgust I remembered John Flowerdew, gleeful at the prospect of giving evidence at the inquest into his property.

There was a quiet tap at the door, and Liz entered, Mousy in her arms, fast asleep now after the earlier excitement. She gave me her gentle smile, and said, 'I thought perhaps you might like to take Mousy for a little.' I looked into Liz's clear blue eyes and thought, yes, she, too, remembers what day this is. We had never spoken of her husband's part in the rebellion, nor mine, yet she had divined my feelings.

'Thank you, Liz,' I said quietly. 'I should like to. It was thoughtful of you.'

She said hesitantly, 'I knew, sir, that today would be hard.' As she handed over the sleeping child, our hands touched, and I felt a sudden urge to grasp the soft, plump warmth of hers. Liz reddened, lowering her head. She stood there, but when I did no more she curtsied and left the room.

I held Mousy to me, feeling the gentle rise and fall of her chest. She was getting heavier now. There was a warm fire that heated most of the room, but I returned to the window, despite the cold draught there, and looked out again at the snow, falling in thick white flakes. The wind driving it came from the east. It would already be lying thick on Mousehold Heath, covering the burned-out ruins of the great camp, the bare branches of the Oak of Reformation, and softly blanketing the unmarked mass graves of thousands of brave commoners – old Hector Johnson, Natty, Peter Bone, Toby, Simon. I held Mousy tight, but the warmth of her little body was small comfort against the cold.

ACKNOWLEDGEMENTS

First, huge thanks to my superb agent Antony Topping for all his help in getting *Tombland* into print. Thanks to my editor, Maria Rejt of Mantle, to Marian Reid, Liz Cowen, Josie Humber, Kate Tolley and Philippa McEwan of Pan Macmillan, and to my US editor, Joshua Kendall, and agent Jennifer Weltz.

Roz Brody, Mike Holmes, Jan King and William Shaw again made helpful comments on the manuscript. Special thanks to Roz for accom-panying me on research trips to Norwich when I was not in the best of health.

I am very grateful to friends in Norwich – Colin Howey, Leo R. Jary, Adrian and Anne Hoare and Dr Matt Woodcock, for illuminating discussions on 1549. Thanks to Dr Clive Wilkins-Jones for advice on sources.

I'm also grateful to those who showed me around sites that feature in the book: Adrian and Anne Hoare showed me round Wymondham. Will Stewart, Warden of Mousehold Heath, showed me the surviving section of the Heath. The Kett's Heights Society is doing wonderful work in restoring the Heights, where a part-wall of St Michael's Chapel survives. Nick Williams took me round the Guildhall, and Rod Spokes showed me the surviving city walls. Paul Dixon took me round the Maid's Head, and Cathy Terry discussed textiles with me at the magnifi-cent Strangers' Hall.

Many thanks once again to Graham Brown of Fullerton's for his help, including photocopying and enlarging pieces of sixteenth-century Norwich maps.

Historical Essay

Reimagining Kett's Rebellion

Introduction

In April 1548, the year before Kett's Rebellion, an orphaned minor gentle-woman of around fourteen, Agnes Randolf, was riding over Mousehold Heath with her married older sister and a young servant. They were accosted by John Atkinson, servant to Sir Richard Southwell, one of the most prominent gentlemen in Norfolk, and a companion. Atkinson attempted to abduct Agnes and when she tried to escape tied her on to his companion's horse, saying, 'Sit, whore, sit.' She was taken to Sir Richard Southwell's house and, later that week, forced to go through a marriage ceremony with Atkinson. Then he took her to London.[1]

Agnes's brother-in-law, Thomas Hunne, seems to have been a man of remarkable determination. He went to London and himself presented a supplication to Edward Seymour, Duke of Somerset and Lord Protector of England during the minority of Edward VI, as the Protector entered the council chamber at Westminster. Such direct access to the ruler would have been inconceivable under Edward's father Henry VIII, but it was part of Somerset's style to show himself accessible to those seeking justice. Two days later Southwell was examined before the Council, and Atkinson committed to prison.

Then problems began. Hunne made suit to the Council for Agnes to be restored to him, but was told by William Cecil, Somerset's senior secretary, that he should obtain legal counsel. No fewer than seventeen East Anglian lawyers, however, refused to represent him until Cecil ordered one to do so. Such, apparently, was the fear that Southwell inspired. Cecil tried to persuade Agnes to let the marriage stand but, as determined as her brother-in-law, she refused. Cecil then said she must return the wedding ring, which she immediately did.

Although under suspicion of abducting a minor, Atkinson was released. For the next four years, however, he tried to force Agnes's return through the courts, on the grounds that they had been lawfully married – even after Agnes had, later, married someone else. Norfolk gentlemen could be extraordinarily obsessive.

This story features three people who appear in *Tombland* – Southwell, Atkinson and Cecil. It demonstrates the power wielded, in Norfolk and London, by Southwell, the brutality of which he and his entourage were capable (he had been found guilty of murdering another gentleman during a quarrel in London in the 1520s, but obtained a pardon from Henry VIII), and both Protector Somerset's accessibility and its limits. Were it not for the great courage of Agnes and her family, the marriage would have stood. It is worth noting that Agnes's family had gentleman status; their clothes, bearing and accents would have aided their way into the Protector's court. One wonders how a peasant family might have fared.

It is however the 'non-gentle' classes who feature most prominently in *Tombland*, those who made the huge peasant uprisings that swept England in 1549. Roughly south of a line between the Severn and the Wash, though there were also risings north of there, common people set up camps outside towns and sent petitions to the Protector. It was the largest popular uprising between the 1381 Peasants' Revolt and the Civil Wars a century later. There were substantial pitched battles between rebels and government forces in the West Country, Oxfordshire and Norfolk. The Venetian ambassador estimated that 11,000 died in the rebellions; as a proportion of the population, today's equivalent is almost 150,000.[2] If anything this is probably an underestimate, since casualties among government forces were played down.

Yet most popular histories of Tudor England say little about the rebellions. There are several reasons: their unusual structure – forming 'camps' instead of marching as a single force on London; the misconception among historians, until fairly recently, that the only serious revolts were in the West Country, where they were concerned mainly with religious changes, and in Norfolk where they focused on social issues. However recent studies by Diarmaid MacCulloch, Andy Wood, Ethan Shagan and most especially Amanda Jones have shown the number and the con-nectedness of the risings across southern England.

Perhaps also, in these days of the 'royalization' of popular Tudor his-tory (I do not exempt myself from guilt here) – focusing on the larger-than-life personalities of Henry VIII and Elizabeth I – a rebellion that took place during the short reign of Henry's son, Edward VI, is less likely to gain attention. But the rebellions of 1549 caught my imagination a long time ago, as a colossal event that has been much underplayed.

In *Tombland*, as with all my novels, I have tried to base myself firmly on the source material, although that is scattered, fragmentary and sometimes unreliable. For example, we have no idea what Robert Kett or anyone else on the rebel side actually looked like. When it comes to Robert Kett's great camp on Mousehold Heath, I have had to imagine what daily life could have been like there, day by day; this has thrown up some interest-ing, if speculative, ideas.

THE BACKGROUND: CLASS AND STATUS

To understand what happened in 1549 we must first look at the social structure. The essential division was between the 'gentleman' classes, who did not need to work with their hands to live – perhaps some 2,000 people – and the rest, who did. True, the gentleman classes were divided into a 'society of orders' with social divisions between gentlemen, knights and the various levels of aristocracy rigidly enforced by the 'sumptuary laws' defining what different social ranks could wear.[1] It is also true that gentleman status was not just about wealth, but also rules of gentlemanly behaviour – in the words of Thomas Elyot, a gentleman would have 'more sufferance, more affability, and mildness, than . . . a person rural or of a very base lineage'.[2] That, at least, was the theory.

According to contemporary belief this division was ordained by

God. A 1547 homily stated, 'Almighty God hath created and appointed all things . . . in a most perfect order . . . Some are in high degree, some in low; some kings and princes, some inferiors and subjects . . . masters and servants . . . rich and poor.'[3]

Comparison was often made between social ranks and the human body, with the king as the head, the gentle classes as the arms and hands, and the poor as the feet.[4] Sir Thomas Smith spoke of four sorts of people – gentlemen, citizens or burgesses of cities, yeomen, and artificers or labourers. Only the first two could hold office, although yeomen (the more prosperous small farmers) could hold power in their own villages and towns and so 'must be exempted out of the rascality of the popular'. He admitted however that in villages members of the 'proletarij' were commonly made churchwardens and constables, though this was new.[5]

Economic changes were also taking place. The enclosure of arable land for profit, especially for running sheep for their wool, had been going on since the fifteenth century, bringing a new rural 'gentry' class into exist/ ence, and in the mid/sixteenth century there was a new, assertive gentry capitalism, not least in Norfolk.[6] Enclosure took place at different times in different parts of the country, and indeed the enclosure of common land by landowners would still be a political issue in the eighteenth cen/ tury. In the reign of Henry VIII, however, the sale of former monastic land by the Crown meant that a whole new land market sprang up.

Marx saw capitalism emerging from transformations in both landowner/ ship and the relations of production between around 1450 and 1600. The earlier liberation of serfs from bondage, he argued, resulted in a class of small peasant proprietors who, particularly in the sixteenth century, were then expropriated by capitalistic landowners. Subsequent research con/ firms there is a good deal in this, though Marx pretty much ignored the development of the smaller landowning class, the yeomen.[7] As Jane Whittle has observed, 'we are left with a lengthy period of time which is neither fully capitalist nor feudal'.[8] In the sixteenth century even serf/ dom – the tying of the bondman to his lord's land – was not quite extinct in some parts, including Norfolk.[9]

Thomas Smith's 'labourers' were never, however, completely power/ less. In 1525, when Henry VIII imposed massive new taxation, opposition in East Anglia compelled him to withdraw it.[10] This, however, was a rare success and, like the 1536 Northern uprising, involved the commons and elite classes operating together on issues affecting both – though in 1536 involvement of the gentleman classes was sometimes reluctant.[11] The forces of the State, however, were able to overcome all large-scale peasant rebellions, like the 1381 Peasants' Revolt and Cade's Rebellion of 1450.

While, as some historians stress,[12] common people had wills of their own and would take whatever advantage they could of changing circum-stances, what they could not do, by virtue of their lowly status, was demand a share in the government of the realm. This fact was at the heart of the tragedy of 1549.

THE RULE OF PROTECTOR SOMERSET: INFLATION AND WAR, RELIGIOUS AND SOCIAL REFORM

When Henry VIII died in 1547, his will provided for a Council of six-teen, with alternates (including Sir Richard Southwell) provided in case a member died or left, to rule England until Edward VI, then nine, reached eighteen. Edward was not, as popular culture has often portrayed him, 'sickly'. He was fit and highly intelligent. There was every reason to believe he would grow to manhood.

Within a matter of weeks the Council had devolved power upon the Duke of Somerset, eldest brother of Edward's mother Jane Seymour, who became Protector. Substantial bribes were involved.[1]

There are two views of Somerset. One is that he was 'the Good Duke', concerned for the welfare of the poor, who abolished the draco-nian treason legislation of Henry VIII and led the country, for a time at least, into 'milder climes'. The second, to which I subscribe, is that Som-erset was obsessed with the war he instigated against Scotland, despite its military failure and disastrous economic effects. All other issues were secondary. Meanwhile the 'milder climes' soon turned into a new religious authoritarianism, radical Protestantism.[2] As a man, Somerset was widely viewed as proud, tactless and obstinate.[3] His incompetence speaks of a man promoted beyond his abilities; his performance in dealing with the 1549 rebellions was remarkably inept. Though he often acted like an autocrat, in the end Somerset's position depended on the Council's con-sent, something he realized too late.

Henry VIII had left England in a mess. Since the break with Rome in 1532–3, his religious policy had oscillated between semi-Protestantism and a conservative 'Catholicism without the Pope', leaving an atmos-phere of religious division and uncertainty. His wars with France and Scotland had been costly failures; he made a peace with France in 1546, which included France's Scottish ally, though details remained to be nego-tiated with Scotland.[4] But in 1547 Somerset launched a full-scale war against Scotland. This in turn affected relations with France, making Henry's peace a short one.

THE GREAT INFLATION

Henry's wars had been enormously costly. The state coffers were emptied, heavy taxation levied, and much former monastic land sold. To obtain gold and silver, the silver coinage especially was debased, adulterated with copper. In domestic as well as foreign markets, sellers became reluctant to accept these coins at full value. The result was high inflation, previously unknown in England.[1] In 1549 prices were over fifty per cent higher than in 1540, and in that crucial year spiked by eleven per cent.[2] The poor were worst affected, as wages, limited by statute and local custom, did not rise. The earnings of a semi-skilled workman remained steady at around fourpence a day, a sum whose purchasing power fell by a third in less than a decade, causing drastic impoverishment.[3] Financially, the last thing England needed after Henry died was another large-scale war.

There were two contemporary explanations for the inflation. One, which was wrong, concentrated on agrarian factors – high rents, market-ing problems and enclosure – the replacement of food-producing agriculture by sheep farming. The agrarian situation indeed caused major social problems and huge injustice, but the second explanation, that infla-tion stemmed mainly from the debasement of the coinage, caused in turn by war, was the right one. Somerset, however, determined on his Scottish war, was naturally predisposed to the 'agrarian' explanation.[4]

THE SCOTTISH WAR

Why was Somerset so fixated on Scotland? In 1547 it was no threat to England. However, Henry VIII had wanted to marry Edward VI to his fellow child-monarch Mary, Queen of Scots, thus ending for good the 'Auld Alliance'. Somerset, though, intended fully to unite the two countries. Protestantism was growing in Scotland, and Somerset believed many Scots would support his invasion. He also believed, wrongly, that he had the military key to conquering Scotland – the building of a series of forts in the lowlands on the new Italian model, which would act as local bases for attack and also attract Protestant Scots.

In September 1547 Somerset met initial success at the Battle of Pinkie, defeating a massive Scottish army.[1] However, the number of sympathetic Scots proved to be small, and his fortresses fell one by one to the Scottish Governor, Arran. In 1548 Mary, Queen of Scots was shipped to France, which was already providing aid to the Scots, killing the marriage plan stone dead. By early 1549 the remaining English garrisons, with up to 17,000 men, were under siege, underpaid and ravaged by plague. Conditions in Scotland were so bad that foreign mercenaries refused to serve there.[2]

The Scottish war was a contributory cause of the 1549 rebellions, not only because it made inflation worse but, I suggest, also because of the importance of angry deserters from the English army in helping instigate rebellion. Desertion rates in Tudor armies were about fifteen to twenty per cent and, given the conditions and lack of pay in Scotland, the figure for that war may be higher.[3] Interestingly, the contemporary soldier Elis Gryffydd noted during the 1544 French campaign that it tended to be prosperous yeomen who urged poorer soldiers to desert.[4]

Despite the complete failure of his war, Somerset planned yet another campaign for 1549. This, however, was overtaken by the rebellions.[5]

RELIGIOUS CHANGE

As well as war and inflation, England in 1547–9 faced radical religious change. Some have argued that Somerset's religious changes were fairly moderate, but this is incorrect.[1]

First, people everywhere were affected by the dissolution of the chantries where masses were said for the dead, and government appropriation of their lands and property. Their funding had come partly from guilds who employed a priest to say masses for the souls of dead relatives and members. Robert Kett was involved in several in Wymondham. Most had a little land whose rentals paid for the chantry priests, and a few had sizeable holdings. Somerset put these lands on the market too.

Meanwhile the appearance of the churches was transformed by the removal of stained-glass, ornamentation and images. These altered the appearance of every church in the land, as Shardlake discovers at Whetstone.

The introduction, in June 1549, of the first Prayer Book in English was the biggest change of all, ending the ancient Latin Mass.[2] Like all religious changes since 1533, it was imposed from above. Somerset himself was, I think, a genuine religious radical; he corresponded with European Protestant divines like John Calvin, who influenced him considerably.[3]

Opposition to the religious changes certainly existed, and the abolition of Henry VIII's harsh treason laws was negated by increasing restrictions on preaching – only licensed preachers were permitted by 1548. The introduction of the Prayer Book in services on 9 June 1549 was accepted by the bulk of the country – but in Devon and Cornwall furiously hostile opposition sparked rebellion.

THE COMMONWEALTH MEN

The main cause of revolt overall, though, was the ever-worsening lot of the poor. Somerset portrayed himself as their friend, and their situation was well known to him. But what could be done?

Answers were very much tied to the notion of 'Commonwealth'. This ancient concept, synonymous with the 'body politic', came in sixteenth-century England increasingly to mean the duty of the government to further social welfare,[1] connecting with the medieval 'complaint tradition' where satirical complaint and denouncing of social ills did however not really offer solutions beyond appeals to individual conscience and to the monarch.[2]

'Commonwealthmen' were never a coherent group, though most were radical Protestants. In the 1540s they began complaining fiercely against the 'greedy rich men'. A sermon of Bishop Latimer spoke of how 'covetous landlords, by their enhancing of rents' had produced 'this monstrous and portentous dearth made by man'.[3] Extracts from such sermons were often printed, though they would be the 'best bits', ignoring the often greater amounts of time spent condemning lechery.[4] Simon Crowley's 'Petition Against the Oppression of the Poor Commons' called on the rich to repent, and threatened uncooperative landlords and MPs with the wrath of the Lord, as did Latimer and Becon.[5] Numerous anonymous pamphlets denounced the rich, blaming covetousness for the decay of the Commonwealth.[6] Acquisitive landlords driving the poor from the countryside were particular targets.

There is another, contrary, strand in Commonwealth thinking, particularly where it penetrated government circles. This was that the 'maintenance of good order and obedience' was its very basis. Anarchy among the commons was greatly feared.[7] Thus 'Commonwealth' acquired a double meaning. For gentlemen who supported it – like Shardlake, at first – it was about restoring the natural balance and harmony between the classes; for others, however, it came to mean simply the welfare of the commons.[8] After the rebellions, the Commonwealth writers were the first to condemn the rebellions, often in ferocious terms.

THE ENCLOSURE COMMISSIONS

To be fair to him, Somerset did attempt practical solutions, albeit half-baked. Little help could be expected from Parliament, composed of members of the gentry and urban elite. A series of radical bills, intended to reverse the conversion of arable land to pasture, failed to pass the Com-mons.[1] Parliament did pass one reform measure: a tax on sheep and cloth production, the former taxing owners of sheep according to the numbers they owned, disadvantaging large-scale farmers. The need to raise more revenue to fight the Scottish war was the argument used on reluctant MPs.

Somerset turned to royal proclamations to deal with the enclosure issue, bypassing Parliament – government by proclamation was a notable feature of his rule. In June 1548 a proclamation ordered a 'view and enquiry' on illegal enclosures to be made, to begin with a commission to investigate enclosures in the Midlands. The proclamation recited laws against enclosures ignored since Henry VII's reign. In each place visited, a jury of twelve was to be empanelled under a commissioner, who could make wide-ranging orders including forcing land illegally turned to pas-ture to be returned to tillage. The leading commissioner was John Hales, a strong-minded, fierce MP, the only serious Commonwealth-minded reformer to find an executive government role. However, Hales empha-sized to commoners that they must not take it upon themselves to pull down enclosures. By concentrating on illegal enclosures Hales brought this particular issue to the fore, at the expense of other rural issues.

The practicality of the idea must be doubted – to reverse illegal enclo-sures going back sixty years, far beyond the lifetime of most potential witnesses, against the opposition of landlords and local officials would have been a gigantic, probably impossible, task. No arrangements were provided for enforcement, and appeals by landlords to the courts could have kept the matter tied up for decades. However, without getting further than preliminary enquiries in the Midlands, the commission adjourned, probably because Hales, as an MP, had to return to Parliament for the new session, and nothing more happened for a year. All this indicates how low a priority the matter really was for Somerset.

In May 1548, the month before Somerset's proclamation (perhaps influencing its timing), a sizeable insurrection took place in Hertford-shire.[2] The cause was an impending commission (separate from Hales's commissions) obtained by Sir William Cavendish to authorize enclosure of part of Northaw Great Waste, a very large area of common land. Vil-lagers who used the land, together with outsiders, took action that in many ways prefigured what was to happen the following year, setting up a camp on Northaw Common led by substantial yeomen and local office-holders, creating an infrastructure to supply and run it, and petitioning the Protector. However when local magnate Roger Chomley offered assurances and promises of reform, the rebels dispersed. Several were subsequently prosecuted.

It is worth pausing here to consider what 'enclosure' meant.[3] The English village used the three-field system, where each year two fields were farmed and one left fallow. The fields themselves were divided into strips, with villagers owning several, positioned in a haphazard way. Additionally there was an expanse of village 'common land'. This was of central importance to poor villagers especially, used for grazing their own animals as well as a source of game, wood, fish and reeds. Milk from cows and bacon from the pigs were crucial sources of nutrition.

The village was not an undifferentiated mass of peasants. There were several types of holding – copyhold, the commonest, which had replaced serfdom; tenancies at the landlord's will, often on land occupied long ago by squatters; and freehold, where the freeholder effectively owned the land, subject to a lord's or the King's suzerainty.

Sizes of holdings varied greatly. Many 'cottagers' had only a few acres, not enough to live on, and worked part time as tradesmen or labourers. Often they relied heavily on their rights on the commons, particularly in the 1540s as inflation ate away at their earnings.

WAS ENCLOSURE A MAJOR PROBLEM?

There were two types of enclosure. The first was where tenants, by exchange or purchase, brought their strips together into a single holding, making for more efficient farming. Often such people profited and were able to expand their holdings. This was the rising class of yeoman from which it was possible, though rare and tricky, to rise to acceptance as a 'gentleman'.[1] Most yeomen kept their share of the common land, though some were not above undertaking illegal enclosures of the land themselves.

The second type of enclosure was quite different, and this was the target of Hales's commissions. Here landlords, often non-resident, actively sought to expand their sheepfolds and squeeze out smaller farmers, mainly by attacking the commons. Sometimes they grazed additional sheep or cattle to crowd out other users; sometimes they simply enclosed the commons illegally. Without its commons a village could not survive, and though established rights to use the commons could be enforced in court, this was extremely difficult in practice.[2]

Many landlords entered the land market by purchasing monastic land in the 1530s and 1540s on terms of 'knight service' to the Crown, which meant paying feudal dues to the King. Sometimes – with the aid of unscrupulous royal officials responsible for such dues, the feodary and escheator, or their agents – they attempted to pass these burdens on to tenants.[3] Then they would force the tenants out, or buy them out at knockdown prices.[4]

In the 1540s inflation was reducing the value of landlords' rents at a time when demand for wool was insatiable – in 1548 the price doubled.[5] Sheep required only a shepherd, a boy and a dog, and those turned off their lands at a time of rising population were often reduced to joining the ranks of impoverished 'masterless men' heading for the towns. Others tried to stay put in increasingly impossible circumstances. The 1540s was only one phase of enclosure, limited to certain parts of the country, but it frequently placed those affected in a nightmare position.

1549: A PERFECT STORM

1549 began badly for Protector Somerset. His younger brother Thomas Seymour, always a wild card, had married Henry VIII's widow Catherine Parr in 1547. After her death in childbirth in September 1548 Thomas embarked on a course of action – taking bribes from the Channel pirates who, as Lord Admiral, he was supposed to be clearing from the seas, blackmailing the keeper of the Bristol mint into giving him coin, and stocking weapons at his home, Sudeley Palace – indicating an intention forcibly to take the Protectorship from his brother. He also paid court to the Lady Elizabeth through her servants. His activities quickly became known, and in January 1549 he was arrested and charged with treason.

Elizabeth was put under severe questioning but, having made no commitment to marry Seymour, was released. However the other evidence of
treason was clear, and the Protector had no alternative but to execute his
brother in March 1549. This could only weaken him.[1]

There is another important factor about 1549 to consider – the weather.
There had been three good harvests between 1546 and 1548, but the winter
of 1548–9 had been hard,[2] and by spring 1549 it would have been clear that
the next harvest would likely be poor.[3] It was, indeed, disastrous.

THE MAY 'STIRS'

In April 1549 Somerset again issued a proclamation, stating that the King
intended to enforce the enclosure laws, made since Henry VII's time,
across the country and 'to see them executed against all such as shall be
found culpable, without indeed pardon or remission'. The commissioners
were ordered to proceed 'with all speed and earnest endeavour' to the punishment of offenders throughout the country.[1] Had this proclamation ever
been implemented, it would have destroyed the expansion of large-scale
sheep farming. The proclamation was publicized across the country, and
would have given food for thought, and hope, to the peasantry, who must
however also have noted that, as in 1548, there was a complete absence of
provisions for enforcement.

In May, a spate of rebellions and demonstrations broke out across
southern England. There were disorders at Landbeach in Cambridgeshire over landlord overstocking of common land,[2] and outbreaks of
revolt against landlords and enclosures in Hertfordshire, Northampton-
shire, Suffolk, Kent and Hampshire. Most were small-scale and easily
dealt with by the local elite through conciliation or force;[3] in the most
notorious incident, when the park of Sir William Herbert in Wiltshire
was destroyed, he attacked with 200 men who 'slaughtered the rebels like
sheep'. It is worth noting that emparkment of land for deer-hunting was
very fashionable among the gentry and aristocracy, but again took large
amounts of land out of cultivation.

Another proclamation in late May condemned those who had taken
the King's authority upon themselves; subjects were reassured that the

King intended to reform enclosures but commanded them to cease unlawful activities, and warned that those who did not would be prosecuted 'by
the sword, and with all force of extremity'.[4] The commissions would not
set out until disturbances had ceased. Here is the mixture of conciliation
and threat that, with different emphases, dominated Somerset's approach
to rural unrest until mid-July.

THE WESTERN REBELLION

In early June all seemed quiet again, but when the new Prayer Book came
into use on Whitsunday, 9 June, it immediately sparked a ferocious rebellion in Devon, which quickly spread to Cornwall. Perhaps 10,000 men
were involved. The traditional account that 'the Prayer Book Rebellion'
was solely concerned with reversing religious reform has been challenged
by subsequent writers, notably Joyce Youings.[1] There were no enclosure
problems in the two counties, but there was serious resentment against the
power of the gentleman and officials. There were very few of gentleman
status among the leaders of the Western Rebellion, while some gentlemen
were killed and most seem to have kept out of the way. The other leaders
and the rank and file ranged from priests to yeomen and labourers. On
2 July the rebels began besieging Exeter, but the Protestant elite retained
control of the city. Exeter's high elevation and strong defences meant the
rebels got bogged down there, the city being too large to bypass. Very sig-
nificantly, the men of neighbouring Somerset refused to join forces with
them, although there were risings there from May through July.[2] This was
crucial in containing the Western Rebellion; its religious conservatism,
violent opposition to the government and the hopelessness of their siege
strategy may have given the men of Somerset pause. And they may have
known that, across the south, quite different tactics were already under
consideration.

The Western rebels resembled the later camps only in sending petitions enumerating their grievances to Somerset. Twelve have survived, and
have been meticulously studied by Aubrey Greenwood.[3] While they show
a growing preoccupation with reversing religious changes, they also complain of the sheep tax, inflation and how the King's officers and magistrates

'are not trustworthy' because of newly acquired wealth and lack of accountability. One petition included a demand for the number of each gentleman's servants (meaning enforcers) to be limited to six, which would have destroyed local seigneurial power. Interestingly, one petition denounced 'wasting resources on prolonged, failed foreign wars'.

To begin with, the government showed little understanding of the scale of events in the West. They tried a policy of conciliation, while gathering military forces to prevent any further advance. Outside Devon and Cornwall, there was in June what the Earl of Arundel described as 'a quavering quiet'. On 1 July the Protector summoned much of the nobility and gentry from the Thames Valley and South-East to consult him at Windsor, probably to discuss forming an army to march against the West.[4]

THE REBELLIONS OF COMMONWEALTH

Then, in the first week of July, rebellions exploded all across southern England and the south Midlands. Apart from one slightly later, isolated rebellion in Yorkshire, northern England remained quiet: it is unclear why, but firm government control established through the 'Council of the North' after the 1536 rebellion, lack of serious enclosure problems and fear of Scottish invasion are all likely factors.

The strategy of the southern rebels was to set up camps, often several in each county, usually outside towns, and send petitions to the government setting out their grievances. According to Amanda Jones there are sixteen camps whose location is known, with a question mark over another three, and very possibly other smaller ones. Ten were in East Anglia and Cambridgeshire.[1] The range of grievances encompassed both opposition to the religious changes and social discontents, but the East Anglian rebellions concentrated almost exclusively on social issues and stressed loyalty, not opposition, to the government and its religious policies, saying that they were not rebels at all, merely seeking to help implement the Protector's own agrarian policies. Numbers in the camps varied, and are hard to pin down, but several thousand were certainly involved both in Oxfordshire and Mousehold Heath. Local 'stirs' continued until the end of the year.[2]

The rebels in Oxfordshire and Buckinghamshire complained both about religious innovations and enclosure, high rents and prices.[3] Priests were among the leadership, but everyone defined themselves as the 'poor', and targeted the rich. They were well organized. It seems likely they moved headquarters from Enslow Hill in Oxfordshire to Chipping Norton as 1,500 men, detached from the army sent to deal with the West/ ern rebels, were sent to put them down. Interestingly, this was the same number as the first army sent to deal with the Norfolk rebels two weeks later, implying the camp at Chipping Norton also numbered several thousand. The rebels were defeated in battle on 18 July. Fifteen were later hanged, including five priests from their steeples. Most of the rebels seem to have been husbandmen. The authorities certainly regarded the Midland rebels as anti/government and anti/hierarchical.

Studies by Diarmaid MacCulloch in the 1980s showed that while much the largest in numbers, Kett's camp outside Norwich was only one of several linked East Anglian camps.[4] His work, and Amanda Jones's work on the 'lesser stirs' of what contemporaries were soon calling the 'commotion time', are the most important correctives to the long tradition of seeing what happened in 1549 as comprising only the Western and Kett's Rebellions.[5] Jones has suggested that in localities where the authori/ ties were unable to deal with disorder, or perhaps, as in Norwich, reluctantly forced to cooperate with rebels for a while, smaller rebellions may have gone deliberately unrecorded.[6]

REBEL COORDINATION

That rebellions should erupt across the country in the same week, just when many of the local leaders who would normally be the organizers of local forces were absent, cannot possibly be coincidence. All seem to have adopted the 'camping' strategy and avoided armed violence. In June, it seems clear, men had been coordinating and preparing for a new sort of rebellion.

Who were they? The importance of deserters from the Scottish wars is, I have suggested, more central than previously suggested. The military/ organizational skills of soldiers, particularly officers, were I think to be important especially in Kett's huge camp. Among the confusing blizzard of proclamations by the government in July, one referred to 'criminals, deserters and loiterers' as spreading 'rumours' that misled people to gather in unlawful assemblies,[1] while in a letter to Philip Hoby talking of the rebels, Somerset wrote 'the ruffians among them and the soldiers, which be the chief doers, look first for spoil'.[2]

Meanwhile Thomas Smith, Somerset's Chief Secretary, was terrified of the spread of the 'camp-men', as they were already being called.[3] There was an abortive plan for a large Hampshire-Sussex Rebellion, with a conservative religious hue, led by Garnham, a Winchester carpenter, and one Flint of Sussex. However, Flint failed to appear at a crucial meeting and was probably captured.[4] This raises another interesting issue, the question of government agents among the rebels; in Kent a man called Latimer (not the Bishop) travelled the county claiming he had Somerset's approval to take bills of complaint. But he also received money from the government and may have been used by Somerset to try to pacify the rebels with money.[5] In other words, he became a double agent. Elsewhere, the authorities sent Edward Loft to the Thetford camp in south Norfolk 'as a scout watch', fearing the Cambridge commons were about to join the Norfolk rebels.[6] So the presence in the Mousehold camp of a government spy, which I have portrayed in *Tombland*, was perfectly likely.

MacCulloch, however, has emphasized the importance of substantial yeomen and townsmen in leading the rebellions, arranging meetings under cover of the sporting competitions so popular throughout the year, and refers to the regular paranoia exhibited by the gentry about such gatherings.[7] To the sporting competitions may be added plays and religious festivals, such as the Wymondham Game Play where Kett's Rebellion began. I would suggest that yeomen and 'runagates' played complementary roles in instigating the rebellions.

What were the aims of the 'camp-men'? Both those in the Midlands who opposed the religious changes, and those in the east who supported them, expressed the same hatred of 'gentlemen' and government officials, and wanted reform of rural conditions. Although only fragmentary evidence has survived, the camp-men sent numerous petitions to the Protector. I would suggest that part of the motivation for this strategy, especially in the east where religious questions mattered less, was the promise of the arrival of the enclosure commissioners. Indeed Somerset, on 8 July, at last announced the formation of the new commissions, pre, sumably as a gesture of appeasement.[8] I suggest that the 1549 camp/men, only too aware of the commissioners' lack of any enforcement powers, set up the camps partly to provide exactly that muscle, as well as a force to influence their strategy. I have shown the Norfolk rebels initially following this plan in *Tombland*. It is also true that petitions from the camps were overwhelmingly made to the Protector, not the commissioners, but they had not been named yet. The petitions were not limited to grievances about enclosure. Nicholas Sotherton, our main contemporary source for Kett's Rebellion, considered that it was the very failure of the Protector to set a date for the commissioners to start work that caused the commons of East Anglia and Kent to decide to take matters into their own hands. I suggest however that setting up the camps was designed rather to force their coming, pre/emption not bypassing, and this ties in with the East Anglian rebels' emphasis on their loyalty to the King.[9]

However, as July continued there was no sign of their coming, except in Kent where they arrived at the large camp outside Canterbury on 17 July, after a royal Herald had been received rudely. Conciliatory letters, money and beer were distributed to encourage the rebels to disperse, rather than dealing with their grievances, although this failed and the camp remained in place until mid/August.[10] Elsewhere they disappeared from the picture as, from mid/July, the Protector, urged by the Council, moved to a strategy of confrontation.

EAST ANGLIA: BACKGROUND TO REVOLT

Norfolk and Suffolk had a long tradition of rebelliousness. Suffolk espe, cially had been central to popular rejection of Henry VIII's 'Amicable Grant' tax in 1525.[1] A decade later, during the Pilgrimage of Grace, copies of the Yorkshire rebels' petition were found in Norfolk, and some tried to begin an insurrection at Walsingham; Richard Southwell, who played an important part in suppressing the conspiracy, was one of those picked as a target three years later by John Walter, who was hanged for attempting to start another rebellion. Norfolk commoners were also notoriously litigious, well used to clubbing together to go to court where their lords were consistently presented as a network of mutually supportive gentlemen.[2]

Why was East Anglia so radical? Geographically, much of Norfolk and Suffolk had poor, 'light soil', where sheep dung provided the fertility needed to raise corn through the 'foldcourse' system, where landlords ran sheep on the fields in winter.[3] In the 1530s and 1540s, however, landowners were increasingly keen to get the tenants off their lands. As noted above, their principal tactic was to encroach on common lands, taking the oppor- tunity to abuse the foldcourse system, for example by running very large numbers of sheep on both tenants' fields and on the commons.

Politically, the fall of the Duke of Norfolk in 1546 had removed the figure at the apex of local government, a religious conservative and a harsh and unpopular landlord, who still had bondmen on some of his estates. Another central authority figure, William Rugge, Bishop of Norwich, equally conservative and unpopular, was by 1549 weak, his diocese in financial trouble (after the death of his predecessor, it appears a good deal of cathedral property was embezzled by Sir Richard Southwell as a Crown official). Under Rugge's rule ecclesiastical office-holders remained conservative.[4] So, very likely, did the priesthood.

Finally, to understand Kett's Rebellion one must look at the situation in the city of Norwich, England's second largest and with one of its big- gest markets, although the population may have been as little as 8,000. In the mid-sixteenth century it had serious problems, due largely to decline in the long-established worsted cloth trade, which had a knock-on effect on other city trades.[5]

The governing structure was similar to other English cities, with 'common' councillors and above them aldermen, drawn from a few wealthy commercial families, with a mayor at the apex. The gulf between rich and poor was enormous, with the richest concentrated in the central wards of the city; it was widening in the sixteenth century. According to the survey for the 1525 Amicable Grant, twenty-nine men owned more than forty per cent of the taxable wealth, and around a quarter of the population was too poor to be taxed at all. With the inflation of the 1540s more must have fallen into desperate poverty.

There were signs that trouble was feared in early 1549. In May

Norwich became the first English city to legislate for compulsory contri/ butions to poor relief.[6] At the June Assizes, which feature prominently in *Tombland*, the judges were welcomed not with the usual feast but only with beer.[7] Both imply a fear of popular disturbance. And the poor of Nor/ wich were to be vital participants in Kett's Rebellion.

WYMONDHAM

As Diarmaid MacCulloch has pointed out, much writing about Kett's Rebellion is based on one source – the short account, written just after the rebellion, by Nicholas Sotherton, member of a wealthy Norfolk mer/ chant family. It is short, and hostile to the rebels. Nonetheless it contains much useful information. This was supplemented in 1575 by Alexander Neville's *Norfolk Furies*.[1] Neville was secretary to Archbishop Matthew Parker, and as a younger man had visited the camp. It was written in Latin, in a classical rhetorical style, and was not merely hostile but splen/ etic. Although he was far from the only one to do so, Neville persistently refers to the rebels as 'boys', 'clowns', 'dogs' and similar epithets – ani/ malizing and infantilizing them. In 1582 the Elizabethan Privy Council ordered it to be used in all schools in the kingdom to teach Latin prose style. It was translated into English in 1615.[2] However, it too contains useful information. Other contemporary material on the rebellion is frag/ mentary, though useful work using other contemporary data has been done in recent years.

The rebellion began at the annual Game Play and Fair in Wymondham, the third largest town in Norfolk, held from 6 to 8 July 1549. There were festivities, pageantry and a play.[3] From the speed at which rebellion spread from here, it can only have been planned. Meanwhile, other static camps were set up outside King's Lynn and Downham Market, with two in Suffolk.[4] There was also a camp at Thetford in Norfolk.

On 8 July a group from Wymondham went to knock down the fences enclosing sheep runs of John Hobart of Morley, who had enclosed part of the village commons. Next, a group went to Hethersett, where part of Wymondham Common had been enclosed by John Flowerdew.[5]

Flowerdew embodied everything the commoners hated. A serjeant-at-law like Matthew Shardlake, he was a very senior lawyer who seems to have devoted himself to seeking profit in Norfolk: he had been Cromwell's agent in the dissolution of Wymondham's large abbey. As was common in monastic buildings, the parish church was an integral part of the abbey and, opposing Flowerdew, leading townspeople petitioned Henry VIII to be granted those parts of the buildings essential to maintain the church, together with other property. They succeeded. Flowerdew, however, had already pulled down the south aisle of the church and misappropriated lead and stone from the building, for which the parishioners had already paid.[6] Neither can have been worth that much to a wealthy man, and Flowerdew seems to have been a petty man who enjoyed conflict.

Some sources have named Flowerdew as feodary in 1548–9. However the Norfolk feodary throughout Edward's reign was the Lady Mary, and the escheator in 1549 was Henry Mynne. Nonetheless in such a large county it is likely that both delegated their duties, particularly to lawyers; Flowerdew gave evidence regarding Kett's properties at his inquest and in *Tombland* I have made him local agent of the escheator, while Southwell is agent for the Lady Mary (he was steward of her properties).

When the group arrived at Flowerdew's house, he paid them to redirect their attentions to his old enemy Robert Kett, who had himself recently enclosed a piece of common land. Robert Kett and his brother William had been among the leading townspeople who opposed Flowerdew over the fate of the abbey properties. The family had been minor men of property locally for centuries. In 1549 William was sixty-four and Robert fifty-seven – both elderly by Tudor standards, although, as the next two months were to show, Robert certainly still possessed extraordinary political skills, energy and charisma. William was a butcher and mercer owning considerable property, while Robert was a substantial farmer who also owned a tannery. After the Dissolution, like many others, he had purchased ex-abbey land that came on the market. His property at his death was valued at £750.[7] Economically this could have placed him on the lower end of gentleman status (though well below Flowerdew). However his personal identification seems to have been with the Wymondham townspeople – as well as being prominent in the town guilds, he was active in the society that organized the annual Game Play. He was thus a very experienced local politician and organizer. Educated by the monks, he had been a friend of Loye, the last abbot of Wymondham.[8]

Given this history, Robert Kett seems an unlikely candidate to lead a popular rebellion, let alone one with a strongly Commonwealth and Protestant flavour. A possible explanation is that he may have had a late, but profound, conversion to Protestantism. Henry King, vicar of Wymondham from 1539 to 1553, was a noted evangelical reformer and may have influenced Kett.[9] This is speculative, but I think the most plausible interpretation and the one I have chosen in *Tombland*.

When the group arrived at Kett's property, he not only agreed to his enclosures being pulled down, but assisted in their removal.[10] He then accompanied the party back to Wymondham. Next day, 9 July, the rebels began a march to Norwich, pulling down enclosures along the way, including those of Flowerdew who must have run away as he does in *Tombland*, as he was not heard of again until after the rebellion. Already Kett seems to have been accepted as leader, and he made a speech outside Hethersett where, according to Neville, he promised 'that they should have him, not only as a companion, but a Captaine: and in the doing so great a worke, not a fellow, but a leader, Author and principall . . .'[11] Thus Kett effectively took an oath to the rebels, rather than, as would have been usual for a leader, the other way round. Kett was undoubtedly leader of the Mousehold camp during its existence, but he was no dictator. Unfortunately, we have no direct descriptions of his manner and personality – I have had to invent these, as well as his appearance.

NORWICH TO MOUSEHOLD

Arrived outside Norwich, the rebels were joined by supporters from the city carrying little boughs as a sign of support,[1] and together they proceeded to pull down the newly enclosed Town Close. It is likely that by now the rebels had decided on their destination: Mousehold Heath, on the other side of Norwich, a barren area of grassland stretching six miles eastwards.[2] This followed the pattern of setting up camps outside towns. The heath rises steeply from the River Wensum, making an ideal defen- sive position. Mousehold also had a large wooded area, Thorpe Wood, to the south, giving access to a source of timber. The heath, however, suf- fered the disadvantage of being waterless, rain being quickly absorbed by the light soil.

Mayor Codd and the city council refused a request by the rebels to march through Norwich to Mousehold. Rather than attack the city walls they went the long way round, via Drayton Wood, going up to the heath from there, where it was more accessible. They arrived on 12 July. En route an attempt to get the rebels to disperse, accompanied by an offer of hospitality (a traditional way to check riots), was made by Sir Roger Wode- house, but it led only to him being stripped (this was to be a common humiliation, removing the fine clothing that represented gentleman status) and cast into a ditch, where he would have been killed but for the inter- vention of a servant.[3] This is the only account of serious violence against gentlemen, as opposed to humiliating them and taking them prisoner.

Who Were the Rebels?

According to Neville, 2,600 rebels were present at the foundation of the camp.[1] People now flocked there from all over north and central Norfolk. There are contradictory accounts of how many were there once the camp was fully established, varying from six to twenty thousand. During the seven weeks the camp existed numbers would have varied, probably increasing during July and decreasing in August when the camp, origin- ally part of a huge network, became isolated as other camps went down, and the threat of a very large army being sent against Mousehold grew. It is important to realize that the camp was a dynamic, not static, entity. In August, as the more fearful perhaps left, and the hard-core rebels from other camps that had been put down arrived, Mousehold probably became more radicalized as well as smaller.

The *Historical Atlas of Norfolk* suggests a county population of 112,000 in the 1520s, one of the densest in England.[2] Given national population rise since then, this could have taken Norfolk to around 136,000 by 1549.[3]

The camp was drawn from twenty-five of the thirty-three regional Norfolk Hundreds, plus one from Suffolk. Men from the other Hundreds may have gone to camps in south Norfolk. This would reduce the population pool for the camp to say 100,000. The adult male population would have been around 36,000 but would include the old and infirm, and those who needed to remain behind to look after farms and businesses. I suggest an average camp population of around eight to nine thousand.

To this of course must be added the number of supporters among the poor of Norwich, perhaps 4,000, who would likely have gone to and fro between camp and city once the rebels annexed Norwich, and who certainly participated in the three military actions.

Were there women in the camp? Large-scale rebellion would not have been considered women's business, though women were often involved in Tudor riots. However two pieces of evidence suggest some women were present. There is a reference in Neville to an adder falling from a rotten tree onto the breast of Kett's wife just before the Battle of Dussindale.[4] More significant is a hitherto unnoticed reference in F. W. Russell's nineteenth-century history of the rebellion, citing a document where, after the rebels' unsuccessful August attack on Great Yarmouth, city constables were ordered to find out the names of those who had joined the camp and also 'how many of the rebels wives are in the camp, and how many be at home'.[5] I suggest that a minority of wives followed their husbands into the camp – I have portrayed this in *Tombland*. The majority of rebel wives would, I think, have stayed behind to deal with children, businesses and farms.

As for the class and occupational structure of the rebels, two important studies, by Aubrey Greenwood and Jane Whittle, have contributed to our understanding, although both authors agree this is still limited since where rebels' names and occupations are traceable, they tend to be the most prominent members.[6] Of a sample of 121 leading rebels, three were yeomen, twenty husbandmen, thirty-three poorer peasants and no less than forty-two artisans – though this ranges from butchers, who were usually wealthy, to a shoemaker and a rat-catcher, probably poor village artisans partly dependent on the village commons.[7] Whittle has studied manorial records, which show the rebels as a cross-section of the tenant population, but as she points out, manorial documents do not record the very poorest.[8]

Whittle's study also looked at the ages of her cross-section: eleven per cent were over fifty, fifty-four per cent between forty and fifty, and thirty-five per cent between twenty-five and forty.[9] She concludes that while the impetus for the rebellion came from the poor, the richer farmers took over the leadership; although they, like Robert Kett, were potentially in conflict with the poor rebels, especially over their share of the commons. For the time at least they had common grievances over issues of gentry encroachment on common land – and the corrupt exactions of the escheator and feodary.[10]

The unrecorded majority of the rebels were likely to have been poorer and younger. Twenty to twenty-five per cent of the rural population of Norfolk were landless labourers.[11] Those most likely to come to the camp were, I think, those with little to lose; small-scale village artisans, cottagers, labourers and bond men as well as unemployed 'masterless men' like Simon and Natty in *Tombland*.

ADMINISTRATION OF THE CAMP

At the top of the escarpment facing Norwich, from which Mousehold Heath stretches away, stood the executed Earl of Surrey's vast Italianate mansion, Surrey Place, now empty except, probably, for caretakers. It may be symbolic that while the great mansion was used for storage and imprisoning some of the detained Norfolk gentlemen, Kett did not make his headquarters there but at the nearby, much smaller, St Michael's Chapel, a survival from the old St Leonard's Priory which was demolished to build Surrey Place.

Members of the gentleman class played no part in the government of the camp. As the rebels sent parties out into the countryside to requisition goods, more gentry prisoners were brought in. They were stripped, beaten, humiliated, subject to trials – but not killed. The rebels must have been well aware from the start of the revenge they would wish to wreak on their tenants if things went wrong. This made the enterprise an all-or-nothing venture from the start.

Robert Kett was undisputed leader of the camp, and a highly effective one who knew how to delegate. Two 'governors' from each of the thirty-three Norfolk 'Hundreds' were elected, although the franchise is not known. Like much else in the camp, the use of the Hundred subdivision mirrored official structures – two high constables had been chosen annually for each Hundred to report local offences to the court. We know the delegates' names, and several, like Kett, had been involved in previous disputes.[1]

This was an effective way of subdividing the huge camp, which I have portrayed as being laid out according to Hundreds. Many groups came in waving village banners, and I have had these kept flying, useful markers for people finding their way around a vast camp composed mostly of strangers.

Throughout the camp's history, as even Sotherton and Neville admit, good order was kept and there was a lack of violence. Organization was clearly effective. Public debates, religious services, trials of the gentlemen and offenders against order in the camp all took place at the camp's focal point, a gigantic, ancient oak tree which they named the Oak of Reformation (the name may have been intended to have a double meaning, reformation in religion and in society). They constructed a roofed wooden stage, the floor of which must have been raised at least six feet (otherwise, when Matthew Parker visited the camp and made an angry speech there, men would not have been able to stand underneath and prick his feet with spears).[2] It is likely that supplies brought in by foraging parties were surrendered to the common store here, and perhaps also distributed.[3] Speeches were made, and the leadership, according to Neville, used the Oak to criticize the more radical elements in the camp.[4] In the early days at least, opponents of the rebellion were given a voice too.

The trials held at the Oak involved gentleman prisoners being tried for offences committed against the poor. In *Tombland* I have portrayed these as following the procedures of a court of law, so far as rules of evidence are concerned, which I think was likely given rebel 'mirroring' of state institutions. There was no jury of twelve, however, guilt or innocence being decided by acclamation.[5] Despite calls from the crowd to kill some of the gentlemen, none are known to have been executed, though certainly there was some severe roughing up, notably of one particularly unpopular lawyer, Robert Wharton.[6] There was probably an element of letting off steam in the trials, but also the opportunity to gather detailed evidence against offending landlords and lawyers.

The immediate issue, for thousands camped on a waterless heath, was food and drink. The communities from which the rebels came supplied this, to begin with at least – it is important to remember this was the hungry season of the year, just before harvest. In an oft-quoted example, the North Elmham churchwardens sent fish, butter, bread and other food-stuffs to their people at Mousehold and also paid two people to brew for the rebels, another to be their cook and a third to be their spit-turner.[7] This implies that the camp established its own breweries and other infrastruc-ture early on.

Food from supporters outside was supplemented by requisitions from the gentlemen. There seems to have been an initial explosion of indul-gence – according to Sotherton the rebels took 3,000 cattle and 20,000 sheep, and deer from parks as well as 'swans, geese, and all other fowl', setting the price of mutton at a penny a quarter. Neville states that only the best cuts were eaten; heads and entrails were thrown away.[8] Rabbits and doves would likely have been taken too.

Raids on gentlemen's houses also brought in money and weapons. Horses, carts and fodder would also have been taken. Soon warrants to supply food were issued to the gentry, signed by Kett and the governors in the name of the King.[9] It is notable that weapons, including cannon, appear to have been sought from the beginning. Receipts were given, at least in some cases – yet another example of the Mousehold camp claim-ing loyalty to the King and following ostensibly legal procedures.

Another early example of remarkable organization – and a huge amount of work – was the building from scratch not merely of the scaf-folding around the Oak of Reformation, but an enormous number of makeshift huts to accommodate the population.[10] (I have imagined what these might be like in *Tombland*.) The wood came from Thorpe Wood. The skills of countless labourers as well as many carpenters would have been involved.

To create all this from scratch was a huge achievement. Meanwhile, though the Kett brothers and most governors were probably literate, if they were to follow legal forms they needed to prepare documents, and would have required a secretariat and people with legal knowledge. Certainly there were scriveners in the camp, but given the hostility to lawyers in general, the skills of sympathetic ones would have been at a premium. One lawyer, Thomas Godsalve, was captured early on and made to assist, but soon escaped. I have given my fictional lawyer Matthew Shardlake the role of an (at first reluctant) legal adviser in *Tombland*. There is no evidence that he had any real equivalent.

What was done by the common people on Mousehold, in a short time, was remarkable. I believe, however, that one important element is missing from most discussions of camp organization – the importance of military skills. 'Captain' is a military term, and it is interesting that Kett adopted it from the beginning. The title was also adopted by leaders of the requisitioning parties sent out into the countryside.[11] And only men with experience of war, from Scotland and from Henry VIII's French wars, could have had the experience of organizing and victualling such an enormous camp.

Only one actual soldier is mentioned by the contemporary chroniclers: Miles, Kett's 'master gunner',[12] appears to have been one of the nine principal rebel leaders executed at the Oak of Reformation the day after the rebel defeat.[13] The role of deserters from the Scottish war in organizing the national 'camping' strategy is mentioned above. If Miles was a master gunner, he had been a very senior officer, in charge of a group of cannon, each requiring a team of men to operate it – loading, priming, sighting and firing. If such matters were not handled very precisely, the cannon could explode. Given that cannon of differing calibres, and presumably many different types of shot, were brought to the camp it seems unlikely that Miles would have been able to train the several teams needed to operate them on his own. I suggest that he was assisted by other skilled deserters.

The rebels fought no fewer than three engagements during their seven weeks on Mousehold, against successively larger forces. During the 1540s, England's 'decade of war', villagers would have been involved in compulsory archery practice. They would also have been reviewed and sometimes sent for military service at the periodic musters. Nonetheless, to obtain the very high degree of skill that they were to demonstrate, the archers must have received constant training, and this would have been needed even more where 'pole weapons' – halberds, pikes and half-pikes, and agricul- tural implements adapted as weapons – were concerned.[14] Training would also need to be given in fighting in large formations. Only men with mili- tary experience could have provided this; Robert Kett had no such background. Seven weeks is an extremely short time to turn a relatively unskilled fighting force into what was, by Dussindale, an extremely effect- ive army. Experienced soldiers must, I think, have been there to train them.

There is another hint at military involvement. Given the rudimentary Tudor knowledge of hygiene, any large camp was likely to suffer from disease, especially dysentery, that great killer in Tudor army camps which often spread with terrifying rapidity, killing thousands. The Mousehold camp presented many features that would have encouraged the spread of disease – it was high summer, there was no ready source of water, and in the early stages at least the camp was probably full of rotting offal. Yet there is no evidence of any outbreaks of disease at Mousehold; one may be sure the hostile chroniclers would have mentioned it had there been. Military men would have had at least some experience and knowledge of the best ways to avoid disease spreading, especially in the construction of latrines and burial of food remains.

I would argue that a significant military presence was involved in the organization, preservation of hygiene and above all training in the Mouse- hold camp. Training would likely have been carried out by a parallel organization, subject to control by the civil administration. Otherwise, I find it difficult to see how the largely untrained men of Mousehold could have achieved the military successes that they did, and that is how I have reimagined the camp in *Tombland*.

RELATIONS WITH NORWICH

With the establishment of the camp, equal or possibly even larger in num- bers than Norwich itself and going from strength to strength, the city authorities had no alternative but to become involved. The mayor, Thomas Codd, a leading alderman, Thomas Aldrich, and the preacher

Robert Watson attended the camp and soon assumed administrative roles themselves, Codd and Aldrich even, we shall see, becoming signatories to the '29 Demands', the surviving petition from Mousehold. They spoke, and Watson preached, at the Oak of Reformation, Codd and Aldrich seeking to moderate rebel behaviour so far as they could.[1] This did not prevent them sending a leading citizen, Nicholas Sotherton's brother Leonard, to the government to make a full report on the situation.[2] The Norwich elite and the Mousehold men must both have been well aware that this was a temporary alliance of convenience; the rebels could prob/ ably have taken Norwich even at this early stage, but the walls, although not in good condition, were in most places over twenty feet high and with room on the battlements for archers to defend the city.[3]

The rebels seem however to have had free access to the city, and some gentleman prisoners were moved to Norwich.[4] It is clear the rebels were walking freely round the city in mid/July when Matthew Parker arrived.[5]

Meanwhile the radical Norwich preacher Robert Conyers was appointed to preach twice daily at the camp. No opposition was expressed to his evangelical Protestantism or to the religious settlement; as Green/ wood suggests, this probably meant that Norfolk people generally accepted the Reformation, without necessarily wanting it.[6] This was all of a piece with the Mousehold leaders' strategy of proclaiming that they were not rebels at all, merely carrying out the King's wishes with regard to agrarian reform, and with no complaints about the religious settlement. Kett, and others, may well have been evangelicals, but this can hardly have applied to the whole camp, even if they might have been hostile to trad/ itionalism given its association with the Duke of Norfolk.

FINANCING THE CAMP

To begin with, the camp supported itself through provisions brought by local villages and requisitions from the local gentry. Later, after occupying Norwich, they took more weapons, and the money of rich city gentlemen. However it must be doubted that these resources alone could support eight to nine thousand people for seven weeks. The rebels cannot have immediately eaten the 20,000 sheep quoted by Southwell; after an initial celebratory gorging, it is likely that the remaining sheep, together with cattle and other animals, would have been penned in for later slaughter. There was no shortage of room on Mousehold Heath. This is how I have portrayed matters in *Tombland*.

Diarmaid MacCulloch has noted two possible further sources of finance – Archbishop Rugge and Sir Richard Southwell. Although both were enemies to religious and political reform, each were actively involved in discussions with Kett.[1] The content of his talks with Rugge are unknown, but possibly the archbishop offered Kett money in return for leaving diocesan lands and property – and possibly himself – alone. Certainly Rugge was dismissed in disgrace after the rebellion.

Even more interesting is the conduct of Southwell who, as has been noted, was an alternate member of the Council, a leading and highly unpopular Norwich encloser, and a ruthless man. He had been a key figure in providing evidence against the Duke of Norfolk, his former patron, and the Earl of Surrey, in 1546. He was also, as noted above, steward of the Lady Mary's estates – a link that would continue after Mary became Queen.

In each of the rebellions outside the West Country, leading county figures were sent to negotiate with, or put down, rebellions. With the Duke of Norfolk gone, Southwell was the nearest Norfolk had to a senior political figure. After the Rebellion, he was accused of giving £500 (very roughly £250,000 today) to the rebels. This was far more than other camps received in attempts to buy them off. Of course the Mousehold camp did not disband, although they got the money. After the Rebellion Southwell ended up in the Tower and was then fined £500 for writing 'bills of sedition with his own hand'.[2] Such an action would normally have resulted in execution for treason, yet somehow Southwell, as always, survived.

I suggest in *Tombland* that he may have done a private deal with Kett to give him the money in return for leaving his own flocks, and the lands of the Lady Mary, alone. In the early days of the Rebellion some fences were pulled down around her Kenninghall estate, but she was then left in peace; remarkably, she sat quietly at Kenninghall, in the middle of rebel territory, throughout the summer. It would be interesting to research what happened to Southwell's estates during the Rebellion.

If, as I have argued, the rebels had money, where could they spend it? This leads to another vital question – did Norwich market, the heart of the city's economy, continue to function during the Rebellion? I think it must have done; without a venue to sell their products, Norwich traders and citizens would have found themselves in desperate straits. There was no reason for the rebels to close the market, and every reason to keep it open – they could use the money they had obtained to purchase necessities such as candles, shoes, warmer clothes when the weather got colder, and above all food and brewery supplies. The occupation of the city, to cut the rebels off from the market, may be the true explanation of the 'blockade' that forced the rebels to give battle in late August, of which more below.

REIMAGINING LIFE IN THE CAMP

Trying to understand what daily life in the camp might have been like is an exercise in imagination. However, I have tried throughout to base my portrayal on what few indications the sources give, and on the lives and pastimes of the Tudor commons.

Where one matter, which would have been of vital importance to those camping out, is concerned – the weather – we have clues from Sotherton and Neville. July seems to have been hot and sunny, facilitating the early construction work and camp organization. When Matthew Parker visited, he found the men drunk and exhausted due to the great heat.[1] When the Earl of Northampton's army arrived on 31 July, they had to rest in Norwich for the night due to heat exhaustion.[2] The fine weather was interrupted by at least two very violent thunderstorms. The first was probably during the first fortnight of the camp, because gentlemen were still being brought in from the countryside and one, newly captured, was dragged into the camp in the middle of the storm;[3] the second on 1 August, which was severe enough to douse the fires raging in Norwich after the defeat of the Marquess of Northampton.[4] The thunderstorm on 1 August seems to have heralded a change in the weather. Afterwards, Sotherton records the rebels taking shelter from rain in the city churches at night.[5] The picture, therefore, looks like a hot, dry July punctuated with severe thunderstorms, followed by a cooler, wetter August. This is the picture I have given in *Tombland*. The sandy soil of Mousehold Heath would have quickly soaked up rain, but intense thunderstorms would be disruptive, while in hot weather the lack of water would have been a risk to health and a serious discomfort.

I have pictured the camp as setting up its own breweries and bakeries, with barber-surgeons and country craftsmen. There must have been pens for livestock and also – essential in the forthcoming battles – horses, which would themselves have needed training in their new environment.

There were probably elements of fiesta, especially in the first days of the camp. It would be easy to reproduce the games and pastimes of the villages – storytelling, cockfighting, wrestling – and entertainers from Norwich may have come up to stage larger events – pageants, acrobats, bear-baiting, puppeteers and players. The 'camping game', a Tudor sport strong in East Anglia – a violent version of football with far more players and fewer rules – may have been played. The camp would no doubt have attracted peddlers with their trinkets and other easily transportable goods – and news of how the rebellions were going elsewhere.

Drunkenness was an issue that could have been more disruptive than it was. Again, if it had been a running problem Neville and Sotherton would have mentioned it. There was a great difference between Tudor 'small beer', with its low alcohol content and drunk by everybody, since to drink water was known to risk illness, and 'strong beer', far more potent. The beer most commonly brewed in the camp would likely have been 'small beer', with the camp authorities likely keeping the supply of strong beer to a minimum.

There is only one recorded incidence of drunken behaviour, when as noted above Matthew Parker came to preach, but decided against it because the men were drunk.[6] However he returned the next morning and gave an angry sermon against the camp. Although much has been made of this story, nothing serious happened to him – men went under the stage at the Oak and pricked his feet with spears; not seriously, or he would have been unable to walk away. The purpose was probably to make him dance. For all the indignation with which Neville related the story, it was a minor comic episode, fiesta not violence.

THE 'PROPHETS'

There were other, unofficial preachers at the camp – what Sotherton refers to as the 'prophets'. We know almost nothing about them. The term could refer to several different ideological types, all of which could have been present at the camp.

First there is the 'fantastical' prophecy, often claiming to be inspired by Merlin and other ancient writers real or imagined, frequently prophesying the overthrow of the State. They had featured prominently in the 1536 Pilgrimage of Grace, notably an adaptation of the ancient 'Mouldwarp' prophecy, which had also featured in the Peasants' Revolt and Cade's Rebellion, and was reworked in 1536 to foretell the fall of Henry VIII.[1] Sotherton spoke of 'faynid prophecies which were phantastically devised which prophecys they . . . often cawsid before to bee openly proclaimed in the (Norwich) market and other placis'.[2] Who knows what ancient prophecies were remoulded in 1549?

Second, very popular among radical Protestants in the 1540s was the 'biblical' prophecy – people selecting texts from the Bible and claiming God had revealed their true meaning to them. This was not limited to the unlearned. John Knox regarded himself as one selected by God to be a prophet.[3] In the atmosphere of the camp, any number of amateur Bible readers might have believed themselves chosen to be prophets.

Third was the great bogey of the 1540s ruling classes: the Anabaptists, a radical German Protestant group who believed all good should be held in common.[4] Although the Anabaptists later renounced violence and by the mid1540s their numbers in England were few, if any, their egalitarianism had made them greatly feared. However, as the leading historian of the Anabaptists in England notes, there is no indication of Anabaptists at Mousehold.[5] Two Anabaptists were burned for heresy under Edward VI, but for arcane theological, not social beliefs. It seems likely that by 1549 they had petered out as a socially radical movement, despite elite fears.

Finally there were the socially radical Commonwealth men. It has been noted above that they envisaged complaints being remedied by the King, not the people themselves. However their opposition to the 'greedy rich men' must have influenced the 'camps of Commonwealth' which at first expected the Protector to remedy their grievances, and when it became clear this was not going to happen some may have developed their complaints to justify rebellion.

These four strands of opinion probably mixed and melded in the camp. Sotherton has only identified the first; this emphasis may reflect his desire to portray the rebels as simpletons, but the 'fantastical' prophets were obviously very important. There were precedents from 1536 of them forecasting the fall of the realm. Two were among the nine leading rebels executed for treason at the Oak of Reformation immediately after the final battle.[6]

12–21 July: Days of Hope

While Leonard Sotherton was in London, messengers from Kett were also at the Protector's court. On 17 July Somerset said the delegation had arrived and he was hopeful that 'some of the light sort remaining tickle' about Norwich would soon be appeased.[1]

At the same time, the Mousehold rebels were preparing a petition to the King known as the '29 Demands'; although it is worded as a petition, each section was headed 'We pray . . .'[2] Petitions, to some of which Somerset replied, were also sent by the Thetford and Suffolk camps, though the original petitions have been lost.[3] The Mousehold petition seems to have been composed in a hurry, the items not being set out in any organized fashion.

The document has been interpreted in two ways. First, as representing a 'conservative rebellion' seeking a return to an idealized past of mutual obligation between landlord and tenant, without acquisitive enclosers.[4] Alternatively, it has been seen as demanding a permanent voice for the commons in running their communities.[5] Arguably the document is both, but with the innovative extremely radical and novel, some Articles calling for a say in local government for commoners.[6]

The document does not mention urban grievances, despite the rebels' links to the Norwich poor, with whom they had worked to remove the enclosures round the Town Close. This is not as surprising as it might seem. The alliance of convenience with the Norwich rulers would discourage including urban complaints, while, most important, the peti-tion was framed to appeal to the Protector, to whom loyalty was still claimed, and the grievances that he had promised to redress were rural. A second petition may have been planned, although it is unclear whether even the first reached Somerset.

The grievances are best discussed by subject area. Regarding enclos-ure, Article 29 wished to simply prohibit gentleman from farming livestock for profit. This is very radical indeed.

Articles 3 and 11 sought to end abuse by the manorial lord of his rights over common land, Article 3 stating flatly that 'no lord of no man shall, common upon the commons', although the rights of tenants and freeholders are protected. This was more than a return to the past. Other articles restricted the keeping of rabbits and doves.

The petition objected to manorial laws imposing feudal dues includ-ing wardship on their tenants, which connects with articles upbraiding local royal officers, particularly the feodary and escheator, for abusing their duties. The solution here was radical and innovative indeed, asking for commissioners – *chosen by the Commons* and approved by the King – to 'redress and reform' laws and statutes concealed from the commons by royal officials (and, no doubt, lawyers employed to work with the land-lords). This implies commissions, possibly permanent and certainly including commoners. Such commoners were to be paid fourpence a day (a labourer's wage) while sitting.

Articles 6 and 14 deal with the abuse of manorial rents and rights. Famously, Article 16 prayed that 'all bond men may be made free for God made all free with his precious blood shedding'. This may have been thought likely to appeal to Somerset, who had freed serfs on his own estates.

Parish priests were heavily criticized for their ignorance, absenteeism, involvement in land purchase, and failure to preach. Such priests should be 'put from their benefices and the parishioners there to choose another or else the patron or lord of the town'. Here was another request for involvement of the commons in rural institutions.

The petition, then, wished to keep the manorial system intact, and end the 'seigneurial offensive' against common land. However in the provi-sions dealing with the abuses of royal officials and members of the clergy,

it looked to a substantial step forwards in popular representation and participation in rural institutions.

An interesting trio of articles has examined Somerset's dealings with the
rebels through surviving letters to them.[7] Ethan Shagan has argued that
letters between Somerset and the rebels showed a dialogue in which Somerset made some substantial concessions. M. W. Bush and G. W. Bernard,
however, more plausibly argue that Somerset was being disingenuous,
and while he probably had some sympathy with some rebel demands – as
we have seen, he had accepted the 'agrarian' explanation for inflation and
believed in reform – he was as ferociously opposed to commoner assertive-
ness as Henry VIII would have been. He made it plain in his letters, at
length and in fierce language, that commoners had no right to set up
camps and make demands – that it was a defiance of the true order of
society – but that if they dispersed they would receive pardons, while their
grievances would be dealt with by the commissioners or Parliament. In
some ways this recalled Henry VIII's initial conciliatory response to the
Pilgrimage of Grace, but as with Henry the threat of force always lay
behind the promises, and sometime around mid-July the policy of
appeasement changed to one of destroying the camps by military force
unless they agreed to disperse.

I do not think Somerset ever intended that commoners should have a
say in running things. Though he made occasional concessions to the
camp-men – such as agreeing to reform of the fee-farm of tolls on his own
land at Thetford – these were very minor. There has been argument over
whether another letter to the Thetford rebels actually acceded to the commons' desire for a role in appointing commissioners, but the letter is so
garbled that it is impossible to gather its meaning.[8] Somerset, by then,
must have been under tremendous strain. Shagan's argument – that the
camps and Somerset were engaged in a dialogue, a mutual feedback
system – flies in the face of the facts. What was happening was the reverse
of a dialogue; it was a deception, an attempt by Somerset to buy time, and
around 17 July (interestingly, the date the commissioners arrived in Kent
but failed to get the Canterbury camp to disperse) he turned from appeasement to confrontation. False hopes had been created – in these
circumstances it was not unreasonable for Robert Kett to hope for a

sympathetic response, so that when the royal Herald arrived at Mousehold Heath on 21 July, the confrontational nature of his message can only have caused shock and anger, as I have portrayed in *Tombland*.

The coming of a royal Herald had been preceded by the delivery of a letter to Kett the day before. If, as is possible, this was Letter No. 2 appended to Shagan's 1999 article quoted above,[9] it consisted of a particu-larly fierce diatribe, stating that it would allow the rebels to petition the coming Parliament with their grievances provided they dispersed. Other-wise it offered nothing new.

The Herald's visit to the camp was a moment of high drama. He rode up to Mousehold from Norwich, accompanied by Codd and Aldrich and the city sword-bearer, Pettibone; he allowed himself to be led to the Oak of Reformation, and there delivered to the massed camp-men a proc-lamation that roundly abused them as traitors and, particularly, 'Kett, man of mischief'. It offered a pardon to those who dispersed – and noth-ing else. Kett responded angrily that 'hee had not offendid or deserved the Kings pardon and soe requird as many as would . . . to take his part and remain'.[10] Neville reports Kett asking the company 'not to leave him, nor to be fainthearted, but remember with what conditions they bound them-selves, either to other, and that he for his part was ready to bestow his life (if need were) for their safetie'.[11] The Herald then accused Kett of high treason, and ordered Pettibone to arrest him, but the threatening demean-our of the camp-man forced the Herald's party to flee. A minority (we do not know how many) did accept the pardon and left the camp, but the great majority remained.[12]

Back in Norwich, the Herald ordered Codd and Aldrich to shut the gates against the rebels 'and keepe them from victual'.[13] This emphasizes the importance, mentioned above, of Norwich market in feeding the rebels.

ARMED CONFLICTS: 21 JULY TO 1 AUGUST

The Herald's order to close off Norwich, almost certainly a fallback pos-ition ordered by Somerset, was extremely foolish, for it left the camp-men with no alternative but to invade and breach the weak city walls. The Herald remained in the city, proclaiming his message there, perhaps hoping for the townspeople's support, but once again he was gravely mis-taken; Sotherton reports that 'soon after they perceived that through ye falsehood of many of their citizens the said rebels were entried [entered].'[1]

Next morning, 22 July, the camp-men launched a full-scale invasion, having first attempted and failed to negotiate a peaceful entry.[2] Half a dozen cannon from the castle had been brought within range of the rebels, but neither the city's gunners nor the rebels with their own guns showed (at this stage) any skill in aiming, although the city bowmen on the walls (probably servants of leading citizens, constables, and soldiers from Nor-wich Castle) caused many casualties. There were two huge charges down the hill towards Bishopsgate Bridge, the crucial strategic point: the first failed but the second succeeded by force of numbers. According to Sotherton, 'vagabond boys . . . came among the thickett of the arrows and gathered them up when some of the seid arrows stuck fast in their leggs'.[3] 'Boys' in Tudor usage meant young unmarried men; the story of pulling out the arrows is plausible if, as is likely, practice arrows without barbed heads were used. The charges displayed the fierce courage that the rebels were to display from now on. They were helped by supporters in the city calling out that the enemy were within the walls, to distract city forces from Bishopsgate Bridge.[4]

The whole of Norwich was now annexed to the rebel camp; its six cannon were taken up to Mousehold. Codd, Aldrich and other leading citizens were taken prisoner, except for one leading Alderman, Augustine Steward, whom Kett appointed his deputy in the city to keep order (though no doubt aware of the limits of his loyalty.) After an initial few days of looting, the city, like the camp, was kept in remarkably good order; the defenders on the walls were now from the camp. The Herald fled back to London. Trials at the Oak continued, now including senior citizens of Norwich, where according to Neville 'if they [the camp-men] found nothing of the man in question, cryed out, A good man, hee is a good man; and therefore ought to be set at liberty. But . . . if . . . hee had offended any one of them . . . The common sort followed, as it were stirred up of the furies, "let him be hanged."'[5] Given that no gentleman was ever named as hanged at the camp, either Neville was romancing or, more likely, the camp leaders refused to allow it to happen.

The number of Mousehold men who perished in the fierce assault is not known, but is unlikely to be less than a hundred. Now a new reality must have entered camp life – sudden death, grief for fallen comrades, family or friends. But they remained determined not to budge.

It is not known how much territory Kett controlled from Mousehold; Land suggests fifteen to twenty miles.[6] Attempts were made to expand into north and central Norfolk in July. Late in the month a camp was formed near King's Lynn, probably aimed at its capture. However the local gentry – who, having recovered from their initial shock, were now becoming organized – managed to dislodge the insurgents, who withdrew twenty-five miles south to Watton, on the road from London, possibly to try and impede the army that was now expected to come from there. Early in August they abandoned the site and joined the Mousehold camp.

A separate camp was formed at Hingham, fifteen miles from Norwich, again perhaps to protect the road to London; however they were attacked and dispersed by a local force under Sir Edmund Knyvett.

Meanwhile a small group from Suffolk marched against Great Yarmouth, but the townspeople refused to admit the rebels. Thus all attempts to spread the camp's area of control, including what would have been the significant prizes of Norfolk's two major ports, failed. And news soon reached the camp of the preparation of an army in London.

What were the rebels to do now? Kett's original strategy (not unreasonable given Somerset's promises of reform) had failed. The camp had two choices: fight or surrender. If they fought and won, they might win concessions from Somerset and even spread rebellion further. London was quiet, but martial law had been declared and rebellion there was feared.[7] If they surrendered, many must have feared, given what they had done to the gentry, that they would be massacred. And as we shall see, there were many who believed the forces coming against them had not been sent by Somerset at all, but by local gentry and their sympathizers on the Council. Among many, the failure to realize what sort of man Somerset actually was persisted to the end.

Command of the army sent from London was given to William Parr, Marquess of Northampton, who had risen solely because he was Queen Catherine Parr's brother. He was a courtier, not a soldier. The same is true of his deputy, Edmund, Baron Sheffield. Sheffield seems to have been a young gentleman thug – he and three relatives once attacked his brother⁄in⁄law's mistress, disfiguring her to break up their relationship.[8]

The army probably consisted of a mixture of professional soldiers and men conscripted from other areas.[9] Local gentry who had fled returned, together with some high government officials, and formed the junior leadership. Interestingly Sir Richard Southwell, who can only have returned to London recently from Norwich, was also there. The army not only lacked serious professional commanders, but was far smaller than the camp – around 1,500, and including a number of Italian mercenaries.[10] Most government forces were engaged in Scotland and against the West⁄ern and Oxfordshire rebellions, and Somerset perhaps thought that as 1,500 men had put down the Oxfordshire rebels, the same number might suffice for Norwich.

On 31 July, having possibly put down the camp at Thetford along the way, Northampton arrived outside Norwich. Another Herald was sent to call for the city's surrender: Augustine Steward smartly passed the buck to Mayor Codd, under guard at Surrey Place, who agreed to allow Northampton's forces in. As he was a prisoner this must have been with Kett's authority. Northampton's forces entered without resistance, South⁄well bearing the city sword before him, and settled down for the night.[11] They had walked into a trap.

Before nightfall, a small group of Italian mercenaries scouting outside the Norwich walls encountered a group of rebels. One was captured (the episode is reimagined in *Tombland*), and he was hanged from the walls of Surrey Place.[12] The mood on Mousehold was becoming fierce, hardly surprising given the prospect of a savage battle the next day. Northamp⁄ton's armies settled down for the night, the majority of them in the Market Square which was lit by a huge bonfire, while others patrolled the city and attempted to strengthen the walls. The patrols, in the narrow, hilly streets in pitch darkness, faced a formidable task. Now the trap was sprung; rebels opened fire with their cannon against the city's eastern defences, fol⁄lowing this up with a mass night assault through the streets. However, despite fierce street fighting, the rebels failed to dislodge the soldiers and were forced to retreat.

Next morning Northampton made another offer of pardon. It was reported that a crowd was gathered outside Pockthorpe Gate to the north, but when the Herald arrived there his offer of pardon was rejected, the argument being repeated that the rebels were loyal subjects in no need of pardon.

This was a feint; just then the rebels had entered the city across Bishop-sgate Bridge. To avoid being trapped in Holme Street, with the fifteen-foot-high walls of the Cathedral Close on one side and the walls of the Great Hospital on the other, the rebels brought down the Great Hospital walls.[13] This would have needed artillery, fired this time with some skill. The rebels were thus enabled to reach the broad square of Palace Plain. Here Northampton's forces were soundly beaten, Lord Sheffield killed, and the remains of Northampton's army fled, together with many richer inhabitants of the city, some in their lightest garments to disguise their status. Sotherton reported that a large part of the city around Bishop-sgate Bridge was set alight, but the violent thunderstorm late on 1 August doused the fires. Northampton and his army retired to Cambridge.

The government army had been too small and poorly commanded, while the Italian mercenaries proved disappointing. The rebels had shown considerable skill as well as courage. Sotherton puts the rebel death toll at about 400. This might be as many as one in twenty of the camp-men, and again must have brought much grief to the camp.

Growing Isolation: 1–24 August

The defeat of Northampton's army was the high-water mark of the rebellion. Throughout August, in sometimes rainy weather, the rebels retained firm control of Norwich, but neighbouring camps were going down, and a second, major attack from Mousehold on Yarmouth failed on 17 August, a counter-attack capturing six cannon and thirty rebels. Meanwhile news of the preparation of another army from London, far larger and better commanded, would have reached the camp. The Mousehold men must have felt increasingly isolated.

Norwich was now thoroughly occupied, with Augustine Steward back in formal charge, but men from the camp holding all important positions.[1] The cathedral was occupied. Again, there were several days of looting; rebels calling out 'a Cod's head for a penny' to frighten the richer citizenry, while houses were broken into and looted, sometimes under the pretext of search being made for Northampton. Augustine Steward's own house was broken into; however, the men were ordered off by a rebel in authority, indicating that Kett soon re-established control over his men in the city; indeed Steward was authorized to send sometimes unsympathetic preachers to the camp – although the richer citizens of Norwich must have remained in a state of considerable fear.

On the 11 August a proclamation declared forfeit all the property of the Western rebels, who were decisively defeated at Sampford Courtenay on the 16th – savage reprisals against the population followed. Pardons and money were carried to the three camps in Essex, and two in Kent. Six leaders of the Essex camps were later executed.[2] The majority of the smaller camps were going down.

The Coming of Warwick's Army

Around 20 August the Earl of Warwick's army set out from London. Again, numbers vary according to the sources, but 10,000 men is a reasonable figure. The army consisted of local levies but also professional soldiers, including Captain Drury, who had experience of the Scottish wars, and some 1,500 landsknechts. These Swiss or German mercenaries were among the most feared troops in Europe, and were the strongest and most experienced of soldiers, employing heavy horses, long pikes and arquebuses, which in close formation could deliver deadly volleys.[1]

The original plan had been for Somerset himself to command the army, but he changed his mind and placed John Dudley, Earl of Warwick, in command. Dudley was the second man on the Council, an experienced and highly successful soldier both on land and sea, a very different prospect from Northampton. It may be that Somerset changed command since leading the force against the rebels himself could finally have destroyed his reputation as a 'friend of the poor', but if so, it was another mistake, because Dudley's victory greatly enhanced his own reputation. The army set out on 20 August, linked up with the remnants of Northampton's army at Cambridge, then moved on to Norfolk and by the 23rd had reached Wymondham.On Mousehold the mood must have been a mixture of fear, anger and above all determination. Given the skill the rebels were to show against a serious professional army, good use must have been made of the month of August for intensive training. This would only stiffen the resolve of those about to fight.

But what of those unable to do so – those wounded from earlier battles, the unfit, the elderly and women? In *Tombland* I have imagined these groups as being sent away before Dudley arrived. This is reinforced by the fact that the rebels planned to burn the camp beforehand if they had to give battle.

How hopeful were those who remained? There had been every chance of defeating Northampton's small, weak army, but Warwick was a very different prospect. Determination to do or die must have been mixed with doubt, especially among the betteroff yeomen, who had most to lose. It is quite possible that August saw a shift in power in the camp towards the younger, more radical element, with the least to lose. Kett retained his leadership throughout but, as we shall see, there are signs that perhaps by the very end he was no longer fully trusted.

There must, inevitably, have been deserters who preferred to go home rather than face death – this too may have shifted the balance of power in the camp. It would be easy for them to get out, as the wide frontiers of Mousehold Heath were impossible to police effectively.

What would the rebels do if they won? It is interesting that, when it later became clear that they would have to give battle outside Norwich, they brought down the walls of the northern part of the city.[2] This denied the walls as a position from which government forces could attack them. In *Tombland* I have speculated that they may have further intended, had they won the final battle, to sweep on into north Norwich, where they had support among the citizens, then perhaps afterwards to try to reinstate the camps of the SouthEast, possibly even march on London to face the Protector himself. This seems the most likely plan that the optimists might have envisaged.

As Warwick approached the city, the rebels shored up the walls.[3] This does not mean that they did not envisage more street fighting in Nor- wich – they did, and were to be extremely effective – but it presented an extra barrier for Warwick's forces. If he broke in and fighting inside Norwich failed, the fallback was to give battle in open country, where the rebels had the advantage of being able to choose the site, which must have been well prepared.

There has been discussion in recent years over where the battle site might be, focused on the discovery by the archaeologist Anne Carter of a site named 'Dussing's Deale', three miles east of Norwich, in eighteenth- century records, which she argued presented suitable terrain.[4] Previously most writers followed Sotherton, who states that the site of the battle was at 'Dussens Dale' which was 'not past a myle of[f]'.[5] Since Warwick left from Coslany Gate in the north of the city, however, the destination was surely likely to be to the north – if he had intended to follow a rebel march to the east he would have left from one of the southern gates. Such a long march would have been hard for him, but equally so for the rebels. I think Leo Jary's argument that the battle site was directly north of Norwich, and a mile from Kett's headquarters at St Michael's Chapel, is correct. It accords with the sources and makes military sense. He also points out that the name Dussin is not uncommon in Norfolk.[6] Meanwhile the idea, ori- ginating with Sotherton, that the rebels were influenced in their choice of battle site by a prophecy can be dismissed: everything we know about the rebels in battle indicates their decisions were based on careful planning.

> *The country gnoffes, Hobb, Dick, and Hick,*
> *with clubs and clouted shoon,*
> *Shall fill up Dussyn dale*
> *with slaughtered bodies soone.*[7]

The Final Battles: 24–27 August

On 24 August Warwick, camped three miles from Norwich where he was awaiting the arrival of the mercenaries, once more sent a Herald to Norwich. Augustine Steward suggested that another offer of pardon be made to the rebels. Warwick agreed to this, and sent the Herald back to try and negotiate it.[1] Steward must surely have acted on Kett's instruc/ tions. Kett sent some forty horsed rebels, who returned to the camp with the Herald, a trumpeter and two aldermen (and, from what transpired, clearly some soldiers as well). When the Herald arrived outside Bishop/ sgate Bridge the sound of the trumpet fetched a large number of rebels. Kett himself was not present at first.

The Herald addressed the group. Many removed their caps and cried 'God save King Edward' (the camp's loyalty to Edward had never been in question). He was then joined by Kett with a further body of men. The Herald announced that the King had sent down the Earl of War/ wick with power to suppress the rebels, but 'if they would . . . humbly submit themselves to ye Kings mercy hee woulde graunt to them his Highness pardon for life and goods Kett only excepted'. If they refused, Warwick would not depart until he had 'vanquishd them with the sword'.

Sotherton records that although many trembled, others said that they might seem fair words but that afterwards they would be hanged, others again that the Herald was not sent by the King at all but was an agent of the gentleman 'putting on him a piece of an old cope for his cote armour'. Clearly, the camp was in no mood to surrender. However, Kett was allowed to lead the Herald to another part of the camp to repeat his message.

Then a tragedy occurred. A boy in the crowd bared his backside at the Herald; as shown in *Tombland*, this was a standard Tudor insult, but one of the men with the Herald immediately shot the boy dead with a currier (a small arquebus). He must have been a soldier, with a fire already lit. I have made Simon Scambler the victim of this real event in *Tombland*. We have no idea who the boy actually was.

This was the end of any slim prospect of negotiation. Rebels rode through the wood calling out 'our men are kylled by the water syde'. The Herald rode back towards Norwich. Kett accompanied him, apparently intending to return with him to Warwick, but he was followed and sur/ rounded by a rebel company saying 'whither away, whither away, Master Kett; if you goe, we will goe with you, and with you will live and dye'. This sounds like suspicion on the part of the camp/men that Kett had decided to try and carry negotiation further despite the will of the camp. The Herald told him to stay with his men, and rode away.

Warwick now brought his army up to the gates and, having been apprised by Augustine Steward that entry could easily be gained through one gate, the 'Brazen Gate', quickly broke through, while Steward ordered the neighbouring Westwick Gate to be opened.

This (hardly unexpected) about-face by Steward allowed Warwick to make a surprise entry into the city. He and his troops reached the market square where some fifty rebels were captured and later hanged. At about three in the afternoon of this eventful day, the baggage carts and artillery entered the city.

The rebels gathered in Tombland and divided into companies to begin street fighting. The government forces' lack of knowledge of the streets had already caused their artillery train to lose its way, and in Tomb-land it was subject to a rebel assault. Most of the artillery was captured and taken to Mousehold, and later used by the rebels. By now there was fierce fighting in the streets; in one encounter near St Andrew's Hall rebel bowmen gave a good account of themselves, but were surprised by Captain Drury with a band of handgunners and set to flight. Elsewhere, the rebels shot down the tower off Bishopsgate Bridge, but after a further skirmish Captain Drury won back the position. At the end of the afternoon they had been driven from the city, retreating to Mousehold. To the south of the city large areas were set on fire.

Next day, the 25th, Kett's forces attacked again and at one point gained control of both the north and south of the city, although fierce fighting forced them again to withdraw. At this point Warwick planned to blow up the bridges connecting the north to the rest of the city, and the city authorities, seeing no end to the destruction, begged him to leave. If he had, this would probably have given victory to the rebels, certainly bringing Norwich back under their control. However, he refused, demanded the authorities' loyalty, and compromised by blowing up only one bridge. He also set up a system of billeting troops on householders.

On the 26th the landsknechts arrived. There was no fighting that day; the rebels realized that having lost Norwich and, critically, access to supplies at the market, they would soon run out of necessities. Somerset confirms this was his strategy in a letter to Philip Hoby, ambassador to the Holy Roman Emperor.[2]

On Mousehold Heath, therefore, the rebels decided to give battle at their chosen site of Magdalen Hill, on the lower slopes of the heath, not far from the city's northern walls – marching over mainly even ground to a spur of the heath that gave them the advantage of high ground, with the sun behind them and in the eyes of Dudley's forces.[3] Probably as a symbol to friend and foe that there was no turning back, on the night of the 26–27 August they burned the camp. They had erected a defensive line of stakes facing the direction government forces would take, built protective earth-works to prevent a flanking movement from the west, and had erected a gun-flat for their twenty cannon,[4] which now outnumbered Warwick's. Behind the stakes, facing the front rank of the army, the gentleman prison-ers were chained together as a human shield.[5] Early in the morning of 27 August, the landsknechts having arrived, Warwick's army marched out of Coslany Gate and turned right to face the rebels.

There is dispute about the numbers involved in the battle; certainly Warwick kept his English footmen in Norwich, going into battle with the horsed English forces and landsknechts.[6] I therefore suggest a figure of some 5,000 men, mostly professional soldiers, well horsed, armed and armoured, some with handguns, facing perhaps 6,000 rebels, less well armed, less well armoured and with fewer of the vital junior officers, but with a crucial advantage in artillery, and on the high ground.

With troops drawn up, a final offer of pardon was made (perhaps because of the looming fate of the gentlemen) but instantly rejected. Battle was joined, first blood going to the rebels when Gunner Captain Miles shot and killed Warwick's standard-bearer. The chained gentlemen man-aged somehow to escape and run away.[7]

It is important to stress that Dussindale seems to have been a narrow victory. It lasted from early morning until around four in the afternoon.[8] Rebel prowess was admired by Warwick's son, who later wrote, 'the battle was so manfully fought on both sides, it could hardly be judged which side was likely to prevail.' It involved savage, close-quarter fighting, until the rebel lines were finally broken and large numbers fled, being pursued and cut down by Warwick's troops. Kett himself fled the field. However, a large body of rebels, seeing the others cut down, continued fighting for some time behind makeshift defences until Warwick himself came and granted a pardon.[9]

Neville estimated there were 3,500 dead at Dussindale; Edward VI's Journal gives 2,000. Vengeance on the rebel leadership was swift and harsh. The following day trials under martial law were held, and nine leading rebels were immediately hanged, drawn and quartered for treason at the Oak of Reformation. Many others were hanged. Heads were set on poles around Norwich, as I described in *Tombland*.[1] Meanwhile the earl ordered the bodies of the slain to be buried. The bodies were stripped, in accordance with the practice of the time, and the rebels' property was afterwards sold in Norwich Market.[2] This implies that somewhere under the battlefield, now part of suburban Norwich, there may lie mass graves containing the bodies of those slain at Dussindale. At a guess, these would have been buried six feet down, deeper than the twentieth-century foundations of the modern houses. There may be nothing left but bone; it would be interesting to know if advances in forensic archaeology may allow these to be traced.

Robert Kett, meanwhile, was captured some miles away; his brother William was also taken. For the time being they were held in the Guild-hall prison. The rulers of Norwich celebrated victory with a church service and possibly a masque on the 28th (an annual church service at St Peter Mancroft church was to continue until 1667). Dudley's emblem of the bear and ragged staff was set over the city gates.

Many of the now freed gentlemen demanded, as the rebels had feared, a ferocious revenge on the survivors. Warwick admonished them severely: 'He knew their [the rebels'] wickednesse to be such as deserved to be grievously punished, and with the severest judgement that might be. But how far will they goe? Will they ever shew themselves discontented, and never pleased? Would they have no place for humble petition; none for pardon and mercy? Would they be Plowmen themselves, and Harrow their own lands?'[3]

This actually seems to have settled things; afterwards the surviving

Mousehold men returned home, and for the most part landlords seem to have been content to return to the status quo ante, although no doubt unrecorded acts of private vengeance were taken.[4] Somerset remained in Norwich until 7 September, dealing with claims for compensation, hearing accusations, and dealing with convicted prisoners.[5] Robert and William Kett were taken to London and tried for treason; afterwards Robert was hanged in chains from Norwich Castle, and William from the steeple of Wymondham church.

This was the end of the rebellion, but not of its consequences. Within weeks, Warwick led an effort to overthrow the Duke of Somerset. Somerset took the King to Windsor and called on the common people to support him. Amazingly, after the destruction of the rebellions, several thousand still answered his call. However, with the return of the leaders of the Western army, he had no chance. He surrendered the King to the Council in October and was put in the Tower. He was later released and returned to the Council until a somewhat murky plot resulted in his execution in 1552. His achievements may be summarized as galloping inflation, 11,000 rebel dead in England, 15,000 Scottish soldiers at Pinkie and an unknown number of English and Scottish soldiers, and Scottish civilians killed thereafter, during his failed war. Nothing else.

The Protectorate was abolished and authority returned to the Council, although Warwick was now the acknowledged leader of England. If the fall of Somerset was one unintended consequence of the summer rebellions, the second was a rapidly negotiated end to the wars with Scotland and France. Thomas Smith's opinion that inflation must be cured by reversing the debasement was accepted, and in 1551–2 the Council began reforming the coinage.

Warwick in power showed himself to be very much the classic, competent Tudor hard man.[6] There were further, smaller rebellions in the winter of 1549–50, and considerable anxiety about another large-scale popular rebellion. The definition of riot was tightened, making it treasonous for forty or more people to break down enclosures, and a felony for twelve or more to destroy parks, or seek to lower rents and prices. In December, interestingly, an Act against 'fond and fantastical prophecies' was passed by Parliament.[7] Government control in the localities was strengthened, particularly by the introduction of county Lord Lieutenants to supervise the suppression of unrest. Warwick's regime did pass some legislation to ameliorate poverty, but this was very limited: allowing settle, ment on waste land to alleviate the lot of the poor peasant, and also to galvanize local authorities into introducing poor laws.

Many in Norfolk remembered the rebellion with longing, and, like Ralph Claxton in the epigraph to *Tombland*, were prosecuted for saying so. John Oldman was prosecuted in 1550 for stating 'he wished that he was still in the rebel camp on Mousehold, eating stolen mutton'.[8] John Red, head quoted two men as looking towards Kett's body hanging from the top of Norfolk Castle, one saying, 'Oh Kette God have mercye uppon thy soule and . . . trust in God but the kings Majestye and his Connsaill shell . . . Of their own gentylnes thou shalbe taken downe and by the grace of God and buryed and not hanged uppe for wynter stoore.'[9]

There were, however, to be no more large-scale popular rebellions, and the power of the Tudor State against the poor was strengthened. Andy Wood has argued that 1549 was decisive in shifting the loyalties of the yeoman class towards aspiration and gentleman status, valuing literacy for their children and becoming stalwarts of the Elizabethan State.[10] Meanwhile, the poor got poorer.

And yet. Almost a century later, in 1644, during the English Civil Wars, the New Model Army arose from the Eastern Association, made up of men from the South-East, especially East Anglia. The New Model Army would later produce radical movements such as the Levellers. It is perhaps not too fanciful to imagine that some of the soldiers of the Eastern Association, great-grandchildren of the 1549 rebels, brought with them memories of a past attempt to create a more equal society.

ENDNOTES

Introduction

1. The full story is told in Holbrooke, R., 'A Mousehold Abduction, 1548', in Rawcliffe, C., Virgoe, R. and Wilson, R. (eds), *Counties and Communities: Essays on East Anglian History* (1996), pp. 115–28.
2. Jordan, W. K., *Edward VI: The Young King* (1968), p. 493.

The Background: Class and Status
1. Hayward, M., *Rich Apparel: Clothing and the Law in Henry VIII's England* (2009), chapter 2.
2. Elyot, T., *The Book Named the Governor* (1531), quoted in Wood, A., *Riot, Rebellion and Popular Politics in Early Modern England* (2002), p. 26.
3. Hayward, p. 42, quoting Elton, G. R., *Tudor Constitution* (1960), p. 15.
4. Hayward, p. 43, quoting Hale, J., *The Civilization of Europe in the Renaissance* (1993), p. 465.
5. *De Republica Anglorum*, quoted in Wood (2002), pp. 29–30.
6. Wood, A., *The 1549 Rebellions and the Making of Early Modern England* (2007), p. 14.
7. For an interesting discussion of the virtues and limitations of Marx's analysis, see Wood (2007), pp. 14–16.
8. Whittle, J., *The Development of Agrarian Capitalism: Land and Labour in Norfolk, 1440–1580* (2000), pp. 97–8.
9. Wood (2007), p. 181.
10. Fletcher, A. and MacCulloch, D., *Tudor Rebellions* (2004), pp. 22–4.
11. Ibid., chapter 4 and Wood (2002), pp. 49–54.
12. See particularly Shagan, E., *Popular Politics and the English Reformation* (2003).

The Rule of Protector Somerset: Inflation and War, Religious and Social Reform
1. There is an interesting discussion of the circumstances of Somerset's rise to power in Skidmore, C., *Edward VI: The Last King of England* (2007), chapters 1–3.
2. Jordan, W. K., *Edward VI: The Young King* (1968) expresses the first view; Bush, M. L., *The Government Policy of Protector Somerset* (1975) the second.
3. See e.g. Jordan, p. 39, Skidmore, pp. 239–40.
4. Merriman, M., *The Rough Wooings: Mary Queen of Scots 1542–1551* (2000), pp. 218–19.

The Great Inflation
1. Chalis, C., *The Tudor Coinage* (1978), pp. 68–95.
2. Wood (2007), p. 30.

3. Youings, J., *Sixteenth-Century England* (1984), p. 135.
4. See discussion in Bush, pp. 41–2.

The Scottish War

1. This account is based on Merriman, chapter 10.
2. Ibid., p. 342.
3. Hodgkins, A., 'Reconstructing Rebellion: Digital Terrain Analysis of the Battle of Dussindale (1549)', *Internet Archaeology* 38 (2015), p. 20.
4. Phillips, G., 'To Cry "Home! Home!": Neutrality, Morale and Indiscipline in Tudor Armies', *Journal of Military History* 65 (April 2001), p. 320.
5. Fletcher and MacCulloch, chapter 13.

Religious Change

1. Jordan, chapters 4–5.
2. Fletcher and MacCulloch, p. 240, fn. 9.
3. Jordan, pp. 125–6.

The Commonwealth Men

1. Jones, W. R. D., *The Tudor Commonwealth* (1970), chapter 1.
2. Woodcock, M., 'Thomas Churchyard and the Medieval Complaint Tradition', in King, A. and Woodcock, M. (eds), *Medieval Into Renaissance: Essays for Helen Cooper* (2016), pp. 123–41.
3. Jones, p. 214.
4. Quoted in Elton, G. R., 'Reform and the "Commonwealth-men" of Edward VI's Reign', in Clark, P., Smith, A. G. R. and Tyacke, N. (eds), *The English Commonwealth 1547–1640* (1979), p. 27.
5. Bush, chapter 3.
6. Jones, p. 214.
7. Ibid., pp. 43, 50.
8. Fletcher and MacCulloch, pp. 12–14.

The Enclosure Commissions

1. Discussion of the 1548 enclosure commission and the sheep tax follows Jordan, pp. 427–36.

2. The discussion of the 1548 Northaw rising is based on Jones, A., *'Commotion Time': The English Risings of 1549*, University of Warwick PhD (2003), chapter 2.
3. For the issue of enclosure, see Cornwall, J., *Revolt of the Peasantry* (1977), chapter 1; Hammond, R. J., *The Social and Economic Circumstances of Kett's Rebellion* (1934), chapter 1; Kerridge, E., *Agrarian Problems in the Sixteenth Century and After* (1969); and a particularly good summary in Youings, J., *Sixteenth-Century England* (1984).

Was Enclosure a Major Problem?
1. Youings, p. 171.
2. Kerridge, chapter 4.
3. Fletcher and MacCulloch, p. 83.
4. Hammond, p. 64.
5. Ibid., p. 75.

1549: A Perfect Storm
1. Jordan, chapter XIII.
2. Jones, p. 253.
3. Bush, p. 59.

The May 'Stirs'
1. Heinze, R. W., *The Proclamations of the Tudor Kings* (1976), p. 217.
2. Ravensdale, J. R., 'Landbeach in 1549: Kett's Rebellion in Miniature', in Mundy, L. M. (ed.), *East Anglian Studies* (1968).
3. MacCulloch, *Thomas Cranmer: A Life* (1996), p. 429.
4. Heinze, p. 217.

The Western Rebellion
1. Youings, J., 'The South-Western Rebellion of 1549', *Southern History* (1979), pp. 100–22.
2. Jones, pp. 89–90.
3. Greenwood, A., *A Study of the Rebel Petitions of 1549*, University of Manchester PhD (1990), Part 1.
4. MacCulloch, *Thomas Cranmer*, pp. 430–1.

The Rebellions of Commonwealth

1. Jones, Map 1.2.
2. Ibid., pp. 69 and 183–238.
3. Ibid., pp. 194–222 for discussion of the Buckinghamshire and Oxfordshire rebellions.
4. MacCulloch, D., 'Kett's Rebellion in Context', *Past & Present* 84 (1979).
5. See for example Cornwall, op. cit.
6. Jones, p. 5.

Rebel Coordination

1. Heinze, p. 218.
2. Somerset to Hoby, 24.8.1549. Quoted in Bush, M. L., 'Protector Somerset and the 1549 Rebellions: A Post-Revision Questioned', *English Historical Review* (February 2000).
3. MacCulloch, 'Kett's Rebellion in Context', p. 47.
4. Jones, pp. 115–20.
5. Alsop, J. D., 'Latimer, The "Commonwealth of Kent" and the 1549 Rebellions', *Historical Journal* 28.2 (1985), pp. 379–83.
6. Cooper, C. H., *Annals of Cambridge* 2, p. 43, quoted in Jones, p. 146.
7. MacCulloch, 'Kett's Rebellion in Context', p. 43.
8. Fletcher and MacCulloch, p. 77.
9. Sotherton, N., *The Commoysion in Norfolk* (1549), reproduced by Beer, B., in *Journal of Medieval and Renaissance Studies* 6 (1976), p. 1.
10. For discussion of the Canterbury rebels, see Jones, pp. 169–74.

East Anglia: Background to Revolt

1. Fletcher and MacCulloch, p. 23.
2. Wood (2007), pp. 58–9.
3. MacCulloch, 'Kett's Rebellion in Context', pp. 53–5.
4. MacCulloch, D., 'A Reformation in the Balance: Power Struggles in the Diocese of Norwich, 1533–1553', in *Counties and Communities*, pp. 97–114.
5. Information on Norwich is taken from Pound, J. F., *Tudor and Stuart Norwich* (1988).

6. Wood, A., 'Kett's Rebellion', in Rawcliffe, C. and Wilson, R. (eds), *Medieval Norwich* (2004), p. 294.
7. Wood (2007), p. 59.

Wymondham
1. Neville, A., *Norfolk Furies* (1575), translated from the Latin by Richard Woods, 1615. Pagination follows that of the edition held in the Norfolk and Norwich Millennium Library, Norwich.
2. MacCulloch, 'Kett's Rebellion in Context', p. 43.
3. Hoare, A., *An Unlikely Rebel: Robert Kett and the Norfolk Rising, 1549* (1999), p. 22.
4. MacCulloch, 'Kett's Rebellion in Context', pp. 41–4.
5. Land, S. K., *Kett's Rebellion: The Norfolk Rising of 1549* (1977), p. 144.
6. Hoare (1999), pp. 16–23, on Flowerdew.
7. Land, p. 144.
8. Hoare (1999), pp. 20–22.
9. Communication from Adrian Hoare, 2017.
10. Sotherton, p. 80.
11. Neville, p. 9.

Norwich to Mousehold
1. Neville, p. 13.
2. Sotherton, p. 81.
3. MacCulloch, 'Kett's Rebellion in Context', p. 61.

Who Were the Rebels?
1. Neville, p. 105.
2. Ashwin, T. and Davison, A. (eds), *An Historical Atlas of Norfolk* (2005), p. 100.
3. Coleman, D. C., *The Economy of England 1450–1750* (1977), p. 12.
4. Neville, p. 70.
5. Russell, F. W., *Kett's Rebellion in Norfolk* (1859), p. 102.
6. Greenwood, Aubrey R., *A Study of the Rebel Petitions of 1549*, University of Manchester PhD (1990); Whittle, J., 'Lords and Tenants in Kett's Rebellion 1549', *Past & Present*, no. 207 (May 2010), pp. 3–51.
7. Greenwood, pp. 320–1.

8. Whittle, p. 23.
9. Ibid., p. 26.
10. Ibid., p. 41.
11. Greenwood, pp. 320–1.

Administration of the Camp

1. Whittle, pp. 37–8.
2. Neville, p. 18.
3. Land, p. 20.
4. Neville, p. 17.
5. Sotherton, p. 84.
6. Ibid.
7. Greenwood, p. 327.
8. Neville, pp. 25–6; Sotherton, p. 84.
9. Russell, p. 47.
10. Blomefield, F., *An Essay Towards a Topographical History of the County of Norfolk (1739–75)*, chapter 2.5 18/29, British History Online edition.
11. Greenwood, p. 306.
12. Neville, p. 65.
13. Ibid., p. 75. (Land quotes Sotherton as mentioning Miles's name in this connection, but this is not in the *Journal of Medieval and Renaissance Studies* edition.)
14. Sotherton, p. 87; Jary, L. R., *Rewriting the Rebellion* (2018), Part 2, 'Weapons'.

Relations with Norwich

1. Sotherton, p. 83.
2. Ibid., p. 85.
3. Jary, L. R., *Through Ancient Gates: the Medieval Defences of Norwich* (2011) for a discussion of the walls.
4. Sotherton, p. 82.
5. Neville, pp. 20–1. (Parker's visit must have been on 18–19 July, since he spoke at the high scaffold round the Oak on a Friday. This could not have been the 12th, since that was the date of the rebels' arrival; and by the 26th Norwich had been occupied.)
6. Greenwood, p. 305.

Financing the Camp

1. MacCulloch, D., 'Kett's Rebellion in Context: A Rejoinder', in Slack, P. (ed.), *Rebellion, Popular Protest and the Social Order in Early Modern England* (1984), p. 75; Fletcher and MacCulloch, p. 85; MacCulloch, *Thomas Cranmer*, pp. 437, 451–2, 456; Skidmore, pp. 130–1. This would be a fascinating area for further research. For example, it would be interesting to see whether his flocks were raided during the Rebellion.
2. Skidmore, p. 131.

Reimagining Life in the Camp

1. Neville, p. 19.
2. Ibid., p. 43.
3. Ibid., p. 27.
4. Ibid., p. 51.
5. Sotherton, p. 92.
6. Neville, pp. 18–23.

The 'Prophets'

1. Morehouse, G., *The Pilgrimage of Grace* (2002), pp. 40–1, 72.
2. Sotherton, p. 97.
3. Dawson, J., *John Knox* (2015), chapter 3.
4. Horst, I. B., *The Radical Brethren* (1972), chapter 3.
5. Ibid., pp. 103–7.
6. Holinshed, R., *Chronicle* (1577), The Holinshed Shared Project (http://english.nsms.ox.ac.uk/holinshed/), Vol. 4 (1613), p. 69.

12–21 July: Days of Hope

1. Greenwood, p. 211.
2. Land, pp. 63–6, reproduces the demands.
3. Greenwood, p. 211.
4. Land, chapter 11; Cornwall, p. 145.
5. Greenwood, p. 143; Wood, p. 64; Beer, B., *Rebellion and Riot: Popular Disorder in England During the Reign of Edward VI* (2005), p. 111.
6. My argument is largely based on that of Greenwood, pp. 214–36.

7. Shagan, E. H., 'Protector Somerset and the 1549 Rebellions: New Sources and New Perspectives', *English Historical Review* (February 1999); Bush, M. L., 'Protector Somerset and the 1549 Rebellions: A Post-Revision Questioned', *EHR* (February 2000); and Bernard, G. W, 'New Perspectives or Old Complexities?', *EHR* (February 2000).

8. Shagan, op. cit., Letter 3; op. cit., p. 58; Bernard, op. cit., p. 116.

9. Shagan, op. cit., pp. 55–7.

10. Sotherton, p. 85.

11. Neville, p. 31.

12. Ibid.

13. Sotherton, p. 85.

Armed Conflicts: 21 July to 1 August

1. Southerton, p. 85.

2. Russell, pp. 78–80.

3. Sotherton, p. 87.

4. Russell, p. 81.

5. Neville, pp. 40–1.

6. Land, chapter 16, is a good summary of attempts to spread the rebellion.

7. Jones, pp. 264–73.

8. Hoare, A. and A., *Mystery, Drama, Scandal and Ruin – Exploring the Lives of Some Families Whose Coats of Arms Were Found at Number Nine, Town Green Wymondham* (2018).

9. Land, chapter 14. Land is good on the military aspects.

10. Sotherton, pp. 89–90.

11. Ibid.

12. Ibid. The account of the battle is based on Sotherton, pp. 89–91, and Land, chapter 15.

13. Groves, R., *Rebels' Oak* (1947), p. 57.

Growing Isolation: 1–24 August

1. Sotherton, pp. 91–3.

2. Jones, pp. 163–4.

The Coming of Warwick's Army

1. Miller, G. J., *Tudor Mercenaries and Auxiliaries 1485–1547* (1980), esp. p. 44.
2. Jary, L. R., Part 2, 'Destruction of the North Wall Gates', has a very useful discussion of this.
3. Sotherton, p. 95.
4. Carter, A., 'The Site of Dussindale', *Norfolk Archaeology* Vol. XXXIX, Part 1 (1984), pp. 54–62.
5. Sotherton, p. 98.
6. Jary, L. R., Part 4.
7. Neville, p. 70.

The Final Battles: 24–27 August

1. Description of events between 24 and 26 August is based on Sotherton, pp. 92–7.
2. Somerset to Hoby, 15.9.1549, quoted in Russell, p. 214.
3. Jary, L. R., Part 3, on which my discussion of the Battle of Dussindale is largely based.
4. Neville, p. 71.
5. Sotherton, p. 98.
6. Russell, p. 144, referencing journal of Edward VI.
7. Neville, pp. 71–2.
8. Sotherton, p. 99.
9. Neville, pp. 73–4.

The Aftermath

1. Neville, p. 76.
2. Holinshed Shared texts, Vol. IV, p. 1613, 69.
3. Neville, pp. 75–6.
4. Whittle, Part V.
5. Land, p. 126.
6. This account based on Loach, J., *Edward VI* (1999), pp. 105–6.
7. Skidmore, p. 152.
8. Wood (2007), p. 77.
9. Ibid., p. 78.
10. Ibid., chapter 5.

BIBLIOGRAPHY

Until comparatively recently, little was written about the rebellions of 1549 as a whole or about the Western Rebellion; there has been more on Kett's Rebellion, but not that much.

As Diarmaid MacCulloch has said, much of what was written about Kett's Rebellion before the 1970s was derived from the only contemporary narrative, *The Commoysion in Norfolk* by Nicholas Sotherton. Written in the immediate aftermath of the rebellion, it is very short, and viscerally opposed to the rebels.

The next narrative to appear was Alexander Neville's *Norfolk Furies* (1575), translated from the Latin by Richard Woods in 1615. Neville was secretary to Archbishop Matthew Parker, who briefly visited the camp in 1549. Neville's opposition to the rebels is ferocious, but a lot of useful information can be garnered from his longer account. Holinshed's *Chronicle* (1577) discusses the rebellion but adds little to Neville.

Almost two hundred years passed before the next discussion of the rebellion, in Francis Blomefield's *An Essay Towards a Topographical History of the County of Norfolk (1739–75)*. Again, it adds little.

Almost another century passed until the first 'stand-alone' history, F. W. Russell's *Kett's Rebellion in Norfolk*, was published in 1859. It is a first-rate work of scholarship, incorporating many new sources unearthed by Russell, though not very readable now. Russell was the first writer to show at least a little sympathy for the rebels.

In the first half of the twentieth century two writers brought a socialist perspective to the rebellion. Joseph Clayton's *Robert Kett and the Norfolk Rising* (1912) effectively takes the existing story and turns it on its head, the rebels being good and the landlords bad. It is the first book that is written to be accessible to the general reader. Short, but thoroughly researched and with useful insights, is R. Groves' *Rebels' Oak* (1947).

There is then another gap until 1977, when S. K. Land wrote *Kett's Rebellion: The Norfolk Rising of 1549*. This is a useful introductory book, though dated now given subsequent study, and aims at impartiality. All these books portray Kett's Rebellion as an independent entity – though other south-eastern camps are mentioned, it is only incidentally.

In the same year came J. Cornwall's *Revolt of the Peasantry*, written by an academic but very readable. Paradoxically, this first modern book to discuss the 1549 risings as a whole also portrayed the Western Rebellion and Kett's Rebellion as separate entities, with the 'commotions' in between as incidental.

In more recent years several academic writers have added greatly to our knowledge. Diarmaid MacCulloch's 'Kett's Rebellion in Context' (*Past & Present* 84, 1979) was the first study to put Kett's Rebellion in the context of the other risings. Andy Wood's *Riot, Rebellion and Popular Politics in Early Modern England* (2002) and *The 1549 Rebellions and the Making of Early Modern England* (2007) are interesting and thought-provoking. Amanda Jones's '*Commotion Time': The English Risings of 1549* (University of Warwick PhD, 2003) has greatly deepened our understanding of the rebellions' connectedness. Ethan Shagan's *Popular Politics and the English Reformation* (2003) also contains useful information. A. Greenwood's *A Study of the Rebel Petitions of 1549* (University of Manchester PhD, 1990) is an excellent study of the Mousehold petition, and also casts light on rebel leadership and membership of the Mousehold Camp, as does Jane Whittle's 'Lords and Tenants in Kett's Rebellion 1549' (*Past & Present* 207, May 2010).

These works have all greatly deepened our understanding of the 1549 rebellions and their consequences, but are aimed, necessarily, mainly at an academic audience. However, the flame of thoroughly researched but highly accessible work on the Rebellion has been kept alive by Adrian Hoare, working with his wife Anne; notably *An Unlikely Rebel: Robert Kett and the Norfolk Rising, 1549* (1999) and *On the Trail of Kett's Rebellion in Norfolk 1549: Places, People and Events* (2016). Leo R. Jary's *Rewriting the Rebellion* (2018) adds greatly to our understanding of the military side.

Other books I found particularly useful were Barrett Beer's *Rebellion and Riot: Popular Disorder in England During the Reign of Edward VI* (2005); M. L. Bush's *The Government Policy of Protector Somerset* (1975); and

Bibliography

Marcus Merriman's *The Rough Wooings: Mary Queen of Scots 1542–1551* (2000) – I think the outstanding work on England's wars against Scotland in this period. One book that was of special help to me in recreating the trial of the fictional Thomas Boleyn was J. S. Cockburn's *A History of English Assizes 1558–1714* (1972).

I hope that *Tombland*, which is fiction but based on primary and secondary sources, may help carry the story of Kett's Rebellion and the 1549 rebellions as a whole to a wider audience.

ABOUT THE AUTHOR

C. J. Sansom was educated at Birmingham University, where he took a BA and then a PhD in history. After working in a variety of jobs, he retrained as a solicitor and practiced in Sussex, England, until becoming a full-time writer.

Sansom is the internationally bestselling author of the critically acclaimed Shardlake series, as well as *Winter in Madrid* and *Dominion*. He lives in Sussex.

MULHOLLAND BOOKS

You won't be able to put down these Mulholland books.

KILLING EVE: NO TOMORROW *by Luke Jennings*

THE ELEPHANT OF SURPRISE *by Joe R. Lansdale*

CROWN JEWEL *by Christopher Reich*

TOMBLAND *by C. J. Sansom*

SEAL TEAM SIX: HUNT THE LEOPARD *by Don Mann and Ralph Pezzullo*

DECEPTION COVE *by Owen Laukkanen*

CONVICTION *by Denise Mina*

THE CHAIN *by Adrian McKinty*

THE GOMORRAH GAMBIT *by Tom Chatfield*

PLAY WITH FIRE *by William Shaw*

SAVIORS: TWO NOVELS *by Malcolm Mackay*

Visit mulhollandbooks.com for
your daily suspense fix.